ELEANOR THOMSON was a teacher before she took up writing. She is married to an army officer and lives in Wiltshire. *A Time Before Oliver* is her first novel.

A Time Before Oliver

ELEANOR THOMSON

HarperCollins*Publishers*

HarperCollins*Publishers*
77–85 Fulham Palace Road,
Hammersmith, London W6 8JB

A Paperback Original 1996
1 3 5 7 9 8 6 4 2

Extract from *Van Diemen's Land* from *Shanties from the Seven Seas*
ed. Stan Hugill published and copyright 1984 by
International Thomson Publishing Services Ltd, reproduced by kind permission

A catalogue record for this book
is available from the British Library

ISBN 0 0 00 649714 4

Set in Plantin Light
at The Spartan Press Ltd,
Lymington, Hants

Printed and bound in Great Britain by
Caledonian International Book Manufacturing Ltd, Glasgow

AUTHOR'S NOTE

The strange love story of Sikes and Nancy was never fully explored by Dickens and *A Time Before Oliver* is an attempt to cover the ground prior to Dickens's story.

Wherever possible I have integrated Dickens's characters and timescale. Some events from *Oliver Twist* are hinted at, so that some continuity is achieved.

To the best of my knowledge, the slang and canting language used is appropriate to the period and Partridge's *Dictionary of Historical Slang* has been invaluable for this purpose. Only in a very few cases have I stretched a point.

For those who do not know *Oliver Twist*, the epilogue of *A Time Before Oliver* follows Sikes's brutal murder of Nancy, his pursuit by the law and the accidental fall to his death as he attempts to escape across the rooftops of Jacob's Island in Southwark.

E.T.

I wander thro' each charter'd street,
Near where the charter'd Thames does flow,
And mark in every face I meet
Marks of weakness, marks of woe.

In every cry of every Man,
In every Infant's cry of fear,
In every voice, in every ban,
The mind-forg'd manacles I hear.

How the Chimney-sweeper's cry
Every black'ning Church appalls,
And the hapless Soldier's sigh,
Runs in blood down Palace walls.

But most thro' midnight streets I hear
How the youthful Harlot's curse
Blasts the new-born Infant's tear,
And blights with plagues the Marriage hearse.

William Blake, *London*

PART ONE

BILL
1813–1827

My mother groan'd! my father wept,
Into the dangerous world I leapt:
Helpless, naked, piping loud;
Like a fiend hid in a cloud.

Struggling in my father's hands,
Striving against my swadling bands;
Bound and weary I thought best
To sulk upon my mother's breast.

William Blake, *Infant Sorrow*

ONE

He sat silent and crossed-legged at the side of the low bed, his chin resting on his fists, his elbows making tiny hollows on the insides of his knees. His eyes never moved from the lifeless body before him as he sat hour after hour, watching and waiting. The night wore on and the chill, damp air of the room made gooseflesh of his skin, scantily clad as he was. Once he got up and went outside to the communal privy to relieve himself. A light rain was falling and for a moment the boy raised his face and let the fine drops spatter over him. Then he hurried back to the room.

He was eleven. He had watched as his family left him, one by one, over the years, until all he had left was this poor broken creature whom he had called Mother. She had been young and pretty, with a spark in her eye and a great mane of dark brown hair when Charley Sikes had first noticed her. She had been employed as a laundry maid in a nearby lodging house and had fallen for the big fellow who occasionally stayed there. No one was quite sure what he did for a living and no one asked. But Fanny went willingly enough when he beckoned and they set up home together in a room in the southern corner of the parish of Shoreditch, a place of close yards and alleys and evil-smelling ways.

Fanny bore a babe every couple of years, but most of them had not lived more than a few weeks. Young Charley survived, but he had always been delicate and died of diphtheria when he was twelve. Johnny was another who lived past infancy; he had been such a humorous, mischievous little lad, but he had met his end last year under the wheels of a passing wagon. And there was Billy, who sat now in silent mourning for his mother.

3

He didn't cry, his face was set like stone, but his mind was in turmoil and his heart ached with a physical pain. It had been different with Johnny. Johnny had been close in age to him and they had done everything together and he had wept bitterly for his lost companion. But his mother had held him tightly to her and whispered into his dark curls, 'Only us two left now, Billy. We must look after each other.'

And he had looked into her face and seen not the ravages of a life of poverty and neglect, but eyes which spoke of love and devotion and a fierce maternal protection. He had dried his eyes, determined to be the man of the house, to watch over his mother and somehow to make up to her for all she had lost. But it was difficult with no bread-winner. His father had gone to the gallows three years before for robbery with violence, and his mother had never really recovered from the shock. She flitted from one trifling job to another, match-making here, sack-making there, never earning more than a few pence a week, and in the winter, she and Billy had had to take refuge in the workhouse. They had got out of the terrible place as soon as the weather improved and between them had scraped together enough money to rent a room to live in.

Billy used to earn an occasional penny, holding a gentleman's horse or running errands; he was quick and strong, despite his tender years and his lack of sustenance. He was tall, too, for his age, and his mother could see the strong resemblance to his father. But she fervently hoped he would steer clear of his father's line of business, though she doubted it. Already she guessed that the odd pie or loaf, which found its way into their lodging, was not honestly come by.

The summer came and at least the walls of their room no longer streamed with moisture. But the air became stifling and the alleyways stank of human filth. Children played in the runnels. Dirty little hands went into little mouths. Fanny shuddered. How many of those children would survive till next summer?

4

Autumn set in with constant rain. Fanny caught a cold and coughed and wheezed, shivering and burning by turns under her blanket. Billy bathed her head, brought her the cleanest water he could find and fed her with what little he could muster. But today she had given up the struggle and when the death-rattle sounded in her throat, Billy knew he would walk life alone.

Now he sat thinking. Where was the fairness in all this? He had given her his all and she had been taken from him. There was no one to turn to, no one to love him any more. He was on his own. His resolution hardened into an iron will, which was never to leave him. He was filled with a bitterness and impotent rage against life, against the world and against the people around him.

Dawn, silver-grey and cold, lightened the cracked and grimy window pane. Bill was cold. He rocked stiffly to his knees. He bent over the corpse and gently kissed the cold lips and marble forehead. Then he drew the blanket over the body because he knew this was the right thing to do, and went quietly from the room, ignoring the grindings of hunger in his belly. He knew what he had to do and the sooner he did it, the better. But he trembled at the thought of approaching the workhouse once more.

He slipped like a shadow from the lodging house and into the maze of yards and alleyways outside, walking steadily until he came out into Shoreditch, where trade was already brisk and working people were abroad, despite the early hour. Here he turned north and headed along the Kingsland Road, the porticoed church of St Leonard on his right. He wondered where they would bury her and he stopped for a moment to peer through the railings surrounding the churchyard.

At length he came to the gate of the workhouse, which stood vast and foreboding on the west side of Kingsland Road. Dashing across the street between the wheels of drays and the hooves of horses, the boy rang the bell without hesitation. It seemed to make a tremendous din within the fastness of the building, but he had to wait some minutes before a gaunt and bent old pauper shuffled to the gate and peered at him with rheumy eyes.

'Wotcher want, sonny?' he enquired in a high, thin, cracked voice.

'Please, I want ter see the beadle,' replied Bill.

'Huh!' laughed the old man. 'But does the beadle want ter see you, eh?'

'My name is Bill Sikes an' I want ter see the beadle. It's very important.'

The gatekeeper narrowed his eyes and thrust his face nearer the bars in order to get a closer view of the boy before him. What he saw was not a cowering child, but a determined lad with clenched fists, a set jaw and a dangerous glint in his eye. He was rather frightened of his dark good looks, too. He grunted and fumbled with the huge bunch of keys dangling from a large ring in his gnarled old hand. He selected a key of giant proportions and unlocked the gate, swinging it just wide enough to admit the boy and hastily locking it again behind him.

Bill stood irresolute for a moment. Memories of this place were too fresh in his mind. The old pauper cuffed him roughly on the shoulder, bidding him follow him. They walked along a dark and gloomy corridor, which reeked of carbolic soap and stale cabbage. Bill's stomach churned dangerously. He had eaten nothing since yesterday morning.

They fetched up outside a heavy oak door, upon which the old man beat twice with his knuckles.

'Come!' called a weary voice from inside.

The gatekeeper opened the door and pushed Bill inside. '*Mister* Bill Sikes ter see yer, sir.'

He laid mocking emphasis on the first word and then retreated, banging the door behind him. The beadle winced at the noise and looked up from his desk into Bill's determined face. Impressed by what he saw, he leaned back in his chair, surveying the boy; he was used to seeing cowed bodies and dejected expressions. This lad had neither.

6

'Well, young Sikes,' he said, almost smiling. 'Come back for another holiday?'

Bill's face did not crack.

'No, sir,' he replied. 'Me mother's dead an' I want 'er buried – please,' he added as an afterthought.

The beadle sighed. He was not totally without feeling and he held a grudging admiration for the boy.

'Where is she?' he asked, quite gently.

'In our room – in Crown Alley. 'Ouse in the corner. Second floor up. I covered 'er up. She died yes'day.'

'I will tell the vicar of St Leonard's and send someone to fetch her away.'

He looked at the boy and felt moved to follow this with, 'Are you hungry?'

'Yus, sir,' replied young Sikes.

'You can join the queue in the casual ward and have a bowl of gruel. And I think we can replace those tatters you're wearing.'

Bill dreaded the thought of entering the casual ward again, but the gnawing in his belly won him over and he shuffled along with the inmates to the large eating hall. One or two familiar figures hailed him, but not with any enthusiasm, and he bolted his bowl of gruel in silence.

Making his way to the outer door, he was accosted by a lean, scowling woman, who pinched his arm and ushered him into a side room lined with tall cupboards and clothes presses. There was a smell of old clothes about the place, despite its obvious scrubbed appearance, but Bill did not even notice it; he was, after all, one of the Great Unwashed.

'Take those off!' commanded the dame, her hands folded over her waist, her large, thin nose held high.

Bill looked at her, not understanding.

'Get them rags off your back.'

Slowly, he pulled off his torn clothes and stood cold and shivering, naked and ashamed, in front of this termagant. She looked him up and down, assessing him. Then she raised her eyebrows at some inward comment to herself, sniffed and walked away to a chest of drawers under the high window, where she proceeded to riffle through a mass of clothes. At last she emerged with a pair of knee breeches of a doubtful colour, a shirt with no collar, a blue woollen jacket, with large pockets and shiny buttons, a pair of grey stockings and some rather grey-looking drawers.

'Put 'em on and I'll find you some boots,' ordered the woman.

With trembling hands, Bill pulled on the clothes, all old, all someone else's, but riches for a boy who had never had anything. And here was a pair of stiff and cracked half-boots, which he had trouble lacing. The woman unbent herself so far as to tie them for him.

'Well?' She waited, grimly.

Bill was worried. Did he have to pay?

'What d'ye say, boy?'

'Oh, thank y'ma'm,' he replied in relief and was then ushered from the building.

Bill fairly raced back down the Kingsland Road. Just wait till Mother saw him. He stopped in his tracks. Mother would never see him now, would never admire his new togs. He could have been almost a gentleman, except that he had no hat. He could probably find a hat. But what did it matter? Mother was dead, quite dead and cold and deaf and lifeless. His eyes blurred, but he would not give way. Instead, he kicked hard against the wall of a house he was passing, kicked again and again in his rage and frustration, until the owner came out to see what the thumping noise was about and chased him off, brandishing a large stick.

He couldn't go back to the house. Instead, he crept into St Leonard's churchyard and crouched on a bank of grass at the side furthest from the road. He thought they might eventually bring her here – the beadle had mentioned the vicar – so he would wait. He rested his arms on his knees and his head on his arms.

Whether he slept or not, he wasn't sure, but he was suddenly aware of a gentle pressure on his arm and a man's voice saying, 'Hello, boy, what's the trouble? Can I help?'

He looked up, blearily, into the kindly face of the vicar of St Leonard's. He was a tall, thin man, just as thin and gaunt as the majority of his flock. Not that many of them attended church more than the required occasions of baptism, marriage and burial; and few troubled themselves with the second. Bill had seen him about on the streets of Shoreditch, vainly trying to steer some of his black sheep back into the fold.

When he received no reply but a somewhat defiant stare, the vicar crouched down to the boy's level and said, 'What's your name?'

This seemed to goad some life into the child.

'My name's Bill Sikes an' me mother's dead an' I bin ter the work'us an' they're a-goin' ter let yer know an' send someone ter take 'er away.' His voice broke on the last few words and he swallowed hard.

'Poor boy,' murmured the kindly old man, 'poor boy. Is there no one else at home?'

'No,' came the reply. A pause; then, 'Where will they take 'er, Rev'rend?'

'Will here do?'

The vicar made a sweeping gesture with one hand. They both looked around God's acre, with its neat, ordered green mounds, its few inscribed headstones and one or two grandiose, tomb-like structures erected over past Shoreditch worthies, now all reduced to the same state as their poorer neighbours beneath the sward.

'Yus please, sir,' whispered Bill. 'She'd like that. Can I stay 'ere till she comes?'

'Of course, Bill, but you may have to wait till late in the day.'

Bill nodded and resumed his former position while the vicar made his way back to the vicarage, reflecting on the sad plight of the poor in general and of his own parish in particular.

The sun got round behind St Leonard's and then began to sink beyond the tall buildings opposite. Bill dozed from time to time, but never for long. At length he was alerted by a movement at the entrance to the churchyard. The vicar came first, saw Bill and beckoned him over. Bill picked his way carefully between the graves and came to where the vicar and two sour-looking individuals had stopped with a rough coffin between them. At their feet was a gaping hole. He hadn't heard the gravedigger, being on the other side of the church all day. But here was his mother's resting place, all ready for her.

The vicar came and put his arm about the lad's shoulders while he read a short burial service over the departed woman. The coffin was lowered into the ground and the vicar threw in a handful of earth. Bill thought this a useless gesture; after all, she was going to be covered with the stuff soon enough. The vicar patted his shoulder, sighed and walked away with one of the coffin bearers. The second man went to a little shed in the corner of the graveyard to collect his spade.

Bill crouched at the edge of the hole. He wanted to be with her, there, in the dark, cool earth, to be wrapped in her gentle arms for ever, with no more fear, no more hurt, no more anxiety. Instead, he was up here with life stretching out long and bleak before him. They had all gone, every one of them, and left him behind.

And finally, Bill wept.

TWO

'Yer can't stay 'ere, sonny. Yer've got ter pay, yer know. This ain't a charity.'

The lodging-house keeper was not unkind, but he was very firm. Bill took a last look round the appalling hole that had been his home for the past two years and stumped dejectedly down the rotten staircase and out across the courtyard into the harsh light of a November morn. He had nothing but the clothes he stood up in, nothing of use, nothing from his past, not even a pathetic bundle to sling over his shoulder. His hands were free and he was unencumbered.

He wandered off towards Whitechapel. There was always plenty going on there. Today, being Thursday, the Hay Market was in full swing and as Bill turned into Whitechapel Road, he saw a stream of heavily laden carts rumbling along past St Mary Matfelon's. Although the market was mainly for hay and straw, which was brought in from Essex and Hertfordshire, other street vendors took advantage of this thrice-weekly event and a range of stalls would appear on either side of the street, selling all manner of goods and produce.

Bill ambled along in the wake of one of the big haywains. The smell was fresh and wholesome after the stench of the lodging house, but Bill was painfully reminded of his brother's death. He quickly put the memory from him; no good letting himself think of that now. He'd got to be a man, he had to be firm with himself. But the smell of the hay persisted in reminding him of the tenter grounds in Bethnal Green, where they had sometimes played as small children. They were building over all that now, row after row of drab, cheap housing for all the labourers beginning to flood into the capital.

11

Like most boys of his age, Bill was constantly hungry; being poor meant that hunger was rarely satisfied; but poverty had taught his stomach to cope with waiting. However, delicious smells issued from a nearby stall and while the owner was engaged with a customer, Bill neatly lifted two small meat pies and slid them into his pocket. He rather regretted having to do this, because the pastry crumbled and he feared he might lose some of the precious contents, and because the grease would be bound to make an unsightly mark in the pocket of his newly acquired jacket. He cast a furtive glance round him, then darted off down the side of St Mary's and found a secluded corner of the churchyard in which to indulge his hunger. The pies were good, lean and succulent and when he had finished them both and licked the last vestige of gravy from his grubby fingers, his belly felt as though it would burst. He leaned back against a listing tombstone.

'Thass better,' he said to himself. 'A good 'ot pie puts the 'eart back into a man.'

He'd heard his father say this and he thought it sounded grand and grown up. He spared a thought now for his departed father, hanged for his crimes. Charley Sikes had not been much of a father to his offspring, he was rarely there. But he was proud of his boys and had taught them a great deal when he *was* home. By the time each of his three sons was eight, they could pick a lock, make a fair go of removing a pane of glass from a window, handle a knife and a jemmy, and dip the odd pocket or two. As far as Charley Sikes was concerned, these were enough skills for his sons to get along in life. He had also taught Johnny and Billy to fight with their bare fists, though young Charley was too delicate to fight. The two boys had gladly practised on their pals and hardly a day went by but their mother wasn't bathing cut lips or finding raw meat for black eyes.

Bill sighed. Johnny had been a really good friend. Why in hell's name had he had to be taken from him? He felt the tears rising once more and was angry. He walked on, aimlessly, down Adler Street. On his left was the large grim edifice of the German Catholic church of St Boniface and its adjacent school. Some children were filing into the school and he stood and watched them. He had never been to school, there had never been enough money to pay the weekly fee and his parents had not deemed it necessary for their boys to be 'hedicated like toffs'. He would have liked to be able to read and maybe to write. But he knew he would never have the chance. He looked up at the church. What did they do in there? He didn't know much about Catholics, let alone German ones. Some of his mates were Catholic Irish boys and the only thing that seemed to mark them out was a tendency to a different vocabulary of oaths; they appeared to have an endless supply of saints on whom to call.

He crossed the road and glanced up at the big arched doorway, wondering if he dare look inside. He lifted a hand to try the heavy iron ring, when suddenly the door opened and the priest came out. Terrified, Bill turned and ran as fast as his long legs would carry him, leaving the kindly man of God surprised and saddened on the steps of his church.

Bill ran on down into Commercial Road, then doubled back along Church Lane. When he reached Whitechapel High Street again, he crossed over and sauntered up Brick Lane. On the corner of Thrawl Street was a jolly-looking public house, called The Frying Pan. It was not yet open, but a brewer's dray was parked outside and the heavy wooden barrels were being rolled down into the cellars. The great grey horses were restive and Bill sidled up to them. They towered above him and he felt very small. He caught the eye of the sweating drayman.

''Old yer 'osses for yer, sir?' he called out.

'Aye. I'd be grateful if yer would, laddie,' came the reply. 'On'y watch that near one. 'E's a bugger this mornin'. Don't know wot's got into 'im.'

Bill stood by the great creature. The horse tossed his head and rolled his eye, fidgeting, pawing the ground, whickering to himself. The boy put up a hand, tentatively, and the beast

13

jerked its head up, snorting as it did so. Its mate took no notice and appeared to have drifted off to sleep.

'Summat wrong 'ere,' muttered Bill, half to himself, half to the horse; and he laid his hand firmly on the great arched neck, smoothing and patting, talking all the while.

He cast an eye over the harness and ran his fingers under the heavy collar. Halfway down, the leather was snagged and had balled up, ever so little, but enough to irritate the creature's skin. He managed to lift the collar enough to free the offending piece of leather and smoothed it out, stroking the hair beneath before replacing it.

'Thass better, innit?' he murmured.

The great horse rubbed its long nose against Bill's breast and blew gently down its nostrils. Bill laughed and patted him, resting his hand gently on the bridle.

When the drayman had finished, he came up to Bill with a smile.

'You talked 'im out of 'is silliness, then?' enquired the man.

Bill explained what he had done and showed the man the damaged harness.

'Thass my new groom, blast an' burn 'im. I'll tan 'is 'ide when I gets back.'

He was grateful for Bill's concern and pressed a sixpence into the boy's hand, before climbing on to the dray and driving off. Bill's mind was awhirl. A whole sixpence! Why, it would keep him in food for a week, if he was careful. And 'blast an' burn 'im!' What a wonderful phrase. He would store that one up and use it when the time was ripe.

Clutching the coin tightly, Bill Sikes, feeling quite a little swell, walked on and turned into Flower and Dean Street. He had a friend who lived in Three Cups Alley, and this was a short cut. He wanted to share his good fortune with Nat, if he was around.

Halfway down this rather insalubrious street, he was suddenly confronted by several boys of various ages and sizes, who seemed to have appeared from nowhere but who

14

materialized in front of him. He glared defiantly at them and tried to make a dash through their ranks, but their tactics were well-tried and he could find no way through. Now he was encircled. The mob was laughing at him and the biggest boy, taller than Bill by a head, and much older, drawled, 'Come on, tiddler, 'and over yer blunt.'

Bill shook his head. The big boy took a step forward.

''And it over, I say.'

'It ain't yours. It's jus' bin giv' me.'

'Ef yer don't give it 'ere, I'll –' and the bully boy made a grab at Bill's hand.

Bill had not unclenched the fist which held the precious sixpence and he swung it now with all the force his thin body could muster. It hit his tormentor on the nose and there was an immediate gush of blood, which went over both of them.

Seeing their leader thus immobilized, the pack fell on Bill and set about beating him up. He returned their blows with a fury which surprised his assailants, but they were too many and eventually they pinned him down, bloodied and bruised, and prised open his fingers to release the coin. With a howl of delight, they made off, leaving Bill angry and hurt and whimpering in the filthy gutter. He lay dazed for some minutes until a woman came out of a front door, her basket on her arm, and she bent over his prostrate form.

'Wot's up, boy?' she asked roughly. 'Them ruffians giv' you an 'ard time, eh?'

Bill nodded miserably and crawled painfully to his knees. The woman helped him to his feet and offered to bathe his wounds. But he shook his head, dashed his hand across his eyes and staggered away.

There was a brewery not far away, with troughs and pumps in its yard. Bill had often stood at the gates and watched the horses drinking and the men busy about their work. He made his way there now, wiping his bloody nose and split lip from time to time on the back of his hand. He turned into the brewery yard and made for the pump in the corner.

'Crikey, young'un!' called a cheery voice. 'Yer in a bit of a mess, ain't yer?'

A gangling apprentice boy was just crossing the yard and he saw Bill sneaking in. He came over and worked the pump, while Bill held his head beneath the icy water. The apprentice tipped back Bill's head and surveyed the damage.

'Yer snitch is all right now, but yer lip's a good size an' yer'll 'ave an 'alf mournin' suit by lunch-time,' he added, referring to Bill's purpling right eye. 'You got an 'ome ter go to?'

Bill shook his head. The lad sighed and thought himself mighty lucky.

'Well, yer'd best come an' 'ave summat warm inside yer.'

He took Bill's arm and steered him up an outside staircase to a small room over the stables.

'This is my little pad,' he announced proudly. 'I'll brew yer summat warm.'

Bill looked about him. There was a small fire in the grate and a table and chairs and a bed, everything very neat and clean. He crouched by the fire and stretched out his hands to the warmth. He hadn't realized how cold he was.

The brewer's lad, who introduced himself as James, put a large pewter mug into Bill's hands. It was warm, and a strange yet not unpleasant smell arose from its clear contents. He stared into its depths.

'Garn, young'un. Sup up,' the older boy admonished him.

Bill sipped at the liquid. It was bitter and warm, but its pungency was attractive. He took a gulp and spluttered. James laughed.

'Ain't yer 'ad 'ot gin afore, boy?'

'No,' said Bill in a small voice. 'But I think I remember the smell. Me father used ter drink it.'

'Don't let it get cold then.' A pause. 'Wot's yer name, littl'un?'

'Bill. Bill Sikes. An' I ain't little,' he added defiantly. 'I'm eleven.'

'Yus, but I'm seventeen,' laughed James, 'an' I'm older *an'*

16

bigger 'n you. Still, yer must 'ave put up a good fight. Flahr Street gang?'

Bill nodded.

'Bloody menace, they are,' continued James. 'The Runners is always arter 'em. They need boatin', the lot of 'em.'

'Wot's boatin'?' asked Bill.

'It's transportation. Bein' sent away from England to the other side of the world. Orstralia, usually. Or a place they call Van Diemen's Land. An' never comin' back, least, not fer a long time.'

Bill shuddered. James warmed to his subject.

'They say it's 'orrible there. Wild animals. Savages. Ain't no towns. No civvylization. Nothink. Big spiders. Big snakes. Terrible weather. Bakin' 'ot or rain all the year. Depends where yer go.'

'Wot do people do wot get boated, James?' He couldn't remember the big word.

'Oh, thievin', burglin', robbin', fightin', knockin' people about, all them sort o' things. But don't you worry yer 'ead about things like that, Bill. Jus' keep out o' trouble.' He leaned across and ruffled Bill's hair.

Bill finished his drink and stood up, but whether it was the drink or the result of the recent blows he had sustained, he swayed, grabbed uselessly at the table and fell on the floor. James laughed uproariously and putting his hands under Bill's armpits, lugged him unceremoniously to his feet.

'You ain't used ter such med'cine, are yer?' he chuckled. 'Come an' sit outside fer a bit. No one'll bother yer.'

And he helped Bill down the stairs and sat him on the bottom step. There he left him and strode off back to his work.

Bill leaned his head against the wall behind him and felt the watery sun on his face. The air was cold, but there was a warm, pleasant glow inside him and he slept.

THREE

In the weeks that followed, Bill scrounged what food he could from market stalls, shop fronts and the refuse of the gutter. But the biggest problem was shelter. It was nearly Christmas and the days were short, the nights very long and the weather growing progressively colder. Bill's hands were permanently blue and chilblains began developing on his fingers and toes. At night, he would creep into a corner, perhaps a church doorway or the ruins on a demolition site. Once he'd even crawled into a broken tunnel. There was water still flowing at the bottom, but it was wide enough to accommodate Bill and several other street urchins and not a few rats. There were hard frosts at night and the tunnel became a regular refuge for them all.

Bill found an old woollen scarf on a refuse tip and tore this in half, wrapping a piece round each hand, leaving the tips of his fingers free for picking pockets and pilfering from street stalls, activities which were becoming a regular part of his daily survival. He had made friends, after a fashion, with a hardware dealer on Petticoat Lane and he brought his pickings to him, in return for a few pennies; enough to buy him food three or four times a week.

That winter was to prove so intensely cold that an extraordinary phenomenon occurred, which Bill was to remember all his life. The River Thames froze. The Londoners could scarcely believe their eyes when they saw the sluggish waters around the bridge beginning to ice over and by early February, the river was a solid highway of ice from London Bridge well upstream, beyond Westminster. There was even a little icing up below the bridge. Quick, as always, to take advantage of a situation, the London tradesmen soon had a full-blown Frost Fair set up on the slippery surface and Bill and his friends thought themselves in heaven as they slid for hours to keep warm, filched hot chestnuts and hot sausages from the many stalls and had the whole world's pockets open to them for the daily acquisition of silk handkerchiefs, loose coins and even the occasional watch. Life was wonderful, colourful, precarious.

One evening, a huge ox was roasted on the ice and the boys gathered in a little knot savouring both the glorious smell and the penetrating warmth from the fire. Bill stood with his muffled hands deep in his pockets, staring at the flames. Despite his new-found friends, he felt alone. He wished Johnny were here to share the fun with him. He wished he had a home to go back to when it was all over, where he could at least be dry and warm for the night. His mouth watered as the juicy carcass revolved steadily round and round on its spit. Suddenly, one of the older boys brought the attention of the gang to the sound of music some little way away, and they all moved off reluctantly in his wake to see what the next excitement might be. The new attraction proved to be a pair of swingboats set up between iron scaffolding, and a man at the side turning a little barrel organ to attract customers. Bill and the other youngsters stood open-mouthed as they watched the brightly painted boats being swung high in the air, back and forth to a tremendous height, by two strong men, one at each end of the boat. He would have loved to have a turn in the boats, to feel as free as a bird, high up and out of reach of the world; but he knew he couldn't afford the price of a go, not when he needed every penny to keep himself alive. He turned reluctantly away, the music and the rusty squeaking of the boats loud and clamorous in his ears.

He was just moving off, when he felt a hand on his arm and a woman's voice said softly, 'You'd like a go on that, wouldn't you?'

He turned sharply, his eyes suspicious, his body poised to run. But the face he looked into held him. She was young and she was the most beautiful creature he had ever seen. She was

19

also very handsomely dressed and at her elbow was a tall, bewhiskered young man, who looked on rather disapprovingly.

Bill gulped and didn't know what to do. The beauty smiled and her voice purred.

'I saw you looking so longingly at the swingboats, I felt sure you wanted to go on them.'

Somehow Bill found his voice and said, rather shakily, 'Yus, but I ain't got any blunt.'

The young woman glanced up enquiringly at her escort.

'He means money, my dear,' the gentleman said.

The woman's laughter was like the rippling of the wind through myriads of icicles and Bill felt a sudden thrill at the sound of it.

'Wait a moment,' she continued and pulled open her small velvet reticule, felt inside with her elegant, gloved fingers and pulled out some coins.

'Here you are,' she said softly, 'now you can have several turns on the boats or buy yourself some hot food.'

As Bill took the money from her, his eyes round and sparkling at this unlooked-for windfall, the woman put out her hand and stroked his cheek.

'So good-looking,' she murmured, half to herself.

But Bill heard her and felt his cheeks redden. He was glad of the night with only the lights from the booths to illuminate the scene. He muttered his thanks and went over to the swingboats, his heart beating wildly, his stomach churning in anticipation.

He had to queue for some time and he stamped his feet up and down to keep warm and blew on the ends of his fingers. He liked watching his breath drift out into steamy clouds on the cold night air. Sometimes he would open his mouth wide and let a great blast of breath go white and misty, drifting up into the dark sky above; at others, he would whistle softly and then the mist came out in a long thin stream. At last it was his turn. He climbed in with another boy and two girls. At first, they didn't seem to be moving very far or very fast, but soon they were soaring high, high above the heads of the onlookers and Bill could see the lady and her partner way below the swinging vessel. The girls squealed with delight, but Bill was in his own little world and he barely heard them. How his heart leaped every time the boat reached its zenith and how his stomach heaved when they descended again, ready to swing up on the other side, almost upside down.

'So this is wot bein' a bird's like,' he mused. 'Cor! Lucky blighters.'

He looked over the side and the beautiful woman was still standing watching him. She waved her black-gloved hand and Bill waved back, laughing.

At last the boat was allowed to swing lower and lower and the earth gradually drew nearer and nearer, until the little vessel was pulled to a final halt by the two burly men who had kept its momentum going. Bill stepped out and his legs felt shaky as the young woman hurried over to him.

'Did you enjoy it?' she asked, smiling her beautiful smile.

'Yus, thanks, it was smashin'. Jus' like bein' a bird.'

'Will you go up again?'

'Nah. Got ter get meself summat ter eat. Gets cold at night in the tunnel.'

The young woman's smile faded. She held Bill's arm gently.

'What tunnel, child?' she asked.

Bill was immediately on the defensive, but judged her pretty honest.

'Where me an' me mates live at night.'

He threw the information lightly at her. She looked horrified and to his dismay Bill saw the lovely eyes fill with tears. They were like deep pools, he thought, but he couldn't fathom their colour; only that they were quite fascinating to him. She looked again at the man with her.

'Francis,' she said in a low voice, 'can't we take him back with us?'

The young man thus addressed let out an exasperated sound.

'Angela, my dear,' he said, trying to be patient. 'We have had all this before. You are not going to bring home every child you find on the streets. Look around you; there are hundreds of them here tonight. If you brought home one, you'd want to bring the lot. Besides,' he added, lowering his voice, 'look at the state of him. He's probably crawling with vermin and you don't know what disease he might bring with him. No. You can't. And that is my last word on the matter. Give him money if you wish, but let it finish there. Whatever would our friends say if we were to start off our married life by setting up our home as a refuge for waifs and strays?'

Miss Angela listened to all this sensible talk with her eyes on Bill. And Bill looked steadily into those pools. He didn't want to go off with some toff couple, but he wanted to look at those eyes for ever. When the gentleman had finished speaking, there was an awkward silence for a moment. Then the young woman reached out and in an impulsive gesture, caught Bill to her tightly laced bosom and held him close, laying her smooth cheek on his dark, tousled locks. He was so surprised that he made no attempt to resist and simply savoured the smell of her, his face buried as it was against the rich velvet coat. She smelled divine, like the flowers in spring which he had often smelled in Covent Garden Market. And he felt strangely disturbed, a feeling not unlike that which had assailed him when the swingboat reached the height of its arc. He trembled and the young woman thought he was cold. He pulled away gently from her arms, his pale face looking up enquiringly at her. She kissed his cheek and her lips felt warm and soft. He turned and ran into the night, leaving her staring after him.

'I didn't even ask his name,' sighed Miss Angela, while her young fiancé took her arm and steered her very determinedly away from the scene.

Bill had lost sight of his mates, but he didn't particularly want to share the moment with anyone; he wanted to hug the adventure to himself. She had been so beautiful, a real angel stepping into his life.

22

He sauntered now between the rows of stalls, pushing his way among the crowds and getting elbowed in his turn. He thought about turning in and began to make his way slowly back to the tunnel. It was a long walk and he was glad to keep moving to circulate some warmth around his body. The streets were more deserted than was usual, since so many folk were down on the frozen river. There were always the bawds, though, hanging around on street corners and outside the public houses; Bill knew what they were and what they did for a living. He had grown up wise in the ways of the city and he was no innocent. All the same, he tried to keep clear of these women; he was rather frightened of their brazen way of talking and their very bright clothes and heavy make-up.

There were prostitutes now on his route back to the tunnel and one of them spoke to him as he passed.

'Give yer a nice time, ducky,' she murmured.

Bill was so tall for his years that she did not realize how young he was. He looked at her in disgust and took to his heels, her cackle ringing in his ears. He couldn't understand how two women could be so different. Yet he supposed that was the consequence of being rich or poor.

He gained the shelter of the tunnel at last and found most of the other boys curled up inside. He wriggled in and lay staring into the darkness, listening to the breathing of his companions. His belly made a gurgling sound and he realized that he had forgotten to buy his supper. Cursing himself, he hugged his arms around his shrunken stomach and eventually drifted off into a sleep, where his dreams were peopled with angels in swingboats.

FOUR

There were seven young sewer rats in the tunnel, all orphans like Bill. One boy had run away from a harsh master, where he had been serving a parish apprenticeship; four of the boys had been on the streets for two or three years already; they were older and made a point of resenting the presence of 'small fry'. They often disappeared, especially at night, and then, on their return, they would brag of their sexual experiences and the younger boys would listen to their talk with wide-eyed wonder. Sometimes they brought back measures of gin, or broken pipes with shreds of tobacco still in the bowls, which they might, or might not, share with the others. When they did share, the atmosphere became relaxed, and if they were sharing spirits or beer, then the company became almost congenial. The younger boys would feel grown up and part of a man's world. They would listen to the talk and the bragging and then, on occasions, watch in fascination as their elders worked away at themselves, their hands inside their breeches. There would be little groans and grunts of satisfaction and then they would all laugh together, their eyes bright, their hearts beating fast; and the air in the tunnel would be warm and sharp with sweat. It wasn't long before Bill and the three younger boys were joining in; it seemed an amusing way to keep warm on cold nights and he enjoyed the glow that spread through his loins. He always thought of 'his angel' at such times and would be filled with such an overpowering urge that he was often frightened by his own feelings.

Meanwhile, life was a matter of living from hand to mouth. One of the older boys was caught pilfering from a shop; he was tried and sentenced to seven years in Botany Bay.

The little group was devastated by the news and sat miserably inside the tunnel one evening, discussing the disaster.

'I told 'im not ter do shops,' said one of his associates, nearly in tears. 'It's too risky; but 'e would go fer it. Nah look where it's landed 'im. You be careful, you young'uns. You 'as ter learn by others' mistakes.'

''Ow do they take yer ter Bot'ny Bay?' asked Bill.

He had visions of people in Thames barges, or wherries, being rowed across the sea.

'Bloody great ships wiv sails, Bill. You 'as ter cross the Hequator, an' you gets bleedin' 'ot. Then it's 'eat all the way to Orstralia.'

Bill wondered how the lad knew so much, but he didn't interrupt. He remembered what the brewer's apprentice had told him.

The boy was in full spate and went on, musing, 'Cor, mus' be 'ell on board a ship. Takes weeks ter get there, yer know. 'Spec most of 'em die afore they reach Bot'ny Bay.'

Bill looked at him and shivered.

'You cold, mate?' the older boy asked. 'Come 'ere an' I'll give yer a cuddle.'

His friends laughed, but Bill was wary.

'No thanks,' he said, 'I ain't cold.'

But he kept a weather eye on the big boy. There was something odd about him and Bill couldn't define it.

The year progressed and the young rats left their sewer. The days and nights warmed up and they were able to sleep rough on the streets again. But in the middle of May, when no one in the least expected it, there was a sudden cold snap and the boys abandoned their open-air resting-places and made, with one accord, for their old shelter. But to their consternation, it had been filled in and the tunnel had been paved over. So they searched about for doorways and arches and eventually they all found shelter.

Bill and his friend Joe found themselves squeezed into the crumbling remains of a cottage at the back of the Clothworkers' Hall in Fenchurch Street, along with Perkins, the older boy whom Bill had endeavoured to stay clear of since the winter. He found Perkins's presence embarrassing and talked as little as possible to him. They shared a small piece of cheese, half a loaf and a couple of wrinkled apples between the three of them. Then, wrapping their coats tightly round them, they settled down to sleep.

Bill had not been asleep long, when he was aware of someone's hands on him. He started up, his eyes wide and terrified.

'Who's there?' he hissed into the dark.

'It's all right, Billy. It's me, Perkins.'

Bill went hot round the neck and a fine sweat broke out on his lip.

'Don't wake Joey,' whispered Perkins.

He slipped an arm about Bill's shoulders and pulled him close, his lips mouthing against the younger boy's cheek while his other hand groped its way beneath Bill's coat, searching him out.

Struggling free, Bill leaped to his feet, shouting, 'Burn an' blast yer, yer filthy bastard! I ain't a judy!'

'My, my!' chuckled Perkins. 'Wot a lot o' naughty words we know. Now, come back 'ere, Billy, an' let's keep warm. I ain't goin' ter hurt yer, yer know.'

'I ain't stoppin' 'ere with you,' persisted Bill, feeling thoroughly sick. 'You're weird. Queer in the 'ead!'

And he shot away into the night, retching and choking as he ran. He didn't stop until he came to the river, where he stood, bent double, panting, still retching and thoroughly shaken.

At last, he grew calm and could think straight again and he walked along by the wharves, until he found some planks piled up, waiting for carting. There was just enough space for him to crawl in and curl up and he fell into an exhausted sleep, until the sounds of river business woke him.

When he awoke the tide was out and he squelched his way through the mud towards London Bridge. He was learning fast that not all folk were the same, they didn't all act in a conventional manner. He hoped there weren't many people like Perkins about. He walked with his head down and his hands in his pockets and occasionally he picked up little artefacts from the mud: a delicate glass scent bottle – Mr Finegold on Petticoat Lane would like that; he might give him sixpence for it – a piece of old pottery, dull russet, green with age, black with slime; he threw it down again; a big bronze cartwheel penny, some ten years old; he pocketed that and it weighed heavy in his coat. He came up the West Stairs of the Custom House, between that government building and Billingsgate Market. Here the aroma of fish was enough to make a man blanch. Bill wrinkled his nose, but was nonetheless fascinated and wandered among the stalls.

All seemed slimy, slippery, silvery chaos and the din of the men auctioning was almost overwhelming in the confines of the narrow street. Great crates of cod, whitebait, smelt, herring and flounder filled all the market space. There were live eels, too, and Bill stood watching them, writhing in their boxes, fascinated by the heaving mass of snake-like bodies. He remained transfixed, until a porter moved him on.

Bill walked slowly, scuffing his boots along the cobbles, his hands thrust deep in his pockets. He stared at all the bustle and activity around him and stopped for a time to watch two men fighting bare-fisted in a narrow courtyard. A little knot of spectators had gathered and Bill squeezed his body to the front of the crowd. The men were small, rather scrawny individuals and were battling out a personal difference of opinion. The sound of knuckles making contact with flesh and bone evoked a strange feeling in the boy. It was a satisfying sound – provided you weren't on the receiving end of it, but they weren't very professional fighters, Bill could tell. He remembered what his father had taught him. One day, he promised himself, he would fight well and maybe take on chaps like Belcher and Mendoza. Meanwhile, there was dinner to be found. And he hadn't even had breakfast yet!

He wandered on up into the City, bored, but not willing to seek out his old friends again just yet. Halfway along

Cheapside, he found a shop with an outside stall attached to it, selling hot currant buns, sticky with sugar, smelling enticingly of spice and peel and plump fruit. His mouth watered, his belly ground within him. There was, momentarily, no one in attendance on the stall, and with a shifty look over his shoulder, Bill grabbed four buns and began to run, stuffing them into his pocket as he went.

But he had reckoned without the observation of a maid at an upper window opposite, and she now shrieked out, 'Thief! Stop 'im! Thief!'

All heads were turned, hands shot out to clutch him, but he wheeled and dived and evaded them all, turning this way and that, dodging barrows and bodies and stalls, and he might have got clean away up a side street had he not tripped on a cobble and pitched over on to his head. He lay stunned for a moment, unsure of what had happened. Then twenty hands seized him, the stall holder among them. He had Bill by the scruff of the neck.

''Ere, young'un. Wot d'yer think yer playin' at?' He appealed to the bystanders. 'I can't turn me back fer 'alf a minute an' one o' these urchins 'elps themselves. They're a bloody menace!'

His audience growled in agreement.

''As anyone gone fer a Redbreast yet?' asked the stall holder, Bill struggling in his grasp.

'Yus,' called someone from the back of the onlookers. 'There's one comin' now.'

A sleek and important-looking Bow Street Runner came striding up, the messenger hurrying breathlessly beside him. He stood looking down at Bill, his red waistcoat a dazzling blaze of colour against the drab inhabitants gathered about him.

'Pilferin', eh?' he demanded.

Bill said nothing, but the irate owner of the buns had plenty to say. The Runner held up his hand.

'That'll do, thank you, Mr Bapton. Let's get this lad off the streets where 'e can't do any more harm.'

And Bill was marched away.

The nearest prison was Newgate and through those dreary portals he was taken. He stared about him in fright. Yet he was awed by the place. He had seen it often enough from the outside. He and his mates often passed the Debtors' Gate and watched the poor inmates begging through the windows for alms.

And now, here he was, on the other side of the great wall. The place was vast and dark, full of narrow corridors and dim recesses, rattling chains and the cries and moans of the suffering prison population. He felt very small and very scared as he was escorted between two turnkeys to a large communal cell, which stank of urine and sweat and rotting food. It contained a large number of prisoners, ranging in age from about fourteen to some thirty years or so.

Bill sat on the bare floor, his head throbbing, trying to collect his thoughts. A trickle of blood oozed from the cut on his forehead, but it was congealing fast and the skin felt tight and dry. He put his hands in his pockets and his heart sank; no buns, no bottle which had reminded him of his 'angel', and no cartwheel penny; all had been taken from him. He rested his arms on his knees and dropped his head on them, thankful that none of the other inmates had bothered him.

How could he have been so careless, so stupid? It was such a basic thing – check all round and above before you lift. But he hadn't remembered to glance up. Well, he was learning fast about life, that much was certain. He sighed and raised his head. The other prisoners were either talking among themselves in low voices or, like him, sitting dejectedly against the wall, awaiting their hearing.

Eventually, the oldest man detached himself from the group and came over to sit by Bill. He was small and wiry, with a foxy face and whiskers to match. He leaned back against the wall.

'Wot they run you in for, lad?' he asked.

'I was 'ungry an' I took some buns,' replied Bill in a small voice.

The foxy man threw back his head and laughed; a short, sharp bark of a laugh. Bill glanced nervously at him.

Foxy said, with a snort, 'They'll be locking up babes fer takin' their mothers' milk next! 'Ow old are yer?'

'Twelve.'

'Cor! An' they run you in fer that? There ain't no justice left in the world. Now me,' he made a grand gesture with his hand, 'I'm in fer makin' a good job of it. Leastways, it would've bin a good job if I 'adn't blundered into a bloody table.' He became melancholy at the recollection.

'Wot job wos you doin'?' asked Bill, all innocence.

Again the fox barked. 'Hah! Ever 'eard of a cracksman, young'un? They're the elite wot bust into toffs' 'ouses. Yer know,' he added, frowning at Bill, 'sharin' out this world's goods a little more even, like.'

He fell to musing and Bill listened with open-eyed wonder.

'Ah, I've seen some wonderful cribs in me time. All them bits o' silver an' brass, delicate china, bootiful paintin's; and the joolery, oh my! The ladies do 'ave some bootiful joolery. All glisterin' an' bright an' shiny; an' sometimes there's gold, too. An' there's often cash lyin' loose. Ah, it's a grand life.'

'You mus' be very rich,' remarked Bill, eyeing the man's good but well-worn clothes and boots.

The fox frowned again. 'Thass the trouble. You 'as ter get rid o' the stuff. An' yer never git top prices; the fences are a tight-fisted race.' He brightened suddenly. 'But I gets enough ter live on an' I've got a couple o' decent rooms an' I keeps meself in wittles an' gin – an' women,' he added, winking. 'I'd like ter join the 'igh swell mob if I can.' He stopped, remembering his position. 'But I doubt if I'll make it now.'

'Wot will they do to yer?' enquired Bill.

The man shrugged. 'Dunno. Boat me? 'Ulk on the Thames? Jug with 'ard labour? Who's ter say?' He drew a deep breath. 'Or I could be topped. Yer know,' and he pulled his neckerchief up to one side in the age-old imitation of hanging.

Bill looked at him in horror. 'Wot? Fer burglin'?' he breathed.

'Oh yes, sonny. But it all depends on the beak an' whether yer've bin 'ere afore or whether yer well known.'

He fell silent. Bill sat thinking how unjust it seemed to hang a man for stealing. It didn't often happen, but it wasn't unheard of. And what if a man was so poor he couldn't buy the necessities of life? What if he had to take things because he couldn't afford to pay for them? But at the same time he thought what a fine line of business the foxy man was in and he hoped with all his heart that he would get off lightly. His thoughts turned again to his father, hanged for housebreaking. He had never really thought a great deal about that. But now he realized, with a faint thrill, bordering on horror, that his father's last hours might have been spent in this very prison.

His father never seemed to have had much money to bestow on his family; food and clothes had always been in short supply. Yet there was usually enough to pay the rent for their meagre, seedy lodging; Bill's mother saw to that. He supposed his father hadn't been paid 'top prices' for the goods he acquired. Bill was sure that his father had been a good cracksman. Hadn't he taught his sons most of what he knew about the subject? Bill knew where his future lay, if he ever got out of this place. It was obvious, it was in his blood.

He must have dropped off to sleep while thinking these thoughts, for he was suddenly awakened by the turnkey hauling him to his feet. He rubbed the sleep from his eyes and blinked, surprised to see daylight still filtering into the grim building. He was marched along passageways, through great doors and across a courtyard and was eventually admitted to a small and stuffy courtroom. It was crammed with the curious public and presided over by a magistrate in a black flowing robe and a powdered wig, assisted by two clerks. Bill was ushered unceremoniously into the dock, where he stood, his hands gripping the ledge in front of him, his legs trembling. He was frightened and he stared hard at his knuckles, concentrating his thoughts upon their bony whiteness. The magistrate looked at him over the top of his pince-nez; and continued to regard him for a full minute, while the public grew restless and the clerks coughed and shuffled their papers. Bill felt uncomfortable and kept his eyes lowered. At last the magistrate spoke.

'What is your name, boy?' he asked.

Bill looked up now. 'Bill Sikes,' he answered. Then added, 'Yer Worship, sir.'

'How old are you?'

'Twelve, sir!'

'Where do you live?'

'Where I can, sir.'

This was getting easy. Bill relaxed a little.

'No mother or father?'

'No, sir.'

'Dead?'

'Yes, sir.'

'When did your father die?' The magistrate had a sly look about him.

''Bout four years ago, sir. He was h–'

He stopped abruptly, aware of the magistrate's intense scrutiny. So this was it. They recognized his father in him. Was he so like him then? He'd never thought about it before.

'I thought so.' The magistrate looked pleased with himself. He turned to the nearest clerk and said in a low but audible voice, 'Charley Sikes's son. You remember the fellow? Hanged for robbery with violence. House in Pentonville.'

The clerk nodded. He remembered that colourful character only too well and the defence he'd put up for himself. The magistrate turned back to the younger Sikes.

'I understand you stole three buns from Mr Bapton's stall in Cheapside?'

'Four buns, sir,' corrected Bill.

The public tittered.

'Why did you steal them?'

'I wos 'ungry.'

The public groaned in sympathy. Most of them knew all about hunger.

'But food must be paid for, boy.'

'I 'ad no money.' Murmurs of support from the public. ''Cept an old penny I found. An' they took it off me.'

'Quite right too. You probably stole it.'

'No I didn't.' Bill almost shouted, but managed to control his voice in time. 'I found it in the mud along the tide-line.'

The magistrate spoke to the clerk.

'First offence?'

'Yes, sir.'

'A month with hard labour in Coldbath Fields should sort him out. Next prisoner.'

The public drew its breath as one.

'Not the 'Steel?' they whispered among themselves. 'Poor little bugger.'

Bill was hurried away and passed Foxy on his way to the courtroom. The man winked. Silently Bill wished him luck. He was escorted back to Newgate, but this time was assigned to a small cell with two other boys about his own age. They greeted him desultorily and asked his name. A turnkey brought in a tray with a flagon of water, three hunks of bread and some rather dry and crumbly cheese. The boys fell on the food like animals and soon cleared the tray, then settled down to talk away the evening. Tomorrow would be time enough to begin their sentences.

FIVE

The next day, the three boys were removed by coach to the House of Correction in Clerkenwell. At Coldbath Fields, their names were taken by a clerk and they were presented before the wily old Governor, Mr Thomas Aris. Mr Aris looked them over, silently, through slitted eyes.

'Not much to be made 'ere,' he remarked out of the corner of his mouth to the clerk. He was renowned for his avarice.

'Where d'ye come from?' he added loudly.

The boys glanced nervously at each other, wondering who should speak first. Bill spoke up.

'Please, sir, I ain't got no father or mother. An' I ain't got no 'ome.'

'Nor me,' added the boy next to him.

'Me father's in the jug an' me mother ain't well. So I bin tryin' ter bring in a bit.' This from the third boy.

'Ye-e-e-s.' The Governor drawled out the word and leaned back in his chair, the slightest hint of a smile on his pasty-looking face.

Bill had a sudden urge to decorate that pale expanse with his fist and had to hold his hands tightly behind his back.

The Governor seemed to be contemplating what he should do with these three young miscreants, but suddenly he tired of the game, sat upright and said sharply, 'Turn 'em out in the yard. They can pick oakum later.'

The boys were hustled from his presence and conducted to a cobbled yard, enclosed on all sides by grim brick buildings, but open to the air. This place of recreation was teeming with the whole gamut of London's criminal classes. Young children, of no more than six years of age, scuttled about among the hardened rogues and vagabonds and dodged about the skirts of the very worst kind of women. There were young people of Bill's own age, too, and the three new boys soon gravitated towards them.

They had to shout to make themselves heard above the rabble and when Bill and his new acquaintances, Ned and John, asked what they were supposed to do in the yard, the established group laughed shrilly and slapped their thighs.

'Do?' shrieked one of the girls. 'We don't do anythink 'ere, 'cept talk an' learn useful things fer when we gets out!'

Bill was impressed by this female. She must have been three or four years his senior and she looked as though she knew a lot. He thought he might listen to what she had to say. There were two other girls and six boys, all in their adolescence, all of them pickpockets, petty thieves, and worse.

The new arrivals were soon accepted and they fell to exchanging information on the different lays they made. Bill had little to offer. He had only forked with any determination since his mother had died; these others had mostly been at it for years and had been up more than once before the beak.

'Tole me I'd get boated next time,' bragged the eldest lad. 'Course, it won't stop me. Besides, I think it might be rather pleasant ter go ter Bot'ny Bay an' make a new life. Ticket o' leave fer good be'aviour, then yer own bit o' land.'

He turned to the girl who had spoken to Bill, and put his hands round her waist.

'You comin' with me, Doll?' he asked and bit her shoulder.

She squealed and slapped him round the head and a brawl ensued. Several adults gathered, roaring and encouraging the couple. Eventually, the boy removed his belt and gave the girl a thrashing. Bill watched, wide-eyed, fascinated, horrified. His father had hit his mother on occasions, but he had never taken his belt to her. At this point, one of the guards sauntered up to see what the noise was about. The boy's mate, seeing him approach, slipped over to him and passed him some coin.

'You ain't seen nothink, 'ave yer, mate?' he said in a low voice.

The guard looked at his palm, shook his head, winked at the lad and returned to his post. Bribery was rife in Coldbath Fields.

Meanwhile, Dolly had been rescued by her two confederates from further beatings and an older woman was taking her inside to bathe her stripes.

'Wot d'yer do that for, Evans, yer silly sod?' asked the boy who had bribed the guard.

'You shut yer face, Carter, an' let me mind me own business.'

'It was 'ardly your business,' retorted Carter, 'more like Joe Public's.'

Evans replaced his belt and took a mock swing at his mate. Carter ducked. ''Ere, wotchit,' was all he said.

A great bell now sounded and the heaving mass of filthy humanity made a dash for the one entrance to the eating hall. Eventually they all found a place to sit down and the meagre rations of boiled potatoes and thin soup were quickly devoured. When all had finished, the women prisoners returned to their rooms, while the men and boys were sent to the oakum sheds. Here they sat on long wooden benches until late in the evening, their hands torn and bleeding from the wicked spike on which they teased out the tarred and tangled rope. By nightfall, their backs were aching and their hands were smarting. Tomorrow would bring stone-picking in the nearby fields or the useless exercise of shot-carrying. And there was always oakum to be picked.

After a supper of watery gruel, evening prayers were conducted amid a constant barrage of noise, over which the prison chaplain did not even attempt to raise his voice. Then that mass of low, lewd viciousness slunk off to its sleeping quarters, where the guards turned a blind eye to the bed-sharing. The day could be spent in bullying and hatching future plots, but the night was for all manner of immorality.

Bill huddled miserably under a coarse, lice-infested blanket and scratched. He wondered how he would endure four weeks of this torture. And he was not a little afraid of the proximity of so many blackguards and scoundrels. Merciful sleep gave him temporary release from his worries, but the days ahead would be difficult to bear.

Within a week, however, the young people had formed a loose gang and had planned to work together on their release, which would come at roughly the same time for them all. They would work certain areas of London, pickpocketing and thieving, operating in threes and fours, and to this end they began practising in the exercise yard. They had no possessions, but made do with stones, bits of oakum, stale crusts, small scraps of bedding, anything to serve as material on which to practise their forking. Soon they were all adept, taking turns at being the 'victim'. The older boys, already experienced, trained the younger ones to use their fingers sensitively. Bill became quite an expert and Evans and Carter, who seemed to be the natural leaders, praised him in their abrupt fashion.

If the older members in the yard knew what was going on, they made no comment. But one day, Bill had just lifted a makeshift handkerchief from Dolly's pocket, when he glanced up to see a pair of steel-blue eyes under shaggy grey brows watching him closely. The man was seated on a nearby step and beckoned Bill over. Bill strutted across, belligerence written on his features, but the man did not admonish him. On the contrary, he nodded and grunted, 'Good work, young 'un. Yer'll go far. I bin wotchin' yer. Yer've got the 'ands for it.' He looked hard at Bill and added, 'But yer don't want ter stop there, do yer? Yer wants ter go fer the big stuff, like wot I done.'

'You a cracksman?' Bill asked.

'Yus.' He spat out a piece of grass he had been chewing. 'You int'rested?'

Bill looked at the man and his eyes sparkled.

'Me father was a cracksman,' he said, 'a bloody good one. 'E taught me a lot. But I know I ain't strong enough yet.'

'D'yer fight, boy?'

'Sometimes.'

'Yer must fight, lad. Build up yer muscles. Ain't no good bein' a cracksman if yer mealy. Yer've got ter be a bully-boy, haggressive, stick up fer yerself.'

Bill stood up, annoyed.

'I ain't mealy an' I ain't afraid o' no one. Jus' let 'em try me. My father was Charley Sikes an' 'e were topped fer 'is livin'. No one ain't goin' ter bully me around!'

'So you're Charley's son, are yer? Well, dam' me eyes. I should've known. Gawd, yer like 'im, boy. No wonder yer good at the old game!'

He chuckled and called to several of his mates. An evil assortment of villains sauntered over, their hands in their pockets. They stood menacingly round young Sikes.

'This 'ere,' said the grizzled man, 'is the son an' heir of our departed friend Charley Sikes.'

The others looked impressed.

'Wot's yer name, lad?'

'Bill,' said the boy.

'Now there's a name ter remember; Bill Sikes. Ah, me boy, I bet we'll be 'earin' a lot more o' you in time ter come.'

'I 'ope not,' replied Bill. 'I intend ter be careful.'

The grizzled head came close to his ear. 'Then keep out o' gangs. They don't work. Three's plenty. Two's enough. An' don't keep canaries,' he added significantly, although this last was lost on the boy.

'But I ain't big enough ter make cracks yet.' Bill recoiled from the blackened teeth and putrid breath. 'I'm stickin' ter fogle-'untin' an' the likes until I've growed.'

The men laughed.

'Thet won't be long, by the look o' yer,' remarked one.

Bill turned and walked away. The grizzled man came after him, grabbed his arm and the pungent aura assailed him again.

'Don't ferget, Bill. You foller in yer father's footsteps. 'E were a brilliant cracksman; one o' the best. But 'is temper ran away with 'im. That's wot led to 'is downfall. You keep calm, an' bc clever. Yer'll be one o' the best, too. Yer've got the makin's of it.'

He released Bill's arm and the boy went back to his friends. Evans pounced on him.

'Woss that ole codger want?'

Bill was non-committal. 'Jus' int'rested in wot I wos doin',' he said. 'Give me some advice.'

'Yus. Well, let me give you some advice,' said Evans, importantly. 'Don't listen ter them ole fogies. We works diff'rent nahdays. Safety in numbers, me boy. We can all 'elp each other.'

Bill said nothing, but throughout the miserable month in the 'Steel, he thought of the old robber's words and about his father. And he wondered why he should want to keep a canary, anyway. He thought, too, about the new 'family' he was to have when they all got out.

The day came at last and Bill, Ned and John were unceremoniously ejected from the dirty House of Correction on to the equally grim streets of Clerkenwell. They were the last of the gang to go and the others had left them strict instructions as to where they could be found. The three boys set off for St Giles's and the Seven Dials rookeries. It was not a long walk, but they were tired and thirsty by the time they reached the centre of that hubbub of vice and they began to look for sustenance. It was easy enough to lift in the rookeries and within five minutes, they had apples, pies and a bottle of beer between them.

Seven Dials was like a rabbit warren. No law held here, except that of the criminal. No Bow Street Runner ever penetrated its depths. It was as tight a community as ever existed in London and Bill and his companions had some difficulty finding the gang's hideout, a public house called The Fig Tree. Eventually they found a cross street, which led into a courtyard between the backs of the houses. The court was alive with ragged children like themselves, mangy dogs, gin-sodden men and sad apologies for the female sex, all heaped together round the midden, staring balefully out at the world through a mist of alcohol and dejection. Rising from this imbroglio was a seedy public house, whose battered, peeling sign proclaimed it to be The Fig Tree.

Inside, it was almost pitch dark. A couple of candles burned low in tarnished metal candlesticks, set on tables at either end of the small, airless room. The boys stepped down and stood blinking, waiting for their eyes to become accustomed to the dark. When they entered, there had been a murmur of voices. Now, suddenly, it was very quiet. Someone pushed back a chair and it grated on the stone floor.

A voice said softly, 'Bill Sikes?'

'Yus,' replied Bill, 'an' Ned an' Johnny.'

'Good. Come an' sit down.'

They joined Evans and the others at the long table in the middle. More spirits were called for and the landlord brought more candles. Dolly sat close to Evans, evidently back in favour and Bill had difficulty keeping his eyes off her blatantly exposed breasts, which Evans fondled from time to time.

'Well, boys,' announced Evans. 'Welcome to the rookery. 'Ope yer'll be werry 'appy.'

Everyone laughed. Evans banged the table with his tankard.

'Nah then. Business. First – who's takin' charge o' these three young forks?'

'I am,' said Dolly, covering her bosom with a shawl, more in deference to the boys' tender years than to their sex. 'I've got a little nest ready for 'em in the room next door to Em's.'

'Good,' said Evans, and looked up at her admiringly. 'Nah, you three. We've got a job planned an' we need some good dippers – clever ones, mind you – ter make a diversion. So this is wot we do.'

And he proceeded to elaborate the plan in which Bill and his young mates were to create a stir by pickpocketing, while the more experienced members set about relieving a certain shop of its more valuable items.

When they had the plan thoroughly in their heads, Carter, who up till now had said little, was detailed to show the boys the lay-out of their expedition, while Evans and Dolly disappeared through a door at the back of the bar. The rest drifted away and the three lads went out into the bright sunlight again with the usually amiable Carter. He remained morose, however, and Bill wondered if Evans and Carter had fallen out, perhaps over Dolly. She really was rather pretty, thought Bill. And he remembered with a thrill the small, bare, swelling breasts, with their tiny protuberances.

A short walk brought them into Dean Street, where some newly erected shops sported bright awnings as protection against the sun. Here they took in the aspect of shop doors, side roads and the odd archway or pillar. When they were all satisfied with the scene, Carter pointed to a jeweller's shop on the opposite side of the road.

'Thass the crib we're goin' for. Pretty things in the winder, ain't they?'

The boys nodded, wide-eyed.

'Come on, then,' continued Carter, 'afore we gets noticed,' and the little group moved off.

SIX

The hoist-lay on the jeweller's shop came off better than they expected. The boys made a marvellous picking job and took to their heels in a matter of moments, a group of outraged citizens hot on their trail. But they quickly lost them in the courts and alleys which led to the rookery and there, no man would follow. They arrived at The Fig Tree panting and laughing and were seated at the table swigging gin and examining their haul when the older boys and girls turned up with their treasures.

That night, the drink flowed freely, the landlord joining in with the celebrations. It was late when they finally dispersed. Two of the older lads fell asleep with their heads on the table, Evans and Dolly disappeared again and Carter followed them, turning to Emily to say, 'Get those three off to bed, will yer? I'll be waitin' for yer.'

And he chucked her under the chin. Emily smiled and put up a hand to his cheek. Then she bade the boys follow her and led them to a dingy room on the top floor of the lodging house adjoining the tavern. Here she had strewn some rough straw mattresses on the floor, together with an assortment of moth-eaten, malodorous blankets.

''Ere y'are, boys. See yer in the mornin'.'

And Emily slipped away, leaving the boys with a candle. They were so tired that they fell on to the straw and were asleep within minutes. But some time later, Bill was awakened by noises from the room next door. The partition was thin and he could hear low murmurings and a rhythmic creaking of the bed. Suddenly, he heard a girl's voice cry out, several times; then there was silence. Bill lay rigid, sweating, the straw pricking through his coarse clothes. He knew who it was and he knew what they had been doing. He pictured them lying there together, perhaps naked. He wondered if Emily's breasts had the same tiny protuberances as Dolly's. Em was plumper, so maybe they were bigger. His entrails felt hot and his small rod stirred. He shuddered in anticipation.

Life with the Lumber Court gang was heady. They had numerous successful forays out into the world beyond Seven Dials and made enough money between them to keep them all in drink and victuals. The following summer, Napoleon was finally defeated at a battle in Belgium, which everyone called Waterloo. The world seemed to go mad with joy and London was in a perpetual state of celebration until late into the year. There were many gatherings of jubilant crowds, which events were greeted with great glee by the inhabitants of all the London rookeries. Here were treasures for the taking, and the lodgings at Lumber Court became transformed daily with festoons of gaily-coloured silk handkerchiefs. The landlord fenced most of their more valuable hauls, the pocket watches, the snuff boxes and the ladies' jewellery; and no questions were asked. Life was good, or so it seemed to Bill Sikes and his peers.

Over the next three years, Bill grew in stature until he was taller and broader than any of his peers.

'Blimey!' said Evans one day. 'I'm 'avin' ter look up ter talk ter yer, Bill!'

They laughed about it, but secretly Evans was jealous. He was a short young fellow and had always felt inadequate. He was intimidated by the big lad, and he feared, too, that he might be passed over by the women in favour of Sikes.

Bill Sikes himself never thought much about his size. He was fit and strong and he would box and wrestle with the other boys and that was enough for him. The fact that there was almost six feet of him he only saw as an occasional advantage, when he wanted to see above the heads of a crowd. He thought it more important to keep his great frame fit and agile, so that it would be of use to him. A man needed to move fast if he was to keep one step ahead of the Law.

But one thing threatened to undermine his strength and that was drink. Since joining the youngsters in Lumber Court, Bill had readily taken to drinking and when he became bored with beer, he switched just as readily to spirits. By the time he was nearly sixteen, he had suffered innumerable hangovers and Ned and John had put him to bed more times than they could remember.

One day, in that year of his sixteenth birthday (he never knew the exact date, since birthdays had not been kept in the Sikes household, but he knew it was some time in the autumn, September or October, he thought) Carter was shopped, caught with cash in his pocket and a silver watch and chain in his hand. Within the month, he was incarcerated in a prison hulk lying off Woolwich, on a seven-year sentence. Emily was inconsolable, weeping openly for a week after Carter was taken. When news of his trial filtered through, Bill offered to go down to the Sessions House for her, to hear what Carter's fate was to be. For the first time in her grief, Emily smiled and touched Bill's hand.

'Thank you, Bill,' she said brokenly through her tears. ''E was your friend, too, wasn't 'e?'

Bill nodded and strode away to the Magistrates' Court in Clerkenwell Green. He arrived late, but managed to push his way into the public gallery, just as the magistrate was summing up. Bill looked across to the dock and tried to catch Carter's eye, but Carter stood, tall and erect, staring straight at his judge. He looked pale and his eyes glittered brightly. When sentence was passed, Carter's face seemed to sag; was it relief that he was not going to the gallows or to Botany Bay? Or was it horror at the thought of seven interminable years on the filthy, stinking hulks? Perhaps he felt that transportation would have been preferable. Bill felt the press of people closing in on him and his neck began to prickle. Carter was being led away and he had to get out of the place, get back to his quarters, back to Emily.

He paused in his headlong flight from Clerkenwell. Why was he suddenly so concerned about Emily? She was nothing more than a friend to him, a sister in crime. But who would look after her now? He laughed to himself; she was perfectly capable of looking after herself and would probably take over Carter's place in their small community and organize their activities just as Carter had done. After all, hadn't she spent most of her earlier years on the streets, looking after herself?

Emily rose to greet him and grasped his arm. He stood with his hands resting on the table, trying to recover his breath. Evans sauntered over to the landlord and ordered a pint of beer for their runner. Bill looked up when he could speak, straight into Emily's anxious face.

'Seven years,' he gasped. 'On a Thames 'ulk!'

He watched as Emily's eyes flooded again with tears. But she turned away and went to sit alone in a corner of the room, quietly brushing aside anyone who came to offer her sympathy. Bill sat and drew thankfully at his tankard, while Evans and the others plied him with questions. But he kept a watchful eye on the lonely figure in the corner.

That night, Bill heard Emily weeping alone in her room. He crept in, feeling his way in the dark. No words were spoken. He lay down by the girl and took her in his arms. And she clung to his body, raising her tear-stained face to be kissed. Bill tasted the salt on her cheeks and on her mouth. Here was his chance at last to prove himself a man. His mind was thrown back to his beautiful benefactress on the frozen Thames and there was a strange association of sensations within him, mingled with pictures in his brain; pictures of a swingboat climbing to its height; of a bawd's enticing words; of boys in a tunnel; of hands groping about his body. He was clumsy and untried, but the surging power he felt carried him on its crest. In a sudden spasm, he found release and the pictures in his brain burst again and again in a series of exploding sparks. It was over in a moment. He lay panting, his head against Emily's breasts.

'I weren't much good, wos I, Em?' he whispered.

Emily smiled to herself. She was aware of the brush of his hair against her face. It was the first time she had seen the top of his head and she fingered the dark waves. To her he was still childlike, his first fumbling efforts expended in the briefest of climaxes. She didn't mind. She knew how to teach him.

'Oh yes, you wos, Bill,' she said. 'An' yer'll get better with practice. Wos that yer first time?'

He nodded and was glad his face was hidden from her. He wondered whether this would be the beginning of something between them, or whether Em would gently dismiss him with the daylight.

But when dawn broke and he slipped from her bed, she stirred and called his name.

'Bill. You will come back ternight, won't yer?'

'Yus, Em,' he said gruffly.

Nothing was said among their confederates, but it was obvious to all that Bill was Emily's new lover. He now received a new deference from the others. Em was the eldest of the group and her word held much weight. The little group waxed and waned, as new members arrived or disappeared. They were usually lost to the gaols of the city and its suburbs, to Newgate, Clerkenwell and Coldbath Fields.

One late November evening in 1821, Sikes was sitting alone in a tavern, working his way steadily through several bottles of beer, liberally interspersed with measures of gin. The others were out on a lay and he had told them he would catch them up later. However, he was so tired and irritable from the previous night's celebration of Dolly's twenty-first birthday, that he had risen much later than he intended and had spent the day kicking his heels around St Giles's High Street and the local taverns. His capacity for drink meant that he could hold his own with the best, though it made him irascible and people steered clear of him at such times. He didn't care. He didn't much like people anyway. Few of his fellow beings had ever brought him anything but misery, he reflected, wiping a trickle of beer from his mouth with the loose ends of his neckerchief.

Suddenly, the door swung open, letting in a blast of cold,

damp air, and a young soldier lurched into the bar, his arm about a plump and pretty, if somewhat dishevelled young woman. Sikes raised his head at the interruption and for a moment stared in disbelief. There was his Emily, her ample breasts exposed, the soldier lurching over her, his hands pawing and searching. Some of the clientele of the tavern now cheered at the spectacle and ribald words of encouragement were bandied about.

Sikes staggered to his feet, his head reeling.

'You bloody well get off my gal,' he shouted. 'Dam' yer bleedin' eyes. Wot the 'ell d'yer think yer playin' at?'

He stood before the stranger, swaying slightly, wishing the room would keep still. Emily's laughter had died and she was unsure and frightened of Bill. She covered her breasts and disengaged herself from the soldier. She put out a hand towards Sikes.

'It's all right, Bill,' she said softly, 'really it is. We all met up tergether down the road an' we come back 'ere fer a drink. The others are on their way.'

Sikes ignored her and gave the soldier a push in the chest.

'Garn, get out, will yer!' he growled.

The soldier, who up till now had looked mildly amused, suddenly turned belligerent.

'Who the 'ell d'yer think you are, yer young pup?' and he doubled his fists and squared his body at Sikes.

'Oh no, please, no fightin',' cried Emily, genuinely frightened. 'Please, Bill, don't!'

But Sikes didn't hear her. He advanced a step nearer and breaking through the other man's defence, struck his fist at the man's chin. The soldier's head shot back and he reeled under the impact. There was a general hubbub from the crowd and the landlord bustled up, flustered and alarmed.

'Ef you please, young gen'lemen,' he whined, wringing his small hands in his large apron. 'Houtside an' hoff the premises, ef you don't mind.'

The two young men eyed each other, the soldier rubbing his bruised jaw. They moved rather stiffly out into the street, like a couple of curs spoiling for a fight. The drinkers from the tavern followed them out and amid cheers of encouragement and howls of sympathy, battle ensued. Sikes cursed his fuddled state, but his blows rang true and he made short work of the soldier, who was all mouth anyway. While the loser's seconds picked him up off the street and bore him away, Sikes seized Emily by the arm in a cruel, tight grip and marched her back to their room in the rookery. Inside, he took off his belt and thrashed her soundly. He never spoke a word, but he felt his whole body shaking, and pictures of his dead mother burst through his brain as his hand descended with each stroke. He hated Emily for her disloyalty, yet he felt passionately about her. Not love, he didn't know what that was, except where it had existed between his mother and himself. He couldn't fathom his feelings and the frustration made him angry.

That night, he slept alone and Emily disappeared from Lumber Court. Sikes missed her; he had enjoyed her generous body and she had taught him much. But his pride had been badly hurt and he felt that perhaps he was well rid of her.

No one reproached him for his actions. No one dared, not even Emily's female friends. Sikes was second only to Evans now. But that dissolute young man seemed to be collecting more women in his lodgings than lifted goods and he left all the working of the little community to Sikes. He nearly always deferred to Sikes and Sikes in his turn would brook no thwarting of his plans, once he had made a final decision. There was no doubt about it, Lumber Court was frightened of the young Bill Sikes. And though the women were attracted by his dark good looks, they fought shy of any intimate association with him. Emily was having her revenge. So he went elsewhere for his women; to Whitechapel, Stepney and the Ratcliffe, among the lowest and the poorest. And he hated them and he hated himself.

Then one day he found himself with a dose of the clap. He went tentatively to the parish doctor, who merely told him it was all he could expect and gave him laudanum and mercury and strict instructions to keep away from the stews.

'Silly ole fool,' said Sikes to himself. 'Wot does 'e think I am? A bloody monk?'

All the same, he was very careful where he distributed his favours in the future.

Then open warfare broke out between Lumber Court and the inhabitants from a small rookery in St Martin-in-the-Fields; an age-old rivalry that had found a contemporary grievance and had spilled over on to the city streets in brawls and ambushes and beatings. It was rumoured that one of the St Martin's swell-mob, the very highest of that order, had been burgled by one of Lumber Court's cracksmen. And then, on a bright spring morning in 1825, when even London had thrown off its winter shrouds and was rejoicing in the clear sky which peered down through the serried ranks of grim housing, word came that the St Martin's gang were on their way. A pot boy from The Fig Tree came bursting into the parlour of that tavern, where a few unshaven faces, Sikes's among them, hung over a late breakfast.

'St Martin's lot,' he panted, jerking his thumb towards the door. 'Comin' this way. I think that sodjer's with 'em, Mr Sikes. Any'ow, they've got chivs with 'em an' they don't 'alf look dang'rous.'

He laughed nervously, but stopped abruptly as he caught the glitter in Sikes's bruised and blackening eye. He wondered idly how many black eyes a man could take. Mr Sikes seemed to be permanently in 'half-mourning'.

The clientele of The Fig Tree rose as one and advanced into the cobbled court outside. Men from the neighbouring houses came out and joined forces with them, mustering what staves and knives they could find. The rival gang turned into the courtyard at this juncture, thinking they had cornered their opponents, and closed in.

Pandemonium broke loose. Women screamed abuse and encouragement from doorways and upper windows, leaning out at the most dangerous angles. Knives and fists flashed in the bright air. Roars and cries, blasphemies and curses filled the narrowness of the rookery and the noise reverberated from the walls all round. The mob swayed back and forth and the filthy cobbles soon became slippery with blood.

No one was ever quite sure of what happened in the end, but suddenly there was a little clearing and the outsiders melted away. Several bodies lay inert on the ground and the women folk at the windows set up a chilling wail. One figure remained on his knees, his hands gripping his thighs, his head bent forward, a knife-hilt protruding from between his shoulder blades. He made a move to reach the knife with his hand, but the effort was too painful and with a cry of agony, he pitched over into the midden.

To an observer in an upstairs room, the women who ran to Sikes's aid might have looked like so many spiders scuttling to inspect a fly caught in their web. In health, he frightened them; injured and vulnerable, he was fluttered round, bathed, comforted, cosseted. With difficulty, they got him to his feet and up to his lodgings, where one of the oldest and least attractive women insisted on putting him to bed and tending his wound. She shrewdly selected her band of helpers and they laid him on his stomach, the knife still embedded in his flesh.

'Floss!' bawled old Mother Legg. 'Get me some 'ot water. Mary Fleet, go an' see wot you can find ter bind 'im up with. An' you, Annie.' Here she poked a finger at a young woman with bloodshot eyes and her hair in disarray. 'You can go an' fetch some brandy from the lan'lord. Tell 'im it's ter cut the pain. Maybe the ole miser'll let us 'ave it free o' charge!'

Having issued her orders, she rolled up her grubby sleeves, summoned the assistance of the two remaining women and, with hands that had not seen soap for some time, removed the offending weaponry from Bill Sikes's broad and muscular back.

Floss and Mary had by now returned with water and bandages and between them they cleaned and bound the wound, pulled Sikes into a sitting position and with a minimum of persuasion got some brandy between his teeth. He spluttered, swore and then cursed again at the pain in his back. Mother Legg laid him on his side and looked at him critically, her head on one side, like an old hen, her eye bright and knowledgeable.

'You ain't ter move, Mr Sikes. D'yer understand? Yer've got ter keep werry still, until that flesh knits tergether again. I'm goin' ter make an 'erb dressin' for yer an' I'll come an' put it on later. It'll take a bit o' time ter prepare. I'll leave someone with yer, jus' ter keep an eye on yer.'

Sikes opened his eyes and stared up defiantly into the old dame's fleshy face. He knew he wouldn't be able to take orders from this hectoring old woman. He'd seen her about the courtyard many a time and knew her for a bossy creature. Beyond her he saw, through the haze, the befuddled features of Gin-Annie and his heart sank. She was always hanging about the entrance to his lodgings; the only local woman who did. What a state he had come to, that he was laid so low that he had to be ministered to by the wretched women of Lumber Court. He tried to speak, to protest, but although he formed the words, they wouldn't come out. Everything was swimming before his eyes. The voices faded. Only the occasional word drifted back to him; until he suddenly felt himself falling down into the black oblivion of unconsciousness.

For a week he lay, poised precariously betwixt life and death. He tossed and turned, sweated and shivered in his fever, babbled incoherently in his delirium. There was no shortage of volunteers to sit by his bed now and someone from The Fig Tree tiptoed up to his room every day to find out how he fared. As the week ended and they had all given up hope of his ever recovering, Sikes came out of his fever and his wound began to heal. In another week, he was sitting up and grudgingly taking medicine and thin, unappetizing invalid food from the hand of Old Mother Legg.

'I'm all right now,' he grumbled one morning, as she placed a bowl of calf's foot jelly in his shaking hands. 'I don't need anyone ter fuss round me.'

'You ain't nowhere near recovered yet, young man,' retorted Mother Legg, her hands on her broad hips, her feet planted wide on the bare boards. 'An' if it 'adn't bin fer us lookin' after yer, yer'd 'ave bin dead the day they struck yer down. Nah. You jus' do as yer told an' eat this good food. Yer'll be no good to anyone unless yer build up yer strength again, now will yer?'

Sikes glared at her. He had an irrepressible urge to laugh in her face. But he knew he dared not. She would think she had some hold over him then and he didn't want to be anybody's fool. Instead, he looked at the congealing mess in the bowl in front of him and felt sick. He leaned back gingerly against the wall behind his bed and shut his eyes.

'I'll eat it,' he mumbled. 'Presently.'

Mother Legg fussed about and Sikes was glad when she eventually took herself off. He knew that but for her he would be six feet under by now, but he wasn't used to expressing gratitude. He supposed he ought to say something grateful now to these women who clustered round to save his life. They wouldn't normally come near him. He was certain Emily's word had ensured that. They stood far off, admiring him, eyeing him, making believe, but they wouldn't come any closer. They were frightened of his temper. They were all used to boxed ears and slapped cheeks, but they only expected it from couples of long-standing, not from a young chap like Sikes. He thought about that now. Wasn't it usual for a man to beat his woman, whoever she was? Why had Emily resented it to the extent that she had left him and spread her poisoned word among the local girls? He was too insensitive ever to know that Emily had been less hurt by the beating than by Sikes's unwarranted jealousy of her. She had loved him and the beating had crushed that love. She was older than Sikes, too, and her pride had been hurt to think that he could treat her so. She had been proud of the tall, dark young man who had stepped into Carter's shoes and she had felt humiliated by his treatment of her.

Outside, the women of Lumber Court, both young and old, were marvelling at Sikes's recovery.

''E's not nat'ral,' mumbled an old crone, her mouth decorated by a single yellow tooth.

The other women, grouped about her doorway, listened with interest.

'You mark my words,' she continued. 'No one could 'ope ter live with a wound like that. I know. I seen enough o' them in me time an' doctored 'em.'

'Well, 'e is a lot bigger an' stronger'n most of our men folk, ain't 'e?' suggested a pretty woman in a drab brown frock and blue apron. 'P'raps 'e's just 'ealthier than them.'

The crone bent her back further and peered up at them all. In a harsh whisper she said, 'Devil's spawn, my dears!'

A shiver shot through the little knot of women and there were gasps of disbelief.

'No one believes that sort o' thing any more,' announced a brazen hussy in a tight and dirty print frock.

The old woman's eyes held her. 'Time will tell, duck. Yer've only ter look at that brow – yer knows that foretells the 'angman, don't yer?'

Several of the older women nodded knowingly and the younger ones began drifting away; they didn't like talk like that. It was disturbing. Besides, Jack Ketch was a bogeyman they preferred not to think about.

Sikes's recovery continued and by mid-summer he was back on the streets, fighting, drinking and well into the burglary business. He and his confederates were making enough to buy themselves little luxuries and Sikes acquired a good velveteen coat and a hat, which, although they had seen better days, nonetheless had sufficient life left in them for him to cut quite a dash in the locality.

There was no doubt about it. Sikes was the unspoken ruler of Lumber Court and he was shown a healthy respect by his neighbours and often given a wide berth if folk met him at close quarters. He became more surly as he grew older and men steered clear of him when he had imbibed more than two or three pints of beer. His aggression he released by a constant round of fighting with those who crossed him and by beating the few women brave enough to share his company. And yet he was known and admired in that dim underworld for his powers of master-minding burglaries. Sometimes he took part, sometimes he detailed others. Always he was successful. Always there was money in his pocket. Ned was still with him, but Johnny had moved on to other pastures. Evans and Dolly had eventually disappeared and Sikes later heard that they had been transported to New South Wales. He thought ruefully that Evans had got his wish at last, but the thought of transportation brought him out in a cold sweat and he resolved always to be vigilant and careful.

SEVEN

On a hot, sticky afternoon in July of the following year, when London seemed to sleep and the putrid streets fairly simmered in the heat, Sikes wandered down towards the river. If he felt deeply about anything, it was about London's river. It was an old friend. He loved its strange, sharp smell, its raucous watermen, the wonderful flotilla of craft always plying up and down; laden barges moving with the tides, small ferry boats shooting the dangerous arches beneath London Bridge; ochre-sailed wherries bringing cargoes from Kent and Essex; and the big merchant ships and tea clippers, which brought in the odour of the Orient.

When he had nothing better to do, or when life left him feeling particularly sore and bruised, he would automatically drift towards the river and lean on the bridge, or sit on one of the many stairs leading down to the water's edge and just watch the continual flow of life along that highway. It never failed to restore him and he would return to the Rookery revitalized.

On this particular afternoon, Sikes sat at the top of Custom House Stairs. He was nursing yet another black eye, earned the previous evening when he fell out with his next-door neighbour in the lodging house, and his face felt bruised and tender. He had a headache and wanted to be alone. He sat watching a Thames barge unloading on Hay's Wharf on the Surrey bank opposite him. The shouts of the stevedores drifted across on the still, humid air and the green-brown waves slapped softly below him. He leaned his aching head against the wall of the stairs, closed his eyes and let the continuity of river life flow over him, soothing him, easing his mind.

It was at times like this when he vaguely wondered whether he wouldn't be better off doing an honest job and earning a regular wage. But wages were so low that he doubted if he would be able to live as well as he was doing now. That was one of the reasons so many in that great city turned to crime, driven to it by sheer necessity. No, he was born and bred to the business and he would remain there. But he would break away from petty thieving. He was twenty-three now, time to think of following in his father's footsteps, time to set himself up as a serious cracksman, to work on cracks that really paid off. But he might need a good contact to get him started, a reliable partner.

He was almost on the point of drifting off to sleep, when his peace was shattered by a cheery but strident voice near his left ear.

'Bonjooer, mate! Wossup? Y'ain't got troubles, 'ave yer? On a fine day like this, too. Dam' me, a man should be up an' about an' enjoyin' hisself.'

Sikes opened his eyes and looked sideways at this intruder, but did not take his head from the wall. All he said was, 'Bugger off! I want ter be alone.'

But the bouncy newcomer was undeterred and sat on the step level with Sikes's shoulder, where he fancied he could command a hold of the situation. He continued his stream of prattle.

'Like I said, a man shouldn't turn in on hisself. Get up! Scurry around! Now me, I ain't sat down all day, savin' to eat me wittles. Too much ter do an' see ter waste time thinkin' an' dreamin'.' He lowered his voice. 'Too many cribs ter be cracked.'

Sikes glanced up sharply and the fellow winked his eye and nodded knowingly, tapping the side of his nose as he did so.

'Oh yus,' he continued, 'I knows a thing or two about that, an' I knows all about you. You're Bill Sikes, ain't yer?'

Sikes turned to look fully at this extraordinary personage.

'Who the 'ell are you?' he demanded.

The other man shot out a hand.

'Tobias Crackit, hesquire. Hat your service, m'sieur.'

Sikes studied him for a moment. He was tall and thin, not much meat on him, and he was probably older than Sikes by some six or seven years. But he had a boyish countenance which made him look younger and his wispy fair hair blew around his head in a kind of cherubic nimbus. He was dressed in good clothes, with a great many ruffles and laces about him, and anyone less like a felon it would be hard to imagine. Reluctantly Sikes shook his hand.

'Wot d'yer want with me, Crackit?'

'Toby ter me friends.'

'I ain't yer friend. Wot d'yer want?'

Unabashed by this rebuttal, Toby Crackit leaned over Sikes's shoulder.

'I 'ear you need a good partner, Mr Sikes.'

'Well, you've 'eard wrong. I'm quite 'appy with meself an' me mates.'

Sikes was not going to give anything away just yet, not till he had the measure of this cove. Toby murmured agreement.

'But they're not a clever lot, the Fig Tree crowd, you must admit. Bin causin' you a bit o' bother lately, 'aven't they?'

'Strike me blind!' exploded Sikes. ''Ow the blazes d'yer know so much about my business?' He felt his fists doubling up.

'I keeps an ear ter the ground,' replied Toby. 'Come on, think about it. I knows yer good at yer job, but I bet yer could do better gettin' away from that lot. Set up on yer own, like. An' yer'd need a good contact, lookout man. Someone ter nose out the lie o' the land for yer. If yer need someone like that – then yer lookin' at 'im.'

Sikes did indeed look him up and down, while Toby Crackit lapsed for once into a comfortable silence, during which he smiled covertly to himself, smoothed his elegant buff waistcoat over his thin belly and stretched out his long legs, crossing his booted feet at the ankles. He stared across to Hay's Wharf, much as Sikes had done, a small smile playing at the corners of his mouth. He waited.

'Where d'yer live?' Sikes snapped out the question.

'Mary'bone.'

'Gawd. Wot yer doin' livin' in a toff ken?'

''Ow d'yer know I ain't one o' the swell mob?' came the rejoinder.

'Well,' replied Sikes, 'yer wouldn't be comin' ter me if yer were.'

Crackit relaxed again. 'All right. But it's a useful place ter be. Yer can watch all the comin's an' goin's an' work out ev'rybody's movements. Werry useful.'

Sikes nodded and made a sudden decision. 'I'll take you on, Toby. On approval, like. See 'ow we gets on tergether.'

They shook hands again and sat for a while in silence, watching the barge opposite swing round with the tide. But Toby Crackit could not sit still for long.

He soon leaped to his feet, brushed down his pale grey breeches and said, 'Well, I'll be off, Mr Sikes. Shall we meet somewhere?'

'Not The Fig Tree,' warned Sikes.

'Nah. There's a good tavern, The 'Are an' 'Ound, in Soho, corner o' Marshall Street, by the work'us. See yer there. 'Bout ten o' the clock?'

Sikes nodded. 'I'll be there. An', Toby –'

Crackit turned in the act of mounting the steps.

'No Misterin'.'

'Fine by me – Bill!'

And he swung away into Upper Thames Street, heading for the City, whistling loudly and tunelessly.

Sikes returned to his former contemplative position. He felt hot and sticky and took off his coat. His neckerchief felt as though it were choking him and he undid it and stuffed it into a pocket. He wondered how long his headache would last and whether he would be able to cope with the inevitable drinking session that evening. He cursed himself for a fool and made a note to keep his fists to himself for a while.

There was no point in staying here. The advent of Toby Crackit had destroyed his peace and, besides, the sun was uncomfortably hot. He swung his coat over his shoulder, pushed his hat to the back of his head and strolled leisurely through the City, thinking about the strange turn of events. He wondered if he had made the right decision in telling Crackit that he would join forces with him. He knew nothing about the man, but he seemed likeable enough, although he thought his mannerisms might grate on his nerves after a while. Still, that was not to be held against the man. If he were clever and quick, not afraid of trying anything; if he was good at nosing out information; then he was just what he needed. He would have to give the fellow a chance, anyway, but tonight he would find out all he could about him.

EIGHT

Thunder rumbled in the distance as Bill Sikes and Toby Crackit made their separate ways towards The Hare and Hound. Toby, always one to pay attention to his dress, was buttoned up to the neck, with a high collar and grubby, once-white stock. His dark blue, cutaway coat revealed an extraordinary pair of loud checked trousers, strapped down under his shoes. He strode along swinging a walking cane and whistling loudly. Several heads turned at the slightly eccentric figure he cut and he winked saucily and tipped his top hat at several young ladies, whose gaze followed his progress.

Sikes, on the other hand, presented a more sober appearance. His linen was no cleaner than Toby's and his drab cord breeches ended below the knee, favouring a style which was no longer the height of fashion. Beneath the breeches he wore grey stockings and a pair of laced half-boots. In this attire he felt comfortable. In deference to Joe Public, he retained his beer-stained waistcoat, but he still carried his coat slung over one shoulder, his hat perched at a rakish angle. Thus attired, he made his way in no great haste towards the Soho tavern and arrived a little after St Anne's had struck the hour of ten.

Darkness was almost complete as he reached the door and he saw flashes of light coming from the South. He was glad he had brought his coat.

Inside, the bar parlour was dimly lit and crowded, the smell overpowering with so many unwashed, sweating bodies, but it was no worse than The Fig Tree. One or two pairs of bleary eyes were raised to Sikes as he walked in, but no one hailed him and he soon found Toby comfortably ensconced in a high-backed settle, a pipe in his mouth, beer and victuals before him.

'Bonsoir, Bill!' Toby's accompanying expansive gesture hit the bottle of beer, which Sikes caught just in time. 'Be seated and let me order you some wittles.'

Sikes sat down in the high-backed seat opposite.

'I'll 'ave a daffy o' gin,' he said, 'an' me belly could certainly do with fillin'.'

These delectable items having been brought by a red-haired serving wench, who dallied a while under Toby's attentions, the two men were left to discuss their proposed merger.

'I ain't comin' ter live in no toff district,' warned Sikes. 'I want ter be able ter disappear when I want. The rookery serves me very well fer that.'

'Oh, I don't blame yer,' replied Toby. 'But 'ow yer goin' ter break free o' The Fig Tree mob? Eh? They ain't goin' ter like losin' their leader, are they? You'd do better ter cut loose an' move helsewhere. There's plenty of other places wot'll do; like Whitechapel, or round by Clerkenwell (good rookery there), or Shoreditch. Nah, there's a good spot. I could tell yer –'

'I know, I know!' interrupted Sikes. 'I was born in blasted Shoreditch. I ought ter know the best places.'

Toby wondered at Sikes's tetchiness and began to doubt whether he had chosen wisely after all. He himself was happy-go-lucky and rarely succumbed to bad temper. He was silent as Sikes attacked his cheese and half-loaf of bread. He puffed thoughtfully at the long clay pipe, sending up a coil of smoke to join the general haze which hung over the room. Sikes finished his meal and sat staring at the pot of gin between his hands.

'You leave me lodgin's ter me,' he said quietly. 'I'll sort out somethink. You tell me about these great cribs yer got in Mary'bone.'

Toby, thus encouraged, forgot his partner's churlishness and launched into an enthusiastic tour of the delights of his district. Sikes let him ramble on, occasionally glancing at him, more to let him know he was listening than as any sign of encouragement or interest.

61

When Toby eventually paused for breath, Sikes asked, 'And 'ow d'yer go about gettin' into these toff kens?'

'Oh, that's where I use me charm,' smirked Toby. 'I chats up the maids an' gets invited down ter the kitchens. Sometimes takes a week or two, but it's worth it.'

''Ow many cracks yer made on yer own?' enquired Sikes.

Toby looked abashed and his reply was almost inaudible. 'Only two this year, Bill.'

'Dam' me!' exploded Sikes. 'Yer'll be a bleedin' pauper at that rate. Wot 'appened? They get wind o' yer?'

Toby shrugged in what was to become a familiar gesture. 'Dunno,' he said. 'Never seemed ter get further than the kitchen or pantry an' some ole codger'd come bumblin' along an' I'd 'ave ter leg it smartish.'

'You ain't very clever, are yer, Toby?' said Sikes ruthlessly.

Toby looked down his long thin nose.

Sikes continued: 'Yer bloody lucky you ain't bin shopped.' He paused and Toby was silent. 'Or 'ave yer?'

Toby nodded miserably.

'Oh ma Gawd!' Sikes leaned back against the settle and shut his eyes.

'Only 'alf a stretch,' ventured Toby.

'When?' persisted Sikes.

Toby was becoming uncomfortable under this cross-examination. 'Las' summer.'

'Yer bad luck, Toby. I don't think it's a good idea fer us ter go into business.'

Toby leaned forward and looked urgently into Sikes's face.

'Please, Bill. Please take me on. I can't work on me own, but I know I could be useful.'

He laid a hand on Sikes's arm, but Sikes shook it off irritably.

'I'll think about it,' growled Sikes.

Toby looked relieved and ordered more spirits for them both. But this time Sikes insisted on paying.

Outside, the storm had broken. Now and then, lightning

illuminated the dingy corners of the tavern and there was much squealing from the female company present. By the time Toby and Sikes emerged, the rain was falling in a continuous sheet and the gutters were overflowing, carrying all sorts of stinking filth. The two men parted, in a rather constrained fashion, and Sikes heaved on his coat, turned up his collar and splashed off towards home. By the time he reached Lumber Court, he was soaked through and the midden had flooded, making a lake in front of the tavern and its attendant lodging houses. Cursing roundly, Sikes splashed through the foul-smelling liquid and gained the shelter of his lodging.

Back in his room, he stripped off his clothes and hung them up around the room to dry. Then he wrapped himself in a blanket and lay down on his bed. But sleep eluded him. First the blanket hairs irritated his naked body, then he felt the movement of the tiny vermin, ever present in the rookery.

He scratched at them and thought about Toby Crackit as a partner. Really, if he was honest with himself, the man was a bit of a fool. And yet he liked him. In an odd way. The fellow's seniority made Sikes wonder what he had been up to in the intervening years. Well, he wouldn't pry any further. It didn't always do to uncover a man's past. He would try to work with him and maybe he could make good use of Toby's patience and his so-called charm. They were certainly attributes which Sikes himself did not possess and they might be a useful foil to his reticence and taciturnity.

'Yus,' he decided at last. 'I'll take 'im on. If nothink else, 'e'll be good comp'ny in a tavern!'

NINE

As it turned out, Toby Crackit and Bill Sikes made a good working pair. At first, Sikes was reluctant to lose his hold completely on The Fig Tree clientele; they had been useful individuals over the years and they had all had a large degree of success. So he kept his lodgings there and ran a loose gang of petty thieves, occasionally using one or two of them on his more difficult ventures. Toby proved as good as his word when it came to insinuating himself into grand houses. And by Christmas, he and Sikes had made several profitable hauls, which, in fact, had proved somewhat difficult to dispose of. The landlord had to go through other means to realize hard cash for the silver and jewels that Toby and Sikes brought to him. But he was a good fence and kept his mouth shut.

But someone in the rookery had not kept silent, and little by little tales began to filter back that the name of Bill Sikes was known to the Bow Street Runners. Sikes wasn't too bothered since the Runners were mostly concerned with detective work outside the City. But it did worry him that there might be an informer in the midst of their little community. He wondered if someone was plotting revenge and thought of whom he might have offended. He gave up, the task was too great! Well, he would have to be even more circumspect than ever.

Since he and Toby had teamed up, Sikes had used the proceeds of their hauls to supply himself with a pistol, a large jemmy, skeleton keys, a glass cutter and a length of rope. These he kept beneath his bed in a black leather bag which never saw the light of day. He was careful never to be caught with such incriminating evidence upon him. His sheath knife, however, he carried with him always, in an inside pocket; he needed some form of weaponry in the places he frequented. Toby used to bring along another barker and a well-shielded lantern. Occasionally, a very small boy, a snakesman, was needed to go through a narrow window to open the door from inside and there was a reliable source of these in Lumber Court, with no questions asked.

Life was proceeding smoothly for the two cracksmen and so far they had evaded the Law. But a hiatus to this existence came abruptly, late one night in the autumn of '26, after Toby and Sikes had made a successful crack over in Charter-house. They had left the goods, by prior arrangement, with a Mr Solomon in Cripplegate, whom the Fig Tree landlord knew, and made their way to The Rainbow in Fleet Street to celebrate their achievement. They were both rather flush with coin at this time and by the end of the evening they were in that inebriated state which lowers the barriers of inhibition and makes fools of men.

They left The Rainbow, and it wasn't easy walking over the uneven paving stones of Fleet Street with several pints of beer in their bellies, to say nothing of the gin with which the evening had begun. And soon these two rogues were propping each other up, shouting directions to each other for the progress of their journey. Toby began singing, but Sikes quickly shut him up.

' 'Ave the 'ole blurrystreet 'wake,' he slurred, clapping a hand over Toby's mouth.

Several windows had opened and irate and sleepy inhabitants shouted admonitions and shook their fists, threatening to call out the constable.

'Go ter bed, yer thund'rin' ole dudder!' Sikes bawled to one particular gentleman, whose head, decorated with a long tasselled nightcap, appeared at a window.

The outraged gentleman almost exploded and withdrew immediately to don his outdoor clothes and call the constable, or whoever he could find.

Meanwhile, Sikes and Crackit had progressed a little further on their tortuous journey and for no apparent reason turned up Shoe Lane. Here their voices were flung back at them from the narrow way and high buildings on either side.

'Need a good piss,' mumbled Toby. 'Pity there ain't a jakes around.'

'Bit fussy, ain't yer?' remarked his companion. ''S always gutter, orawall.'

And the two men found an alleyway in which to relieve their overloaded bladders.

Unfortunately, this call of nature gave the disturbed gentleman on Fleet Street ample time to find a man in authority. He hurried up Shoe Lane in the wake of the parish constable, who called to the two men as they staggered across into St Bride's Street. They tried to increase their pace, but their legs would not keep up with their fuddled brains and Toby Crackit fell down in the middle of the road. There was a shout from behind and an answering one ahead and even in his inebriated state, Sikes could discern the smart and determined advance of four Bow Street Runners. He lugged Toby to his feet.

'Gettup!' he hissed. 'Isser Redbreasts!'

But Toby was too far gone. For one minute, Sikes panicked. He thought of legging it through a side street. But he knew that in his state he stood little chance of escape. So he stood his ground and waited.

The Fleet Street citizen began babbling at the officer in charge.

'If you please, my good sir,' the officer interrupted, 'we'll 'ear wot you 'ave to say on the morrow. In court. Now, gentlemen,' he continued, addressing his two drunken charges, 'if you'll kindly step this way, we can give you a bed for the night!'

And Sikes and Toby were taken firmly by the arms and marched off to Newgate, which was only a short walk away. Inside the prison, they were thrown into a cell and the door closed behind them with an echoing crash.

' 'Ave a good night's sleep, gen'lemen!' laughed the turnkey, as he shuffled away.

'Oh Gawd,' moaned Sikes, more to himself than to the inert form of Toby Crackit. 'Nah we're in the shit!'

Early the next morning, both men were dragged from their cell and shortly found themselves with their heads under the icy water issuing from the Newgate pump. They gasped and spluttered and spat, and Sikes added a few epithets to round off the proceedings. Then they were led away to a dim corridor which connected the prison to the Sessions House. Here they waited miserably in silence until they were called to step up to the dock, where they appeared together.

'Names.' The magistrate had a loud, hollow voice.

'Bill Sikes.'

'Toby Crackit.'

Suddenly the courtroom was abuzz. Every eye was turned on the two men in the dock and the magistrate sat up, very alert.

'Did I hear aright? Did you say Bill Sikes?'

Sikes felt nervous, but stood his ground. 'I did, Yer Worship.'

The beak smiled and stared at him with eyes which bore into him. So this was the fellow whose name kept cropping up lately in connection with so many robberies from the fine houses about the city. He studied the prisoner with interest.

'Well, well, well. And to what, pray, do we owe the pleasure of your company?'

Silence.

'What are they charged with, officer?' roared the magistrate, glowering at the unfortunate Bow Street Runner.

'Drunk an' disorderly be'aviour halong Fleet Street, Yer Worship.'

The magistrate could hardly believe his ears. Here was a notorious robber, together with his accomplice, within the confines of the Old Bailey, and they could charge him with nothing more than being drunk and abusive. He sat in stony silence, while the clerks looked embarrassed and the public kept up a murmur of interest and admiration. Toby saw a female acquaintance and winked at her, which caused some tittering among the other ladies gathered near her. Toby nudged Sikes, who looked in the direction of the public gallery. The brazen hussy pouted her lips and tossed her head at Sikes and a smile began to twitch his lips as she thrust out her bosom towards the dock. The two men were rudely recalled to the proceedings by the strident voice of the magistrate.

'A week in prison should sober them up,' he announced angrily.

And as the guilty parties were led away, he looked across to the officer.

'Keep an eye on them will you, officer. And try to get them on a better charge next time. Bill Sikes is one of the best cracksmen around. Remember that.'

The officer looked embarrassed and affirmed his intention of doing better in the future and then hurried off to supervise the detention.

A week of kicking his heels in prison was pure frustration for Sikes, although it was a familiar enough routine for Toby. Sikes grumbled incessantly and he strode up and down the cell like a prowling tiger. Sometimes he shouted at the four walls, sometimes he shouted at Toby. More than once he beat his fists against the rough walls and never seemed to notice how they bled. Toby sat through it all, silent and patient, waiting for the anger to subside. After five days, the rage suddenly went out of his companion, who came and sat down quietly beside him in the straw. Neither man spoke for a while.

Then Sikes said, 'Who was that fancy piece in court?'

'Eh? Oh, 'er? Thass Charlotte. See 'er around occasional like.'

'She seemed to know you quite well,' continued Sikes.

'Yes. Well. I 'ave 'ad some dealin's with 'er. We used ter fogle-'unt tergether when we was small. She taught me a lot, did Charlotte.'

'I bet she did,' remarked Sikes. 'An' it weren't all pickin' pockets, I'll be bound.'

'Well, she's pretty 'ot in bed, I can tell yer.'

'Yes. She looks it.' Sikes leaned his head against the wall.

Toby went on, 'D'yer want ter meet 'er, Bill? She's cracking good comp'ny.'

'Not at the moment, Toby. Thank you. All I want ter do is get back 'ome an' lie low fer a bit.'

Toby nodded in agreement. Charlotte could wait another day. But he thought she and Sikes might make a good pair. She was handy on cracks, too, and might be a useful asset. He wondered if she were still on the Ratcliffe Highway. When the two men were finally released from Newgate, Toby took his leave of Sikes in Ludgate Hill and turned east to try to flush out his former doxy.

TEN

After his brush with the Law, Sikes decided to lie low for a while. He hung around Lumber Court and The Fig Tree and slept late in the mornings. He hated this inactivity and after a week, took himself down to the river again. He needed a long walk and a change of scenery. There was cash in his pocket and he took the ferry down to Woolwich, with the intention of walking the eight miles or so back. As the little boat plied in and out between the larger craft, Sikes watched, fascinated, at the vista of hulls and masts around him. Looking up from the low boat, the sky above seemed full of rigging and he stared like a small boy, awe-struck, at the sailors swarming over the decks and shrouds, and stevedores heaving and lugging beneath the great cranes on the quaysides.

When the little craft entered Woolwich Reach, another sight met his eyes. There were two, huge, rotting hulks anchored in mid-stream and the men who lived on them were working in the docks alongside, under the supervision of an armed guard. The hulks themselves presented a depressing sight, reduced to a hull and a broken mast each, with ramshackle shelters perched on the built-up fore decks like a pack of cards; washing, strung about the decks to dry, flapped lazily in the smoke which belched from a stove pipe.

Into each vessel would be crammed up to four hundred miserable wretches, sometimes chained, often flogged, always hungry. Sikes had heard fearful tales of those aboard the hulks. It was said that transportation, or even hanging, was preferable to such a fate. He wondered if his old mentor, Carter, had survived. Sikes shivered involuntarily as they slid through the water in the shadow of the *Dolphin*, which already listed to port and which was shored up all the way round with wooden piles.

When the little ferry put ashore at a jetty just beyond the hulks, Sikes turned west towards Silvertown. It was a pleasant walk, along roads which ran through open countryside. At the Isle of Dogs, he had to swing north and cross the River Lea by Bow Bridge, then on through the little villages of South Bromley, Poplar and Limehouse and eventually entered the sprawling skirts of the Metropolis, although one could look to the north and still see open vistas of trees and green fields. He came at last, through a maze of little streets and alleys, to the water-front at Wapping, where stood an ancient public house, The Town of Ramsgate. He climbed the wooden outside staircase and entered the bar-parlour, which looked out over the busy waterway. He ordered an eel pie and a draught of beer and settled down in a seat by the window to enjoy his lunch and the view.

Looking obliquely upstream to the Surrey bank, Sikes could just make out the wharves of Jacob's Island. The tide was out and a great swathe of slimy, green-grey mud was exposed in the creek which formed one side of the Island. Thames barges listed in the mud alongside the quays of this creek and men were busy loading and unloading. Cranes stood out like grasping skeletons against the sky, waiting and watching.

He couldn't have said why, but there was something faintly disturbing about Jacob's Island, something menacing. He felt a shiver down his back and the hairs on the back of his neck stood up.

'Damn an' blast it, Sikes!' he muttered to himself. 'Yer gettin' fanciful. Too much confinement an' not enough hactivity.'

He drew his eyes away and concentrated on his meal. But every so often, his glance would involuntarily seek out that distant prospect, he would see the great predatory cranes and the same shiver would run down his spine.

He was about to leave the place in disgust when an eruption

71

at the door announced the arrival of Toby Crackit and Charlotte. Sikes's heart sank, but he endeavoured to tolerate Toby and his companion and at least he no longer felt drawn to look out of the window.

'Bonjooer, me ole cock!' announced Toby. Sikes almost squirmed. 'Hallow me to hintroduce the charming Miss Charlotte.'

Sikes took the proffered hand and nodded perfunctorily over it. He wasn't used to such niceties, but he thought it would be churlish to act otherwise.

Miss Charlotte was indeed a beauty, but her voice betrayed her origins. She was of average height and slim, without having that undernourished look about her common to most women of the lower classes. She had an almost childlike face, lightly sprinkled with freckles, which she evidently tried to disguise with powder and paint. But her crowning glory was her hair: a mass of wavy, chestnut locks, scooped back from her face and caught with a comb glittering with sparklers. Sikes wondered if they were genuine or paste. He wondered, too, at her attire, which was of excellent quality and very clean. She was not one of the usual class of females who frequented the Ratcliffe. He wondered what she was doing here and even why Toby had attracted her attentions. But the blue eyes held him and he felt already that he shared Toby's interest.

'Fancy meetin' you 'ere, Bill,' said Toby, as he and Charlotte seated themselves at Sikes's table. 'Bit out o' yer depth 'ere, ain't yer? I thought you was lyin' in lavender fer a bit?'

'I was,' replied Sikes. 'An' I've done that now. I came out fer some exercise. I bin up ter Woolwich by boat an' walked down as far as 'ere.'

'Crikey!' exclaimed Toby. 'Nothink better ter do?'

'No,' said Sikes, his tone a touch belligerent.

'Yer must 'ave bin lonely, Bill.' Charlotte's voice held none of the former brazenness which she had displayed in court. She sounded genuinely sympathetic.

'Nah,' replied Sikes. 'I don't get lonely. Plenty o' people about. Plenty goin' on.'

Toby thought the subject needed improving and ordered refreshments for Charlotte and himself. Sikes had another pint of beer. Charlotte was seated next to Sikes and as Toby turned to call the pot boy, she shifted slightly, so that below the table she was squeezed up tight against Sikes's leg and she hooked her foot around his. Sikes was used to such games. He had had enough dealings with women by now to know their wiles. But there was that about Charlotte which made his heart beat faster and which brought a fine sweat to his lip. If Charlotte noticed, she said nothing, but presently she removed her fine walking shawl to reveal what seemed a vast expanse of nakedness. Her dress was cut so low as to be barely decent and Sikes had only to glance sideways at her to see straight down her bodice.

Toby was obviously familiar with all this, for he struck up a conversation with Sikes, upon which the latter could only half concentrate and to which he could give only vague replies. Toby was extolling Charlotte's virtues as a canary, one who kept watch on cracks, and indeed she had, before now, entered buildings and helped with the removal of goods herself, he assured Sikes.

'She's quick, quiet and werry efficient,' he pointed out, 'an' I think we should take 'er on.'

'I ain't sure I want ter split three ways,' replied Sikes.

'It won't be on ev'ry job,' said Toby, 'only really big cracks. Ones where we could do wiv the hextra lookout or pair of 'ands.'

'Well, maybe,' said Sikes. 'But I ain't promisin'.'

Charlotte looked unconcerned.

They finished their drinks and stood up to depart. Toby led the way, clattering down the outside stairs. Charlotte delayed her exit by the simple means of dropping her hand-kerchief, which Sikes retrieved for her. Their hands touched and it was like an electric shock between them.

'Where do I find yer, Bill?' whispered Charlotte.

'Next door ter The Fig Tree. Seven Dials. But it's too far fer you ter come. Where's yer lodgin'?'

'Anywhere an' ev'rywhere,' was the reply. 'I'll find yer.' And she pursed her lips in a kiss and hurried after Toby.

A group seated on a nearby bench had observed this. Now one of the company chuckled and remarked, 'Lucky you, mate. She's fussy where she throws 'er favours, is that one!'

Sikes wasn't at all sure he wanted to be thus singled out, but back in the city, the familiar hum of noise and stench of middens greeted him and he felt less conspicuous. All the same, he hurried home towards Seven Dials, for he had no wish to be spotted by a Redbreast. As he turned into Lumber Court, his heart sank for the second time that day. A brawl was ensuing in front of The Fig Tree. It involved several of his associates and the women were joining in, too, screaming like Furies, kicking, scratching and tearing at any head of hair which came within their reach.

'Wot the blazes is goin' on 'ere?' shouted Sikes above the din and pitched in to separate the main combatants.

For his trouble, a fist came up and bloodied his nose for him. But eventually his presence was felt and the protagonists sheepishly fell apart, while others, who had been egging them on, slunk away to their holes like rats.

Sikes stood surveying them, blood trickling over his lip, a long scratch down his cheek.

'Yer goin' ter bring the Redbreasts down 'ere if you ain't careful,' he announced.

'Since when was you worried about the Redbreasts, Bill Sikes?' demanded one aggressive young man.

'Since I got shopped fer a week. I don't want ter repeat the experience. An' nor will you, if yer've got any sense. The Runners'll be keepin' a close watch on us.'

There was general agreement and the fighters shrank back.

As he walked to his door, Sikes almost tripped over a small, dirty object which moved and revealed a pair of winking black eyes. It was a puppy, scavenging in the filth on the street. It had several cuts on it and was bleeding. Sikes would have kicked it out of the way, but he was suddenly aware of a small group of boys nearby with stones in their hands, waiting. He looked at them defiantly.

'Mind yer don't get 'it, Mr Sikes,' yelled one cheeky urchin.

'It'd be tough fer you if I did,' replied Sikes. 'An' leave the dawg alone. It ain't done you any 'arm.'

'Nah. But it's good sport,' countered another boy.

Sikes turned on him. 'You'd do better ter train yer muscles an' learn ter fight prop'ly,' he said, 'not brawl like the rest o' this mob.'

'Who's goin' ter teach us, then?' they wanted to know.

'I will.' Sikes felt reckless. 'If yer leave off stonin' that there dawg.'

'All right, Mr Sikes. But wot yer goin' ter do with it? Bash its 'ead in, or drown it?'

'Neither,' said Sikes. ''E's mine from now on. So you jus' remember it.'

He whistled shrilly through his teeth and the puppy's ears twitched, though it didn't move.

'Come on, dam' yer,' growled Sikes and the watching boys laughed.

Sikes glared at them and they dispersed. He bent over the dog, wondering if he had gone mad to take on an animal; it could only be a nuisance. But he couldn't leave the thing crawling in the gutter. It was, he thought, a white dog, but it was now such a mixture of blood and dirt, that it was difficult to tell its original markings. He picked it up roughly and carried it up to his room, where he deposited it on the floor and gave it a bowl of beer to drink, in the absence of any milk.

'Yer'll 'ave ter wait till termorrer fer the milkman, mate,' he pointed out to the puppy. 'That'll keep yer goin', though.'

He raked up the embers of the fire and put on a log and a few precious coals, for the evening was growing chilly. Soon he had a good blaze going and the puppy settled in front of it.

'You ain't 'alf a mess,' remarked Sikes.

He heated water in a kettle and used one end of his towel to wash the puppy's wounds. The small creature remained quite still under these unusual attentions, simply winking its bright little eyes at Sikes all the while.

'There,' he said at last, sitting back on his heels. 'Yer look a bit better now. You goin' ter stay 'ere?'

The animal winked again, its head on its paws.

'I'll 'ave ter give you a name, I s'pose.'

He pondered this while he prepared his simple supper and he was still contemplating the matter as he idly fed scraps of bread and cheese and cold bacon to the new arrival. The puppy sat very close to his feet and looked up at him, ready to snatch up whatever he chose to let fall.

The light was fading and the room grew dark, but the little dog's eyes continued to twinkle in the firelight. Suddenly, Sikes slapped his thigh.

'Of course! Why didn't I think of it before? Yer look jus' like the bleedin' lamp the Redbreast carried when I was shopped the other week. Thass yer name. Bull's-eye!'

Bull's-eye sat up and pricked his ears. This sounded good. Did it mean a large, juicy bone, or a dish of succulent beef and gravy? Sikes leaned over and pulled at the puppy's ears. Bull's-eye looked disappointed.

'Yer not a bad little thing, are yer?' Sikes said roughly. 'Yer'll 'ave ter learn ter do as yer told, though. No muckin' about an' no makin' a bloody nuisance of yerself.' He regarded the animal thoughtfully. 'I'd better start trainin' yer now, 'adn't I?'

ELEVEN

Charlotte became a regular visitor to Sikes's lodgings, but she would never let him visit her. He was not really troubled by this and asked no questions of her when she had been absent for several days; he simply assumed she was working the Ratcliffe as a regular beat. So far, the two men had not included Charlotte on any cracks and she had made no protest. But a little before Christmas, she begged to be allowed to help. She wanted to show her worth, she said.

'Oh go on, Bill,' she wheedled, 'let me 'elp. I'm a real good gal at it.'

Sikes looked across the table at Toby. They were sitting in the tavern and had broken their usual rule to discuss the next crack together. Sikes was not at all keen to include a third party, even if it was Charlotte. It was not a big job, but it needed careful planning and perfect timing. He didn't think an additional member to the gang would make for a smoothly run operation.

Toby shrugged. ''S up ter you, Bill. It's only a small job. We don't really need a third pair of 'ands. But she can stand stooge.'

'All right,' agreed Sikes reluctantly, 'but yer'll 'ave ter dress down a bit, yer know. Dark clo'es an' sof' shoes.'

Charlotte smiled and slipped her arm through Sikes's, squeezing it as she did so. She seemed easy to please and he liked having her around.

Their plan was straightforward. An alley gave access to a brick wall, which was easy enough for the men to climb, though they had their doubts about Charlotte.

'I'll wear breeches,' she announced.

The men stared at her, grinned, then burst out laughing.

'Well, wot d'yer think I'm goin' ter wear?' she demanded hotly.

Sikes was in danger of choking on his gin, but Toby said, 'Thass all right. Clever gal. Best thing ter do.'

Charlotte looked defiantly at her partner, but there was a sparkle in her eye.

Once over the wall, they would let themselves in through a rear window, which Toby had already examined, and would then remove cash and valuables which they knew were kept in a small wall-safe behind a picture in the study. Toby had covered the groundwork well and had even discovered the whereabouts of the safe key. It was a simple yet audacious crack and could not fail to work.

Nor did it. Charlotte kept cavy for them at each stage and they came away with their deep coat-pockets laden. They reached Sikes's lodgings exhilarated, breathless and extremely pleased with themselves. Their takings were better than they had hoped. Among the bundle of banknotes was a small ebony and mother-of-pearl box. It was locked, but it took Sikes only a few seconds with a fine knife-blade and his skilful fingers to prise open the lid. Inside was treasure indeed. A pearl and coral necklace, several rings set with diamonds and other precious jewels and a pair of exquisite earrings, small, solid gold, three tiny pear-shaped pearls, surmounted by a sky-blue sapphire. Charlotte gasped as Sikes lifted them from their bed of sapphire velvet.

'I reckon yer could 'ave these,' he said to her. 'There's enough stuff 'ere ter share between us. Only watch where yer wear them, won't yer?'

'Oh Bill!'

Charlotte's eyes misted over for a moment. It was the first thing he had ever given her. She put her arms round his neck to kiss him, but he was embarrassed in front of Toby and shook her off, muttering, 'Not now, gal, fer 'eaven's sake!'

They repacked the jewel box and put it with the cash in Sikes's leather bag and he took it down to the landlord. When he was gone, Toby sat contemplating Charlotte. He felt a little stab of jealousy.

'Yer 'appy with 'im then, Lottie?'

Charlotte nodded.

'Very, Toby.'

'Ain't 'e beaten yer yet?' Toby wanted to know.

He was talking out of turn, he knew, but he couldn't stop himself.

'No!' she replied, surprised and a little annoyed. ''E wouldn't do that, would 'e?'

''E might, if yer crossed 'im. Yer wants ter talk ter some o' the natives o' Lumber Court. They'll tell you a tale or two 'bout Bill Sikes.'

Charlotte looked faintly uneasy.

''E don't brook no nonsense,' continued Toby, 'so yer wants ter be werry careful. Werry careful indeed.'

It sounded like a betrayal of his friend and he regretted the words immediately. Charlotte decided to ignore him and looked at the dainty earrings lying in the palm of her hand.

'It's an 'an'some present, ain't it, Toby?'

Toby nodded glumly and she sensed his despondency.

'Wot's up, Toby? No love life, eh?'

'Never bin good since you left, Lottie.'

Charlotte came and sat on the side of Sikes's bed, close to Toby. She put her arm round him.

'I can always come an' keep you 'appy fer the odd night,' she whispered. 'After all, I ain't ezackly 'is woman, yer know. I still shares meself around.'

'I know.' Toby's gloom deepened. 'An' whoever it is keeps you bloody well-dressed, my gal. You 'ardly need them gee-gaws fer yer lugs.'

'No. But it's somethink from him, innit?' she reasoned. 'So it's special, like.'

Toby pulled a face. ''S'pose so,' he agreed.

Charlotte leaned over and kissed his cheek just as Sikes opened the door. He stood stock still, his eyes narrowed and glittering.

'It's all right, Bill,' Charlotte assured him. 'I'm just tryin'' ter cheer Toby up. ''E's such a dismal fellow ternight an' 'e ought ter be celebratin'.'

Sikes grunted, relaxed and came into the room. Toby hadn't moved.

'We'd best go an' 'ave a drink, then,' announced Sikes and they all trooped down to the inn.

On the strength of their success that evening, Sikes ordered a bottle of port and the three of them sat drinking steadily till late into the night. But there was a tension in the air between them. They were not at their ease and what humour there was in their talk was forced. Toby continued to look downcast, a most unusual state of affairs for him, and Sikes eyed Charlotte with suspicion. For her part, with neither fellow putting himself out to be gallant or even charming towards her, she reflected ruefully upon her other lover and wondered why she bothered with the rookery.

At last, Toby Crackit rose unsteadily to his feet, announcing his intention to return to his dwelling and assuring his companions he would see them before many days had passed.

After he had gone, Sikes seized Charlotte's wrist and hissed at her, 'Wot the 'ell were you up to with 'im while my back wos turned?'

'I told yer, Bill. I wos only tryin' ter cheer 'im up.'

Sikes's angry, smouldering expression scared her and she remembered Toby's words. He continued to hold her with his stare for several seconds. Then suddenly, he lurched to his feet, dragging her with him. She was thoroughly alarmed now, as she bumped into chairs and tables in the wake of Sikes's long stride. The sudden flurry of snow which met them outside made her gasp, but in a moment they were inside the lodging house and she was being dragged up the stairs to Sikes's room. Once inside, he flung her from him and locked the door, leaning his back against it, breathing heavily. Charlotte felt outraged.

'You've never bothered before about my activities outside this room, 'ave yer? Never asked no questions. Never wanted ter know wot else I do with me time. Why you so concerned now?'

Sikes glared at her, his eyes bright with anger.

'I don't care wot yer do out o' my sight,' he growled. 'But yer don't start yer dallyin' with mates o' mine. D'yer hear?'

She laughed at him then. A short, mirthless laugh.

'Dallyin'? With Toby? I wos 'is mistress long, long afore I ever 'eard the name o' Bill Sikes. 'E wos good an' kind an' generous, but 'e couldn't afford me no more, see? I usually only moves in 'igh circles. I'm only 'ere as a favour ter Toby, as an ole friend of 'is. I don't need you, Bill, so don't treat me like you owns me.'

It was a long speech for Charlotte and she sensed she was on dangerous ground. Sikes looked as though he would explode with anger. He walked slowly towards her, an almost devilish expression on his face. She shrank back until she touched the wall and could go no further. He struck her then, hard, once on each cheek. She reeled under the weight of his hand, but kept her balance.

'You'll regret that, Bill. You see if yer don't,' she said quietly.

'An' wot ezackly is that s'posed ter mean?' snarled Sikes. 'Anyone who crosses me gets the same treatment.'

'I ain't ezackly crossed yer, 'ave I? I only told yer a few 'ome truths.'

'They wosn't arsked for,' replied Sikes. 'So you keep yer potato-trap shut in future.'

He went to stoke up the dying fire. Bull's-eye pottered up to him expectantly, but received a kick for his trouble. He crept away under a chair, his eyes winking at this strange master of his. He was learning quickly to sense when Sikes had been on the booze.

Sikes himself, though, was on dangerous territory, for unbeknown to him, Charlotte's other fancy man was a magistrate for the Middlesex Sessions and he was paying her handsomely to play Sikes well and truly into the hands of the Law. Therefore it was necessary that Charlotte should contrive to be contrite and subservient to Sikes and peace was once more restored between them.

In early February, the ground froze solid and there was little housebreaking. Charlotte went pickpocketing and brought in a steady, if meagre, flow of cash, supplemented occasionally from her own private resources.

Confined to his lodgings on account of the winter, Sikes spent much of his time training young Bull's-eye to come to his whistle, to sit, to lie down, to seize, and to guard, all of which activities the dog learned to obey with alacrity and enthusiasm, often accompanied by ferocious and threatening growls. Sikes was well pleased with his new companion.

By the spring, Sikes had almost broken away from his old gang, no longer their regular leader. He had moved to an altogether higher plane. He was deferred to in matters of 'technique' and the youngest prigs and fogle-hunters went in awe of him, but it was with Toby and Charlotte alone that, when the days lengthened, a new crack was planned.

TWELVE

As usual, the job was Toby's conception and was centred on an elegant house standing in its own grounds in Chelsea. It would be a dangerous and difficult crack, involving high, spiked iron railings, guard dogs and a jittery butler with a blunderbuss, all of which Toby had seen with his own eyes during days and nights of careful watching. But Toby had also managed to insinuate himself into the lower regions of the house and so knew the movements and daily routines of the family and domestic staff alike. He had even managed to obtain strategic keys for long enough to take casts and so there would be no need for broken windows.

On a warm May evening, Toby, Sikes and Charlotte sat round a small table in The Fig Tree and laid their final plans. Charlotte was to go ahead at each stage and signal when the coast was clear. She would then stand canary and keep a sharp ear and eye open for any untoward intrusions. The time was fixed for three nights hence and they would wait until midnight, since the evenings were light now.

Charlotte disappeared the next day and did not reappear until late in the afternoon of the appointed day. Sikes was not unduly worried, although he would like to have been sure that she was within calling distance. But Toby fretted about the place. They were in Sikes's room, checking their tools and cleaning pistols.

'Where the 'ell's she got to?' Toby wanted to know. 'She said she'd be 'ere terday in time fer some grub an' a final run-through o' the plan. She should 'a bin 'ere hours ago.'

'Fer Gawd's sake, Toby, siddown will yer, an' stop jitterin' about!' snapped Sikes. 'She's gawn missin' afore an' always turns up like a sore thumb. She ain't a bad gal really. Bit 'oity-toity sometimes, but nothink a bit of a swipe don't put right!'

Toby nodded but said nothing. And at that point they heard a woman's tread upon the stairs and Charlotte came in, breathless, glowing, a little dishevelled and with a strong smell of cigar smoke hanging about her clothes. Sikes sniffed and pulled a face.

'An' where the blazes 'ave you bin, miss?' he demanded. 'Yer've 'ad Toby sweatin' blood 'ere over yer.'

'Not you, then, Bill?' The glance was coy yet challenging at the same time. 'I bin visitin' – as usual. Nothink odd about that, is there?'

There was no reply.

'Well? Any objections?' She stood, threatening, her fists on her hips.

Sikes was unmoved. He turned his head away and asked, 'Did yer get the sackin' fer the spikes?'

For answer, Charlotte threw down the bag she was carrying upon the table. Sikes picked it up and drew out two large hessian sacks, which would buffer the spikes when they scaled the railings. Sikes had been particularly worried about those spikes!

'Good,' was all he said now.

They packed away their equipment and hid it under Sikes's bed. Then they took themselves off to the tavern, where they stoked up with a good meal for the evening. But for once, they drank with caution. For this job, they needed clear heads and ready wits.

Toby's good humour seemed restored with the eventual appearance of Charlotte and even Sikes was in good spirits. But Charlotte herself was as jumpy as a cat. The men teased her, but put it down to nerves, on what was to be a challenging escapade. By half-past eleven, the tavern was full and very noisy. The air was heavy with tobacco smoke and the cries of sharpers, thieves and whores. The three partners slipped out separately and met up in Sikes's lodging again, where Charlotte donned a pair of drab breeches, boots and a large coat, and tucked up her hair under a battered felt hat. Sikes and Toby secured their pistols in their belts and the necessary tools into their deep inside pockets. Charlotte was to carry the travelling bag which would hold their haul.

The three rogues stepped out into the warm night air and set off towards Chelsea at a determined pace. Halfway down King's Road, they saw a pair of Redbreasts sauntering along and quickly turned up a side street. Sikes was not familiar with this part of London, it seemed alien and threatening to him and he began to wish he had not agreed to this particular crack. Charlotte had hardly spoken and Sikes had an odd feeling about the whole affair, a feeling he had never before experienced on a job. He felt oppressed; and the nearer they drew to their target, the worse he felt. Toby, on the other hand, was enjoying himself immensely. He knew the area like the proverbial back of the hand and led them through a grid of neat streets, with clean-fronted dwellings, smart new paint and tree-lined pavements. Sikes wondered how folk could live in such clinical surroundings.

They came at last into Flood Street and here Charlotte was to go ahead and signal them at each corner until they reached the house at the end by the river. From here, the two men proceeded with caution, but there was neither sight nor sound of another human being.

They were drawing close to the river now. Sikes knew the smell and heard the familiar slap, slap of wavelets on the shoreline. But it failed to reassure him. He felt distinctly uncomfortable, as though the night were full of eyes, watching, waiting. Charlotte whistled and the men moved on. Sikes clutched Toby's sleeve.

'D'yer hear anythink?' he whispered, so low that even Toby barely heard him.

'Nah.' Toby's whisper was less practised.

Sikes frowned and peered into the dark. 'You sure there ain't no one watchin' us?'

'Bloody well 'ope not!' chuckled Toby.

Sikes was not amused by Toby's flippancy.

They reached the end of Cheyne Walk, on the very bank of the river and Toby nudged Sikes and pointed to a grand house at a little distance from them, where the lane followed the course of the river and swung south. It was a new house, tall and elegant, with a stuccoed white façade and high bowed windows. There were shallow steps leading up to the front door and a shell porch looked down on them. Well-polished brass lanterns hung on either side of the door, though these had been extinguished. But there was enough of that eerie reflected river light to see that it was indeed a very promising crib. The men could see Charlotte standing outside the front garden, which was surrounded by those fearful spikes which had caused Sikes so much concern. The girl was waving a handkerchief to show the coast was clear. They were about to move on, when Sikes saw a light on their left, moving steadily along the water. The two men drew back into the shadows and waited for the little vessel to pass. Low voices floated up to them and they heard the rhythmic dipping of oars.

The sound faded and they walked stealthily along the lane towards the white handkerchief. Sikes had never felt so uncomfortable in his life. The hairs on the back of his neck stood up and his spine quivered. He could feel eyes boring into his back, but whenever he turned there was nothing to be seen. The lane was not very long, but to Sikes it seemed the longest he had ever walked. His legs ached through trying to step quietly along the rutted way and his body oozed the sweat of fear. He cursed himself for his misgivings, but it didn't help and as they drew level with Charlotte, he sensed that the crack was going to go horribly wrong.

It was at the moment when his eyes met Charlotte's and he saw her glance slide away from him, that the world came down about his ears. A very young and untried Bow Street Runner was so overcome by the wanted man passing him within inches that his unbridled enthusiasm set the action of the Runners prematurely in motion. He leaped from his well-concealed hiding-place and pinioned the big man's arms to his sides, yelling for the rest of the detachment, as he struggled to hold his captive. Sikes, enraged, fought back violently and managed to secure a hold on his pistol, which he fired. It failed to find its mark, but it served as a spur to utter confusion for the next few minutes. Bow Street Runners appeared out of the dark from all directions, lights went on in the house, dogs began barking, windows were thrown up and night-capped heads emerged in a mixture of outrage and curiosity.

Outnumbered, Sikes and Toby were eventually over-powered and handcuffed, amid volleys of curses from Sikes and useless placations from Toby. As they were led away to a carriage, waiting in a side street, Sikes passed the treacherous Charlotte and down the years floated the voice of the old robber in Coldbath Fields: 'Don't keep canaries.' The old rogue had been right about everything. Charlotte stood lean-ing against a pillar in front of the house and stared at Sikes with such an enigmatic expression on her face, that he could not tell what she was thinking. He thought she must have friends in high places and that she was being well paid for this filthy business. He wondered if she was pleased with her efforts and whether she really hated him so much.

The would-be burglars were hustled into the coach and driven away to Marlborough Street to await their hearing. Two sullen Redbreasts sat opposite them and not a word was exchanged between the four men. Above the grinding of their carriage wheels, Sikes and Toby heard the young Runner outside being berated by his superior.

'You bloody young ass! You knew damn' well we was to wait till they was inside the 'ouse. Caught red-'anded, they could've swung!'

Sikes glanced across at Toby, but he couldn't see his expression in the dark.

The man continued: 'As it is now, we've only caught 'em with tools and pistols in their pockets. We got no proof they was a-goin' to break in. 'Cept the judy's word. An' who'll believe the word of an 'ore? Eh?'

By the time the carriage drew up outside the Marlborough Street Court House, the young man was suitably chastened and Sikes and Toby knew exactly how the whole episode had been planned and how it should have culminated.

They stepped down on to the street and Sikes glanced up at the portals of the Sessions House. At that moment, he felt an uncanny calmness, amounting almost to a numbness inside. His brain refused to work and he felt neither fear nor anger. Toby, on the other hand, was reduced to a whimpering heap and Sikes could smell the fear emanating from his accomplice. But, as yet, they had exchanged no word or glance.

Inside the building, their particulars were noted and they were handed over to a pair of prison officers, who marched them through the dim, echoing corridors of despair and flung them, without ceremony, into a low-ceilinged police cell, occupied by half a dozen other felons awaiting trial. Toby lay cowering in the filthy straw, but Sikes retained his balance and leaned against the cold wall. He toed Toby, none too gently, with his boot.

'Get up, yer chicken-'earted pillock! We ain't in the salt box yet.'

Toby came slowly to his feet and lay back against the wall beside Sikes, his eyes closed, a pained expression on his face. There was a light burning beyond the bars and Sikes swept his glance over the other inmates of their cell. They were mostly asleep, although one pair of very young and scared eyes looked balefully out at him from a huddle in the far corner. The place stank of human excrement and urine and Sikes felt a momentary wave of nausea. But it passed and he tried to collect his thoughts. He turned his back to the bars and the turnkey sitting guard outside and addressed Toby in a muted whisper.

'Yer know who blew the gaff, don't yer?'

Toby nodded miserably. His eyes remained shut.

'I thought she wos trustworthy.'

'So did I,' moaned Toby.

'Well, we know now who 'er fancy bloke wos – the bleedin' beak!'

Sikes spat out the words in disgust. The anger which should have been there earlier was creeping in now and with it, the first faint waves of fear, though he would never show it.

'Bloody little 'ore,' he muttered. And, 'Hell's fire an' damnation!'

He shouted these last words and several heads lifted sleepily and frowned at him for disturbing their slumbers. He bent close to Toby's ear.

'We bin nibbed, but we ain't bin topped. An' with any luck, we won't be, neither. They ain't got a lot to 'old us on.'

Toby stared straight into Sikes's eyes. 'Only your name, Bill,' he said quietly.

THIRTEEN

The light streaming through the tall arched windows of the great courtroom fell in tangible shafts upon the barristers' polished desks and the magistrate's high bench. Dust motes rose lazily, as a busy clerk shifted papers and ensured all was ready for the morning's session. To him, it was another day, like all the rest in his monotonous life. But word of the impending trial of Bill Sikes and Toby Crackit had spread fast and when the doors to the public gallery of the Marlborough Street Magistrates' Court swung open two days after the would-be robbers had been taken, there was a surge into the courtroom, a press of sweating bodies, a buzz of expectant humanity. There was a good cross section of the community represented, but there was also a large number of women present. The regular old crones were there, the ones who had little better to do than satisfy their morbid curiosity. And a handful of younger females, who had undertaken the walk from Seven Dials to Marlborough Street that morning. They had been drawn to witness the fate of one of their number. No matter how they felt about him, no matter what he had done, or how he had treated them, he was one of them. And they would give their support.

As a distant bell struck ten, a side door opened to admit the magistrate and jury and numerous court officials. The public rolled its eyes at the flowing robes and antique wigs. The gentlemen of the court seated themselves and there was shuffling of papers and some low discussion. Then the first prisoner was called. Toby Crackit, looking pale and drawn and not a little frightened, stumbled into the dock. His eyes looked wildly round for a familiar face, but they saw nothing and nobody. The bright light from the tall windows was blinding after the half-dark of his cell, where he had spent the last forty-eight hours.

'Name?' The magistrate's voice was sonorous.

'Toby Crackit.'

A murmur of recognition from the public gallery. Toby didn't live in the rookery, but they knew him for a friend of Sikes. The magistrate now called for witnesses.

The first was the officer in charge of the Runners who had effected the arrest in Chelsea. When he had been sworn in, the officer was asked for an account of the night's events. He launched into a lengthy narration, which the magistrate was obliged to interrupt from time to time.

'My youngest recruit, Yer Worship, Mr Josiah Spoils, was, you will understand, within a few inches of the haccused and being an henthusiastic young man, like most young men, you will understand, he could no longer contain himself and so seized the hopportunity which presented itself.'

He paused for breath and the magistrate leaped into the breach.

'And your man apprehended one of the accused?'

'Yes, Yer Worship. The big feller. The one we've been after.'

'But you found nothing on him?'

'No, Yer Worship. No stolen goods, that is.'

'And what did you find on the accused?'

'They both carried a pistol and various housebreaking tools.'

He indicated the barkers, which Sikes and Toby had so lovingly polished the day of the crack. They lay now on one of the tables in the middle of the court – exhibits for all to see, along with the other equipment they had taken with them. Toby fixed his eyes on the pistols now and kept them there. They were like old friends. The only friends he had in that impersonal place. He studied the polished wood and the metalwork. It had taken him a long time to clean his. Sikes's was easier. It had silver mountings and was really a very fine duelling piece. He was not a little envious of his friend, but it

91

seemed irrelevant now. Neither of them would get their property back again. Toby was filled with a sadness, a regret, a longing. But he didn't know what for. Only that he wished he could go back in time and undo the preparations for that crack. He would have left Charlotte out of it as the number one priority of his plans.

The officer was droning on again.

'This man carried a bull's-eye lantern, too. But it was obvious what they was up to and we know from the woman exactly what was planned. However, she was found holding a travelling bag, Yer Worship, so she should be held an accomplice.'

'Leave the woman out of it!' roared the magistrate.

There was a stunned silence and the Bow Street officer looked abashed. The magistrate lowered his voice.

'We know about her,' he said, dismissing Charlotte with a flick of his hand.

Toby shifted uneasily in the dock. He hoped Sikes would not be able to hear from where he was waiting in the dim corridor below. He remembered only too clearly their conversation that morning as they broke their fast. Sikes had seemed sullen and seething with an inner, bitter hatred.

'If I ever get me 'ands on that woman,' he had growled between his teeth, 'I'll slit 'er throat, s'welp me God I will. I mean it, Toby.'

Toby had shuddered. He didn't doubt Sikes's word, but he hoped no one would overhear, or it would not go well for Sikes. He was recalled now by the magistrate addressing him.

'Toby Crackit, did you plan to break into Lord Barrage's house on the night of May the twenty-fourth?'

'Yes, Yer Worship.'

'With what intent?'

'To relieve 'Is Lordship of some of 'is waluables.'

Laughter from the public gallery. Toby hadn't meant to be funny. The magistrate glared first at the public and then at Toby. The tittering ceased.

'Did you plan this alone or with the other accused?'

Toby hesitated. But there was no point in denying anything. They had been caught red-handed and Charlotte had supplied the beak with every detail, even down to how they would fence the swag.

'With the other accused, Yer Worship. An' Miss Charlotte,' he added.

The magistrate said nothing, but Toby squirmed under his icy stare.

'You may stand down. Call the next prisoner.'

Thankfully, Toby descended the stairs in the company of his gaoler, his knees shaking. He passed Sikes on his way up. They exchanged glances, but no word. Toby could not help but admire Sikes's confident manner. He wondered what was going on inside his friend's head.

As Sikes appeared in the dock there was an excited murmur among the public and a great deal of interest shown by the female members. He stood, with an insolent air about him, looking defiantly at the sea of faces. There was a moment's delay as the clerk and magistrate conferred together and Sikes had time to view the lofty room, with its tall, arched windows, the faintly ecclesiastical air about the place, with its congregation in tiered rows.

'What is your name?' asked the magistrate, without even looking up.

'Bill Sikes, Yer Worship.'

There was a renewed murmur. The magistrate's head came up and he quizzed Sikes through narrow, reptilian eyes.

The same questions were thrown at Sikes as at Toby and the Bow Street officer was delighted to be given the opportunity to recap on the activities of the night in question. The young recruit who had pre-empted the proceedings was also invited to give his account of events. Thinking it over, Sikes was grateful to the young man. For if the Runners' plan had gone ahead, he and Toby would be facing a much more serious charge than he hoped would be brought. There was more evidence given by the owner of the house and by his various servants, who had been disturbed by the fracas. Sikes was bored and let his gaze drift across the earnest faces in the gallery. He spotted several acquaintances there and nodded to them. Suddenly, he was aware that he was looking at a very familiar face. He couldn't believe it at first, but there she was, sitting in the public gallery as bold as brass. The woman who had shared his bed and who had sold him to the Law. She wasn't even being called to give evidence. He felt the anger and hurt and resentment boiling up inside him like an earth tremor. He thought he would explode. He knew he was shaking and he was deaf to the drone of witness and magistrate alike.

'Hell's fire!' he bawled across the courtroom, almost crying with rage. 'Wot in Gawd's name is that bloody 'ore doin' 'ere?'

There was a horrified silence. Sikes stood trembling from head to foot, his manacled hands gripping the dock so hard that his knuckles shone like naked bones.

'You bitch!' he roared again. 'You bloody, two-faced, lyin' bitch. I 'ope ter Gawd they lock you away. 'Cos if they don't an' I gets my 'ands on yer, they'll really 'ave somethink ter swing me for.'

'Silence!' The magistrate's voice matched Sikes's own. 'How dare you speak out of turn! And to address a lady so in public. Officer, take him away.'

'She ain't no lady, an' well you know it!' retorted Sikes over his shoulder, as he was bundled down the stairs.

Toby, waiting below, shut his eyes and his heart sank. They might have got away with a fairly short prison sentence if only Bill had kept his mouth shut. This latest outburst might cost them dear.

Sikes sat down on the bench beside him, shaking, sweating and breathing heavily. Toby looked at him, but Sikes's head hung down, his arms across his knees, and he said nothing. They waited some three-quarters of an hour or more, while further evidence was heard and the jury debated the case. At last, they were summoned back together. Charlotte was no longer in the room.

The magistrate summed up in a few words and passed sentence.

'Tobias Crackit, you have been found guilty of intent to enter and burgle and of being in possession of such tools which would assist you in such a crime. You are therefore sentenced to two years' imprisonment, with hard labour.'

A little groan from the gallery. Was it approval or disappointment or even sympathy?

'William Sikes.'

The public leaned forward in expectation.

'You have been found guilty of intent to enter and burgle and of being in possession of such tools which would assist you in such a crime. You are also charged with contempt of court. Neither is this your first offence.'

Sikes thought back to the day he was shopped for stealing buns. It seemed a long time ago. Surely they would have forgotten by now. Someone was setting the magistrate up, he was sure. And he could guess who it was.

'It is therefore ordered and adjudged by this court, that you be transported upon the seas, beyond the seas, to such place as His Majesty, by the advice of His Privy Council, shall think fit to direct and appoint, for the term of seven years.'

If the public gallery was surprised, Sikes's surprise was even greater. Shock might better describe his reaction. He stood staring at his judge, a pained, almost questioning expression on his face. And, oh God! he could feel the hot tears smarting in his eyes.

'Stand down,' ordered the magistrate.

And Sikes and Toby were once more ushered along the cheerless stone corridors to their cell. Sikes moved in a numb daze, trying to come to terms with his sentence. Toby seemed to accept his. After all, he would be a free man again in twenty-four months. But seven years! I'll be thirty-one when I gets back, reflected Sikes. If I live. If I ain't ship-wrecked or eaten by savages or don't get some 'orrible disease.

''Ow the 'ell did we come ter this pass?' he murmured as they were thrust into the cell and the gate was secured on them.

Toby shrugged his thin shoulders. He didn't want to think about it any more. He already felt guilty for having introduced Charlotte to Sikes and for agreeing to let her into their work. He might almost be said to have urged her participation. But how could he know she would turn King's Evidence? She had been an old friend, they had grown up together on the streets. How could she do such a thing to them? He avoided Sikes's eyes. He couldn't begin to imagine what mental torments his friend must be enduring, but he knew that they must be far worse than his own. And Sikes was not a man to take such things lightly. He wondered if Sikes would ever come back from wherever they sent him, whether he would ever see him again. He glanced across at the silent figure opposite and felt a stab of pity and not a little fear for himself.

Sikes sat slumped against the wall, a figure of dejection, his elbows on his knees, his head against his great fists. His thoughts were in turmoil. He kept seeing a picture of the hulks on the Thames and he could hear snatches of conversation from the dim past: 'Yer 'as ter cross the Hequator, Bill, an' yer gets bleedin' 'ot.' 'Takes weeks ter git there.' ''Spec' most of 'em die afore they reach Bot'ny Bay.' He shuddered involuntarily and looking up, met Toby's mournful gaze.

'I 'ope someone looks after the dawg,' he said irrelevantly.

Toby nodded. 'One o' The Fig Tree'll take 'im in, no doubt. If anyone comes from there, I'll make enquiries.' Toby hesitated. 'An' Bill . . .'

Sikes's eyes bore into him and he cringed before their fiery glitter.

'Good luck,' he added weakly.

FOURTEEN

On a day of blue sky and brilliant sunshine, William Sikes was taken from his cell and conveyed, by means of an official coach, to the docks at Woolwich. He barely had time to bid farewell to Toby. They shook hands and Toby noticed the set of Sikes's jaw. The man was evidently struggling with his emotions. Toby's turn would come later that day, but as he watched his friend walk from the cell, he wondered when he would see him again; if ever. How quickly they had come to all this. Was it really only four days since he had been fretting about Charlotte's failure to turn up on time? So much had ended in such a little while. But he must not allow himself to become maudlin. At least he had a foreseeable goal to work towards. Not like poor Bill. Oh Gawd, he thought, 'ow will 'e ever manage it?

At Woolwich, Sikes was handed over into the charge of a military officer who was given his particulars. The officer looked him over, a sneer on his face.

'Bet you give 'em plenty of trouble,' he said, noting Sikes's belligerent expression.

The big fists doubled automatically. The officer called for the services of his farrier and Sikes was shackled, an iron band secured round his waist, two more about each ankle, connected by a chain; and a second chain running up from the first to the band at his waist. Thus, his long stride was curbed and he would have found it impossible to effect an escape, even if he could have evaded the many guards about the place. His strong physique was to make him the target for all kinds of heavy lifting and carrying and he was immediately turned into the dockyard and set to work with a multitude of other miserable souls, working hoists, humping great planks of wood and shovelling barrowloads of stone.

It took Sikes some while to accustom himself to his shackled legs and he suffered the ignominy of numerous falls before he learned to adjust his stride. But it was difficult in the extreme to lift a heavy load and keep his balance, weighted down and restricted as he was by the chafing irons. By the end of the day, his ankles were raw and his back ached. He had begun work in the early afternoon and had not stopped until dusk. He had tried to strike up conversation with some of his fellow prisoners, but received only desultory grunts or nods for his trouble. Their dejection was beyond belief and Sikes feared for his own sanity.

When the order to halt work came, an audible sigh of relief went up from the men and they shuffled into ranks to be counted. Sikes could see a little flotilla of rowing boats streaming out from the hulks to the shore and presently, he found himself on one of these, passing into the shadow of one of the great wrecks, which was to be his home for the next eight weeks. He gazed around him. The hulk was big, certainly, but there was a vast number of men to be accommodated on it. Sikes was allocated to a group to make up a mess of six and he shuffled down to the galleys with them, where they prepared their supper. This consisted of ship's biscuit, a small piece of ox cheek each and a helping of rice, all of which they were permitted to take up to the decks to eat, if they so wished.

The water accompanying their repast was clean and cool, one concession the authorities had made, and the men downed copious quantities after their day's labours.

'Beer termorrer, chaps,' remarked one of the group in an attempt at cheerfulness. 'An' porridge, bread an' cheese.'

'We 'as two burgoe days a week 'ere,' explained a small, wiry man, much given to coughing and wheezing. 'They're sort of feast-days.' He grinned, displaying more gaps than teeth. 'Wot's yer name, mate?'

'Bill Sikes.'

The cheerful fellow leaned close to Sikes. 'Wot you 'ere for?'

Sikes regarded him with some disdain. How could these men discuss their guilt as though they were on a Sunday outing! Sikes no longer felt like talking anyway. His neighbour shrugged, but pursued his questioning.

'You 'ere fer good, or Bot'ny Bay?'

'Dunno. I bin boated, I know that much.'

The man sighed. 'Lucky cuss,' he breathed. 'Most of us is 'ere instead o' gaol. Mind you, it ain't so bad really. Place is inspected reg'lar, an' the food's 'olesome – usually. Quarters is a bit cramped, but yer gets used to it. An' once yer used ter the chains, the fresh air's good ter work in.'

'Don't they unshackle us at night?' Sikes wanted to know. His new companions laughed.

'Swipe me, no,' replied his informant. 'They used to 'ave 'ammicks 'ere. But they was so okkard an' so many of us fell out o' them, they give us straw beds an' a blanket instead. Not much room though. Bit cosy, like.'

And his listeners all roared with laughter. Sikes did not share their amusement. He did not relish the thought of sharing all his hours with his fellow prisoners.

The thin man now had a coughing fit and had to be slapped on the back and given water. Two of his mates took him to his sleeping quarters. Sikes sat on a bench, staring into his empty mug. The two remaining members of the mess seemed to have forgotten their mirth and gloomily introduced themselves.

'Will Spiring.'

A tall, gangling young fellow, with a clear, open mien, thrust out his hand, which Sikes took and was surprised at the strength of the grasp.

'I've been boated, too, so we may be seeing a lot of each other.'

Sikes looked into his face for a moment. The expression he found there was almost calm. There was none of the wild, hunted expression about this young man. He certainly didn't look like a criminal and he didn't speak like an East Londoner. He seemed a cut above the others and, although he couldn't have said why, Sikes found himself warming to Wilfred Spiring. And he smiled – the first smile on his face for many days.

Spiring continued, 'This is George Biddulph.'

George did not shake hands, but looked up and nodded at Sikes. Spiring winked and Sikes guessed there was something about George which he would hear in due course.

'An' the other fellows?' he now enquired.

'The thin one, who coughs, is Matthew,' replied Spiring. 'Matthew Dancy. Nice chap, but he won't last long. The hearty fellow is Charlie Finch, the cheerfullest rogue out. And the other one is Jack Garlick. You need to watch him; he's quick and sharp as a razor.' Spiring frowned. 'Bit shifty, too,' he added, 'but they're all here to serve their sentences. You and I will only be here for a few weeks, please God.'

They finished their supper just as Jack and Charlie returned.

'How is he?' asked Spiring.

Charlie pulled a face. 'Coughin' blood again. 'E won't last long, poor bugger. Ship's surgeon's with 'im now, tryin' ter pour physic down the poor blighter's throat. Kill 'im quick, they will.'

They all sat silent for a few moments, while Charlie and Jack finished their half-eaten meal. The evening glow was fading and out on the shores of the river, little globules of light winked, crazily reflected in the rising tide. Sikes listened to the water slapping at the hulk and to the desultory talk around him. He looked up at the soft velvet sky and had a sudden urge to sleep out in the open, knowing his sleeping space was going to be cramped and airless, but presently he saw the guard emerge from the fore deck, and in a few moments they were all being hustled below.

The deeper into the bowels of the ship they descended, the closer the air became and a foul stench reached Sikes's nostrils. As they clattered and clanked their way to the very bottom of the ship, Sikes realized he was to be housed in the bilges themselves. His stomach heaved and he fought down the rising nausea. The mess to which he belonged was hurried along to the far end and Sikes was shown his bed – a straw mattress, covered in grimy, striped ticking, and a coarse, grey blanket. He thought fleetingly of his room in Seven Dials and it seemed he had been living in luxury before now.

Physically and mentally exhausted, he lowered himself carefully on to the mattress and closed his eyes, hoping for oblivious sleep. But sleep was evasive that night. A lantern burned at one end of the deck and Sikes was able to study his surroundings. The height between decks here was only a little over five feet, and most of the prisoners had to walk bent double. He had a sleeping space of some eighteen inches, with Spiring on his left and the wily Jack Garlick on his right. Beyond Spiring was George and then Charlie; and on Garlick's right was the ailing Matthew Dancy, whom Sikes could hear wheezing and bubbling alarmingly. His other bed-mates seemed to have dropped off to sleep straight away and Sikes lay listening to the varied sounds of breathing. Occasionally, there was a rustle of straw or the clank of iron, as someone tried to find a more comfortable sleeping position.

Sikes lay and his thoughts drifted. Would anyone look after Bull's-eye? He was fond of the little brute and would miss his companionship. He hoped no one would kick him out on the streets again. Perhaps Toby would be able to look after him when he got out. But that would be two years hence. Poor old Toby. Sikes really shouldn't have taken him on. He was bad news. Yet he liked the fellow immensely. He could say he was his best friend, though he would never admit to it. They had got along so well since that day when Toby had discovered him sitting by the water's edge. It seemed a lifetime ago now.

The warmth was uncomfortable and the smell was overpowering. Sikes wondered how long he would be able to stand it. He was sure he could feel the occasional lurch of the hulk as it settled in the mud, the tide licking around her creaking timbers. He felt a cold pain in the pit of his stomach and he began to sweat. He struggled up from his mattress and shuffled down towards the guard sitting sleepily by the lantern. The soldier looked up.

'Where you goin', mate?' he asked.

'I want ter be sick,' muttered Sikes, breathing heavily.

The soldier indicated a porthole on his right and Sikes staggered over thankfully to the open window and fresh air.

FIFTEEN

The days which followed brought no respite to the spell of hot weather. The nights were a little cooler, but Sikes dreaded them. To return each day, after hours in the open air, no matter how hard he had been worked, nor how exhausted he might feel; to return to the bilges, reeking of stagnant water and human outflow, and to the tiny, claustrophobic sleeping space, filled him with fear and loathing and it became a constant dread with him. After a few nights, he managed to overcome the sickness, but there were others who didn't and the sleeping hours were punctuated by snores and mutterings, coughings and retchings, and the incessant creaking of the rotten timbers. Sikes had lived in plenty of hellholes before, though this was surely the worst. He could hear rats scampering along the deck joists at night, squealing and grunting, and more than once felt the scuttle of a small body across his legs. And after two days on the hulk, he was covered in flea bites and his hair was already crawling with lice.

But though the nights were a torment, the days were a mixed blessing. Under the glare of the sun he toiled, but at least he had been issued with a hat to protect his head, a sailor's bonnet, which, with his dark stubbled chin, gave him a faintly nautical air. At half-past six each morning, Sikes and his fellow prisoners were roused from their slumbers and they filed to the upper deck, where they sluiced their heads in buckets of cold water. This was followed by a breakfast of bread and water. Sikes stared at the hunk of bread in his hands on the first morning, but Spiring nudged him.

'It's all you'll get, Bill, and it's wholesome. Food's the one good thing here.'

They spent most days digging ballast from the Woolwich bank and wheelbarrowing it to waiting carts. Sometimes Sikes and other big men would be required to heave and carry timbers and Sikes was glad to put his muscles to good use, though it was not easy work with the encumbering irons.

On a particularly warm night in late July, Sikes lay on his mattress looking up at the timbers above him. Sleep had eluded him again. The sounds around him drifted into the background of his consciousness, apart from Matthew, whose terrible wheezing and coughing punctuated his thoughts every now and again. He was thinking how stupid he had been to trust Charlotte, and he cursed himself for being softened by a woman. He had not understood until his trial just how devious a female could be. She had been in liaison with the very beak who had tried him and she had wormed her way into Sikes's confidence over the months, surely getting encouragement and orders from her pet magistrate. Certainly she reaped rewards from him, for it must have been he who supplied her with her finery and it was obviously with him she had spent the missing days when she was not with Sikes. At first, Sikes had raged and fumed at the knowledge, then he had put it completely out of his mind. Now he could think rationally – and quietly curse the woman who had trapped and betrayed him with her sensuous body. One thing he vowed: he would never trust a woman again. Never.

He dragged his thoughts away from Charlotte and listened to Matthew Dancy. Poor devil, he thought, 'e ought ter be in isolation. Give us all the spit!

Suddenly, there was a terrible noise from Matthew. Sikes and Jack Garlick shot from their beds, their chains bruising their legs, and came to his side. The poor man's eyes were staring and he was trying to speak, but his lungs were full of blood and a fearful rattling was all that issued from his throat. Sikes and Garlick sat him up between them to try to ease the pain and pressure on his chest. Several of their neighbours roused sleepily, curious to know what had disturbed them. The guard hurried towards them and Jack called over his shoulder to him, 'Fetch the surgeon, quick!'

But the surgeon's offices would not be required. For, as Jack turned back, Matthew gave a last cough and the blood poured from his mouth in a torrent and the poor fellow fell back dead in his mates' arms.

Sikes stared unbelievingly at the lifeless body he now held. 'So much blood,' he whispered in astonishment.

Jack Garlick looked across at him. 'Yer'll see plenty more if yer 'ere long enough,' he growled. 'Come on, lay 'im down. No more we can do.'

Both men were spattered in Matthew's blood and the guard ordered them on deck to make use of a bucket of water. Having rinsed their clothes as best they could, they stood a moment looking over the river. Jack glanced round furtively, but there was no chance of escape. There were guards every few yards around the hulk and they were certainly not asleep.

There were no lights on the shore now and they could see the faintest pink haze over the eastern horizon. The ever-moving waters around them were dappled with its reflection. And Sikes wished Matthew could have died up here in the fresh air, with dawn breaking around him. He shook his head to rid his brain of such sentimental thoughts and carefully descended to his sleeping quarters once more, Jack following in his wake. The surgeon was there and Spiring and Charlie Finch were preparing to remove the corpse. There was a hush about the place, although by now most of the men were awake, and a hundred pairs of eyes were turned towards the little knot of activity at the far end of the deck.

Matthew's body having been removed, Sikes and Garlick settled down on their mean beds again without any expectation of sleep. Wearily, Sikes began scratching beneath the iron band at his waist, where the fleas had created a girdle of bites. Even in his lodgings in Lumber Court the vermin had never been this bad. And at least there he had one change of clothes and could put a comb through his hair to rid himself of some of the ubiquitous lice. He could feel them now, wriggling on his scalp, just moving the strands of hair sufficiently to create a constant irritation. He scratched again, heaved a sigh and shut his eyes. Perhaps sleep would come after all.

SIXTEEN

By some quirk of his human make-up, Man can adapt to the strangest things, although an individual will swear on oath that he can never accustom himself to extremes. And yet, by the end of that hot July of 1827, Bill Sikes had fallen into an uneasy routine aboard the prison hulk at Woolwich. Perhaps he had just naturally fallen into the terrible dejection which was so much a part of the hulk convicts' lives. He worked hard and long and silent. And if his fellow convicts thought him unduly morose, they refrained from saying so, but left him to his thoughts. Spiring he did talk to and Sikes learned that the young man had been convicted of fraud. He was the youngest son of a respectable trader in Piccadilly, but had been cut off by his father for proposing to marry a milkmaid from a farm in Kensington. Wilfred, left without an allowance and with no trade to his name, since he had refused to become an apprentice, seized the first opportunity of making money that presented itself. It was unfortunate that the opportunity came in the guise of a couple of rogues making ill-gotten profit from a false lottery scheme. He had met them in a club and they had, at first, seemed the essence of respectability and they soon won the young man's trust and confidence. By the time he realized what their undercover activities were, it was too late. Before long, the three were arrested in the very club where they had first met. All three were sent for trial at the Old Bailey and the two perpetrators were hanged. Wilfred, when it was proved that he was a minor accessory to the crime, a mere tool in their hands, was committed to seven years' transportation.

'I don't think I shall be able to survive it,' remarked Spiring one day, as the two men sat eating their dinner, a little apart from the rest of their mess. 'Leaving Sarah was bad enough. But to leave everything one has known and grown up with . . .'

Sikes nodded gloomily. 'I wouldn't grieve over a wench if I were you,' he advised. 'Never trust a woman. Thass the reason I'm 'ere. Betrayed by a bloody female, I wos.'

Spiring looked at him with interest. He was the complete antithesis to Spiring. He had been brought up on the streets of London, an orphan from an early age, worldly wise from his tenderest years and surviving by a life of crime. And he looked it. Spiring, on the other hand, was a respectable, middle-class citizen, who had been educated, gently reared and had had the opportunity to better himself even further. Neither knew what had made them drift into each other's company, out of all the hundreds of men on that hulk. But there was an empathy between them, which they both felt.

'What exactly were you done for, Bill?' Spiring asked tentatively, for he had not yet got the measure of this dark and silent man.

' 'Tempted burglary,' said Sikes quietly.

He proffered no more information and Spiring asked for none. He nodded and drained his mug, his chains rattling against the rim as he raised his arm. He was about to rise, when a captain of the guard, flanked by two soldiers, approached him and Sikes.

'Prisoners William Sikes and Wilfred Spiring?' he asked sharply.

Spiring stood up smartly. 'Yes, sir!' he answered. 'Wilfred Spiring.'

Sikes looked up languidly, holding the officer with his eyes.

'Are you William Sikes?' repeated the captain.

'Aye,' growled that gentleman.

One of the guards seized him roughly and hauled him to his feet.

'Stand to attention when addressed by an officer,' he barked.

Sikes's eyes blazed and his jaw was set. He clenched his fists in an effort not to hit the wretched soldier.

'I have orders to convey the two of you to the barque *Asia*, now riding at anchor in the Port of London,' continued the captain, sensing trouble. 'She will sail from there on the first of August under Mr Edman, and is bound for Hobart.'

The two prisoners exchanged glances.

'Where the 'ell's that?' demanded Sikes.

The officer surveyed him with contempt and said menacingly, 'Van Diemen's Land.'

PART TWO

NANCY
1817–1835

Excess of sorrow laughs. Excess of joy weeps.
Joys impregnate. Sorrow brings forth.

William Blake: *Proverbs of Hell*

ONE

◆

St Leonard's church stands in the south-east corner of the parish of Shoreditch and casts its shadow over the boundary with Bethnal Green. Those who lived within that shadow would, if they deigned to attend church at all, make their way there of a Sunday, rather than walk the quarter of a mile or so to their own parish church of St Matthew. The vicar of St Leonard's was glad to see them there, though the ravaged grey faces ranged before him in the cold, hard pews saddened him deeply. He was an old man now and had seen so many of those pinched and ragged sheep arrive in his poor parish – and seen them depart after an all-too-short sojourn there. The churchyard was full of them. And those who did survive clung to the pits of life with their raw fingertips, struggling to keep their heads above the edge, to breathe the air of freedom. But too often they fell back into the great chasm of crime, their grimy hands clawing at the empty air. There were few of his parishioners who had not brushed with the Law at one time or another. They all knew want and hunger, and they knew, too, the dreadful temptations offered by crime – a full belly, coins to jingle in the pocket and a quenched thirst.

A stone's throw from St Leonard's, lying in the neighbouring parish, was a dirty, ramshackle alley, which went by the enigmatic name of Sweetapple Court. It contained some twenty tenements, ranged on either side of its cobbled street, with a row of eight more at its far end. At its entrance was a seedy-looking ale-house, whose doors and windows were as caked in grime and dust as any of the tenements. Down the centre of the alley ran the inevitable midden, thick and blocked. And strung from one side to the

113

other, high overhead, were lines of cheerless washing, hanging limp, cold and damp on a bleak December afternoon in 1817.

A long-legged, mangy dog snuffled about in a pile of garbage halfway down the court and there was intermittent shouting from a noisy group of men at the ale-house door. A few ragged children, cold and miserable-looking, hung about, waiting to seize any chance of a dropped coin, an unguarded pocket. But the natives here were too careful with the little they had. It was not a good hunting ground and the children knew they would do better further afield. But they had no shoes and it was so cold on the cobbles. And soon it would be dark. They would stay in the court and play; throw stones at the scavenging dog; or pick over the same pile of refuse. There might be a stale crust to eat or an old withered apple.

A cry sounded from below the street level. It was a woman's voice, a voice in distress. The children looked at each other, their eyes large and vacant, lacking in lustre. A girl turned her head in the direction of the sound, but the others shrugged and turned back to their desultory waiting game. The cry came again, urgent, painful.

'Thass the girl wot's got a bun in 'er oven,' drawled the child who had first taken note of the sound. 'Reckon she's 'avin' it. Muvver says she needn't expect no 'elp from 'er. Muvver says she's got wot's comin' to 'er.'

The children's eyes followed the source of the sound and they nodded sagely. They weren't interested in another entrant to their dismal world. There wasn't enough food to go round as it was.

In the basement of one of the tenements, a young woman was labouring to give birth. She was frightened and alone, having neither husband nor family. She was not even sure who the father of her baby was. All she knew were the great waves of pain which enveloped her and the uncontrollable urge to expel what had grown in her belly over the months. When at last she thought that her body must split asunder, the baby's head emerged. She struggled up and looked with

114

wonder at the bloody sphere between her legs. She stretched out her hands and touched it. It was warm. There was life there. Another spasm. Another great surge down and the baby slithered out and on to the reddening sheets of her bed. She lay back exhausted, tears of relief streaming down her face. She wanted to sleep, to let her tortured body recover, but she knew there was much to do. She took a length of narrow ribbon from her hair and tied it tightly round the cord. Then she looked about her squalid room for something with which to cut it. Almost to hand was the small knife with which she had been preparing food when her pains had started. She had dropped it on the floor. How long ago that seemed. If she could stretch out from her low bed . . . Yes, she could just reach it. The lifeline severed, she lifted her baby and smacked its back. With a gasping intake of air, the tiny mite screwed up its face and wailed. The young mother smiled through her tears and held her daughter close, in a possessive, protective embrace. There was an old shawl lying on the bed and she wrapped it round the infant and held her to her breast. The baby rootled greedily at the source of nourishment offered. The mother winced as she felt her womb contract within her. In a little while, she put the babe to the other breast and again came that painful but natural process, which begins the restoration of the female body after birth. At last the child fell away from the nipple, her eyes closed, a thin trickle of watery milk running from her rose-bud mouth. The mother gazed at her, her eyes full again with hot tears. So much trouble to bring into the world, she thought, so much trouble to keep alive. 'Ow am I goin' ter do it? There was another contraction within her and she felt the afterbirth slip away from her. She was tired, so tired. And the babe was asleep. She lay back on the pillow, the child in her arms, and blessed sleep enveloped her.

She was awakened by her daughter's cries for food again. It was dark outside and she felt cold and uncomfortable. She must try to clean up a little and wash the baby, too. Shakily she rose from her bed and fumbled for the tinderbox. With trembling hands she lit a candle and then poured water from the ewer into a basin. She unwrapped her child and began gently washing off the traces of birth. But the water was icy cold and the baby screamed. The young woman sighed and removed the worst of the stains, before bundling her baby up again. Her own poor body needed washing, too, and there were other things to be cleared away. But she was still so tired and so cold. And the baby needed feeding again. While the infant suckled, she thought of what she must do. She knew she could not keep the child and she had formed a plan, which she must carry out soon, or her resolve would soften.

But she felt bad inside. Something was wrong, a deep, grinding pain, when she thought all the pain was over. Nevertheless, this other business must be seen to first. She would worry about herself later. As the babe drifted off to sleep again, she pulled from the bed an indescribable garment, which might have been a man's overcoat. It had been of good cloth once and still afforded her some warmth at night. She parcelled up the baby and staggered up the rickety flight of stairs with her to the front door of the house. She looked to right and left, but there was no one in sight, although she could hear voices nearby. She stumbled over the cobbles until St Leonard's church loomed up before her, dark, but not unwelcoming. It had stood for Christianity for centuries, although the building itself had been replaced more than once. Its tall, porticoed spire reached up into the night sky and it seemed to carry her hopes with it. She knew the vicar to be a kindly man and that she could trust him. Him and their Maker.

Looking furtively about her all the time, she went up the shallow steps to the main door of the church. Suddenly, she saw the flash of a lantern and moved back behind one of the great pillars which supported the porch. It was the parish constable going his rounds, but he had not noticed her and thankfully she watched as he went out through the iron gate of the graveyard. If she were seen now, her plans would be foiled and she would be sent to the workhouse, from which there was little chance of escape.

When the constable was out of sight, the young mother laid her sleeping bundle by the great oak door of the church. She stood up but did not move away. It was a cold, dark night, she reflected, and the child might take a chill. She looked towards the mass of the vicarage, so secure and comfortable, and she changed her plan. Gathering up her burden and gasping with the mounting pain in her belly, she staggered to the vicarage door. A last look at the little one she had given life to; one kiss on the soft cheek. Momentarily, she laid her own cheek against the warm golden down of the baby's head. And then laid her gently on the doorstep, rang the bell and melted away into the night.

TWO

The next morning dawned bleak and cold and an icy wind blasted its way down Kingsland Road. In her filthy room in the Sweetapple Court tenement, the abandoned baby's mother lay dead in a great pool of her own blood. No one found her for two days and then she was hastily shovelled into a pauper's grave.

The baby was removed to the parish workhouse, the vicar's wife herself insisting on swathing the tiny mite in copious shawls and carrying her up the long road to the same formidable pile that Bill Sikes had bravely entered a little over four years earlier. She was shown in with some deference, and conducted to the matron's quarters. Here, the vicar's wife reluctantly handed over the infant, who had slept throughout the rocking motion of the journey, but who now objected to being transposed, and set up a feeble wailing.

'I'm afraid she's taken little nourishment,' admitted the good lady from St Leonard's. 'I doubt the mother fed her more than once or twice, if she managed that.'

The matron scowled down at the red, puckered face almost lost in the superfluity of shawls. She pulled some of them off and thrust them abruptly towards the vicar's wife.

'Too 'ot, that's wot she is, ma'am. You've made 'er too 'ot, bundlin' all them wrappin's round 'er. I'll pass 'er over ter the baby farm. She'll be well looked after.'

The vicar's wife handed over two silver coins with a brief 'Thank you'. The matron stared hard with her little bird-like eyes, bit the coins and pocketed them. The vicar's good lady touched the baby's soft hair and turned away.

When her visitor had departed, the matron of the workhouse called for the maid, who brought thick cloaks and bonnets. Together they set their faces against the wind and carried the infant to the baby farm. This was no more than a none-too-clean cottage off Rope Walk, in an area bordering on Hackney, which was still pleasantly rural in aspect. The cottage, large and substantial, had been acquired by the parish some ten years earlier. It stood in its own plot of ground, but at this time of the year, the garden looked dead and untidy, with the remains of vegetables drooping and yellow in the cold air, and unpicked fruit rotting and shrivelled on the tree. The gate was broken and had to be lifted to be opened and the path was unswept and slippery with green slime and fallen leaves. Up this uninviting path the matron and her maid stepped cautiously and rapped at the door. It was opened a crack by a very small child with tangled hair and frightened eyes. Its mouth was surrounded by sores and it sucked a dirty thumb, no doubt the cause of the sores. The child was dressed in frocks and its wispy hair curled down its neck, so that it was impossible to decide on its gender.

The matron pushed her way imperiously into the room beyond, followed by the maid clutching the baby. The room was squalid and made dim by ragged curtains drawn across the windows. There was an all-pervading stench of stale urine and the air was full of cries coming from an assortment of infants, ranging from three babes in wooden cradles, set close to the big iron range, to a sharp-looking, pinch-faced kinchin of some seven years. Two young ladies of drab appearance seemed to be in charge of these orphaned chicks, but an older, grey-haired woman bustled forth from an adjoining room and greeted the workhouse matron obsequiously.

'Another one on the parish,' announced the matron. 'A girl child, a day or so old. Don't s'pose it'll live. Looks a puny little thing. But I dare say she'll do all right in your 'ands, Mrs Grey.'

'Oh that she will, ma'am,' replied Mrs Grey, 'if I 'ave anything ter do with it.'

The baby was handed over, yet again. In her short life, she had changed hands four times and barely known her mother's breast. No wonder she writhed and screamed in her cocoon of shawls, beating the air with her tiny fists. Mrs Grey took her with surprising gentleness into her arms.

'Poor little mite. She's 'ungry, no doubt. Lottie! Fetch some warm milk an' a cloth.'

One of the drab young ladies complied and began dribbling milk into the baby's mouth with a corner of the cloth. Soon the child began to suck and, although the procedure was slow, presently the long-lashed lids drooped, the tiny mouth closed in a perfect bow shape and the baby slept. The matron, meanwhile, took her leave, her job well done, her conscience salved.

The baby did not die, but against all odds clung to life with a stoutness and tenacity which surprised all the inmates of the baby farm. Not least among these was a pretty four-year-old, called Betsy, who took a particular delight and interest in the latest arrival. The other babies were boys and Betsy had no interest in them. She wanted a baby sister and had prayed every night for one, ever since she had been taught to form the words which would ascend to her Heavenly Father. And now, at last, it seemed her prayer had been answered. A tiny baby girl had arrived and she would be Betsy's very own sister.

She soon learned how to feed the baby and, on rare occasions, helped with its bathing. But on the whole, bathing was not a regular practice at Mrs Grey's cottage, although the children must wash their hands before meals and before going to bed. And a quick swill of cold, sometimes icy water over the head was deemed good for the constitution, if not for the cleanliness of the inmates.

One day, when Betsy was helping one of the older girls to change the baby's napkins, she stopped suddenly, her little hands hidden in the soapy water with which they were cleansing the child.

'Meg,' she lisped, 'wot'th 'er name?'

'Don't think she's got one, Bet. Wot shall we call 'er?'

Bet thought for a moment and then said, 'Can we call 'er Annie? I like that name.' She gazed at the baby. 'Pwetty Annie,' she crooned.

Her companion laughed and called out, 'Mrs Grey, young Betsy 'ere wants ter name the babe Annie. Is that all right by you?'

Mrs Grey came into the room, a pile of grimy clouts in her arms.

'That'll do nicely,' she agreed. 'That's a good name for 'er, Betsy.'

And so Annie she became. She was christened on Christmas afternoon that year at St Matthew's church in Bethnal Green, along with the three boy babies with whom she shared the warmth of the kitchen range.

After the service as they trudged back to Rope Walk, Betsy clung to the edge of Mrs Grey's cloak, as the good woman clutched Annie to her bosom in protection against the icy blast.

'Mrs Gwey,' Betsy said, her voice low and confiding, 'Annie will be *my* sister, won't she?'

'Why, bless the child,' laughed Mrs Grey. 'She'll be sister to all of you.'

Betsy frowned. 'But I want 'er to be *my* sister.' Her voice trembled and faltered. 'Just mine. I pwayed for a sister and God sent 'er ter me. Please let 'er be mine. Please.' And her blue eyes filled with tears.

Mrs Grey was a sentimental woman at heart and she looked down fondly on the small girl, so independent in her way, yet so desperate for affection and attachment. She nodded now.

'All right, Betsy. She's *your* sister. But, mind, you mus' share 'er, yer know. And,' she looked at the eager, upturned face, 'you must always 'elp ter look after 'er.'

Betsy clasped her small hands together and her face shone.

'Mrs Gwey, I s'all always look after 'er. As long as I live.'

Mrs Grey smiled and nodded. As long as she lives. Ah me, she thought. I wonder 'ow long that'll be!

Annie proved that she was a survivor. When fever carried off two of the boy babies and one of the older children, Annie's fight for life was astonishing to all concerned. The parish doctor declared that she should have died along with them, but here she was in the spring of the following year, sitting up, sprouting teeth and getting under everybody's feet. Betsy adored her and even the other children found her an endearing child and as Annie was weaned on to more substantial food, they would save little scraps from their meals with which to ply the baby, to show their own favour. Betsy kept a watchful envious eye on little Annie, but she did not resent her foster-siblings' attentions. Hers was a generous and loving heart, and her delight in her new sister overflowed into a generosity with others.

And so Annie's early years passed more tranquilly than her departed mother could have possibly hoped for. She was fed and clothed, kept warm and loved. And if she was not always clean, at least her little heart was pure and for the time being her mind was unsullied by the great world which lay beyond the confines of the cottage garden.

THREE

As the years passed, Annie and Betsy grew even closer. They were like true blood sisters and Annie had no reason to doubt that Betsy was anything different. The children at Mrs Grey's cottage were lucky. They had a roof over their heads, clothes for their bodies and plenty of noisy company. If their meals were wanting in substance, then at least they fared better than the workhouse inmates, and Mrs Grey's babes grew up healthier than many in the parish. By the time they left her at seven or eight years of age to enter the dreaded workhouse, they knew their prayers and had some idea of what was right and what was wrong. But this upbringing did not prepare them for their launch into the world of the pauper, the world of the streets and the gutter, the backways and the under-cover places of London, where most of them would end their days. Sometimes Annie and Bet used to peep between the gaps in the neglected garden hedge and watch the passers-by. They would see farmers and labourers, carters and trades-men, poor tramps and evil-looking vagabonds. They saw it all from the safety of the Rope Walk cottage, never dreaming that they could ever become part of that passing parade of humanity outside.

When she reached seven, Betsy should have gone on to the parish workhouse, but since she and Annie were so insepar-able and Annie was too young, Mrs Grey pleaded with the beadle and the matron for her to be allowed to stay. So it was agreed that Betsy should remain at the baby farm until Annie was seven, at which time both girls would be handed over to the workhouse.

Bet's relief at this decision was so great, that she went immediately in search of her little companion to impart the

good news. Annie, being just three, did not really understand, but she knew that something good and special had
occurred to make Bet so happy.

When Annie was five, Betsy explained it all again to her.

'But I don't want ter go ter the work'us,' wailed Annie.

''Ush,' whispered Bet. 'We don't want no one to 'ear us.'

They were hidden behind a large and shady clump of
rhubarb, growing in a corner of the garden, its stems huge
and woody and quite useless for consumption. But it made a
wonderful secret den for the two children.

'Can't we run away?' asked Annie, her blue eyes round
and wide with anticipation.

'Wot, leave 'ere? Leave Mrs Grey? Anyway, where d'yer
think we'd go, silly?' replied her companion.

'Well,' Annie continued, warming to her subject, 'we
could slip out o' the garden one day, run across the fields
and down into the City. We'd be a long way from the
work'us there and no one would ever find us.' Her eyes took
on a dreamy look and she rested her chin on her interlaced
fingers. 'I'd love ter see the City – all them 'uge 'ouses an'
churches. Oh, an' all the ladies in their beautiful dresses,
like in the songs Mrs Grey an' Lottie sing to us. An' markets
an' shops an' fings ter buy . . .' She trailed off, aware that
Bet was frowning at her.

'Don't be daft, Nan. Lunnon ain't like that. It's dirty an'
noisy an' the posh folk ain't ter be seen much on the City
streets. They keeps ter their carriages an' the West End. I
know,' she added importantly, 'Meg tole me so. She's been
out there. No, we'd best go the other way, out into the
country. I think it's Essex and you can get ter the sea that
way. Maybe we could get on a boat an' sail across the sea.'

She paused, aware that this was just as unlikely an idea as
that suggested by Annie. She went on, 'I've never seen the
sea. Would yer like ter see it, Nan?'

Annie nodded. She didn't really know what 'the sea'
meant and besides, she was much more attracted to the idea
of the City. It was closer to home and it was more real.

'Well,' announced Betsy, jumping to her feet, 'we'll 'ave ter make plans an' watch our chances. I expect we'd miss old Mrs Grey, though. But I s'pose if we didn't like the City, we could always come back.'

'Ter the work'us?' Annie asked simply.

Betsy did not reply. The girls sauntered up the overgrown path hand in hand. Whatever they decided to do, they would do it together.

Suddenly, Annie's hand tightened on Bet's. She said now, very low, 'Look at that funny ole man over there,' and she nodded towards the hedge.

Shuffling slowly along Rope Walk was a very strange figure. He was quite tall and seemed thin, a little stooped at the shoulders. His hair and beard, which looked very ragged and tangled and appeared to be part of each other, were an indiscriminate reddish-grey colour and his blue eyes peered out from beneath a battered wide-awake hat, which had seen better days. He seemed to be searching. He moved quite slowly, his head turning frequently in the direction of the garden, until his piercing eyes came to rest on the two girls. He stopped, quite still, and studied them, while they stared back. Then his craggy face broke into a smile, which somehow frightened Bet and Annie, for he had several teeth missing and his nose was long and slightly hooked. He spoke across the hedge and his voice was wheedling and soft.

'Good day to you, my pretty dears.'

He gave a slight bow and the girls giggled and looked at each other.

'What a delightful day it is,' continued the stranger. 'Such a day to be out and enjoying the sun and the air. And you're walking in your garden. That's nice, my dears. And do you often walk in your garden?'

'Oh yes!' Annie was anxious to please and answered up quickly. 'But it ain't our garden. It's Mrs Grey's. She looks after us.'

'Does she now?' asked the wily old gentleman. 'And I'll

warrant she doesn't often give you treats. Sweetmeats or cakes or lemonade?'

The girls shook their heads, though Bet was wary of continuing the conversation. The old man delved around inside the deep pockets of his overcoat, which garment must have caused him to swelter on such a fine day as this, and eventually produced a screw of paper containing a few sticky bull's-eyes. He extended a long arm over the hedge, keeping a sharp lookout all round him.

'Here. Have a sweetie.'

Betsy hesitated, not sure what would happen if they were caught. But there was no one about and she and Annie took two bull's-eyes each. They were hard and shiny and reminded Betsy of the swirling colours of the marbles the boys played with. She put one in her mouth. It was large and sweet and the sharp boiled corners cut the roof of her mouth. But the glorious sensation of having her sweet craving satisfied for once overrode all discomfort. Annie, too, was savouring the moment. The stranger chuckled.

'I'll come again, my dears. Soon. I'll bring you something else.' He paused. 'But don't you go telling anyone. The grown-ups won't like your talking to strangers.'

And he shuffled off in the direction of Shoreditch, stopping at the end of the lane to turn and wave to the little girls. They waved back, giggling again, and Annie nearly choked on her bull's-eye. Betsy patted her back and they returned to the rhubarb patch to finish their sweets in secret.

The old gentleman, although he was in reality no more than five and fifty, was very pleased with his find and came again many times during the summer and autumn of that year. He always brought some little nicety and always admonished the girls never to 'let on' where they had got their little treasures from. He usually brought sweets, a different sort each time, though once he brought them each a tiny silk handkerchief. When Mrs Grey found these pretty wipes at the back of a cupboard, it started a long enquiry and the two girls were frightened that their old friend would be discovered. When it was finally ascertained that Bet and Annie were the owners of these delectable silk objects, Bet quickly told Mrs Grey how they had found them one day by the garden gate. Whether Mrs Grey believed her was a matter of some doubt, but there were no more walks in the garden that year. The weather had turned, anyway, and the children were all glad to stay indoors.

Betsy and Annie were now the two eldest girls at the baby farm, with the exception of Lottie, who had stayed on as Mrs Grey's assistant. There were five children under the age of seven, excluding Annie and three tiny babies. Two more were brought in during the winter and the girls were kept busy looking after them.

Annie used to love to hold the babies and would spend hours fondling and playing with them. When they cried, she would be the first on the scene, gently lifting them to her thin, flat breast, rocking them, singing softly to them, till their tiny heads drooped against her shoulder. Then she would rest her own baby face against their warm heads and a look of such happiness would come into her eyes that Bet would smile and call her 'little mother'.

One chilly January evening Annie sat with a sleeping babe in her lap, studying its perfect features and playing gently and idly with its tiny fingers.

She was thinking what a beautiful piece of creation a baby was and she was moved to say to Bet, 'What did I look like when I was born, Bet?'

Betsy smiled up from her place on the floor.

'You was beautiful, Nan. An' I was so 'appy. I always wanted a sister.'

Annie smiled absently and was silent for a minute. Then she said, 'Bet, why don't we call Mrs Grey mother? I mean, we're all brothers an' sisters 'ere, ain't we? An' who's our father?'

Betsy sighed. She would have to tell Annie the truth.

'Nan, dearest,' she said, 'we ain't got no mother nor father. We're most of us orphants.'

127

Annie stared back at her for a moment.

'But, Bet,' she whispered, her voice trembling, 'ev'ryone 'as a mother an' a father. I know that. It's in the Bible wot Mrs Grey reads to us.'

'Yes,' said the patient Betsy, 'but sometimes parents die. Sometimes they can't afford to look after their children. Then the children gets 'anded over ter the parish. That's why we're 'ere. That's why there's a work'us.'

Annie stared in horror. The tears began to roll down her cheeks.

'But didn't no one ever see me mother or father, Bet? Doesn't no one know who they were?' Her voice held a touch of desperation in it.

Betsy's heart sank.

'Nan, dear, they say you was left on the steps of St Leonard's church one night an' the vicar's wife took you ter the work'us an' they brought you 'ere. A couple o' days later they found a very young woman in Sweetapple Court, what had died givin' birth an' they think it was your mother. But no one ever knew who yer father was.'

Annie sat in stunned silence staring at the baby lying in her lap. She tried to picture the young woman, alone and afraid in a dark, dirty room, having to part with her new-born baby because she was too poor to keep it. She thought her mother must have died of a broken heart at having to give up her new daughter. It comforted her to think that her mother must have loved her so much. The baby on her lap stirred and she picked him up and held him close.

If I 'ad a baby, she thought, I'd never part with it. I'd find some way to keep it.

She said no more on the subject and Betsy thought the moment had passed off tolerably easily. But Annie was to keep alive in her heart the picture of the young woman who died of a broken heart for love of her child and it was to forge a great maternal urge within her body as she grew and matured.

FOUR

When spring came, the girls were at last allowed out into the garden again, and on the first really warm day of the year, in the middle of April, the strange old gentleman reappeared, furtive as ever. The girls were pleased to see him and told him their news, and how, later in the year, Annie would be seven and they would both be going to the workhouse. At this, the old man's eyes narrowed and his expression hardened.

'The workhouse, my dears?' he said sharply. 'But you don't want to go there. You'll be treated very harshly. No walks in the garden, no friends to visit you and bring you presents. Gruel to eat and beatings if you're naughty. You won't like that, will you, my dears?'

The girls looked alarmed and shook their heads. Annie glanced at Bet and spoke her thoughts.

'We'd acshully thought of runnin' away,' she confided, drawing close to the hedge. 'I'd like ter go down ter the City, but Bet 'ere wants ter go ter the sea. Is it a long way ter the sea, sir?'

'Oh yes, my dears, a very long way. You have to follow London's river for miles and miles until it opens right out into the ocean.'

' 'Ave you ever bin down the river, sir?' Annie clasped her hands in excitement.

'No, my dear; but I've been *up* it!' and the stranger chuckled. 'I sailed up it when I was a very little kinchin, no bigger than you. I came on a very big ship, with my parents, from across the water.'

His eyes seemed to mist over for a moment and the girls watched him, awed by this information.

Then he shook himself and said, 'I could certainly show

you the river. And the big ships. They're not so far away as the sea.'

'Oh yes, please,' gasped Annie; then her face fell. 'But Mrs Grey would never let us out without her.'

'No. But you could – ah – slip away with me. You could come and live in my house if you like.'

The old gentleman seemed nervous. The girls exchanged glances again. This was a new departure from their plans.

'Think about it, my dears,' went on their friend. 'Tell me next time I come. I've other children in my house. You'll be quite happy. Plenty to eat – and drink. Just a little work to do for your board and lodging. But you won't mind that, eh?'

The girls agreed this would be a good bargain and scampered off to their private retreat to discuss the old man's proposal. Betsy, being older, was not entirely sure. The prospect of the workhouse loomed very large and real, but Mrs Grey had been a good guardian to them in many ways, when she wasn't full of gin.

'I don't know as I'd like ter leave Mrs Grey,' said Bet doubtfully.

'No,' agreed Annie, 'but it'd be better than the work'us, Bet, wouldn't it? After all, we'll 'ave ter leave 'ere the end of the year anyway.'

Bet said nothing. Her mind was racing. She couldn't decide whether it would be better to endure the workhouse or to escape to the relative comfort of the old man's house. But they knew nothing about him, not even his name. But he had promised them plenty to eat and drink; and there would be other children at his house; he had said so. She wondered what work they would have to do. But neither of them would mind a bit of hard work. They had worked about the house here and helped with the smaller children, and the old man didn't seem to be the sort who would be a hard taskmaster. Eventually, Bet agreed and both girls decided to run away next time their friend called.

The following week they saw him lingering under the big chestnut tree at the end of the walk. Annie was to remember the sight for the rest of her days: the tree full of great fat sticky buds, promising a myriad bright green umbrellas within a few weeks, and the old man waiting, as though expecting the shade to grow any minute. The girls quickly collected their few belongings – their little nightdresses, their cloaks and bonnets, with which all the parish children were supplied – and crept furtively out of the house. Mrs Grey was at the wash tub, singing tipsily to herself, her arms deep in suds, several babies crawling round her feet. She did not see her two eldest charges slip away into the garden.

There was a small gap in the hedge which had been roughly blocked some years ago with a piece of hurdling and the grass and brambles had grown round it, holding it in place. The girls managed to free it, careless of the clawing brambles and spiteful nettles. They were excited, exhilarated by their own audacity. At last, they were out on the lane, their bundles under their arms, and the old gentleman was hastening towards them. But he looked angry and the girls were frightened.

'What do you mean, coming away now, in daylight, when all the world will see you?' he cried in despair. 'Oh my, oh my, what am I going to do?'

Annie began to cry and Bet put her arm round her.

The old man thought for a moment. Then he said, more kindly, 'Can you walk well, my dears?'

'I think so,' replied Betsy. 'But you see we don't often go far. We ain't ever bin further than the church.'

'Well, we'll go for a little walk round before going home,' went on the old man. 'And maybe I'll show you the river!'

Annie stopped crying and looked up in awe at the shabby figure before her. His coat was exceedingly long, stained and patched, and his knee breeches and stockings were equally dull and second best. His ancient, pointed boots were very down at heel and he wore no collar to his shirt, although he did sport a somewhat fancy waistcoat. This had likewise seen better days. The blue eyes beneath the slouch hat twinkled at her and he held out his hand, which Annie took trustingly.

Betsy carried both bundles and walked silently at his side as they moved off in the direction of the fields.

For some time, they followed lanes and cut across fields until they came by a circuitous route to the little village of Bethnal Green. They did not enter the village for fear that someone might recognize the children, but took a narrow path which skirted the dwellings and so struck south towards Shadwell and the river. They now left the fields behind and there were ugly warehouses and grim tenement buildings, close and secretive.

'Now, my dears, there is the river,' announced the old gentleman at last. 'And look at all those masts and all that rigging. See the cargoes being loaded and unloaded. Isn't that a pretty sight?'

The two girls stood spellbound, their mouths like Os, their eyes never leaving the bustle and activity spread out before them on the crowded water.

'Now,' continued their companion, 'I expect you're tired, so we'll sit down here for a bit below Shadwell Stairs and rest. Are you hungry?'

The girls nodded and from his copious pockets he produced a large piece of cheese and some cold sausage. Betsy picked some grit and fluff from her share of the cheese, but Annie pitched in immediately. What was a peck of dirt when you were hungry?

It was now time for the pleasantries of introduction and when Bet and Annie had given their names, their captor said pleasantly, 'What lovely names, my dears. Bet – and Annie.' He pointed to each in turn, so that he should not forget. 'And my name is Mr Fagin; though precious few people "Mister" me these days,' he added ruefully.

The unlikely trio sat below Shadwell Stairs until the noises of the day gradually gave way to the sounds of eventide. Flocks of starlings wheeled noisily overhead as they flew to roost and a coot made a loud craking noise from a tuft of reeds further along the bank. And the human noises were different, too. Coarse shouting, a brawl outside an inn on the opposite bank at Rotherhithe, men on the boats, swearing, laughing loudly, calling lewdly to women appearing along the dockside. The girls shivered.

'Come, my dears.' Fagin spoke quietly. 'We'll get along home now.'

And he led the way up a smelly alley to the Ratcliffe Highway, where overdressed and brightly painted women appeared and disappeared like the winking lights on the river banks. As they went along, the children perceived that they were now heading for the City, for the area was becoming more built up and they could see the spires and domes of churches silhouetted against the western sky. They were still close to the river, but travelling by the most roundabout route Fagin could think of. They wove in and out of lanes and alleyways, courtyards and squares. Fagin knew his way like a wily fox. The girls' feet dragged and their little bodies were weary. They plodded on in Fagin's wake, not even chattering now.

At last, he stopped outside a very seedy-looking lodging house set in an equally run-down street, which went by the name of Field Lane. There were no fields and it was no lane; but at some time in its history it had been, no doubt, just that. Fagin let himself in with a large key and Bet and Annie followed him sleepily up a wooden staircase to yet another door, upon which he knocked softly.

'Jem,' he called, his long nose against the edge of the door. 'It's me.'

The door was unbolted and the girls were ushered in. The door was locked again behind them and they stood blinking in the bright glow of oil lamps.

'Oh criminee!' exclaimed the youth hailed as Jem. 'Wot *'ave* yer got there, Fagin?'

Fagin smiled and bowed to the girls, sweeping his hand towards the rest of the inmates.

'Boys,' he said, 'I have two sisters for you – Miss Betsy and Miss Annie.'

The two girls stared, horrified. There were seven boys of

varying ages and sizes. All looked uncouth, all sat grinning at the new arrivals and all had either long clay pipes in their mouths or small tankards in their hands.

'My dears,' said Fagin to Bet and Annie, 'these will be your new friends.' And he began introducing them.

Jem seemed to be the eldest and Fagin's right-hand man; he looked about fifteen. There were two slightly younger boys, both evil-looking, called Sam One and Sam Two, who constantly swore and grumbled. Fagin called them his Terrible Twins. The other four boys ranged between nine and thirteen; there were Fred, Dicky, George and Tom. There was nothing special about them, nothing to mark them out. They all had thin, pinched faces, with thin, hard mouths and each bore an expression which reflected the sort of lives they lived – lives of constant evasion and trickery, of lies and broken promises.

'Come, boys, make the young ladies feel at home.'

Fagin ushered them to seats, while Jem brought a large frying pan of sausages to the table and Tom poured drink from a brown glass bottle. Fred, the youngest, found a plate for the girls to share, and unceremoniously dumped two hunks of bread on it. Jem dished up the sausages and they all fell to hungrily. Fagin responded to the insistent questioning of his boys between mouthfuls of sausage and gulps of beer. The girls thought the boys sounded angry, resentful at their intrusion, but Fagin knew how to quell their indignity.

'They'll be an asset to us, boys. You mark my words. Girls are just as quick. And they're less conspicuous.'

'But, Fagin –' one of the Sams attempted to object.

'No! No more! They're here and they're staying. You'll be civil, every one of you. And look after them till they know the ropes.'

Bet and Annie barely uttered a word, squirming under the censorious looks of the boys. The beer was strong and made them cough. It was not at all like the diluted liquid they had been used to at Mrs Grey's.

Soon Annie's eyelids began to droop and Fagin showed them where they might sleep. This was a very small area of the room curtained off from the boys, and there was a jug and basin for washing. The bed was no more than a large, straw-stuffed cushion on the floor, but there was an ample supply of blankets and the girls quickly cuddled up together.

'Goodnight, my dears. Have a good sleep.'

Fagin's face disappeared behind the curtain and the girls were alone. They lay silent for a few minutes listening to the hushed but anxious voices of the boys. They could hear the two Sams grumbling away and Fagin's sharp reprimand, which resulted in silence. The girls dared not even whisper their fears to each other.

FIVE

When they awoke the next morning, the girls found themselves alone except for Fagin. They washed their faces and
emerged shyly from their makeshift boudoir. Fagin clasped
his hands together and looked at them.

'You slept well, my dears?'

They nodded, their eyes on the toast which stood warming
by the large kitchen range. Fagin chuckled and waved them
to the table, where he brought them toast and eggs and
bacon. The girls' eyes widened. Never had they had such
food before. There was the same strong beer again, but they
thought they would soon get used to it. Fagin watched them,
a paternal smile on his thin face. He knew how to bind
kinchin to his side, to keep them loyal. Good food, warmth,
security. That was all they needed. And they were his for
good then.

He viewed Betsy and Annie now as potential workers. He
would start teaching them straight away. Girls made good
prigs. They were careful at flimping. They took no chances.
They made sure they got it right first time. Not like the boys,
who wanted to show off. And girls aroused less suspicion,
especially two innocent little faces like these. He rubbed his
hands together and thought of all the extra goods he would
have to fence, the extra money to come, maybe some more
little trinkets to add to his growing store of treasures.
Suddenly, the oleaginous smile disappeared from his face.
These two wouldn't be innocents for long. Another three or
four years and Bet would be looking elsewhere to earn her
living. And if he wasn't mistaken, Nan would follow in her
wake soon after. It was a shame, but a fact of life, especially
when you lived in Field Lane.

Fagin got up from the table and crossed to a window which gave on to the back of the house. Looking down, he watched the foul Fleet Ditch snaking uneasily between mouldering banks. He could see the bloated, almost naked corpse of a cat, caught among the flotsam of the sewer, for sewer it had become. It was a general rubbish tip for everyone in Field Lane and those streets which backed on to it. There had been talk of covering it over, but nothing had been done. The chutes from the houses poured out their unspeakable effluent into it and even darker, more sinister secrets had been consigned to its shallow, filthy waters before now.

But this morning, the sun was shining and Fagin was happy. He would begin teaching his latest pupils the art of fogle-hunting. First, however, he would take them on a little tour of their new home. When their little bellies could take no more and they had wiped the egg and grease from their mouths, the two girls followed Fagin out into the street. They held each other's hands while Fagin walked beside them, waving his arms in the direction of the pastry-cook's shop, the butcher's, the pawnbroker's and the many second-hand shops which lined Field Lane. It seemed to Bet and Annie that the narrow street was festooned for a fair, but Fagin assured them that it was always thus. Such an array of clothes and shoes, furniture and china, pictures and hardware, brushes and brooms, they had never seen before. Zinc baths, earthenware pots and lace tablecloths jostled for space above poky doorways and crowded windows. Lines and poles attached to the shop fronts sported swatches of silk and cambric handkerchiefs, the riot of colour rippling in the gentle breeze. Higher up, at the very top of the tenements, more poles extruded washing, which flapped among the smuts from chimney smoke. Annie squinted up at the path of blue above them between the rooftops. It was a different world up there. A world free of squalor, a world where the air echoed to the distant cries of the street beneath. She wondered what it would be like to look out across the rooftops and chimney-pots.

Here, though, Fagin was shouldering his way through the jostling crowds. Occasionally, someone would nod at him or grunt a greeting. They were mostly close-visaged, secretive individuals, and the girls shrank from such men and kept close to each other, their eyes wide and fearful.

All that morning, Betsy and Annie trailed round after Fagin, through all the backways of Field Lane and Saffron Hill, until they felt they had come to live in a rabbit warren, one mean street looking much the same as another. When they returned to Fagin's den, they found that the boys were back. The lads produced a plentiful array of items from their pockets and the girls watched in amazement as silk handkerchiefs, coins, a purse, a wallet and two tiepins were laid out on the bare wooden table in the centre of the room.

'Well done, all of you,' cried Fagin. 'A good morning's work! Now, a little refreshment and we must show Betsy and Annie how it's done.'

And so, when hunger and thirst had been assuaged, Fagin proceeded to enact a pantomime, in which the boys endeavoured to relieve his pockets of the items which they had just brought home. It was done with such cheek and nerve, and not without a little panache, that Bet and Annie clapped their hands and laughed.

'Now,' said Fagin, seriously, 'the girls must practise.'

Some time was spent that afternoon showing the two innocents the skills that would stand them in good stead over the years. But the girls found it hard at first. If Mrs Grey had taught them little else, she had taught them what was right and wrong. But in this new place, with strange people, who was to keep them on the straight path?

'It ain't right,' Bet kept whispering to Annie. 'Stealin's wrong.'

'Yus, but 'ow else we goin' ter earn any money? Any'ow, the toffs 'ave got lots o' nice things. They wouldn't miss a pin or a 'kerchief.'

'I know, but . . .'

There was nothing really Betsy could say. At least it was

better than going to the workhouse. At least they would have freedom to move about here. And, if their meals so far were any indication, they would be fed far better than at Mrs Grey's.

By the evening of that first day, the girls had pleased Fagin with their skills and had even won a little grudging admiration from the boys. And by the end of the week, they felt quite at home in their new surroundings.

As the months went by, the girls went further afield to pick pockets and they enjoyed the excitement of exploring the streets of London. There was so much to see and the noise was unbelievable. They saw some sights, too, and would rush home breathless to Fagin with news of a chained bear dancing on the streets, or a band of dark-skinned musicians in bright clothes. One day they came home with a tale of a giant, who reached to the first floor of a shop in Ludgate. Fagin laughed and they knew he didn't believe them. But it was all exciting and such fun and the thrill of drawing out the fine handkerchiefs from the fine coats cancelled out any inhibitions which they had entertained about their new work.

There was a keen spirit of competitiveness between the girls and the rest of Fagin's gang. Sometimes it spilled over into aggressive jealousy and there would be fisticuffs. Then Fagin would separate the main protagonists and there would be a beating for each of them. Not very hard; the old man was fond of his adopted family. But they had to be taught their places. The girls were not exempt and many a time Fagin had had to pull Annie, small as she was, away from one of the boys, where she clung scratching and spitting like a little she-cat.

No one ever came looking for Bet and Annie, but on several occasions, Fagin had taken himself off towards Shoreditch or Bethnal Green and kept his ear to the ground. One day, while taking refreshment in a public house near the girls' old home, he heard two men discussing the disappearance of some parish paupers.

'Young girls, they was,' remarked one man. 'Jus' disappeared off the face o' the earth. Never bin seen since.'

'Remarkable,' put in his companion. 'And when was this?' He was evidently a visitor to the area.

'Oh, I should say four, five months ago now,' replied his informant. 'They say the woman wot runs the 'ouse where they lived nearly went out of 'er mind with worry. She thought the parish officers'd turn 'er out. An' she do love them babies she takes in. Mind you,' he added conspiratorially, 'she loves the bottle, too!'

And the two men dismissed the subject with much laughter. Fagin did not hear of Mrs Grey's subsequent fate, if indeed she had been brought to book. But at least now he felt secure in the knowledge that the girls were no longer being sought, though he would not mention any of this to Bet or Annie. It could serve no purpose.

So summer passed into autumn and winter and Fagin's family muffled themselves in scraps they picked up from the second-hand stalls. Gin and water heated with the poker served to warm their blood, as the middens and puddles froze outside. At first, the drink had made the girls cough and splutter and they preferred the beer, but Annie grew to like the strange aroma from the colourless liquid in her tankard and she welcomed its gentle, numbing warmth.

One night, at the beginning of 1825, Annie stood at the window looking out across the Fleet Ditch. She could see a mean light in the house across the street and she watched shadows moving about in the flickering candlelight. She craned her neck and looked upwards to the night sky beyond the high tenement rooftops. It was black and dusted with stars and the street below reflected the stars in frost. Fagin sat warming his hands by the fire and she came across to him. He looked up and smiled at her.

'Fagin,' she began, 'I wish – I wish I could go right to the top o' the 'ouse an' look out at the roofs an' the sky. There's a lot o' stars ternight. They'd look beautiful from up there.'

Fagin raised his eyebrows. 'If that's what you want, my little Nan, you shall go.'

And he rose straight away and beckoned her to the door. She glanced at Bet, but Bet was busy unpicking initials from the latest batch of wipes and was too warm to move.

So mentor and pupil left the room, Fagin shrugging on his threadbare winter coat and helping Annie with her cloak.

'Up here, my dear,' he murmured.

Together they went up one flight of wooden steps after another, their trudging feet sounding hollowly on the treads. At last, breathless and warmed by their exertions, they came to a door at the top of the last flight of stairs and Fagin took from his pocket a heavy key and unlocked the door. It swung open on to a dusty lumber room with a small window on the far side. Fagin led the child across to where the bright night filtered through, but she was not tall enough to see out, so he lifted her up and sat her on the open sill, holding her thin frame tightly, lest she should fall. He was out of breath and the exertion of climbing had made his heart thump unnaturally within him. But he felt it had been worth it when he saw the sheer delight in Annie's face as she gazed at the scene before her. Rooftops, grey and red and green, shiny and sparkling with frost, stretched away in a tumbled landscape as far as the eye could see. Chimneypots of all shapes and sizes and colours punctuated the landscape at impossible angles. And the sky!

'Oh Fagin, look at the sky!'

It was a vast, indigo velvet dome, pierced in a million places to let the light of the stars shine through.

'It's beautiful,' she breathed.

And then she looked down. Down, down, such a long, long way.

And the street shone in the frost-light and the distance between the vault of heaven and the floor of the earth was enormous. She shivered.

'You're cold, my lambkin,' whispered Fagin.

'No,' replied Annie, her eyes still resting on the faraway

141

street. 'I'm just thinking what a long way down it would be if you fell.'

Fagin chuckled as he lifted her down from the sill.

'That's why I keep this door locked,' he said, suiting his actions to his words. 'Then nobody will be able to fall.'

That night, as she lay curled up against Bet's warm body, Annie thought about the world above the rooftops. It had been beautiful to see, but it had been spoiled for her when she realized its dangerous potential. And she vowed never to go up there again. It was safer and warmer down here on the first floor and she was happy. She had Bet and she had brothers and a father-figure, of sorts. She was sure they had been right to leave the Rope Walk cottage before the workhouse drew them inexorably into its grasp. Picking pockets wasn't really so bad and they lived quite well in the house in Field Lane. But she wondered what was beyond, out there in the world of grown-ups. Out there beyond the shining rooftops and the frosty alleyways; beyond the diluted gin and the swags of coloured handkerchiefs. She supposed she would find out as she grew older. After all, she was only seven and she had a long way to go yet.

SIX

In the year she was fourteen, Bet suddenly found herself the centre of attraction with the older boys. Jem spent less time at Field Lane these days, preferring to follow his own inclinations, but when he did, he took an inordinate amount of interest in the girl. The other boys resented his attentions and Jem's visits usually ended in fights. In his absence, the two Sams fought between themselves for Bet's favours, but she brushed them all aside. She preferred the mystery of Jem, who was out in the wide world. She would sit moodily in the evenings, patching the boys' clothes or unpicking the tell-tale embroidery on the handkerchiefs. At such times, Annie would sit beside her and try to draw her out, to make her chatter as she used to. But Bet was growing up. She was unsure of herself and her feelings. How could she talk to Annie, who was still a child?

One day, Annie returned alone from working the pockets of Fleet Street, to find Bet and Jem making love on the floor of the deserted kitchen. She stood in the doorway watching, horrified, fascinated, as the two bodies urged and thrust together. She felt her cheeks flush scarlet, but it was too late to move. Bet had seen her.

'Go away, Nan,' Bet panted. 'You ain't s'posed ter be 'ere.'

Annie turned and fled from the house and hid herself away down by the river. She found a secluded spot beneath some stairs and sat watching the river traffic. To the east she could just make out a big, three-masted ship slipping away with the tide. She wondered for which far-distant land it was bound and she wished fervently that it might take her too. She felt sullied by what she had seen in the house. Yet she knew that she should not have been surprised. Jem had made no secret of his desire to have Bet as his special girl. He always had his hands somewhere beneath her clothes and Annie wondered why Bet let him take such liberties. She supposed Bet must like it. Perhaps, she thought sadly, this was the beginning of that world beyond the rooftops, the secret world of adults. She sensed life was about to change again.

Three weeks later, Fagin himself disturbed the two lovers. He was infuriated and would have turned them both out on the streets but for Annie's desperate pleading. Who would she have if Bet went? Who would she turn to, who would be her friend in that house full of males? Fagin relented so far as to let Bet stay on, but Jem was banned from the house for good and Bet had to promise solemnly that she would always work in company with Annie and never be on her own. Bet complied and her misdemeanour was soon forgotten. But Fagin kept a hawk-like eye on his little flock and he worried about the vulnerability of both his boys and his girls as they grew towards maturity.

Bet had learned a lot from her escapades with Jem and she missed the heady sensation of his lovemaking.

'Wos it so good?' asked Annie one day, rather tentatively. She was almost fourteen herself now and she and Bet had taken to secret talks again at night or when they were alone together. It was almost like being children again at Mrs Grey's, only now their talk was serious and grown up.

Bet nodded and smiled. 'Oh yes,' she said, her voice low and husky. 'It was good, Nan. And Nan . . .' She hesitated a moment. Then went on. 'You know there are girls out there earnin' money fer doin' it. Only you 'as ter be prepared ter share yerself around a bit.'

Annie stared at her disbelievingly. 'Oh Bet, you don't mean . . .'

Bet nodded. 'I reckon that's wot we'll be doin' soon, Nan. Fagin won't want us 'ere much longer. 'E thinks we disturb 'is boys. I know. I bin watchin' 'im.'

'Well, 'e brought us 'ere in the first place,' retorted Annie indignantly.

'Yus, but we've served our 'prenticeship. 'E's bin a good master an' 'e's made us into 'is best pickpockets, 'asn't 'e? But you mark my word, Nan, we'll be out on them streets afore long.'

Annie wouldn't believe it. Fagin had been kind to them all these years. He wouldn't just turn them out. In the weeks ahead, she became obsessed by the unspoken threat of their future and she grew more and more depressed. She fretted at her nails, she was waspish with everyone and then, as though to blot out the awful fear, she let Fred's attentions get out of hand. And there was the gin, the panacea to all her worries. And she imbibed more and more of it. Already she was on the slippery, downward path.

On a blustery March evening in 1833, Bet and Annie sat at the big kitchen table. Supper was brewing on the range and they were waiting for Fagin and his boys to return. Annie reached for the gin bottle. Bet put out her hand.

'Ain't you 'ad enough already, Nan?' she asked softly.

Annie looked up at her. She felt so tired, so drained. But the gin was a friend. She poured a generous measure and began sipping it. Bet frowned.

'Annie!' she exclaimed. 'You're drinkin' that without water. Fagin'll be angry. 'E wos wond'rin' where 'is gin was disappearin' to. Blamin' the boys, 'e wos.'

Annie shrugged. 'I don't care,' she said. 'I like it. Makes me feel better.'

'Why? You ain't ill, are yer?' demanded Bet.

Annie shrugged again. 'Oh, jus' worried wot'll happen to us. Wond'rin' where we'll end up in life.'

Bet looked very hard at her foster-sister.

'Nan,' she said, 'you ain't bin up to anythink, 'ave yer? I mean, with the boys?'

Annie had the grace to blush and hid her face in her tankard. Bet sighed and sat back in her chair.

'Oh Nan, wot a pair we are. Wot 'ave we come to? After all these years, priggin' an' dippin' fer ole Fagin an' now we're goin' down ter the bottom of the barrel.'

'We ain't there yet,' Annie reminded her. 'Only, I jus' wanted a bit of excitement in me life. I'm fed up of liftin' wipes ev'ry day, jus' ter bring the ole devil a few pennies. I know,' she added, seeing Bet's expression, ''e feeds us well an' looks after us; but I want ter do somethink on me own. I don't want ter thieve fer 'im all me life.'

Just then there was a commotion downstairs and the men folk of the house returned, hurrying to the fire to warm themselves.

'Supper smells good, my dears,' remarked Fagin, bustling up to the table.

Bet went over to the range and began to dish up plates of food for the boys. Annie sat where she was, frowning into her tankard.

'What's this, Nan?' asked Fagin. 'Come along, my dear, give Bet a hand.' He peered at her. 'Are you ill, my dear? Come and sit by the fire.'

Annie raised her eyes to him and smiled. 'I'm all right, Fagin,' she slurred.

She stood up and staggered across to the chair by the fire, taking her gin with her. Fagin frowned, but refrained from comment. Annie did not join the family for supper and she was left to sit on her own. But from time to time, one or more of the boys cast covert glances at the figure huddled over her tankard.

Annie took herself off to bed early that evening. She and Bet now slept in a room separate from the boys, and Fagin followed her.

'May I come in, my dear?' he asked, insinuating his body round the door of the room.

'I ain't got much choice,' Annie flung over her shoulder. Fagin stood irresolutely in the doorway.

'Well, come in if yer comin'.'

Annie's voice sounded weary. Fagin shuffled a little way into the room.

'Nan, my dear,' he began. 'You've always been my best little prig. Always clever, always good at your job. I've looked after you, haven't I? Over the years? Saved you from the workhouse, you and Bet? Kept you here together? Taught you a trade – of sorts?'

He smiled ingratiatingly and Annie turned her head away.

He went on, 'Is this how I am to be repaid?'

Annie looked at him in defiance. 'Wot d'yer mean, Fagin? Repaid?'

'Come, come, Nancy. You know what I mean.'

She had noticed that of late he was calling her Nancy. She didn't mind the name. It sounded quite pretty. But it had other connotations, as though he were almost expecting her to follow some other way of life.

'The gin for a start, my dear,' he said. 'I thought the boys were tippling it for a lark. But no. It seems that our Nancy is pouring it down her young and tender throat. Neat, too. It's not a good example to the others and I can't afford that sort of luxury for you all, my dear.'

He paused and Nancy shrugged. She wished he'd go away and leave her to sleep. But he hadn't finished.

'And Nan, I can't have you playing around with my boys. Not here. Oh yes, I know what's been going on.'

Nancy had sat down very suddenly on the edge of her bed and was staring at him with wide, vacant eyes. Fear clawed at her stomach. She knew what must come. Yet she still could not believe it of him.

'I can't run a thieves' den and a brothel, my dear. You do understand?'

He thought how pretty she looked, her fair hair streaming loose about her shoulders. He wished he could have been one of his boys that night. He knew the temptations and that was why he must say what he had to say.

'You and Bet must go, Nancy. I can't let you stay any longer. It's not fair on any of them. You understand, Nancy my dear?'

Oh yes, she thought. I understand all right. We'll be turned out on the streets an' we'll thieve or starve. An' if we don't thieve, there'll always be ourselves to sell, just ter keep a roof over our 'eads.

147

She suddenly didn't care any more. She was tired. Her brain was fuddled with too much gin. She'd talk to Bet in the morning. She laid her head wearily on the pillow and Fagin slid out of the room.

But the next morning brought no opportunity to talk. The boys left for work and Fagin bade the girls gather their few belongings and depart. He slipped five shillings apiece into their hands, patted their shoulders and ushered them out. As they stood blinking in the bright spring sunlight filtering down into Field Lane, Nancy's eyes filled.

'Bet,' she said, her voice wavering, 'it's 'appened. Jus' like you said. But I never believed 'e'd do it, did you?'

'Oh yes,' replied the elder girl. 'I knew 'e would. I can see the way 'is mind works. And I think we were becomin' a source of temptation to *'im*, too, yer know, Nan.'

'Wot? 'Im? Ole Fagin?' Nancy scoffed.

'Yes. Ole Fagin,' echoed Bet.

Nancy was silent for a while. Then she said, 'Where we goin', Bet?'

'Ter find a lodgin',' came the sensible reply.

They spent the morning looking for a suitable lodging house. It was not easy. They wanted to stay fairly close to the areas they knew, but so many of the lodging-house keepers were lewd and beery men, who would have been only too glad to have such young chicks beneath their roofs.

At last they found a room in a house which stood in the shadow of Coldbath Fields. Neither young woman liked the view, but the lodging-house keeper was a woman and they felt safer with her. They paid their first week's rent and stood looking about their sparsely furnished room. The floor was bare and there was a rickety table, a chair and a stool. The two beds felt damp and the whole place smelled musty. Nancy wandered over to the window and looked out at the high wall surrounding the prison. Its drabness depressed her, even on such a sunny morning, and she sighed deeply.

'Well,' said Bet, 'this is 'ome now, Nan. It ain't much, but it'll do.'

She looked at Nancy, small and very young and very vulnerable. She hoped and prayed they could both keep off the streets. The tears stung her eyes and she gathered the child, for she was little more than that, into her arms and held her tightly.

'We'll manage, some'ow,' she whispered, more to herself than to Nancy. 'Come on,' she continued with false cheerfulness. 'Le's go an' find somethink ter brighten up this place!'

And laughing with a levity she did not feel, she flew down the stairs with her foster-sister in tow.

For a while they *did* manage. They carried on what Fagin had taught them so well and once a week they took their little treasures to him to fence. He never gave them a good price, they knew that, but he was reliable. Their visits were always welcomed by the boys, but Nancy found Fred's presence embarrassing. She was unsure of their standing now and would take more notice of Fagin's other youngsters. He had a new lad, a dapper young fellow, who called himself Mr Jack Dawkins and who dressed in the most outlandish clothes he could lay hands on. He was the clown of the establishment and Fagin was obviously very fond of him.

'He's a cove, is that one,' he chuckled one day. 'Cunning as they come. In fact, I call him my Artful Dodger. Lives up to his name, he does.'

The young women smiled and hoped The Dodger would not overstretch himself. It didn't do in this trade.

Sometimes Fagin would offer them a little refreshment, or he would ask solicitously after their progress.

''Ardly progress,' grumbled Nancy one day as they left Field Lane. 'We ain't goin' nowhere. We ain't earnin' more. If 'e doesn't give us a better price next week, we're goin' ter be stumped fer the rent.'

Bet bit her lip. She knew that already. She had hoped Nan would not realize the truth. But Nan was not stupid. When she wasn't full of gin, she was sharp and quick. But Bet knew they could just afford to live on their pickings, if only Nance would keep off the drink. The trouble was, they sometimes found employment for an evening or two at a run-down tavern in Little Saffron Hill, called The Three Cripples, and then the gin was to hand. Nancy didn't always get free drinks, but she drank nonetheless. And the little she earned was soon dissipated.

When Bet finally confessed that their money had run out, Nancy was irritable and querulous. She was fifteen now and didn't want her life dictated by money. Nor did she like being taken to task by Bet. Bet sat silently under the tirade, saying nothing, thinking much. When Nancy eventually stopped, she saw the tears on Bet's face and flung her arms round her.

'Oh Bet, dearest. I'm sorry, I'm sorry. I'll make it up ter you, some'ow.'

The words were empty, Bet knew, and she dreaded what must eventually come. The landlady promised a week's credit, but no more.

Somehow they survived on the very little that came each week. But it would not last for long. The items they lifted fetched such miserable prices; it was barely enough to buy their bread. They would have to move into cheaper lodgings and that meant going into the worst areas of London. When the landlady told them firmly that she would give no further credit, they sadly bundled up their few belongings and trudged off through the rain of a particularly cold, wet April evening. They had little idea of where they were going and little hope of finding a shelter that night. Both girls were hungry and Nancy began to cry.

'I'd give anythink fer a swig o' gin an' a pork pie,' she sobbed.

Bet was cross. They'd be lucky to find some scraps on a sausage stall, let alone swigs of gin. She took Nancy's arm very firmly and hauled her along through the mud and puddles. She knew lodgings were cheaper to the east of the City and she was making for the area beyond the Tower.

The rain came on in a deluge and they were forced to take shelter in an ale-house. It was smoky and noisy inside and the place seemed to be seething with bronchial sailors and rough-shaven vagabonds, women in bright dresses and snarling dogs underfoot. They stood in the doorway, dripping and bedraggled, peering through the haze of tobacco smoke. A sailor with an accordion struck up a shanty and his moll leaped on to a table, kicking tankards out of her way, and began to dance, displaying a generous amount of leg as she did so. The men roared their approval and stamped and clapped for more.

While the girls stood staring at this spectacle, a woman in a purple dress with tinsel at her throat, sidled up to them and said, under cover of the noise, 'Lost, ducks?'

Bet turned to look at her. The woman was obviously a whore, but she had a kind face and was smiling at them in a friendly fashion.

'Not really,' replied Bet. 'But we're lookin' for some cheap lodgin's. A room to ourselves. We ain't got much money.'

The bawd laughed, not loudly, and she said, 'I know of jus' the place fer you. Go on along the 'Ighway until yer come to Wappin' Lane. Fifth 'ouse down on the left. Tom Filkins. Tell 'im Polly sent yer.'

Bet opened her mouth to thank Polly for her kindness, but the woman was gone, lost in the seething crowd.

'Come along, Nance,' she said, hurrying out of the tavern and into the fresh air.

Nancy was for staying and drying out, but Bet would rather face the rain than spend longer in that stuffy house of ill repute.

They ploughed on through the wet and finally arrived like two rats at Mr Filkins's front door. He was slow to respond to their knock and when he did, he viewed them with distaste.

'You say Ole Poll sent yer?'

'Yes,' said Bet. 'We're lookin' fer a room fer the two of us. Only we can't afford much.'

She refrained from saying that they could afford nothing at this moment. Thomas Filkins stood surveying them for a moment, heedless of the rain falling on them.

'Thruppence!' he said suddenly.

The girls looked enquiringly at him.

'Thruppence a night,' he expanded.

Bet opened her worn reticule and took out six pennies. There were three left.

'Here you are, sir,' she said. 'That's fer two nights. We'll pay you for the week when we get some work, if that's all right with you.'

'Aye,' grunted Thomas Filkins. 'You'll likely need a bit o' credit, though.'

Bet could have fallen on his neck there and then, except that she didn't know the man. Instead, she said politely, 'Thank you, sir.'

Thomas Filkins opened wide his door and led the girls to a room at the very top of his house.

'It ain't much,' he said, 'but it'll keep the rain off yer 'eads! Prowided the roof don't leak again. I'll get my boy ter bring in another bed. An' you'll be wantin' summat warm, no doubt? No hextra cost ternight.'

Bet and Nancy could hardly believe their luck. They sat side by side on the edge of the one rickety bed and Nancy clasped Bet's hand.

'Oh Bet.' She smiled for the first time that day. 'Ev'rythink's goin' ter be fine now, ain't it?'

'I 'ope so,' replied Bet, though she doubted it.

SEVEN

The Ratcliffe Highway ran for nearly a mile parallel to where the new docks were being constructed and was connected to them by numerous streets and alleys sloping down to the wharves and quays, upon which were unloaded the source of the nation's wealth. Other cargo was offloaded here, too: the sailors who manned the great tall-masted ships. The Ratcliffe came alive on such occasions and at night, amid the flares of gas lamps, groups of overdressed prostitutes would fill the streets, drifting towards the docks, where they met the sailors coming ashore. The air would be full of laughter and hoarse shouts and the taverns would be crammed to bursting point. Fights would spill out on to the muddy streets amid a flurry of fist-blows and petticoats. And quietly drifting among the newcomers with their fat wage packets, were the thieves and pickpockets of Ratcliffe, who vied with the rats for superiority in numbers, and who relieved many an unwary sailor of his six months' pay.

Into this licentious neighbourhood, Bet and Nancy found themselves inexorably drawn. At first they went out tentatively, lifting their food from street stalls, picking the odd pocket or two. But there weren't many fancy goods to be had in the Ratcliffe. Everyone was poor here, apart from the sailors. And they soon went away with their pockets lightened. Competition was intense. There were so many thieves on the streets that the girls found themselves having to travel much further afield and they would return home in the evenings tired out with walking and little better off than when they set out. They grew thin and gaunt and Bet's pretty plumpness disappeared. And now their resources were so low that they had run up three weeks' debt with Mr Filkins.

'Wot we goin' ter do, Bet?' asked Nancy in despair one evening.

They had been working around the Pentonville area and it had been a long walk back. They both looked worn out, dusty and very dirty. Nancy drew out a small bottle from her reticule and unstoppered it. Bet stared at her in horror.

'Nancy!' she cried. 'Where did you get that from?'

Nancy lowered the bottle from her lips and glared back defiantly.

'I earned it. It's mine. It's me own money.'

'No,' said Bet, almost in tears. 'It's our money. You can't do this, Nan. We need every penny we've got. You can't waste it on gin!'

'It ain't wasted, Bet. I need it.'

Bet grew angry. She made a sudden decision.

'Nancy, from now on, I'm taking charge of any money we make. And you'll 'ave to ask me for it when yer want any. I'm sorry, dearest, but we're in a desp'rit sitiwation.'

Nancy looked at her, her eyes full of tears and hurt. But she said nothing. In her mind she knew that she must be independent of Bet. And there was only one way to do that.

Now she said, 'I'll take those things ter Fagin. You stay 'ere an' rest. You look all in.'

Bet looked at her sharply.

'It's all right,' went on Nancy. 'I shan't pinch the money. I promise yer.'

'You can't go floggin' over ter Field Lane ternight, Nancy. Not after terday's work. Yer'll be a wreck come termorrow.'

Nancy thought this very likely, but refrained from saying so. She knew that the night would change her completely. She would never be the same again. She was almost at the bottom of the barrel.

She finished off her gin, carefully corked the empty bottle and replaced it in her bag. Then she splashed cold water over her face, repinned her hair and kissed Bet very lovingly on the cheek. For a moment, Bet held her tightly in her arms. Nancy wondered if Bet had any idea of what her sister was about to do.

'Tell Fagin we're on the bread line,' laughed Bet. 'P'raps 'e'll cough up the odd shillin' or two extra.'

'P'raps 'e won't!' returned Nancy, grimly, and she set off for Field Lane.

In the early hours of the following morning, Bet was awakened by the opening of their door.

'Is that you, Nan?' she whispered, half fearing the reply.

'Yes.'

Nancy's voice sounded strange, choked and quivering. Bet sat up and watched Nancy's featureless form drift ghost-like into the room. She watched her take off her bonnet and shawl and boots, lay some coin carefully on the table and then climb silently into her bed. Neither girl spoke. But in the morning, Bet rose as soon as the sun was up and stood looking at the money. There were two piles. Three shiny shillings from Fagin, for yesterday's trinkets. And three dull copper pennies. Bet stared, the tears pricking her eyes. Was that all her little sister was worth? Had it come to this at last? She turned and looked at the sleeping girl. So young, so innocent-looking. Yet now she had joined the ranks of the frail sisterhood. And Bet knew it was only a matter of time before she, too, succumbed.

Within the month, they both had a patch on the Ratcliffe. They were both young, both attractive and there was no shortage of clients. But some of the older-established members of the profession resented their presence and more than once they found themselves the centre of fierce squabbles and even physical abuse. But they stuck firmly to their ground and most of the bawds of Ratcliffe tolerated them. At least now they had enough money to pay for their lodgings and for a modicum of food. Nancy spent much of her earnings on gin, which worried Bet. She feared for the girl's health more than her pocket. But Nancy was intractable over her drink. It was her standby, she said, her friend.

'But, Nancy,' Bet pleaded, 'ain't I yer friend? Surely yer don't need ter drink so much of it?'

'I dunno, Bet,' Nancy answered. 'I can't seem ter do without it. I get so down sometimes.'

They were both silent for a moment with their unspoken thoughts.

Then Nancy leaned back in her chair and said, 'You know, Bet, I just wish I could find some good man as'd marry me an' give me children. I know I'd be better then. I just need someone ter love me, ter make me feel wanted.'

Bet nodded. She knew the feeling. She often wished for a husband herself. She was twenty and most respectable girls of her age were married and starting their families by now. She sighed.

'I doubt we shall ever find that sort of 'appiness now, dear,' she said. 'We've blowed our chances, 'less we're very lucky.'

Luck seemed to be playing a game with the two young women these days and they never knew when it was going to run out. They were making a reasonable living at present. Their earnings were good when the ships came in and the two girls had bought coloured shawls and dresses and gaudy shoes, all cheap, all second-hand, but bright and cheerful and guaranteed to attract attention. One sailor had given Nancy a pair of enamelled clips for her hair, a gift from the East, where they specialized in such artistry. Nancy was thrilled and they became her most treasured possession. Bet acquired her first decent boots from an indulgent nautical man, who had expressed his concern when she revealed feet muddied and wet from the streets after a particularly heavy rainstorm.

Their biggest worry, however, was that of disease. Sailors were notorious disease-carriers and since they formed a large proportion of the Ratcliffe clientele, it was inevitable that the clap threatened their health as much as cholera and typhoid. Nancy was infected twice during the autumn of that year and she loathed the doses of mercury medicine with which the parish doctor supplied her. He shook his head when she went a third time.

'You're ruining your body, my dear,' he said. 'It's unlikely you'll ever bear a child, you know.'

Nancy had stared at him in disbelief. The man must be a quack. He didn't know what he was talking about. Of course she would have a babe – sometime. She wanted one. But not yet. She needed to keep working. There was so little cash to spare. So it was necessary to try to avoid a pregnancy. It wasn't easy. The old whores on the Ratcliffe were full of ideas and advice and plenty of old wives' tales. Few of them worked. Small sponge devices, soaked in vinegar, seemed the most effective, but they were no guarantee. Copious amounts of gin were advocated. But gin was more likely to help abort a baby than prevent its conception. Despite all this, Nancy needed a baby. She needed a child to pour all her dammed-up love into. And when her monthly courses ceased for six weeks, she rejoiced and knew she had been right. But when her elation and joy terminated in a mess of pain and gore, she began to believe the doctor's words.

But what could she or Bet or anyone do? There were thousands like them, there always had been and there probably always would be. Bet had said that if they got themselves into a brothel, they would be safer. Brothel-house keepers usually made sure their girls and their clients were clean. But they would lose their freedom. Their earnings would all be handed over to a madam and even their clothes would not belong to them. They would be virtual prisoners in the establishment. Bet knew. She'd met a girl on her patch who'd been immured in a bordello for almost a year. Eventually she had escaped with the connivance of a client, and here she was, on the streets again.

Winter came and went and Bet and Nancy felt they had spent their entire lives on the streets. They hardly ever went to Field Lane now. They had no need. They no longer picked pockets. They had a regular income, if not a very large one. But it was enough to keep a roof over their heads and to buy their food. They had been accepted by their colleagues and there were no more fights. They knew their place and their patch and kept to it. They frequented the taverns of East London in the company of their partners and even Bet got a liking for beer. But Nancy indulged her gin-craving and never had as much spare cash as Bet. It was not a balanced relationship. But Bet was so kind-hearted and could not forget the child that Nancy had once been. And she often lent money to her. Usually it was for mercury medicine or gin, but occasionally Nan would ask a penny or two for a length of bright ribbon or lace. Sometimes, to supplement their small wages, the two young women would earn a little extra by helping out in one of the taverns and they enjoyed the bustle and general goodwill of the customers. They were the happiest days for Nancy. Sometimes she would pick up a client, always she and Bet would get a good supper and very often she would be treated to measures of gin.

But it seemed impossible that life could go on like this indefinitely. Nancy would anticipate the next day or week or month almost with held breath. She knew that change bedevilled her life and the end of the year brought a change for the worst. It was a particularly vicious winter and the ground froze solid from December till early March and there were fewer ships entering port. So the old squabbles resumed, the girls of the Ratcliffe all fighting for business. Bet and Nancy noticed the slump in their income and began supplementing their few pennies with a return to pickpocketing, once a week traipsing over to Fagin's lodgings to fence their pickings. The old man was delighted to see them and the boys would cluster round, glad of a diversion. But Bet and Nancy remained distant and sceptical with him. They could not forget how he had driven them out on to the streets. But they had to return to him. He was the only fence they knew. And he was a good one. He had that hold over them.

Life on the Ratcliffe became progressively more wretched. The sailors were a rough and brutal bunch, much given to thuggery and strange habits, picked up in the ports of China and the Far East. But they formed the backbone of business. And the girls could not afford to be choosy. A drink in a tavern, an hour or less in some squalid room in a lodging house, a few pennies at the end of it all. And a feeling of having sunk a little further into the pit.

In the spring, Nancy miscarried again. Bet looked at her as she lay in the narrow little bed in their tiny lodging. The girl looked much older than her seventeen years. Her face was drawn, her eyes lacked sparkle and her hair, once a shining mass of gold about her infant head, was now a straggling mane of dull yellow. Bet could have wept for her, but she knew there was little chance of their improving their lot. And Nancy stood even less chance with her constant adherence to the bottle.

Bet's earnings did not stretch to buying coals and the cold spring nights were miserable. The two girls huddled together for warmth in one bed and pooled their bedclothes in an effort to keep out the cold.

But summer came at last and Nancy went back to her work just as Bet had to visit the doctor. She came away with a long face and a bottle of medicine.

'You ain't got the clap, 'ave yer, Bet?' Nancy put a sisterly arm about the older girl's shoulders.

Bet nodded miserably. Somehow she had managed to keep clear of it all this while.

'Well, yer'll 'ave ter take it easy for a bit. Lay off the job fer a while. Yer'll be better soon. I know,' she added, smiling.

Bet turned wild eyes on her. 'I can't,' she said desperately. ' 'Ow would we 'ave enough money ter live on? I've got ter work, Nance. I ain't too bad, 'e said.'

'No, but yer soon will be if yer don't give over fer a few months,' replied Nancy, her fists on her hips and a truculent expression on her face. It was a change for her to take control of a situation and she was quite enjoying herself. 'Now. Yer goin' ter stay at 'ome fer a few days an' I'll look after yer. Don't you worry, Bet.'

Having delivered this piece of advice, Nancy escorted her old friend back to their lodgings and immediately put her to bed, though Bet protested strongly.

'You jus' stay there, Bet. Yer'll feel a lot better. 'Ere, 'ave a little of yer medicine, too.' And she pushed a spoonful of

159

laudanum at Bet. 'I'm off ter Petticoat Lane. See wot I can find!'

Nancy did remarkably well down Petticoat Lane. She was still quite small of stature and her fingers had remained sensitive enough for her to continue picking pockets to a profitable end. She came back at the end of the day with several good silk handkerchiefs, a purse with some coins in it, and a silver stick pin from a lady's coat. The money they could keep, but the other items would have to go to Fagin. She decided to hide them away and wait for a few days until she had a fair collection. She had ready money now with which to buy food and coals and to pay the rent on their mean lodging.

When she returned home, Nancy found Bet in a state of depression. She had been weeping, her eyes were red and swollen and her face was blotchy where tears and dirt had coursed together.

''Ere, wot's up, luv?' asked Nancy as she breezed into their little room at the top of the house.

'I jus' bin lyin' 'ere, thinkin',' said Bet in a small voice, 'an' wishin' we didn't 'ave ter live like this. I 'ate it!' And she beat her fists on the bedspread. 'Oh, how I wish some kind man'd come an' carry me off out of it an' marry me an' give me a decent 'ome!'

Nancy sat down rather abruptly.

'Yus,' she said quietly. 'I feel like that, too. Only I'd be 'appy if a man jus' took me under 'is roof. I'd like ter marry an' 'ave children, respectable like, but I know I never will. Our sort don't, do they? But to 'ave one man as I could love an' care for an' call mine. That'd be somethink. That'd be enough ter content me.'

She gazed into mid-air, dreaming of no longer having to sell her body, no longer worried where the next meal was coming from; happy and contented. She knew it was a futile dream. No one lived like that, she was sure. She and Bet were trapped in a downward spiral of vice and poverty.

EIGHT

Business picked up again during the summer and a new fence arrived on the scene. His name was Levi Blumberg and he was a dealer in old clothes. He was tall and might have been thin but it was difficult to tell, for even in the hottest weather he maintained layers of clothing, which had all seen better days, but which were, no doubt, the best pickings of his trade. He was a man in his early thirties and had a quietly humorous air about him. No one knew his background, no one asked, no one really cared. Word soon got round that he was a good fence and much business was put his way.

Levi Blumberg had the makings of a good-looking man. His features had a chiselled appearance and his skin, or what one could see of it, was of a dark olive hue. His black hair was worn rather long and stuck out at angles from beneath a tall black hat. His whiskers grew in a fringe around his jaw-line and a long, aquiline nose dominated his face. He rented a small shop with rooms above it in Commercial Road, so that, to the casual eye, he was a respectable shopkeeper. But he had numerous connections with the market and, once in his hands, goods disappeared with remarkable speed. One might have found one's missing pocket watch 'christened' and up for sale in Petticoat Lane within three days of its disappearance. Levi Blumberg was fast building a reputation for himself. And Sir Robert Peel's New Police Force had its watchful eye on him.

While the police were keeping Levi Blumberg in their sights, Levi himself had his eyes on an attractive target. He had begun to notice her when he first started to frequent The George, which stood on the corner of Commercial Road. He went there to make himself available, since the landlord ran a gambling den in his back parlour and Blumberg rightly guessed the man to be up to his neck in vice. It had proved a profitable move, for cracksmen and pickpockets came and went at all hours, in what seemed a never-ending stream.

When he had first seen Nancy, she had been in the company of Bet, and Blumberg was shy of breaking into what was obviously a close friendship. So he admired from afar, biding his time. He would sit night after night in the tavern, a dark familiar figure hunched in his dim corner, following Nancy everywhere with those lustrous eyes of his.

Bet noticed him after some nights and nudged Nancy as they were standing at the bar.

''Ere, that dark bloke's bin watchin' you all evenin', Nance.'

Bet nodded in Levi's direction and Nancy frowned into the gloomy corner. The brown eyes swung away momentarily, unable, after all this watching, to make the contact. Nancy turned away.

'Wot, 'im? Gawd 'elp us, 'e gives me the creeps.'

'Well, 'e mus' fancy yer, gal. Why don't yer go an' talk to 'im?'

'Not likely, Bet. I want ter know who 'e is first.'

Presently they saw the landlord slip furtively over to Blumberg's table. There was a hurried, whispered conversation, and something was exchanged between the two men. It was skilfully done, but it was enough to make the girls aware that the newcomer might prove useful.

Soon after this, they were both borne away by some very drunk young men and found themselves in the midst of an impromptu party. Nancy was prevailed upon to sing and was then pulled to the nearest available male lap amid much laughter and clapping. The young man in whose arms she found herself began exploring the contents of her bodice with his rather fat hands, forcing them down into the tightness of her dress until he had revealed one smooth, rounded breast at the expense of the torn fabric. He immediately latched on to the enticing nipple, egged on by the loud cheers from his mates. Nancy tried half-heartedly to fight him off, but she was tipsy herself and laughing, and tonight she could not have cared less. But as she struggled feebly in her companion's arms, she caught sight of the still figure in the corner.

''Ere,' she said on a note of seriousness, 'don't do that in public. We're bein' watched.'

The ardent young man raised his head from Nancy's breast and glanced over his shoulder.

'What, him?' he said loudly. 'Old Hawk-Eyes? He won't bother. He don't move from his corner. Ever.'

The other lads laughed.

'Come on, Levi,' called one. 'Come and have a go at this lot. This'll move you if anything will.'

There was more laughter, but Levi never stirred nor answered, and his tormentors soon forgot him. But Nancy kept glancing across her partner's shoulder and found her look answered by that mysterious gaze in the corner. She felt exposed, censored, no matter how much she tried to lose herself in her young man's exploits.

Eventually, the revellers moved off, taking Nancy and Bet with them, together with the other young bawds in the tavern, and the dark presence in the corner was forgotten. But he was there the next night and Nancy was serving drinks.

'Oh Gawd, Bet,' she whispered, 'I can't go to 'is table, not after 'e saw me all undone last night.'

Bet scoffed. 'You getting prudish or somethink, Nance? Why should you worry wot 'e thinks? Garn. Take 'is drink over to 'im. 'E's probably shy.' She peered towards Levi's corner. ''Ere.' She nudged Nancy. ''E ain't so bad-looking really. Lan'lord says 'e's a fence. Pretty reliable one, too, so 'e reckons. Might suit us, yer know. Save draggin' the ole trotters over ter Field Lane ev'ry time we wants cash.'

Nancy had to admit the sense of this, and reluctantly moved to the murky corner where her admirer sat. She smiled nervously as she poured out his spirits and set the glass down in front of him.

'Is that all yer'll be wantin', sir?' she enquired.

He nodded and then spoke, a scratch across rough parchment.

'Vot is your name?'

His voice was heavily accented, but not unpleasant. And he was younger than she had thought.

'Nancy. And yours?' she ventured.

'Levi. Levi Blumberg. Please – sit down.' He indicated the seat opposite him.

Nancy sat down, half afraid of where this encounter was taking her. This was not an ordinary pick-up and she marvelled at her fear.

'That was not good last night. I like not to see you – how you say? – exposed?'

'Oh, that!' Nancy permitted herself a laugh. 'That's nothing. That goes on all the time 'ere. If you don't like it, there's another tavern down the road. They don't let us in there.'

She hadn't meant to be unkind, but Levi looked hurt.

'I come here to do business,' he said quietly. 'The landlord – we have an – understanding.'

Nancy nodded. She leaned across towards him and noted with satisfaction how his eyes travelled down to her breasts. She was wearing a particularly low-cut purple gown, decidedly out of fashion, but she liked the colour and it drew men's eyes to her.

'Would you be willin' ter do business with me, Mr Blumberg?'

'Of course. You haf only to find me here in the evenings. I gif you goot price for watches, rings, brooches.'

'We get a lot o' silk wipes,' confessed Nancy, 'but not much in the way of jewellery. Sometimes a wallet or a purse. It's all we bin trained to.'

'And who trained you, Miss Nancy?'

'Ole Fagin, over in Field Lane. 'E's a crook, if ever there was one!'

She laughed as she said it, but the laughter died on her lips when she remembered the nights she and Bet had spent on the streets since Fagin had turned them out.

164

'He was, perhaps, not kind to you, this Fagin?'

In the tight-knit family of the underworld it didn't do to say too much, so Nancy merely shrugged and said, 'Oh, 'e was all right. A real good fence. But we 'ad some disagreements. So we parted comp'ny, like.'

There was an awkward lull in the conversation, so Nancy seized the opportunity to free herself.

'I must go an' 'elp Bet,' she said. 'Give us a shout if yer wants more drink.'

And before Levi could reply, she had slipped away to the lights and smoke of the bar, leaving him alone with his thoughts in his dim corner.

Nancy had no opportunity to talk to Bet again until the tavern had shut up for the night. There were no interested clients, but the landlord had offered them a night's lodging above the tavern and they staggered up the dark staircase at the back, tired but grateful for his kindness.

Bet placed their candle on the table by the bed they were to share and began to take off her shoes.

'Whatever're you thinkin' about, Nance?' she asked in some surprise, as she looked up to see her companion sitting idle on the side of the bed.

'I was thinkin' about that dark chap. The one in the corner.'

'Oh?'

''E's called Levi Blumberg.' She laughed. 'Bit of a mouthful! 'E's quite young, actually. Bit of a prude, I reckon. But 'e was nice, Bet. A gen'leman, I s'pose, even though 'e's a furriner.'

'Well, wot *did* 'e want?' Bet was always practical.

'I dunno really,' said Nancy, frowning. ''E said as 'e'd fence fer us.'

'That's a bit o' luck.' Bet was pleased.

Nancy went on. ''E seemed ter want me ter keep away from them lads an' 'e wanted ter know who taught us ter dip.'

'Gawd, you ain't told 'im about Fagin, 'ave yer, Nance?'

165

'Course I 'ave. I couldn't say otherwise, could I? But I ain't told 'im wot Fagin done to us, not 'ow 'e turfed us out on the streets.'

'Good,' said Bet, relieved. She climbed into the bed. 'Because if Fagin ever got ter know, I wouldn't fancy Mr Blumberg's chances – or ours!'

In the weeks that followed, Levi fenced for the two girls and they were pleased with what he gave them for their meagre pickings. Sometimes it was Bet who went quietly to his corner and slipped the few items across the table to him. He would secrete them in the pockets of his enormous coat and the next night, a few coins would pass in the opposite direction to whichever girl brought his drink.

Sometimes Nancy would be in demand with a rowdy group and would have to sing and entertain. Afterwards there would be a scramble to appropriate the star turn and Bet would melt away into Levi's corner.

'I like not to see her like zis,' he remarked on one such occasion. 'It is so – cheap. She made to look like a slut.'

Bet looked at him in surprise.

'But you know wot we do fer our livin', surely?'

'Ah yes, I know. But I like not to see it. But I must sit here vaiting for my custom and I haf to vatch you girls vaiting for yours. It make me very sad.'

Bet thought him a strange fellow.

'You could always join us,' she ventured, slipping into her coquettish voice.

Levi regarded her in horror, his eyes very large and flashing.

'Ah no!' he exclaimed. 'How could I do that? It is not right for me. Or for her,' he added sadly, nodding towards the oblivious object of his interest. 'I do not want – chance events?' He was still unsure of the language. Bet laughed. 'Chance meetings, yer mean,' she offered helpfully. 'Casual pick-ups. One-night stands.'

'Plees, plees!' Levi was distracted. 'You must not talk so. Among my people we luf and marry. This – this sort of thing we do not tolerate. It is not to be found.'

166

'I don't believe you,' scoffed Bet.

'Is true,' replied her companion. 'It goes under the ground. No one sees. No one knows. We do not haf to look at it.'

'Well,' sighed Bet, rising, 'I'm sorry, Mr Blumberg, but in London you'll see an awful lot of it. It don't go underground 'ere. All the same, we keeps out the way o' the peelers, just in case. Yer never know when they're goin' ter show up. Mindjoo, most of 'em are too scared ter come round our neighbour'ood. So we're fairly safe. On the 'ole.'

And having delivered this piece of philosophy, Bet flounced away, back to the lively group under the lights. Levi remained motionless and his face bore one of the saddest expressions in the tavern that night. But his mind was embarking on a new venture, a momentous idea, a gamble which he was prepared to take, because he was so sure he would win.

He took to shadowing Nancy when she was out during the day. It began one morning of blustery wind and rain. Levi was about to open his shop on Commercial Road when he saw, through the thick curtain of motley coats and trousers hanging in his window, a figure hurrying past, head wrapped in an old grey shawl, shoulders bowed beneath the onslaught of the elements. But he recognized her in an instant. Without pausing to consider his actions, he pulled on his greatcoat and rammed his battered top hat on his head, locked his door and set out after her. Keeping close to the lee of the buildings, he trailed the girl for half a mile or more, then stood, partly hidden, in an alleyway, as she crossed the road and entered a lodging house opposite. Obviously she and the other girl had earned enough recently to afford a roof over their heads, he told himself. But what a lodging! With bulging walls and sagging roof and windows so thick with dust they were barely discernible from the bricks which supported them.

Levi turned and walked home thoughtfully. He could not bear this. His Nancy, as he thought of her, should not have to live like this, but what could he do? His moral rectitude dictated that he could not give her shelter; he, a bachelor with a single woman of dubious character beneath his roof? It was not to be contemplated. But he could marry her.

This notion of permanent and accepted respectability appealed to Levi's sense of enterprise, as well as to the humane side of his character. It gave him a new purpose in life, too. He felt already that he was the girl's unofficially appointed guardian and he spent more and more time away from his shop, so that he might catch a glimpse of the fair face he was coming to adore. He would trail her for miles, hiding in archways and shop doorways when she stood on the streets hoping for custom. And when she was successful and walked away on the arm of another man, Levi would grind his teeth and clench his fists in a passion of grief and jealousy and take himself off to the tavern. There he would drink a whole bottle of gin or vodka in an evening and would need a cab to take him home afterwards.

The wet spring gave way at last to a hot, dry summer.

Down by the Port of London a devastating disease had broken out among the brothels and several prostitutes and sailors had died. Some said it was typhoid, others cholera. Whatever it was, no one was frequenting that part of the capital if they could help it.

Levi had not seen the two girls for a week or more, nor had he spotted Nancy on the streets. He worried, he fretted, but he dared not ask after their whereabouts. He went every night to the tavern, drinking, watching, waiting, and at last his patience was rewarded.

It was a sultry night in the middle of August and the clients of the George were not particularly disposed to merriment. Levi looked about desperately for Nancy as he made his way to his corner but failed to see her. Bet came over to him, smiling, and deposited his bottle and glass on the table in front of him. Levi raised his doleful eyes to her.

'Where haf you been zis week? Where is *she*?'

Bet laughed and Levi felt she was laughing at him.

'Us? We've just 'ad a change o' scenery. Don't do to get too familiar with the landmarks, yer know. Besides, I ain't bin too well, either.'

'I am sorry. But Miss Nancy? She is well?'

'Oh yeah, she's fine. She's over there, chattin' ter that sodjer.'

And Bet nodded towards the back view of a large beefy fellow in the uniform of a foot soldier. He was so big that he masked the girl he was talking to. Levi viewed the man's scarlet back with disgust and something akin to hatred, which was alien to him. But such was the strength of his feelings of late. He pulled his thoughts sharply to a halt. What was he doing, letting his mind run away with him like this? He, who was always renowned for his gentleness and tolerance. What worm had crawled inside his brain to make him feel so strongly? I am in luf vith her, he told himself. I am deeply in luf. And I must save her. She is too precious to be left on the streets, to go down into the abyss. I can save her and I will.

The soldier moved away and Levi found himself gazing straight into Nancy's eyes. She smiled and came across to him and his poor heart beat unbearably in his overclad breast. Nancy was dressed in a thin muslin gown and Levi could see every detail through the tight bodice. He forced his eyes to meet hers.

'I haf not seen you since a week,' he said, his voice trembling slightly. 'You are well?'

Nancy was already a little drunk and took a swig from the bottle she was carrying before she answered.

'Me? I'm right as rain. Bet wasn't too well, so I 'ad ter look after 'er fer a bit. She's all right now. I shall 'ave ter dip a few pockets ter make up the cash, though.' She put her head on one side. 'Or step up the ole pavement lark,' she suggested, laughing. ' 'Ow about you, Mr Blumberg? Are you interested in a bit o' sport?'

Levi stared at her as though he had been slapped round the face.

'Plees, Miss Nancy,' he begged, 'do not say such things.

169

You are too goot for that. It makes me very sorry ven I see you to sell yourself to men.'

Emotion made him forget the intricacies of the language and Nancy smiled, but not unkindly, at his efforts. She lowered her gaze to the table and ran her finger through some spilled beer, tracing a shape. She stared at her handiwork. There was a letter there, but she couldn't be sure what it was. She laughed.

''Ere! 'Ave I writ' somethink?' She drew Levi's attention to the mark.

'Yes, my dear, you haf drawn a B.'

Nancy laughed again in sheer delight.

'B fer bottle,' she announced, 'an' booze an' bed – an' blokes!' She sobered momentarily and cast her eyes down again. 'An' baby,' she added wistfully and left the table.

'And Blumberg,' murmured Levi gazing after her retreating figure.

He was sad and angry, because he had failed to speak his mind and because she was being so capricious with him. He must speak soon, or she would be lost to him for ever. He would give her another week and he would not come to the tavern in that time, just to see if she missed him.

Before the week was up, Levi had his chance. The sultry weather continued, and people seemed to be more careless of their belongings. Nancy and Bet did a little pocket-dipping to supplement their income and Nancy was elected to take their pickings to Levi Blumberg. He had not been in the tavern of late. Nancy wondered if she had shocked him out of his corner. So it was with some sense of embarrassment that she made her way to his shop. It was that hot and sticky sort of air which presages a thunderstorm and brings on irritating head-aches, and Commercial Road was quiet.

The outside of Blumberg's shop was festooned with second-hand overcoats, frock coats and smocks, all hanging from an army of pegs fixed up around the shop front. Nancy was reminded for a moment of her first sight of Field Lane. It seemed a lifetime ago. There was a small opening among all these cast-offs, which looked far from inviting and which plunged her into darkness for a moment. She stood blinking. At least the coolness was welcome.

'Goot afternoon,' came Levi's nasal tones from somewhere in the depths of the little shop. 'Can I 'elp you, my dear?'

Nancy blinked in the direction of the voice. It was unnerving to know that he had the advantage of seeing her clearly. She could just make out his swathed form behind a table, on which stood a bottle and a little glass.

'Mr Blumberg,' she said, 'I've brought some pickin's for yer. Can yer fence 'em for me? We ain't seen yer recently, so I 'ope yer didn't mind me bringin' 'em 'ere?'

Blumberg reached for his tinderbox and lit a large oil lamp, which stood on a shelf behind him. The soft light threw his features into eerie relief and Nancy was startled by the youthfulness of his expression.

'Vot haf you got? It's Miss Nancy, isn't it?'

She smiled and lifted from her basket several silk handkerchiefs, a silver brooch, two leather wallets and a velvet reticule embroidered with tiny seed pearls. She laid the goods in a row and Blumberg's eyes glittered as his long hands fluttered above each item in turn.

'Pretty. Very pretty,' he breathed.

Nancy waited, while the almost black eyes darted from end to end of the row, assessing, rejecting, calculating.

Finally he said, 'I gif you two pounds, my dear.'

'That'll do,' said Nancy, well satisfied. They could put that by for the winter.

Blumberg swept the goods together and carried them to the back of the shop, returning a moment later with the cash. He stood very close to Nancy, the coins in his open hand, offering them. As she took them, the long fingers closed and held her hand tightly. Perhaps it was the sudden rumble of thunder outside that made her gasp. Or perhaps some spark of emotion had been emitted in that dark and dusty hole.

Blumberg's arm was round her, holding her tight. His

breath, smelling strongly of spirits and garlic, hit her squarely in the face, so that she all but recoiled.

'I haf luffed you since I first see you,' he whispered. 'I need a vife. You come 'ere? Marry me? Live vith me? Ja?'

Nancy's mind reeled. The man who a moment ago had named a price for her pickings, was offering her the security of marriage, almost in the same breath. She nearly laughed at his audacity.

'Mr Blumberg – ' she began.

'Levi. Please.'

'Levi, then. I – I really don't think it'd be a good idea. Yer see, I live off the streets. Well, yer knows that.' She looked at him very hard. 'An' I ain't of your faith. So we ain't very well suited.'

Levi Blumberg put both his arms round her, bent his head and kissed her very gently, but very long. When he released her, Nancy felt she really had no argument left. He was obviously kind and gentle, virtues she had never experienced from any man, and his proposal was an answer to all her dreams and problems.

'Give us a little time ter think about it, Levi,' she said softly. 'It's jus' that yer've taken me a bit by surprise, like.'

'You vill be at the tafern tomorrow, ja?' asked Levi.

'Yus. I'll be there,' replied Nancy, 'an' I'll let you 'ave yer answer.'

She smiled encouragingly at Levi and he closed her fingers around the coins. They were warm from his touch and she kept them clasped in her hand.

Outside, the bright sun hurt her eyes and another rumble of thunder threatened to break the long spell of heat. The streets reeked in the rising hot air and garbage festered in the gulleys. But Nancy neither saw nor heard nor smelled any of this, as she hurried back to Wapping Lane. She was walking on air and felt as though her heart would burst. Dear, kind, funny Levi Blumberg. A man with a legitimate trade, a shop with lodgings and he himself a respected fence in their twilight world.

Bet was less enthusiastic.

'Yer don't even know 'im prop'ly,' she pointed out. 'An' 'e's a furriner. They got funny ideas, yer know. Do funny things ter their menfolk –'

'I know, I know,' Nancy interrupted impatiently. 'But if I wait fer Mr Perfick, I'll likely wait fer ever. 'E's not likely ter come round the corner termorrer, or even nex' week, is 'e now?'

Bet looked away, disgruntled. If she were truthful with herself, she was very glad for Nancy. Her future would be as assured as it could be in this life they led. But she knew she was envious and not a little sad to think that she might soon be living on her own. But I mustn't be selfish, she thought. After all, it's Nancy's 'appiness wot's at stake.

And so she said, 'Leave it a day or two, Nance. Think it over. Yer mustn't rush into these things.'

'I told 'im I'd see 'im in The George termorrer night an' let 'im know me answer.'

'Well, you think it out very careful, my gal,' replied Bet. 'You don't know nothink about 'im, do yer?'

Nancy sat down and took Bet's hand.

'Bet, dear,' she said, smiling, 'do we ever know anythink about the men we take on? They're all like a lot of oysters: clam up if you asks 'em anythink. No, Bet. I'm sure 'e's a good'un. An' I won't leave yer completely on yer own, 'cos I know that's wot yer worritin' about, innit?'

Bet hung her head and nodded.

'Well, don't you worry,' continued Nancy. 'I'll see yer ev'ry day an' make sure yer've got the necessary.' Her eyes sparkled. 'I might even ask Levi ter find you a job in 'is shop! It's pretty smelly in there, though!'

And both girls laughed.

NINE

What was there for girls on the streets, what future? What had they to look forward to? The simple answer was – nothing. Marriage eluded them. Happiness, if it came at all, was transitory. Comfort came in the shape of a gin bottle. And down into the ever-spinning maelstrom they whirled over the years, health and life disintegrating, the pitiful earnings of their profession the only means of keeping body and soul together. Sooner or later, disease or drink would overtake them and they would end their days in a pitiable state, no more than a bundle of rags in a doorway. Such was the destiny of most of London's street prostitutes. Unless they were lucky enough to be lifted out of the pit, before it was too late, by some well-intentioned man. Levi Blumberg was such a man; but the B Nancy had unwittingly traced on the table top did not refer to him.

That same night, there was a tremendous storm. It began about ten o'clock and raged overhead for several hours. The clientele of The George were forced to stay put and the landlord did a roaring trade. In his back parlour, a gambling table had been set up and some thirty to forty assorted characters were gathered around it, some playing in earnest for high stakes, others watching listlessly, as they downed their beer and spirits. All the dregs of the Ratcliffe were represented here: dippers, cracksmen, magsmen, shofulmen, and even the youngest members being trained up to fine-wire and flimp. And interspersed among them all were the sad jades of the streets. Some were young and still pretty, others heavily rouged to disguise their flecked and pocked faces.

One man stood over the table, a lamp at his elbow, dealing cards and calling the stakes. It seemed that there were two factions present, for there was much disparagement in the conversation and curses and taunts flowed freely back and forth across the table.

Into this hot-bed walked Levi Blumberg. He slipped quietly in at the door, the landlord securing him a place at the table.

'Oh Gawd! Look wot's jus' blown in,' remarked a ruffian at the opposite end of the table. Heads turned and surveyed the tall, well-clad figure as he brushed the rain from his coat and sat down.

'If it ain't bloody Moses hisself,' jeered another. 'Come ter moralize on our hactivities, I s'pect.'

'Yeah. Wonder wot 'e keeps under all them clo'es?'

'Got a few money bags there, I reckon.'

There was much laughter at this, but little further notice was taken of Levi. He was greeted by those who knew him well with a little more respect and friendliness and he acknowledged them with a nod. And he laid his bets.

He had played a little before and it was an amusing way to pass a dark, wet night. But the large crowd had a bad feel to it and he felt nervous. There were too many faces here which he did not recognize.

Blumberg won the next round, much to the annoyance of the outside party, and their noisy indignation brought the landlord hurrying in.

'Please, please, ladies an' gen'lemen,' he cried. 'No noise, no noise. I don't want no p'licemen 'ere ternight!'

'Bah!' shouted a stranger. 'Who's goin' ter turn out on a night like this, I'd like ter know?'

'The peelers'll come in all weathers, if they think there's cause enough,' warned one of The George's regulars.

He was rewarded for his troubles by a gob of spittle which hit him on the cheek. There was a minor scuffle, a few blows and then the landlord prevailed upon both sides to keep the peace, upon pain of being ejected, one and all, into the storm.

Play continued for a while amid oaths and grumbles, until Blumberg had won four hands in succession and was going for yet bigger stakes. Suddenly, the anger of the outside element overflowed.

''E's some bleedin' toff, comin' in 'ere with all that tin.'

'Wher's 'e keep all 'is blunt, then? Under all them bloody clo'es?'

'Come on, le's get 'em off 'im. 'E's probably got money bags all round 'is waist!'

They leaped in, fighting towards their prey. Blumberg rose quickly and his chair toppled over behind him. He eyed the door, but there was no clear way to it. Several locals closed in protectively around him, but his assailants were determined fellows and put up a fight to get at him. Blows rained down in all directions. Chairs were overturned. Tankards flung about the room. Bottles were smashed and the contents spilled on to the floor and table in shining pools.

Blumberg called out over the heads of his attackers, 'Oh please, gentlemen, ve must be more civil. Ve must not fight over little things. It iss not vorth it!'

A blow caught him on the side of the head and he reeled under the impact. Someone made a grab at the scarf at his neck, another knocked off his hat. In a moment, he was besieged on all sides. He was a mild man by nature, but he fought back surprisingly viciously, and landed a neat hook on the jaw of a fellow tugging at his shirt front. This further enraged his assailants.

The landlord burst in, but his entrance went unnoticed, until he suddenly cried out in alarm, 'Look out, Mr Blumberg. 'E's got a chiv!'

His warning came too late. Blumberg disappeared amid the flailing arms, but the landlord had seen a knife flash above his head. It was unclear who held it, but it was driven hard into the foreigner's chest with an upward thrust, slicing through his layers of clothing. Blumberg doubled over, gasping. It went in again, slipping with ease between his ribs. His eyes stared and he cried out in some foreign tongue. The crowd fell silent and now the landlord's urgent voice was heard.

'The p'lice is comin'. Oh Gawd, gents, get out, quick!'

The press of people fell back and as they did so, the blood welled and gurgled in Blumberg's throat. He slid silently to the floor and lay still.

A boy cried out, ''Ere they come! We'd better move!'

They all made for the back door in a concerted rush. But the band of policemen had split into two and, while one section approached by way of the taproom, the other had gone to the back entrance, so effectively stopping any escape. They now rushed in, wet from the storm, and the erstwhile gambling party knew that the game was up. The landlord stood shaking and stuttering as they clapped him in irons. He watched, terrified, as one after another, his clients, his customers, his friends and his enemies, were handcuffed and taken roughly to the waiting coaches outside. This was the end for him, he knew. The end of his legitimate trade and his comfortable sidelines. Murder had been committed that night and he was part and parcel to its setting.

The bleeding corpse on the floor was given scant attention. The police had been watching Blumberg for weeks and had been about to take him. They had been tipped the wink that very evening, but too late to save him. Still, reflected the officer in charge, they had hauled in a good many other troublemakers. And the Ratcliffe would be better off without them.

The police made arrangements for Blumberg's remains to be laid out decently in the parlour and sent for the parish undertaker. There would be an inquest, of sorts, held here in a day or two, though the officer doubted that an accurate charge could be brought. It was always difficult pointing the finger in a large crowd. But justice must be seen to be done.

TEN

The following day dawned bright and clear, the storm having quite blown itself out. But the streets were still wet and as the sun gathered strength, steam rose from the ground, as though the Ratcliffe were built over the fires of hell itself. The gulleys and runnels were blocked with refuse and dirty, reeking water gathered in large pools, which in some places spread right across the road, making passage impossible. Bet, on her way to buy bread and cheese for the day, encountered such a puddle and was forced to turn up a side street and divert her route. As she did so, a small urchin cannoned into her, almost throwing her off balance. He looked up fearfully. Then recognized her.

'Oh, Miss Betsy,' he panted. 'I'm sorry. I wos jus' comin' ter tell yer. The George.' He gasped again. 'They've all bin taken. Least, some of 'em 'ave. An', an', Mr Levi – 'e's dead, miss!'

Bet grabbed his arm. 'Wot d'yer mean, dead?' she demanded angrily, shaking the boy.

He screwed up his face and she relaxed her hold.

''E wos up the George las' night. In the back parlour. They wos all gamblin'. Loads o' them. Then a gang o' coves from Mile End, they set about 'im an' knifed 'im. Cor! 'E didn't arf bleed, miss. Even frough all them clo'es 'e wore!'

Bet found her eyes misting over. Poor, poor, eccentric Levi, with his surfeit of clothes, which hadn't been enough to protect him. He had been kind and generous to them all and he had been a good fence. But what was she going to tell Nancy?

Bet returned dejected to Wapping Lane.

Nancy's heart turned over as soon as Bet opened the door.

'Wot's 'appened, Bet? Gawd, you looks awful. Wot is it?'

Bet set down her basket and took both of Nancy's hands. She looked steadily into her eyes. There was no point evading the question.

''E's dead, Nancy. Levi. 'E were murdered by a gang up at The George last night.'

Her voice broke and she clung hard to Nancy's hands, more to give herself strength than to fortify her companion.

Nancy stood motionless. Her face betrayed nothing yet of what she felt. He couldn't be dead. She had only spoken to him yesterday. He had wanted her to marry him. She was going to see him tonight, to give him her answer. And yes. She would marry him. She would be his wife. She would bear his children. She would be happy. She stared beyond Bet's shoulder, her face white, her lips compressed. She could see him so clearly, his face illumined by the oil lamp in his dark shop. Bet took her in her arms and stood rocking her as she had when they had been children.

'Go on, gal, cry, for Gawd's sake.'

Bet herself was choking back the tears and she bit her lip in an effort to control them.

''Ere,' she said after a moment, 'we'd best 'ave a nip o' gin. Do us both the world o' good.'

She sat Nancy in a chair and busied herself with a bottle and tankards, glancing sidelong at the younger woman's face. The tears stood in her eyes, but Nancy was silent. Bet wondered how she managed it. She put a small pewter pot into Nancy's hands, but they were shaking so much that Bet was forced to take it from her. She sat now on the edge of the table and smoothed Nancy's hair and brow. Nance looked up through her tears. Her voice was broken and faint.

'Oh Bet, why? Why 'im? Wot 'ad 'e done? 'E was 'armless, Bet. Wot they pick on 'im for?'

Bet shook her head sadly.

'I dunno, luv. Life's wicked sometimes. It just ain't fair. We gets born into the rough end of it and then when a bit of

'appiness comes along, it gets snatched away, like. Seems to
'appen a lot to us types, dunnit?'

For answer, the tears suddenly flowed from Nancy's eyes
and both young women wept, until there were no more tears
left. They drank their gin. Then more. And the morning
passed and the level in the gin bottle fell.

'Le's leave this bloody place,' slurred Nancy, some time
later. 'I 'ate it. Nothing's gone right, 'as it? Le's go termorrer.'

'Where s'll we go?'

'Back 'mong friends, I reckon. Le's try Clerkenwell again.'

'Yus,' agreed Bet. 'Fagin'll give us a room fer a bit, I s'pect.
'E's a good sort really.'

They made their way rather slowly to Field Lane, on
account of their having emptied the gin bottle, and knocked
hopefully at Fagin's door. But Fagin would not let them stay.

'No, my dears,' he said, a dash of regret in his oily voice.
'How can I possibly take in two young ladies, pretty young
ladies, with all my lads growing up? Wouldn't be right, now,
would it? I shall be pleased to see you when you visit. Give
you the occasional victuals and drink. But no lodgings, I'm
afraid, my dears. You must find your own lodgings.'

And he waved his sinewy hands in the general direction of
the street. Bet and Nancy pleaded, promising to keep house
and wash and cook for Fagin and the boys, but the old man
would have none of it. And at last the two young women went
away dejectedly.

It was a warm night and they hung around the streets of
Clerkenwell, hoping for pick-ups. Several well-established
ladies sent them packing for trespassing on their beat and the
girls drifted off towards the Three Cripples. But nobody
there was interested. Nancy asked if there was any work for
her behind the bar. Barney said they weren't short-handed
just then.

'Cub back id the autub, luv, an' we might take you on to
'elp wid the servin'.'

This was as far as the nasal Barney could promise. He

watched them depart and was genuinely sorry he could not help.

The girls wandered back to the Ratcliffe Highway. They were both lucky and picked up sailors who had just come ashore. But their hearts were no longer in the job, if indeed they ever had been.

By October, money was low for Bet and Nancy and they eked out their remaining savings with the occasional foray into a City pocket. The end came when Mr Thomas Filkins, who had been so kind to them, went to live with his sister in Colchester and sold his lodging house to a new landlord, who increased the rent to such an extent that Nancy and Bet had no means of meeting the increase.

So they moved themselves out on to the streets once more and headed for Whitechapel. Here, at least, business was a little brisker and one or other of them usually managed to secure a room for the night. But as the weeks wore on and the weather became colder, they found little custom. When they thought they had found an unoccupied beat for a few nights, they were rudely ejected by the regulars and driven from the district. The community of the streets was a tight-knit one, if you didn't fit in.

'Bethnal Green any good?' suggested Bet wearily.

Her companion nodded. And so they trudged on, back and forth across London, sleeping in doorways or under bridges when they weren't able to secure a room. They looked so down at heel that few men were interested in them and no man would pay them more than a mere pittance.

From time to time, they drifted back to The Three Cripples, when they had scraped together enough pennies to buy a hot supper. It seemed a haven in the rough storm of life. There were a few familiar faces there and sometimes Barney would quietly refuse their proffered coins. But they couldn't expect too much of his kindness. Sometimes they would just sit in the tavern to keep warm. It was on one such occasion that Bet noticed a young man eyeing her from a nearby table. She looked at Nancy and slid her eyes meaningfully in his direction. Nancy followed her look and smiled at her friend.

'You know who that is, don't yer?'

Bet frowned and shook her head.

'Thass young Tom Chitlin', wot used to be with us at Fagin's afore we left. 'E's quite grown up, ain't 'e?'

Bet looked back and smiled and Tom Chitling coloured noticeably, even in the heat of the bar parlour.

'I think 'e fancies you, Bet,' whispered Nancy. 'Maybe yer luck's changin'.'

Bet looked down into her stew and toyed with the lumps of meat in it.

'I couldn't sell meself to 'im, though, could I, Nance? I mean, we know 'im. 'E's sort of one of us.'

Her dilemma was obvious. Nancy patted her hand.

'Yer don't 'ave to, yer know,' she said looking very directly into Bet's bright eyes. ''E can always be a – friend. 'E might even take you in! Yer never knows yer luck!'

At that point, the young man in question was ushered away by some high-spirited youths whom Bet and Nancy did not recognize, and Bet was left without an answer to her problem.

It was several nights before they were in the tavern again and this time, Bet was sitting on her own, while Nancy helped to serve drinks. Barney had managed to find a use for her at last. Bet watched her now as she whisked in and out between the tables. She thought how pretty Nancy was beginning to look again. It didn't take much to pull a girl up from the bottom of the pit. She just needed to have something to work for, no matter how menial the task. And Nancy seemed to be happier than she had seen her look for a long time. All she needed now was a little colouring on her wan cheeks and for her hair to be swept back more tidily from her face. Well, they could work on that in time. As she sat dreaming thus, Tom Chitling, greatly fortified by spirits, slipped on to the bench next to her and slid along it until he was almost touching her. She turned and smiled and his heart turned a complete somersault. He reached out, took her hand, and whispered through her chestnut hair.

'Bet, will yer let me walk you 'ome ternight?'

His kindness and gentle voice brought the tears to Bet's eyes.

'I ain't got a 'ome now, Tom,' she murmured, ashamed. 'Nance an' me is out on the streets fer good an' proper.'

Tom looked at her askance. And she misjudged his reaction, thinking him shocked at how low she had sunk. But he was all concern.

'Then come 'ome with me, Bet. I've only got a very little room. But you're welcome ter share it – whenever yer want.'

He wasn't offering a permanent refuge, but it was more than she could have hoped for. She looked up into his brown eyes and smiled her thanks. She found it difficult to reconcile this gentle lad with the thief and rogue he was reputed to be. But she knew appearances could be deceptive. And she had a feeling that Thomas Chitling was not a very clever thief. Perhaps he needed a guiding hand. She saw herself as his mentor. After all, hadn't she been one of Fagin's best pupils for dipping, along with Nancy, of course? She could teach him a thing or two about thieving. She laid her head on his shoulder and he held her as close as he dared in that crowded room. Then quietly they slipped outside and Tom caught her in his arms.

'I don't want the rest o' the mob ter know about us,' he said, his voice trembling a little. 'Least, not yet.'

Bet nodded and raised her face. And Tom kissed her, so gently and so lingeringly. She wasn't used to such consideration and she felt the laughter bubbling up within her, so that she was forced to pull her head away and give vent to her mirth in the crook of his neck.

'Wot's amusin' you?' he asked, not sharing her humour.

She pulled herself free and skipped away up the road, throwing her arms wide.

'Oh Tom, I'm jus' so 'appy,' she called back to him.

Relieved that she wasn't laughing at him, Tom hurried

after her, caught her round the waist and bore her away to his lodgings in the City Road.

Nancy, busy with drinks at The Cripples, did not see the departure of her friend. But in a little while she noticed that both Bet and Tom had gone and she felt pleased for them. At least Bet would have a roof over her head tonight. And perhaps for a good few nights to come. Which was more than she could expect for herself. She sighed and began collecting empty pots and tankards. Perhaps her time would come one day too.

PART THREE

VAN DIEMEN'S LAND
1827–1834

They marched us off like hosses, an' they
sold us out of hand,
Then yoked us to the plough, me boys, for
to plough Van Diemen's Land.

Sea Shanty: *Van Diemen's Land*

ONE

A freshening breeze filled the sails as the *Asia* floated downstream with the tide. She nosed her way like a great swan through the flotilla of little ochre-sailed Thames barges and scurrying ferries. Recognized for what she was, a few fists were shaken in her direction accompanied by cries of, 'Good riddance ter the lot o' yer!' The muttered prayer of one lighterman, 'God bless yer, yer poor buggers,' went unheard in the hissing wake of the barque, as she passed the Bow Bridge over the Lea.

The day was warm, but not yet uncomfortably hot, as August in London could sometimes be. It was the first day of that month in 1827 and for the 158 convicts on board the *Asia*, it was the start of a whole new chapter in their existence. Most of them would never see England again and had they seen the familiar landmarks of London, its docks, its water traffic, its soaring spires, its watery highway, drifting away for ever, then many must have wished themselves sinking in the flood which bore them oceanwards. For this very reason, they were all chained in their sleeping quarters until the ship should be far out to sea and well clear of any last glimpse of England.

But for Bill Sikes, sitting dejectedly in his allotted space, the timbers of the barque might not have existed. His eyes could almost see every detail of the north bank, sometimes slipping across to the Surrey side to pick up a familiar sight, a tall warehouse or a church spire, then back again to the Middlesex bank, with the Ratcliffe Highway running alongside, with its accompanying taverns, The Town of Ramsgate, The Prospect of Whitby and their associations: Toby, Charlotte! He dropped his head into his hands. All this because he had trusted one woman. Or was that the reason? If he was honest with himself, was he not just as much to blame for coming to this pass? He didn't have to live a life of crime. Could he not just as easily have found some honest employment? He wondered what it would be like to work at a trade. To feel secure in a job. To earn a regular wage. But what could he do? He was strong, brave, quick-witted, he knew. But he doubted he would ever have the ability to endure hour after hour, day after day of the same thing, working long set hours. He shook himself free of such thoughts. No, he knew that wasn't his way of life. He'd been over all this before. But meanwhile, he would have to accustom himself to routine and obedience to rules. And he knew it wasn't going to be easy.

His time on the hulk had given him an unpleasant taste of captivity and he was determined that he would do all he could not to exacerbate his situation. He knew he would hate the new life to which he was sailing and he dreaded the sea voyage. He would begin ticking off the weeks and months as soon as he could. And he would come back! Of that much he was sure. He had no family, no ties, and he should have welcomed the antipodean prospect as an adventurous new beginning. But there was that about England, and about London in particular, which pulled him, as if by an invisible thread. It was as though London had been the womb which had borne and nurtured him, the cradle which had lulled him, the parent he had lacked all these years. And the yearning began before the ship was even clear of the river mouth.

He raised his head. All around him men sat in various attitudes of misery and dejection. There were several young lads of fourteen or fifteen, and they wept openly. One man rocked back and forth, beating his head against a ship's timber, moaning quietly to himself. Two evil-looking characters sat hatching trouble together in a dark corner, muttering and glancing round at their neighbours.

Sikes looked across at Will Spiring, sitting cross-legged a few feet away from him. The weeks on board the hulk had done nothing for the lad's health. He looked thin and gaunt and his dark eyes stared out blankly from his sallow face. He returned Sikes's glance with a look of such despair, that Sikes feared for his sanity. He shifted over towards Spiring and took his wrist in a strong grip.

'Don't give in, Will,' he whispered harshly. 'We'll see it through. 'S only seven years, after all. Wot's that when yer young? Nothink. We'll work our way through it an' get back to England again 'ventually.'

Spiring raised his eyes to Sikes's. And Sikes saw they were brimming. He looked away and bit his lip. This was bloody awful and they hadn't even put to sea yet. Still he could feel the draught of the ship's passage, and was thankful for the fresh air.

For once in his life, he was clean. When he and Spiring had been taken from the hulk, they had been conveyed to a building on the water's edge near the Custom House, where they had been thoroughly inspected by the ship's surgeon, Mr Campbell France, and then stripped of their clothes, made to bathe and given a new set of clothes for the voyage. They were coarse but strong, and should last him the long voyage. Too much like a bloody uniform, thought Sikes, looking ruefully at his long legs clad in shiny black duck trousers, grey yarn stockings and stout black shoes. He wore a blue kersey waistcoat and jacket over his check shirt and with a red kerchief knotted at his neck, he felt stifled in the warmth of the prison deck.

As they progressed downstream, the barque began to roll and a number of the men were turning pale and groaning. In a short while, the prison deck echoed to the sound of men retching and the air reeked with the smell of vomit. Sikes was unaffected by the gentle rolling of the ship, but the smell made him gag and retch for a while, until his nostrils had accustomed themselves to the stench. Oh Gawd, he thought. Four months o' this. 'Ow the 'ell am I goin' ter stick it?

They were now approaching open sea. Sikes felt the ship shudder slightly as she swung south. They would follow the line of the southern shore to the great North Foreland Point.

And he could smell the salt air as it gusted through the tantalizingly inaccessible porthole above him. He heard the echoing cry of gulls somewhere above the ship. 'Free!' they cried. 'We and the air are free. To come and go as we please!'

The men were summoned for supper. They had partaken of a substantial dinner at noon, having left the Port of London around ten of the clock that day. Once again, they had been divided into messes of six men and one man from each mess was issued with the rations for his group for the day. They had eaten steak and kidney pies and cabbage, a treat while fresh food was still available. There would be plenty of salt meat in the days ahead.

The prisoners sat now in their messes, only a low murmur of conversation accompanying the clatter of metal mugs and plates. There was a small allowance of beer and a round of bread and cheese. Sikes thought longingly of the hearty meals he had tucked away at The Fig Tree and wondered when he would eat the like again. He thought, too, of the friendly, noisy, smoky atmosphere of the inn. When it had become too much for him, he had been able to slip away back to his lodgings. Here, there was no sneaking off quietly to be alone. Your business, your likes and dislikes, your feelings, were everybody else's, too.

Lanterns were lit and swung from beams at intervals along the decks. When eating had finished and the messing tools cleared away, the prisoners were ordered to sit on their beds and await the visit of the Captain. Mr John Edman was a short, stout man, with sandy whiskers and brown eyes. He stood with his hands clasped behind his back, rocking back and forth on his heels. Bag o' nerves, reflected Sikes. But Mr Edman was a shrewd and experienced sea captain and knew exactly how he wanted to run his ship. He cleared his throat and looked around at the sea of wary faces disappearing into the dark recesses of the deck. He made no preamble, but plunged straight in.

'There are one hundred and fifty-eight prisoners on this ship. My crew and my men, including your guard, constitute another nineteen men. My duty is to get us all safely to Hobart in as short a time as possible, for all our sakes. I can do that, with the co-operation of every man on board this vessel.'

He cast his stony gaze over them all and it rested briefly on the two rebellious characters who had sat plotting in the dark corner.

'You have already been divided into messes of six and each man will take his turn to lead that mess – collecting rations, sharing them out and organizing his men. This ship is a good ship. She has made similar journeys before and she will carry us safely there with God's help and your obedience and, as I say, co-operation. I need say no more, except that daily routine will be explained to you by the crew as we proceed.'

And he turned sharply and disappeared up the ladder, the First Mate stepping in to take his place. A lean, hard man, in his mid-thirties, when he opened his mouth to speak, the heavy Scots accent rendered his words almost unintelligible.

'Ah dinna ken what ah done tae deserve a bunch like yoo,' he began. 'Bu' ah'll tell ye one thing. Any disobedience, any whisperr o' rebellion, an' it's the cat forr ye. An' if the cat isna gude enough, then we've a'ways the box or the irons. So it's up tae ye.'

He glared maliciously at his charges and many hearts sank even further that night.

'Right, noo. Taemorra mornin' ye'll be up a' dawn an' the cooks we've selected will come up tae the deck. Ye'll be given ye' instrructions then. While they're a-cuking, the rest o' ye'll come up an' wash. Ye'll then send ye' messmen tae collect breakfast, while the rest o' ye swab the decks and bring up ye' beds fer stowin'. Ye'll eat at eight an' we'll instrruct ye further frae there. Rememberr! Ye've go' a guard on ye a' the time an' we're in ten fathoms o' water. We pu' in tae Plymouth taemorra an' the ship'll be inspected. After that, we head forr Biscay. Gude-nicht tae ye!'

The prison doors were hove to with a mighty thud and locked and bolted. There was silence for a few minutes, then a low murmuring began among some of the convicts and two of the boys began quietly sobbing again. Sikes lay back on his bed. He knew there were difficult times ahead. The routine alone would be enough to kill him.

Gradually the prison deck settled down and the lanterns were extinguished. The air was close and warm and the constant movement of the ship made sleep elusive. The men still wore chains, so there was as yet no question of shedding any clothing. But they had hopes that their fetters would be struck off some time after leaving Plymouth and most bore the discomfort in silence. Now and then a stifled sob accompanied the snores of sleepers, or the mutterings of the poor disturbed creature, who, even in the night, sat up on his bed to strike his head mournfully against the timbers. The sharp rattle of his chains disturbed those around him, who flung curses and shoes alike in his direction. The poor fellow would yelp and whimper like a dog and sink back on to his bed and peace would reign for a while.

Eventually, Sikes drifted off to sleep, but he was thankful when the first hint of the new day penetrated the porthole opposite to rouse him from his troubled slumbers.

TWO

The *Asia* and its human cargo left Plymouth on a sunny morning, with the sky reflected brightly in the waters of the Sound. The breeze filled her sails as the tall ship turned her bows southwards and westwards to head down the Channel and out into the Atlantic beyond.

The transport ships differed considerably in their organization from other vessels, in that the surgeon on board was responsible, not only for the health of the prisoners, but for their welfare, their occupation and their exercise. And, to some extent, their discipline. Mr Campbell France was a good man, and one of the most humane surgeons on the run between England and Hobart. He handled the *Asia's* prisoners with fairness and understanding, a fact which surprised many of them, in view of the treatment they usually received at the hands of those in authority. With seasickness rising again among the men, Mr France deemed it time to begin occupying the many idle hands. A full and constant daily routine was, in his opinion, the finest remedy for seasickness, homesickness, despair and any ideas of rebellion. For the benefit of all, there was to be daily school, where prisoners could learn to read and write, and religious instruction for the betterment of their wayward souls. They carried a chaplain on board for this purpose. Those with a suitable trade behind them were quickly picked out and made use of. Tailors would be detailed to mend clothes, shoemakers would repair split seams and worn soles and the carpenters were always found jobs among the timbers of the ship. There was even a sailmaker on board and his presence would be especially useful later on the voyage. Bakers were in demand at mealtimes and there were two shepherds, who disappeared periodically to tend to the livestock on board. But the majority of prisoners were unskilled labourers and they would be set to the most menial tasks: swabbing and holy-stoning the decks, helping the crew to carry stores. And when there was no work, they would pick oakum.

Oakum! For Sikes the very word conjured up his time as a youngster in Coldbath Fields with awful clarity. Once again, he snagged his fingers, fumbling the rope with unfamiliarity on the wicked spike, and the blood ran down and mingled with the coarse fibres in his hands. Mr France noticed him and ordered bandages for Sikes and two others with similar wounds. Sikes cursed to himself and felt frustrated and inadequate. He couldn't stand this for four months. He would end up raving, like poor Barty, or he would somehow cast himself overboard and put an end to it all; a difficult feat in view of the chains he still wore. No, he thought, I must find somethink useful ter do.

'Why don't you learn to read and write, Bill?' asked Spiring, as he watched Sikes adjusting the bandage on his hand.

Sikes looked at him as though he had suggested Bill should swarm up the rigging and swing by his feet.

'Wot the blazes d'yer take me for?' he said, half laughing. 'Me? Read an' write? Yer've got ter be pullin' me leg, Will.'

'Well, you're bored already, aren't you? You don't enjoy picking oakum. Why don't you do something useful?'

'Don't be daft, Will! Can you really see me sittin' at a school desk, scribblin' on some bloody slate?'

Spiring dropped the subject and said no more for the time being.

One evening, soon after leaving Plymouth, when the sky was a mass of fire and thunder cloud and a chill wind had sprung up, most of the prisoners made their way back to their sleeping quarters. Sikes always stayed on deck as long as he could, breathing in the fresh salt air, filling his lungs with the tempting scent of freedom. Now he toyed with the remains of his supper, poking pieces of gristle about his plate with a fork. Spiring watched him, sensing he was about to speak. In a moment, Sikes dropped the fork with a clatter on the tin plate. His hands hung loosely between his knees and he stared, unseeing, at the deck.

'Yer know, Will,' he began, 'there's summat wrong with the British justice system. I know I bin on umpteen cracks an' never bin nibbed. I admit, I bin lucky up till now, an' I s'pose this is punishment fer all those times I got away with it. But, yer know, we wosn't even over the railin's o' that 'ouse. Of all the things they could've shopped us for . . .' He was silent for a few moments. Then went on: 'I don't like the toffs gettin' the better o' me. They got so much o' this world's goods. It ain't fair. Thass why I do wot I do.' He grinned. 'Well. I get a bit of a thrill out of it too, yer know. The plannin', the excitement, the danger . . .'

His voice trailed off and he frowned. Will was studying him.

'I know how you must feel, Bill,' he said, 'but you could do something to fight back against society, you know. If you feel that strongly about it.'

'Wot d'yer mean?' grumbled Sikes.

'Well, I know all about that crack. I know what they said about you and Toby Crackit. And the part the woman played. And all the background of skulduggery that went on.'

''Ow could yer?' Sikes was looking at him incredulously.

'I read it in the papers.'

'You . . .' Sikes stopped and Will smiled.

'That's just what I mean, Bill. You learn to read and you'll be one up on your associates and you'll be a lot wiser as to what's going on about you. Don't let them get the better of you.'

Sikes was silent. He was thinking hard. He hadn't realized the case had made the newspapers, he hadn't dreamed he would be written about. He was angry to think that his name, and Toby's, had been read by hundreds of people across the capital and beyond. And their names had been linked with that jade, too. Somehow he felt cheated. It reinforced his feeling of no longer being in control of his own life. Spiring was right. He needed to fight back and the best weapon was education. Well, they'd never educate the likes of Bill Sikes, but if he could learn to read and write a little, it would give him an enormous advantage. It would also occupy his time on this confounded ship. And it could open up endless possibilities in the future. He looked up at Will, smiling.

'All right,' he said. 'I'll try it.'

And so it came about that Mr William Sikes, robber and thief, attended daily classes with the schoolmaster, Mr Cox, and within a week of leaving England he had learned his letters and could just scrawl 'W Sikes' on his slate; the William would come later.

He had begun with some trepidation, feeling belittled at attending school at his age, but when he saw the numbers of other prisoners eagerly queueing up each day for their tuition, he gradually lost his self-consciousness and threw himself wholeheartedly into this new activity. Will Spiring had been to school for many years and now and again he came into the lessons to assist Mr Cox. At first Sikes had been appalled at the thought of displaying his childlike efforts to young Spiring, but the latter gave only praise and encouragement and when the ship's library was opened to those prisoners aspiring to literary tastes, Spiring would select books and listen with infinite patience while Sikes worked his way painfully through the text.

The *Asia* put in briefly at Tenerife and collected fresh supplies of water, sugar, good Spanish wine and lime juice, which would be issued daily to the men to combat scurvy, the scourge of past ocean voyages. The prisoners were allowed on deck in the evening, when they tramped noisily and dejectedly round the perimeter of the ship for an hour, most with their heads hanging down, their shoulders slumped, their feet dragging, poor outcasts of society. Sikes, though he could not stride out, did not slouch, but looked ahead and feasted his eyes on the magnificent sunset over the sea. He had never seen anything quite like it before. His life had not been one of aestheticism, but he found the sight strangely moving, almost exciting. He wanted to grasp it and keep it within his sight for ever, to capture those subtle hues of pink and purple and almost green lying like a great bruise across the whole western horizon. If only he could have come on this voyage as a free man, as a merchant, or even as a sailor or a marine . . .

They sailed from Tenerife early the next morning and headed down the west coast of Africa. The weather was becoming hotter and hotter as they neared the equator and tempers frayed in the heat. Exercise was kept to a minimum and water was strictly rationed. The men rigged up awnings during the day so that a little shelter from the white-hot sun might be gleaned, and the surgeon ensured that every man on board wore a hat while he was on deck.

And then came the glorious day when Mr France ordered all chains to be struck off. He had been closeted with the Captain for some long time and rumours were rife among the crew.

'Reckon they'll be hackin' off the chains o' you lot,' remarked one of the Irish sailors to Spiring.

Immediately, he was surrounded by a mob of eager, sweating bodies, demanding to know the truth of this tale.

'Aye,' he sang, 'they usually do hereabouts an' your Captain doesn't shut himself up wi' the surgeon for no reason. They'll be discussin' of your behaviour so far.'

He laughed, and the sea of faces around him laughed too. And word flew round the ship as she sailed serenely on across the glassy waters of the Atlantic.

Ten minutes later, Mr France and two soldiers stood before the men and a blacksmith, from among the convicts, stood with them. The men on deck crowded anxiously to watch the fetters struck from the legs of the first man. A cheer went up and with it lifted 157 hearts. The one hundred and fifty-eighth sat rocking on his bed.

THREE

As the long days dragged on, the men slipped back into their previous apathy. Water was closely rationed and closely guarded and bartering and bullying for extra rations had begun. The food was as wholesome as could be expected under the circumstances, but it was in short supply and its very monotony was the cause of much dissent among the prisoners. Sikes for one was feeling the pinch and in particular was missing his regular intake of alcohol. He and several others had created a monopoly among the convicts, whereby they bartered wine from those desirous of more food. Invariably this led to tipsiness and, although never seriously drunk, Sikes was warned that any drunken behaviour would be very seriously dealt with. He became more circumspect after this and moderated his intake, sharing much with Spiring, in whom he had a close friend. He wondered, too, if it might not be worth getting on the right side of one of the crew. He reflected on the possibility of this one morning as he took his turn at swabbing the deck. The water was blessedly cool on his bare feet and he was thankful to put his back into some physical labour. He was stripped to the waist and had rolled his ducks to the knee. The African sun burned his shoulders and the muscles rippled under the tanned and sweating skin.

He stood for a moment, leaning on the broom handle, and as his glance swung over the deck, Sikes became aware of the two evil-looking characters he had first noticed on the day they left the Port of London. One had a badly broken nose and a great scar down his left cheek. The other had a rat-like appearance, with teeth to match. They sat now in the shadow of a great cask of oatmeal, their heads close together, deep in whispered conversation. The 'rat' kept looking furtively round and when he encountered Sikes's penetrating gaze, he returned the stare with such venom that Sikes feared the fellow might suddenly leap up and sink his teeth into him in truly rodent-like fashion. He turned back to his swabbing and dismissed the incident. But that evening, he heard them again, hiding beneath a dark staircase between decks. He sank back into the shadows and snatches of conversation drifted towards him.

'. . . later, when we're all bedded down.'

'. . . need others to 'elp . . . too many crew.'

'. . . big, dark-'aired fellow?'

Mutiny! It wasn't unknown on the convict ships, but they rarely got away with it. Sikes turned hot at the thought. But there were only the two of them. They must be going for the stores. He ought to let the Captain know, but he would never blow the gaff on his fellow men. Besides, the ship was too confined a space in which to live with them afterwards. No, he'd let it go. They wouldn't get away with it. He crept away and found Spiring.

'I reckon there'll be a rumpus 'ere afore long, Will.'

Spiring looked up from the book he was reading. His eyes looked tired and he was not weathering the heat as well as Sikes.

'Mmm?' he murmured wearily.

'I 'eard them two rough types talkin' agin,' hissed Sikes. 'I think they're after the wine rations. I reckon we're in fer a right shindy ternight. Best keep yer eyes open an' yer wits about yer, Will.'

Wilfred Spiring nodded. 'You do that, Bill,' he said sleepily. 'I'm too tired to stay awake watching.'

'Don't be so . . .' Sikes began, but stopped.

Spiring was obviously exhausted and it wasn't fair to pester him.

'Sorry, Will,' said Sikes. And then in a sudden surge of helpfulness, 'I'll do yer turn at supper ternight. You stay 'ere,' and he hurried off to collect the rations for his mess.

That night Sikes forced himself to stay awake, blinking up into the darkness. He heard the guard outside changed and far above them the coarse tones of the First Mate's voice. There was some humping about of ropes and barrels, a door slamming here and there in the stern as the officers took themselves to their berths. And then the ship was quiet, save for her night noises as she drifted through the warm seas towards the equator.

The heat was almost intolerable and Sikes continually tossed and turned, trying to find a cool spot. After what seemed like a couple of hours, there was a scuffle outside the door and the heavy slump as of bodies falling. He lay rigid. The sweat trickled unmercifully over his temples, down his neck and under his arms. He listened intently, his head turned towards the distant door. He heard metallic scratchings and grindings and then a pale shape appeared in the blackness of the doorway. He waited, tense, ready to spring. The figure was joined by another, and the pair were making their way to his end of the deck. He watched through half-closed eyelids and saw them stand at his feet. Mentally bracing himself, he waited. The 'rat' tiptoed up the narrow space between Sikes and his neighbour, ducking his head beneath the bed above. Sikes could see the glint of metal in his hand and as the wretched little fellow bent over him, no doubt intending to put the knife to his throat and a hand over his mouth, Sikes thrust himself upright, grabbing the man's wrist and sending the weapon skittering across the boards. With a deft movement, he had a brawny arm across the man's throat and a knee in the small of his back. The 'rat' was trapped.

His confederate started to run, but by this time a number of the sleeping men had awakened and rallied to Sikes's cry of, 'Catch 'im, someone!' The man with the broken nose was floored by a flying tackle and the young man who executed this move now sat on him, with his arms pinioned tightly behind his back.

'Someone fetch the guard!' bellowed Sikes.

And the young boys, who slept near the door and who were glad of some action, sped away to find the military, it being apparent that their own guards had been rendered unconscious by the villains.

Lanterns were lit and the Captain himself appeared, his greatcoat thrown on hastily over his nightshirt. The miscreants were taken away and boxed for the rest of the night in tiny wooden cells, where they could only stand. Tomorrow there would be a flogging. Sikes was commended for the speed of his reactions, but dismissed the praise of his fellow men. He hated public attention. He threw himself back on his bed. At least he might now get some sleep.

The following morning, after the sleeping quarters had been holystoned, the entire ship's company gathered on the upper deck, an awful and expectant silence hanging over it. The Captain stood on the fore deck and his officers were lined up alongside. The two culprits of the previous night were brought out of their boxes, looking much the worse for wear, blinking and squinting in the brilliant sunshine. Two crew members fastened their hands to the fo'c'sle bulwarks and another two delivered twenty lashes to each man with a cat-o'-nine-tails. Sikes, along with the rest of the convicts, watched in awed silence, as the leather thongs cut into the two thin, bony backs and rendered them bloody messes. It was all they deserved, but the sight made him wince none the less. Afterwards, the two men were taken away and put back into chains, in which state they were to remain for the rest of the journey.

The company, subdued by such a practical warning, slunk away and picked up the threads of the day's routine. But every man had been affected to a greater or lesser extent by the morning's flogging and work was carried on in a chastened mood that day.

By evening a storm, first sighted many hours earlier as odd-looking cloud on the horizon, and a welcome fresh little breeze, had met the ship. As the *Asia* started to buck in the swelling waters like a fractious horse, the crew and prisoners forgot all about the attempted mutiny.

FOUR

For three days the storm raged. Sikes was awed, yet excited by it. It was an entirely new experience in his life. The ship pitched and rolled, bucked and yawed, and fairly leaped from the sea at times. The wind snatched breath and voice away, and within minutes of the rain starting every man above deck was soaked to the skin.

Many of the prisoners were sick and the majority were confined to the prison deck, where they were less likely to be swept overboard. Even here, the water seemed to follow them and disturbed the odours of the bilges just below them, adding to their discomfort. The Mate, catching sight of Sikes skittering about on the slippery deck, commandeered his help in securing battens and winding in the mainsails. His strength and stamina were a welcome addition to the hard-pressed crew and Sikes himself was glad to be occupied once more.

It was difficult in the extreme to haul on ropes saturated with water, even to handle the wooden hatches, and Sikes developed a new admiration for the crew of the *Asia*. It seemed strange that for the past week they had been constantly on the lookout for a freshening of the wind to speed their journey. Now it seemed as though they must be blown all the way to the Antipodes.

There had been some distant rumblings of thunder and several times the ocean around them was lit up by lightning. But they had escaped the very centre of the storm. While it raged, darkness fell and lanterns now swung crazily from brackets on the bulwarks. Sikes helped pump out sea water with a two-handed pump. His partner was a small, thickset, bow-legged little sailor with the strength of an ox. He didn't waste his breath trying to talk above the uproar, but swung

202

into an easy rhythm with Sikes. Between them, they kept the water from the lower decks. Sikes looked at the scene. It was like something from a nightmare. The men's faces loomed ghostly from the recesses of the ship, highlighted by the streaming rain. And the noise all around was terrifying.

By the early hours of the third morning, the storm was beginning to die down and the exhausted crew and the few prisoners who had helped them sank thankfully on to their beds and slept till noon.

They anchored for two days in the calm waters of Table Bay to take on fresh stores. There was plenty of work for all on board the *Asia* in the days that followed the storm, but by the time the stores had been replenished, the ship was ready to put to sea again. The officers and crew had gone ashore by turns and the military guard, too, had been allowed to feel firm land again beneath their feet. Sikes looked enviously out over the blue-green water and watched the Captain and the First Mate step ashore from the lifeboat. The water was crystal-clear and only just deep enough to anchor in. He could easily dive in and swim ashore. He laughed at himself. He had never swum in his life and had not the first inkling of how to keep afloat. Besides, the drop from the bulwarks was considerable and the resultant splash would immediately alert the guard.

After the storm came the heat and when, a few days later, the *Asia* entered tropical waters, the convicts lay tossing in their bunks at night in temperatures which they thought must boil their blood. This is it! Sikes thought, lying in a bath of sweat. This is 'ell fires themselves. We'll all burst in this 'ere 'eat an' that'll be the last anyone 'ears of us!

The bilges stank, the prison air was stifling and oppressive, but they survived, simply by sitting still or lying patiently on their bunks. There was little activity on deck during the day, for the sun beat down remorselessly and even between decks, the tar melted and dropped sizzling on to their naked flesh. After sunset, the surgeon would allow them on deck until ten at night. No man had the energy for more than a slow shuffle round the deck for half an hour, but the air here was marginally cooler than in the prison and at least they weren't under the glare of the sun.

Sikes and Spiring were engaged in conversation one evening after they had crossed the Line. They shuffled slowly in the heat. There was no sound but the lapping of waves around the ship's bows. They were almost becalmed.

'I don't think I can stand much more of this, Bill,' said Spiring quietly. 'It's like a nightmare. All that celebrating and nonsense when we crossed the equator. You'd never believe we were the same company.' He sighed. 'If only there was just a little wind.'

Sikes nodded and stared out to sea. The sun had long since sunk beyond the horizon, but there was still a faint, eerie glow between sky and sea. He strained his eyes in search of a cloud. He thought longingly of the storm off Africa. There was a gentle, periodic creak of timber, as the ship rocked very, very slowly in the water. The men's voices were hushed, saving energy.

'Well, it can't go on for ever.' Sikes's voice was husky. 'But lor', wot I'd give fer a pint o' good English ale!'

His throat ached and his lips were parched dry. The water ration wasn't due till morning. Even then, it would be only a quart of stale, warm fluid, downed in a few seconds. There would be the daily ration of lime juice, too, and a little wine. But these did nothing to slake the terrible thirst from which they all suffered.

Now the two men stood against the rail, their eyes restlessly searching the profound emptiness before them. Sikes rubbed a hand over his face. It came away salty and wet.

'Yer know,' he pointed out, 'we must 'ave bin through more troubles in the last four months than we' bin through in a lifetime.'

Spiring nodded sadly. He was thinking of the hundreds and hundreds of miles between him and Sarah, and he wanted to weep, to beat his head and fists on the rail in his impotent anger. There was nothing he could do. All the time, they were drifting further and further away from all he had ever loved. He glanced at Sikes and wondered if the man had felt love, too. Perhaps his tough exterior was simply a façade for a deeply emotional soul within. Yet somehow he doubted it. Sikes himself had told him he had been on the streets as a child and had lived the low life ever since. After all, he'd been shipped for housebreaking. No, he thought, Sikes is a hard nut to crack. Nothing sensitive about him. He wouldn't understand what there was between Sarah and me.

He ran his fingers through his hair and scratched his bare and sweating back. Sikes moved reluctantly away from the rail and the two men descended into the oven-like bowels of the ship to snatch what little sleep they could.

About three in the morning, the prison deck was roused by shouting outside. Those who had slept fitfully woke rapidly, but no one knew what had happened. Suddenly, the ship lurched and men who had got up to stretch their legs found themselves having to grab at the sleeping partitions.

'Christ!' shouted someone. 'We struck a bloody rock or summat?'

When the ship tilted in the opposite direction, a nervous cry went up.

'Wot's 'appenin'? Why can't we 'ave some light? Someone tell us wot's goin' on!'

Sikes's voice growled across their fear. 'Wind's got up. Thass wot's 'appened.'

'Really? You reckon so, Bill?'

He could sense their eager eyes and grinning mouths. A cheer went up and the convict nearest the prison door bawled through to the guard, 'Wot's afoot then, mate? Wind got up?'

'Yes!' came the reply. 'We're moving proper now.'

Again the great cheer. Now they could carry on, they could survive. Whatever the alien country ahead of them had in store, they would meet its challenge and survive. Little pockets of animated conversation broke out, but most of the men were happy to drift back to sleep. Sikes turned and cuffed gently at Spiring's shoulder, his aim uncannily accurate in the dark.

'There y'are, Will,' he whispered. 'Yer'll be all right now.'

Spiring declined to answer. He didn't trust his voice.

After her long drift in the South Atlantic, the *Asia* now made good headway to Cape Town to replenish her water supplies. But, once again, only the crew were allowed ashore for a few hours and the military had the task of bringing on supplies and watching the prisoners.

As they left the Cape behind them, the Captain called his crew and human cargo together on deck. He stood on the bridge surveying them for a moment. He thought they looked a sorry bunch, thin, gaunt, some with great burn blisters, others suffering from scurvy, since they had run out of lime juice not long before their landfall. But they were survivors, he felt, every one of them. Even Barty, who had ceased his head beating and who had sat docilely throughout the long hot days, giving trouble to no one. Some of these fellows had been big, brawny chaps when they started out, reflected Mr Edman. His eye fell on Sikes. Well, they would recover. England's loss would be Van Diemen's Land's gain, he was certain.

'We're on a straight run now, men. Straight across the Indian Ocean to Hobart. It's another six thousand miles, but once we get the Westerlies behind us, we should make good running. We'll return to activities and I think you'll find the time will pass tolerably quickly.'

There was a movement among the convicts and a hand was raised.

'Yes?' the Captain asked warily.

''Ow much longer will it take, Cap'n?'

The Master of the *Asia* smiled and looked relieved.

'Impossible to say exactly, but about another two months.'

And he went back to his cabin, while the surgeon dismissed the convicts to their various tasks. Sikes was detailed to dry-holystone the deck that morning and as he and some dozen others bent to their task, he determined that he would master his reading and writing before they reached Hobart. It was the only thing he envied the toffs for; well, that and all their blunt! But he could see what an advantage it was for a man to be able to read and write. He grinned to himself and didn't even notice how the crumbly stone scoured his hands. And when it was time for his lessons, he went more willingly than any grammar school boy.

When they entered the Southern Ocean, the Westerlies backed them and they fairly raced towards the Antipodes. And on the last day of November, the *Asia* nosed her way up the River Derwent and lay still at last, nudging the quay at Hobart Wharf. It had taken 121 days and not a man had been lost. The Master and surgeon were cheered as they went ashore, leaving the military the task of disembarking their charges.

FIVE

Sikes had had no idea what to expect when he first laid eyes on the land of his exile. The morning of 30 November 1827 was one of bright summer sunshine. The sky was a vast dome of blue, pierced by a soaring, snow-capped mountain, the little settlement of Hobart gathered at its mighty foot. Sikes fairly gawped at the orderliness of it all. Neat, stone buildings edging the spacious quay and wide, clean streets stretching away from it.

They had all been chained again before the ship entered the mouth of the Derwent and the mournful clank of irons became a backdrop to their arrival on the other side of the world. They were briskly ushered off the ship, stumbling and staggering at the unaccustomed stability of the ground beneath their feet. Many of the convicts found their legs giving way under them and Sikes felt his own weak and useless as he was bumped and jostled against his neighbours.

Eventually, all 158 men stood together on the quayside. One hundred and twenty-one days had brought them to this far distant shore, twelve and a half thousand miles from home. And most of them stood, awed and wondering, and not a little fearful of their future. The voyage had taken its toll and the men looked thin and sickly; some still bore the burns of the Tropics; all were scorched by the relentless equatorial sun.

Chained one to another, this sorry-looking band were marched away under their military escort, through the streets of the little town. Here, early risers stared in undisguised contempt for the latest shipment of cheap labour. Children ran alongside, jeering in their clear, piping voices. Sikes stared straight ahead and ignored the settlers. Ahead of him he saw, on rising ground, the grim building of the penitentiary. Gawd, he mused, my 'ome fer the next seven years!

It was a squat, single-storeyed, stone affair. The two adjacent sleeping wards each held two tiers of sloping bed platforms, with a messing space in front. For ventilation, there were three high, heavily barred windows and opening on to the general scene was a stout wooden door, heavy with bolts and locks. Adjoining these wards were the kitchens, the Superintendent's office and the guard house for the military.

Sikes and his brothers-in-crime were marshalled into some semblance of order in the yard outside and, three at a time, were marched, clanking and disconsolate, before the Superintendent. A clerk was kept busy recording every detail of each man, from the colour of his eyes to his date of conviction. Never had such records been kept anywhere in the world before. Governor Arthur was going to shake up this colony and run it according to his own dictates and the Superintendent knew better than to attempt any cutting of corners.

A fussy little man with a measuring device ran circles round the prisoners.

'Name?'

The Superintendent was getting tired and didn't look up.

'Bill Sikes.'

'Age?'

'Twenty-five.'

'Height, Mr Cook?'

'Six feet and two inches, sir.'

The Superintendent's head came up and he fixed Sikes with a keen eye.

'Where are you from, Prisoner Sikes?'

'Lunnon,' came the surly reply.

The Superintendent raised his eyebrows. How had this one survived the poverty of the streets to reach this sort of height? He was a giant among his fellows, although the thin young fellow who had just gone through (Spire? Spring? it didn't matter) was only a little short of this one's height. London was breeding a new race, it seemed.

When his details were all written in the clerk's ledger, Sikes and his two companions were unchained and led into an adjoining room, where they were stripped and then poked and prodded by a doctor. Clothed once more, they were returned to the yard to wait in the hot sun. When all had passed through the hands of the receiving officials, the Superintendent stood before them and read out the names of those assigned to free settlers, and Sikes watched in envy as they were escorted to their new homes by small detachments of soldiers. Sikes was not among the next category, either, the twenty-odd men guilty of crimes which had earned them time in a penal settlement. They had another journey ahead of them and they were rechained. He waited in a fret of anxiety. What the hell were they going to do with him and Spiring? They were reserved for 'government projects', it seemed. Road-making, bridge construction and the erection of new buildings. They would be based here in Hobart, but for some projects they would be housed in huts on the job.

Their work began in the stone quarry, a little way outside the town. Again they were chained together and they stumbled with difficulty along the unmade path. Sikes looked around him as they went. The sun was hot, and he wondered irrelevantly why the great mountain, towards whose foot they plodded, was capped by snow. He'd never seen a mountain before and the last snow he'd seen had been brown and slushy on the streets of St Giles's.

In the quarry, they were set to work smashing up great slabs of sandstone with sledgehammers. It was strenuous work for men much depleted in strength and stamina, and despite his size, Sikes had great difficulty in making much effect on the stone. Like his mates, he was tired and exhausted from the voyage and from the contrasts in climate through which they had passed. He was undernourished from the poor rations on board ship and weakened by days of inactivity. But he was only one among hundreds and in a short while he would recover and rebuild his strength. It was only a matter of time, he told himself. Meanwhile he put as much energy into his work as possible. But by the time a halt was called for their dinner-break, he felt completely drained and his head swam in the heat.

'They ain't goin' ter leave us in these fer good, are they?' queried the middle of Sikes's threesome.

He was a fellow in his mid-thirties, very small and thin, with a pinched, sallow face and large staring eyes. He wore a permanently surprised look. The third man in the party was nearer Sikes's age, of medium height and build, his thin brown hair plastered close to his head.

He seemed better-informed than his two companions and now said, in an unmistakably Irish accent, 'To be sure, young Jacky. An' they'll leave yer trussed up at night, too. Yer in them tings fer the rest o' yer days, me lad!'

And he winked across at Sikes. Sikes felt too tired to join in the banter, but he smiled none the less and Jack caught sight of him.

'Garn!' he laughed, elbowing Paddy in the ribs. 'Yer both 'avin' me on. I weren't born yesterday, yer know.'

Paddy Phelan relented. 'Not a bit of it, young Jack,' he chuckled. 'I'm told they'll be havin' the irons off us in a week or so. Once they've got the measure of us. Now, tuck into yer food, man, or yer'll be complainin' they don't feed yer!'

Sikes listened in silence. He hoped Paddy wouldn't prattle all the time. They would need a little respite from his tongue. Still, he would probably keep them cheerful, provided he didn't open his mouth too wide or too often.

When they returned to the prison that night, they were unshackled from each other, but the fetters on their legs remained. Supper was a noisy affair, with men scrabbling for places, talking loudly, nervously, still unsure of each other, and grumbling in harsh whispers. And over all was the incessant clank of chains. Sikes looked at his plate. It held a congealed mass of salt beef and a large helping of grey-green peas. In his mug was his ration of watered beer. Seven years of this, he thought. Seven years afore I gets a decent meal again. He picked up his fork and toyed doubtfully with the mess.

His neighbour had been watching him covertly. Now he spoke from the side of his mouth.

'Ain't goin' ter get anythink diff'rent, mate. Might as well get on with it.'

Sikes eyed the fellow but felt no reply was required of him.

'Wot's yer name, mate?' pursued the man, stuffing his mouth with the unappetizing victuals as fast as he could.

Sikes told him.

'Yer look pretty fit. Wot's yer line o' business?'

Sikes was non-committal. 'Second-'and business. Get around visitin' quite a lot. Y'know.'

'Yeah. I know.' The man grinned. 'I'm in a similar line meself. Well, sort of.' He lowered his voice. 'Only reason I'm 'ere is because me 'oss stumbled an' threw me.'

'Yer 'orse?'

The fellow laughed and stuck out a hand.

'Yus. Thomas Oxbrow, dragsman, at your service!'

Sikes stared in amazement. 'You? An 'ighwayman?'

'Wot's so strange about that, eh?' retorted Oxbrow. 'I bin robbin' coaches an' carriages along Mile End long afore you wos pickin' pockets, young buzzer.'

Sikes made a sudden move, but Oxbrow waved a hand at him.

'All right, all right. Let's not get aggerywated. We've got ter spend too long tergether ter start off argyfyin' at this early stage. But I've spent a lifetime on the drags an' a rare life it's bin, too. Bin livin' in clover, the last ten years or so.'

He smiled to himself and stared across the long room. Sikes studied him sideways for a moment. He must have been a good twenty years older than Sikes and years of adventure and law evasion had taken their toll. The lean face was hard and brown, the shifty eyes a cold clear blue. Oxbrow's hair was silver and he seemed to have more on his cheekbones than on his head. His hands were thin and gnarled, callused from reins. Oxbrow felt himself being watched and turned his head, grinning openly.

'Cheer up, Bill,' he chuckled. 'A purtin' glumpot ain't good fer man nor beast. Now, if yer game, I can teach you a thing or two.'

Sikes nodded. He was not averse to picking up knowledge from another's experience. If he was going back to England one day, then he wanted to return with his head full of ideas. He would follow in his father's footsteps. Maybe move up a notch or two. Money, new clothes, good food and drink and his pick of the best women.

His thoughts were rudely interrupted by the strident voice of the duty sergeant.

'I said, on yer feet! Smartish!'

Sikes drained his mug and stood up. As they shuffled away from the table and prepared to bed down for the night, Oxbrow nudged Sikes.

'There's women 'ere, yer know.'

The small man's eyes glinted and Sikes could have sworn his mouth watered.

'Over the river,' Oxbrow went on. 'Loads of 'em. I'll interduce you, if yer like.'

He raised his eyebrows and Sikes nodded.

'Ain't too easy, of course,' said the little highwayman. 'Depends on who's on guard. Might mean 'andin' over some o' yer rations now an' again.'

Sikes thought it might be worth the sacrifice, and in time, he became familiar with the route out of the prison, across the footbridge over the river and into the women's quarters. He didn't go as often as some of the men, since his food and drink meant a great deal to him. But the occasional visits satisfied his natural desires and the change of company was welcome.

The months progressed through stone-breaking to road repairs, from summer to winter. It still seemed odd to Sikes that here they were, in May and June, with the weather closing in like any English autumn and leaves dropping from the trees outside the penitentiary. Sikes would watch them blow in dry little circles in the wind, much as he had seen them chase each other in the corner of Lumber Court. And his mind would go back, relive all those good times. He could see now they had been good times. Why hadn't he clung more securely to them? Why hadn't he been more careful? He was a fool, he told himself. A stupid, naïve fool. Well, he wouldn't let it happen again.

Life on the prison camp was hard and unyielding, like the ever-present military surveillance. Just occasionally, a soldier could be bribed to let in extra rations of beer or tobacco. But if he or any of the prisoners were caught, there was hell to pay.

Once Sikes and Spiring had persuaded a young soldier to bring in a small quantity of spirits for them. Sikes was missing his gin and he thought it might revive Spiring's sinking morale. But Spiring was seen receiving the bottle from the soldier and both of them received fifteen lashes apiece. Sikes watched miserably, knowing that he ought to have been there too at the end of the cat. But self-preservation was particularly strong if you had been brought up on the streets of the harshest, dirtiest city in Europe.

SIX

After that, Spiring seemed to descend into a pit of abject misery. One cold morning in early July Sikes saw him sitting alone on a half-built wall in the compound. They had just breakfasted and were waiting for the guard to escort them to a farm some three miles distant, where they were to dig ditches and clear scrub for the day.

Sikes watched his breath drift in a white cloud on to the still, blue air. He stepped over the low wall and sat down by Spiring, chafing his hands to keep warm. For a few moments he said nothing.

Then, casting a sidelong glance in Spiring's direction, he said quietly, 'You got problems, Will?'

There was no indication that Spiring had heard him. He remained with his head bent and his shoulders hunched. Sikes did not push further and the two men sat in silence, a silence of mutual understanding. Sikes thought he knew what was troubling his friend; it was surely the woman he had left behind. Poor Will was devastated by the loss of his Sarah.

The sound of gathering troops brought Sikes back to the present and he glanced over his shoulder.

'Come on, Will,' he chided. 'It's time ter move off. Yer comin'?'

Spiring shook his head and a sob escaped him.

Sikes felt uncomfortable. 'Yer can't stay 'ere. Yer'll get another floggin'. Come on, lad, move yerself.'

'I can't. I can't do any more, Bill. I want to die. Leave me alone, for God's sake. I don't want anyone else involved.'

Sikes's hand shot out and grabbed Will's shoulder.

'Don't be daft, Will! Yer can't just give up like that. Come an' do some work an' we'll talk about it later.'

Spiring shook his head again, but Sikes hauled him to his feet and all but dragged him over to where the other prisoners were gathering. Since they were going outside the compound to work, the men were chained together to prevent their escaping. As Sikes was locked into his irons, he looked across at Spiring, being shackled alongside him. He was horrified by the look of sheer desperation on the man's face.

The gang moved off, stumbling over the rutted ground, the heavy irons rubbing at their ankles. There was much coughing and hawking; many of the men were suffering from colds and bronchitis. By the time they arrived at the farm, most of them had wet feet, their boots providing little protection against the deep puddles they had encountered. Some of the gang were left chained together to clear out undergrowth around the perimeter of the farm. But Sikes, Spiring and half a dozen other tall fellows were given spades and pickaxes and ordered to construct drainage ditches in the fields.

As usual, Sikes welcomed the strenuous activity, glad to exercise his muscles. But Spiring stood with the pickaxe in his hand, staring at the ground.

'I want to be down there,' he murmured. 'Dig a hole for me, Bill, and bury me in it.'

He was almost talking to himself. Sikes looked up in mid-swing.

'You gone crazy or somethink? You must be sick, Will. 'Ere, I'd better get the surgeon to yer.'

He dropped his pickaxe and ran towards the sergeant who was lounging against the field gate, smoking a cigar.

'Sir!' he called. 'Will Spirin' needs a doctor, quick. I think 'e's sickenin', got a fever or somethink.'

The sergeant looked unperturbed.

'We have no surgeon here, prisoner. He'll have to wait till we get back this evening.'

'But look 'ere, the bloke's really ill. 'E might be goin' ter die,' interposed Sikes.

The sergeant grinned. 'I doubt it,' he drawled, nodding in Spiring's direction. 'Seems to have made a speedy recovery.'

Sikes followed his gaze and to his embarrassment saw Will Spiring wielding a spade at the hole Sikes had been making. He hurried back and grabbed his own spade.

'Wot the 'ell you playin' at, Will?' he growled. 'Made me look a bloody fool!'

'I'm digging myself a hole,' replied Spiring, his voice low and sonorous.

Sikes decided to ignore him. He worked feverishly at the ditch and in a little while had to remove his coat and jacket, despite the cold, since the sweat was beginning to trickle down inside his shirt. But his feet remained encased in soggy boots and he watched the ditch slowly filling with water as they dug. With every spade stroke the water seeped in, until they were all standing ankle-deep in icy water. For four hours they worked thus, heaving and grunting at the thick, water-logged soil, until at last the sergeant on duty gave orders to break for dinner.

Sikes clambered from the trench, anxious to escape the watery bath in which he had stood all morning. But Spiring remained standing still, resting on his spade, staring at the oozing earth.

Sikes looked back, then leaned over and held out a hand, saying, 'Come on out, Will. Yer'll feel better fer some grub.'

Spiring took the proffered hand and Sikes heaved him out of the ditch. The man's hands were icy cold and he was shivering from head to foot. Unlike Sikes, he had removed none of his clothing while working. Sikes, alarmed at his friend's deterioration, took his coat and threw it about Spiring's shoulders, making do with his own thin jacket against the chill air. He collected their rations and the two men sat a little apart from the others.

'You goin' ter tell me wot's up then?' Sikes spoke in a low voice. 'You ain't well, are yer? You got a fever? Or jus' makin' yerself mis'rable?'

Spiring looked up, his eyes bright and dilated, fearful, searching.

'It's Sarah,' he said simply. 'I can't live without her. And I know I'll never see her again. So it's best if I die. I'm sure I've got a fever coming on anyway, so maybe it's all for the best.'

Sikes did not reply, but regarded him with a worried expression. He couldn't understand this. Dying for love was the sort of thing you heard women talk about when they giggled in corners or were the worse for drink. But it didn't really happen. Not to young men like Spiring. He was educated, sensible. He'd be going home in less than seven years now. What the hell was he playing at? Spiring was talking again.

'Bill, if ever you get back to England, will you do something for me, please?'

'Course I will.'

'Find Sarah and tell her what happened. Rixon's Farm, Kensington. That's where she'll be. Tell her I let myself go because I couldn't face life without her. Tell her I loved her right to the end. And Bill – give her this, will you?'

He reached deep inside his clothes and brought out a small package. He opened it to show Sikes the contents. There was a brief letter, written in Will's neat hand, a small lock of his hair and a button cut from his coat. Sikes disliked the sentimentality of the moment, but he said nothing. Spiring had been his only friend, ever since they left London, and the least he could do was to go along with what might be the younger man's last wishes. He stowed away the package and the two men ate their meal in silence.

As the gang trudged back to Hobart that afternoon, there were others who, like Spiring, stumbled and fell, and the military became angry at the slackening of pace. It was a sorry sight which finally staggered into the prison compound that evening as the lamps were being lit, the sick prisoners supported by their comrades.

Sikes overheard the words 'marsh fever' and inwardly shuddered. He ate his supper in silence and walked dejectedly across the yard to his sleeping quarters to see if Will was there. A depressing sight met his eyes as he entered the ward. Six men had been brought low by fever, sweating,

218

ranting in their delirium and retching in their brief moments of lucidity. The surgeon was there and a couple of military medical men. But there was little they could do.

Sikes went over to Spiring's bed. The young man was unconscious. He lay still, deathly pale, a dew of sweat gathering on his brow. Sikes crouched down by his side.

'Don't die, Will,' he whispered hoarsely. 'I ain't got no one else 'ere ter talk to. I ain't got any other friends. I think they're scared o' me or somethink.'

He smiled briefly. Then went on in a desperate attempt to stem the flow of life from his companion, 'Yer can't go yet, anyway, Will. We ain't finished that ditch we started!'

There was no reply, but Spiring's hand moved slightly where it rested on the crumpled blanket. Tentatively, Sikes closed his own hand round it. It was very cold and clammy and Sikes knew a moment of fear. He was reminded of another cold, damp hand, over fourteen years before, which he had sat and held until the life had drifted out of its owner, leaving him an orphan. Will's face blurred before him and he started nervously when the surgeon's hand descended on his shoulder.

'He's gone now, lad. I'm glad he had a friend by him at the end.'

Sikes blinked hard to clear his vision and saw that Will's breathing had ceased and his head had dropped to one side. He drew a deep, deep breath, gave a last gentle squeeze to Will's hand and went outside.

Here, it was bitterly cold, but the overcast sky of the day had cleared and the air was brilliantly clear with frost. Sikes looked up and marvelled at the myriad stars above him in this southern sky and he wondered, childishly, if Will were up there among them.

SEVEN

For the next two and a half years, Sikes allowed himself to settle into a grudging routine of heavy labour, punctuated by the deaths or sickness or punishment of those around him. He felt himself immune to all that; he led a charmed life, he thought. As long as no one bullied him into work, he was a strong and efficient labourer, and he found that life was safer and marginally more comfortable if you refrained from insolence to the overseers, if you didn't lose or damage your tools, or if you didn't refuse to work. Oh yes, he'd seen what happened to those who did. You could be imprisoned for a week on a minimal diet; you could be flogged, more than once, your back never having a chance to heal between sessions; you might be shackled for months, at a time when many of the prisoners were now free of irons. Or you could be sent to a penal settlement. Macquarie Harbour was the place whose very name brought terror to the inmates of Hobart Penitentiary. It was the wildest, wettest, cruellest spot in the territory. Some said in the world. And woe betide any man who was sent there. You never came back the same man you went out.

So Bill Sikes was keeping clear of trouble to save his skin, not through any wish to be a model prisoner. But it was difficult, with so much corruption and influence to hand. The overseers, drawn from among the prisoners, were the most corrupt men, and a little power went to their heads. They were almost spies in their own camp, and they would create trouble, simply to make a show of crushing it. Sometimes it was difficult, if not downright impossible to know who was friend or foe. Sikes trusted no one any more. It was safer that way, he felt.

By the end of the first year, the convicts had completed the road which ran along the side of the River Derwent to Hamilton. This was followed by the construction of bridges across the river at various points. Sometimes they would be away from Hobart for weeks at a time, up in the wilder parts of the valley, where the thickly wooded hillsides were full of strange beasts and noisy, brightly coloured birds. Sometimes they would disturb a troop of kangaroos gathering to drink by the water's edge. The men would stop and stare in wonder at these extraordinary creatures, who never went far away. Until the soldiers found that they made good sport for their guns. Sikes was sorry to see the creatures shot. And only the soldiers benefited from the meat. The convicts were never offered any variety in their diet.

Sometimes there would be a bold escape. Usually, the culprits were soon brought back, miserable and chastened, then rarely seen again. At such times, Macquarie Harbour would be the byword. And there would be no more outbreaks for some time. But just occasionally, men would get away and the prisoners left behind would look at each other and there would be an unspoken cheer between them, a wishing of God speed. It took guts and determination to escape and then to exist in uncharted territory, up there in the hills. There were natives, too. Aboriginals, they called them – wary people, very black with a white bloom to their skin and wild, flashing eyes. Sikes had seen them occasionally, crouching in the bushes and perched up in the eucalyptus trees like predatory birds; watching, studying the prisoners' every move.

In the autumn of 1830 Sikes was put with a gang to work on a farm. Here he was happy, hedging, ditching and building dry-stone walls. For a towny he adapted remarkably well.

Jacob Owen, the farmer, was a convict who had worked his time and earned himself a plot of land, to which he had added over the years, until now he had a sizeable farm, on which he ran a flock of some three hundred sheep.

Sikes worked hard on the farm, his labours occasionally punctuated by a return to building work for the Government. He won grudging respect from his fellow prisoners on account of his artisanship, but never made a close friend. No one seemed able or willing to break through the enigmatic reserve which surrounded him.

As the days lengthened and warmed and the calendar year drew to its close, work for the prisoners ceased on the farms and Sikes reluctantly went back on the road gangs. Jacob Owen was sad to lose him. He, of all his convict labour force, had been the most valuable. But now that winter maintenance was finished for the year, there was no need for the extra hands. He hoped he would have Sikes allotted to him again next year. But you could never tell. The prisons were strange places and convicts an unpredictable species. He knew that from bitter experience.

That summer the weather had become unusually hot and, inside the penitentiary, sleep was almost impossible at night. The overcrowding had reached such proportions that the men were jammed in tightly, one by another, their eighteen inches of sleeping space a mere memory. The heat generated in such conditions was considerable and the air became reeking and stale. They asked for the doors and windows to be left open at night, but the guards merely laughed at such a preposterous suggestion. Several of the prisoners fell sick and the emanations from their bodies added to the foetidness of the air. There was growing resentment and fear and a small delegation took itself to the Superintendent to complain. This effort earned them a week in solitary confinement and a reduced diet. When they came out, the whole prison was seething with unrest, for each ward suffered the same overcrowding.

The end came when a new shipment of prisoners was offloaded and an influx of numbers drafted to each ward. Sikes, for one, had had enough. He sat talking with a group of prisoners on the evening after the new draft had arrived.

'We'll 'ave ter do somethink,' he said, without much idea of what that would be.

222

'Wot d'yer suggest, Bill?' said Tom Oxbrow, the highwayman. 'Guvner don't listen. Don't want ter know. Who's goin' ter take note of our plight?'

Sikes shrugged. 'All we need is some more room. Why don't we suggest we build some 'uts ourselves?' Tom looked around the little company, grinning. ''Ere, thass a good idea, innit?' he chuckled. His mates nodded in agreement. ''E can't complain about that, now can 'e?'

''E'll find somethink wrong with it, yer can bet yer rations on that,' remarked Jack Frier gloomily.

'Ach, shut up, will yer?' Paddy Phelan cuffed him on the shoulder. 'Have yer got any better suggestions, young Jackie?'

Jack shook his head and Paddy continued: 'I think Bill's idea is a bloody good one, only 'tis no good hopin' fer too much now. Will we be sendin' another delegation like last time? Or will we just send a couple o' lads? What d'ye think now?'

Several voices struck up an overall cry in favour of sending one or two men. All eyes turned to Sikes, who had made the original suggestion.

'All right,' he agreed. 'You can come an' 'elp, Tom.'

Tom Oxbrow's eyes twinkled wickedly. He liked an element of danger. Hadn't he spent all his life living on the brink of disaster?

The following morning, the two men requested of the guard if they might be taken to speak with the Governor, who was said to have lately arrived in the town. Reluctantly, the two soldiers on duty agreed. And for the price of a rum ration, Sikes and Oxbrow were duly re-ironed and escorted to the Governor's office.

It was a grand affair in white stone, built on classic lines, with an imposing entrance. The two convicts waited anxiously in a lobby, listening to the hushed, almost reverent sounds around them. An official enquired of the guard the purpose of their presentation and after casting a disdainful look at both prisoners and escort, disappeared through tall double doors with ornate brass knobs and finger plates on them. It was a long time since Sikes had seen anything of worth and he eyed the brass and wondered how much it would fetch with a fence. Not as much, he felt sure, as the paintings on the walls, the crystal lights hanging from the ceiling, nor the costly pieces of furniture displayed about the room. Suddenly, his thoughts were interrupted by an angry voice from beyond the doors.

'I tell you I won't have them here. I don't care what they want. You are not to allow such scum to enter the Government buildings. Do I make myself quite clear?'

There was a subdued murmuring from the official, but no further outburst from the Governor and a moment later, Sikes and Oxbrow found themselves standing in a sparsely furnished room before a large desk, behind which sat the Lieutenant-Governor of Van Diemen's Land.

Sir George Arthur was an unsmiling man, whose eyes would fix and hold another with their calm, cold gaze. His was a zeal fired by moral and religious duty and he knew exactly how he wanted to run the colony. He did not like boundaries to be crossed and he was annoyed that prisoners had been ushered, unbidden, into his office, without due notice. He caught Sikes's impudent look and held it with his own steady gaze. The two men were well matched.

'You have a complaint?'

The Governor's voice was low, his eyes still on Sikes. It was the latter who spoke up, while Oxbrow shuffled and twisted his hands nervously in their unaccustomed shackles. He didn't look quite the intrepid highwayman he claimed to be and Sikes was secretly disappointed with him.

'Yes, sir,' Sikes replied, almost defying his superior. 'It's about our sleepin' quarters. When we arrived, we 'ad precious little space fer each man. About eighteen inches, no more. Nah we don't even 'ave that. Wot with the new harrivals crammed in with us. We wos 'opin' you could at least get 'em put somewhere else, like. Or p'raps we could build some new 'uts . . . sir,' he added grudgingly.

The Governor stared at him, unblinking, for several moments. Sikes stared steadily back and Oxbrow glanced anxiously from one to the other. At last the Governor sat back in his chair.

'New huts are out of the question,' he said laconically. 'There's to be a new penitentiary built in the next two years and we are certainly not going to litter the compound with a surfeit of wooden huts. You must use the floor to sleep on.'

'With respect, sir –' Sikes began.

But the Governor held up his hand for silence and signalled to the official to show them out.

'Bloody lot o' good that was,' grumbled Oxbrow, as they clumped back to the compound. 'Still, at least we didn't get punished for it like the last lot. You must 'ave made a good impression on the Guv, Bill!'

But Sikes was strangely silent.

By evening, word had spread round to every convict in the penitentiary that the delegation had failed and that if they wanted to achieve anything, they would have to make some sort of demonstration to draw attention to their plight. The plan was to keep up a barrage of shouting through the fence. There was to be no violence and no abuse. They were just to shout about their grievances. A palpable tension grew throughout the following day.

When the guards came to lock and bar the doors at night, the prisoners were ready for them and rushed the doors, knocking the guards to the ground in their zeal. It had been timed well and the men collected at the compound fence, chanting, 'More space! More space!' and shaking their fists. Several soldiers, recovering from the initial onslaught, staggered to their feet and tried to remonstrate with the men at the back of the mob. But tempers were high and the night was hot. Scuffles broke out and blows were exchanged. Next door to the prison, lights went on all over the guard house and a platoon of soldiers came running, pulling on their jackets and shakos as they came.

And then above the yelling and shouting of the men, there

was a crackle, a rush and a roar, and flames spurted from the windows of one of the sleeping wards. Almost immediately, fire leaped from the other ward and the mob howled delightedly. But when Sikes turned from the fence and saw the blazing wards, his heart sank and he experienced a feeling of dread such as he had not had since he had stood in the dock at the Old Bailey and heard sentence passed on him.

'Christ!' he muttered. 'Stupid bastards! No one said nothink about firin' 'em. Now we'll be in the shit!'

He turned and fought his way back through the press of prisoners.

'Who ordered the firin' o' them wards?' he bawled above the racket.

'Dunno, guv,' shouted a man from his own block, 'but we'll 'ave ter sleep outside now, won't we? Lot cooler!'

It was then that Sikes saw Oxbrow, a burning brand in his fist, almost dancing with glee, as he made his way towards the kitchens and the prison offices. Sikes pounced.

'No yer don't, Oxbrow!' he roared. 'You bloody idiot! We wanted a quiet protest, not a bleedin' riot on our 'ands!'

Oxbrow grinned at him with goblin-like delight on his face.

'But the power, Bill! The feelin' of power. We'll make them bastards sit up an' take notice.'

'Yes,' shouted Sikes, his temper sorely tried, 'and good notice they'll take, too. They'll notice ev'ry detail of ternight an' who was responsible. An' whose are the first two names they're goin' ter fix on? Eh?'

And he seized Oxbrow by the throat and shook him. The highwayman began spluttering and blubbering under Sikes's stranglehold. Sikes viewed him with disgust. To think this milksop had once terrorized the Mile End Road. He was a disgrace to the names of Jack Sheppard and Dick Turpin. He doubled his fist and planted it hard in the middle of the man's face. Oxbrow's mates had gathered to watch and when they saw Tom sprawl bloodied and crushed on the ground, they leaped on Sikes and began swinging their own fists.

Other convicts joined in. Sikes was lost in the middle of the fracas when his own mates pitched in to help him. The noise was tremendous and the smell of sweating bodies overpowering on the night air.

Soldiers came swarming in from all directions, firing over the prisoners' heads. When the first rifle shots rang out, there was a surge of panic and men began detaching themselves from the fights which had broken out all over the compound. In a few minutes, fighting had ceased and the mob had split up and scattered, shrinking nervously to the perimeter of the yard. A sergeant began barking orders, his voice echoing strangely in the sudden silence. There were bodies lying in the dust who were beyond discipline and others who staggered blindly, their faces bruised and bleeding. Sikes bent down to inspect one of the fallen, a young lad from his own ward. It shouldn't have been like this. This wasn't what he had intended. His own face was a mass of cuts and bruises and blood ran from a gash on his head. A heavy hand descended on his shoulder and he was hauled to his feet and snapped into handcuffs. He stood, with several others, waiting while the military elicited the ring-leaders. They found Oxbrow, but he would never talk again. Whether Sikes's blow or the subsequent riot had killed him, was now impossible to say. Sikes looked down at his thin prostrate form and felt not the slightest twinge of remorse.

When the guard had rounded up some fifty prisoners whom they deemed responsible for the riot, they marched off with their charges to the gaol. Sikes had a dragging fear, deep in his bowels and he dreaded the outcome.

Well, he reflected, sitting in the communal cell of the prison that night, if I'm topped, then all me troubles is over. I ain't got much ter lose. Though I'd as soon as departed this 'ere world in me own country.

He thought of what he'd leave behind: the cruel labour and punishment of his long sentence; the poverty; the misery; the uncertainty. And who would mourn his passing? Was there

227

anyone? Toby? He didn't even know if Toby was still alive. Toby was careless enough to have swung by now. But he hoped not. For Sikes there was nothing to lose – except life itself. And that suddenly seemed unbearably sweet to him in that dirty prison, in the deep of the hot night, thousands of miles from home.

Macquarie Harbour! The name was on everyone's lips next day as sentence was passed on each of the prisoners: a sound flogging and a two-year stint in that godforsaken hell, the penal settlement that held as much fear as the gallows.

'William Sikes. As prime instigator, agitator and leader of the riot in question, twenty-five strokes of the lash and three years in the penal settlement of Macquarie Harbour.'

Sikes stared at his knuckles as the magistrate spoke. They stood out white and bony, scarred by his labours, bloodied by last night's fighting. There was a bruise where he had struck Tom Oxbrow. It was spreading, purple and yellow from his middle knuckles across the back of his hand and it was painful. The words went echoing emptily, dizzily round his head. And still he kept his eyes riveted on the backs of his hands. Three years! The others only got two! I didn't order the firin'. It ain't fair! He wanted to shout the words out, but nothing came from his mouth. His eyes blazed and he felt suffocated by his own breath. He was shoved unceremoniously out of the dock by the guard and his place taken by another. He stumbled blindly from the courtroom, prodded along by the butt of a soldier's rifle. Back to the stinking cell, where they were to await a ship bound for Macquarie Harbour.

They waited a week in the dimly lit prison, during the course of which they were taken out, one by one, to receive the first part of their punishment. As each man returned, his back like a butcher's slab, the fear and the resentment grew, so that the men became something not quite human, something wild and dangerous. Sikes spoke hardly a word in all this time and took his vicious punishment in silence. He had not realized how the pain built up with successive strokes, each lash biting into the raw wounds of the previous stroke. When he walked away, the back of his trousers clung to him and his shoes felt sticky with blood.

That night, the cell reeked of blood and the putrefying skin of those flogged earlier in the week. Sikes rested his shoulder against the wall and fought down wave after wave of nausea. The surgeon had washed them all down with cold water and spread a little lard on each back. But if it soothed the pain somewhat, it did not prevent infection in that unhealthy place.

Two days later, a ship was ready to convey them to the west coast. She was loaded with stores, mostly destined for the garrison and officials on Sarah Island, the miserable chunk of land in Macquarie Harbour on which the penal settlement was built.

And so, a week after the abortive riot, fifty sorry-looking individuals were paraded down to Hobart Wharf. Most of them carried their shirts and jackets, since their backs were still too raw to bear clothing. And on some, the maggots had hatched already and seethed in their foul activities. The men blinked up at the bright sun and gulped in the brief taste of fresh air. But they were very soon hurried aboard the waiting ship and thrust down into the hold. Once again, the close air became fouled by infected backs and sweating bodies. It was the beginning of the hell called Macquarie Harbour.

EIGHT

It took five weeks to reach the penal settlement. Despite fair sailing all along the South Tasmanian coast, once they struck up the west side of the island it became a nightmare of tacking back and forth, sitting and getting nowhere, battling against the Roaring Forties from the north west and waiting for the winds to abate a little. When her bows were finally swung towards the entrance of Macquarie Harbour, the little brig began plunging on the turbulent waters, before she had even drawn near.

The entrance towards which they struggled comprised two steep rocky headlands with a bare fifty yards between them. The water ran treacherously shallow over a sandbar, swirling glaucous and menacing between sheer rocks streaked with iron ore. The crew counted off the fathoms as they drew inexorably nearer to the tiny strait. Every man on board tensed his body and strained every nerve, keeping his eyes rigidly fixed on the ever decreasing distance. They could see the sandbank now, lying brown and glistening in the shallows. It awaited their arrival, reptilian in its watchfulness. A pair of albatrosses circled overhead, their sad cry emphasizing the awesomeness of the place.

They had reefed the vessel's sails as they turned her bows, leaving only a single mizzen to give her enough momentum across the bar.

'Eleven fathoms.'

The roar of the wind beat on his eardrums and it was difficult to draw breath. He felt helpless. Many of the convicts had been sent below, but Sikes had asked to remain on deck. There was little he or any of the others could do. But if he was going to die, he wanted to be in the open air, not cooped up like a chicken. He watched as the nightmare drew ever nearer and felt his last moments had come. He leaned back into the wind and felt the buck and surge of the ship, as the combined force of the elements was hurled against her. But the captain and his helmsman held her straight.

'Five fathoms.'

Sikes felt sick. It was fear as well as the pitching of the ship. This was a much smaller vessel than the one on which he had travelled out from England. He clutched at the rail. It was sodden and slopping and the rain and salt stung his knuckles.

'Two fathoms.'

They were almost there. The roar of the wind and the foam and spray spewing high into the air echoed eerily from the rocks ahead. The men were counting in feet now.

'Ten feet . . . Eight feet . . . Seven feet . . .'

With a sudden tremendous surge, like a babe expelled from the womb, the brig shot forward across the bar into the deep waters of Hell's Gates, the sea boiling and foaming around her, the captain and helmsman clinging to the kicking wheel. The worst was over, but the passage was far from smooth. Sikes looked up at the towering cliffs on either side. Great stacks of iron ore and basalt, with the sea thundering against them and the cry of the albatross for ever echoing between them. He hadn't known such things existed. There was nothing like this near London, nothing similar within his narrow experience.

As they drew into the great harbour, the men began to relax and the crew exchanged their own secret laughter with the false levity born of fear. One grinning sea dog came lurching past Sikes. He cocked his head on one side and scratched into his beard.

'Not bad, not bad!' he chuckled.

Sikes stared at him in disbelief.

'You want to see it in a winter gale, mate. That'd really make you shit in your shoes!'

And he lumbered away, still laughing, wagging his head at the naïveté of these new boys.

Many of the convicts had been overcome by sickness and remained below. For those who came to catch their first glimpse of Macquarie Harbour, it was a soul-destroying experience. This long, narrow arm of the sea reached obscenely inside the mainland through the tiny bottleneck of Hell's Gates. It swirled brown and peaty below them. Either side of its twenty-mile length was edged with a decaying yellow lace of froth, which slapped and licked at the shore. Thick spiny scrub covered the shoreline. Range upon range of featureless grey mountains stretched away beyond, their heads lost in the grey mist, which hung suspended from a grey sky. A steady, wetting drizzle fell as they sailed up the long body of water. They were in full sail, the Roaring Forties backing them. The men huddled, cold and miserable, pulling their inadequate jackets and bits of old sacking tightly round them in an effort to stay warm. Morale, never very high, plummeted. Despair hung over the ship with a tangible palpability. It deepened as a distant range of tiny islands loomed out of the mist.

'Is that it?'

The speaker had a North Country accent and his face stared out grimly from his tattered clothing.

'Looks like it,' Sikes returned with equal dourness. 'I wonder which perwerse sod thought this one up.'

The two men relapsed into gloom. As they neared the largest of the islands, they could see great thirty-foot-high palisades around its perimeter, effectively cutting off their view of the island itself.

'What's that for, then?' The Northern lad addressed one of the crew and nodded his blond head in the direction of the great fence.

The sailor laughed. 'You'll be glad o' that, soon enough, when the ole wind comes a-whistlin' down the 'arbour. You'll spend 'alf your time replacing it, too, after the winter gales.'

The men nearby glanced at each other. Winter gales? And this was supposed to be summer time! They shivered.

232

'Any women 'ere?' shouted a fellow from Sikes's home town.

The sailor laughed again.

'You must be joking, cock. You've seen the last o' women for the next two years, or however long they've sent you 'ere for! Unless you wants to go off into the jungle and find an abo girl. I'm told they like the white men! I wouldn't know, mind you.'

Any attempt at lightening the moment was gone, lost in a horrified, deep despondency. At least in Hobart there were women to be had, if you were brave enough to run the risk of being caught. How could the men possibly survive? Sikes suspected they wouldn't.

Meanwhile their vessel had swung around the north-east tip of the island and was running parallel to the shore. Here there were few wind defences and the prisoners could make out a signal house with a flagstaff behind, the British flag flapping stiffly in the wind. There were grass plots marked off by low fences and a great saw-pit. Then came a cluster of buildings, a few of brick and stone, but many constructed of the local wood. Wharves jutted out at intervals and at the largest of these their ship came alongside. Sailors on shore caught the ropes thrown to them and bound them fast, until the ship's side was nudging provocatively against the quay wall. The anchor was dropped with a splash of finality and a gangplank lowered on to the wharf. The armed guards hustled their charges ashore and they trudged up to the penitentiary buildings which had been erected on the windward side of the island. Typical! thought Sikes. How much worse could things get?

His dejection did not prevent him from taking in his surroundings and he noted the various buildings with their notices outside proclaiming their function. The military barracks were obvious and there was a guard house just beyond. Then came the gaol for further offenders on the island. Sikes wondered how much lower a man could sink. Adjoining the gaol were a tannery and a bakehouse, the smells of their products vying with each other in sickly combat. The small, unmarked hut, they were told, was the ship builder's house. And this was followed by the substantially constructed edifices of the administrative block.

The prisoners' quarters consisted of an L-shaped building of brick and wood, roofed in slate. Here the men were to be crammed in, much as they had been in Hobart, with a blanket their only protection. The sleeping platforms, though, were only on one storey, so there would be none of the clambering over others as there had been in their former quarters. The messing area was in front of the sleeping platforms and consisted of the usual long trestle tables with wooden forms behind them. They always reminded Sikes of the Shoreditch Workhouse.

The new prisoners had arrived early in the afternoon and after a hasty dinner of bread, beer and salt pork, they were rounded up into working gangs and plunged straight into their labours. Those who had suffered sickness on the journey staggered outside and would have willingly spent the rest of the day on their mean beds.

'Bit o' fresh air, that's wot you wants,' shouted a sergeant, as he waited for the shuffling crowd to stand still. 'You'll get plenty o' that in this 'ere place, I can tell you!'

The trees on Sarah Island had already been felled, so there were no natural windbreaks. The topsoil had rapidly eroded away, so nothing could be cultivated. And there was no source of fresh water on the island. So supplies of timber, firewood, topsoil and water were boated or rafted over daily from the mainland. It was to these everlasting chores that the convicts on Sarah Island were allotted. Sikes found himself part of a felling gang and was ferried to the mainland in a dubious-looking craft with some dozen other convicts. The boat made several trips back and forth to convey all the men and their guards. They tramped up the shore and along a well-worn path through dwindling forest. The aroma of pine was overpowering and the floor of the forest was soft and springy with fallen needles. The wind soughed in the high branches, but there was little other sound. Even the birds seemed to have deserted this godforsaken place. The pines growing here were big but there would be even bigger ones, they were told, when they worked along the Gordon River. Here there would be great stands of thousand-year-old Huon pines, their timber the best in the world for ship building. There were other valuable trees to be harvested, too; light-wood, celery-topped pine and myrtle, all of which found a use in the shipwright's yard.

The men were mostly too cold and too miserable to notice the lush vegetation around them or the soaring mountains clothed in great swathes of forest. As they tramped along the muddy path to their destination, an old man, who had said his name was Walter, nudged Sikes and pointed to a tiny bird skulking in the undergrowth.

'Honeyeater,' he remarked. 'Seen plenty of those in my time.'

Sikes watched the bird hovering over a bush of waratah, its bright eye fixed on the dark pink flowers full of nectarine promise.

'You bin 'ere before?' Sikes asked, surprised.

'Aye, you might say so.'

'Christ!' exclaimed Sikes. ''Ow 'ave you survived?'

'Willpower, boy,' replied Walter, 'and an iron nerve. That's what you need out here. No good letting it get on top of you. Here, this is where we start work.'

They were standing at the top of a steep slope, littered with the bark and chippings of a hundred other casualties of the axe. The overseers split the men into rough groups. They were to begin felling, three men to a tree at a time. When they tired, three more would take their place, until the tree was down.

'While you're waiting your shift at felling,' said the over-seer, 'the rest of you can start constructing rollers. Choose the straightest of the smaller trees and clean them down so they're smooth as a baby's arse. The trunks won't move unless the branches are hacked off cleanly. So be warned.

235

And any sloppy work will earn a flogging. Tomorrow, *if* you've managed to get one of the buggers down, you'll start shifting it.'

''Ow many of us will that take?' muttered Sikes under his breath. 'Wot do they think we are? Bleedin' cart'osses?'

'Yes,' came Walter's succinct reply, 'and you'll be harnessed like one.'

Sikes picked up his axe and weighed it in his hands, thoughtfully. Walter eyed him.

'I wouldn't if I were you, Bill. They've got gallows here, too.'

Sikes smiled lopsidedly at the older man, wiped his nose with the back of his hand, spat on his palms and swung his axe. Their third member was a raw youth with a stutter. He had huge hands and big-boned limbs, but Sikes didn't think he looked particularly strong. However, he soon set up a good rhythm of axing with young Chris.

Midway through the afternoon, while Sikes and his two companions were taking their turn again, the final wedge was cut.

'Timber!' cried Christopher in his excitement and the men scrambled to safety higher up the slope.

There was a creaking sound from the depths of the tree and as they looked up, it seemed to hang suspended above their heads. Then, with a prolonged crashing and snapping, the giant toppled to the forest floor, bringing down a shower of loose needles and twigs as it did so. Sikes was acutely aware of the pungent, resinous smell about them and as the afternoon wore on, the forest seemed full of it and their clothes and hair were impregnated with it.

The branch-stripping took them until the light began to fade. By this time, their tree was a clean, naked trunk, waiting to be floated across to the island with its ancient sisters. Beside it was a growing pile of smallwood and firewood. Sikes doubted if they would see any of that in the penitentiary.

Here in the forest, the men had been fairly well protected

from the wind and rain. But as they tramped back to the boat, they were hit by the full force of the elements. Sikes stood looking at the small rowing boat bobbing at anchor in the lapping waves on the beach. He wondered if they would reach the island in this weather. But he was quickly to learn that in this place, nothing stopped for the weather. And so they eventually arrived back at their barracks, shaken, aching, but safe. At supper, the talk was desultory, but the loggers were obviously the envy of those who had been shipping stores all day. And they all viewed with a jealous spite those few who had been selected to work in the shipwright's yard. *They* were privileged indeed.

That night, they lay cramped and obscenely close to each other and listened to the Roaring Forties whistling from Hell's Gates and battering at the palisade outside their sleeping wards.

Sikes lay on his back, rigid, silent, loathing the feel of his fellow prisoners on either side of him. There was no way of avoiding them. The best you could do was to wrap yourself in your blanket, turn on your side and hope your neighbour didn't decide to roll in your direction. Sikes turned now, only to feel the stinking breath of his neighbour on his face. He moved his head in order to be out of range of the poisonous blast and struck it on the wall behind him. He cursed and there was a burst of laughter from nearby.

'Thass Longfellow's 'ead again! 'E used to do that reg'lar in 'Obart.'

And there was general banter at Sikes's expense. He ignored them, pulled the blanket over his ears and went to sleep.

NINE

The men awoke the following morning to a sky washed clear of cloud and rain. It was one of only a handful of days in the year when the rain didn't fall in Macquarie Harbour and the soldiers made a point of letting the convicts know how lucky they were. 'Ow much store we set by little things! Sikes thought as he sat toying with his bread and lard. He let his mind drift homewards.

He wondered, for the hundredth time, what Toby was doing now. He hoped he had survived his imprisonment. It would be a pity to lose Toby. He would be the only friend he'd have when he got back. He closed his eyes. How many more years? It must be four. He wasn't even halfway through yet.

''Ow's Longfeller this mornin' then, eh?'

The comment sliced through his thoughts and he raised his eyes to the speaker. It was the Cockney who had complained about the lack of women the day before.

'Got a bump on yer noddle, eh?' continued the incorrigible little man. ''Ow d'yer git that then? Too much of an 'urry ter git ter bed, were yer?' and there was further laughter.

Sikes stood up suddenly, his eyes blazing, his fists clenched.

'I don't know wot you're implyin', mate,' he growled, 'but if it's wot I think, then you'd better steer clear of my fists!'

The Cockney, nothing daunted, strutted up to Sikes, his hands shoved in his pockets. He stood looking up belligerently at the tall man, baiting him, daring him. The others watched, a mixture of amusement and apprehension on their faces.

'Garn, Jockey, belt 'im one. See if 'e notices.'

Sikes was about to move when a low voice spoke near his shoulder.

'Leave him, lad. He's not worth the effort. And the guard's just outside the door. Solitary confinement if you're caught assaulting another prisoner.'

Sikes breathed hard in an effort to control his temper. Then he turned and flung away from the table. The guard looked up as he strode out into the yard, but made no move to stop him. A man couldn't go far here. Sikes went and stood against the great palisade.

'Hell's fire!' he breathed, beating his head against the timbers. 'If I'd bin back 'ome, 'e'd 'ave 'ad 'is face rearranged by now! 'Ow am I goin' ter cope with this fer three years?'

Walter Barley hailed him over and he joined his fellow loggers as they trooped down to where the boat was moored. Full of pent-up rage still, Sikes grabbed the oars and began to row like a madman. But the shouts of the accompanying sergeant soon put paid to his erratic stroke and he calmed down sufficiently to let the other rowers set the pace. By the time they reached the mainland, his temper had evaporated and he was impatient to start work.

But first, the great trunks had to be dug out from where they had fallen. More rollers were needed on which the giants could be shifted. And all the while the men sweated in the clammy atmosphere of the forest. The mosquitoes tormented them and great spiders and insects threatened their safety.

When their overseer judged that enough rollers had been laid to start the trunk moving, half the gang, Sikes and Walter and young Christopher among them, strapped themselves into the harnesses with which they had been issued. The other ends were attached by long chains to the trunk. In a concerted effort, some fifty men strained every muscle in their bodies. The forest was filled with the groaning and panting of men exerting every ounce of their strength to combat the great beast which lay inert behind them. But eventually, the tree was dislodged. Slowly, they manoeuvred the trunk so that it began to slide over the platform of rollers.

The remainder of the gang scurried back and forth, taking out rollers from behind and adding them in front. It was a major task, but one which must be repeated for every felled pine.

By dinner time, Sikes and his team had their tree down at the water's edge, where it lay alongside another. The water lapped between them, little shards of red bark and moss breaking off and jerking away on the tide. Sikes sat down to his dinner flexing an arm and working his shoulder round in circles. Walter looked at him with concern, but Sikes was dismissive.

'It's nothink,' he said, but Walter saw him wince.

The guard brought round flagons of weak beer and water and while the men recovered, the soldiers sat and talked to some of them. Sikes and his fellow loggers were joined by a square-set man, about Sikes's own age. He came from Kent, he said, and had enlisted some three years before.

'I was looking for adventure, but I never expected to get sent out here.'

He pulled off his shako and leant back against a tree, a beaker of beer in his hand, his rifle across his lap.

'It's not too bad this time o' year, but you wait till winter comes. You'll wish you'd never been born.'

The men were not amused by this forecast and Walter growled, 'That's enough, my lad. We've all got to learn to cope with it out here. No need to rub salt in the wound.'

He glanced at Sikes, sitting steely-eyed and breathing more easily now; and at Chris, still red-faced and panting. He wondered if the boy were ill.

'Wot we s'posed ter do with these bleedin' tree trunks nah?' Sikes enquired of the soldier.

'You've got to lash 'em together and float 'em across to the island.'

Sikes looked at him, very hard. 'Oh yes? An' wot 'appens then?'

Walter examined the contents of his mug. He knew what was coming.

'Ah! Well!' The soldier looked flustered. 'They have to be manhandled ashore with long hooks.'

Sikes still held him with his eyes and the lad felt uncomfortable.

'Go on,' growled Sikes.

The soldier's eyes flickered desperately round the group, looking for a way out, but the sergeant was summoning the men to work again.

'Time's up, I'm afraid,' he said, the relief in his voice obvious. 'Back to work!' And he strode away, ramming his shako on his head as he went.

Sikes stood up, staring after him. His nostrils flared and his mouth was compressed into a thin hard line.

'Tell me, Walter.'

The words seemed to emanate from the side of his mouth. Walter laid a hand on his arm.

'No, lad. Nothing like first-hand experience. You'll learn better that way.'

Sikes jerked Walter's hand away and went silently to where they had left their tree trunk. He stood at the side of it and gazed out across the peaty waters of the harbour. He felt more captive here, in this hostile climate, than he had ever felt behind bars. He shivered, as the wind blew his sweat-sodden shirt against his body.

'Come on,' he said quietly to the others. 'We've still got to get this bugger into the water.'

They began the difficult task of roping the trunks together, the old hands showing the newcomers the intricacies of safe lashing.

Sikes watched, but the pain in his shoulder distracted him. He didn't think anything was broken, because he could still move his shoulder. But it hurt like hell and there was a bruised feeling in his chest every time he drew breath.

The journey back to the island was one blur of pain. Sikes was ordered in as a rower again and each movement was agony, especially with the added weight of timber behind the boat. When they reached the island, Sikes shipped his oars and made as if to step ashore. But a soldier on the slipway placed a hand firmly against his chest.

'Oi! In the water, mate!'

Sikes looked blankly at him.

'In the water, I said!'

Sikes stared at the soldier and then at the murky water lapping just beyond his feet.

'Wot d'yer mean?' he asked.

'What the hell d'yer think I mean?'

The soldier hit him round the head and Sikes staggered sideways towards the freezing water. He lost his balance, went under and fought frantically for the surface. As he came up, gasping and spluttering, he found old Walter beside him, handing him a grapnel.

'The sooner we get these logs stowed away, the sooner we can get out of this water.' The water was up to Sikes's armpits and he was shaking with cold, so that he could scarcely hold the grapnel. But somehow, through sheer determination, he managed to contribute a fair amount of help with the manoeuvring of the logs. It wasn't easy work. The grapnels didn't always hold and a log rolling back into the water could knock you under. He didn't want that experience again. It was the first time he had ever been in water, and he had been genuinely frightened.

It took another three hours to get the two logs up the slipway and stacked in the shipwright's yard. By which time, Sikes was so cold and numb that he could scarce hold the grapnel. And he thought his genitals must have shrunk away to nothing. No wonder they don't 'ave no women 'ere, he thought wryly. But he was not alone in his misery. A hundred other men were suffering similarly and at supper that evening, there was little conversation. Sikes wondered how long it would take for this regime to break them all.

TEN

The summer wore on and the felling gangs became accustomed to the arduous labour. They learned to avoid accidents, to keep their axes sharp and how to fell correctly. They even learned to tolerate the water in which they spent so much time. But winter was drawing close and the wind and rain increased in frequency and intensity. The men developed coughs and colds and many of them were already in pain with rheumatism.

Only one thing gave Sikes any peace of mind or pleasure and that was a visit to the shipwright's yard. Occasionally, he would be detailed with a few others to go to the artisan's sheds to collect seasoned wood or to fetch something which had been made for the barracks. He wished he could work there. He felt he could make better use of his hands and his brain by making something, instead of destroying. One day, when he had heaved himself from the water and stacked the last of the logs for the day, he wandered along to the workshops. No one stopped him and he knew he wouldn't be missed till supper time. No harm in having a quick look round. He needn't stay long.

There were two new ships in the process of being built. Sikes walked round them, letting his eyes follow the lines of their magnificent hulls, gazing up at the jutting bowsprits. The smell of the worked timber was wonderful and he breathed deeply, looking enviously at the men working there now. The atmosphere was one of calm industry, no overseers with the cat in their hands. No soldiers with a rifle butt at the ready.

His attention was caught by a recently carved figurehead, awaiting its coats of colour. It was a woman, her eyes wide

243

and blazing, her hair in wild coils streaming from beneath a naval crown. Her draperies began somewhere near her waist and her bulging breasts thrust out to meet the sea. Sikes looked at her for several minutes and then laid his hand on the smooth wood and let it slide down over those unyielding protuberances. He felt a thrill of pleasure and turned quickly away, but the carpenter had seen him.

'Ah, they all do that, my boy!' he chuckled and hobbled over to where Sikes stood, embarrassed at having been seen. 'She's mine,' continued the old man, 'all mine. Till she goes up there, under the bowsprit. And none of you lads'll get your hands on her then.'

And he laughed, but not unkindly and his old eyes twinkled.

'Are you a wood-carver, then?' Sikes asked.

'Oh, aye. But I do other things as well. Spar shapin'; balustradin'; anything as needs a bit of artistry about it. You interested in carpentry, lad?' he piped.

'I dunno,' replied Sikes, shrugging his shoulders. 'But I like the feel o' worked wood. It's better than them bloody logs we 'ave to 'aul about.'

'Ah, well you work at it a bit longer, lad, and maybe you'll get a chance to come down here to work. What you out 'ere for?' He thrust the question at Sikes without preamble.

'Riotin'.'

The old eyes twinkled knowingly.

'And back 'ome?'

''Tempted burglary.'

'Hah!' The little carpenter slapped his hands on his aproned thighs. 'Nothing too serious there. Behave yourself and I'll see if I can get you down here. I like a lad who's got an interest in the job. What's your name?'

'Bill Sikes.'

'Well, Bill. I like the look of you. I'll take you on if they'll let me have you. Hoy's the name. Samuel Hoy.'

'Thanks, Mr Hoy,' replied Sikes, though he didn't hold out much hope for the little man's enthusiastic plans.

He hurried away to rejoin his gang, but the beautiful figurehead remained in his mind and strangely disturbed him.

They thought logging would stop in the winter, but it seemed nothing prevented the steady destruction of the cloak of pines which enveloped the lower slopes of Mount Sorrel. There were deaths, there were accidents and there were chronic diseases – rheumatism, bronchitis, salt-water boils, pneumonia or dysentery. Every few weeks there would be another sorry shipment of secondary offenders and the island would be back to full strength once more. On one particular day of tremendous gales in the winter of '31, when the wind came wailing up from Hell's Gate like a banshee, one of the rowing boats overturned and two lads were lost. Their bodies were recovered the following morning, washed up on the mainland, a little further down the shore from the landing place. Three days later there was another near accident, when a gale blew up in the afternoon.

Sikes and two others were in the water, struggling to lash together some dozen logs, which kept leaping from their grasp as the tide surged back and forth. Walter was wheezing a little and moving stiffly.

'Rheumatiz,' he remarked, when Sikes frowned at him.

'You shouldn't be workin' 'ere,' Sikes said.

'Don't you worry about me, Bill. I'm used to all this. Been through it so many times.'

They heaved themselves out of the water and into the boat. Their breeches and shirts clung to their thin cold bodies, the pine bark scraped at their bare, numb feet. The overseer that day was a particularly bullying character who insisted on Walter taking the pole to steer the raft behind the boat on its trip to the island. Sikes immediately protested.

'Walter's too old fer that job,' he said belligerently. 'It's a young man's job an' he's already wheezin'. It'll kill 'im. I'll do it.'

'You get back to yer own bloody place, Sikes!' shouted the bully above the noise of the rising wind. 'Or you'll wish you 'adn't bothered to open yer gob!'

Sikes would dearly have liked to have hit the fellow, but he was fast learning the diplomacy of keeping his fists to himself.

They all pulled on the oars and the great natural raft began to move towards the island, the sea churning wildly round them. They were only halfway across when a lashing came undone and the logs began to jostle each other. There was pandemonium as men shouted, the bullying overseer screamed orders and the wind roared in their faces.

Suddenly, there was a cry and Sikes saw Walter disappear between a gap in the logs.

'Jesus!' he breathed, dropped his oars and leaped into the seething cauldron.

The waves crashed over his head and he spat and spluttered. He couldn't see Walter anywhere and he knew that he must be under the logs. He filled his lungs with a great gush of air and thrust himself down into the murky shadows beneath the tree trunks. He encountered Walter's body almost immediately and hauled him clear.

They burst through the surface together and Sikes flailed desperately for the boat. But the distance was increasing between him and safety and he could barely hold Walter and himself above the water.

'Rope!' he bellowed. 'Quick!'

Two men grabbed a length of rope from the bottom of the boat, flung one end to Sikes and began to pull him in. He and the old man were hauled aboard and a considerable amount of filthy harbour water was pumped from their lungs. The overseer, thoroughly alarmed, closely supervised the rest of the journey, but the logs had had to be cut free and someone would have to answer for their loss tomorrow.

Sikes and Walter were both taken to the little hospital building and Sikes revelled in the warm bath, the single pallet bed and the quietness around him, punctuated only by old Walter's coughing and wheezing.

Gawd, thought Sikes, 'e's a rum one. 'Ow could any man of 'is age survive that?

And Walter did survive. He spent a little longer in the

respite of the hospital than Sikes, but he was back with his fellow prisoners within a fortnight.

They were both lucky to escape the requisite flogging which naturally followed any absence from work. Sikes thought the surgeon may have had a hand in the matter. He was learning that, on the whole, surgeons were among the few people you could trust. It must be something to do with their seeing so much of the quick and the dead, he thought. They were closer to humanity. Mr France on the *Asia* had been a humane man. So had the surgeon at Hobart. And Mr Matthew Burnside here on Sarah Island had listened to him when he been brought in from the accident.

'Don't let 'em flog ole Walter,' Sikes had whispered through his chattering teeth. 'It wasn't 'is fault the rope snapped. 'E ain't strong enough fer this sort of work. Please, Mr Burnside. They can flog me if they want, but not 'im. Don't let 'em flog 'im.'

His urgency and loyalty had impressed the surgeon. The fact that Sikes had rescued the old man stood him in good stead, too. So it wasn't difficult to procure a reprieve for both men. But when he returned to work, the overseers looked as though they couldn't wait to get their hands on him. Sikes felt a marked man.

ELEVEN

With the prisoners reduced to little more than draught animals and human machines, morale was non-existent on Sarah Island. The men rarely talked to each other now. They were withdrawn, turned in with their own self-pity. And any communication between them was likely to result in snappish exchanges and blows.

In the spring, a pit-man was required in the huge saw-pit on Sarah Island. They needed a big, strong chap, with plenty of stamina, said the shipwright. The overseer of the timber yard laughed.

''Ave you seen 'em recently, Harry?'

The overseer was a convict himself, but had spent years out here and had gained a position of authority for himself. He fancied himself on good terms with his superiors. The shipwright frowned.

'Why? What's up with them? They're no different to the hundreds of others we get, are they?'

'No,' replied the overseer, 'but you've 'ad reg'lar chaps in the yard for some time now. You're a bit out of touch. Like a bunch o' sweet peas, this felling gang. 'Ardly a leg to stand on between 'em.'

'Oh come, come, Fred,' said the shipwright. 'They're still bringing in the timber regularly. There must be *some* strength in them. I mean, you can't do that job unless you're fit.'

'Precisely,' returned Fred. 'And there's precious few still 'ere completing their time. The turnover's pretty high.'

The shipwright raised his eyebrows and sighed.

'Well,' he said, 'you must be able to find someone to replace young Beech.' He paused. 'Tragedy that.'

'Aye. Well, it's a dangerous business. We all know that.

248

But at least it weren't the top-man. Go a long way afore you find a hexpert like 'im.'

The shipwright was about to return to his workshop, but at this he swung round again.

'You know my thoughts on that matter, Fred,' he admonished. 'Strict discipline's one thing. Safety is another.'

And he walked away, leaving the overseer with a look of disdain on his face. The shipwright was too soft, he reflected. He wandered down to the timber yard, where the convicts were in the throes of hauling logs ashore.

He stood staring at them, his eyes moving critically over the cold, thin bodies, the hollow eyes, the beaten expressions. Was there any man here capable of the brutishness needed in the saw-pit, especially if he was to be bottom-man? Bodies white and blue with cold, backs knotted and scarred by flogging, shoulder blades and ribs protruding. What a choice! 'Hang on, Fred!' he muttered to himself. 'That one ain't too bad.'

His eye had alighted on Sikes. He watched as the man heaved and grappled, lifted, pulled and manoeuvred, the muscles still prominent, his body still strong. That one's got some staying power, he thought. Wouldn't take much to build up his strength.

He strolled along the quayside until his feet were level with Sikes's head.

'Oi! You!' he shouted.

There was no response.

'I'm talking to you, mate!'

The green eyes flashed up towards him, darkened by a frown.

'Out! I want to talk to you.'

Sikes looked enquiringly across the great log towards Walter. The old man gave a slight nod.

'You'd better go, lad. No need to court trouble.'

Sikes slung his grapnel into the log and made his way slowly to the slipway. He dragged himself out, water streaming from him. The overseer came up, wrinkling his nose at the smell of harbour water surrounding the younger man.

'What's your name, prisoner?' he asked.

Sikes told him.

''Ow long you been 'ere?'

Sikes shrugged. He'd lost count of the months. He didn't think he cared any more.

'Ten months. A year. I dunno.'

'You look strong,' pursued the overseer. 'Are you?'

'Strong enough . . . Seein' as 'ow!'

The overseer ignored the remark.

'We need a pit-man in the saw-pit. Last lad met with a haccident. You'll do. You can start now.'

He turned away and made for the saw-pit. Sikes stood staring after him. The overseer turned and jerked his head. Reluctantly, Sikes followed.

The saw-pit had been excavated alongside the timber yard, where the pine logs were stacked ready for sawing. It was a formidable structure, some twenty feet long and about six and a half feet deep. Along the top were laid two logs, which formed the supports, or strakes, with shorter sill-pieces across their ends. There was already a huge log in position, secured by iron-dogs to the strakes, and it wanted only two sawyers to begin work on it.

As the overseer approached the timber yard, a man of average height and stocky build emerged from the shed. He was wiping his hands on a dirty rag and his rolled-up shirt-sleeves displayed hard, brawny muscles and big-fisted hands.

'I've brought you a new pit-man, Jake,' announced the overseer. 'His name's Bill Sikes.'

Jake Varrow stood quite still. He was not a good-humoured man at the best of times and the sight of the belligerent Sikes standing wet and dripping before him did nothing to improve his mood.

'What am I supposed to do with 'im?' he enquired.

Fred frowned. 'What d'yer think? Stick 'im in the pit an' teach 'im to saw!'

The overseer walked away in exasperation and Sikes could hear him shouting at a gang of men inside the timber sheds. He looked at Varrow and noted the turned-down mouth and brittle eyes. He and Varrow were dangerously well matched.

'What're you waiting for, Sikes?' snapped Varrow. 'Get in that pit and I'll set up the saw.'

Sikes jumped down into the pit. The top of it was higher than his head, and with the log in the middle there was little light to see by. He was surrounded by the smell of peaty earth and pine resin and he suddenly felt trapped, like a man buried alive. He wanted to get out, to breathe fresh air, to see the sky, no matter how grey and murky it was. His heart was racing and he felt the ominous darkness creeping up on him. He put his hands up on the edge of the pit. But Varrow's boots were there already.

'Oh no you don't!' he growled. 'You just stay put an' do as you're told. Then we'll all get along fine.'

Sikes sank back and leaned against the pit wall. There were small recesses here and there, where candles or lamps could be shelved when the light grew too dim.

Varrow was fitting the seven-foot saw into the starting kerf, which had already been made. He threw the bottom handle down to Sikes.

'That's the box,' he said. 'Position it on the tail of the blade and then knock the wedge into it.'

He followed his words with a wedge and a mallet and watched critically as Sikes carried out his instructions.

'Now,' he went on, 'I sets the pace. So you follow me. When I stop, you oil the blade with that rag down there.'

He pointed to a deep recess in the wall of the pit, which contained a pot of oil and a rag on a stick. As Sikes looked where he pointed, his eye took in a dark red patch on the sawdust covering the bottom of the pit. Varrow saw his gaze.

'Young Beech.' Sikes waited to be enlightened. 'Timber shifted last night. Come down on 'is 'ead.'

There was silence for a moment and Sikes felt the pit closing in on him again. But Varrow was up on the log now and had the tiller of the saw in his great hands. He called out to Sikes and made the first down-thrust.

The blade came through quicker than he had expected, its wicked teeth bared at him, inches from his face. He carried it up again and it returned, grinning at him and sending a fine shower of dust over his head. Once he looked up and was rewarded by dust in his eyes. For several minutes, he continued lifting the saw blindly, trying to blink away the particles. He was thankful when Varrow called a halt at last and told him to oil the blade.

The two men continued at the pit all afternoon. As the light faded, Sikes lit a small oil lamp and he watched in fascination as his shadow leaped about the interior of the pit. It helped to take his mind off his aching arms and sweating body.

When Varrow finally called a halt to the day's work, Sikes climbed wearily from the pit and staggered up the hill to the prison with the convicts from the timber yard. They were still talking about Tim Beech's death, the only thing in weeks which had fired them into conversation.

'Should never of 'appened. Varrow ain't too clever when it comes to securin' things. Thinks 'e can get away with it.'

'I 'ope 'e larns 'is lesson.'

'Unlikely. Anybody complains, 'e uses 'is fists.'

Sikes listened in silence.

It was difficult to know which was the worse torment. Dragging the trees and grappling them ashore, up to your chest in cold water for hours. Or standing in the bottom of a claustrophobic pit, feeling that your arms would drop off if you dared to stop thrusting them upwards towards the insatiable appetite of Varrow and his end of the saw. At the end of each day, Sikes would be coated in a layer of sweat and fine sawdust. The dust got into his ears, up his nose, down his throat and into his lungs.

'Good for yer!' shouted Varrow, when Sikes began to cough and complain. 'Pine's the best remedy for blocked lungs. Especially Huon pine.'

'The smell might be,' retorted Sikes, 'but the bloody dust ain't. Can't I 'ave a bit o' fresh air?'

'No you can't! We got too much work to do.'

And he thrust the grinning saw-blade down towards Sikes again. Sikes wasn't ready for it and it passed so close to his face that he felt the rush of air it carried with it. He swore and failed to return the blade. The two men glared at each other, nurturing resentment.

'I'll 'ave you flogged if you get difficult with me,' threatened the top-man.

Sikes's eyes blazed back at him and he felt his fists doubling. He returned to his work grudgingly and didn't speak to Varrow again that day.

Day after day, Sikes stood in what he came to regard as his grave. He grew more surly, more churlish, until his conversation with Varrow was reduced to a series of grunts. Sullen he might be, but he was ever on the alert for Varrow's nastiness. The odd tool kicked into the pit, which hit him on the head. The extra shower of sawdust which descended on him one day. The saw, angled to come dangerously near to his face. He wondered why Varrow had singled him out for such torments. But perhaps he hadn't. Perhaps he always treated his underdogs like this. Well, he's a fool, thought Sikes. There can't be many of us who could stick at this job for long.

But the real cause of the antagonism which had grown up between them was a result of Varrow's lack of care. The overseer had said he was an expert, but then Fred and Jake were old friends. Sometimes it seemed as though Varrow were drunk, though where he obtained enough drink was beyond Sikes's comprehension.

One day, they were nearing the end of a cut, dividing the last piece of a trunk into two planks. Varrow had not bothered to insert the necessary wedges as he went along, which would have damped down the vibrations, although he had roped the two planks soon after they had started. It was almost as though the business of routine procedure was all too much for him. Sikes was worried. The iron-dogs were shaking alarmingly as the planks vibrated more and more.

'Oi! Varrow!' he called, squinting up at the sawyer. 'You ain't put in any wedges recently.'

'Nah. Don't matter,' slurred Varrow.

Sikes was convinced he was drunk.

'Well, get some in quick. The 'ole pit'll collapse in a minute.'

Varrow stopped sawing and peered down at Sikes's up-turned face.

'Listen. If you're chicken, then that's your lookout. But no one's goin' to tell me 'ow to do my job.' And he spat full into Sikes's face.

There was no time for recriminations. The saw-blade was tearing its way down towards him again and the planks were shaking dangerously. Sikes grabbed the box and thrust the saw upwards again, his anger fuelling the strength in his arms.

Suddenly, one of the iron-dogs juddered loose. Too late, Sikes saw it lift and on the next down-stroke it seemed that the whole pit had collapsed on him. For a few seconds he lay senseless, darkness all around him. But gradually he was aware of a pain in his right knee and of a movement in the pit, as if someone were struggling to get out. He opened his eyes and saw Varrow clambering over the fallen strakes and planks. He sat up and found that one of the iron-dogs had fallen across his knee. He freed himself and struggled to his feet. His knee hurt badly, but he was determined to deal with Varrow while he had him down here in the pit. He made a grab at the sawyer as the latter was preparing to heave himself over the side.

'Oh no you don't, you bastard!' growled Sikes. 'You ain't gettin' away that easy. You nearly killed me that time.' He pulled Varrow down into the pit and fetched him a hefty blow. Varrow jerked away with the impact and swung back at Sikes with a viciousness which Sikes had not been prepared for. Perhaps the man wasn't drunk after all.

By now, the opening of the pit was surrounded by convicts from the timber yard, who had heard the collapse of the timbers. Any deviation from their daily routine was welcome. The sound of bare-fisted blows elicited shouts of encouragement and it was only a few minutes before the overseer himself came over to investigate. The convicts shrank back and Varrow and Sikes were ordered out of the pit. They climbed out in silence, shaken and bloodied. Sikes's knee felt bruised and swollen and he had difficulty walking.

The overseer sent for the guard and the two sawyers were bundled away to the office of the Commandant, Major Pery Baylee.

He demanded their names, then said, 'You know fighting is a punishable offence out here? Have you any excuses?'

Varrow's nose was still dribbling blood and he sniffed constantly. He glanced across at Sikes, who had his eyes fixed on a point on the white wall behind the Commandant's head. His lip was cut and swollen and there was a bruise spreading along the side of his jaw. Neither man spoke. Baylee lost patience and slammed his fist down on his desk, making both men wince.

'I *will* have an answer!' he bellowed. 'You!' He turned to Sikes. 'What happened in that pit?'

Sikes opened his lips. They felt heavy and bruised. It hurt him to speak, but he wasn't going to let Varrow get away with this.

''E spat in my face, sir.' Sikes spoke steadily. 'I don't take kindly ter that sort o' thing.'

'Why the insult, Varrow?' Baylee looked towards the top-man.

'Sikes was fussin',' he said. 'Tryin' to tell me my job. 'E's a new boy. Don't know anything about sawing. Kep' on an' on about safety.'

Baylee's interest was roused. Turning back to Sikes, he asked, 'What had you said to Varrow?'

'I told 'im ter put more wedges in as we worked through

the plank. The 'ole works wos vibratin' an' the iron-dogs wos shakin' loose. 'E didn't seem ter care. But I wos the cove on the bottom! I could've bin killed. I told 'im about it, but 'e spat in me eye. Then the 'ole thing come down on me.'

'And the fight?'

'Ah! Well!' Varrow seemed to have found his voice. 'I was climbing out of the pit – to get 'elp, you see. I thought Sikes 'ad been 'it by the timbers. 'E was lyin' very still. Then suddenly, 'e jumps up and lays into me. I 'ad to defend meself, sir.'

Baylee could imagine the scene. Varrow had been a fool, a careless one. And Sikes had been overhasty with his fists. They must both be punished.

Sikes received a flogging and took it stoically enough. But in addition, he was placed in solitary confinement on Grummet Island for a week. He thought he had reached rock bottom as the pain of the lash descended again and again on his broad back, but when he saw where he was to be incarcerated, he felt a great wave of despair. He was rowed across to the tiny island by half a dozen soldiers, who would bring him food and water once a day. As they approached the dark cavern at the foot of the rock, Sikes felt emboldened to ask, 'Ain't Varrow gettin' the same treatment, then?'

'Oh yes,' replied a cheerful young soldier. 'He'll get his turn after you!'

Sikes and the soldiers splashed through the shallow waters licking round the foot of the island and the shadow of the cavern enveloped them. The short path sloped upwards and the entrance to the cell was above the tide-line. No daylight penetrated here and there was no living thing to be seen. Even the sea birds seemed to have deserted this part of the harbour. Sikes was ushered into the cell and the heavy door was locked upon him. He listened to the receding sounds of the soldiers returning to Sarah Island. And then there was silence. A thick, black blanket of silence, closing in on him. Like the saw-pit, only worse. Like the grave. They'd buried him alive! He couldn't even see the inside of his place of detention. A faint chink of evening light found its way through the close grille in the door. That was all. His head thrummed. He couldn't swallow. He sweated. His breath came in short snatches. He beat his fists against the door. He cried out to any who might be there to hear him. But there was no one. Nothing. Only the silence and the occasional, faint whistle of the wind above. He couldn't even hear the sea!

'Oh Gawd!' he cried. 'Let me out of 'ere. Let me out afore I suffocates!' He crashed his fists on the door again. 'Let me out!' he screamed. 'Let me out!'

He could hear wheels in the darkness. The creaking of carts along Whitechapel Road. He could smell the sweet pungency of hay, the sweat of horses.

'No, not that!' he whispered fearfully. 'Not that again!'

He sank down on to his knees, his face scraping down the hewn rock of his cell. But he felt no pain. His body was numb and he knew no more till the following evening.

TWELVE

After a week in the blackness of the cell on Grummet Island, Sikes greeted his release with an uncanny calm. He stood at the entrance feeling slightly light-headed, and screwed up his eyes against the light. The cloud had lifted from the sea as a concession to the summer season, but the rain fell continuously. He picked his way painfully to the boat, his damaged knee and flayed back giving him the gait of a much older man. He was rowed straight to the mainland to resume work among his old felling gang. It was not thought prudent to return him to the saw-pit. He sat slumped in the boat, breathing in the fresh air and he looked towards the oncoming shore and wondered how he would struggle on. Perhaps he wouldn't, he reflected. He needn't. He could end all this misery. He almost wished he had met his death under the timbers of the saw-pit. He marvelled at his escape. But he seemed to survive most things. Was he destined for something else? Something more devious? More horrific?

Ashore, two soldiers left him in the hands of the felling overseer and he was set to work immediately, stripping logs for rollers.

He did not speak to the men he worked with, but now and then he would look about him, trying to locate Walter Barley and Chris Freeman. When they stopped for dinner, he wandered off and found his former mates further up the hillside. They were seated with their backs against a recently felled pine and were making short work of their rations. They looked up as Sikes approached and Chris greeted him with spaniel-like joy. Walter nodded. He saw signs in Sikes's expression which he did not like. Sikes sat down and Walter broke off a piece of his loaf for him. Chris offered his own drink, talking all the time. What was it like in the saw-pit? Was it better than felling? Was it really as brutal as they said it was? His questions tumbled out over each other. Sikes didn't reply, but kept his eyes on Walter.

When Chris drew breath, Walter interposed, 'We heard you'd been in trouble, lad.'

Sikes looked at the ground and ran his fingers through the soft earth, idling with a piece of bark by his foot. The others waited in silence. At last he spoke.

'I wos in a fight. I wos flogged. An' I bin in solitary on Grummet fer a week.'

Walter watched the jaw muscles working. Chris made as if to speak, but Walter frowned and shook his head. Sikes, he knew, was suffering his own private hell and would not welcome platitudes from his mates.

They went back to work and Sikes stayed near Walter for the rest of the day, stripping the fallen trunk, preparing rollers and piling the smallwood. Walter watched him covertly, and was alarmed by the change in Sikes. The man hardly spoke at all. He was still in pain, that much was clear. But there was something else, a kind of shadow over him. Walter couldn't quite pinpoint it, but that seemed to describe what he saw in the younger man. He wondered what had caused the change. Was it the week's confinement? He himself had never been on Grummet Island, but he'd heard enough gloomy tales about it to make him think this was behind Sikes's manner.

Next morning, the felling gang moved further upstream, where the Gordon River fell swift and steep on its rocky bed before levelling out into the marshy plain below. It was one of those rare days when the wind had dropped, the rain had ceased and the sun shone, warm and welcome. The ground steamed and the scents of the forest lifted with it. It was a lengthy trek to the felling stand and they were all sweating long before they got there. They split up into their working gangs and Sikes took off his jacket and shirt and picked up the axe he had been carrying. Carefully he felt its edge. It

259

needed sharpening. He went away to ask the overseer for a whetstone. As he turned to go, Chris caught sight of his back and stood open-mouthed.

'Come on, lad,' called Walter, 'we'd best get started.'

He looked up when there was no reply and saw the boy standing stock-still, tears on the his face.

'What is it, Christopher?' he asked softly.

'His-his b-back. D-d-did you s-see his b-back, Walter?'

Walter watched the retreating figure and sighed. 'Oh aye, lad. I've seen it. And plenty worse. That's why it's used as a punishment. Looks bad; feels bad. Warning to others.'

Chris had no answer and Sikes was coming back. But he was a simple soul and so hero-worshipped Sikes, that he would gladly have borne his pain for him. He watched now, in amazement, as the muscles rippled under the healing flesh with every stroke of the whetstone against the axe-blade. He envied the man his strength and stamina and wished with all his heart he could fill out his own raw frame.

By midday, the prisoners were all running with sweat as the temperature rose a little and the forest floor steamed. Morale was dropping again, despite the temporary let-up in the weather. Sikes had spoken hardly a word, except to grunt in reply to a question of Walter's. The old man was worried.

They sat down gratefully to eat their dinner and swigged greedily at their watery beer. Sikes finished his meal, wiped his mouth and stood up. He seemed on the point of speaking to Chris, who was still eating, but walked away without doing so. Walter watched him from where he sat, leaning his weary back against a tree. He feigned sleep, but was following Sikes's path with half-closed eyes.

The sound of voices grew faint and Sikes found himself on steeply rising ground. If he could just get up to that point ahead, where the sun was filtering weakly through, he should be well away from discovery. Beneath his feet, the scrubby undergrowth had given way to bare boulders which burst through the mossy ground. At length, he emerged into sunlight and found that he was high up the hillside, above the tree line, on the edge of the gorge through which the Gordon River had cut its path. He had the strangest sensation that here he was above all the misery and squalor of life, above its vice and its crime, its dirt and tears. Here the air was clean and pure. No human soul in sight. He could have been the only man in the world at that moment. Carefully he climbed a little way over the edge of the cliff. There was a small slope here, covered with short tufted grass and hillocks of thrift. He sat down on a small ledge of rock. There was a sheer drop beneath his feet now. He had reached a decision point, but he wanted to breathe in this view before he took it.

The distance across to the other side of the gorge was considerable. The cliff was more sheer there and the sun glanced off the tiny crystals of granite in the extruding boulders. Small trees grew from the cliff at impossible angles, hanging precariously as though to pluck any wayward traveller from the cliff face. He could see brown birds flitting in and out of crevices in the gorge walls and their piping was the only sound which came to him. That and the rush of water far, far below him. He rested his elbows on his knees and let his hands hang down. His back was sore and his gums were bleeding. Supplies of limes had run out yet again and scurvy was rife. Even up here his dejection would not leave him. How could he go on? It just wasn't possible. He'd been here less than a year and there were at least two more to do if he didn't put his foot in it again. No, it would be better to get it over with now. He gazed down at the river far below, boiling and thundering between the jagged rocks. It would be a messy business and his mates wouldn't like fishing his remains out of the harbour, but he couldn't go on in this torment – generated by this miserable existence and fuelled by his flogging and the terrible week on Grummet Island. He didn't think he would ever get over it. The darkness, the silence, the walls forever closing in on him. And the nightmares. God! He'd had more nightmares that week than in his whole life. He couldn't endure the anguish any longer.

Something in the recesses of his mind told him he was

being a fool. He answered it back, the tears starting to his eyes: I ain't a fool. It's the best thing ter do. It ain't ever goin' ter get any better. An' I don't even know that I'll get back to England eventually. This was rock bottom. He had never let himself think that before. Always there was the vision of England to carry him forward to the next day, and the next. Now there was doubt. And with it came despair. He thought about his past life. What had he done with it? What bright spots were there? Nothing and none, were his answers. He thought of the women he had known. All whores, every one of them, except his mother, and he doubted whether she had been married to Charley Sikes. And his friends? All thieves and criminals. 'What about Toby?' asked the small voice inside his head. ''E's just as much a criminal as you. Knows the inside o' Newgate better than you do. An' I bet 'e's rakin' in the blunt – an' the lush – an' the women.'

His head dropped at this melancholy thought. Then he suddenly stood up. He would never do the deed sitting on a rock contemplating it. Action was needed. He stared down at the yellow-edged froth below. It was a friend, beckoning. He swayed; it made him giddy, watching the thundering water. 'Right, Bill Sikes,' he muttered to himself. 'This is it, mate. This is the last we'll see of you.' He took a step forward, his body poised to jump, and drew breath. Someone took his arm, gently but firmly, and pulled him away from the edge of the precipice. He turned his head, but his vision was blurred. He dashed the heel of his hand across his eyes and found himself looking into the deep and troubled eyes of old Walter.

'Don't, Bill. Don't do it. You're young yet. Don't throw away your life. This won't last for ever. And think of the mess your mates'd fish out of the harbour tomorrow.'

He smiled as he said this, trying to break the tension, but Sikes did not respond. Walter felt the young man's body tight as a bowstring under his grasp.

'Come and sit down. Over here.'

Walter steered him away from the threatening leap and they sat together on the grass. Sikes leaned his head on his arms and there was silence between them for some while. Below them and out of sight, they could still hear the roar of angry waters.

''Ow did yer know I was 'ere, Walter?' He spoke quietly, without looking up.

'I followed you. I knew something was up. You weren't yourself this morning.'

'Why did yer stop me? I've got so low, one more drop wouldn't 'ave made much difference.'

Walter reflected. He must be circumspect.

'It's a long drop, Bill. And you'd have probably changed your mind halfway down. And it would have been too late.'

'But wot am I goin' back to? A bloody awful, unjust system, full o' madge culls and putty coves. And work as'd tear the guts from a hefelant.'

There was no answer to that.

Sikes wondered why it was always Walter who came to his rescue or advised him, put him wise, set him on the right path. Walter was almost like a father to him and Chris. He wondered, not for the first time, why Walter was here. Now seemed like a good time to ask.

'Me?' laughed Walter. 'I was a doctor.'

Sikes stared. Walter was joking.

'No, Bill, it's true. I trained at St Bartholomew's. I expect you know it?'

Sikes knew it all right. How many times had he walked through Smithfield and seen the ancient hospital and its great Norman church?

Walter went on. 'I had my own theories about medicine. I wanted to put them into practice. But there were so many quacks around. Whenever I offered my own ideas, I was laughed out of town, or worse. I was interested in why people behave the way they do. What makes them commit crime. What makes them become insane. Even what makes them kill. No one ever gives much thought to this sort of thing,

Bill, but I'm sure there are answers to these problems, just as there are to sickness and disease. Well, I prescribed a sedative for a woman in the London Hospital and refused to have her committed to an asylum. I knew she wasn't mad. She needed some better treatment than to be locked away. I was adamant about it. When she turned savage and killed one of the nurses, I was held responsible. The hospital brought a case against me and I was transported. Fourteen years. I had a young wife and a child.'

He fell silent. Sikes was overawed. He didn't know what to say. Presently Walter went on.

'When I went back, my wife had married again. The child was dead. I felt reckless and maddened. I tried to get a job back in St Bartholomew's. I had much research to do on diseases of the brain, but I met so much opposition, I had to give up even applying. I fell in with a gambling lot and made a little money. But then there was a forgery case. I got another fourteen years. And out here? I get sent here every so often. Sometimes it's things I've done; sometimes I think they've just got it in for me. I can't bear injustice, or inhumanity. I get sent here for a "holiday". I suppose I'm a nuisance in Hobart.'

He turned to look at Sikes. 'How long have you got to do now, Bill?'

'Wot, 'ere, or back in 'Obart?' His voice was husky.

'Time out here, in Van Diemen's Land?'

'I wos boated fer seven. I've done four – just about.'

'Then you're over halfway, Bill. Don't give up now. Besides, what would your folks back home think of you for doing that? Eh?'

Sikes raised his head and looked at the old man. 'I ain't got any folks,' he said gruffly, 'none at all. So there'd be no one ter bother about me.'

'No lass?'

Sikes shook his head. There was silence again.

Then Walter said, 'Well, if you had jumped, Bill, I would have had a gibbering lunatic on my hands.'

264

'Wotcher mean?' Sikes frowned.

'Young Chris. He thinks the world of you. If you'd gone over, he'd have gone to pieces.'

'Burn an' blast me! Not a perwert?'

And the big hands doubled up into fists. Walter laid his hand on his arm again.

'Don't worry, Bill. He's not like that. He's a very simple lad. But he sees you as the man he'd like to be. Don't spurn him, Bill. Indulge the boy a little. Look after him. He's a good lad at heart.'

'Wot's 'e doin' out 'ere, then?' demanded Sikes.

'He was boated for stealing plums from the local squire's orchard. A schoolboy's prank. Then he was sent out here for some trouble cooked up by some bullies.'

Sikes thought about what Walter had said. He wasn't sure he wanted any hero-worship, but he would certainly look after the boy with Walter. Together they might be able to save him from the clutches of the other prisoners.

'Now,' said Walter, rising, 'if you're feeling better, we'd best return, or they'll be out looking for us.'

He stood in front of Sikes, waiting. He sensed that Sikes's mind was racing desperately. He still might make a dash for the edge and he would be powerless to stop him this time.

Wearily, Sikes lifted his head from his arms. He felt as though he were slowly climbing out of the pit into which he had sunk over the past week. Perhaps there *was* a point in going on. There was still the pull of old England; there would probably still be Toby, if he hadn't done anything really stupid by the time he got back! Perhaps Toby would be pleased to see him – alive and home again. And young Chris? Well, he was only a pup. But yes, he would humour him, he'd teach him how to use his muscles properly; how to fight, maybe.

He got to his feet and Walter held his arms.

'You all right now, Bill? You sure?'

Sikes nodded. He was battling inside. There was some natural reaction he wanted to make – something connected with his father. But he didn't understand the feeling and stood quite still as Walter clapped at his arms with his gnarled brown hands and muttered, his voice thick with emotion, 'Good lad. Good lad. Come along now.'

And the old man turned and stumbled away through the undergrowth. Sikes watched him in silence. Then plunged after him, his long legs slipping and sliding down the hillside, until he caught up with him, just before they reached the felling grounds.

'Walter!' he panted.

Walter turned, his old eyes sparkling.

'Walter. I – I wanted ter say "thank you".'

Sikes stuck out his dirty hand and Walter grasped it, surprisingly tightly, with his equally grimy one.

'You saved my life once, Bill. It was the very least I could do.'

He turned away and the two men went back to their work with renewed vigour and a strong bond between them.

THIRTEEN

Helped by Walter's tactful advice and Christopher's friend-ship, Sikes gradually found a modicum of restored faith in himself. He saw the end of his sentence as a goal to strive for. Meanwhile he filled his days with labour and in secret, he taught young Chris to use his fists. The boy wasn't very good, but Sikes didn't mind. It amused him and gave him the chance to do something he enjoyed. And Chris blossomed under his tutelage. His thin body filled out, as much as the prison diet would allow, and his muscles found a new strength. Even his stutter grew less noticeable. Walter nodded and approved of it all.

In May the weather closed in again for the antipodean winter and Macquarie Harbour echoed to the wailing of the wind. The palisades shook and rattled and collapsed in places. One day, having returned early from the mainland, the felling gang was employed to mend the breaches. They sawed and hammered well into the night, battling with wind and rain, their bodies soaked to the skin, their hair plastered to their heads.

By the time they had finished, they were all shivering with cold, wet, exhausted and thoroughly dejected. They trooped into their barracks, dripping water in an endless trail, and sat down to their meager supper in pools of moisture.

Sikes was sitting next to Walter and he noticed the old man's hands shaking. He watched him from the corner of his eye for a moment. The old fellow could scarcely hold his mug and he was wheezing badly. Sikes steadied the mug for him.

'You ought ter be wrapped up warm somewhere with that chest o' yours, Walter,' he murmured.

Walter tried to speak, but only succeeded in making

strangled noises in his throat, which led to a coughing fit. Sikes leaped to his feet.

'Chris!' he called. The boy was seated opposite and he jumped up immediately. 'Go and fetch the surgeon, quick. Yer know 'is 'ouse?'

Chris nodded, scooped up his sodden coat from the floor and plunged out into the storm again. When Walter had finished coughing, Sikes took the blanket from the old man's bed and wrapped it tightly round him. He pulled off his own and put that on him too. The other prisoners looked on, glassy-eyed, helpless, glad to let Sikes take charge.

The surgeon arrived quicker than Sikes had hoped and having listened to Walter's chest, decided to take him into the little hospital there and then. A cart was ordered and poor Walter was trundled off into the dark. The guards refused to let Sikes and Chris accompany him. Sikes had felt bitter about that and Chris had been near to tears.

As Sikes had been helping to lift Walter into the cart, the old man had fumbled beneath his blankets and croaked, 'Bill! Come here!'

Sikes had leaned closer and Walter had struggled to free his hands from the enveloping warmth.

'I want you to have this,' he wheezed. And he pressed a small box into Sikes's hand.

The large hand closed round the smaller, gnarled one and Sikes felt the chill in it and shuddered. The old man's eyes were rheumy and glazed.

Sikes leaned close and whispered, 'Thank you, Walter. I'll keep it safe for yer. But yer'll be back 'ere soon.'

But the look in Walter's eyes told him otherwise.

Sikes lay drifting in and out of a fitful sleep that night. He knew, with sinking heart, what the day would bring. He crawled from his bed and walked slowly to the barred window. He would have liked to wander outside, but the door was firmly bolted and barred until six. He could see little from the window. It was dark outside and the flicker of the guards' lamps was wetly reflected in the puddles of the yard.

Between the other buildings, he caught a glimpse of water: the black harbour, with its white reflections twinkling subtly in the lights from the quayside.

He wondered whether Walter would die, or if he had died already. One more death out here. What difference did it make? Nobody cared. No one grieved. It was a blessed release from the miseries of this place. He had seen men sent back to Hobart for execution, cheered on by their envious mates. It was not unknown for a man to commit murder here so as to be hanged and spared the torments of further earthly punishment. So you never knew when someone would be driven to strike. You were always looking over your shoulder, wondering if it would be your mate. Wondering whether you would be the next victim, plunged into eternity alongside your desperate killer.

The next morning, the surgeon's boy came up to the penitentiary to tell them that Walter Barley was no more. Sikes received the news in silence, while Chris sat sobbing over his neglected breakfast. He kept close to Sikes all the way down to the quay and in the boat and across to the trees. But never a word did Sikes say.

Another convict was appointed to take Walter's place and he, too, was a surly individual; so like Sikes that they both knew immediately that they would never work well together. Between their grunts and the briefest of sentences, Chris worked miserably, watching Sikes with his big doleful eyes. He yearned for just one word of comfort, but it never came. The man was too wrapped up in his own sense of loss.

Sikes was tempted to go up to the gorge once more, but he knew Walter would be there, watching, waiting for him. He couldn't let him down. It wouldn't be fair to the old man's memory. And so he threw every ounce of vicious energy into his work, though he never smiled and he rarely spoke. And Chris's boxing lessons were forgotten.

By the time spring was with them again and Walter's grave on One Tree Island had grassed over, Sikes felt he would go mad if he had to fell and haul trees much longer. He thought longingly of the shipwright's yard and he sought an interview with the Commandant. Baylee was sceptical, but Sikes had kept out of trouble since his flogging and he saw no real reason why the man shouldn't learn an honest trade. He still had a year's sentence to work.

And so it was with a sense of profound relief, in that October of 1832, that Sikes found himself as a temporary apprentice to Mr Samuel Hoy, the carpenter who had taken such interest in him the day he had lingered in the shipwright's yard.

The old man shook Sikes's hand with delight and chuckled as he showed him round his workshop. Sikes stared at everything, wide-eyed, like a child.

'You're lookin' for the lady, an't you, boy?' said old Samuel, laughing.

Sikes nodded.

'Well she sailed for England back in August last year, so she's out of your reach!'

He cackled and nudged Sikes in the ribs. But there was no response. He frowned and peered at his new pupil.

'Here, you an't so 'appy as last time I saw ye. You an't in trouble, are ye?'

Sikes shook his head, but did not answer.

'Well, I 'ope ye an't goin' to be a purtin' glumpot.'

Sikes had no intention of sulking, but he didn't feel like smiling.

'One o' me mates died back in the winter,' he confessed. 'I ain't really got over it.'

The little carpenter patted his arm and turned away, knowingly.

'You'll be better when you can occupy your mind,' he said quietly. 'Come along. I'll get you started.'

He led Sikes to a workshop bench, littered with wood shavings and heavy with the scent of resin. He showed the younger man how to use the bewildering array of tools and gave him a virgin piece of wood to work on.

'I want a hatch cover made up, Bill. Here's a drawing;

those are your measurements; now see what you can do. If you make a mess of it, don't worry. It an't the end of the world. An' there's plenty more where that came from!' And he went away to an adjoining room, chuckling to himself.

Sikes stood and looked around him. The workshop was quite large and there were other workmen here, free and convict alike. They looked up from their work and nodded at him, but no one spoke to him. He stared at his plans and the supply of wood in front of him. He picked up a piece and felt it, his long fingers tracing the grain. He put his nose to it. He didn't think he would ever forget that smell.

By dinner time, he had made slow, but accurate progress and Samuel was pleased.

'Come an' see what I've been doin' this mornin',' he offered.

Sikes took his dinner with him into Samuel's private workshop, gazing about him in admiration. This man was an artist, without doubt. There were carved figureheads leaning out from the walls, shapely rails and balustrades, a chest or two hanging from the rafters, and mundane frames of varying sizes and in varying degrees of completion. On the bench were small figures, 'little trifles', as Samuel called them, 'knocked up in my spare moments'.

Sikes put his hand in his pocket and drew out the box Walter had given him.

'Did you make this, too?' he asked, holding out the box to his tutor.

Samuel eyed it and laughed.

'Oh yes, I remember making that for old Walter Barley last year. Said he wanted to repay the lad who'd saved his life.'

He stopped and stared at Sikes.

'Was that you?' he asked quietly.

Sikes nodded and said, 'Wot's the carvin' on the top?'

'It's a copy of a paintin' found up in the caverns in the mountains beyond here. Somethin' done by the Western Tribe. Can't tell you what it means, Bill, but it's a good picture, I think. I enjoyed makin' it into a carvin'.'

271

Sikes looked at the little box in his palm and the curious pattern seemed to reach out to him from the distant mountains. He didn't really want to keep such a strong reminder of this place, but Walter had wanted him to have it and it was a tiny link with his old friend. He would keep it for ever.

Later that day, he took the little package which Will Spiring had given him before he died and fitted the contents into the box. Together, they stayed constantly inside his breast pocket.

During his year with Samuel Hoy, Sikes learned a great deal and was glad he had been allowed to come. Chris had been upset at his departure, but he still saw Sikes in the evenings and he was one of the few people Sikes ever talked to.

At the end of the year, Sikes was recalled and bade farewell to his master. The old man was sorry to see him go and Sikes left with a strange mixture of feelings. In an odd sort of way, he had enjoyed his time in the workshop and he had profited by the old artisan's expertise. He had even managed to carve a little figure for Chris. It was a rough representation of a wallaby, the curious animals they often saw down in the plain. It was crude but recognizable and Chris was speechless.

'It's – it's beautiful, Bill. But why are you giving it to me?'

Sikes looked straight into the lad's eyes. The boy had become a man over this last year and Sikes was pleased to see how strong and fit he looked compared with some of his fellow prisoners. But he hated what he had to say to him.

'I'm goin', Chris. Back to 'Obart. Me time's up.' Christopher stared.

Sikes plunged on: 'You'll be all right. Yer big an' strong now. When yer gets out of 'ere, yer'll be fit fer anythink.'

Chris clutched at his hand.

'N-n-no, B-Bill.' His stutter was back again. 'I-I d-don't want you to g-g-go. I've got another y-y-year to do h-here.'

Sikes was brutal.

'Yer've got plenty of comp'ny 'ere. Yer know which ones ter steer clear of. This time next year, we'll both be on our way back to England. Thass summat ter look forward to. You set yerself a goal, lad. The time'll soon go.'

That night, the last in the dreadful penitentiary of Macquarie Harbour, he heard someone crying, softly. Someone else flung a boot and growled, 'Shut up!' Sikes sighed. He feared for the young man, but he wasn't going to lose sleep over him. He had his own future to look to. And tomorrow he was to sail for Hobart!

FOURTEEN

The summer weather held and improved during the four-week journey back to Hobart, and the vessel nudged Hobart Quay amid warm sunshine and a cloudless sky. The occasion was marred only by the fact that the men had been chained again before disembarking.

'Woss this for?' Sikes had grumbled angrily when the blacksmith had come aboard to fetter every convict.

'Stop you runnin' off, mate,' chuckled the blacksmith.

'You know where I've spent the last three bloody years?' demanded Sikes.

'I know, I know. And you can't escape easily from Macquarie Harbour. But you can from 'ere!' and he winked at Sikes.

Sikes wondered; was it worth the risk? He probably had no more than six months to do and he would then be free anyway. He put the thought away. It wasn't worth the effort, not at this stage.

The returning convicts trooped up the hill under armed escort and were allotted new quarters in the penitentiary. Much had changed since the last time they were here. But the old barrack wards were the same: cramped, two-tiered sleeping quarters and everyone fighting to get a place at meal times.

The most urgent need of the men, that first night back in Hobart, was for women. After dark, shadowy figures might have been seen slipping to or from the women's quarters across the stream. For the most part, the guards were content to turn a blind eye, except where minor scuffles broke out. The sudden influx of males put pressure on the smaller number of females and the already established male population.

Sikes readily found a willing partner, but like so many other attempted couplings that night, it was not a success. The years of abstinence and the months in an aqueous clime had rendered him almost impotent. He cursed and raged, but Susannah was kind. She had been here a long time and understood the problems. She lay with him and held him close as he shook with anger and frustration. She murmured into his hair and stroked his body. At last he slept and when he awoke in the early dawn, she smiled and talked to him again and made him pour out the whole hideous episode of Macquarie Harbour.

For his remaining time on the island, Sikes was allotted to a settler, Stephen Brewer, to help him on his small farm up on the side of Mount Wellington. He was to return to the penitentiary each night and was therefore under a certain amount of trust. It was as if the authorities, knowing he had almost worked his time, also knew he would not try to escape, so ruining his chances.

Stephen Brewer had emigrated to Van Diemen's Land some eight years before and had built up a thriving small-holding for himself. He had a wife and four children, horses, poultry and a good-size flock of sheep. But his boundary fences were in need of repair and Sikes already knew something of dry-stone walling. The Deputy Governor thought that Sikes would make an ideal farm servant for Mr Brewer.

When Sikes, his fetters removed, arrived with his military escort, Brewer stood looking him up and down for some minutes without speaking. Then he examined his papers. Sikes felt like an animal in a market. Brewer chuckled to himself as he read where Sikes had spent the last three years. Macquarie Harbour broke most of the devils who went there. He had not reckoned with Sikes, though.

'I'll take him on,' said Brewer to the officer who had accompanied his new servant. 'He'll get his dinner here and he'll be back with you come sundown.'

The soldiers marched off and Sikes and Brewer eyed each other for a moment, uncertainty on one side, wariness on the other.

Suddenly, Brewer clapped him on the shoulder and said, 'Welcome, Bill! I'll take you round my modest estate.'

Sikes breathed a sigh of relief and followed Brewer into the small but solid farmhouse.

'This is Betty. My wife,' announced the farmer proudly.

She turned from the kitchen range, wiping her hands on her apron. Something lurched inside the very depths of Sikes's being. He thought he had never seen such a beautiful sight before. She was not young by the standards of the day, but such an aura of fecundity and contentment emanated from her smooth, flushed face and liquid brown eyes. Tendrils of still-dark hair escaped from her lace cap and she was dressed in a comely gown of pale grey and cream lace, which set off her surprisingly trim figure. Sikes had an overwhelming desire to be enveloped in her embrace. And he was suddenly, irrationally jealous of Brewer.

He followed the farmer out to the byres, tripping over chickens and cats and puppies on the way. Crossing the neatly swept yard, they were almost mown down by a sudden eruption from one of the barns, an eruption which separated and re-formed itself into four squealing children.

'Here! Here! What's all this?' said their father, as they picked themselves up and stood breathless before him.

There were three boys and an older sister. The boys looked up sheepishly at their father. The girl stood with her eyes cast down, but Sikes was watching her and those insolent eyes kept sliding up to look directly into his. Oh Gawd! he thought. More trouble, if I ain't careful. The boys listened dutifully to their father's mild admonishing, but Elizabeth's mind was obviously elsewhere.

'Now,' said Brewer, 'this is Mr William Sikes, who is going to help me repair my boundary walls up on the hills. And Mr Sikes will be taking Digger out each day with the cart, to load up with the stones we need. You can help him load up if you want something useful to do.'

'Is he staying here?' Elizabeth looked at her father very directly, almost defiantly.

'He'll come up here each day after breakfast and return to the town at sunset.'

'Is he another convict?' the youngest boy asked in a hushed voice.

Sikes bit his lip and looked at his boots. Never before had he felt so ashamed of his status. He could feel the girl's eyes on him and he dared not look up.

'Yes,' replied Brewer, in his mild, steady voice. 'He is. But he's only here for six months and then he'll be a free man.'

The boys were not really interested in a felon who had almost worked his time. They liked the dangerous proximity of real criminals, fresh from England. Sometimes men turned up in irons and they would dog their footsteps, knowing exactly where they were. This man had no such adornments. Besides, the two older boys didn't like his surly expression and the younger one was a little afraid of him. The boys ran off, but Elizabeth lingered behind the two men as they made their way to the stable. Sikes felt her eyes raking his back.

The stable was dim, with that warm, rank smell of horse. There were two massive shires stabled here, each in his own loose box, and Sikes was suddenly put in mind of the day he held such a creature's head for a drayman, and the man giving him a whole sixpence, which he later lost in a fight.

'I keep the two for ploughing,' Brewer was saying. 'They're good chaps. Digger and Furrow. I had 'em shipped out as two-year-olds when I left England. This is the feller you'll be dealing with. He's big, but harmless. Soft as a kitten, but strong as an ox. You won't have no trouble with him.'

Sikes reached up and patted the great neck and stroked the long nose with the white blaze. The horse turned and rubbed its nose against him, nearly knocking him over.

'You have to watch his feet, though,' continued Brewer. 'Has a habit of planting 'em where you least expects 'em, he does!'

Sikes looked down at the huge hooves, the feathers almost covering them. He didn't fancy his chances if his own foot got in the way.

Elizabeth now spoke. 'Do you know anything about horses, Mr Sikes?' The question was a challenge.

'No,' he replied, 'but I ain't frightened of 'em. An' I ain't afraid to learn 'ow to 'andle 'em.'

Elizabeth sniffed and flounced out of the stable. Brewer smiled after her retreating back.

'She's my pride and joy,' he said proudly, 'but she's a naughty lass. You'll have to watch her. Let me know if she starts any nonsense.'

Sikes thought it very likely she would start something and he was prepared to be on the alert as far as Miss Brewer was concerned.

The two men spent the rest of the morning ensuring that Sikes knew how to harness the horse to the wooden cart and Brewer was pleased with his quick assimilation of knowledge.

At midday, they went back into the farmhouse and sat round the big pine table, Sikes and the family together. As he sat waiting while Betty ladled out vast helpings of stew and dumplings into thick earthenware bowls, his fingers wandered over the wood.

Elizabeth, seated immediately opposite him, leaned across and said mockingly, 'Haven't you ever seen Huon pine before, Mr Sikes?'

Her father frowned. 'Elizabeth!'

It was a single word of warning. Sikes's feelings were aroused by the girl's words, but he kept his voice level.

'I've just spent three years fellin' the b–' He stopped and corrected himself. 'Choppin' down 'undreds of 'em. An' a year workin' the wood in a shipwright's yard. I've only ever seen 'em made up into ships. Never into anythink useful about an 'ouse.'

Elizabeth was temporarily suppressed. She glared at Sikes. Her eyes were the same colour as her mother's, but Elizabeth's were hard, brittle, defiant. Sikes disdained to look at her and instead let his eyes rest on the more placid figure of Betty Brewer. That was where his interest lay and he was perversely thankful that he was not lodging under the same roof.

The afternoon was warm and Brewer and his new labourer took off their jackets as they harnessed Digger to the cart and went down to the quarry to collect stones. They sat in the cart together and Brewer taught Sikes the rudiments of driving.

'He knows his way, anyhow,' laughed Brewer, 'but he just needs keeping on the straight and narrow. Likes to fill his belly on the way!'

The cart rumbled and jerked down the path to the quarry and when they reached it, the horse stopped of his own choosing.

'Walk him on a bit, Bill,' advised Brewer. 'He's got a habit of stopping where he feels like it.'

With difficulty, Sikes got the brute moving again and when he jumped down from the cart, he felt hot and his arms were aching. Brewer pointed to a pile of rough-hewn stone. Sikes bent and picked up a shard. It was a strange colour, a damp-looking, old, mossy colour.

'Greenstone,' Brewer informed him. 'Quite a bit of it round here. Then we've got slate just south of the town. Very handy for building purposes.'

There were quarrymen swarming over the piles of hewn rock, many of them fettered convicts. Sikes recognized one or two, but did not acknowledge them. He wanted to keep work separate from the penitentiary. Brewer showed him the best stones to select.

'Some of them'll need further chipping,' he warned, 'but I'm sure you can wield a sledgehammer.'

Sikes grunted assent and the two men began piling stones into the cart. When Brewer was satisfied they had enough to work with, they climbed back into the cart and set off on the long, lonely path back to the farm.

For a while they drove in silence, Sikes concentrating on keeping the horse from wandering off to find its dinner in the hedgerows, Brewer viewing the landscape around him with a practised eye.

Presently he said to Sikes, 'Am I allowed to quiz you, Bill?'

Sikes shrugged. 'Depends wot yer want ter know.'

Brewer pressed on. 'Where d'you come from, Bill?'

'Lunnon. Shoreditch.'

Brewer was silent for a minute. Then, 'You'll stay here when your time's up?'

Sikes turned his head briefly to look at his new master.

'Wot, 'ere? In Van Diemen's Land? Nah! I want ter get back to England. It's me 'ome, after all.'

'Mine too, Bill. But I find it a better life out here. More opportunities. Less crowding. Less temptation.' He hesitated. 'You could come and work for me. You're a quick learner. You're obviously fit and strong; and any man who can survive Macquarie Harbour for three years must have an iron constitution.'

'Kind of you to offer, Mr Brewer,' Sikes said gruffly. 'But me mind's made up. It's wot's kep' me goin' all these years, the thought o' goin' back ter Lunnon. I miss it. It's got a special life of its own, 'as Lunnon.'

There was silence again, except for the creaking of the laden cart and the heavy snorting of Digger as he laboured up the rutted trackway.

Suddenly, Sikes said, 'Where do *you* come from, Mr Brewer?'

Brewer was taken aback for a moment by the sudden turn of questioning. But he was an indulgent man and he laughed and said, 'Oxfordshire.'

'I thought you 'ad a country accent. But I ain't very good at tellin' where folks come from.'

'I guessed you came from London,' replied Brewer, 'but I wouldn't have been able to tell you were from Shoreditch. So I suppose that evens us out!'

Sikes smiled. He liked Brewer and thought he would be reasonably happy on the farm.

When they reached the farm gate again, they took a left-hand path which wound away up the lower slopes of Mount Wellington, and Sikes saw the hillside littered with sheep. They gained the edge of the great field and began unloading the stone, piling it beside a short stretch of half-constructed wall.

'This is where the last chap finished,' remarked Brewer. 'He was took ill at the end of spring and I haven't heard nor seen him since. He wasn't very suitable. Bit thin and weedy-looking. No strength at all.'

The afternoon wore on and Brewer was impressed by Sikes's building skills and as Sikes jumped down from the cart at the gate at sundown, Brewer said, 'You've done well, Bill. I'm pleased with you. Come back tomorrow, won't you?'

'Of course,' Sikes said, patting Digger's neck.

They said goodnight and Sikes strode off down towards the lights of Hobart. At the gate of the prison barracks, he reported to the guard and made his way to the supper table. He thought ruefully of the genteel meal he had shared earlier in the day and his mind went back to Brewer's daughter. She was up to no good, he was sure. But it was Mrs Brewer who interested him. That was the line of danger he must watch.

That night he went again to Susannah, but he thought of Betty Brewer and imagined it was her generous body into which he plunged, his manhood restored.

'You've recovered quickly,' remarked Susannah, laughing afterwards.

Sikes kept his face in the crook of her neck.

'I ain't sure it's permanent yet,' he mumbled.

She stroked his hair thoughtfully.

'Wot you bin up to today, then?' she asked quietly.

He told her about the farm and the horses, the quarry and the stone walling. But she was more interested in the family.

'The boys don't like me,' he said, 'I know that much. The littl'un takes to 'is 'eels when 'e sees me. S'pose 'e thinks I'm a bogeyman!'

Susannah laughed. 'An' what does the daughter think of yer?'

Sikes was silent.

'Come on now, luv,' she wheedled. 'I bet yer've given 'er the once-over.'

'She's a troublemaker,' Sikes admitted. 'I ain't too int'rested in 'er.'

'But the mother?' Susannah left the question hanging in the air.

Sikes rolled on to his back. 'Time I went,' he whispered.

Susannah smiled. 'Come back termorrer,' she said softly.

'Oh I will, don't worry!'

And he was gone. Susannah lay still. Bill Sikes was an odd cove in many ways, but she understood these lads just back from Macquarie Harbour and they always blossomed under her care. She lay in the pale dimness of dawn and listened to the sounds around her. Somewhere, not far away, one of her companions was having second helpings and she could hear the rhythmic chink of fetters on the man's legs. She was glad Bill wasn't ironed. It made life a lot more comfortable. There were snores and sighs and rustlings all round. The men were beginning to shift themselves to go back to their own quarters. There was a stealthy creaking of boards and the muffled chink of held chains. Susannah smiled and hugged herself. She really did like Bill Sikes.

FIFTEEN

After a week, the wall-building had progressed faster than Brewer had hoped for and he was glad he had accepted the offer of this new labourer.

Sikes had seen little of the children, except at dinner, although the older boys had helped load stones once. They hadn't spoken to him; in fact, they treated him as though he didn't exist. But it didn't worry him as much as having to sit at table with Betty Brewer only inches away from him. He ignored the eyes of her daughter.

Most days Sikes and his employer would harness up one of the heavy horses and make their way down to the quarry. Sikes liked the hard work in the fresh air. The air had a sweet and bracing quality about it. It permeated his body, and his bones and muscles benefited from its restorative powers. Macquarie Harbour began to slide into second place in his tortured mind. Here there was temperate weather, a reasonable standard of living, a measure of freedom and hours away from the almost incestuous climate of the barracks. And against this backdrop there was a woman. She was removed from his grasp, unattainable, but an object of ardent adulation, none the less. Time and again he saw her gentle features superimposed upon the hard rock faces he handled and he would stop work and stare in disbelief.

'You all right, Bill?' asked Brewer one day.

Sikes did not hear him. Betty Brewer's face shimmered in the unyielding surface before him. He stretched out tentative fingers to trace the contours. 'Not fer you, lad,' he whispered.

Brewer's hand touched his shoulder and he started.

'Nothing wrong, is there?' Brewer was anxious for his new labourer.

Sikes resumed his work, saying gruffly, 'No, sir. Nothink. Just day-dreamin'.'

It occurred to Brewer that maybe Sikes was troubled by visions of his nightmare on Sarah Island. He nodded sagely to himself and determined to make the younger man feel entirely at home in his domain.

He spoke of it to Betty as they sat by a small fire in the parlour that same night.

'Betty, my dear,' he began. 'That young Sikes. He's suffered, you know.'

Betty tilted her head to one side, her eyes wide and compassionate.

'I know, Stephen. But they all do; those who have been in Macquarie Harbour, I mean. I should think most of them are damaged for life. Poor lads.'

She let her hands drop from her crochet work and turned her full eyes to the fire. She was an unusual woman, with a love of all humanity. Had it been possible, she would have gathered all these poor broken souls under her roof and rehabilitated every one of them, setting them on the right road, feeling loved and cared for. What she didn't realize was that at not yet forty years of age, she was still an extremely attractive woman and might well further disturb the 'poor lads' in her care.

Brewer took a draw at his tankard and wiped his mouth.

'What I was thinking,' he went on, continuing his train of thought, 'was that we could perhaps make him feel more at home here. He could spend his weekends with us and come to church with us. More like a family servant would be, back in England.'

'Oh yes,' exclaimed Betty, her eyes shining with fervour. 'That would be wonderful. Perhaps then we'd get him to talk, exorcize those dreadful times for him. Make a new man of him.'

Her enthusiasm knew no bounds and Brewer wondered if he had made the right suggestion.

Next day, the sun burned from a cloudless sky, a herald of

summer. Sikes and Brewer were working far up on the exposed hillside. It wasn't long before they were both down to their shirtsleeves. By midday, Brewer had stripped off his shirt, revealing a hard, sinewy body, still strong, despite his advancing years. He suggested Sikes follow suit.

'No one here to see you, Bill. I should work comfortable if I were you.'

Sikes hesitated, afraid for Brewer to see the marks of punishment, but he was already sweating and the temptation to feel the air on his naked torso was too great. He peeled off his shirt and slung it over the piece of wall they had just finished. He turned to pick up another stone slab and Brewer caught sight of his back. He inhaled sharply through his teeth.

'Is that what they did to you, Bill?' he asked gently.

'Yus.'

The reply was cursory and Brewer ventured no further, feeling he was on sensitive ground. They went on working a while in silence until Sikes happened to straighten up from his work and gaze out over the valley below them. He loved the view spreading out into the sea beyond. As a child, he and his brothers had never seen the sea. Johnny would have loved it. He could almost hear his brother's squeals of delight. He screwed up his eyes; the sun was too bright and brought a kind of blackness to his vision. He could hear wheels grinding again – the old nightmare returning. 'Oh Gawd, not 'ere.' Not up here where the air was pure and unsullied. He forced his eyes open and saw a small trap labouring up the hill path below them, the pony stumbling and straining up the sharp incline. Brewer had heard the sound too and turned his shaded gaze towards its source.

Digger, roaming loose and contentedly among the sheep, lifted his head and whinnied and began to trot downhill towards his stablemate.

'That's my Betty in the trap,' announced Brewer proudly, studying the nodding sunbonnet and capable hands on the reins.

Sikes had already spotted the driver and stood as one mesmerized, all thoughts of Johnny forgotten. There was an ache in his back and a wicked ember burning in his loins as the trap approached. Brewer reached for his shirt and went forward to hand his wife down from the brightly painted vehicle and Digger thrust his head over the gate to converse in his own language with the pony. Sikes stayed where he was, watching jealously.

'Oh, what a hot day!' exclaimed Betty. 'I've brought you men a flagon of beer. It's been standing in the stream all morning to keep cool, but I fear it will be heated to boiling point in this weather.'

She laughed and her eyes flashed and swept up Sikes in their glance. But those same eyes rested appreciatively on his still unshirted body. He was suddenly aware of his nakedness and turned to retrieve his garment. As he did so, a small cry escaped his master's wife. Brewer frowned and laid a finger to his lips. But Sikes knew she had seen. He turned round, buttoning his shirt, and gratefully took the flagon she proffered. In doing so, his fingers momentarily covered hers and the shock of contact made him start slightly. Either Betty had not noticed or she was sufficiently shrewd enough to refrain from comment, but Sikes felt sure his passion must be evident in his face. However, nothing was said and Brewer fetched a rug from the trap and laid it on the grass for his wife to sit on. He was delighted to find that she had brought a small feast with her as well as the cool beer and busied himself with the basket, while his young labourer tied up the pony.

Sikes felt this was a family affair and though he accepted his portion of fine wheat bread and succulent cold meat with a good grace, he took himself a little way off to eat it.

'Mr Sikes,' called Betty and Sikes's heart leaped. 'Don't eat alone. Please come and join us. We'd much rather you thought of yourself as one of the family,' and she patted the tussocky grass beside her.

Sikes felt embarrassed, uncouth, yet elated, all at once.

He hesitated, but Brewer said, 'Come on now, lad. You might as well be near the picnic basket.'

He grinned and his wife laughed, but not at Sikes's expense and the latter felt emboldened to join them. He picked up his tankard and came over, unsure of where to seat himself. But Mrs Brewer had no such doubts and patted the ground beside her again.

Sikes lowered his long body on to the springy turf and leaned back against the wall. He was inches from the woman he silently adored and he could almost feel the vibrations from her body. A light breeze lifted the tendrils of her hair and wafted a delicate perfume beneath his nose. Gawd, he thought, I'm done fer nah. I ain't bin 'ere a coupla weeks an' I'm fallin' fer the missus.

Boldly he let his eyes study the set of her head and the contours of her body. He could have put out a hand and caressed her shoulders from where he sat. It was a good job Brewer was there or he would not have been responsible for his actions. As it was, he hoped she would not take his surliness amiss; it was Sikes's way of covering up his emotions, which at this moment were so highly charged that he felt she must see into his very soul.

A morsel of bread dropped from the piece she was eating and her hand followed it automatically, brushing Sikes's leg in doing so. The fire which shot through him burned and seared. Betty turned her head and smiled, unaware of the effect her proximity had on the man at her side.

Sikes could stand it no longer. He leaped to his feet, returned his tankard to the basket with a muttered, 'Thank you, ma'am,' and went back to his walling, aware of two pairs of eyes watching him.

'Poor lad,' Betty said in a low voice. 'He seems very disturbed.'

'Oh ah,' agreed Brewer, reverting to his native dialect for a moment. 'I've seen some strange 'uns here in my time. But he beats 'em all. I can't make him out.'

They sat watching Sikes labouring under the hot sun.

'He must be so hot in that linen shirt,' remarked Betty.

'Well, he won't shed it while you're here, my dear,' countered her husband. 'He may be a rough cove, but he's enough sense where a lady's concerned.'

'He needn't worry on my account,' said Betty.

'I know that, but he doesn't. So leave him be.' Brewer watched in silence for a moment. Then he said, 'You know, there's something strange about Bill. I don't know as I can put my finger on it. But there's something troubling him, that's for sure. And it seems to be getting worse. He never has talked much, but he's rarely opened his mouth these last few days.'

'I'm not surprised, Stephen. If you'd been through the horrors of Macquarie Harbour, I don't suppose you'd want to talk. And we only hear a fraction of what must go on out there.'

'I suppose so, my dear,' Brewer said, getting somewhat stiffly to his feet and extending his hand to her. 'It was good of you to bring nammet. But I must get on with this job. We're planning to finish this stretch by sundown.'

Betty smoothed her skirts and gazed across to where Sikes was working with feverish energy.

'If he goes on like that, you'll have the whole field completed by sundown!' she remarked.

Sikes saw her climb up into the trap, though he did not stop work. But he kept glancing down the hillside till she was a mere white speck on the dusty path and the pony's hooves no more than an imagined sound.

The hillside was very quiet after Betty's departure, and the only sounds to break the silence were the harsh chink of the wallers' tools and the grating of rough stones against each other as they were eased and cajoled into their allotted places. Sikes could not rid his head of Brewer's wife and the older man expressed concern over his churlishness when he spoke.

'Must be this 'eat,' said Sikes. 'I ain't used to it. It rained a lot where I was.'

No more was said, but Brewer had been successfully, if only temporarily, diverted.

Sikes was truly worried by the strength of his feelings for Betty Brewer. Every waking thought was for her and he had reached the stage where he hardly dared to open his mouth for fear he would tell the world of his longings. If only she were not married to Stephen Brewer. If only she were free. If only *he* were free. If only . . . if only . . .

One morning, when he had been on the farm some three or four weeks, he arrived to a very quiet farmyard. His boots echoed across the newly swept flagstones and he looked all round for signs of activity.

'Mr Brewer and the boys have gone down into Hobart this morning, Mr Sikes.'

Betty's voice sent an agonizing thrill through his body and his heart lurched. He spun on his heel and there she was, standing outside the kitchen door, a basket over her arm, her face twinkling and smiling at him. He came over to her, feasting his eyes on her. He wanted her so much and he knew he ought to turn away.

He must have been scowling with the effort, because she laid a hand on his arm – Burn my body, he thought, if I don't blow somethink! – and said in her soft country burr, 'Aren't you happy here, Mr Sikes? Nothing's upset you, has it?'

He drew a deep breath and somehow answered her levelly.

'No, ma'am. I'm all right. Woss Mr Brewer want me ter do terday?'

'He asked for you to bring up another load of stone from the quarry. He'll be back come noon.'

Sikes nodded and strode away to the stable. He took off his jacket, his face set and his eyes wild. He picked up a brush and began grooming the great shire with big, angry strokes. Digger didn't seem to mind at all and stood with half-closed eyes, snorting gently through his nose.

Suddenly, Sikes stopped and rested his head against the huge warm shoulder, his hands in fists on either side. Woss got inter me? he thought. I'm playin' with fire 'ere. She's far too good an' pure fer the likes o' me an' I couldn't hurt Brewer. He's a good guv'ner to me. He was surprised and annoyed to find himself trembling and he bit his lip in an effort to still his emotions.

Since his thoughts were with Betty, he was totally unprepared for the hands which slid over his back the next minute. He jerked round, thinking she had followed him into the stable. But it was Elizabeth's wicked, flashing eyes into which he found himself staring.

She kept her hands on his arms as she said, 'You thought it was her, didn't you? I can tell, you know. But you won't get her.'

Sikes stared down at the girl. She was quite tall and she was standing very close to him. She dropped her hands and found his, twining her fingers among his own, so that the grooming brush fell to the floor and was lost under the straw.

The girl went on. 'Why don't you take me instead?' And she tilted her head a little to one side, almost enquiringly, and pursed her lips gently.

'You 'aven't ezackly bin very friendly since I come 'ere,' said Sikes, battling to keep his voice steady. 'Yer've bin pretty damning in yer comments.'

She smiled slyly. 'I'm always like that with men I like,' she confided, 'especially exciting ones.'

Sikes ignored the last comment.

''Ow many men 'ave you 'ad, then?' he asked, frowning.

'That'd be telling,' she said.

And now she was leaning against him and sending a flame of desire through his veins. Somewhere in the back of his head he heard Brewer's voice: 'Let me know if she starts any nonsense.' The danger signs were up and he knew he must be strong. He tore himself away and retrieved the brush from the straw. He heard Elizabeth breathing hard behind him, but he went over to the door where he had left the horse's bridle. She was there again, her hands on him.

'Bill!'

He was surprised that she used his name. He swung round

and found her in his arms. He knew resistance was imposs-ible. He bent his head and met her mouth in a hard and vicious kiss. She pushed her little tongue into his mouth like a tiny snake. Their need was desperate. The world disappeared in a haze of straw. But he was horrified when she emitted a stifled scream and clung to him, sobbing desperately into his ear, 'Bill, Bill, it hurts so much. I didn't think it would hurt.'

He couldn't stop, not now, not after these pent-up days of wanting the mother. Release was being offered. He seized and took, but he tried not to be too rough with her and it was over in a moment. She lay weeping in his arms, her eyes closed, the salt tears sliding over her cheeks. He looked down at her and in that instant his whole world collapsed about his ears. He knew what would happen, he could see it all in dreadful detail. And there began a little growth of fear in the pit of his stomach.

'Why didn't yer tell me?' he asked, his voice shaking. 'I thought you was 'andy with the men.'

She shook her head miserably. 'Father doesn't let me near them. He knew Mother was here this morning, but she's so good and simple, it wouldn't occur to her that I might go looking for you. I wanted you from the first moment you came here, Bill. But I didn't know it would be like that, so awful.'

'It ain't really awful,' he said gruffly. 'Yer gets used to it. An' then you enjoys it. But I didn't intend to 'urt you. I'm sorry. I didn't know you was a – a virgin.'

The word sounded odd on his lips.

He stood up and helped her to her feet. He brushed the straw from her hair and her dress and she reached up and kissed his cheek. He didn't respond. He was too shocked.

The following day, when he reached the farm gate, Brewer was standing waiting for him. His face looked cold and grey and there was no one else in sight. Sikes walked up to him and waited. Brewer did not open the gate. 'I told you to let me know if she started her larks, didn't I, Sikes?'

He spoke slowly and carefully, no trace of anger in his

291

voice; just regret and an infinite sadness. Sikes was immediately on the defensive.

'I didn't 'ave a chance,' he said. 'It all 'appened so quick.'

'But you must have known she was an innocent.'

'She didn't be'ave like one. Thass why I thought she was game.'

Brewer nodded his head slowly. 'Well, I'm sorry to lose you, lad. I like you. You're a good worker. She could have chosen much worse. But you'll understand, I can't keep you on. It wouldn't be right. I'll come down now to the barracks and tell them.'

Sikes stood back from the gate, a picture of misery.

The two men strode down into the town together and Sikes stood in embarrassed silence while Brewer told the Deputy Governor why he was handing back his convict labour.

'Of course, if there's a child, we shall have to talk again,' he said.

Sikes felt the cold sweat of fear creep up his back. He sensed he was being cornered. What the hell was the old fool saying? He couldn't marry Elizabeth. He'd be going back to England in a few months. He wasn't going to saddle himself with a wife and child. Worse, it might mean he'd have to stay out here! It wasn't to be contemplated. Brewer was droning on.

'But please, sir,' he urged, 'no punishment. I think it'll be punishment enough that he's no longer working on the farm. I think he enjoyed it.'

The Deputy Governor looked at Sikes, his steely eyes boring into him.

'You know it's a flogging offence, don't you, Sikes?'

Sikes winced at the word and said miserably, 'Yus, sir.'

'No, please. No flogging. I-I insist.' Stephen Brewer was flustered.

He was beginning to wish he had ignored the whole affair. It was only because Elizabeth, for reasons best known to herself, had seen fit to confide in her mother that night and Betty had insisted on his getting rid of Sikes that he was here at all. Her indignation at her daughter's deflowering would have cut Sikes to the quick, had he witnessed it.

Brewer didn't approve of the brutal punishments meted out by the Government. He was a mild man. And if his wayward daughter had got herself into this scrape, then they would find a peaceful means to get her out of it. He wouldn't mind having Sikes for a son-in-law, if it came to that. He enjoyed having him on the farm and Sikes was a good worker, one of the best he'd had. And the man had almost finished his time. He would be free in a few months. The stigma of his conviction was almost expunged.

The officer stared at Sikes, then jerked his head.

'Get out!' he said. And to the guard at the door, 'Iron him and put him with the chain gang on the new road.'

Sikes ignored the troubled gaze that Brewer threw after him. He was marched to the smithy and the wretched fetters were put on him again. He hoped to God the incident would not count against his time out here. By noon, he was at work again with his dirty, smelly, grumbling mates. He missed the clear air that blew down the hillside of the farm. He missed the companionable warmth and smell of the horses. He missed the feel of the rough stone in his hands. And above all he missed Betty Brewer's serene presence over the household. Elizabeth's face he let fall in a painful mist of guilt and he was thankful to blot out her memory. He worked with a feverishness which surprised his fellow prisoners.

''Ere, 'ang on, mate,' said one man. 'Yer've got plenty o' time ter do this job. All year, if yer stayin' that long.' The other prisoners laughed at this wag.

Sikes replied hotly, 'I ain't,' and brought his sledge-hammer down with tremendous force, completely shattering the stone he was working on.

The overseer strolled over and stood watching him.

'That's no good,' he said. 'There's too many small pieces there. We wants the stones split in 'alf. Not minced!'

Sikes glared at him, while his mates laughed outright. Life

293

was going to be awful again, he knew. And he fell into a despondency he had not known since Walter Barley died.

He sought comfort in Susannah's bed. She made him tell her everything and was rather inclined to take Sikes's part over the Brewer affair. But Sikes would not blame the girl entirely.

'I should've known. I should've seen it,' he murmured, while Susannah massaged his aching shoulders. 'She was barely fifteen. She was too young to 'ave 'ad any experience.' Susannah smiled.

'Ain't you fergettin' somethink?' she asked gently. 'Wot about all them London girls? Wot age d'yer think they start at? Wot age d'yer think I started at?'

Sikes raised himself on his elbows and looked into her eyes.

'But she ain't on the streets o' Lunnon, Susan,' he objected. 'She's in the 'eart of a decent fam'ly. Thass wot I can't fergive meself for. If only I'd bloody stopped ter think.'

'Well, she's learned her lesson, an' you've learned yours. Or have you?' she asked him, smiling wickedly.

'It ain't funny, Susan. I lost a really good job 'cos of it.'

She laughed out loud.

'You?' she spluttered. 'Bill Sikes? You, enjoying a job? I thought you was a convicted fel–'

'Shh!'

He laid a finger over her lips. She met his eyes above his hand and he bent his head and kissed her.

SIXTEEN

Fate, which had dogged Sikes's footsteps throughout his life, was not to pass him by on this occasion either. Just before Christmas, on a day of soft summer rain showers, Stephen Brewer mounted his cob and made his way down to the Governor's office in Hobart. Now that it had come to the moment, he felt less confident. After all, he was content to let the matter rest. But Betty had insisted. Their daughter must be made a respectable woman and the expected baby given a name. It was all so unfortunate, more so because he had liked the young rogue. But he knew, too, that his daughter was far from blameless.

He was shown into the Governor's office and faced those same steady eyes which Sikes had faced. The Governor looked hard at him for a moment, then smiled and invited him to be seated. Brewer was, after all, a farmer of some consequence in the community, and a free settler.

'Well, Brewer, how can I help you? I presume you want my help?'

Brewer looked at his hat, licked his lips and said quietly, 'It concerns my daughter, sir.'

The eyebrows were raised. The interest was there. But would he comply?

'Beginning of October, sir, you was kind enough to appoint a young man to help with work on my farm.'

'That's the one up the side of the mountain, isn't it?'

Brewer nodded.

'You've made a splendid job of that farm, Brewer. No one else would take it on. But you've obviously got a keen eye for these things.'

Would he ever let him get to the point? It was as if the man

295

knew what was coming and was stalling for time. Brewer pushed on.

'He was a very good worker, sir, very good indeed. I'd like to have kept him on. Only there was the matter of his seducing my daughter.'

The Governor's eyes narrowed, but he said nothing.

'I had to return him to you, if you remember, sir. I saw your Deputy at the time. I couldn't keep the man on my farm. It wouldn't have been fair, to him or to my daughter. You see,' he hesitated; Betty had told him not to say this, but he was an honest soul and the truth must out. 'My daughter encouraged him; I think he thought she was a fast one, sir, but in actual fact, she'd never had a man before.'

'What was his name?' The Governor sounded less affable now.

'William Sikes.'

A sound of exasperation escaped the Governor's lips. 'Not that man again,' he muttered to himself. To Brewer he said, 'Well? What do you want me to do with him?'

'My daughter carries his child. Will you release Sikes to marry her?'

Governor Arthur sat back in his chair and surveyed Brewer in silence. Then he rang a small bell on his desk and a uniformed officer immediately appeared at a side door.

'Fetch me the papers on Prisoner William Sikes, will you,' he said without taking his eyes from Brewer's anxious face.

Brewer lowered his gaze once more. He could feel Governor Arthur's eyes on him still and he felt uncomfortable, though for the life of him he could not imagine why he should. Perhaps it was just the man's direct gaze.

The door opened and the officer came in with a thick sheaf of official-looking papers in his hands. He put them silently on the desk in front of the Governor and retired from the room. Governor Arthur leaned forward and began examining the papers. Brewer waited in silence.

Presently, the Governor looked up and said, 'Are you sure you know what you're asking for?'

Brewer looked surprised. He was, in some respects, a rather naïve and trusting man.

'I – I don't follow you, sir. I'm only asking that things be set right.'

'This fellow, Sikes. He has a record as long as the Derwent. He's nothing but a rogue and a scoundrel. He was sent out here for attempted robbery. Attempted, mind you. If he had been caught in the act, it would have been the hangman's rope for him. He was well-known to the London peelers and the magistrates, it would appear, and had been up before the courts as a child.' He glanced down at the papers again. 'No parents. On the streets from an early age. Sent to Coldbath Fields House of Correction at the age of eleven.' His voice rose. 'Occupation – cracksman!'

He put down the papers and stared hard at Brewer. The man must be out of his mind. Governor Arthur had daughters of his own and he would never, ever entertain the thought of one of them marrying a convict, just to save her good name. Better to hush it up and have the baby adopted. But then, he would never have allowed his daughters to become enmeshed with such a man as Sikes. He thought Brewer was looking miserable. Silly fool, he thought. Doesn't know when to let go.

'But surely, sir,' Brewer managed, 'he has had a good record out here. He was recommended to me.'

The Governor sighed. He would have to explain carefully to this simpleton.

'Mr Brewer, Prisoner Sikes was sent from this settlement to Macquarie Harbour for causing a riot. I remember the man standing here in this very room, demanding more sleeping space. And because he was rightly refused his request, he stirred up the whole camp and there was a riot, in which several men died and I don't know how many were injured. He was flogged and sent to the penal settlement for three years. While out there, he earned himself another flogging; fighting, this time. He has a record for being surly and insolent and he doesn't get on well with his fellow prisoners.

He was sent to you because he had some skills in dry-stone walling, which you required at the time. Now you tell me he has seduced your daughter and left her with child. And you want him to marry her?'

The question hung in the air like the echo of a knell sounding. Brewer felt a fool. He knew he should not have listened to Betty. She was a good wife and he loved her dearly, but he had been right here. How could they possibly take such a man into their respectable home?

'I see what you mean, sir. I didn't realize he was quite such a bad party. Thank you. I'm sorry to have wasted your time, sir.' He rose to go.

'You haven't wasted my time, Brewer,' the Governor said. 'You have brought the prisoner to my attention and he will be dealt with accordingly. The offence is punishable. Good day to you.'

Brewer hesitated, his mouth half open to protest. But the Governor's dismissal was final and he walked slowly from the room, feeling like an executioner. He knew what they would do to Sikes. If only he hadn't come here and stirred it up, the man would have been safe.

He mounted his horse and rode slowly back to the farm. They would have to find a home for the baby now. Or could they keep it there, on the farm? He brightened at the thought. He had four young children of his own. Betty was still just within child-bearing years. Perhaps they could pass the child off as their own. It would need very careful consideration, but it was a hopeful alternative. He pushed the cob into a trot.

When Sikes was hauled roughly before the Governor later that day, he felt angered and bewildered at such treatment.

'Why the 'ell 'ave I bin dragged 'ere?' demanded Sikes, before the Governor could speak. 'Wot 'ave I done? Why ain't I bin told wot I'm wanted for?'

The Governor looked at him in disgust. 'If you'll just calm down for a minute, Sikes, I will tell you.' And he fixed his prisoner with a look that brooked no nonsense.

Sikes said no more. He stood breathing heavily, waiting. The Governor was looking at a paper on his desk.

'A certain matter of a bastardy order.'

'What!' The word escaped Sikes like a gunshot. 'I bin on the chain gang fer the last three months. 'Ow could I 'ave . . .' He sensed that what he was about to say would have been indelicate to the Governor's ears and he knew the guards were grinning to themselves.

The Governor decided to ignore his outburst and went on: 'Farmer Brewer was here this morning. You worked for him for a while. Left in rather embarrassing circumstances, didn't you?'

Oh Gawd, thought Sikes. So this is it. She's knapped.

'. . . and her father wants you to marry her,' the Governor was saying.

Sikes went rigid. He could feel the sweat trickling down his forehead. This was a continuation of the wretched nightmare. Soon he would see the great wheels again and the crushing darkness: and someone would die. The room seemed to tilt and he closed his eyes for a moment. When he opened them, the Governor was still there, the room was steady and he was evidently expected to say something.

'I – I don't think I'd make a very good 'usband.'

It was a lame excuse, but the Governor seemed satisfied.

'Nor do I, Sikes, which is what I pointed out to Mr Brewer when he came here this morning. I suggested he gets the baby adopted when it's born.'

Sikes visibly relaxed. But the Governor was playing a cat-and-mouse game with him.

'I think it has been mentioned to you before, Prisoner Sikes, that the seducing of free women is a flogging offence. You were spared that at the time on account of Mr Brewer's plea for mercy. However, he is not here today to plead again for you and the girl is pregnant. I have no choice but to punish you as you deserve.'

The darkness was there again at the edge of his vision. He

could hear the rumble of carts, could almost smell the carnage on the road.

'Forty lashes of the cat. I shall oversee it myself.'

The Governor rose and the soldiers came smartly to attention. Sikes stared at the blank wall beyond. Dazed. Numb. The guards took his arms and he went with them, unresisting, to a small cell to cool his heels until dusk. There were few to witness a flogging at the moment. They must wait until the men returned from work in the evening. The prisoner must be made an example of.

Sikes sat on his haunches in the corner of the cell and rubbed absently at the sores on his ankles. The basils were bad in hot weather. The sweat got under them and when they chafed, they made great ulcers in the skin. He tried to think straight, but his mind flitted from one nightmare image to another. He saw Elizabeth's face, distorted in pain; he saw Brewer dismissing him from his service at the farm gate; he saw the wicked cat-o'-nine-tails descending on his back; and he could feel the raw, burning pain even before it began. And always, the darkness and the wheels threatened to hem him in.

The small shaft of light which found its way through the bars on his cell door began to fade and dim. He heard the sounds of the returning men, the sharp metallic clink of their tools. No one had been near him all afternoon, no one had brought him food or drink. And he was very thirsty. He waited in a sweat of fear for the turnkey's tread. It seemed they had forgotten him. But at last he heard the sound of voices and the heavy crunch of boots. His gaoler unlocked the door and jerked his head in the direction of the corridor beyond.

'Out!'

Sikes struggled to his feet, stiff with sitting, and went past the turnkey to be confronted by four soldiers and an officer. No one spoke and he shuffled along as fast as he could in his chains, trying to match his stride with that of his guard. They came outside to an evening sky washed clear of rain. The air smelled fresh and welcome after the close atmosphere of the cell. But he was still very thirsty and he knew he would find it hard to endure his punishment without slaking that thirst. When they reached the yard outside the penitentiary, he saw that the men had all been drawn up in lines to witness his humiliation. One or two smirked and there were audible guffaws from the back. As his irons were removed and his shirt stripped from his back, Sikes asked one of the soldiers if he might be permitted some water.

'Sorry, mate. You'll have to wait till afterwards.'

Afterwards! Forty lashes later! So much pain to be endured before he could taste the coolness of water on his tongue. And his mouth would be doubly parched by then.

He was roped to a hurdle, similar to the one used for punishment in Macquarie Harbour, his body spread-eagled, his arms already aching. He turned his head and saw the Governor approaching in the company of the surgeon and a clerk. They conferred for several minutes and someone was sent back to the barracks for something.

'For Gawd's sake get on with it!' muttered Sikes, more to himself than to anyone standing by.

The flogger heard him and laughed. 'That's my sentiments exactly, mate!'

And he took another swig at the bottle he carried in his left hand. Sikes closed his eyes. What he would have given for just one gulp from that bottle! The flogger lurched a little closer to him. Sikes could smell the beery breath. The man nodded his head in the direction of Sikes's naked back.

'You bin through this before, 'aven't you? Wot was it that time?' He stuck his head close to Sikes's face and winked. 'Bit of a lad, are yer?'

Sikes turned away and saw with relief and yet fear, that the Governor was now ready.

'Is that man drunk?' The Governor's voice was imperious.

The flogger threw his bottle away behind him and called back, 'No, Yer Honour. Not at all. All ready when you are, sir!'

'You may begin!'

Sikes tried counting the strokes on his fingers; four double handfuls that would be. He gave up at eight. He tried to count how long an interval there was between each stroke. He tried to concentrate his mind on all manner of things. But the pain cut through him again and again. He wondered if there was any skin at all left on his back. At the twenty-fifth stroke, he doubted if he could endure much more. After all, he'd never received more than that. His lips were bleeding from where he had bitten them in an attempt to stem his anguish and the salt fired the dreadful thirst in his mouth and throat. If only they would let him have some water. Or beer. Or gin. He could pay them for it. He would be getting money for his latest crack, very soon. The landlord at The Fig Tree had promised him. He was a good fence. Weren't many around like him. It was getting dark, too. He could hear a rumbling in the distance. Perhaps they were in for a storm. It grew nearer and the darkness crept up from the edges. There was Johnny, standing by the wheel of the great wagon and he could see his mother behind him, and Walter, too. They could all come down to The Fig Tree with him and have a drink. He could hear someone sobbing, a gasping, desperate sound. He knew it was from nearby, but it was too dark to see who it was. Only it was a very insistent sound. It seemed to be right in his ears and he didn't like it. He opened his mouth to protest and was violently sick.

He had not been prepared for the sudden douche of cold water which was thrown over him as he hung suspended by his wrists. He gasped and came to with a great spasm of his body. But his legs would not hold him up and he swung by his wrists, his head lolled back. Then he heard orders being given and was aware that men were being marshalled back to their sleeping wards. The soldiers who had accompanied him out here now untied his wrists and ankles and caught him as he fell. It was only then, when the muscles moved on his back, with such resulting agony, that he realized fully what had been done to him. He was hauled back to his barracks, his feet dragging in the dust of the yard, and was laid face down on his bed. No one spoke to him and he was only dimly aware of the sounds around him. The men were sitting down to their supper, but few had the stomach to eat. Glances were cast across at the bloody mess which lay on the sixth bed from the left and there were murmurs of sympathy.

'Bit 'ard on the poor bloke, wasn't it? I mean forty's a bit much. Ain't it?'

'Just for screwin' some ole farmer's daughter.'

'Lucky devil. I'd 'ave taken fifty lashes for the opportunity.'

'Says you. Look at 'im. An' they don't come much tougher than that. He's a Macquarie 'Arbour survivor, too.'

''Ere. Is 'e tryin' ter say somethink?'

The last speaker got up from the table and went over to the bed. Sikes's voice was faint and hoarse, but his meaning was clear.

'Want a bloody drink.'

The man went back to the table and poured a mug of water. When he returned to the bed he stood irresolute, staring at the awful sight of Sikes's back.

'I've got yer some water, Bill, but I don't know 'ow yer goin' ter drink it.'

Slowly, painfully, Sikes raised himself on his elbows and put out a hand for the mug. His hand shook, but most of the water went down his throat as he drew greedily at it.

'More.'

Several mugfuls later, his thirst was temporarily slaked and he sank back on to the bed. Sleep drifted over him, like someone spreading a blanket and then dragging it away again. The surgeon came in just before the lights were extinguished. He examined Sikes's back and spread a thick layer of hog's lard over it. He thought, not for the first time, how barbaric it was to continue punishments like this. He would have to speak to the Governor again about it. It was against all his principles. He was here to heal sick prisoners, and here was the system creating the artificially sick for him. He could do little for the flayed back in front of him. Only time would heal that. Time would never heal the scars on the young man's mind, he thought, as he gently spread the lard over the exposed muscles. He was reminded of his time at medical school; they had made dissections on bodies and had had to expose the muscles, just like this. His hand hesitated. He studied the closed face turned towards him on the bed. The man's eyes were shut, his brow furrowed in pain, but he had not uttered more than an occasional hissing intake of breath. The surgeon admired his constitution, but it would be wasted on the authorities here.

He leaned close and whispered in Sikes's ear, 'Have you had anything to drink?'

The eyes remained closed, but the blood-caked lips moved and he caught the words, '. . . gave me water.'

'You must have plenty to drink, you know. You've lost a lot of fluid and you were pretty sick out there. I'll send for some extra small beer for you.'

The face relaxed a little and he took this as thanks. The surgeon packed his bag and left and the men settled down for the night.

Soon a soldier came in carrying a jug. He stood at the foot of Sikes's bed.

'Surgeon says you're to drink this.'

Sikes struggled up again and took the jug from the soldier.

'Thanks,' he muttered and tipped it to his lips.

It was beer. Small, rather weak, but beer none the less. He gulped it down gratefully and didn't stop until he had almost drained the jug. He wiped his mouth with the back of his hand and held the jug out to the soldier.

'Thank Mr Osborne, will yer? He's a good surgeon.'

The soldier nodded and let himself out again. Sikes sank back and waited for sleep. The wagon was lodged in its byre tonight. He had no more need to fear its lumbering passage yet awhile.

SEVENTEEN

Summer slipped away into autumn and slowly Sikes's back healed. He struggled on, labouring from one day to the next, knowing that his time would soon be up. He hated the place with a cold and vicious hatred. He hadn't thought himself capable of such a feeling. But it was growing all the while. The years of degrading treatment, the unhealthy conditions, the nightmare of Macquarie Harbour, and now this latest flogging. He would never be the same again. How could any man not be touched by such experiences? Meanwhile, he must get through these last few weeks.

He still went to Susannah's bed when he could. She had coaxed his body back to normal and he was grateful to her. He felt a man again. But disease was rife amongst the women and he had no desire to return to England with the clap. Susannah assured him he was safe with her; she was very fond of him.

One night she said, 'Bill, dear, I haven't had anyone else since you come back 'ere. An' I don't intend havin' another as long as you're around. So there's no need for you to worry.'

He was touched by her concern and comforted by her words. He looked on her as one of the very few friends he'd made in all his seven years out here. And he thought he could make it to the winter.

And so, on a bright winter morning, when the hillsides around were sprinkled with the first fall of snow and the roofs of the houses sparkled in the sunlight, the police magistrate appeared at breakfast and read out the list of names of those convicts who had been pardoned – there were precious few – those who were to receive ticket of leave, and those whose time had expired and were free to go. The name of William Sikes was among them.

If he had thought he would feel some great surge of emotion or joy or satisfaction, he was disappointed. He was a name on a list; as he had always been. He would be put on the next ship back to England and that would be the last he'd see of this accursed place. He went about his work that day with a lighter tread, his head held a little higher, almost defiantly: defying the wretched island to crush his spirit, defying the blasted Government to change their minds, defying fate which lurked at every corner of his life. He waited anxiously for news of a ship and a fair wind.

It came a week later, as they trooped in to their supper, one cold, miserable winter's night. The police magistrate was standing in the room and they shuffled nervously to their tables, casting sidelong glances at him. But he was here, for once, on amiable business. He called aside Sikes and four others who had elected not to stay on as settlers.

'There's a ship sailing on tomorrow's tide, eleven of the clock. Your irons will be removed after breakfast and we want you on that ship clean and with your new clothes by half-past ten. You'll collect your clothing from the stores after your visit to the blacksmith and you'll be brought to the police court for your papers. And,' he added, not unkindly, 'be prompt. The ship won't wait for stragglers!'

The men grinned at him and looked at each other. There was a growing tension in the ward. It always happened when a batch of prisoners came up for release. It was as though a barrier grew up suddenly between them and the men who were left behind, a barrier born of resentment and envy, and sometimes genuine loss.

That night, Sikes persuaded the guard to let him across to the women's quarters. He wanted to see Susannah one last time.

'I won't ever see you again, Bill, will I?' she asked, stroking his hair as she always did.

'It ain't likely,' he murmured, ''less you comes back to England.'

'No,' she whispered. 'I shall never return. I'm here for good, Bill, though I hope to get ticket of leave.'

Sikes wondered what she had been boated for; but he had never asked her and he wasn't going to stir up that one now.

Susannah sighed and went on, 'All my boys go eventually. They all drift off. Become free settlers or go back to England, like you. I've seen so many come and go.'

Sikes felt some word was required of him. 'I'm grateful to yer – fer what yer did fer me – after Macquarie 'Arbour,' he said, slightly abashed.

She laughed and held him close. 'I'm glad you're all right now, Bill.'

He kissed her then; and sadly, but urgently, they made love for the last time. She lay in his arms, and the hot salt tears slid silently from the corners of her eyes. As dawn broke, he took her in a last embrace and she, uncharacteristically, clung to him, desperate to keep him. Gently but firmly he freed himself and swung his still-fettered legs over the end of the sleeping platform, leaving her sitting amid her tumbled blankets. He stood a moment, his smouldering eyes quiescent, his face troubled. She pressed a hand to her lips and held it towards him.

'Goodbye, Susannah,' was all he said.

And he was gone.

'Goodbye, Bill Sikes,' she whispered, as the door closed. 'And Godspeed.'

Sikes felt strangely calm as the five of them were escorted to the smithy after breakfast by two soldiers. The blacksmith was quick and efficient. Sikes rubbed his ankles and felt relief at the absence of the iron about his waist. Their next job was to bathe and obtain a new set of clothes. They would be pretty verminous by the end of their voyage, but the authorities insisted on their starting clean. So, for only the second time in his life, Sikes stepped gingerly into a tub of steaming water and was given a cake of rough soap with which to clean his body and hair.

His new clothes, plain, strong, seafaring clothes, felt stiff and unfamiliar. But he would soon break them in and they

307

would become as much a part of him as his old prison clothes had been. These he handed in to be burned and the armed guard escorted him and his companions to the police office.

The police magistrate was waiting for them and they stood scrubbed and shining like schoolboys before him. They were all young and had all survived their sentence with varying degrees of fortitude. The magistrate spoke lightly.

'I'm not here to lecture you fellows, but I hope your time here, for whatever reason you were sent, has taught you to see the folly of your ways. I trust your journey back to England will be a safe one. And I sincerely hope you will all find profitable employment in your lives.' He looked meaningfully at each of them. 'Good luck!'

The men were each given their papers of freedom and passage, which they stowed away in their new jacket pockets, and then they were free to take leave of their old surroundings. Most of the goodbyes had already been said and the men were out working on the chain gangs or in the quarry. Sikes wanted to be alone. He wandered away from the Government buildings, his bundle of spare clothes in a bag tucked under his arm, and glanced towards the women's quarters. But they were all at work in the factory. He walked on down into the town and, for the first time as a free man, made his way along the main street.

It was a long street, well constructed, and the stonework of the buildings was fresh and clean. Elegant ladies on the arms of sprucely dressed gentlemen gazed into shop windows, for all the world as if they were in Regent Street or Bloomsbury. But there were no ragged street urchins, no beggars, no prostitutes lurking at street corners, and a noticeable absence of rubbish in the street. Sikes felt uncomfortable. They weren't like the streets he had known as a child, they lacked something, for all their cleanliness. He could no more have settled out here than fly. He knew what awaited him at home: dirt, squalor and poverty. And there would be a further misery – the presence of the new police force. Word had filtered through, even to this far-flung corner of the world, that Sir Robert Peel had at last got his Bill through Parliament and a brand-new idea had come into being in 1829. Young men were flocking to become the new guardians of the Law and criminals were having a hard time of it, by all accounts. Still, as long as the populace carried on mistrusting this new force, the underworld would be relatively safe.

On the quayside were tall, substantial warehouses and there were boats and cargoes all the way along its edge. Sikes found the ship which would take him home. She was tall, sturdily built, with graceful lines, beckoning in the cold winter sunshine, rocking gently on the sparkling waters, her timbers creaking comfortably. There was an insistent, high-pitched squealing of pulleys, as supplies were winched aboard. Sikes wandered up to the bows and looked up at the figurehead and the years of Macquarie Harbour poured over him for a few seconds; she was there, gaudy with paint, her pink breasts thrust out enticingly over the water, her coiled hair holding up the bowsprit. Sikes stood staring. Behind the figure's head, affixed to the side of the boat, was a black and gold painted plate with her name: *Moffat*. He couldn't see the connection, but it didn't matter. It was old Samuel Hoy's figurehead, the one Sikes had let his hand wander over when it stood in raw wood in the carpenter's workshop. His heart leaped. Here was luck. He felt sure Lady Moffat would see him safely home.

He made his way up the gang-plank and hesitated. There were two young merchant navy officers leaning on the rail, talking quietly to each other. One of them noticed Sikes's arrival and nudged his companion.

The other turned, raised his eyebrows and said, 'New crew?'

'Yus,' replied Sikes, and he pulled out his papers.

The two young men examined them, looked him up and down and then smiled. The second officer spoke.

'Well, you're a bit early, Mr Sikes. But you can stow your clothes while you're waiting. Follow me,' and he turned on his heel and headed for the open hatch in the deck.

Inside the bowels of the ship, there was that strange mixture of smells which Sikes remembered from his journey out: stale bilge-water: stale cooking: stale meat: only made bearable by the overriding aroma of new tar. But there was something missing. For a moment, Sikes couldn't place it, but as he followed the officer through to his sleeping quarters, he realized that it was the absence of stinking humanity. This ship had docked a week before, and would return to England with Sikes and four others and three women. There was part of a regiment coming, too, so the ship would have a fair quota of passengers. But Sikes could see that it would be a far more comfortable passage home. There would be more room, more food, less rigorous discipline. But three women wouldn't go far, he mused. The ship's officers would soon claim them, if they hadn't already. That was how the women paid for their passage back.

He stowed his bundle away on the shelf above his allotted sleeping space and went back on deck. He leaned against the rail and looked down into the green-brown waters of the Derwent. Bits of wood and bark and weed floated on the waves, and Sikes wondered if the bark had drifted round from the west coast, if it was from the Huon pines. His hand went automatically to the little box in his pocket. He had managed to keep it safe through all his troubles and it nestled against his breast, its hard edges digging into him, reminding him of Walter and Will Spiring and the girl he was to look for in London. A sharp wind sprang up and he lifted his face to drink in the sweetness of its freedom. Mount Wellington glistened with snow.

Somewhere up there on the hillside was Brewer's farm. He squinted into the distance. Yes, he could actually see the farmhouse from here. Betty Brewer's face floated before him. He allowed himself to dwell on her for a moment. If he hadn't been so preoccupied with her, he might have noticed what the daughter was up to and he might have avoided the trouble which had made his last few months almost unbearable. He wondered if Elizabeth had had her baby yet. His child! He had left his own flesh and blood out here, in this place on the other side of the world. He would never see the child, never

310

know his own seed. For a moment he knew panic. He wanted to rush back up to the farm. He wanted to know about the child. He couldn't go away, not knowing. He could marry Elizabeth now, if she still wanted him. He was free. He would give up his ideas, he would stay in Van Diemen's Land!

Someone slapped him on the shoulder. It was one of the prisoners returning with him. The moment was lost. And he was thankful. Elizabeth might have miscarried anyway. Or the child might die, though he hoped not. But it was not his concern any more. The gang-plank was drawn up and he was called to the capstan to help raise the anchor. The great sails rattled down in a billowing rush and the wind immediately bellied them out, like a large-bosomed matron. He felt the ship move beneath him and saw the quayside slipping away. He stood staring, mesmerized, as the town became smaller and smaller and shrank away to the size of a child's toy, the snow-capped mountain towering over it. There was something in his throat which made it ache. He swallowed hard, but it wouldn't go away. He looked across at his mates. Their faces, too, showed signs of strain, their eyes narrowed against the winter sun, gazing at the last glimpse of the land of their exile. Suddenly, they all grinned, slapping one another on the back, shaking hands and laughing at their new-found freedom.

'Free, mates. Free o' that cursed place!'

The fellow who spoke shook his fist at the fading settlement. Sikes smiled, but did not follow his action. He, perhaps more than any of them, had cause enough to hate the place. But he had to be honest with himself. He had left the quick, the dead and the unborn there. He couldn't curse it. Instead, he turned his back on it and gazed out across the vast emptiness of the Southern Ocean. That way lay England and home.

PART FOUR

LONDON
1834–1837

Cruelty has a Human Heart
And Jealousy a Human Face:
Terror, the Human Form Divine
And Secrecy, the Human Dress.

The Human Dress is forged Iron,
The Human Form, a fiery Forge;
The Human Face, a Furnace seal'd,
The Human Heart, its hungry Gorge.

William Blake: A Divine Image

ONE

The brown, riverine smell that was London assailed Bill Sikes's nostrils, as the great three-masted ship nosed her way sedately up the Thames on a cloudless morning in late August 1834. The smell and the old familiar sights warmed his heart as the sun could not do and he knew he had been right to return home. Home? What was home? If it was your own house and a family and a hearth to gather round, then he had none. But he had first seen the light of day in this great sprawling city and he had been reared in the squalor of its streets. So London, he supposed, was his home, its tall, light-obscuring buildings his roof, the thieves and rogues his family, the convivial warmth of a public house his hearth. And so he had returned, his time expired, ready to take up the threads again.

As the ship swung round the bend at Wapping, he stared ahead in disbelief and wonder. There, where the old bridge had stood, ancient, cluttered, a barrier to shipping, hung a new edifice, not yet three years old, gleaming white in the summer sun, its outline clean-cut and challenging, its five arches on their stout piers decorously channelling the water through to the western reaches. By the time he left England, half the structure had been complete, but the old bridge had still stood, a little downstream of the new, masking its successor. Looking at it now he wondered if it was an improvement. Certainly it was wide and strong and easier to navigate. But on top, the roadway was as congested as ever the old bridge had been and he could hear the shouts of the cabbies echoing across the water, to mingle with the hubbub from the water traffic, which ebbed and flowed all round him.

He stood propped against the deck rail, lost in thought, a

tall, lean, broad-shouldered man, the marks of penal servitude evident on his weather-beaten face, giving him the appearance of a man somewhat older than his thirty-one years. He had seen much, suffered much, but he was not the reformed character that the philanthropists hoped he and others like him would be as a result of transportation. He was returning hardened, determined. He would not be seeking out some fancy employment, where he would be working all the hours God sent for a meagre wage. That was not what he had risked the long sea journey back to England for. He knew where his future lay and he knew his limitations. Things would be different, he would specialize, he would be cunning, and he would be his own master. He might keep Toby on, but it would depend on how things stood between them after all this time. But he would make a success of his crime. And if he struck lucky, well, maybe he'd move up into the swell mob; that would be good enough for him.

He looked down critically at himself. He could do with a change of clothes; and he had a beard of some six weeks' growth, roughly cut as close as he could manage in the absence of a proper razor. That would have to come off, he thought, or he would be taken for a villain on his looks alone.

His thoughts were rudely disturbed by the loud clattering of the anchor chains, as they were released into their muddy bed. The ship shuddered and swung a little as the current lapped round her in mid-stream. Watermen, who a few minutes before had been sitting on the Customs House Stairs awaiting business, now gathered in their boats in the shadow of the greater vessel, like ducks at feeding time. The exchange between crew and watermen was of long standing, and their coarse laughter and friendly banter rang on the summer air.

Sikes picked up his bag containing his few belongings, and made his way down the ladder to the waiting boat beneath.

At the landing stage, his papers were checked and he was dismissed. A free man at last! Free to go where he would, to do as he liked, provided he kept within the Law. There was the rub again – the Law. But he knew he had to be more careful this time; no risk-taking, no working in gangs, and above all, no women in the business.

Walking slowly through the busy London streets gave Sikes ample opportunity to look about him and absorb all that he'd missed over the years. At some stage, he wanted to go and inspect the new London Bridge more closely; he knew enough about bridge building now to appreciate the achievement of Rennie and his son. But that could wait. At present, his eyes were too busy with the women. When he had left England, seven years before, women were still wearing dresses with the waistline under their breasts, the flimsy material of their gowns scarcely concealing the lithe bodies beneath. Now the dresses were tightly pinched in at the waist, the skirts wide and stiff and the sleeves puffed out into enormous excrescences to balance the skirts. The men had bowed little to changing fancies, except Sikes noticed many more whiskers about in the form of moustaches and extraordinary beards, which followed the line of jaw and chin. And the hair! Short, swept-up curls!

Blimey! thought Sikes. All them curls an' whiskers. Well, they ain't fer me. Soon as I can get rid o' this lot, the better!

He cut across the City to Holborn and thence by a maze of back roads and alleys, short cuts and sharp turns, which he had never forgotten in all those years, to Seven Dials. It was the same old rookery, crammed with the flotsam and jetsam of the City. He stood for a moment in the very centre and grinned to himself. You could hear Seven Dials before you ever set eyes on the place. If it wasn't children screaming or babies wailing or dogs fighting, then it was men brawling; or, worst of all, gin-sodden women tearing at each other, screeching like night owls or screaming abuse. He was home.

He turned into Lumber Court and hesitated. There was his old lodging, nestling up against The Fig Tree, which looked as though it had fallen several stages further into decay. He stood against the wall wondering if it was wise to return. It was seven years since he had last set foot here. Enough time for the whole population of this hidden corner of London to have changed hands a dozen times over. The youngsters he had known – would they still be here? Would anyone recognize him? He might pass through this place entirely unnoticed. Was that what he wanted? To remain unknown would suit his ends very well, in view of the future he was planning for himself. And yet, there stirred within him a very basic human instinct to talk, to unburden himself of the years. Still, at this moment he needed more than anything refreshment and a base from which to take stock of his newfound freedom.

Several inhabitants noticed him lounging and a couple of young bawds nudged each other and sauntered up behind him. One of them had a wealth of fair hair caught back with a scarlet ribbon and arranged in a crude attempt at artistry over one shoulder. Sikes turned sharply as he heard their whining entreaties.

'I ain't int'rested at the moment, gals,' he said firmly but not unkindly. He couldn't tell them he had barely enough blunt to keep him in victuals for a week.

But as he spoke, he was brought up sharply by the steady blue gaze of the younger girl. He frowned. She was pretty and he felt the stirrings of desire. How the hell had this one come down to street level? He turned away quickly and made for the tavern.

'I wouldn't 'ave minded 'im fer a night or two,' remarked the taller girl, as they stood watching him go.

Her companion was silent. Nancy had felt a sudden rush of emotion as she met that dark visage with the smouldering eyes.

'We should've tried a bit 'arder,' said Bet. 'Funny, 'e didn't look like a sailor. But 'e 'ad that sort of beard, didn't 'e? The sort wot scratches yer, short an' wiry. I bet 'e wos all right under that lot . . .'

Her voice trailed off. Nancy failed to reply and Bet peered into her face.

'Come on luv,' she chided, 'cheer up. 'E ain't the only fish the sea's spewed up!'

Nancy smiled. No, she thought, but 'e would 'ave bin a good catch.

They went back towards the centre of Seven Dials and Sikes made his way through the refuse which spilled across his path and stood at the door of The Fig Tree. He turned, curious to see where the two girls had gone. They had disappeared, but he was left with the impression that his life had somehow been touched by them. He shook off the notion. He was too much given to strange thoughts and conjectures these days.

As always, it was dark, airless and smoky inside the tavern; no sunlight had ever penetrated the bar and it retained its own local climate, whatever the weather, whatever the season. All heads turned towards the stranger and he stood there, staring back aggressively at them. Undaunted and unrecognized, he made his way to the bar and ordered a pint of beer and a plate of chops and potatoes from the scruffy barmaid. He sat down alone at a dirty table, the feel of a pewter tankard in his hands again somehow comforting. His fellow drinkers had not given him a second glance. He had been a fool to think anyone would still know him. He recognized no one here. The old Fig Tree gang had long gone. He was free, but he was entirely alone. And the sense of loneliness suddenly pierced him acutely.

The smell of cooking food wafted into the close confines of the bar and made his mouth water. He'd hardly had a real, decent dinner in seven years, with the exception of Betty Brewer's wholesome cooking. When it was placed before him, his hands shook with the anticipation of the moment. And he was not disappointed. He savoured every morsel of meat and onion and gravy and finally sat back, sated and happy.

He drained his tankard and swung away to the door. As he put his hand to it, he felt a tap on his shoulder.

'You're back, then, Bill?'

He turned in surprise to face his old fence and landlord, Jeremiah Rudd.

'I didn't think I'd be recognized. There ain't no one 'ere as I knows.'

'No,' agreed the landlord of The Fig Tree. 'They've all gone. Dead or moved on. Me an' the missus is the last 'ere in Lumber Court.'

Sikes nodded and made to go out, but Rudd laid a detaining hand on his arm. It was an old man's hand now.

''Ave a drink on the 'ouse, Bill.'

Sikes hesitated. It might be useful to keep in with Rudd. He nodded and followed his former fence to a corner table. Rudd fetched a bottle of brandy and two small glasses.

'Wot you goin' ter do now, Bill?' he asked, pouring out two careful measures of the golden liquid.

Sikes fingered his glass. 'Find lodgin's. Set up on me own.' He looked hard at Rudd, who smiled knowingly.

'Well, you know where ter come if yer want 'elp.'

'Thanks.'

There was an awkward silence. Sikes felt that he was required to contribute something by talking of his past. But now that he had the chance, he couldn't do it. It seemed suddenly too obscene, too private, too much of a nightmare. No one would believe what he had suffered.

Rudd looked at him intently, almost reading his thoughts.

'You 'ad a bad time out there?' he asked quietly.

'Yus.' The simple answer told Rudd everything.

'Ah well,' he said, tossing back the last of his brandy. 'We'll no doubt see somethink of yer, now yer back.'

'Probably,' replied Sikes. He stood up. 'Thanks fer the drink.'

Rudd watched him go with a faint feeling of uneasiness on the younger man's account.

' 'Oo wos the sailor-boy, Mr Rudd?' asked the barmaid.

For some reason, Rudd felt he should cover Sikes's tracks for him. 'Oh, just someone as used ter live round 'ere as a youngster,' and he shuffled off into the kitchen, leaving his young assistant to wonder at her employer's closeness.

TWO

Sikes stepped out into the bright sunlight of Seven Dials, feeling a certain empathy with the life around him. He set off northward, not in any great hurry. There was still plenty of the day left and he was savouring every moment of being back on his native soil. He sauntered along watching the passing traffic: cabriolets, tradesmen's carts and once, a handsome open carriage, coming in from the fashionable suburbs of North London. He was more interested in the pretty young woman seated inside with her parents than the vehicle itself. God, how he'd missed the women! Now he could pick and choose again. No need to be confined to the poor drabs of Hobart Prison. Hobart was a world away. Four months since he'd set sail, with not one regret at leaving the place. Except . . . But he pushed that thought from his mind. He would never allow himself to dwell on Elizabeth and her baby again. Never.

The street was full of busy shops, some sporting bright awnings, many with their wares on display outside the windows. Silly fools, thought Sikes. They never learn. Askin' fer trouble. Flimpers' paradise, this. His beard now felt uncomfortably hot and when he saw a barber's pole he turned into the tiny shop and spent some of his discharge coin on a decent shave and a haircut.

Feeling less conspicuous and a good deal cooler without the black growth round his chin, he continued his journey. As he crossed Compton Street, his eye was caught by a terrace of low, three-storey buildings, mostly with workshops below their living accommodation. On the corner stood a public house. Sikes thought this looked promising and knocked at the door of the first building. There was no reply, so he walked on and entered the open door of a dimly lit workshop.

Inside sat a small man bent over a bench, a jeweller's glass jammed into his right eye and a watch in his hands. The back was off and the moving wheels glittered in the light from the oil lamp on the bench. Sikes stood a moment, watching. He let his gaze swing round the tiny room. The shelves were lined with a variety of clocks and watches and the various tickings made a symphony of their own in this quiet back-water.

The watchmaker turned and looked at Sikes short-sight-edly, waiting for his eyes to refocus on the figure in the doorway.

'Can I 'elp you, sir?'

'I'm lookin' for a room,' replied Sikes. 'You got one?'

The little man, who was balding and had a sickly-looking skin, turned his attention fully on his visitor and opened his eyes wide. The eyeglass popped out of his eye socket and swung from a tape at his neck, leaving its owner with a red circle round his eye, like a monocle.

'Well, sir, as it 'appens, I do haff a room. Not very big, nosink special. But you can haff a look. Com' viz me.'

He rose and Sikes followed in his wake, noting the shabby breeches, the holed stockings and the flapping soles of the man's shoes, as he trailed behind him up the crumbling staircase to the top floor.

'Mind ze second and sird steps,' advised the owner of this seedy establishment, as they approached the final flight of stairs.

Sikes took a large step over the offending treads, only to find the wood creaking beneath him on the following steps. The little man laughed nervously.

'Trade's bad zese days,' he apologized, spreading out a skinny hand. 'No money for repairs.'

Sikes followed him into the room at the top of the staircase and his spirits sank. The walls were peeling and, in places, there was mould growing, despite the warmth of the summer. The floor was bare and splintered, the window filthy and jammed up with paint. It couldn't have been opened for years. Sikes sniffed. The place stank of staleness and decay. But it would have to do until he could afford something more salubrious. He settled on his rent with the watchmaker and paid him a week in advance. The little Swiss handed him a key and left him, stumping off down the treacherous stairs.

'Gawd!' said Sikes aloud. 'Wot 'ave I come to? This place'll fall down around me ears afore long, I shouldn't wonder.'

He went over to the window and tried to look out. A spider's web brushed against his forehead and he beat it away in disgust, turning back to the dismal room. There was a bed of doubtful strength and proportions; a worm-eaten chair and table; and a cracked and dirty ewer and basin. It was all too depressing. Sikes slung his bag into a corner and went out, locking the door and making his way gingerly down the two flights of stairs.

Now he would go and look for Toby. He needed a friend, someone with whom to share this day of his return. And Toby was the only friend he'd had. Of course, there had been Will in Hobart, but he didn't want to think about poor Will. Or Walter.

After taking several wrong turnings, he finally arrived outside the house in Marylebone where Toby had lodged on their last acquaintance. The building had a neglected air about it, as though someone had abandoned it and the others in the row, of which it was a part. The stucco was cracked and peeling like London plane trees and the paint had faded and chipped over the years. The railings around the area were rusty, and broken flowerpots and tubs littered the area yard. The windows were boarded over and the steps to the front door were chipped and unswept. Sikes knocked at the door without much hope. The sound echoed through the building and there was no immediate reply. But just as he was turning to go, the door opened a crack and a wizened face with vacuous eyes appeared and stared at him. The apparition, which might have been male or female, did not speak.

'Does Mr Toby Crackit live 'ere?' demanded Sikes.

The ancient head shook in negation.

'D'yer know where 'e's gone, then?'

Another shake of the head.

'Damn an' blast yer eyes. Yer must know!'

Sikes felt desperate and with his desperation rose his temper. The face of the lodging-house keeper, or whoever it was who lived in that dismal edifice, took on a fearful expression and the door was quickly shut and bolted.

'Dammit!' spat Sikes. 'Where the 'ell do I start lookin'?'

He wandered off, back towards St Giles's, his former buoyant mood quite spoiled by this minor incident. His feet seemed to be taking him in the direction of The Fig Tree again. Suddenly he struck his palm with his fist.

'Bill, you idiot,' he muttered to himself, 'the landlord, of course. 'E'll know.'

Jeremiah Rudd did indeed know. Yes, he said, Toby had gone back to his old lodgings after his two-year stretch, but he had soon moved out and had been changing lodgings ever since. He was at present over in Hoxton, 'quite respectable like'. Sikes raised an eyebrow at this information and wondered what had come over Toby. Perhaps his incarceration had softened his brain.

Sikes fortified himself with a large gin and strode away in the direction of Toby's lodgings, between Hoxton Square and the market. Sikes found the place without difficulty and the lodging-house keeper let him in.

'Second floor up.'

Sikes took the stairs two at a time and rapped smartly at the door.

'Come in,' called a familiar voice from inside. 'Door's not locked.'

Sikes opened the door and stood on the threshold. Toby sat in a comfortable-looking armchair, his long legs propped on the table, a clay pipe in his hand and a beaker of beer at his elbow. He didn't seemed to be engaged in any particular pastime, but there were the remains of a meal on the table, so Sikes assumed he was indulging in a post-prandial smoke.

324

When he saw who his visitor was, Toby stared, speech-less, and slowly took his feet from the table, his pipe from his mouth and stood up.

'Bill Sikes?' He almost whispered the name, a look of sheer incredulity on his face. 'Is it really me old mate, Bill?'

Sikes grinned and held out his hand as Toby advanced to meet him.

'Well, strike me blind. I never expected to see you again this side of the Gregory Tree. When did you get back?'

'I docked this morning,' replied Sikes. 'Done me time, an't I? Got to come back 'ome to earn me livin'.'

'Didn't you get ticket o' leave, then?' asked Toby, direct-ing Sikes to a chair.

He poured out two glasses of red wine from a dusty bottle, 'kept for just such a celebration'. Sikes looked shiftily away from Toby's enquiring glance.

'No,' he mumbled, 'didn't get that far. Got into a bit of a scrape. But you don't want to hear about that. What about you? You managed your stretch without too much trouble?'

Toby laughed. 'Oh yes, Bill. But I don't take too kindly to the mention of 'ard labour these days. Nearly broke me bloody back, it did. Smashing up stones for roads most of the time. I've never 'ad so many blisters on me 'ands!'

No, me old friend, thought Sikes. You never did like the mention of 'ard work. Good job you wasn't boated as well. You'd never 'ave survived. Blisters! I'd like to show you my back. That'd make your two years' hard labour look like Bartlemy Fair.

But it was good to be back with Toby, and he certainly wouldn't make Toby a party to the intervening years.

Now he said, 'You know, Toby, there's something about this place that just drags a cove back. I don't know what it is. But it kept me going all those years, I can tell you.'

Toby nodded, knowingly, hoping that Sikes might expand a little and tell him something of his years abroad. But Sikes simply shook his head as if to dismiss his sentimental ideas and turned the conversation round to Toby's exploits since his release from prison.

It seemed that his old friend had not been entirely idle. But neither had he overworked himself. He was keeping a quiet eye on properties in the northern suburbs and was acquiring a long string of 'acquaintances' of both sexes. Sikes was dubious about Toby casting his net of friendship so wide.

'You want to be careful, yer know, Toby,' he warned. 'Too many irons in the fire an' you'll burn yerself.'

Toby laughed and before long, the vintage bottle of wine was empty and both men were in a comfortable state of inebriation. Presently, in a lull in the conversation, there was a scratching at the door and Toby slowly heaved himself to his feet to open it.

'There's an ole mate o' yours 'ere, Bill,' he said. 'Come ter see 'ow you are after all these years.'

Sikes frowned. 'Who's that then?'

Toby put his foot behind the newcomer, there was a yelp and a rather stiff-legged and very battered Bull's-eye pattered into the room and stood winking at his old master.

'Why, you thunderin' ole varmint!' exclaimed Sikes in a rare show of delight. 'They ain't killed you off yet then?'

The dog padded slowly to his master's feet and stood looking up. He wagged his tail, ever so little and Sikes was moved to stroke the creature's head and pull his ears, none too gently.

''E's a lot quieter,' remarked Sikes. 'That ain't good enough, Toby. 'E should make a noise when a stranger's in the 'ouse.'

'But you ain't a stranger, Bill,' Toby pointed out reasonably.

'Then why the blazes didn't you greet me when Toby opened the door for yer?' shouted Sikes at his old canine companion.

The dog hung its head and slunk away beneath the table.

'Bah!' said Toby. ''E's all right really. Good company, when I ain't got no other sort.' And he winked knowingly at

Sikes. 'But you'd better 'ave 'im back. 'E's yours really.'

Sikes nodded in agreement. He wouldn't mind having the old rascal back. But he'd have to retrain him. He'd gone soft since Toby had had him.

They drank far into the night, following the wine with gin and the gin with beer, until Sikes suddenly remembered his new lodging and stood up to go. Whereupon, he fell flat on his face and remained asleep until noon the next day. Toby had collapsed over the table and was finally roused by Bull's-eye whining to go out. He opened the door and the dog made his own way into the street. Toby, meanwhile, blundered blearily round the room, falling over the prostrate Sikes as he made his way to the ewer of cold water. Pouring some into the basin, he doused his head and face and then glanced down at the form on the floor. He picked up the heavy jug and directed a stream of water over Sikes's head. The latter grunted, stirred, then rolled abruptly out of the line of fire with a round curse.

'Come on, Bill, time to get up,' laughed Toby.

Sikes got as far as his knees and groaned. Toby dragged him to his feet, found his hat, pulled him into his coat and steered him out into the bright sunlight. Sikes swore violently at these ministrations and at the brightness of the day, at his aching head and at drink in general. Toby, more used to his drink than Sikes of late, ignored his comments and conducted his companion to a chophouse in nearby Pitfield Street. Here he ordered mugs of hot coffee and a little bread and cheese each. Sikes could barely see what he was doing, but drank copious draughts of coffee and at length had sobered up sufficiently to ask the time of day and how far they were from Clerkenwell. Toby doubted Sikes's ability to walk all the way to his lodging house, but he had reckoned without Sikes's newly acquired stamina. Within a quarter of an hour of leaving Pitfield Street, Sikes was walking independently of the solicitous attentions of his friend and was able to listen with some interest to Toby's prattlings about the new buildings which had gone up since Sikes was last there and events which had happened in the capital.

So many years to catch up with, thought Sikes. I'll never be able to make up for all that lost time, not if I live to be a hundred. Which ain't likely.

When they reached Sikes's lodging off St John Street, the first thing they saw was a battered white dog sitting before the outer door.

'Well, damn my eyes! If it ain't ole Bull's-eye!' remarked Sikes. 'What a strange cove he is.'

Both men marvelled at the dog's extraordinary, not to say uncanny, ability to trace his master's lodging. They clattered up the stairs, followed by the dog, and Sikes unlocked the door. Toby took one look and whistled.

'Yer can't stay 'ere, Bill. This is bloody awful.'

Sikes looked ruefully around the mean little room. And he had to agree with Toby Crackit. 'It'll 'ave ter do for the time being. I've paid a week's rent already,' he grumbled. 'But I'll 'ave ter look for something else.'

'Leave it ter me,' grinned Toby, tapping the side of his nose. 'I'll find yer something.'

'I ain't got much blunt.'

Sikes looked hard at Toby. Toby returned his gaze unabashed.

'Yer needs a job ter get yer goin' again.'

Sikes nodded.

'You sure?' Toby pressed.

'Of course I'm sure.'

Sikes sounded tetchy, but Toby put it down to the hangover.

''Ow else am I goin' to earn me livin'?' went on Sikes. 'I've got to get started again some time. You flush out something and I'm with you.'

Toby patted him on the shoulder.

'Good man. Come to The Three Cripples ternight. Along Little Saffron Hill. Can't miss it. I'll interduce you to some mates. I've – er – got a good fence, too. 'E might be there.'

After only a few hours in London, Bill Sikes was almost back in business.

THREE

The sun was low in the sky and the warm afternoon had given way to a chilly river breeze when Sikes struck out for Clerkenwell that evening. At The Three Cripples, he hesitated, his hand on the latch. It was as though to open the door would be to open up on to a new future, a fateful future. But life had to go on.

'Come on, mate,' said Sikes to Bull's-eye, waiting loyally at his heels. 'Let's get started.'

The scene which met his eyes was somewhat overpowering, but he stepped down into the smoky gloom and elbowed his way to the bar. The room was full of all that was low and mean, dredged up from the surrounding kens and holes of Clerkenwell and Shoreditch. The eyes that looked out of the haggard heads were sometimes bleary with gin, or calculating with greed. Some were shifty, as though their owners had much to hide. Others were more carefree and made the best of their miserable existences. But over all rose the stench of the Great Unwashed, mingling with the odour of stale beer and tobacco fumes. Even at this relatively early hour, there were heads already resting in oblivion on the tables, but there were enough sober bodies around to fill the air with quarrelsome noise and lewd jests, or with just plain high spirits.

Sikes bought a small tot of gin and looked round for Toby. He did not see him immediately, but within a few minutes, the street door opened and flash Toby Crackit had arrived. A half-hearted cheer went up, as some of his drinking partners saw him enter. He nodded and waved his hands at them, like some prizefighter acknowledging his supporters. Sikes leaned on the bar, watching him. The serving man, who did more work in the tavern than the landlord himself, was a red-haired immigrant fellow, called Barney. He had a permanent cold and pungent breath, but he was a good servant to his master and a close member of the Cripples' fraternity.

He leaned across and confided in Sikes's ear, 'They don'd call 'im the Dook o' Shoreditch fer nuthid.'

Sikes snorted at this information. Toby had certainly moved up a notch or two and was obviously heading for the swell mob. Well, he was welcome to it. Sikes preferred to carry on his trade more covertly, not flash it about in fancy togs.

Toby spotted him and embarrassed Sikes by shouting across the room. Many heads turned. Silently Sikes cursed him. But the moment soon passed and Toby was slapping him on the back and introducing him to some villainous-looking individuals, whom he termed his 'trading associates'.

After an exchange of greetings, Toby steered Sikes away by the elbow and said in low tones, 'My tool-suppliers. You'll need 'em soon.'

Sikes nodded and they went to sit in a corner where they could be more private. Toby ordered up bottles of beer and hot supper for two.

'This joint's a wreck,' he said, 'but the food's 'olesome an' nourishin'. Improved a lot lately. Landlord's remarried an' 'is wife spends all 'er time in the kitchen!'

'Toby,' said Sikes leaning across the table and ignoring his friend's praise of the Cripples' culinary delights, 'I need tools an' I need a crack. Are you goin' to 'elp me?'

Toby grinned and tapped his nose in a familiar gesture. 'Trust me, Bill, me ole mate. Give me a coupla days an' I'll 'ave yer fitted out in no time.' He dropped his voice. 'Can't 'elp yer with barkers, though. Yer'll 'ave ter get those later, when you've earned some blunt.'

At that point, there was a sudden eruption at the big central table, round which was gathered an assortment of characters, including some young lads of twelve or thirteen years. Two of these boys were jabbing away at each other with their fists, cheered on by their friends. Sikes watched in amusement and Toby offered the information that they were two of Fagin's boys and were often at each other's throats.

'Fagin?' queried Sikes. 'Who's that?'

Toby cocked an eyebrow and smiled conspiratorially. 'He's our fence.'

When the fracas had subsided and justice had been meted out, resulting in a bloodied nose and some raw knuckles, Toby called out, 'Dodger! Fred! Come 'ere, will yer!'

The two lads wandered over casually and were introduced to 'Mr Bill Sikes'. They eyed his dark, brooding looks suspiciously, as the young tend to do, but accepted Toby's invitation to join them at their table and drink like men.

Dodger, the ebullient victor, spoke first.

'Mr Jack Dawkins, hofficially. But Artful Dodger to me hacquaintances. Pleased ter meet yer, Mr Sikes.'

Sikes nodded a curt greeting. Dodger grinned and rubbed his bruised knuckles, while Fred dabbed at his nose with a blue silk handkerchief. Dodger suddenly noticed what he was doing.

'Oh my eyes!' he exclaimed. 'Wot will Fagin say when 'e sees wot yer done ter that wipe. Gawd 'elp us, Fred. You ain't got much up top when it comes to it, 'ave yer?'

Fred looked up indignantly. 'Wot else is a cove supposed to mop 'imself up with?'

'Bah!' said Mr Dawkins and dismissed the topic, because he had no answer. He turned back to Sikes. 'May I ask wot is your line of business, Mr Sikes?'

Sikes opened his mouth to answer, but Toby grabbed the Dodger's wrist and hissed, 'No, you mayn't. But it's a profitable little line and Bill's a hexpert. 'E'll be comin' ter do a little – ah – business with Fagin.'

The boys grinned, Toby's meaning clear, and they looked at Sikes with some respect, while they drank their beer.

'That your dawg?' asked Fred, pointing to the patient Bull's-eye, sitting at his master's feet.

'Aye,' answered Sikes, 'an' 'e's waitin' for 'is supper, like me.'

'An' 'ere it comes,' announced Toby, as a slatternly kitchen

331

maid delivered two large bowls of stew and dumplings on the table. She sniffed, wiped her nose with the back of her hand and then wiped her hands on her very dirty skirt. Toby put his arm about her and pulled her close.

'Give us a kiss, sweet'eart.'

The slattern willingly complied and Toby sent her off with a smack on her rump. The two men tucked into their meal, Sikes dropping the odd morsel to his dog, who snapped them up before they touched the floor. The boys laughed, drained their tankards and swaggered off towards the door, the best of friends again. Toby called out, 'Fagin comin' ternight?'

And Fred replied, 'Don't think so. He's – er – busy.'

And he looked at Dodger and laughed. The pair departed chuckling. Toby confided once more to Sikes.

''E's probably passin' on goods for the meltin' pot. We'll visit 'im tomorrer.' He paused, fidgeting with his spoon in the stew dregs. Then went on, ''E's a difficult cove, is Fagin. Slippery as an eel, sly as an ole fox. But 'e knows all the right connections an' 'e's never bin peached on. That shows the sort of respect folks 'ave for 'im. 'E may not pay top prices, but then, who does? But yer gets yer whack an' it's all genuine. Trust 'im, an' 'e'll trust you. 'E's the best fence round 'ere.'

'Wot about them lads?' asked Sikes. 'Do they work for 'im too?'

'Yes, but they're only fogle-hunters and flash coves. None of 'em in our line of business. 'E usually 'as six or seven kinchin in 'is employ. It's a good cover-up for his more serious line. I 'ave 'eard it said as 'e used to 'ave girls, too. Ain't seen any about these days, though.'

Sikes frowned. Fagin sounded a thoroughly shady figure. He wondered how the man had managed to rear boys and girls under the same roof and was not surprised that he no longer entertained the female species.

Someone struck up on a concertina and there was a little sporadic singing. Then one of the drabs was prevailed upon to dance, and very shortly the whole place reverberated to the clapping and stamping and bawling voices of the Cripples' regulars. Toby banged the table with his fist in time with the tune and joined in with the choruses. Sikes sat hunched over his beer, not particularly interested in such entertainment.

Suddenly, Toby leaned across and said, 'Need a woman, Bill?'

'Not really,' lied Sikes. 'Not round 'ere, any'ow.'

He wasn't going to let on to Toby how badly he did need a good lay, and he wanted to keep that sort of activity well away from his place of work.

'Garn!' laughed Toby. 'There's a coupla good blowers over there if yer fancy it. Get yer leg over one o' them an' yer'll be the envy o' Clerkenwell. They're very choosy gals, but I'm well acquainted with 'em an' they'll haccommodate any friend o' mine, if I gives the word.'

'Sorry, Toby. Not 'ere. I ain't got any blunt anyway.'

'Ah well.' Toby Crackit sighed and stood up. 'I must be off. I'll take yer ter Fagin's den tomorrer. I'll pick you up from yer lodgin's – 'bout eleven in the mornin'. Au revoir, me ole cove.' And he swaggered his way towards the door, collecting one of the 'choosy gals' on the way.

Sikes watched him go and had to admire the audacity of the man. But strangely, he envied him only his shiny top boots, an item of some expense; and Toby's were certainly new. Sikes was making do with a battered pair of half-boots. But he needed good footwear, for he would walk many miles in pursuit of his occupation. The top boots remained a priority in his mind – along with the barkers.

FOUR

The weather broke the following morning and Toby Crackit was glad of his new boots as he splashed through the mud and puddles between Hoxton and Clerkenwell. By the time he reached St John Street, he was looking somewhat less flash than usual and he stood in the dim entrance of the watchmaker's shop shaking off the rain like a dog. Bull's-eye himself had heard Toby's voice when the watchmaker let him in and now set up a whining and sniffing, his scarred nose close to the gap under the door of Sikes's room. Sikes, lacing up his boots, growled to him to hold his noise. But Bull's-eye's interest was aroused and he continued to snuffle at the gap until Sikes answered Toby's knock.

'Burn me, if yer don't look like a blasted sewer rat!' was Sikes's greeting to his friend.

He kicked the door closed and resumed lacing his boots.

'Bonjooer, me ole mate,' said Toby. 'A touch wet, certainly, but nothin' much if yer well togged.'

He stopped abruptly as Sikes raised his eyes from his boots. Toby coloured. How could he have been so tactless? He saw how thin and threadbare Sikes's clothes were and his boots would never keep out the water. Had the man come back from down under with them? They certainly looked like it, but Toby didn't dare enquire.

'Ah well,' he bluffed, 'weather 'ad to break sometime. Been so 'ot lately, the pumps was all runnin' dry.'

Sikes finished his lacing.

'I've seen enough bloody rain to last me a lifetime,' he said savagely and rose stiffly to his feet.

'You all right?' enquired Toby.

'Yus,' said Sikes, flexing a knee joint. 'I just gets a bit o' rheumatiz when the weather's like this. That's the price yer pays out there.'

Sikes locked his door and the two men turned up their coat collars and strode away to the Saffron Hill rookery, followed by Bull's-eye, who expertly avoided most of the puddles. The wind blew in their faces and conversation was limited. At length they came into Field Lane and halted before a shabby entrance in a row of equally shabby-looking doorways. Their knocking was answered by Fred, who ushered them wordlessly up the stairs and into Fagin's den.

The old fence was bent over a small tub of hot water and suds, washing silk handkerchiefs. Sikes looked about him. Wipes of every size and hue hung festooned from one end of the room to the other, the steam rising from some and giving the place the atmosphere of a minor laundry. The room was of a fair size and was lined with makeshift beds and bunks. A large table with assorted chairs dominated the centre of the room and there was a capacious kitchen range, which gave out a tolerable heat and served for the preparation of the very necessary sustenance of Fagin's young friends. At one end of the room was a curtained-off area, which Sikes suspected was Fagin's private cell; and there were two flimsy wooden screens which afforded the boys some privacy in their ablutions. Sikes had to admit that Fagin had his accommodation well organized.

The old man turned and stared short-sightedly for a moment, screwing up his eyes. Then his face broke into a thousand crinkles as he smiled, wiped his wet hands in his voluminous clothes and then held them out to his visitors.

'Toby, my dear, welcome. And you've brought a friend I see.'

'Yes, Fagin. This is Mr Bill Sikes.'

Fagin pumped Sikes's hand until the latter was forced to withdraw it.

'Mr Sikes,' he beamed, 'very pleased to meet you. And are you a – ah – business associate of Toby's?'

'Yus, yer might say that,' replied Sikes. He wasn't sure how genuine this old fool was.

335

But Toby whispered, 'Hexpert cracksman, Fagin. Bin in foreign parts fer a bit. Needs a fence. We're old friends. Joinin' forces again.'

'Ah,' said Fagin knowingly and rubbed his hands together. 'Always a pleasure to do business with gentlemen who know what's what,' and he chuckled to himself, turning away to pour drinks for his visitors.

Sikes frowned at Toby, but the latter ignored him, taking off his wet coat and hanging it before the fire. Sikes followed suit and they sat at the table drinking gin, which Fagin had fired with a hot poker.

'Now, my dear,' began Fagin, his head on one side, like an old fox. 'Tell me about yourself and your – ah – travels.'

Sikes did not like Fagin's obsequious manner and was not inclined to divulge his past on such short acquaintance.

'I don't like talking about meself,' he said, 'but yes, Toby an' I 'ave done a lot of jobs together. In the past. Afore I went abroad, like.'

'Ahh!' Fagin nodded. 'Boated, eh?'

Sikes half rose in anger. 'Keep yer bloody voice down, can't yer? I don't want the 'ole world ter know I'm back in business!'

'All right, all right, Mr Sikes.' Fagin raised a long, bony hand, the nails black and broken. 'There's only Fred here and he's a close file. This is a very small community, but we're all friends here, my dear, all friends. And I hope you will become one of them.'

And he fixed Sikes with his eyes half-shut, studying him. But Sikes was not a man to be easily overpowered and he stared back at Fagin, his expression hard and calculating. Antagonism hung in the air and Toby foresaw trouble.

Breaking the silence he now said, 'Well, gen'lemen, if yer've done with the hintroductions, then we'll get down ter business. Anythink on the books, Fagin?'

Fagin thankfully slid his eyes away from Sikes's inscrutable gaze and replied, 'Toby, my dear, I have the perfect crack for you. Young Fred was following up a likely dip the other day and the cove turned into a very nice house in Islington. So he hung about and spied out the land and it's got a beautiful back access. Plenty of servants around, too, so you might make it an inside job.'

'That's your line, Toby,' put in Sikes.

'Suits me,' replied Toby. 'I'll start reconnoit'ring ter-morrer.'

Fagin nodded and drummed his bony fingers on the table. He wanted more information on the newcomer if he was to fence for him. He wasn't at all sure that he liked what he saw. He tried again.

'Mr Sikes,' he began, oiling his way behind Sikes's guard, 'what particular skills do you have?' He glanced nervously at Toby as he said this.

Sikes looked at his friend and said, *'You'd* better tell 'im that one, Toby.'

'Well,' bluffed the inventive Toby, ''e can pick a lock afore you've 'ad time to turn round, an' 'e can lift a pane o' glass an' 'ave the window open in twelve seconds flat.'

For once his inventiveness was not far from the truth.

'Wonderful, wonderful,' crowed Fagin, 'but is he quiet? Is he reliable? Does he get caught?'

He was worming his way round, Sikes realized, and fore-stalled any more from both Fagin and Toby.

'I only gets caught when others don't do their job proper. Or if they runs off afore the job's done. Or,' and here he looked very hard at Toby, 'if other parties is brought in wot can't be trusted.'

Toby coloured, coughed nervously and suggested they depart. Which they did, amid oleaginous entreaties from Fagin to visit him again in a very short while.

Outside it was still raining.

'You don't mean you do business with that old bag o' bones?' Sikes grumbled.

Toby was on the defensive.

'I don't particularly like Fagin,' he said, 'but he's a bloody good fence and we're safe with 'im.'

'I reckon 'e's got you all in the palm of 'is greasy old 'and,' Sikes said. 'I ain't sure I want ter be permanently obliged to 'im. 'E likes ter know too much. 'E could ave the upper 'and over us any time. It's too risky, Toby.'

Toby grabbed at his arm.

'Don't be a fool, Bill. Everyone round 'ere fences with Fagin. 'Course 'e knows our business. Stands ter reason, don't it? But you keep quiet about 'is activities with the kinchin and 'e won't let us down.'

'You hope,' returned Sikes. 'I still don't like trustin' 'im.'

Toby slapped him on the shoulder and suggested dinner in a tavern in Holborn, which idea went some way to restoring Sikes's good humour. A bottle of port and a huge dish of liver and bacon between them completed the restoration. Sikes was a man who was on better terms with the world when his belly was full.

'Well,' said Toby, leaning back comfortably in his seat.

He brushed crumbs from his lap and picked at a spot of congealed gravy on his waistcoat. He was feeling pleased with himself. His old friend was back and life was looking up again. And he wasn't going to let his disappointment with Sikes's reaction to Fagin spoil their reunion. He smiled across at his companion.

'Let's 'ear about life in the Hantipodes then.'

Sikes scraped his plate clean and said nothing for a moment. Then he pushed the plate away, wiped his mouth and looked very hard at Toby.

'It wasn't an 'oliday, yer know,' he said quietly.

'No,' replied Toby, 'but yer must 'ave seen some sights out there, Bill, wot no one else 'as seen.'

'Oh yes,' muttered Sikes. 'I've seen some sights all right. Sights as'd make yer 'air stand on end. Sights as'd make yer sick as a dog. Sights as'd make yer wish you was dead!'

The smug, comfortable look disappeared from Toby's face. He wasn't sure how to proceed and there was an awkward silence between them. He studied his friend's face. Sikes had changed. There was a closed look about him. Of course he was older, his face had lost the look of youth; he was gaunt, tired-looking; there were grey hairs in his head now. But there was something else. Maybe it was the eyes. They still burned when Sikes was roused, but the old roguish flash had gone, to be replaced by something infinitely older and wiser; pained; knowing. Toby knew Sikes would tell him little of his years of exile, so there were probably untold horrors to account for the change. Sikes had always been different, always a bit close, secretive.

But Toby was not to be entirely disappointed. Presently, Sikes set down his glass of port and reached inside his breast pocket. He brought out a small package wrapped in a piece of sailcloth and set it on the table in front of him. Toby sat watching as the wrapping was undone. The little pine box lay between them. Sikes said nothing, but his long fingers idled over the carving and it was obvious to Toby that his friend's mind was many thousands of miles away.

Suddenly, Sikes looked straight at Toby and spoke very earnestly.

'Do you know where Rixon's Farm, Kensington, is, Toby?'

Toby frowned, failing to see any connection.

'Never 'eard of it. But then I don't often go that way. It's pretty rural there still. I shouldn't think it'd be difficult to find.'

Sikes gave a curt nod and pushed the box across to Toby.

'Smell it,' he said, smiling, 'but don't open it, or the contents might fall out.'

Toby reached out and carefully lifted the box to his long nose. The aroma was strong, even in the smoky atmosphere of the tavern bar. It gave him a curious sensation. He could feel the mystery, the foreignness of the object; even of Sikes's lost years. He could say, of Sikes himself.

'I spent three years of my sentence working with them pines,' Sikes was saying. 'Bloody great things, thousands of years old. Huons, they called 'em. Surrounded by that smell every day. Got into yer hair and yer clothes. Even yer skin! Funny; I almost miss it.'

339

He smiled to himself and Toby felt excluded. Sikes wrapped the box again, stowing it safely, almost lovingly, in his jacket. He leaned forward.

'I promised a dyin' mate out there I'd try an' find 'is gal. Give 'er a message an' some things of 'is. She used ter be a dairymaid – at Rixon's Farm.'

'Well, don't ferget about it, Bill. Why don't yer go terday? Plenty of time. D'yer want me ter come too?'

Sikes thought for a moment. Then shook his head.

'No, Toby. I'll do this on me own.'

They finished their port and made their way outside. The rain had ceased and the warm, late-summer light fell on Sikes's face. And for a moment Toby saw the old Sikes behind the new, strange façade. He wanted to capture that fleeting look, to hold on to that moment of their lost youth. But it was gone as quickly as it came. Sikes hailed a cab and Toby sauntered off towards Hoxton. The cab took Sikes as far as Bayswater, where he paid the driver, and walked into the village of Kensington.

Mean cottages lined the village street and smoke spiralled lazily from crumbling chimneys poking through the patchwork of thatch and tile. The air of poverty was masked by the presence of several grand houses in their own grounds, but these had been judiciously set on the outskirts of the village, awaiting the spread of the metropolis. Sikes eyed them with interest. He was surprised Toby had not been this way already. There were bound to be some good pickings here.

There were several farms in the village and, rather than make his face and presence known at all of them, he stopped a passing drover.

'Oi, mate! Any idea where Rixon's Farm is?'

The drover scowled, but jerked his thumb in the direction of the church. Sikes was almost there. He could see red chimneypots jutting up from behind a curtain of tall pine trees. Pines! The sight of them, small and English as they were, brought the memories flooding back again, just as the box had done in the tavern. He wondered if these images were going to plague him for the rest of his life.

He tore his eyes away and plunged through the muddy farmyard. He could hear the clatter of pails and the swash of water in a sink. And the laughter of women. He followed the sounds. The door of the dairy stood ajar. He hovered on the threshold, uncertain. He hadn't even thought about what he would say. For several minutes he watched, unseen, as the women went about their work. There were four of them and he wondered which was Sarah. She would be in her mid-twenties by now, so she wouldn't be the very young girl washing pannikins at the sink. There was a hefty, rather hirsute wench turning the handle of the butter churn and two others standing by with pails of milk. He studied them in the dimness of the dairy. Both were attractive girls and either could have been Sarah.

The woman churning butter stopped suddenly, wiped her forehead in the crook of her arm and said breathlessly, ''Ere, Sarah, your turn, ducks. I've 'ad enough.'

The girl addressed as Sarah smiled and Sikes's heart contracted. No wonder Will had thought so much of her. He watched as she took her turn at the handle. Tendrils of hair escaped from her cap. He noted the fine sweat glistening on her brow, the way her breasts moved beneath her tight bodice as she turned the handle. All the old longing was back.

'You want summat, sir?'

The large woman had at last noticed him loitering in the doorway. Now they were all looking at him and even the youngest at the sink stopped and stared. He had been caught unawares and felt a fool.

'I – I'm looking fer a Miss Sarah Fallows, wot works 'ere.' His voice was gruffer than he had intended, because he felt embarrassed.

There was silence in the dairy. Sikes could hear the tap dripping in the sink. The slop of cows' feet outside in the yard. The shouting of farm hands. The distant caw of rooks. Every sound was amplified in that cool, dim silence.

Bewildered, he looked at the faces ranged before him.

'Ain't you Sarah?' he asked the girl who had been thus addressed.

'Yes,' she replied. 'I'm Sarah. But not Sarah Fallows.'

Her voice was very soft and had the faintest of country burrs to it.

'Well, where is she? Where can I find 'er? Don't she work 'ere any more?'

The women exchanged nervous glances. Then Sarah came over to the doorway and stood looking up at him.

'Who are you?' she asked. 'What do you want?'

'My name don't matter. I was with Sarah's young man, Will Spiring.'

Something akin to pain passed across the fresh young face and the girl said, 'You'd best come with me, sir.'

Sikes stepped back and let her through the door and followed her across the farmyard to a gate in the wall. The girl said nothing and Sikes was puzzled. They went through into the churchyard and the iron wicket clanged noisily behind them. Its ring had a certain finality about it and Sikes thought he understood. He followed where the girl went, to the far corner of the plot, where the grass, which had grown tall and rank all summer, now hung bent and brown; bryony berries cascaded red and green from the tangled hedgerow above. He found himself looking down at a green mound. There was no headboard or stone, just a small clay pot with a few late roses in it.

'This is where Sarah is now,' said her namesake, 'and has been these past six years.'

Sikes stared at the mound. Someone kept the grass trim and the flowers fresh.

'Wot 'appened?' he asked gruffly.

Sarah clasped her hands over her white apron and her eyes filled.

'She died of a broken heart, sir. Can you believe that?' Sikes wasn't sure and shrugged.

The girl went on, 'After Will was taken and put aboard the

342

Thames hulk, she thought a pardon might be secured for him. God knows how. She used to go down to Woolwich every Sunday. Along of the sightseers.'

Sikes remembered the sightseers. It was one of the biggest humiliations of his time on the hulk.

'She went there just to get a glimpse of him. She felt she could get through the years like that, just keeping him in sight. What she hadn't realized was that he was to be transported later and he was only waiting for the next ship out.'

Sarah turned to Sikes. 'They treat them terrible bad on them hulks, sir. She used to bring back the most dreadful tales.'

'I know,' said Sikes quietly. 'I was on that 'ulk with Will.'

The girl looked at him with interest. 'Was you boated, too, sir?'

Sikes nodded.

'And you've come back?'

'Aye. With a letter from Will for Sarah. But it seems she'll not be needin' it now.'

'But where's Will? Didn't he return with you?'

'Will and Sarah 'ave been together fer six years now,' said Sikes grimly. 'There's no need for messages any more.' He stood looking down at the little grave. ''E gave up the will ter live, jus' like she did. Love's a funny ole thing, ain't it?'

His question hung unanswered in the still August air. He glanced across at his companion.

'Are you the one wot puts flowers on 'er grave?'

Sarah nodded and smiled. 'We were friends,' she said simply. 'She and Will had such plans. They were very much in love. Will's father didn't approve. But you must know the story.'

'Yes,' said Sikes, 'I know the story. Thanks for showing me this.'

He turned away and went back through the farmyard with the dairymaid. At the farm gate he hesitated. He couldn't think of anything appropriate to say. So his parting words were, 'You'll keep flowers on 'er grave, won't you? Will would've liked that.'

The girl nodded and Sikes went back through the village with a strangely heavy heart. He had hoped to find Sarah, to be able to give her Will's letter, to be able to offer her some comfort. Now they were both dead. He thought they must have died about the same time. Could love do that? Real, deep love? He didn't know. It was all a bit beyond him. He'd never experienced anything remotely like that. He put his hand in his pocket and his fingers closed over the pine box. He wouldn't throw away Will's things. He'd keep them. Always. They would serve to remind him, not only of Will's friendship, but also, if reminder were needed, of the tortuous years in exile. They would enable him to get life into perspective when things got difficult here, as they undoubtedly would.

FIVE

The crack in Islington, which Fagin had suggested to Sikes and Toby, proved remarkably easy. And when Sikes took the haul to Fagin the old man's eyes sparkled and he rubbed his hands together gleefully as he saw the items Sikes took out from his bag.

'You've done very well, Mr Sikes. I shall have to price that little lot before I pay you. Probably tomorrow. You'll be at the Cripples tomorrow?'

Sikes nodded and closed up his bag.

'Toby'll bring his share of the goods round termorrer morning,' he said and departed without another word.

Fagin was left wondering. This new fellow was more secretive than any of his other associates. He still wasn't sure of him and rather wished Toby had not brought him into the circle. But then, he obviously knew the ropes and could do his job well. He was certainly professional if he could bring in hauls like this. And if he was close, then all to his credit. But Fagin wasn't entirely happy.

Nor was Sikes when he received his share of the proceeds and said so, loudly, to both Toby and Fagin. It seemed such a pittance for the effort and the risk involved. Eventually Toby took him aside and assured him once more that they were dealing with the best fence around. Sikes was not convinced.

'I've a good mind ter go back to old Rudd at The Fig Tree,' he said one day when Fagin's payout had been particularly small.

They were standing at the top of Wapping Old Stairs off Wapping High Street. It was late autumn and a thick fog had come down over the river, deadening the sounds that floated

345

across to them from the activities on the water. Although it was midday, they could scarcely see further than ten yards or so in front of them and the damp, clammy atmosphere seemed to penetrate their clothes. Sikes circled his shoulder painfully. He hated this dampness. But he would never admit to Toby the pain it caused him.

For a moment Toby didn't answer. When he did, Sikes was surprised at the intensity in his voice.

'You're a dead man if you do that, Bill.'

'Why? Wot d'yer mean?'

'You've dealt with Fagin now. You're one of 'is "friends" as 'e likes to call us. Leave 'im, an' 'e won't trust you no longer. 'E'll land you in the soup, sure as 'ell. I know, Bill. 'E's done it afore.'

'Yer mean I'm stuck with the old bastard?'

Toby nodded. He watched Sikes trying to control the fury that was building up inside him. He waited for the eruption, but it never came.

Instead, Sikes said quietly, 'So I'm held in 'is greasy palm, like I said? No way out? We both are?'

'Yes,' said Toby, feeling uncomfortable.

'But I could drop 'im in it today.'

'No you couldn't. Because he'd bring the whole lot of us down with 'im. An' if you switch your allegiance to another fence, he'll bring you down alone. 'E's a cunning ole devil; I did warn you.'

Sikes rounded angrily on him.

'Burn me, Toby, you didn't say he'd have us in a corner like this. It's almost blackmail. 'E's taking a huge chunk of the value of goods we bring 'im. 'E must be getting far more than he gives us.'

'Well, that's the way it is,' said Toby gloomily.

For the time being Sikes let the business of Fagin drop and he and Toby concentrated their efforts on a series of cracks, which all ran smoothly and successfully. Sometimes Sikes wondered why he continued to pursue such a course. Surely this wasn't what he had intended to do? But he wasn't sure he knew what he *did* want. He was restless again. He wanted something more out of life.

He had learned to read and write once. Surely he could put that to good use now? But who would employ him in the capacity of a semi-literate hand? Why had he ever bothered to follow Will Spiring's advice all those years ago? He couldn't, after all, take his revenge on society with the written word. He might read 'Wanted' posters or other warnings of predatory criminals like himself loose on the streets, but he was impotent to change anything. The new police force, which had come into existence while he had been away, was gaining too strong a hold. Its presence was felt in too many quarters.

Gradually, over the weeks which followed, Sikes saved enough cash to replace his worn-out clothes with slightly more respectable attire. He also bought new tools from Toby's two rough-looking associates in the Cripples, and his friend helped him find new lodgings in Bethnal Green, in a closed court off Old Nicol Street. It was not far from where he had been born and he was well pleased with his move. The area was not yet the den of iniquity it was to become in later years, but it was shady enough for anyone with a secret to be hidden away in its fastnesses. The tenement itself was of three storeys and Sikes's lodgings were on the first floor. They consisted of a large room in which to eat and sleep, furnished with bed, table, chairs and a grate, and a small store room adjoining, which was lined with shelves and a marble work slab. Here he made his home, adding such small comforts as came his way as he passed through the markets or which took his fancy on a crack. He never kept anything of great value; that would have been courting disaster. He was able to pay his rent regularly and to keep himself in food and drink. Until the winter came.

Winter cracks were rare. Families did not venture abroad and besides, it meant too much hanging around in the cold. You needed to be warm to make a successful break-in. By mid-December, Sikes was feeling the pinch. He skimped meals, drank sparingly and found it difficult to pay his rent

on time. It was amazing, he thought, how quickly the blunt
disappeared. The cold and the damp were getting into his
joints and making his old wounds ache and the pain made
him ill-tempered. He was beginning to doubt the wisdom of
returning from the Antipodes, when one bleak evening,
after an absence of a week or more, Toby Crackit turned up
at his door with a new proposal.

Sikes let him in and gloomily poured out a very small
measure of spirits for him.

'Wot's up, me ole cock?' enquired Toby, looking round
the room.

'Blunt's nearly gone,' replied Sikes. 'No cracks, no blunt.
No blunt, no nothink. Ain't yer got anythink on the cards
yet, Toby?'

Toby sipped his drink, looking thoughtful. Both men
were huddled in their coats and wore scarves and woollen
mittens; the coals had run out three days earlier. There was
a profound silence for a few moments, into which the gust-
ing of the wind and the occasional sigh from the sleeping
Bull's-eye intruded.

Suddenly, Toby looked up. 'You ain't awerse to a
fisticuffs, are yer?'

'No. Why?'

''Cos I knows where you can earn some push with yer
fists.' He waited for this to take effect.

'Oh no!' said Sikes. 'I ain't gettin' involved with the
Fancy. Too many people. Yer never knows when the police
is goin' ter turn out.'

'Not where I'm thinking,' pursued Toby. 'Down at The
Anchor. Shepperton. Little village on the river. Landlord
runs a reg'lar Fancy there. 'E's on the lookout fer new
material. I thought yer might be int'rested. Good pay.'

Sikes didn't answer, but his mind was working furiously.
It was a good idea and might well tide him over the lean
weeks of winter. It needn't be permanent and he could
always leg it back to London if things went wrong, and lie in
lavender for a bit.

'I'm out o' practice.' He hedged a bit longer. 'An' I ain't in great shape.'

'Tell yer wot,' cried Toby. 'I can feed you up a bit an' you can bash about with yer fists. An' then we'll go down an' see the landlord of The Anchor, see wot 'e thinks, eh?'

There was no reply.

'Come on, stand up, let's 'ave a look at yer. Take off yer coat an' get yer shirtsleeves up.'

'Sod off!' grumbled Sikes. 'I ain't takin' my bleedin' coat off in this weather fer no one!'

'Ah well, just a thought.'

Toby was unflappable. He looked at Sikes, covertly. The penal years had given him the edge over his peers. His body looked tough and strong and his muscles must be hard from constant labour. He stood out from the rest with his breadth and height, a good six foot of him, in a time when those around him were mostly thin and bent, weak and pale from lack of nourishment and fresh air, and the evils which constituted their daily lives.

'You'll no doubt do,' continued Toby.

Sikes looked up lugubriously.

'I shall 'ave to, won't I?' he said glumly.

Ten minutes later, the two men were seated in a nearby chophouse over a hot supper and warm ale. Toby expanded on the regular fights at The Anchor.

'There's good money to be 'ad if you're suitable,' he said. 'An' I reckon the landlord'll be 'appy ter back a big cove like you.'

Toby was feeling pleased with himself. If the landlord of The Anchor decided to back Sikes, as he must undoubtedly do, then he, Toby, stood to make considerable gain from the enterprise, on account of his having introduced the fellow.

Back in Sikes's lodgings, Toby finally persuaded him to strip to the waist and in a very short time Sikes was sweating through the effort of punching the air at an imaginary adversary.

'More aggerawation, Bill,' cried Toby. 'Can't you imagine it's someone you 'ate standing there?'

'Much more o' this an' I'll flamin' punch you,' panted Sikes.

Nonetheless, he followed Toby's advice and imagined he'd been given free rein to knock the living daylights out of his chain-gang overseer in Hobart.

'That's much better.' Toby was pleased with his efforts. 'Give it a rest now.'

Sikes sank on to a chair and gulped a measure of what he thought was beer. But Toby had judiciously substituted water. Sikes spat it out, furious.

'Wot the blazes you playin' at?' he demanded. 'A cove needs 'is drink!'

'Adam's ale's better for yer when yer trainin', Bill,' and he threw the aspiring pugilist a grey-looking towel, with which to dry his sweating body.

''Ow long for?' shouted Sikes, splashing icy water over his head and torso.

Toby shrugged. 'It'll 'ave ter be rationed.'

'Oh Christ!' groaned Sikes. 'I shall die.'

Toby laughed, but he thought that Sikes on a limited supply of alcohol might make life rather unbearable and he was secretly glad that the fight he had in mind was not too many weeks away.

SIX

Christmas came and went, almost unnoticed among the fraternity of The Three Cripples. And very early on a bleak January morning, two of that fraternity might have been seen striding out through Holborn and Knightsbridge and along the Great West Road. Creaking market carts plodded past them, their loads swaying dangerously over the hard, frosted ruts. Once, the Bath mail coach hurtled past, the postilion sounding his horn to clear the way, the horses' hooves jarring on the frozen ground.

'That won't do 'em much good,' remarked Sikes.

He had learned enough about horses on Brewer's farm to appreciate the dangers of such treatment. Toby shrugged.

'They've got such speeds ter keep up now an' they makes so much blunt, they can afford ter run their 'orses into the ground.'

By noon, they were at Kew, cold, hungry and caked with icy mud. Despite his empty belly and growing thirst, Sikes was for pushing ahead while the weather held. But Toby, wanting Sikes in good form when they arrived at Shepperton, insisted on finding somewhere to refuel. They spent some minutes arguing as to which lane to take, their breath steaming white and cloudy from their angry throats. At length they agreed to walk down to the river and there found a tavern, where the landlord looked them up and down and silently poured them each a pint of ale.

'We don't get many strangers 'ere,' he remarked eventually.

The heads of the other drinkers turned and stared at the two travellers. Sikes felt uncomfortable and wished they hadn't stopped.

Toby, in his brash way, said, 'Well, landlord, we'll add to yer business by orderin' a hot meal apiece.'

The landlord narrowed his eyes and looked hard at Toby. Sikes kicked him under the table and Toby jerked and frowned.

'Wotcher do that for, Bill?' he hissed angrily.

'Just stop drawin' attention to us, that's all. I don't like it. It ain't good fer business.'

Toby subsided and the two men sat huddled in their greatcoats, waiting for their meal. When it came, Sikes looked askance at the small, cooling pie on his plate. Toby was openly affronted and rose to admonish the landlord. Sikes pulled him back by the arm.

'Fer Gawd's sake, Toby. Let's just eat it an' go. We 'aven't got ter stay 'ere.'

Toby conceded defeat and they ate their pies and finished their beer in silence.

'Come on, let's get going,' growled Sikes, rising to his feet and brushing stale pastry crumbs from his coat.

They left the tavern thankfully, the eyes of the regulars boring into their backs.

'We goin' ter make it by dark?' Sikes asked doubtfully.

'Easily,' replied Toby. 'We're over 'alfway already.'

Sikes was dubious and cast a wary eye at the leaden sky ahead of them. Toby had a strange knack of underestimating things.

They continued along the highway for some four miles, the weather growing colder and the passers-by fewer, and then struck off across Hounslow Heath.

'Bit bleak out 'ere.' Toby laughed nervously. 'I think this is where Claude Duval danced with one of 'is lady victims.'

'Thanks,' muttered Sikes. 'Just the sort of encouragement I needed.'

Hounslow Heath was notorious for highwaymen and robbers and Toby was obviously thinking about it, his thin face tense and nervous. Sikes preferred not to be reminded of the fact. He had nothing in his pockets, but Toby was financing their expedition and carried the money. He shivered. The track here was not very clear and the hard ground gave way every now and then to lightly frozen pools of marsh, which broke under their feet and more than once brought them to their knees. Sikes cursed roundly and remarked that they were making little progress. His joints were aching in the cold and he felt out of temper. By the time they had gained the far side of the moor, the light was beginning to fade and large flakes of snow were drifting into their faces. They now found themselves with the problem of crossing the River Crane.

'There's a crossin' point a bit downstream of 'ere,' said Toby, as they heaved their weary legs over the iron-clad waste. The day was closing in fast and all around them were the skeletal remains of last year's scrub and dead tufts of brown grass, which rustled coldly in the chilly afternoon wind. But it was more than 'a bit downstream' by the time they had found the little white wooden bridge and when they had crossed over, there was still a mile or more of desolate landscape to traverse before they reached the lights of Hanworth.

But Hanworth was tiny, remote and rural, self-sufficient and turned in on itself. It didn't take kindly to strangers any more than Kew did. And its inn was a broken-down hovel, its sign-board creaking painfully in the wind. They could not read the sign, for the paint had long ago peeled off, leaving only patches of doubtful colour, which in this light looked grey. The thatched roof was holed and green with damp, dead willow-herb still standing between the exposed spars. The windows were tight and mean-looking and the doorway so low that both men had to bend double.

'Must be bloody pygmies round 'ere,' observed Sikes.

Toby didn't answer, but surreptitiously kicked at a rat sitting boldly on the doorstep, nibbling at a grey mass between its paws. It leaped away into the darkness as Toby pushed open the ill-fitting door.

Inside the low-ceilinged room were several small trestle

tables, their tops awash with beer slops, which caught the reflection of the guttering candles with which the place was lit. There was no fire, but at least they were out of the icy wind. Not surprisingly, there were few customers. A pair of ancient heads peered round the edge of a settle as Sikes and Toby entered, stamping snow off their boots, and three farm labourers sat glumly over their porter in the centre of the room. They nodded silently as the two men made their way to the bar.

Sikes wrinkled his nose; the place smelt damp and musty and overpoweringly of vermin. He kicked the straw about with his foot and wished he hadn't. The landlord was some time in coming and the travellers had time to take in their surroundings.

'Gawd, this is like a bad dream, Toby,' whispered Sikes. ''Ave yer seen the carpetin' in this place?'

Toby nodded.

'Rats!' hissed Sikes. 'Place stinks of 'em!'

'I know,' agreed Toby, 'but there ain't nowhere else ter go.'

'I 'ate ter think wot the accommodation's like.'

Toby fervently wished Sikes would stop complaining. He, too, felt they had landed themselves in an unenviable situation, but he would make the best of a bad job.

The landlord came through from the back parlour at last and Toby's spirits took an upward surge as he glimpsed the young woman following him. He nudged Sikes, but there was no response. Sikes was cold, hungry, miserable and thoroughly fed up.

'Evenin', gen'lemen,' said the landlord in sonorous tones. 'An' wot can I do for you?'

'We're on our way ter Shepperton,' blustered Toby, 'an' we'd like beds an' a good 'ot meal. An' a hot toddy, of course,' he added, winking at the barmaid, who had draped herself and her ample bosom over the far end of the bar.

'Cost yer.' The landlord was a man of few words. 'If yer wants a fire, that's extra. Back parlour. 'Ot meal, we can do. Fer a price. Got a spare room, with a bed.'

The two men looked at each other. Toby's purse would provide the means, but it wasn't bottomless. They had to decide their most urgent need.

'Two 'ot gin toddies an' the bed,' decided Toby, since Sikes appeared to have temporarily given up on decision-making and had sunk into silent apathy.

He trailed after Sikes, who was making for a high-backed settle in the corner furthest from the door, and sat down opposite him. Sikes pulled up his high collar round his neck, shoved his hands deep into his pockets and stuck out his long legs, so that Toby had to find room for his own to the side of the settle. He looked up tentatively and wished he hadn't. Sikes's face was pinched and cold and his nose was running, so that he had to keep sniffing, and periodically he withdrew his hand from his pocket to wipe the offending appendage on his cuff. But it was his expression which worried Toby. He saw the danger signs in the glitter of Sikes's eyes and knew he must tread warily, or he would lose the man's confidence.

The barmaid sauntered over with two steaming tankards and Sikes's hands shot out of his pockets to clasp the warmth of the vessel, but he ignored the girl. Toby, on the other hand, saw the immediate answer to keeping warm for the night, and pinched her rump, at which she squealed delight-fully and put her arm round Toby's neck. Reluctantly he disengaged himself, but whispered in her ear and she took herself off with a smile on her face.

'Why ain't we got the fire or an 'ot meal?' demanded Sikes.

'I ain't payin' through the nose fer ev'rything,' said Toby in a low voice. 'Wot's it ter be? Fire an' 'ot meal? Or a bed fer the night? I ain't a toff yet, yer know.'

Sikes stared at him, disappointed. He felt something run over his ankle and kicked involuntarily at it.

'This bloody place is swarmin',' he said irrelevantly. And then added, 'I've got to eat if yer wants me ter fight.'

Toby reluctantly got to his feet and stumbled over the heaving floor to the bar. The landlord had disappeared again, but the barmaid smiled broadly as Toby came up and she propped her bosom on the bar, so that he had a fine view into the deep cleft between her breasts. He was cheered by the sight and stood talking idle nonsense to the girl, until Sikes barked from his corner, 'Yer goin' ter stand there drivellin' all night while I starve?'

The barmaid tittered.

'Wot's the matter with your friend?' she asked, her voice soft with the country burr.

'Oh 'e's just cold an' a bit under the weather,' bluffed Toby. 'A good 'ot meal'll soon sort 'im out.'

The barmaid winked and disappeared into the back parlour. Toby had a tantalizing glimpse of a smoke-filled room, which looked warm and crowded, and the heady sound of men with full bellies and warm bodies faded away as the heavy door swung to, blotting out the scene of which he longed to be a part. So this was where the locals all were tonight. He went back to Sikes and the pair sat in silence until their meal was brought. The barmaid had evidently favoured them, because their helpings were generous and hot and the food was wholesome. Sikes poked at it doubtfully with his fork, as if he expected it to move. Toby watched him, exasperated. Sikes looked up and met Toby's gaze.

'Well,' he said defensively, 'yer've got ter make sure. In a place like this they could dish up anythink.'

'Oh Gawd!' breathed Toby, 'just eat it, will yer!'

They cleared their plates in a very short while and Sikes sat back with his eyes closed and his hat pulled down over one eye.

'Are you goin' ter tell me about this crack-brained scheme of yours?' he drawled, hardly opening his mouth.

Toby sat up smartly and leaned across the table, all enthusiasm.

'The real cove, wot backs all these fights, is a Mr Mutchell,' he confided. ''E lives in swell style at The Anchor. An' o' course, the landlord encourages 'im. Good fer business, see? The other patrons, they often collects down at The Anchor if there's a big fight on. Wines an' dines 'emselves summat

356

swell, they do. Then this cove organizes the willagers into sparrin' matches. An' 'e an' 'is mates watch 'em; fer afters, like! 'E's a rare cove, that one. Drives a four in 'and, wot's guarded by a dawg as'd make your Bull's-eye look like a hangel!'

Sikes was mildly impressed, but feigned indifference.

'Where do they 'old the fights?' he asked, the warm victuals spreading a glow of wellbeing through his big frame.

'On a bit o' land called Shepperton Range,' replied Toby. 'It's well outside the village an' they always 'as punts ready on the river. So, if the Law puts its nose in an' sends down a Middlesex beak, the contestants disappear into Surrey! Werry conwenient!'

'Werry!' agreed Sikes, without much conviction. If he was caught in an illegal fight by a Middlesex magistrate, he'd be out of the country for good. He wondered if it was worth the risk. Toby saw the doubt in his face.

'Come on, Bill. They've got it off to a fine art. Yer'll be perfickly all right. Yer'll knock any of 'em fer six an' make a nice little packet into the bargain. If there's trouble, we leg it back through Surrey an' come up over Southwark or London Bridge.'

'An' wot's your int'rest in all this, Toby?' asked Sikes suddenly, eyeing his companion with some suspicion.

'Ah, well.' Toby tapped the side of his nose, took a sip of his drink and stretched.

Sikes leaned forward, the dangerous light in his eye again.

'I want ter know,' he said quietly, through his teeth.

Toby noted Sikes's expression and the great fist doubled on the table and decided to tell the truth, or, at least, a part of it.

'If you wins, I gets a share o' the proceedin's,' he said, 'that's all.'

He didn't add that he was also going to back Sikes heavily with some of his own money, just in case Mutchell wasn't interested. It was imperative not only that Sikes should fight, but that he should win. Toby didn't foresee any problems on that score; he had got Sikes into good form now as far as fitness went and he was sure he would fight well. Toby had seen him in action before he'd been boated and the fellow had impressed him then. It was just a case of getting Sikes to the right place at the right time.

Sikes sat for a moment, only half thinking of what Toby had said. His eyelids drooped and he was feeling cold again. Through the uncurtained windows he could just make out snow falling and as the three labourers tramped off into the darkness, a cold blast came hurtling into the room. Sikes shivered and stood up.

'Well, let's turn in. We've still got a walk ahead of us tomorrer, I s'pose?'

Toby nodded.

'You go on up, Bill. I'll be up later.'

Sikes looked at him. He didn't relish the thought of sharing a bed; it brought back unpleasant memories of Macquarie Harbour. But Toby was an old friend and he supposed he would be glad of the warmth of another body beside him.

Toby grinned rather sheepishly and Sikes saw the barmaid looking across at them, a smug expression on her face. He grunted and opened the side door, which gave on to a dark and rickety staircase. As the door swung to behind him, Sikes missed his footing and barked his shin on the bare step.

'Christ!' he exploded. 'Wot sort of an 'ell'ole is this? Where's a bloody light?'

Toby and the barmaid heard his curses and laughed together, as they squeezed into a corner of the settle. The girl, who was warm and plump and who told Toby her name was Lizzie, said suddenly, ''Ere, I 'ope 'e's all right. I'd better take 'im a light.'

Toby held her tightly.

'Oh no you don't,' he said, pulling her close. ''E's quite capable of lookin' after hisself.'

And he bent his head into the warmth of her neck.

Sikes, meanwhile, had blundered his way up the stairs and across the landing and had found the vacant room. He felt round on the table which stood inside the door and found a candle and tinderbox. His hands shaking with the cold, he eventually managed to strike a light and the candle flame danced crazily in the draught which seemed to emanate from all corners of that dismal room. Sikes sat on the side of the bed, which shifted alarmingly under his weight, and bent to remove his boots. As he did so, he saw a pair of bright, not unintelligent eyes watching him.

'Clear off!' he growled and flung his boot at the rat, who simply scuttled off to a safer vantage point and resumed its watch.

Sikes looked about him and thought longingly of his own lodgings, humble though they were. He looked up at the ceiling, which sported festoons of cobwebs from its rough and dusty rafters; and he was sure he could see a chink of night sky through a dark opening way up in the ridge. There was certainly a damp patch on the end of the bed immediately below it. The corners of the dormer windows were thick with ancient weavings and the dried, papery husks of insects caught there over the years. He turned away, disgusted. He hated spiders. Had done, ever since he'd seen the really big ones out in Van Diemen's Land. They'd never harmed any of the men, but he loathed their bold, bloated bodies. And now he couldn't look at the lesser English varieties without seeing their cousins from the southern hemisphere.

Reluctantly, he peeled off his coat and gingerly crawled between the bedclothes, hoping at least for a good night's sleep. But he lay shivering and miserable under the damp and musty covers and something set up a tickling in his scalp. He scratched and cursed, sat up and shook out the pillow. The tickling sensation continued and he rubbed his fingers briskly through his thick hair. He knew it was lice and he knew there was little he could do about it, except try to sleep. He lay down again, angry that Toby had brought them to this dreadful place, angry that he was uncomfortable, and above all, angry that he was so cold. Where in God's name was Toby? His body shook and his teeth chattered. Something very small bit his ankle.

'Bloody fleas,' he grumbled.

He flung back the bedclothes and tried brushing the sheet with his hand. It made little difference. He could see the little devils hopping about in the light from the candle. He sat on the side of the bed and dropped his head into his hands.

'Oh Gawd,' he moaned. 'I'm so bloody cold and uncomfortable. Where the 'ell's Toby got to?'

He stood up, pulled on his coat, shoved his feet back into his boots and clumped down the stairs to the bar. The place was deserted and dark, so he returned to the landing and cocked his head on one side, listening. He heard suppressed laughter and Toby's deeper tones coming from a room at the far end of the landing. He banged on the door.

''Urry up, Toby,' he said in a loud whisper. 'I'm freezin' ter death 'ere.'

'Be with yer soon,' called Toby.

There was more laughter and the creaking of a bed. It was Sikes's turn to be exasperated now. Here he was, miles from his own familiar creature comforts, cold and miserable, and his one source of warmth was dallying with a girl who looked as though she had never been cold in her life.

'Selfish bastard!' he muttered and went back to bed, where he spent a miserable hour shivering and scratching, and eventually fell into an exhausted sleep.

He wasn't sure how long he had slept, but as the pale light of a winter's dawn filtered through the grimy window pane, Sikes woke, dimly aware of a movement in the bed beside him. The next moment, Toby's arm came round him tightly and he felt Toby's head nuzzling the back of his neck.

'Oh bugger off!' shouted Sikes at this unlooked-for addition to his misery, and he shrugged off Toby's encompassing arm.

Toby came sharply awake, realized what he had done, and said, 'Sorry, Bill, must've bin dreamin'.'

Sikes didn't reply and Toby rolled over and turned his back on his bed-fellow. Sikes lay staring into the room, watching the shadows gradually take shape. He knew Toby was all right; he just spent so much time with women, he forgot where he was sometimes. If he hadn't felt so miserable, he might even have laughed at the incident. But he knew there was worse to come. He would have to put up a good show of fighting for Toby and the more he thought about it, the less he liked the idea. It was one thing to fight when a bloke had taken your woman, or had thrown drink in your face, or had insulted you; it was easy then to land him a quick one between the eyes and settle the score. But to fight a stranger for the sake of it, to earn money; he wasn't sure: he didn't know whether he could work up enough aggression to do that; his stomach contracted at the thought. He rolled on to his back and scratched at his waist. Gawd! how these little pests penetrated your clothes! He wondered how many rats they'd shared the room with, too. He could hear a faint rustling under the bed and there was a constant barrage of scampering up and down the wainscoting. He turned his head and looked at Toby's dormant form. It was comforting to have his warmth still there. He yawned, ruffled his hands through his hair and closed his eyes again.

The world was pure white upon their opening their eyes next morning. Snow lay piled against the corners of doors and windows. It lay thick and virginal on the road, too, except where the smith's boy had ploughed his way up the street from his home to the forge. As the landlord brought breakfast to the two travellers, he cast a knowing eye at the sky.

'There's more to come, I reckon,' he said, his voice full of gloom. 'I wouldn't risk goin' on today, gen'lemen.'

'Well, we'll make a start an' see 'ow we go,' announced Toby.

The landlord raised his eyebrows and went away muttering to himself at the foolhardiness of city-dwellers. The men ignored him and soon emptied the dish of eggs and bacon between them. Then, having paid the bill, they wrapped themselves warmly and set off through the snow.

It was, indeed, very heavy going, with a fresh fall of snow in their faces, and both men were glad of their strong top boots, since the snow was well up over their ankles. It took them a good three hours' walking through lanes deep in the wretched white stuff and Sikes groused most of the way.

'Wot a bloody stupid idea, ter come in weather like this,' he grumbled.

'Sorry, Bill,' panted Toby, 'but I didn't know it was goin' ter be like this, now did I?'

A grunt issued from the depths of Sikes's collar and his face glared out from between his hat and his muffler, which he had pulled up round his chin. Toby thought he looked like a footpad and hoped they wouldn't meet anyone on the road. They came down at last to the river at Sunbury and the snow eased up.

'If we could 'ire a boat, it'd be a lot quicker,' pointed out Sikes.

The old familiar pain was back in his shoulder and he felt he had had enough of this capering about the countryside. Toby brightened. There might yet be a way of placating his friend.

'There's a ferry near 'ere,' he said. 'We should be able ter get a boat o' some sorts.'

They ploughed on and Toby became increasingly anxious with every step, hoping, praying they would find a boat. Otherwise he knew that Sikes would give up and go home. They found the ferry and to Toby's utter relief, the ferryman was down by the water's edge, shovelling snow out of his boat.

'You got a spare boat we could 'ire?' called Sikes, before Toby could open his mouth.

The ferryman looked at the strangely clad pair before him. Toby's fair, open face he could see quite clearly and he noticed his good clothes. The other fellow looked a regular villain, what he could see of him, but the glittering eyes warned him to beware.

'As it 'appens, I 'ave,' replied the ferryman. 'But it'll cost yer. 'Ow far d'yer want ter go?'

'Only ter Shepperton,' put in Toby.

'That's all right then. You can leave it with the landlord of the King's 'Ead. I've got an arrangement with 'im an' 'e'll look after it for me till I can get up there to collect it. It'll cost you two shillin's.'

''E'll pay.' Sikes nodded his head in Toby's direction.

Reluctantly, Toby's hand went into his purse again. He knew Sikes must be humoured if he were to keep him stringing along. The ferryman pocketed his fee and showed them where the boat was moored. When they had shovelled out most of the snow, the ferryman cast them off and they drifted out into mid-stream through the icy mist which hung silent and waiting over the water. Sikes rowed and he could see again the mainland of Macquarie Harbour, the shoreline with its dense covering of pines coming ever nearer. He closed his eyes and heard the shouts of men, the crash of timber, the rush of falling branches.

'Oi! Watch where yer goin', Bill!' shouted Toby.

Sikes jerked his eyes open and scowled. But he was glad to put his strength to some use on this seemingly useless expedition, despite the pain his shoulder gave him. The exercise warmed him, too, and since his stroke was strong and sure, as long as he kept his eyes open, they made excellent headway, and tied up at Church Square in Shepperton a little after one o'clock.

Sikes stepped out of the boat and eased his shoulders. The scene before his eyes would have warmed the heart of any pickpocket, but he was not here to fork, he was here to fight. The square, a small, cosy, cobbled area, ringed by taverns, the church in one corner, was a tightly packed mass of humanity, ebbing and flowing, this way and that, heads bobbing, faces upturned, mouths stretched wide in shouting. And the noise was deafening. Sikes wondered if this little corner of the world had gone mad. It was like Billingsgate and Bartlemy Fair rolled into one. Top hats and lace-trimmed bonnets mingled with battered caps and tousled hair; new broadcloth rubbed shoulders with rough worsted and rustling silk with old wool. All walks of life were here, all bent on the heady pleasures which accompanied the Fancy. They had come in their droves and the village street was awash with slush churned up from carriage wheels and tramping feet.

Sikes stared hard at Toby as they moored the boat, but neither man spoke. Toby knew what his partner was thinking and he felt more and more uncomfortable as time went on. They shoved and elbowed their way through the crowd and stood at last before the white façade of The Anchor. Sikes looked up and saw an eminently respectable, well-kept old inn, the creeper neatly trimmed around its windows, its newly painted sign proclaiming its name in bold colours. Toby went ahead and Sikes followed him. This is an inn fer toffs, he thought. The walls were painted a delicate peach and were decorated with sporting prints. The windows were swathed in brocade curtains and the floors were of good, polished wood. There was a smell of wellbeing and luxury about the place and Sikes felt cornered. But there were all manner of types here and he and Toby fought their way through a motley throng which filled all the rooms and hallways, with people shouting over each other's heads and farmers jostling with squires.

Sikes could see over the heads of most of the crowd and said to Toby, 'There's a cove at a table in the big dinin' room an' 'e looks as though 'e's inspectin' the goods.'

'That'll be 'im,' replied the excited Toby. 'Push yer way through. I'll 'ave ter present yer.'

Sikes didn't at all like this manipulation of his life, but he elbowed his way through nevertheless, and stood before the man at the centre of it all.

Mr Mutchell was a short, thickset man, humourless, with a wary, hunted look about him. Despite the jovial clientele he kept around him, he was a man at odds with the Law and kept a sharp watch-out for any strangers on his patch. He had a florid, shiny head, with a few wisps of dirty, yellow-grey hair brushed across it. He looked up laconically as Sikes and Toby squeezed through the body of the crowd in front of him. He vaguely remembered Toby, much to the latter's relief.

'Well, Mr Crackit,' drawled Mr Mutchell, when Toby had reminded him of his name. 'What have we here?'

'This,' announced Toby proudly, 'is Mr William Sikes. I'm putting 'im forward fer tomorrer's fight, the afternoon one, you understand, not the professionals in the morning.' And he laughed nervously.

'I can see that.' The man spoke somewhat disparagingly. 'How old are you, Mr Sikes?'

'Thirty-two.'

'How tall?'

''Bout six foot.'

'Weight?'

'Dunno.'

''E's quite 'eavy,' put in Toby helpfully.

'How many fights you won?'

Sikes slid his eyes in Toby's direction, but answered steadily, 'Enough.'

The man looked at Sikes through narrowed eyes. He had a pugilistic look about him, but he obviously hadn't tried the Fancy before. Mutchell felt annoyed. Why was Crackit wasting his time with untried talent? There were too many young hopefuls here today; most of them could at least lay claim to having won some fights. This chap wasn't admitting to anything, and Mutchell wasn't going to waste time on him. He heaved himself to his feet and took Toby by the arm, away out of Sikes's hearing.

'This chap hasn't won any fights,' he whispered angrily. 'He hasn't had anything to do with the Fancy before, has he?'

'No – but he's good,' insisted Toby. 'He won't let you down. 'E's very good.'

'Well, I ain't backing him, that's for sure,' announced the Lord of the Fancy.

Toby's face fell. He knew that everything rested on his own backing now and that could cost him dear. He pushed his way over to Sikes and steered him out of the building.

'Wot's up, then?' asked Sikes.

365

'Oh, nothin' much. Just a little matter of who's who an' wot's wot.'

Toby was evasive and Sikes was not easily bought off.

'There's trouble 'ere, ain't there?' he said angrily, as they battled once more through the mêlée. 'I tell yer, I ain't riskin' anythink, Toby.'

'No, it's all right, Bill. Nothink ter worry about. Let's go an' find lodgin's fer the night.'

To stay at The Anchor was out of the question. For one thing it was full to overflowing and for another, it was beyond the means of Toby's purse. He was going to need every penny to back Sikes now.

'We've got ter let the landlord of the King's 'Ead know about the boat, so we might as well try there,' he said.

Sikes nodded sullenly.

They fought their way to the smaller tavern on the opposite side of the square. This was more like the establishments they were used to and Toby's spirits rose as he noticed how Sikes relaxed in the warmth of the bar parlour; only to be dashed again when the landlord said, 'Sorry, gen'lemen. Full up. Yer might try The 'Orseshoes up by Lord's Bridge on the 'Alliford Road; or The Black Swan, by Chertsey Bridge; that's not too far from the Range, you know.'

Toby thanked him, but avoided Sikes's eye. They plunged out into the cold air again, hunched their shoulders and struck out in the direction of Chertsey.

As they had to pass Shepperton Range, Toby suggested they might view the ground. Sikes acquiesced in silence, and Toby could feel the tension in the air between them. He felt Sikes might explode at any moment.

There were many others on the road, walking, riding or splashing through the slush in smart carriages, with snorting horses, who picked up their delicate legs and arched their aristocratic necks. Toby looked at them all with interest, but Sikes never lifted his eyes from the ground. His misery was almost complete.

When they arrived at the common which was set aside for the Fancy, they found a fair-like atmosphere about the place.

There were stalls selling sweetmeats, hot chestnuts, hot spiced buns and mouth-watering pies of all descriptions. There was a fortune-telling booth and a tent advertising the strangest sight in the kingdom. Toby was curious and drifted over, but Sikes was not interested. He stood looking at a long-song seller, who was reciting a ballad which he dangled from a thin, bony hand. It told of the events in Clerkenwell in 1833, when a National Convention meeting was turned into a confrontation with the peelers and a police constable had been stabbed to death. The jury had returned a verdict of 'justifiable homicide' and they had been fêted and honoured, despite the subsequent quashing of the verdict by the Government. The jurymen were seen as the heroes of the working people, the new police as interfering with the rights of all. It was all old news now but still popular, and Sikes had been out of the country when it happened. He stood listening to the details, told in rhyme. Coldbath Fields Riot, they called it. His mind wandered back twenty years. Coldbath Fields! His fingers bleeding from the oakum picking; the old robber who had known his father; he could almost smell the man's breath still. And the youngsters he'd known: Evans, Carter, Dolly, Emily; the faces came flooding back.

He turned round, but Toby had disappeared. So he wandered slowly between the stalls, still thinking about those early days and not really bothered where he was going. There was a hurdy-gurdy playing loud music and some gypsies running a coconut shy, their strange accents ringing out in the cold air. One of the gypsy women swaggered up to Sikes.

'Lucky 'eather, luv?' she wheedled.

He shook his head and brushed her aside. Nothing daunted, she persisted.

'Lucky 'eather fer yer sweet'eart,' she informed him.

He rounded on her angrily and she fell back at the sight of his blazing eyes and melted away into the crowd. An elderly quack doctor had got himself up on a soapbox and had attracted a little knot of people around him by proclaiming the wonders of his latest patent medicine. Sikes was pleased to see the young fogle-hunters busy at work. His own hands were too roughened by labour to be sensitive to forking now, but he was glad there were still skilled lads who could do it. He wasn't tempted by the stalls and their open displays either; that was no longer his line, though he knew he could do it if the necessity arose. 'Well,' he thought, ruefully, 'there's plenty enjoyin' themselves 'ere terday, but I ain't one of 'em.'

He came at length into a clearing and found himself standing by a ring roped off for the boxing. Some friendly matches were taking place and Sikes stood watching a muscular man make short work of the local lads.

His trainer kept calling out, 'Now then, gentlemen, anyone else like ter pitch themselves against Clay Tomkins 'ere? Come on, lads, don't be afraid now. 'E's no bigger than some of you!'

There were laughs among the crowd and mild protests as some local boy prepared to show off to his lass his prowess with his fists.

Toby materialised by Sikes's elbow and sensing a movement from him, Toby seized his arm and whispered firmly, 'Fer Gawd's sake, Bill, not now!'

'Why not?' asked Sikes, without taking his eyes from the ring.

The challenger was standing, stripped to the waist, flexing his muscles and turning round, while his trainer called out, 'Any more, gentlemen? Any more challengers for the great, the one and only Clay Tomkins? Come along now, lads, don't be shy. Step up and see what you can do.'

His eye alighted on Sikes and Toby frantically pulled his friend away. When they were clear of the crowd, Sikes rounded on Toby.

'Burn an' blast yer! D'yer want me ter fight, or don't yer?'

'Yus,' said Toby, flustered, 'but I don't want yer fightin' the wrong man.'

Sikes was exasperated and angry as they strode back to the road in the fading light. Toby persisted, although he knew he was on treacherous ground.

'That bloke would've made mincemeat of yer, Bill. An' then yer wouldn't 'ave bin any good fer tomorrer's fight. Would yer?'

'Is that wot yer think of me?' asked Sikes in disgust.

'No, Bill, 'course not. But you're not ezackly his class, are yer?'

Sikes snorted. He was cold and fed up with the whole business and he wanted to go home. And it had begun to snow again.

They walked along in silence towards Chertsey, where the crowds had thinned out. Toby earnestly hoped they would find a room. Suddenly, Sikes stopped in his tracks and rounded on Toby. The latter quaked in his boots, wondering what was coming.

'Anyway,' demanded Sikes, 'where the 'ell did you get to?'

Toby laughed nervously and made to walk on. Sikes laid a hand on his arm.

'No, seriously. I want ter know where you buggered off to.'

'I went ter see wot was in that tent,' replied Toby nervously. They were walking on again.

'Oh yeah? An' wot did you see?'

'Siamese twins,' came the reply.

'Siamese twins! Wot the 'ell are they?'

Toby hesitated. He had an uncomfortable feeling he knew where all this was leading.

'Well,' he began, 'they're kinchin, least, they was about twelve or so; an' they was joined together, all down one side. They sort of shared a side each . . .'

His voice trailed off as Sikes turned his glittering eyes on him in disbelief.

'Gawd 'elp me,' he breathed. 'We come all this way, in the worst weather we could've picked, we freeze, we're bitten ter blazes by fleas an' lice, yer purse strings are as tight as a virgin, an' yer go off an' waste yer blunt on seein' 'orrors like that!'

Toby had no answer, except to reply lamely, 'Well, I thought it might be int'restin'.'

'Int'restin'?' Sikes exploded.

Toby waited, but the lid was back on the pot and Sikes walked on.

They came at last to Chertsey Bridge and turned off to the left just before it. The ground was dank and marshy along the river bank and the surrounding fields were still white with unmelted snow. The Black Swan stood forlornly by the river, the sole building on this bank, protected only by two or three distorted elm trees. It was in the early stages of decay, with tiles missing from its roof, its once proud stucco flaking away in great patches to reveal the intimate structure of brickwork beneath. The shutters were up and Toby doubted their having any luck here. Sikes was too cold and dejected to take much interest and he sat down on a damp seat outside, sunk within his coat again, a silent foil to Toby's plans.

Toby tried the door. It opened with a swollen protest on to a vaguely familiar scene. The room was dimly lit by oil lamps at either end of a long central table and about this were gathered a number of ruffianly-looking fellows, some with even blacker-looking visages than Sikes's. Den o' thieves, thought Toby. 'Ome from 'ome. And he walked up to the bar. The landlord bustled up, taking in Toby's appearance in a single glance.

'On yer own, sir?'

'I've got a friend outside. We need beds fer the night. Yer got any?'

'Aye,' replied the landlord. 'I might 'ave.'

''Ow much?' The question hurt Toby's pride, but he had to watch his purse.

'You anything to do with the Fancy?'

The landlord eyed him and Toby wasn't sure which way to answer. He decided it might be to their advantage to acknowledge their interest.

'Yus,' he said. 'Me friend's goin' ter fight there tomorrer.'

The landlord's face broke into a wide smile. 'Then you're both welcome. Bring 'im in, bring 'im in out of the cold. Can't leave a fighter out in the snow and ice.'

And he came with Toby to the door and looked out to where Sikes sat in a freezing, miserable heap.

'Bill,' called Toby, 'bed, board an' fire, all fixed fer the night. We're among friends.'

'Yes, yes, all friends 'ere,' chuckled the landlord, as Sikes rose to his feet.

When he entered the bar, the light fell on his haggard features and the landlord took a step back. The faces at the table turned and studied him too, like recognizing like.

'Where's the fire?' growled Sikes.

'Here, sir, here,' and the busy little landlord scurried round and led Sikes to a seat in the great inglenook, where he put another log on the dying embers.

Toby seated himself opposite and the pot boy brought them warm ale. Sikes's hands were shaking as he held the hot pewter tankard and his teeth chattered against its rim.

Presently he looked up and said, ''Ow come you're never as cold as me?'

Toby shrugged. 'I dunno, Bill. P'raps I wear more clo'es than you. Or p'raps you got chilled through out on that island.'

He viewed Sikes's attire. The greatcoat had seen better days and he wore only a thin waistcoat beneath, whereas his own clothing was of good quality, thick cloth, and he wore a jacket under his greatcoat. Toby was beginning to realize just how desperate Sikes's financial situation was; the man needed money now to survive. There would be rent to pay as well. He simply had to win this fight tomorrow.

When supper arrived, Sikes fell on the food like a starved animal and cleared his plate in minutes. Toby, hungry though he was, took a little more time and savoured the tender chops, the tasty gravy, the piping hot potatoes and carrots. Sikes leaned back, picking his teeth, watching Toby eat. He took off his battered hat and shook it and the water from it splashed and hissed in the fire.

'Well,' he said, stretching, his long arms and legs reaching as far away from each other as possible. 'I don't know wot you're goin' ter do, but I'm turnin' in fer the night. I s'pose yer goin' back to the square fer a bit of amusement?'

Toby squirmed. Sikes could read him like a book.

He grinned sheepishly. Sikes stood up, sending a cascade of melted snow into the fire. He took up his hat, cuffed Toby on the shoulder and asked the landlord to show him his room.

Toby sat for some time, soaking up the warmth. He didn't relish the thought of a cold walk back to Shepperton, but he couldn't miss out on this God-sent opportunity of sampling the local beauties, so he sallied out once more into the wintry night.

Despite the continuing snow, there was still much traffic plying between Chertsey and Shepperton and a larger number of pedestrians than usual for the hour. Toby strode along quickly to keep warm and soon gained the centre of the village where there was still much activity and a great deal of merry-making. He caught welcome glimpses of the occasional bared shoulder shining whitely from a doorway. He sauntered down to the landing stage and listened to the water slapping at the sloping cobbles. Little globules of light reflected from the many lamps in the square behind him and they danced and broke crazily and re-formed, as the water rippled and lapped near his feet.

He was aware that he was not alone. Turning, he found a pretty girl near his shoulder and beyond her, two more buxom country wenches. In the light of the lanterns, they looked rosy and wholesome, a welcome change from the drabs of Whitechapel. He thought Sikes a fool to miss such an opportunity as this, but the girl at his side slipped her arm through his, led him into the nearest tavern, and he thought no more of Sikes that evening.

EIGHT

Sikes stood, silhouetted against the window, the drawn curtain still in his hand. He looked at the figure in the bed: Toby Crackit, who was supposed to charm his way into cribs, the flash cove who lived the swell life, who was the essential other half of their business. He noticed the beer-stained waistcoat, which Crackit still wore in bed; the grimy shirt, the unkempt hair; the bristling jaw and the pouches beneath the bloodshot eyes, which were struggling to open in the cold light of morning. 'E looks worse than me, thought Sikes. Fat lot o' good 'e'll be, wormin' 'is way into maids' favours. The fact was that the debauched life Toby Crackit led was taking its toll and he was beginning to look the worse for wear. Sikes was angry with him.

'Toby!' he shouted. 'You gettin' up?'

Toby groaned. 'Oh God, Bill. I can't. Not yet.'

He retreated beneath the bedclothes. His head felt like a large, inflated pig's bladder which might have been kicked around by the village boys. And there were spear-points of pain behind his eyes.

Sikes waited for a further response, but none came. He let go of the curtain, flung open the door, crashed it behind him and took the stairs at a determined gallop.

Outside, the air was clear and biting and the pale winter sun had burst through the shroud of mist and snow which had kept it hidden for the last two days. At least there had been no further snowfalls.

Sikes turned left down the track by the river. It was quieter here, and he breathed in deeply as he walked, in no great hurry. Toby wouldn't be up for hours yet and he needed time on his own. Toby was a good bloke, all things considered, but

374

he had had just a little too much of his company lately and he needed to reassess things.

He felt better this morning, warmed, refreshed with a good night's sleep and ready to tackle any man who challenged him. It was good to be by his old river, too, even if here it was a lot younger and fresher than the river he was accustomed to down in the great City. A piece of driftwood floated past and idly he wondered if it would ever reach London Bridge. He was reminded suddenly and painfully of being a small lad, wandering across the City to Bow Bridge with his brothers, on a sleepy day in summer; he must have been about four or five at the time. They had thrown sticks in on one side of the bridge and then rushed to the other to watch them come through. He heard himself again, squealing with delight.

'Mine's first! Look, Charley, look. I've won!'

And Charley smiling and Johnny grizzling, because his stick was the biggest but had come through last. The memory stabbed him and remembrance twisted the weapon. He leaned back against an overhanging willow and shut his eyes, trying to blot out the past. But he had let it rear its head for one minute and it wouldn't be satisfied until it had wrung his soul to its depths. He let the memory wash over him completely.

They had been watching a toff in a black silk topper and a blue cutaway coat, standing at a second-hand-china stall on the Whitechapel Road. Johnny had nudged his younger brother and nodded towards the man.

'You make a diversion, Billy; git summat in yer eye, anythink to distract 'im. I'll go for 'is fob. You can catch me up round by St Mary's. Only don't git caught, littl'un.'

And so Billy had sauntered up to the stall and suddenly clapped his hand to his eye.

'Oh! Ouch! Summat in me eye! Oh blimey, I can't see!'

The toff had merely glanced at him, not taking the bait, while a passing woman, with a basket on her arm, stopped to inspect his eye.

'Poor child,' she crooned, 'come here an' let me see.'

But he was off. He had seen Johnny running and he had seen why. Two Bow Street Runners, their scarlet waistcoats prominently to the fore, were strolling along between the stalls and drawing close to where the boys were. Johnny had got a beautiful fogle, anyway; Billy could see it hanging out of his pocket and he darted after his brother, longing to know how he had managed it without the planned diversion.

But he never found out. It was market day, when the heavy lumbering haywains swayed and creaked in from the country. And Johnny had darted across the road between two parked cabs and hadn't seen the wagon. The great horses had shied and whinnied and snorted and never touched him, but he had fallen and the inexorable wheels had ground on and . . . Oh Gawd! Why was it all happening again? The screams, the shouts, the confusion! And the darkness creeping up from the edge of his vision.

He turned his face against the damp, creviced bark and rested his cheek against its craggy surface, his three days' stubble rasping as his jaw worked. His face was wet and angrily he brushed his sleeve across his eyes and nose. He looked about him, but no one had seen this unmanning of Bill Sikes.

'Burn an' blast me!' he swore. 'Wot made me go an' think about that?'

He walked on towards the Range, unnerved by the incident. He couldn't understand it. Always when the darkness threatened now, he managed to overcome it. A coot shouted raucously from a clump of rushes and made him start. He looked up and saw that he was nearly at the Range. He could hear the jangling notes of the hurdy-gurdy and he could hear laughter and shouting, a bell ringing, children squealing, children screaming (Oh Gawd, would it ever stop?) and the ubiquitous barking of too many dogs gathered together. Toby had told him that Mutchell bet on anything that fought, whether it stood on two legs or four, whether it was covered in fur or feathers or neither; he suspected there would be dogfights here today.

He was drawn to a dense crowd of people gathered round the boxing ring. He elbowed his way through and planted his tall body almost at the front, where he was afforded a good view of what to expect that afternoon. There were grumbles all round.

''Ere, mate, at least take yer 'at off.'

'Blimey, 'e's a big'un.'

'I say, old chap, d'ye mind? We've been here since nine o'clock, waiting. You can't just barge in front like that. We can't see a thing.'

Sikes turned on them such a withering look that the grumbles immediately subsided. A moment later, a bell clanged loudly and a giant of a man ducked under the ropes and strutted into the centre of the ring. A short, stocky man, in a thick coat and wearing several mufflers, stood beside him. 'Is backer, thought Sikes, or maybe 'is trainer. Did a giant like that need training? It seemed unlikely. The small man cleared his throat and his surprisingly loud voice rang out above the noise of the crowd.

'Ladies an' gen'lemen! Roll up for the first big fight of the day. The mighty Tom Seager, our local lad, will take on Gen'leman Jackson, a mere striplin' from the City, and you will be able to feast your eyes on a splendid performance in this very ring.'

He took Seager's arm and jerked it into the air, then called for Jackson to come forward. But there was no sign of Seager's adversary. The crowd murmured. Bets were still being laid and the patrons were busy. There was big money at stake here and this was to be one of the highlights of the gathering, with two well-known contestants in the ring. People began looking around, standing on tiptoe, craning their necks and calling to each other. But there was still no appearance from the opposition. Sikes could see Mutchell standing on the dashboard of his carriage, looking round frantically for the other half of the fight. He wondered what shade of red the man would turn next.

The crowd was becoming restless and the backers and

patrons were finding themselves the butt of angry demands for a return of their bets.

'We want action, or our money back,' roared the people.

'Where is 'e, where's the chicken? That's what you'd expect from a City type.' This from some local labouring lads.

'Find someone else, then,' retorted an obvious Londoner.

Sikes listened to the mounting ill feeling; then, turning to a scruffily dressed fellow at his side, he asked, ''Ow much at stake?' nodding towards Tom Seager, who paced around the ring, trying to keep warm.

'Three 'undred quid all told. The backer takes a fair cut. You thinkin' of takin' 'im on? Yer might get twenty if yer puts up a good fight. No promises mind. We don't know yer.'

Sikes looked back at the prowling Seager and summed up his chances. Wot the 'ell, he thought. I ain't got nothink ter lose. And he pushed his way to the very front of the crowd, ducked under the rope and stepped into the ring. The little backer looked up at him in surprise, but Sikes spoke first.

'I'll fight 'im,' he said in a quiet but determined voice.

He removed his hat and began to take off his greatcoat. The little man laid a restraining hand on his arm.

'No, sir, you can't do that. 'E's the local champion in these parts; 'ardly a fair match. Besides, no one knows your form. No one'll back you.'

'Don't matter,' replied Sikes.

He wasn't thinking about money. He wanted to fight. He wanted to get rid of all this pent-up tension which had been building up inside him for so long. Maybe it would help him to lay the ghost of his fears, the nightmare creeping darkness, the waking visions. Maybe he could beat them out of his body by fighting.

He stripped off his waistcoat and untied his belcher hand-kerchief. Dropping his clothes into a pile in the corner of the ring, he walked slowly back to the centre, rolling up his shirt-sleeves, the crowd murmuring surprise and interest at this new turn of events. Tom Seager met him in the middle and stood regarding him with utter disdain. Sikes sized him up.

Seager was indeed a big man, some two or three inches taller than Sikes, very broad and very heavy. His legs and arms bulged through his clothes as though they were trying to escape and his head seemed to be a continuation of his enormous neck.

The crowd's mood swung and shouts of encouragement drifted through to Sikes's ears.

'You can do it, mate. Give 'im a good bashin' an' give us a good run for our money.'

'Good for you, lad. Saved the day. Watch 'is left 'ook an' you'll be all right.'

Seager took off his coat, revealing a huge expanse of bare, brawny chest beneath. The man seemed insensitive to the cold and began flexing his muscles. Sikes shivered inside his rough linen shirt and declined to take it off. The backer stood warily between them, not sure he should let the fight go ahead. But he had the crowd to reckon with. He thought it best to take advantage of the way things were turning out.

'Where d'yer come from? What's yer name?'

Too late, Sikes realized he was on public display and he muttered his answers to the backer, as though this would help to deflect interest in him.

'Mr William Sikes, ladies an' gen'lemen. From Shoreditch in the City. Six foot two . . .'

He turned back to Sikes. 'Weight?' he whispered.

Sikes shrugged.

'Well, a match for the reigning champion, Mr Thomas Seager,' he bawled.

The crowd cheered. They waited anxiously, nervously, as the backer stepped from the ring and left Sikes and Seager to battle it out. The two men circled each other. Sikes felt the melting ground slippery beneath his boots. He hoped his grip would hold. Seager shot out his left fist. Sikes was ready and dodged the blow. Around they went. A sudden flurry of blows and Sikes had a cut on his cheekbone. It smarted in the icy air, but served to strengthen his resolve. In another moment, he was under Seager's defence and his knuckles made contact with his opponent's mouth. A roar. And Seager jerked away, spitting out teeth and blood. The backer called the end of the first round. Seager was given copious draughts of water to stem the bleeding, while Sikes watched quietly from his corner, rubbing his knuckles.

Behind him, a man laid a hand on his shoulder and said in a low voice, 'A good start, lad. Keep it up. The people are changing their bets. Don't disappoint them.'

Sikes nodded and returned to the fray. Seager was like an animal gone mad. He came at Sikes with tremendous force and lifted him off his feet in a great bear hug and flung him to the ground. The crowd howled in delight and for a moment, Sikes lay stunned. Gingerly, he got to his feet, his ribs bruised, the wind knocked from his body. As he stood up, Seager came at him again, but he used his half-bent position and the force of his right forearm to crack the giant a mighty blow across the jaw, which knocked both men off balance.

In the third round they were more cautious. Seager was obviously surprised and somewhat dismayed at this new-comer's ability and he knew the fight would be no pushover. The two men now concentrated on straight hooks with the fists and Sikes took several blows about the head without being able to return them. His lip was cut and felt double its normal size. And he could feel his left eye closing up. Somewhere in the back of his mind he thought of Toby and wondered if he were watching. He rather hoped he wasn't. He thought Toby might not be pleased with what he was doing.

Seager was at him again with his deadly left fist, which lashed out like a snake. Sikes could be dangerous with his own right hook, but this fellow was positively lethal, as he was finding to his cost. He was sore and exhausted, but he knew he had a long way to go yet.

The fourth round saw Sikes striking home with several good punches. He was into his stride now and had the measure of his man. The onlookers roared their approval at every blow; and the patrons were so busy with the changing odds, they could scarce keep up.

The end came in the sixth round. Seager struck Sikes in the stomach, well below the belt, and Sikes heaved over, coughing and retching. Seager waited, a sly look on his face. The crowd gasped and there were cries of 'Unfair! Unfair!' Sikes struggled to his feet and stood swaying. The darkness was creeping up again. Surely he would die here before this noisy rabble, here in the public eye. His head throbbed. His nose streamed blood. His shirt clung to the sweat on his body and he felt the chill January air seeping through. He was glad of its sobering sharpness. He felt a gob of blood in the back of his throat and turned aside and spat it out. It lay glistening on the churned-up ground. He saw again the blood on the cobbles beneath the wheels of the haywain. And the screams! Were they his, or Johnny's, or the screams of the women in the crowd? He saw Seager lumbering towards him, his weight slowing him down. Sikes had the advantage. Seager made a dive at the younger man. But Sikes got in over the top and landed him a rabbit punch that brought the one-time champion toppling to the ground. He lay there, senseless, in the mud and snow and sawdust at the victor's feet.

The crowd went wild. The men cheered and threw their hats into the air. The women screamed in delight. The patrons looked angry and embarrassed. Dogs barked and horses neighed. Sikes stood gripping the rope of the ring. He felt bad. The scene before him swam and he shut his eyes. He thought he might be sick. And then, suddenly, a ripple of anxiety swept through the crowd, growing like a tidal wave.

'The beak!' hissed someone.

It was enough. There was a mad flurry of activity, a low anxious murmur of voices, a few shouts of instruction as the ring was dismantled, the ground kicked over and the Fancy dispersed to the river under cover of the obliging crowd, who quietly sauntered away to look at the sideshows. They knew their cue and behaved as though this were any other fair-ground.

A man in a red coat and a stove-pipe hat grabbed at Sikes, thrust a bundle of notes into his hand and said earnestly, 'Git yer clo'es an' leg it to the punts. The beak's bin tipped off!'

Sikes needed no second warning. Bruised and bloodied as he was, he snatched up his clothes, thrust the banknotes into his breeches pocket and stumbled blindly down to the river and safety. Someone pulled him into a punt and he was taken away downstream and round a great bend in the river, with several other small craft in tow. Then, well out of sight of the scene of their activities, the men of the Fancy beached up in a little creek on the Surrey bank. Here they disembarked and made for a local tavern, carrying Sikes along in their midst.

NINE

The Old Crown Inn had stood on the same site, just outside Weybridge, for two hundred years or more. It was small and cosy and conveniently situated alongside the River Wey, just before that river joined the Thames. It was a safe refuge for the Fancy and its doors were accustomed to sudden influxes of desperate men. The landlord, a burly, good-humoured man, when he heard the small flotilla arriving, came bustling to the door, his wife and daughter close behind him.

'Come in, sirs, quick now. I see you've a casualty with ye. Let's be havin' 'im, an' my women folk'll soon be puttin' 'im to rights.'

Sikes was helped from the punt and assisted into the back room of the tavern, where Mrs Molesey and her daughter tended his wounds. Sikes was glad to sink into an armchair by the roaring fire, to close his eyes and to let them bathe and dab and anoint. Only once did he open his eyes, when he felt the scented nearness of Miss Molesey as she bathed his cheek. He found himself looking into a fair, lace-edge bosom, inches from his face. Lifting his eyes, he intercepted her concentrated gaze and noted with satisfaction the blush on her cheeks. Their eyes met and she smiled and dimpled and carried on with her work. Sikes closed his eyes again and regretted the knowledge that he would have to leave here before making the more intimate acquaintance of Mr Molesey's delightful daughter.

When the two women had completed their ministrations and were satisfied that he would live, Mrs Molesey made talk of preparing a bed for their charge. But he would not hear of it and, despite their protests, they found themselves steering him through to the bar parlour, where a great cheer went up and the landlord stood him a hearty meal and a pint of best ale. While he consumed these viands, the men kept up a barrage of questioning. Where did he come from? What did he do for a living? (Well might they ask!) Where did he learn to fight? (Would they believe him if he told them?) He didn't feel like talking and he could barely move his face muscles to eat. At the far end of the room he could see Tom Seager and his backer, their heads together, occasionally throwing covert glances in his direction. He was glad Seager had recovered, but he didn't want to talk. He wanted to be free of them all. He wanted to be back in the City, where he knew the warren of lanes and alleys, where he could lose himself; and above all, where he could sleep peacefully, for days if he wanted to. He wondered what had become of Toby. But he wasn't going to concern himself over Crackit. That flash cove would return in his own time, when he had squeezed out every last ounce of pleasure from his sojourn in Shepperton.

Sikes pushed his half-empty plate from him and thanked his host and family for their kindness. Then, winking at the daughter of the house – a feat which cost him some effort on account of his injuries – he tied his belcher and shrugged on his waistcoat and greatcoat. Walking unsteadily from the tavern, he turned his face towards London.

It was now early afternoon and the sun had warmed the air a little. Even so, his breath floated in front of him in thin white clouds. He followed the lane as far as Walton Bridge and then picked up the tow path by the side of the river. The keen air revived him a little as he walked. Occasionally, he had to make way for a barge horse plodding along the path. One such beast was hauling a family of water gypsies in their gaily-painted home and the entire family stared at the battered fellow on the bank, as he pressed against the alder bushes to let the horse pass. The father, who was at the horse's head, spoke as he passed Sikes.

'Blimey, mate! You all right?'

'Yus. I'll do,' muttered Sikes, hurrying on.

If he looked that bad, he really ought to lie low and travel by night. He would only attract attention to himself, which he could do without. But he wanted to get back to London as soon as he could, he wouldn't feel safe until he did. He must find a carrier and he wouldn't find one here on this lonely footpath. Another hour's walk would bring him to Kingston and he knew he could find transport there.

The river wound on and the fields stretched away on either side. There was still a mist hanging in the distance, but the sun had brought a warm and welcome glow to the countryside. Sikes was sweating now and he could feel every cut and bruise in his body. His nose kept running and he wiped the back of his hand across it and sniffed. He suddenly felt weary and sat down on the next stile he came to. There were cattle in the neighbouring field and they looked up inquisitively, as he took off his coat and slung it over one shoulder. He glanced down at his blood-spattered shirt-sleeves; his waistcoat covered the worst of it, but it was obvious to all what he had been up to. Gingerly, he fingered the swollen bridge of his nose and wondered if it had all been worth it. He remembered his pay and felt in his breeches pocket for the banknotes. There were three of them, three large, crumpled, dirty, five-pound notes. It wasn't what he had hoped for. It wasn't the fortune Toby had predicted. But it would buy him a good brace of pistols, a new shirt and keep him in victuals for the remainder of the winter. He could even afford himself the pleasure of a decent woman; but not with his face as it was. He would have to wait.

He slipped off the stile and walked on. He felt hot inside as well as outside now and he feared he had caught a chill or a fever. His legs began to feel weak under him, but it was imperative that he make Kingston by nightfall.

When at last he came up the east loop of the river around Hampton Court and was in sight of Kingston Bridge, he felt all in and no longer cared whether he found a lodging or lay down where he was.

He staggered into the busy little town and asked his way to the Sun Inn, for he knew there was a good coach service from there to Ludgate Hill. The man he addressed recoiled in horror from Sikes's black eye, swollen lip and cut face, the blood on his shirt and the feverish light in his eye. But he gave him directions nonetheless.

At the inn his luck held out. There was a stagecoach leaving within the hour and the driver, rather reluctantly, agreed to take him on board. This just left him time to purchase a good measure of brandy, which went a little way to restoring his senses.

Sikes found a place on the outside of the coach when the departure time approached, and climbed up next to the driver, who turned his gaze on him with interest. He was waiting for the postilion and struck up a conversation with his neighbour.

'Interestin' mess,' he remarked. 'Who rearranged yer face for yer?'

Sikes was reluctant to reply, but he had to say something.

'A gent wot was bigger than me,' he said.

The driver laughed loudly. 'An' wot did you do to 'im?' he wanted to know.

'Beat 'im.'

The driver's eyes opened wide. 'Did yer now?' His voice was suddenly serious. 'I 'ope yer got well paid.'

Sikes had the uncomfortable feeling that this fellow knew exactly where he had been. A moment later, his suspicions were confirmed, when the driver put his head on one side and remarked, 'I 'ear the beak sent out a warrant fer the Shepperton Fancy today.'

Sikes said nothing, but stared straight ahead and pulled up his collar around his ears. He felt feverishly hot, but he knew the journey would be a cold one.

The guard climbed up and gave the word to the driver. A crack of the whip, a blast on the horn, a creak of harness and carriage springs and they were away; slowly at first, picking their way through the remains of the day's market, now trotting on as they came out into the London Road. In a very little while, they were clear of the town and rattling over the rutted roads towards the capital.

The shaking and jerking of the vehicle jarred every inch of Sikes's aching body, and it was only by keeping his legs braced against the guard rail that he prevented himself from falling. The light had faded now and the coach lamps flung eerie shadows on to the ground in front of the galloping horses. Barring accidents, they should make the City by eight of the clock that night, Sikes was informed above the wind racing past them, and indeed the City clocks were striking the hour as the coach pulled up outside The Belle Sauvage Inn in Ludgate Hill. Beyond was the great Cathedral. 'Ome, Sikes thought – well, almost. He still had almost two miles to walk to his lodgings.

He rose stiffly and climbed carefully from the coach.

The driver called cheerfully, 'Wotch 'ow yer go, mate. I should get them cuts seen to.'

Sikes strode off into the dark night, thankful to be alone again. He passed an apothecary's shop in Cheapside and, after a moment's hesitation, turned back and went inside.

The shop was lit by four small gas lamps and the rows of coloured bottles winked blue and green and opalescent in the unsteady light. The apothecary was matter-of-fact and muttered to himself as he tilted Sikes's head this way and that, felt his forehead and took his pulse.

'You've a fever there, I'm afraid, sir,' he said. 'I'll give you a little laudanum for that. You won't need much. You'll want a comfrey and yarrow balm for your cuts and a little arnica for the bruising.'

He paused and looked Sikes up and down for a space.

'You can pay, I presume?'

The man could be forgiven the insinuation, in view of Sikes's dishevelled appearance. Sikes nodded, producing one of his banknotes. The apothecary looked at it suspiciously and stared hard at his customer.

'It's all right,' Sikes reassured him. 'It's honestly come by.'

Fer once, he thought. And then wondered whether it really had been earned in all honesty. He supposed it hadn't, seeing that the Government had banned all illicit fights. The apothecary took the note and put it carefully away, producing four sovereigns and several shillings and pennies in change. These he handed to Sikes, together with the medications wrapped in a cloth bag. Sikes grunted his thanks, turned on his heel and made for home.

When he reached the door of the lodging house in Old Nicol Street, the keeper's wife let him in. In the light of the hallway she threw up her hands in horror.

'Oh lawks, Mr Sikes! Wot 'ave yer bin an' done?'

Sikes brushed past her without answering and clumped wearily up the stairs, leaving the sympathetic creature to scuttle back to her kitchen. Inside his room, he lit an oil lamp and set a light to the fire, pushing a few sticks of dry kindling into the ashy coals. They glowed a little and he tried to blow on them. But the effort pained his face so much that he gave up. He drew the curtains and shivered as he turned away from the window. He was worried about falling ill, but it couldn't be helped. He would have to manage as best he could. Toby would probably turn up in a day or two. He left his door unlocked and found himself a tankard, into which he poured a little of the laudanum. It was bitter, despite its wine base, and he found a bottle of beer with which to wash away the taste. Then he sat on the bed with a broken piece of mirror propped on the chair beside him, so that he could see where he was putting the ointments.

'Gawd, wot a bloody mess!' he said to himself. 'Wot a way to earn fifteen pound! Still, I proved I could do it,' and he smiled lopsidedly at his reflection.

But immediately he winced and composed his features again. He rubbed the arnica very carefully on his nose. He had thought at first that it had been broken, but the apothecary had assured him, after much painful examination, that it was not. But, hell's fire, it hurt like blazes! He couldn't see out of his injured eye now and his head had started a violent throbbing. He turned down the oil lamp, pulled off his damp boots and wrapped himself tightly in his coat and bedclothes. Thus swaddled, he fell into a troubled sleep, from which he was eventually roused by the landlady, Mrs Waller, timidly entering his room about ten o'clock the following morning, bearing a large mug of beef tea. She advanced cautiously and stood looking down at the rugged dormant form. She touched his shoulder and spoke softly.

'Mr Sikes. Mr Sikes. Wake up. I've brought you some breakfast.'

Reluctantly Sikes opened his good eye, blinked uncomprehendingly for a moment, then rolled over on to his back, his face creasing with pain as he did so.

'Wot's up?' he whispered hoarsely.

'I wos worried about you last night. An' I 'eard you tossin' about an' groanin' in yer sleep. So I brought yer some beef tea. I bet you ain't 'ad anything to eat recently.'

Sikes glanced round him at the tossed bedclothes and feared he must present a sorry sight. He struggled to a sitting position and took the steaming mug from Mrs Waller.

'I'll see if I can find a lump o' steak fer that eye, if you like,' she offered.

'No thanks,' he replied. 'I've got all I need. I'll be all right now.'

The landlady looked at him doubtfully.

'It's all right,' he insisted. 'Mr Crackit'll be along some time. Don't fuss over me.'

The good-natured woman returned to her kitchen, closing Sikes's door quietly behind her. He was an odd sort. She didn't normally take much notice of the lodgers, but there was something strange, compelling, almost sinister about this one. She felt a little frightened by him. And yet, unaccountably fascinated. Had she been a younger woman . . .

Two days after his fight, Sikes was standing unsteadily over the fire, trying to coax some life back into it, when there was a sharp rattle at the door and Toby's voice called out, 'You there, Bill?'

'Yus. Come in. Door's not locked.'

Toby flung open the door. Then stood rooted, as Sikes turned to face him, the poker in one hand, his coat clutched round him with the other. The spectacle he presented was too disturbing for poor Toby and for a moment he stared speechless at Sikes's haggard appearance, his cuts and bruises, his unshaven jaw and the great bruise that seemed to cover half his face. At last he found his voice.

'Swipe me, Bill! Wot the blazes 'appened?'

'Don't ask silly bloody questions, Toby. Ain't it obvious? I 'ad a fight, didn't I? Just like you wanted.'

'Who with?'

'Tom Seager.'

'Bloody 'ell!' breathed Toby. 'You don't mean yer . . .?'

'Yeah! Gen'leman Jackson failed ter turn up, so this 'ere cove stands in for 'im.'

Toby's eyes widened in wonder as he listened in disbelief.

''E weren't 'alf a big bloke,' continued Sikes, 'but 'e weren't very quick an' I got 'im with a rabbiter in the end.'

Toby relaxed momentarily.

'You're 'avin' me on, ain't yer, Bill?' he said. ''Cos that weren't the bloke yer wos down ter fight. I wondered where you'd buggered off to. By the time I'd surfaced an' got down to the Common, there wos 'ardly a trace left o' the Fancy an' ev'ryone 'ad dispersed pretty sharpish. I gather the beak sent out a warrant. I saw three gents in uniform askin' questions among the locals, so I got out as quick as I could. I put up at Sunbury fer the night an' come back 'ere yesterday.'

Sikes was watching him, his good eye glittering dangerously.

'Toby. I wos nearly taken apart back there, while you wos a-sleepin' off yer pleasures. An' I could've bin run in if I'd bin caught by the beak's men. Now listen. Don't you ask me ter play a stupid game like that again, 'cos I ain't doin' it.'

Toby looked so contrite that Sikes relented so far as to smile tightly.

'Well, I lived,' he said, 'an' I won this.'

He held up the remaining banknotes and jingled the loose change in the other hand. Toby brightened.

'You mean, you really did beat 'im, Bill? You beat Tom Seager, the champion? Oh lor', I wish I'd seen yer. It must 'ave bin glorious.'

Sikes turned away, secreting his cash in a drawer by his bed.

'Yus, well, I s'pect it wos,' he mumbled, 'fer them as watched. But it wos a bloody painful way to earn fifteen quid.'

Toby fussed around him, looked at his wounds, decided he was on the mend and offered to fetch him food and drink.

'Well, I need summat,' replied Sikes, sitting down on his bed. 'I ain't 'ad much since I come back 'ere. Barrin' Mrs W's beef tea!' he added ruefully.

Toby chuckled and went off, promising to return with victuals. Sikes stretched out his long body on the bed, feeling decidedly better.

TEN

It didn't take many days for Sikes to feel more like his old self. Within a week he felt he could venture out into the streets again without attracting too much attention. Toby, to give him his due, had, from time to time, called in to ensure that his partner was well supplied with victuals and fuel. But he had interests elsewhere at present and only put in occasional visits to his sick friend. This suited Sikes, since he preferred his own company, especially when he was feeling under the weather.

During the long hours he had lain on his bed, Sikes had spent a great deal of time thinking. The earlier thoughts which had worried him, the distressing scene of his brother's death, had been replaced by the more recent, more vivid recollections of his wasted years in Van Diemen's Land. And the scene he tried his hardest to blot out was the humiliation and agony of his flogging. He eased his back. He could still feel the evil cat, after all this time. And every pain and misery he had endured had been brought about by his allowing himself to be betrayed by a woman. He hoped he would never see her again. He knew now that he would kill her if he did. And that would ensure him the hangman's rope.

One of Sikes's first tasks when he was better was to see about retrieving Bull's-eye from Barney at the Cripples. He had missed the old brute, not through any real affection, but because the animal was company for him; company which didn't answer back, didn't argue with him, didn't gainsay his wants. He knew he mistreated the dog, but somehow he couldn't help it. It was part of his nature now. He cared little for anyone or anything. Looking in on himself, he knew that transportation had changed him irredeemably. Where he had been hard before, now he was ruthless, merciless. Where he had once given the benefit of the doubt, he now gave the proverbial kick in the teeth. And where once he might have just lost his temper and sworn and walked away, now he would lash out in violence with those fists of his. He glanced down at his scabbing knuckles and snorted a mirthless laugh; those fists which had just won him fifteen quid!

There was a light drizzle falling and the streets were a mess of slush and filth. He ambled along in no great hurry, across Shoreditch and down into Clerkenwell. Outside The Three Cripples he hesitated. The noise was tremendous and he could hear the strains of a concertina; someone was celebrating tonight! He walked slowly to the door, pushed it open and stood, half shadowed in the entrance. A few regulars noticed him and gradually all eyes turned on him. The musician came squeakily to a halt and the bawd on the table top stopped her song and dance, her skirt still hitched above her knee. For a moment no one moved and Sikes had the uncomfortable feeling that he was looking at a picture frozen in time and space.

Then just as suddenly, the scene dissolved and there were calls of, 'Crikey, Bill! Wot yer bin up to this time?' and 'Bet the blighter who did that didn't live ter tell the tale!'

Sikes let the adulation pour over him. He swaggered into the room, swinging his tall body between the tables. The women ogled him, their eyes shining, and the men looked at him with a kind of awe, a new respect. He was beginning to enjoy this and made his way to the bar, where Barney was serving. He ordered a large measure of gin. Two old men sat on high stools, drooling and champing over their beer. One of them spoke in a cracked voice.

'Stand yer a round, lad, if yer'll tell us the tale.' And he nudged his neighbour and winked. 'I well remember when I was a young striplin' . . .'

Sikes was spared the necessity of recounting his exploits, as the old man fell to regaling his crony with a story which the latter had no doubt heard a dozen times before. He leaned his arms on the bar and rested one foot on the kick-rail. Barney came over and pushed a bottle of gin towards him, together with a small glass pot.

'Good to see yer, Bister Sikes,' he said quietly. 'But wod on earth 'as 'abbened to yer?'

'I got inwolved with the Fancy, Barney. So inwolved I ended up floorin' a champion.'

Success was making him unusually open. He took a swig of his spirits and Barney's eyes grew round in his dirty face.

'Who was it, Bister Sikes?' he wanted to know.

'Tom Seager.'

'Oh blimey!' exploded Barney, unable to contain himself any longer. ''Ere, gen'lemen,' he announced to the room in general, 'listen ter wot Bister Sikes 'as done. 'E's gorn an' beat Tob Seager. I seed 'im fight back in 'twenty-nine. 'E ain't 'alf a big cove, too. Bigger'n Bister Sikes. An' can 'e fight! 'E's local chambion fer Shepperton. Dow our Bill Sikes 'as gorn an' beat 'im.'

This long and painful speech from the adenoidal Barney brought forth a cheer from the clientele. Sikes turned round to a sea of smiling faces. Not so much smiles of friendship as smiles of admiration and approval. The gin was spreading a warmth throughout his body and he felt reckless, revelling in all this approbation. He was eventually prevailed upon to relate his activities with the Fancy and when he had finished, another cheer went up and several of the listeners bought him drinks.

That night, Clerkenwell was his for the taking. The men offered drinks, the women their bodies. He could have had his pick of women. But he still preferred to seek his pleasures elsewhere. Clerkenwell was too familiar. He collected Bull's-eye from the Cripples' back parlour and strode off towards Whitechapel, where he picked up one of his regular women and hired a room for the night. Here he told her, in a drunken stupor, of his exploits in Shepperton, and spent a night of wild excess with her while Bull's-eye slept patiently outside the door till morning.

In the cold light of day, Sikes felt foolish and angry. He flung himself from the tumbled bed, paid the woman her due and went silently from the house, Bull's-eye padding along behind him. When he reached his own lodgings, he let himself in and found beer and bread and a couple of sausages. He raked up the embers of the fire and coaxed some life back into it, sufficient to cook the sausages on.

'Burn an' blast me fer a fool,' he muttered to himself. 'Wot's got into yer, Sikes? Braggin' ain't yer scene at all. Nor is all that hattention. Wot the 'ell's the matter with yer?'

And he sat himself angrily down at the table to eat his breakfast. He wondered at himself. He shouldn't be feeling depressed and angry; he ought to be elated, with the Cripples community all in awe of him. And half the White-chapel whores would soon know of his exploits. That was it! He banged his fist on the table and Bull's-eye sat up, his head on one side. If the Whitechapel girls knew, then sooner or later the Law was going to know about it, too. Gawd, why hadn't he kept quiet? He ought to have known better. They couldn't do anything to him, not yet, he reflected. But they would be watching and waiting; waiting for him to put one foot wrong. Give a man enough rope and he'd do Jack Ketch's job for him. Sikes felt sick at the thought, as he always did, knowing what his almost certain end would be. And here he was, turning in on himself, reflecting darkly on his life and his future.

'Short life, long drop,' he mused.

Then he banged his tankard down in anger. 'Fer Gawd's sake stoppit!' he admonished himself, and went off to the Farringdon Market to buy himself the much-needed brace of pistols. Work was what he needed, the work he was best at.

ELEVEN

The Three Cripples in Clerkenwell was something of a safe house for the underworld of that area. Safe, that is, in so far as everyone who frequented it was associated in some way with crime and dubious goings-on; and it was one of those public houses where the Law rarely ventured, and then only in large numbers, with a good case in hand. The clientele of the Cripples were as loyal to each other when faced with a posse of peelers as any upright and moral citizen might be for a more legitimate cause. Yet there were often outbreaks of violence and an onlooker could be forgiven for thinking that the crowd within was full of hatred for each other and bent on meting out blows to all their associates. And there was always the occasional stranger to the tavern, doing business with one or other of its shady characters. As often as not, it was with the wily old fence Fagin.

Late one night, in the early autumn of 1835, Bill Sikes might have been seen slipping silently through the shadows of Clerkenwell and entering the Three Cripples. He stood inside the door, obscured by the dimness, his eyes searching out the bent shoulders and scrawny, red-grey locks of his fence. At last he spotted him through the smoke and jostling crowd of drinkers and elbowed his way to where Fagin sat in deep conversation with a fair young man, booted, cloaked and spurred.

Sikes stood by the table, waiting.

'A moment, my dear,' said Fagin to his companion. 'Business,' he added complacently, lifting his shoulders and spreading his hands expressively to the fair young man.

Sikes turned on his heel and the old man followed him to a recess by the door. When they reached its shadows, Sikes rounded on him in sudden fury, grabbing a fistful of clothing at the older man's neck.

'I want the blunt. Where is it?' he snarled, his face very close to Fagin's, so that the latter was afraid Sikes might suddenly bite.

He opened his eyes very wide indeed. 'Bill, dear, you know I don't carry cash on me. I'm always reminding you of that. Come round for it tomorrow,' and he smiled in his oily way.

'I wonder I don't do you a dammidge,' hissed Sikes. 'A week! A whole bloody week since I brought yer the last lot o' goods an' you ain't given me a penny since! I flog me guts out screwin' cribs fer you an' wot do I get out of it? Nuffink!'

He shook Fagin at this last utterance and the old man's greasy locks swung in Sikes's face. He let go of Fagin as suddenly as he had grabbed him and stood looking at him in disgust.

Fagin rearranged his clothes and said quietly, 'Tomorrow, Bill, tomorrow.'

He shuffled back to the young man in the cloak, and Sikes stood watching him a moment. How was a man to earn money with a fence like Fagin? But he knew he was too far in with the crowd here to risk setting up somewhere else. Someone would be bound to blow the gaff and besides, he thought grimly, better the devil you know, even if the devil were a greedy, scrawny old one like Fagin.

The public house had a raised floor at one end, somewhat above the level of the main body of the room, so that it gave the appearance of an old-fashioned gallery. Here were arranged a number of high-backed settles and Sikes sat down in one of these with a bottle of beer and a tankard. As he sat, swigging sullenly, his eyes roving over the heads below him, his glance was attracted by a young woman. He looked again, studying her more carefully. He hadn't noticed her around before, but she seemed well acquainted with a good many of the customers as she swung her way between the tables and sat down opposite a mean-looking fellow with oiled side whiskers, of the sort currently known by the appellation of

'Newgate Knockers'. The girl looked to be in her mid-twenties, but she could have been younger, as so many of her type were. Something in the girl's demeanour disturbed the settled silt of Sikes's mind. There was a familiarity about her which he couldn't place. He didn't recall having seen her before, yet the way she held her head, as though the weight of hair dragged it back, seemed to prod at the carapace of his sentiments.

She seemed engrossed in conversation with her partner, smiling and nodding. Occasionally she glanced up through the wisps of blonde hair which straggled from their gaudy clasps and hung limply over her face. She tossed them back, laughing, and lifted her arms to secure the pins. As she did so, her moth-eaten shawl fell back from her shoulders; and when she lowered her arms, Sikes was treated to the sight of a smooth white shoulder and neck, sweeping down to her breast, which was only just hidden from his view by the edge of the scarlet bodice she wore. The man opposite leered at her with slack wet lips and began pawing her. She leaned over and said something to him. Sikes saw him scowl and push a few pennies across the table to her. She quickly pocketed them and rose to go. The man leaped from his seat and grasped her arm. She winced, but the two left the inn together and disappeared into the night.

He couldn't have said why, but Sikes was disturbed by the incident. Yet he had seen similar a thousand times before, even in this very tavern. He finished his beer, glanced across to where his fence was still deep in conversation, and left the tavern. Outside, a light drizzle was falling and he turned up his collar, pulled his hat over his eyes and thrust his hands deep into his pockets. It was a tidy walk back to his lodgings, but he moved with slow and ponderous tread towards Shoreditch. He couldn't get the girl out of his mind.

The next night she was there again, helping Barney to serve drinks. Although she flirted with every man she saw, Sikes thought there was a look of the trapped animal in her eyes; he knew that feeling only too well. Tonight he sat at a table with

398

Toby Crackit. When the girl brought their drinks, she pressed herself close against Sikes, her breast touching his shoulder as she leaned across the table. He looked up at her and wondered at the large purpling bruises which spread from her shoulder up into her neck. She saw the direction of his gaze and laughed, as she hitched up the wayward shoulder of her gown.

'Don't frown, luv,' she said, 'it don't go well with them black brows of yours!'

And she flounced away to another customer.

'Who's that?' murmured Sikes to Toby, following her progress over the rim of his tankard. 'I'm sure I've seen 'er afore, only I can't think where.'

'Her?' replied Toby. 'That's Nancy, one of Fagin's protégées. At least, she was. 'E took 'er in when she was a littl'un an' 'e taught 'er along of 'is boys. She became a reg'lar little dipper. Till she got a fancy fer the boys an' the gin. Cost Fagin an arm an' a leg, she did. So 'e told 'er to earn money fer 'er own gin. So she did. 'Er an' Bet, as was brought up with 'er. The pair of 'em 'ad a patch off the Whitechapel Road to start with an' then they thought they'd go up market a bit. I don't know the details after that, except they comes back ter Fagin askin' fer lodgin's an' the ole skinflint won't let 'em in. "No," 'e says, "I've got too many young lads 'ere; they might be led hastray." Bet an' Nancy went off in a huff. Well, it weren't very friendly of Fagin. They 'ad to earn their thruppence or fourpence a night just to 'ave a room ter sleep in, otherwise they slept on the streets.' He paused. 'They still do, God 'elp 'em.'

Sikes was staring at Toby in disbelief.

'But – they must 'ave a lodgin' somewhere?'

'No!' Toby snapped out the word with the satisfaction of the man who knows. 'No bus'ness, no roof. Simple as that. They can't earn more than a night's shelter round 'ere, though. But at least they're among their own kind.'

Sikes was quite taken aback. He thought of his own room in the seedy lodging house in Shoreditch. It was sparsely furnished, but it had a bed and a grate and he had coals to burn.

And he made enough money from his ill-gotten gains to pay the weekly rent and to keep himself in food and drink. And the room was his home. He looked again towards the girl and felt a stab of something akin to pity, although he would never have admitted to such a feeling.

'Anyway!' Toby banged his empty pot on the table. 'Wot's next on the hagenda fer you an' me, me ole cove? 'Ow about pushin' out into North London, eh?'

Sikes nodded absently, drained his tankard and hailed Barney for more beer.

Toby went on, 'There's a little village, 'bout seven, eight miles from 'ere. Winchmore 'Ill. Plenty o' good cribs there, I gather. An' the woods to disappear into.'

'Yes. You give it the once-over, Toby, an' we'll plan it out.'

Toby was surprised at Sikes's acquiescence, but felt he hadn't got his friend's complete attention. However, he outlined the plans he had made already, waxing more and more enthusiastic as the drink took effect. Suddenly, Sikes seized his wrist in an iron grip.

'Shut up,' he growled, 'and keep yer bloody voice down.'

Toby cut off in mid-flow. 'Sorry, Bill,' he said in a hurt tone. 'Just got a bit carried away.'

He coloured and looked shiftily at Sikes, but the man's attention was elsewhere again and Toby gave up.

'I'll be off now,' he said, rising from the table. 'I'll let you know the lay.'

He paused, peering at Sikes, from whom there was no response.

'Well, aurevaurie, ole chap,' and Toby lurched off into the street.

Sikes continued to sit over his beer, watching Nancy when he could, without making it too obvious that he was interested in her. He would play this game very carefully.

But Nancy was beginning to have an effect on Bill Sikes. He felt disturbed, watching her swing sensuously between the tables. Several times she glanced across at him and their eyes met. He felt the familiar stirrings of desire and seriously considered propositioning her. But he was short of cash until Fagin paid up. And he was surprised at his own feelings of nicety when he argued with himself that, although he could probably procure the girl for very little, he felt she was worth a great deal more than the usual run-of-the-mill encounters.

The next morning, Sikes had a hangover and slept till gone noon. He knew he must obtain money before he could buy his next meal, but blunt was getting low again and the rent needed paying tomorrow. He needed to make another crack pretty soon, or he really would be in dire straits. So he doused his head in a basin of very cold water, shaking off the drops like a dog, dressed himself, called 'Oi!' to Bulls-eye and went off in the direction of Field Lane.

He took the rickety staircase of Fagin's lodging house two steps at a time and knocked twice loudly and deliberately upon the door. There was a lull in the conversation from within, the sound of young feet hurrying across the room and the door opened to reveal the snub nose and freckled face of Charley Bates. Charley peered up through his fringe of hair and hesitated.

'Who is it, Charley?' came Fagin's voice from beyond him.

'It's me, Fagin,' said Sikes, thrusting young Bates aside and striding into the room. 'An' I've come fer me push.'

'Ah, Bill. Of course.'

Fagin's hands wrapped themselves round each other. There was a suppressed giggle from the other side of the room. Sikes glanced across and saw Nancy with a friend, whom he presumed to be Bet, sitting by the fire. The girls had their skirts gathered up to their knees and were warming their legs.

Fagin followed his look and said hastily, 'Allow me to introduce two of my oldest friends. Nancy, Bet – Mr Bill Sikes.'

The girls smiled. Nancy tossed her blonde hair and Sikes stood silent for a moment. The sight of Nancy's stockinged legs had the effect of rendering him speechless with longing: a longing to possess the girl, to take for himself this jewel off the London streets. With a mighty effort, he kept himself in check and sat down at the large and dirty deal table in the middle of the room.

'Fagin.' His voice was quiet, dangerously quiet, held in check between clenched teeth. 'I am hungry an' I 'ave no money – because you've been a-sittin' on it all week like a bleedin' old 'en.' His voice began to rise. 'Now, are you goin' ter give me the blunt, or am I goin' ter wheedle it out of yer with me chiv?'

And to back up his words, he pulled out the wicked-looking clasp knife he carried, which he brandished in Fagin's direction. He heard the intake of breath from the girls and it seemed to goad him on.

'Well, you misbegotten ole pinch-penny?' he shouted. 'Burn me if I don't stick yer like a pig!' And he advanced on Fagin, seized him by the shirt front and held the point of the blade to his throat. 'The money, Fagin. Where is it?' he asked, his voice now tempered and under control again.

Fagin found himself forced to look into those burning pools and the sight made him shake and gibber. But at last he said, 'A moment, Bill. I must get it from my private bank, you understand,' and he laughed nervously as Sikes released him.

Then he disappeared behind the flimsy partition at the far end of the room. There was the sound of a floorboard being lifted, a box being opened, money being counted out.

'How much, Bill?' called Fagin.

'It was worth a finny at least.'

Sikes heard a sigh, the rustle of a banknote and sounds of box and board being replaced. Fagin emerged with a five-pound note folded small in his hand. He held it between finger and thumb and Sikes quickly relieved him of it.

'Stay and have a drink, Bill.'

He was all smiles now that the bad moment of parting with money was over.

'I'd rather eat,' said Sikes.

'Then stay and have some sausages and toast, my boy. Nancy and Bet will cook them for you. Won't you, my dears?'

The girls exchanged glances, which told Sikes that they hadn't much option, without appearing churlish. Sikes sat down again, as they busied themselves over the frying pan and toasting fork. Fagin pushed a small pot containing gin towards him.

'Any new jobs, Bill?' Fagin asked tentatively.

'Maybe. Toby's on a scout-round now. But if yer goin' ter be so slow with the push, we'll 'ave ter take trade elsewhere.'

For a moment, fear showed in the old man's eyes.

'No, Bill,' he whispered hoarsely. 'No. You wouldn't do that. No need to do that. Fagin'll pay up. Only, I need time, my dear. It takes time to – dispose of these little items.'

'You mind I don't dispose of you instead, then,' returned the big fellow.

He grinned his thanks as Nancy placed a plate of sausages and toast in front of him, brushing his shoulder as she did so. But this time his hunger was more mundane. He fell to, ravenously, swilling it down with swigs of gin; until, in a very few moments, both pot and plate were empty.

'That's better,' said Sikes, rising and picking up his battered hat.

He patted his thigh and Bull's-eye, who had taken up his station in front of the fire, lumbered to his feet and followed his master to the door. Fagin raised a hand in farewell and turned away. Nancy looked up and Sikes winked at her and clattered away down the stairs.

It was a bit of luck, Nancy and her friend being there. Sikes was thinking they might well get acquainted.

TWELVE

The following afternoon the room in Old Nicol Street was the scene of some activity. Bill Sikes sat at his table, which was littered with the remains of his breakfast, the previous night's bottles, two pistols and their accoutrements and the clasp knife. Sikes busied himself cleaning his weaponry and sharpening his knife. A meagre fire burned in the grate and Bull's-eye was stretched in front of it, his head on his paws, his eyes shut, but twitching as he dreamed.

Suddenly, the dog's head came up and a deep growl issued from the depths of his battered old body. Sikes glanced across at him, but said nothing. A moment later, there was the sound of someone running up the stairs, two at a time, and with a peremptory knock, the door flew open and in burst Toby Crackit, his face aglow, a grin stretching from ear to ear. Sikes turned his head and eyed him.

'You look pleased with yerself.'

Toby banged the door shut and fairly skipped across the room to stand before Sikes.

'Siddown, will yer. Yer make me feel nervous, jumpin' about like that.'

Toby pulled up the only other chair at the table, sat on it and leaned towards Sikes in anticipation of telling his tale.

'Bin a long time, 'aven't yer?' enquired Sikes pleasantly. 'Avin' an 'oliday while yer about it, eh?'

Toby's face fell. Why did Sikes always knock the wind out of his sails? Couldn't he share in a man's good fortune and enthusiasm sometimes? He looked somewhat stonily at Sikes, who spat on the butt of his pistol and rubbed it with his sleeve.

'I've found the perfect crib, Bill,' Toby began.

Sikes raised his eyes and Toby cringed under their gaze. But Sikes never uttered a word. He had no need.

Toby went on, flustered, 'A – a fair-sized 'ouse. In Winchmore 'Ill. Stands be'ind a brick wall. Over'angin' trees, gravel path, lawns, sash winders – an' eaps of silver. The owner's away till Friday. I – I bin inside!'

'I can see that,' growled his companion. 'I just 'ope yer didn't open that great trap o' yours while yer were at it.'

Toby blinked, hard, and returned Sikes's stare.

'No, Bill. 'Course I didn't. I 'ad other things ter think about.'

'Yes, but one thing leads to another, dunnit?' hissed Sikes, thrusting his face into Toby's.

'No, 'onest, Bill. It was all right, really it was. An' I know wot's there, an' the layout of all the downstairs rooms.'

'An' the decoration of the ceilin's, no doubt,' laughed Sikes.

But it was a mirthless laugh and Toby had the grace to look slightly abashed, for his access to the house, as Sikes had guessed, had been by way of a very accommodating kitchen maid.

There was a lull in the conversation for a moment. Sikes finished cleaning the pistol, picked up the knife and shut it with a snap.

'Good work, Toby. Yer've done well.' A pause while Sikes thought for a moment. Then, 'We'll do it. Thursday. Now, draw me a plan o' this place.'

Toby relaxed again, his humour restored. This was what he enjoyed best and he was glad Sikes was pleased with his efforts. They shared a jug of beer together, their heads bent over a scrap of paper, while Toby drew in all the details he could remember and they laid their plans.

At noon the next day Bill Sikes and Toby Crackit met up at the Cock tavern on the western edge of Edmonton. Here they idled away a couple of hours, their faces kept in shadow as much as possible so as not to draw unwonted attention to themselves.

When the light began to wane a little, the two men left the warmth of the inn and took temporary leave of each other outside. Toby went on up the hill to Winchmore Hill, where he made his way across the Green and out into the lane which ran back through the woods. On the left-hand side of this lane, just at the entrance to the woods, was the old gamekeeper's cottage. It was now quite derelict, but still afforded some shelter from the cold. Making sure there was no one to see him, Toby slipped inside the building and deposited the large bag he carried. He turned out its contents on to the earthen floor: two bottles of beer, cheese, a tinderbox, bull's-eye lantern, rope and two sacks. This was his contribution. Sikes would bring the tools of the trade in his travelling bag. There was an old box in the cottage and Toby sat down on this to wait.

Sikes took a long circuitous route to the rendezvous and a light, cold drizzle had started to fall by the time he entered the woods. By the time he reached the end of the woodland path, it was quite dark and coming suddenly from the velvety blackness of the trees, it took him a moment to accustom his eyes to the more open darkness of the fields ahead, beyond which he could see the twinkle of lights in cottage windows. And here was the ruin Toby had mentioned. Cautiously he pushed open the door and listened. Not a sound, except a held breath. Too late, Toby's arm was round his neck, choking him, and the pair were sprawling on the hard earth floor.

'Yer bloody fool,' hissed Sikes, when he had managed to free himself from Toby's stranglehold. 'Wot the blazes d'yer think yer playin' at? Who the 'ell did yer think it wos? Eh?'

He got up and hauled Toby to his feet.

'I'm sorry, Bill.' Toby was flustered again. 'I didn't recognize yer tread. 'Ave some beer an' cheese. We've got a long wait.'

Sikes groped his way to the wall and sat down with his back against it. Toby lit the lantern and draped a sack at the window to hide its light.

While they ate their meagre rations, Toby kept a keen eye on the path outside, jumping up every few minutes to peer round the corner of the sacking, ready to douse the lantern if anyone stirred abroad. But the only sound was that of the light rain pattering on the tall trees overhead.

Presently, Toby took out his pocket watch, tilted it towards the dim light of the lantern and deemed it time to push on. Sikes eyed the timepiece somewhat scornfully. He was not envious. He had had plenty of opportunities to furnish himself with some pretty specimens, but he was not a flash cove and did not flaunt the results of his work. He was going careful this time, as he had promised himself. The last thing he wanted to do was to walk the streets wearing stolen timepieces.

The two cracksmen set off towards the Green. It was pitch-dark and there was not a soul abroad. They had picked their night well. When they came into the lane where The Vinery, the house Toby had had his eye on, stood, Sikes stayed on the opposite side of the road, while Toby halted by the gate. Satisfied that all was quiet in the house, he beckoned to Sikes and the pair scaled the wall like a couple of cats and crept carefully across the gravel drive and on to the lawn. And it was only a matter of seconds before Sikes had cut out one of the ground-floor window panes, put his hand through to undo the catch and lifted the window smoothly on its sashes. Silently, they swung themselves over the sill and began systematically lifting all the silver they could find. There was plenty here in the drawing room, but a real surfeit in the dining room. Sikes filled a sack and his bag, while Toby, once his sack was full, began stuffing items into his pockets.

'Come on, that's enough,' whispered Sikes. 'We shall never get rid o' this lot, let alone get it back to Fagin.'

Toby seemed reluctant to end the spree and Sikes had to forcibly march him back to the window. It was more difficult getting their loot out through the window as well as themselves, but at last it was done and they stood on the flowerbed, while Sikes silently lowered the window again. Toby looked up and blew a kiss to the upper storey.

'Thanks, sweetheart!' he whispered.

'Come on, fer Gawd's sake,' muttered Sikes, nudging him with his elbow.

They fled soundlessly over the fields at the back of the house, and so came again to the safety of the hovel. Here they relit their lantern and repacked the bags. It was impossible to get it all safely back to Clerkenwell in one journey and reluctantly they buried the remainder beneath the floor of their shelter.

It was well past the first hour of the new day when Sikes emerged from Winchmore Hill woods and made his way to Southgate. There was a substantial inn here, he knew, but it was too early to hope for transport. He crept quietly into the woods opposite and waited among the undergrowth.

Daylight revealed a small post-chaise bound for Stoke Newington. The driver was stowing other passengers and their belongings on board and Sikes handed up his heavy bag.

'Crikey, mate! Wotcher got in 'ere? The Crown Jewels?'

The coach driver was a native of London and his Cockney cheek went some way to relaxing Sikes's tetchy mood.

'Maybe I 'ave,' he rejoined. 'But you 'andle that bag careful. Tools o' me trade in there.'

The coachman laughed and Sikes climbed into the coach, squeezing his body into a space between a large flustered farmer's wife and an equally large man who declared himself to be a 'bachelor of moderate income', travelling the villages of England for his further 'edification'. Opposite were two young women, who kept eyeing Sikes's dark visage, unshaven jaw and grubby clothing with looks of horror, and a very thin and wasted old man with rheumy eyes, which he turned dolefully upon his fellow passengers in turn, never uttering a word.

The coach lurched and splashed its way along the rutted roads to Stoke Newington and finally came to an unsteady halt outside the Red Lion in Church Street. Sikes was the first out of the coach and was about to retrieve his precious baggage, when he caught the eye of one of the young women. She stared very hard and very defiantly at him and, rather ungraciously, he offered his grimy hand to both ladies as they descended. Sikes's scowl deepened still further when the large and perspiring farmer's wife also hurried from her seat to avail herself of his gallantry.

Gawd! How he loathed these overdressed and prissy females. He thought of the East End girls, as he swung his heavy bag from the roof of the chaise and paid the driver. He was still thinking about them as he strode away towards Fagin's. With a four-mile walk ahead of him, he had plenty of time to reflect.

He was choosy about his women now. Not like poor Toby, who bedded any female he spoke to. Sikes often went weeks without a woman, but when he felt the need, he would go to a house he knew in Whitechapel and there he could be fairly sure that he would not end up the following week with the clap. But that needed money and he had to wait until he had completed a job to afford the better sort of company. With this latest crack, he would be able to afford the very best. He could take himself off to the West End if he wanted. He could splash out on a new suit of clothes. That'd make Toby look to his stocks and collars. He smiled to himself. No, he couldn't see himself doing that. Bill Sikes, a West End toff? He'd be thrown out of the Cripples on the instant. They'd disown him. Funny how he thought of them as his family now. He was too deep in with them to cut away. Toby was right, they'd be loyal to you as long as you were one of them. But move one step out of line and you'd swing come Monday. And what about this girl he'd seen? This Nancy? Why did she keep slipping into his mind lately? *She* wasn't one of the better-class whores. *She* was straight off the dirty streets of Ratcliffe. Still plied between there and Clerkenwell, if Toby was to be believed. He wondered what it was that had made him look twice at Nancy. There was something disturbing about her. Had he seen her before somewhere? He thought it might be her eyes which had held him. He remembered the hunted look in them, the animal waiting to leap away inside them.

The heavy bag was making his arms ache and he stopped several times to rest. Once, as he neared Clerkenwell, he caught sight of a couple of peelers and had to dodge down a side alley until they had passed. Not that anyone had anything on him – yet. But let news of last night's burglary filter down into the City and he would need to go to ground for a while. Christ! What a haul they'd taken this time! Toby was making his own way back with his share and the plan was to retrieve the remainder from the ruined cottage when the hue and cry had died down. Always provided, of course, that Toby didn't get caught on his way back. Things had an unpleasant habit of going wrong for Toby. He'd seen the inside of Newgate a good many times already.

By the time Sikes reached Fagin's den, his arms felt as though they had been stretched from their sockets and the leather travelling bag was straining at the seams.

Fagin hustled him inside with an obsequious greeting. Sikes heaved the bag on to the table and opened it. The fence's eyes glittered wickedly at the contents.

'Beautiful, beautiful.' He almost chanted the words, muttering away to himself a litany of superlatives, as he lifted out the items one by one. Sikes stood watching him.

'Toby's on 'is way with a second load like that – an' we've left another 'aul hidden up there.' He was reluctant to add this last item.

Fagin turned his head sharply. 'You shouldn't have done that, Bill. Too risky, far too risky. Why didn't you bring it all together?'

'Because it was too bloody 'eavy, dam' an' blast yer! Me arms is fair dragged out their sockets carryin' that lot from Stoke Newin'ton!'

And he grabbed a jug of beer and a pewter mug and flung himself in a chair by the side of the fire. Fagin made conciliatory movements with his hands.

'All right, all right, my dear. You have done well.'

'Then there'll be a gen'rous share fer Crackit an' me.'

It was a statement, not a question. Fagin's head nodded up and down automatically.

'Where yer goin' ter fence that lot?' Sikes looked across at the table where Fagin was still pawing over silver salvers, cruet sets and cutlery.

Fagin laid a dirty, bony finger alongside his dirty, bony nose.

'Ah, my dear. You should know me better by now. It'll go, it'll all go. Just give me time.'

'A week,' snapped Sikes. 'That's all!'

Fagin replaced the stolen goods in Sikes's bag and came over to join him by the fire. He sat opposite the housebreaker, who was staring into the blaze. He considered him, trying to fathom this sparring partner of his. He studied his face and thought he saw beyond the hard line of the jaw, the set mouth, the dark brooding expression with the dangerous glint in the eye. He thought he saw a man saddened and embittered by life, a man against the world. Like himself, living on the edge of society, beyond the help of churchmen and moralizers. A man dependent on the trust and goodwill of his confederates. Above all, a man whose temper simmered just below the surface and which could boil over at a careless word or action. Fagin knew that temper. He had been on the receiving end of it, both physically and verbally, more than once during the past year. He was getting wiser now. It was better to placate Sikes than to argue with him; better for all concerned.

He started. How long had those glittering green eyes been on him? Fagin jerked in his chair and cleared his throat. Sikes treated him to a very black look, but was too tired to press the matter further. Instead, he quizzed his fence.

'That gal. Nancy,' he began. ''Ow long she bin around 'ere?'

Fagin smiled slyly. He had been waiting for this. He was a shrewd and wily individual and he had seen the interest in the younger man's eye, last time they met here.

'I brought her up with my boys, her and Bet,' he replied. 'She was with me from the age of six or so, but you weren't around then. Took a liking to my gin, Bill, and I couldn't afford to keep her any more. Pity. She was a good little dipper, too. Better than Bet. But they never earned enough for all the mother's milk they wanted. So they had to make their own way. And I'm afraid they came down in the world.'

He raised his eyebrows and lifted his shoulders in the age-old gesture.

'Yer mean you wouldn't give 'em a roof over their 'eads, yer miserly ole bastard.'

'Bill, Bill, no need for unpleasantness. It was their decision entirely. They can earn more in the West End if they want. They can go into a proper house if they choose.'

Sikes leaned across and grabbed the scrawny wrist in his vice-like grip, making Fagin wince.

'You know bloody well they won't get a look in there. 'Ow can our gals possibly 'ope ter compete with the likes o' the 'aymarket and 'olborn? An' if they was to join a 'ouse, they'd never see daylight again. I know about those places, Fagin, even if *you* don't.'

They stared at each other for a moment.

Then Sikes went on, 'I know that those two gals frequently spend the night on the streets, when they don't earn enough fer their night's lodgin'. An' you're too mean ter let 'em lodge 'ere, after all the thievin' they done fer you! Yes, I know a bit about 'em. Toby told me. So yer needn't look so surprised.'

Fagin spread his hands in the gesture which so irritated Sikes.

'That's life, my boy,' he said, reasonably.

Sikes rose, banged his empty pot on the table and opened the door.

Turning, he said to Fagin, 'A week terday. Blunt, an' empty bag. We'll get the rest when it's safe.'

And he was gone.

Fagin sighed. Bill was such a violent man when crossed, he thought, not easy-going and jolly, like Toby Crackit. Now there was a man he took to. Toby gave Fagin time, plenty of time. He didn't hustle him or bully him as Bill did. But there again, Bill was the reliable one. Bill was the cleverer of the two. Bill kept out of clink. So Fagin was prepared to accommodate both him and his idiosyncrasies.

News of a huge theft in rural North London soon penetrated the kens and kitchens of the East End and Sikes kept to his room during the day, only venturing out after dark. Toby had managed to get his share of the haul to Fagin, but only by the skin of his teeth. He was spotted in Hornsey, lugging not only his heavy bag, but one of the sacks as well, by a couple of shopkeepers idling away a slack hour outside an emporium. They evidently thought he looked suspicious and called out to him. Toby had taken fright and escaped up a convenient alleyway. Sikes had been furious that Toby had taken such risks.

'Why the blazes did yer bring the sack with yer?' he shouted, the day Toby came to see him. 'We agreed we should leave 'em both buried till later. You must 'ave looked a right prat strugglin' along from Winchmore ter London like a bloomin' chapman. Anybody stop you an' buy one?'

Toby ignored the taunts. He knew he had been stupid to take such an awful risk. But he had had a strange feeling that if they left the sacks of silver buried, they would never see them again. But he could only manage to bring one with him.

Sikes went on: 'You're a bloody liability, Toby, you really are. I don't know why I keep you on. We're goin' ter end up in the jug again, if we ain't careful. Correction – if *you* ain't careful.'

Toby had nothing to say. Sikes stood menacingly over him.

'Listen 'ere, Toby,' he said quietly. Toby shuddered at the tone. 'I ain't goin' into any details, but I spent seven years o' my life in the worst 'ole anywhere in the world. An' if I really like to think about why I was there, it all comes down to a certain blower wot you introduced – and trusted. Wot you gave me to understand was a close file. She wasn't, was she? But it was your doin'. Seven years, Toby. Seven years. That's an 'ell of a long time.'

He stopped. Toby stared at him. Sikes seemed to be making a decision. Suddenly, he took off his jacket and waistcoat and began undoing the buttons of his shirt.

'E's gorn mad, thought Toby. 'E's goin' ter do summat daft. He watched in fascinated horror as Sikes peeled his shirt over his head.

''Ere, look at this,' said Sikes and he turned round and presented his back to Toby.

Toby had never seen anything like it. Sikes noted the intake of breath with satisfaction. He put on his shirt again.

'Was that – was that – the cat?' asked Toby nervously.

'It was,' replied Sikes. 'Sixty-five strokes in all. Forty of 'em in one go.'

'Christ, Bill! Why?'

'Never mind the whys an' wherefores. Enough for you to know that that was part of my punishment. While you was kicking yer 'eels in Newgate fer two years.'

Toby thought Sikes was being rather unfair, but the revelation prevented any further comment. Except for Sikes to say, 'So just be careful, me ole friend. Or we'll 'ave ter work alone.'

Toby departed, suitably chastened and temporarily deflated. The vision of Sikes's scored back stayed with him for a very long time and served as a brake to what would have been some of his more foolish moves.

Once the silver was in Fagin's hands, the two cracksmen laid low, until the hue and cry died down. The burglary was reported in several London papers and the police were sent up to Winchmore Hill to augment the searches of the local constables, so there was no question of retrieving the remainder of the silver from the cottage floor.

Fagin fussed and fretted about the hidden goods, urging Sikes and Toby to go back for them. But neither man was going to risk the drop for a surfeit of silver with so many beaksmen about. Then, almost a week after the crack, the hidden hoard was unearthed. When he heard, Fagin set up a loud keening at the thought of such treasures going back to their owner. Sikes merely shrugged his shoulders and opened his third bottle of beer. Toby, who was with him in Fagin's kitchen, was already in a maudlin state and dropped his head on his arms, sobbing softly.

THIRTEEN

It was gone midnight when Sikes finally staggered down the stairs from Fagin's den, followed at a distance by his dog, who knew better than to keep too close to his master's heel after a long drinking bout. Suddenly Bull's-eye's attention was diverted by a huddle in a doorway. He stopped and sniffed, looked towards Sikes's retreating back and barked.

'Burn me, if I don't send you ter perdition, Bull's-eye! Wot the blazes is it now?' But Sikes retraced his steps nevertheless.

In the doorway sat a shapeless hunched shadow. He bent down to look. There was little enough light to see by, but he knew it for a female form and the smell of gin was rank. Tentatively, he put out a hand and felt the body, which trembled beneath his touch. The rain, which had fallen most of the evening, had ceased, but the clothes he touched were soaking. He couldn't see the face, but a low keening came from the depths of the body.

He stood up, looking at this degraded human creature. He couldn't do anything. There were hundreds like her and he wasn't a philanthropist, by nature or habit. He was about to walk on, when the woman shifted, aware, maybe, that someone was near. Sikes was struck by something familiar about her. His stomach contracted with a strange fear and he felt the sweat break out on his lip. He bent down again and spoke.

'You all right, gal?' he asked lamely.

His voice was rough, none of the niceties of gentility about it. The face that was raised towards his own made him draw breath quickly.

'Oh Christ! Nancy! Wot in 'ell's name yer doin' 'ere?'

'Mr Sikes?' she whispered hoarsely.

416

Her body shook with cold and fright. The face that stared out at him from the mass of tangled hair was ghostly in the shadows.

'Aye. Ain't yer got a room ternight, Nancy?'

She shook her head and dropped it back on her knees. Bull's-eye knew that movement of despair and thrust his wet nose under her fingers, but there was no response. He looked up at Sikes and whined. Sikes stared back at him, unseeing, for a moment. His mind was racing, fighting with the fuddled fumes in his head.

'Come on,' he said suddenly, his mind made up. 'Yer comin' 'ome with me,' and he pulled the girl to her feet.

But she fainted away as soon as she stood up and Sikes just caught her before she fell. With ease, he lifted her up and carried her back to Old Nicol Street, only a short distance away, whistling to Bull's-eye to follow.

It was not such an easy matter finding his key and unlocking his door, burdened as he was with the half-conscious Nancy. But at last the door swung open and Bull's-eye shot past him and went straight to the dying embers of the fire. Once inside, Sikes kicked the door closed, laid the girl on the bed, lit a lamp and relocked the door. He threw a handful of coals on to the fire and the dog looked up at him, his eyes twinkling in the orange flames. There was a little brandy in the pantry and Sikes poured some into a tankard and carried it unsteadily to the bed. He stood a moment, swaying slightly.

Despite the tawdry jewellery and spangling on her dress, the kohl and rouge which had smudged on her face like a sad theatrical mask, and the wet hair clinging to her head and shoulders, he saw that she was really quite pretty and he felt the familiar stirring deep inside him. He wondered just how long she had been on the streets. Seeing her now, he reckoned she must be about eighteen or nineteen, so she had probably been living like this for four or five years. He was suddenly filled with self-loathing. He had used girls like her many a time and thought nothing of it. So why was she different?

417

Why had he singled her out? He felt confused. He didn't want complications in his life. He had enough to cope with already, with Fagin on his back over the failure to recover the entire haul from the last crack. Did he really want a woman about the place? Always someone there? Always a bedfellow? He was annoyed with himself. What the hell was he thinking of, anyway? Who said she was staying?

He put out a hand and touched her cheek. She opened her eyes and looked up at the man towering over her. He thought she would dart away like a frightened rabbit. But Nancy saw only concern in his face and she felt she had nothing to fear, as yet, from this man, of whom she had heard much to his discredit. She smiled wanly and Sikes kneeled down and slipped an arm beneath her shoulders, proffering the brandy. She tried to take the tankard from him, but her hands shook and her teeth chattered.

'S-so cold,' she whispered.

Sikes closed his long fingers round hers and steadied the vessel while she drank. She revived a little, resting in the crook of his arm. After a moment, she closed her eyes again and Sikes took away the brandy and laid her down on the pillow. With deft hands, he began to strip away her damp outer clothes. There was a torn lace fichu tucked into the bodice of her dress. As he pulled it away, it tore even further in his hands. He frowned at his clumsiness, but it was a poor, threadbare decoration, anyway, and could hardly have kept the cold from her chest. He looked now to where the fichu had lain and for a moment his eyes were held by the sight of her generous breasts, swelling above the scarlet bodice, in stark contrast to the rest of her body, which lay flat and thin on his bed.

He puzzled for a moment how to undo her dress, but by turning her on her side, he was able to unfasten the hooks at the back and to pull the dress down over her feet, leaving the girl in her shift. Nancy uttered no word of protest, but lay still under his ministrations, which he concluded by pulling the bedclothes over her. Having removed his belt and kicked off his boots, he stirred up the fire, turned out the lamp and slipped fully clothed into the bed, holding the trembling body tightly in his arms. He smoothed her tangled hair with hands roughened by years of hard labour and rested his bristly jaw against her smooth forehead. They were both too far gone for anything more that night, so he might as well lend her the warmth of his body.

It was still dark when he awoke, but dawn was not far away. The palest hint of grey stole through the ill-fitting curtains at the window. Sikes lay looking into the darkness, listening to the steady breathing of the girl beside him. She had not taken a chill and she was no longer cold. In fact, he felt the glow of warmth from her body, which was curled away from him. He turned and stared at her small form hunched beneath the covers. He put his arm around her and gently buried his face in her hair. It was very tangled and in need of washing, but her body smelled all woman and he felt disturbed and excited. He let his hand slip between her breasts and she stirred in his arms and turned towards him. Even in the dark he could sense that her eyes were open. He withdrew his hand.

'Morning already?' she asked sleepily.

'Yus, but it's still early. You feelin' better?'

'Yes. Thank you, Mr Sikes. I – I s'pose I'd better be goin'.'

'You ain't goin' anywhere, my gal. Yer clo'es won't be dry. An' anyway, where would yer go?'

He sensed her smiling into the darkness.

'Oh, I s'pect I'd wander down the tavern. Kick around the markets fer a bit. Find some bus'ness ternight.'

He wanted to touch her again, but hesitated, afraid he might frighten her off.

'Stay 'ere fer a bit, Nancy, will yer?'

'All right. But only till it's light. It was kind o' yer ter take me in last night, but I'll not be a burden on yer time, Mr Sikes.'

'I've got all the time in the world,' he said quietly. 'An' the name's Bill,' he added.

He sensed the smile again and she put her arms around him. He kissed her, slowly and gently, savouring the moment. He felt her body against his own. He wanted her. But there was no hurry. For the moment he was content to explore and caress, waiting for her desire to match his own.

Never had Nancy experienced such pleasure before. Not in all the years she had walked the streets. She had seen them – the timid, the boorish, the perverts, with their endless fetishes. God, how she loathed them all. And always they took her for the same purposes – their own selfish satisfaction. She had learned early on not to expect anything else, no pleasure. She was but a toy or a tool or a vessel, to be played with, used, filled, and then discarded when the game was over. Sometimes the perversions were too much for her, and she would protest or cry. Then she was beaten. Those were the times she hated, even herself and the life which had dragged her so low.

But she had never dreamed it could be as good as this. She had never known her body could rise to such heights. And simply because this man had taken a little trouble with her and had sought to give her a share in the pleasure he so obviously felt. As their bodies met at last in sudden, urgent union, it seemed that some great explosion of electricity was fired between them, fusing them into one pulsating vessel, crying out for release. And all the dammed-up feelings of the years seemed to spill over. And when in her climax Nancy cried out his name, it was as though at last her body had triumphed.

Sikes lay in the aftermath of their lovemaking watching the dawn break, Nancy curled asleep in the crook of his arm, her fair hair strewn across his chest. He was amazed at the speed with which events had happened. He was also very disturbed at his own feelings. Normally once his lust had been assuaged, he thought no more of his woman, and would pay her and leave her. That's what whores were for, wasn't it? What in hell's name, then, had he done, bringing this girl back with him, with no thought of paying her for his pleasure and the feeling that she was going to become a permanent feature in his life? Perhaps it was too much drink; it had addled his thoughts. Or maybe he had sustained some damage to his brain when he took on Tom Seager in that half-baked scheme of Toby's. That was it; he'd had a blow on the head and his brain had gone soft!

But when he thought about it again, he realized this was a new sensation for him. He had bided his time watching this treasure sparkle in the filth of the streets, just out of his reach, waiting for it to drop into the palm of his hand. And now she was here, beside him in his own bed, in his own lodging – his for the taking. Fate had played her into his hands. Perhaps this was what he had come back from Van Diemen's Land for. He was, for a moment, overwhelmed with a sense of protection for the frail creature in his arms.

He turned and looked at her. She was breathing gently, her breasts rising and falling softly. He put out a hand to touch her, but was loath to break her sleep. He let his hand rest lightly on her shoulder and then slid his fingers down over her breast, tracing the outline of the nipple beneath the shift. She woke and their eyes met. He bent his head and kissed her again and she held him close, wallowing in the warmth of his big strong body. And then the gentleness was replaced by a frantic urgency and she wanted him again and drew him on and on and up inside her, until at last they were washed up on the shores of their own passion.

'It's light now,' remarked Nancy, a little later. 'I'd better go. If you'd be good enough ter pay me.'

And she made as if to slip from the bed. Sikes caught her wrist.

'Who said anythink about money? I took you in last night 'cos you'd a' died o' the ague out there. An' wot we done since weren't just fer my benefit, yer know.'

Nancy lay still. Sikes said no more for the moment, but released his hold on her. She was unsure of what to say or do, sensing that perhaps he would make the next move. She had

421

never been in such a situation before. She liked the closeness of his body and turned over to face him again.

'Nance,' said Sikes, lying with his hands under his head and gazing at the dirty ceiling, as though for inspiration. 'I bin thinkin'. I ain't much of a lady's man. I comes an' goes a lot. Sometimes I'm away fer days on end – on bus'ness, you understand.'

Nancy nodded. She lay on her front, her fingers idling with the open neck of Sikes's shirt.

'But I want yer ter come an' live 'ere – with me. I can keep you in wittles an' drink an' a roof over yer 'ead. But yer'll 'ave ter keep yer mouth shut over me job. One word of wot I does for a livin' an' I could be topped.'

Nancy could scarcely believe what she heard. All the hopes and fantasies of her years on the streets were about to come true. This man was offering to give her a home. He wouldn't marry her, she knew that; this sort never did. But he would be her protector and she would be his woman. No, she corrected herself, his lover. She would love him, she was sure. She had no illusions, though. She knew life would be hard, just like it always had been. She knew he was a criminal, living on the edge of the Law, on the fringes of society, like the rest of them. She knew she would suffer, he would probably beat her. But it would be no more than she was used to already and maybe not as bad. She would risk that. He must be older than her by some fifteen years at least; he was experienced, toughened by a hard life, of which she knew nothing. But then, weren't they all hardened by the life they led?

She was aware of his stern gaze on her.

'Can I trust yer, Nance? I mean really trust yer? If I thought yer'd blown the gaff, I'd slit yer throat, no second thoughts. I'm known as a violent man, but only when I'm roused, as yer'll find out if yer crosses me.' He looked at her with something akin to gentleness in his face. 'But I couldn't bear ter see yer sleepin' on the streets ev'ry night. It ain't right fer a gal.'

'I'd like ter stay with yer, Bill,' she said, 'but I'm so used ter wand'rin' the drags, I don't know if I'd be able ter settle to livin' under one roof with one man.' She laughed. 'But I'm willin' ter give it a try. An' I can always dip the odd garret or two to 'elp pay me way!'

Sikes held her face hard. 'Never mind that,' he growled menacingly, 'can I trust yer? That's the most important thing.'

Nancy looked at him with a growing mixture of emotions. 'You can trust me with yer life, Bill.'

Sikes continued to gaze into her eyes for a moment, then released the pressure of his hand and kissed her, lingeringly. Nancy held him tightly. He was her man and she meant to keep him. But she knew she would have to be careful.

They finally rose from the tumbled bed, and Sikes raked up the fire and found bacon and beer for their breakfast. Nancy's dress was still damp and her thin, tattered shawl would afford her little warmth. Sikes pulled a blanket from the bed and wrapped her in it while she ate. She felt a small surge of smug satisfaction, to be sitting here in a man's lodging, eating breakfast and knowing that she had no need to go out on to the streets to earn her next night's roof.

'Yer'd better stay there, at least fer this mornin',' said Sikes, as he took away her empty plate. 'Yer clo'es won't be dry yet awhile. An' them shoes is no good; yer need boots, my gal.'

Nancy laughed and her wan face was transformed.

'Surely I ain't goin' ter need boots if I'm comin' off the streets, Bill?'

Sikes did not answer. He was not sure whether she would stay. He was not even sure if he had done the right thing. But he had given her a temporary home and he would set her up with some new clothes to keep out the cold. It was the least he could do.

When he had cleared away their plates and mugs, Sikes pulled on his top boots and greatcoat and jammed his hat on his head.

'I'm goin' out fer a bit,' he announced. 'I'll see yer later. Don't get cold.' And he whistled his dog.

423

As he opened the door, Sikes took his key from his pocket with the intention of locking the girl in. He hesitated, then replaced the key. He was aware of Nancy's eyes on him as he stood in the doorway.

'Don't yer trust me, then, Bill?' Her voice was low, almost mocking. He turned and she was right behind him. 'I won't run away, yer know.'

And standing on tiptoe, for he was a good head and shoulders taller than she, she put her hands on his cheeks and kissed him briefly and gently. He looked down at her, the faintest hint of a smile playing at the corner of his mouth. Then he swung away down the stairs, leaving Nancy to close the door quietly behind him.

FOURTEEN

Sikes left the lodging house that morning with the intention of filching some items of clothing for Nancy from the markets. But the more he thought about it, the less he liked the idea. He was strangely elated by the events of the last twelve hours and not a little surprised at himself. And the thought of giving Nancy only second best seemed somehow cheap and degrading. He would buy her the best he could afford; Fagin would soon pay him his share of the Winchmore Hill crack and he would easily recoup any expense. And he wanted to show the girl he cared about her.

And so when he turned off into Petticoat Lane, he didn't look for items he could surreptitiously stuff into his greatcoat, but made for the stalls which sold good strong boots and new woollen shawls.

At the shoe stall he stood irresolute. There was a bewildering array of footwear, from men's heavy working boots to children's tiny button-sided affairs, and in between were the light boots favoured by the fairer sex. But he had no idea how big or small her feet were. The coster saw him picking up boots and putting them down again.

''Avin' trouble with the size, mate?' the man called cheerfully.

Sikes looked up and nodded.

''Ow tall's the lady?'

Sikes thought for a minute and remembered resting his face on the top of her head. He indicated a point halfway up his chest.

''Bout up to 'ere.'

The coster reached for a pair of boots at the side of the stall.

'These ought ter fit 'er. Two shillin's the pair. Luvly quality. Last 'er a lifetime.'

Sikes examined the little boots. They were of neat grey leather, with matching buttons up the side. He knew they were a bargain here; he would have paid twice the price in a shoemaker's shop.

'I'll take 'em,' said Sikes.

He handed the coster a sovereign and the man raised his eyebrows and bit the coin. But he made no comment, counted out the change into Sikes's hand, and parcelled up the little boots. Sikes tucked them possessively under his arm.

Most of the stalls here were for second-hand clothing, the speciality of this market, but stalls were springing up of late, like the shoe stall, which sold new items at vastly undercut prices. Sikes, being taller than most of his fellow Londoners, could see above the heads of the crowds and he watched, amused, as young pickpockets had a field day. He thought he saw one of Fagin's young protégés, but he couldn't be certain.

He had travelled almost the length of the street without finding what he wanted and was about to give up, when he found himself by a large stall, selling lace and ribbons, ladies' gloves and stockings, and a colourful array of garters. Hanging at the back of the stall were a number of large, fine woollen shawls in a variety of colours and patterns.

''Ow much yer askin' fer them shawls?' enquired Sikes of the coster, nodding towards the items in question.

'Two shillin's an' sixpence,' came the reply. 'They're luvly, an't they, sir? Made in Hindia, with all the colours of the East. Good quality, too. Finest cashmere. Keep yer lady warm fer the rest of 'er days.'

Sikes thought the woman's patter sounded weary and overworked and he doubted the origin of the shawls. But he asked her to hand him down a cream shawl with a design of glorious poppies all over it and small blue cornflowers round its fringed border. He pictured it round Nancy's shoulders and liked what he saw. He paid his money and the woman wrapped up the shawl in thin paper and string.

Feeling pleased with his morning's purchases, Sikes set off for The Three Cripples. He could have bought food and drink nearer home, but he hoped he would see Toby. He needed to talk to Toby about a new crack and, besides, he wanted to be sure that Fagin was about the business of fencing their latest haul, which Toby would know.

The Three Cripples was emptier than usual, but Barney was there, cleaning up after the previous night's debauch, and he greeted Sikes affably. Several of Fagin's boys were seated round the big central table, ladling hot stew into their hungry mouths, and a familiar figure was propping up the bar. Sikes walked over to him, ignoring the nudges and grins of the boys. He rested his elbows on the bar and Toby Crackit looked up, his long pale face enlivened by an amused expression.

'Hallo, Bill. We was just talkin' about you,' began Toby.

'Oh yeah?' growled Sikes.

Even Barney seemed to bow and scrape obsequiously as he asked Sikes what he wanted. Alerted by all this bonhomie, Sikes became suspicious and his temper rose.

'Stop yer grinnin' an' scrapin', blast yer, an' get me two big 'ot pies an' four bottles o' beer.'

There was a snort of suppressed laughter from the boys and Toby and Barney could not help smiling. They failed, for once, to see the danger signs in Sikes's eyes.

'Wot the blazes are you all smirkin' at?' he demanded, turning a fierce expression on them each in turn. 'Wot's so funny about a bloke orderin' 'is dinner? Eh?'

Charley Bates was at the table and went off into peals of uncontrollable laughter and there was more rib-digging and winking among the lads. Sikes lost his temper completely and banged his fist on the bar, making the glasses jump.

'Christ Almighty!' he roared. 'I'll thrash the life out o' the lot of yer if yer don't shut up!'

The laughter ceased abruptly and Barney scurried in with

the food and beer. Sikes slapped down some coins and pocketed the viands.

'Wot are you up to?' asked Toby in a low voice.

'Strike me blind,' breathed the exasperated Sikes. 'Wot is all this?'

Toby shrugged. 'Search me,' he said. 'But there's a rumour goin' round that you've bin a-screwin' Nancy an' –'

Toby Crackit did not look quite so flash lying flat on his back with a split and bleeding lip and a large swelling developing on his mouth. By the time he had struggled to his feet with the aid of one of the boys, there was no sign of Sikes. Toby's pride and his feelings were hurt as much as his mouth. Sikes had always been a difficult party, and Toby could only think that Sikes was serious about the girl and that the rumours, which had reached the Cripples ahead of him, were true.

'Delicate sitiwation there,' Toby announced to Barney, holding a handkerchief to his lip.

'Hah, hah!' shouted Charley Bates. 'Our Bill's in love!' And the boys began laughing again.

''Ush,' hissed Barney. 'You be careful wod you say id front of Bister Sikes. 'E's a werry daydgerous gedleman when 'e's roused, has you cad see.'

'Yeah, you be careful, Charley,' said one of the boys. 'I thought 'e wos goin' ter take a swing at you. Good job 'e don't know 'oo started the rumour, ain't it, Charley?'

Charley it was who had seen Sikes leave his lodging that morning and had dogged his footsteps through the market, noting the items he bought. When he had rushed into the tavern and announced to all what he had seen, Toby had revealed that his friend was showing an interest in Miss Nancy. And so they had all put two and two together. They sat in pained silence now, the incident having quite dispersed their laughter. They finished their dinner, subdued and chastened for once.

By this time, Sikes was striding away towards Bethnal Green, the bottles chinking in his pockets, the heat of the pies adding to his overheated temper. Passers-by made way for the tall man with the fierce black expression and he knew he was drawing attention to himself. He ought to go down to the river to calm himself, but he wanted to get back to his room, to see *her* again. All the same, he didn't want to go back to her angry. So he continued up the main road and found himself at length by the railings of St Leonard's churchyard. There was no one in the churchyard and he found the gate and went in, his feet taking him automatically to the far corner beneath the row of lime trees, now standing bare and leafless, their branches clawing towards the sky.

There were many green, unmarked mounds, but he knew exactly which was hers, despite the intervening years. He stood for a moment, his heart still racing with anger. Then he crouched down on his haunches, his hands gripping each other, his teeth sunk into his fingers in an effort to control himself.

'Oh Mother,' he whispered, almost inaudibly.

But he sensed her nearness; they had been so close. She alone had loved him, had shown him real affection, and in his worst moments he remembered her still.

Now he muttered through clenched teeth. 'I shouldn't 'ave 'it 'im. 'E's a good friend. But she's mine now an' I won't 'ave no one talkin' ill of 'er, or me. I wonder who saw me take 'er in?'

Whoever it was, their liaison was no secret now and he wondered how he would face the drinkers at the tavern. This was why he had steered clear of the local girls in the past; your business became everybody else's, especially at The Three Cripples. Well, he would show them what he was made of; they wouldn't trifle with him for long.

He wondered what his mother would think of the life he led; he thought she would understand, because he was so like his father. He rested his hand momentarily on her grave and the grass felt wet and cold and springy beneath his touch. A chill little wind sprang up and the dead lime leaves rustled above Fanny Sikes's remains. Her youngest surviving son stood up, his temper restored, his thoughts calmed. He touched his hat and turned away; but it was as though his mother called out softly behind him.

'Keep 'er, Bill. She'll love yer, just as I did. Yer don't need me now. You take 'er into yer 'eart instead. She'll give you all the love an' affection yer've bin without all these years. Just trust 'er. She won't let you down.'

He stood rooted, his eyes dilated. He even turned and looked fearfully behind him. But he was alone and his mother's grave was silent and still.

He hurried home, his collar turned up against the wind blowing from behind, and when he reached his lodging, he leaped up the flimsy staircase, two at a time, and burst into the room, full of joyful anticipation.

It was empty.

He stood irresolute, his eyes suddenly hard and narrowed. Where the hell had she scuttled off to? He emptied his pockets, put the pies and beer in the larder and the packages he dumped unopened on the bed. He looked around again, thinking she might be hiding somewhere. But there was nowhere to hide. He went to the window, but there was no sign of her outside. He clattered down to the courtyard and then back upstairs again. He sat down, he stood up, he poked the fire. He shouted at Bull's-eye. And still she didn't come. He began to panic. He heard a child wail and the sounds of others stumping up the next door's staircase. He began striding about the room. Where in the name of Old Nick was the girl? He couldn't believe she'd run off, just like that. Yet her old shawl and shoes were gone. He glanced across at the pathetic parcels on the bed. He felt a dreadful fear, low down in the pit of his stomach.

'Oh Gawd!' he moaned. 'Why don't I ever 'ave any luck with women? One little ray of 'appiness an' it's snatched away from me.'

He turned away and leaned his head against the mantelpiece, one booted foot resting on the fender. And it was then that he heard her tread on the stair and turned to face the open door.

430

FIFTEEN

After Sikes had left his lodgings, Nancy sat for a long while, wrapped in the coarse blanket, which smelled comfortingly of its owner. She rubbed her cheek against its male roughness, so like his own ill-shaven jaw, and felt again the heady joy of security. She sat in one of the armchairs by the fire and gazed into the flames, watching the changing shapes licking about the lumps of coal. This was sheer bliss; the only time she ever saw a fire these days was on the rare occasions when she visited Fagin's den, or when Barney deigned to light the big fire in the parlour of the Cripples; and then it was always the men who took up all the space in front of it. There was plenty of coal in the scuttle here.

On the mantelpiece was a small carriage clock in a brass case, ticking away quietly to itself, a tinderbox, two candle-sticks with half-burnt candles in them, and a strange box. Nancy's curiosity was aroused. She slipped out of the blanket and lifted the box carefully from the shelf, settling it gently on her lap as she resumed her seat.

It was a small box, one which would fit easily into a man's coat-pocket, and was made of a reddish wood, curiously carved on the top. There was no lock and when she lifted the lid, a strong aroma of pine assailed her nostrils. She closed her eyes and held the box to her nose, breathing in the strange foreign fragrance. The smell conjured up for her deep forests and craggy hillsides, scenes she had only ever seen in pictures or heard of in travellers' tales.

Inside the box was a silver button, its pattern of scrollwork tarnished and black; a lock of light brown hair, tied with a length of fine black thread; and a piece of paper, yellow and faded, folded small to fit in the box. Nancy's hands hesitated, but the box had not been locked and she found herself carefully unfolding a brief letter, written in a firm, educated-looking hand. At the bottom, it was signed 'W. S.' This much she could work out, but the contents of the letter were beyond her capabilities. Nancy refolded the letter thoughtfully. Here was a mystery indeed. Who was W. S.? Not Bill, surely. And anyway, why should he keep a letter from himself? She had no idea, even, whether he could read or write. She replaced the contents as she had found them and returned the box to the shelf. As she did so, her hand brushed the mantelshelf, leaving a clear swathe in its dusty surface. She smiled to herself. The place certainly lacked a female hand, but its furnishings were adequate and comfortable, if not exactly fashionable. The chairs on either side of the fireplace did not match, but both had deep wings and you could sink comfortably down into their depths. They were upholstered in thick old tapestry, one in brown, the other in green and the arms and backs were worn and grubby from long usage. There was a scrubbed deal table in the middle of the room, only it was some time since it had last seen a scrubbing brush on its pitted and stained surface. It contained a drawer full of assorted cutlery on one side. Two Windsor chairs stood at an untidy angle to it.

The bed in which they had slept was too big for a man on his own and Nancy wondered at the frequency of pairs of things in this room; almost as though he had been expecting her, knowing she would come here eventually. She went over to the bed now and plumped up the pillows. On an impulse, she laid her face where his head had been; the smell of him lingered there. She smoothed the rumpled sheets and straightened the blankets and coverlet. As she did so, her foot struck an empty tankard lying on the floor, and it rolled a little way under the bed. She went down on her hands and knees to retrieve it and in reaching for it, her hand encountered a large wooden chest. She peered into the dusty gloom and saw that the chest almost filled the height of the space beneath the bed and had massive clasps and a formidable lock. She pushed at it, but it remained immobile. This was one box she was not going to be able to investigate.

She scrambled to her feet, dusting her shift and her hands, and went back to the fire. She was feeling cold again and the coals were burning low. She was impressed to find a pair of tongs in the scuttle and when she had stoked up a good blaze, she inspected her clothes, which Sikes had draped over the backs of the fireside chairs. Her dress was dry but rather crumpled and she wondered how her lace fichu had become so torn; but it was such a tawdry old thing that she wasted no second thoughts on it. With her dress on again and her shabby shawl wrapped about her shoulders she felt better. Her shoes were still damp and she stood them on their sides nearer to the fire. She didn't remember Sikes taking off her stockings and garters, but there they were, drying alongside her dress and shawl. For an instant, she felt abashed that he had removed such intimate items of clothing from her; she was acutely aware of the relationship between them and it made her realize that this was no impersonal one-night stand. Today she was no longer a prostitute, a common whore, earning her money on the mean streets. Today she belonged to a man; a man who was sufficiently interested in her to save her from certain death, had she remained on those cold, wet streets another night; a man who wanted her to share his pleasure in the very act which had been her livelihood all these years. She thought of him again; so straightforward in his demands, so conservative in his lovemaking, and she thrilled again at the memory of his gentle caresses, caresses which had gradually extended all over her body, seeking out every secret crevice, until, amazed at herself, she could barely wait for him to enter her. A great shudder went through her body at the memory of it and she sighed deeply.

With her stockings on again, Nancy felt warmer and wandered over to the window. There was a bright sky of fast-moving clouds, but the room faced east and the adjoining tenements in Old Nicol street sent black swathes of shadow across this side. It would rain again before nightfall, but the children were taking advantage of the sunshine and she watched them playing in the cobbled yard.

Suddenly Nancy was disturbed by the sounds of angry, raised voices from across the yard. She couldn't distinguish the words, but there was the sound of a sharp smack, perhaps a hand across a cheek, followed by the low sobbing of a woman. A door banged and she heard the clatter of boots down the opposite staircase and a man emerged, his face livid, his fists clenched, and he strode off towards Shoreditch High Street. A few minutes later, a red-eyed woman came out, her four children trailing after her. She stopped to speak to them and then disappeared in the same direction as the man, leaving her offspring in the yard. Nancy felt such a pang of pity for the children, but they seemed happy enough and the youngest found a friend to play with, while the older ones drifted about and eventually took themselves off to play elsewhere. A sudden sound of footsteps outside her door made Nancy turn sharply from the window, but the sound went on up to the next floor and faded away.

It was just after half-past eleven and Sikes would not be back yet, she was sure. She felt the need for air; and, besides, she desperately needed to relieve herself. Wrapping her shawl tightly round her shoulders, she pushed her feet into her shoes. They were warm, but still damp, and felt uncomfortable; but she was used to discomforts and the ground outside was drying fast. She let herself out and made her way down the creaky staircase. In the hallway she found the back door and went out into the narrow passageway, which ran along the backs of the houses. Halfway up the alley stood a very small shed. She could hardly believe her eyes. A privy! Such luxuries were unknown on the streets, where she was accustomed to using the nearest gutter. She picked her way over the mud and filth in the alley and pushed open the door. It was dark and very smelly, but the chance of answering nature's call, in private for once, filled her with unaccountable joy.

Out in the fresh air once more, Nancy drifted along the

neighbouring streets catching glimpses of the busy traffic on the High Road. There were two men lounging on the corner of an alley and they were beginning to take an interest in her. For the first time in years, she turned her back on prospective clients and returned to the relative safety of the lodging-house courtyard. She was about to go back inside when, above the chatter of the children, there arose a sudden wail. A tiny girl was lying on the cobbles, her face distorted with pain and weeping. Nancy ran to her and gathered her up into her arms, cradling the curly head against her shoulder, talking softly, chastizing the 'naughty cobbles' which had tripped her up. Soon the child stopped crying, but her breathing was punctuated by little sobs and her dirty hands had streaked her tear-stained face. Nancy carried her to a nearby step and sat down with the girl on her lap. The other children, who had temporarily stopped their activities to watch, now resumed their games. Littl'uns were always falling down. You couldn't be forever bothering about them. They survived, if they were strong enough. They all did, if disease didn't carry them off first.

'Wot's yer name, luvvy?' asked Nancy, brushing the damp curls from the child's face.

'Annie,' came the small reply.

'That's funny. That's my name, too. Only they call me Nancy.'

'Nice lady.'

The child played with the ragged fringing on Nancy's shawl, winding the pulled ends around her fingers.

'Where's yer mother, Annie?'

'Workin'.'

'You got any brothers or sisters?'

'Yuss. But they gone 'way ter play.'

'Where d'yer live, Annie?'

'Up there.'

The little fingers pointed to a grimy window above them on the top floor. It was where Nancy had heard the row earlier. She looked at the baby face still raised anxiously to her home and had an overwhelming desire to hold the child close. The little mite must have sensed her feelings, for she suddenly threw her thin arms around Nancy's neck and hugged her very tightly. Nancy laid her cheek against the small head and the tears sprang to her eyes. Oh Gawd, she thought, I do so want a babe of my own. But if I 'ad one, 'e'd probably drop me straight away. 'E wouldn't want no littl'uns runnin' under 'is feet.

She sniffed and the toddler sat back and looked into her face with the clear and direct gaze of childhood.

'Don't cry, Nan,' she lisped. 'You un'appy?'

Nancy forced a smile. 'Not really, Annie. Actually, I've bin feelin' very 'appy this mornin'. I was just thinkin' it was a shame you 'ad ter stay on yer own; yer so little. But I s'pect yer brothers an' sisters'll be back soon.'

'Oh yus,' replied Annie. 'They always come back at dinner time.' And Annie laughed, her spill on the cobbles quite forgotten.

She clambered from Nancy's lap and ran off, turning to wave before sitting down to play in a puddle near the midden.

Nancy turned away and climbed the stairs thoughtfully. When she reached the landing, she found the door of Sikes's room standing open and an angry Sikes facing her.

'Where the blazes 'ave you bin?' he roared and now she saw the fierce glitter in his eyes, that dangerous light which she was to learn must not be stoked.

'I – I went fer a little walk. I wanted some fresh air.'

'Wotcher want ter do that for?' He was still shouting at her. 'I thought yer'd run off!'

So, she thought, that was it. He really was in earnest and he had been scared! He really did want her for himself. Secretly, she hugged the knowledge to her.

'Couldn't yer trust me, Bill? I said I'd stay. I meant it.' She lowered her eyes and added quietly, 'Besides, I needed the privy.'

The fire in his eyes went out as surely as though a bucket of cold water had been thrown over it. Visibly he relaxed as he came over to her and stood with his hands resting on her shoulders. How she welcomed his very presence again. He stared into her eyes and then kissed her, holding her face tightly in his hands.

Just as suddenly, he broke away from her, kicked the door shut and said, 'Come an' see wot I got for yer.'

She followed him to the bed and he put the parcels into her hands. She undid the smaller of the two and gasped at the riot of colour which spilled from the paper. Open-mouthed and speechless she stood while Sikes gathered up the shawl, folded it neatly from corner to corner, pulled off the old and wrapped the new round her thin shoulders.

'There,' he said, satisfied with his efforts. 'That'll keep out the cold. An' these'll keep yer feet dry,' he continued, unwrapping the boots. 'Sit down, gal.'

Nancy sat on the bed and Sikes began putting the little boots on her feet. He looked up.

'Fit all right?'

She nodded, her eyes bright. Speech had failed her. Sikes began buttoning up one of the boots and she hitched up her skirts, so that he could see what he was doing. She studied his bent head and the way the hair curled on his neck caused a strange sensation inside her. She wanted to pull his head against her breasts and to hold him there. Sikes must have sensed her thoughts, for suddenly he stopped in the midst of his task and stared at her black-stockinged leg. Then he let his hands slide up her calf and over her knee, pushing up her skirt as he did so. Above the scarlet garter, he met the bare flesh of her thigh and she heard the sharp intake of his breath. Her own body was reeling with the wonderful new sensation of being wanted for her own sake. In a reckless urge, she held his head against her thighs, feeling the heat of his breath on them. Time hung suspended again. He toyed with her, caressed her and touched off those new-found sparks of desire in her. In one swift movement, he had her beneath him on the bed and she was begging for him to enter her. When they both climaxed together, she thought the waves inside her would never cease; she wanted them to go on and on, so that she could live every second in this ecstasy. But at last the spasm subsided and they lay damp and exhausted in each other's arms.

Presently, Sikes raised himself on his elbows, taking his weight from her small body. He studied her thoughtfully, as she traced the outline of his jaw with her finger.

'You always come like that?' he asked.

Nancy smiled at the directness of his question.

'No,' she said softly. 'It ain't ever bin like that afore.' Sikes eyed her doubtfully.

'Honest,' she insisted. And then added, 'No regrets at takin' me in?'

Sikes shook his head. 'Long as you keep your side o' the bargain.'

Here it was again. The doubt, almost fear, in his voice, the anxiety creeping through. The thought crossed Nancy's mind that he was a pretty desperate character; she wondered if he had a price on his head. She rather thought not, but she realized he had not taken her into his home lightly. Well, she would show him how much he meant to her; she could keep a silent tongue in her head when required. Meanwhile, she would make herself useful, so that he would not regret her presence.

SIXTEEN

It was a good ten days before Fagin paid Sikes for the silver haul from Winchmore Hill and Sikes had flung away from the Field Lane lodging angry and disgusted at Fagin's reluctance to pay up on time. However, he had his money at last and it would keep him and Nancy in lodgings and victuals for several months to come. Even so he would have to keep an eye to the future if they were to survive the leanest months of the year.

He returned to old Nicol Street in good spirits, his confrontation with his fence forgotten, sovereigns jingling in his pocket, the paper money fast against his breast. He opened the door and found Nancy mending some breeches she had discovered in the chest of drawers. She looked up and smiled.

'You don't mind, Bill?'

He frowned for a moment, then shook his head. She'd been poking about, but that was inevitable. He had few possessions, but he wondered what she had found. She had his other clothes on the table before her and he saw she had darned his mittens and scarf, ready for winter.

He was taking off his coat, when Nancy said quietly, 'Wot 'appened ter this, Bill?'

He turned sharply. She had his blood-stained shirt in her hand. He did not answer immediately. He hung up his coat on the back of the door, playing for time. He wasn't used to divulging his private life; but Nancy was part of his life now, he had ensured that. He would have to share some of his secrets with her if they were going to live together.

'I took part in the Fancy last January – you know, prize-fightin'. It was a scheme of Toby's. I was short o' blunt. Stood in fer some toff from Lunnon who failed ter turn up. I

439

'ad ter fight the local champion, Tom Seager. Big bloke 'e was. Bashed me about a bit, but I beat 'im.' There was a pride in his voice which he couldn't hide. 'I was in a bit of a mess. That's wot that is. I couldn't get it out.'

He turned and looked at her, sheepishly, almost apologetically, and her heart went out to him. How she wished she had been there to bathe his wounds and wipe away the blood. He was like a young boy, discovered trying to hide some misdemeanour, and she wanted to hold him close. Instead, she lowered her eyes and her fingers played with the spoiled garment.

'Never mind,' she murmured, 'it'll do fer rag, or bandages, or somethink useful.' She met his eyes again. 'Is that where the bruise on yer nose came from?' she asked shyly.

Automatically, Sikes's fingers went to the bridge of his nose.

'Yuss,' he said, 'partly. But I've bin 'it there more than once. I'm surprised it ain't broken yet!'

He laughed and came and stood by her, playing with her hair. His touch thrilled her and she could no longer continue her sewing.

Now Sikes said, 'Fagin's paid up at last, the ole skinflint. So we've plenty ter see us through the winter – if we're careful.'

He went over to where he had hung his coat and retrieved the coins. He dropped them in a careless heap on the table, then felt in the inside pocket of his waistcoat and brought out two folded notes. Nancy's eyes widened.

'Bill!' she breathed. ''Ow did yer get all that off 'im? I ain't seen so much money in all me life! 'Ow much is there?'

'Should be ten quid in notes an' fifteen sovereigns,' replied Sikes and he began counting it through.

Nancy picked up one of the white notes and studied it. There was a little medallion picture of a woman swathed in long garments and she seemed to be holding a palm leaf in one hand and a spear in the other. There was a crown above her head and the date, 1835, split up on either side of her.

There was a great deal of writing, in florid, swirling letters all over the note, some numbers and a couple of signatures.

'Wot does it say, Bill?' asked Nancy. 'Can you read it?'

'Yus. That's Britannia there, an' it's got a number an' the date. See. An' it says as the Guvner of the Bank of England'll pay the bearer the sum o' five pounds.'

He held the note to the light from the window, so that she could see it clearly and their heads touched, ever so little, sending a thrill of anticipation through them both. Sikes pushed the gold coins towards her.

''Ere,' he said, 'you count 'em. Make sure there are fifteen of 'em.'

He watched her covertly, as she gingerly touched the coins, counting under her breath and checking the numbers with her fingers. When she came to the eleventh, she was at a loss. Sikes grinned and placed his hand by hers, the fingers spread out.

'Borrow mine,' he said softly.

She flushed momentarily, but he wasn't making fun of her and she loved him for it. For each of the remaining five sovereigns, she touched one of his fingers. But it was a slow process, for she was distracted by the warmth of his hand and she found herself studying his long fingers, his pared but grimy fingernails, the cuts and scabs on his knuckles. But at last she reached the fifteenth coin and looked up brightly.

'They're all here, Bill. 'E's not made a mistake.'

'I should bloody well 'ope not,' snorted Sikes. 'Now. I'll show yer where I keep it all, just in case anythink should 'appen ter me.'

Nancy laid a hand on his arm.

'Don't, Bill,' she whispered urgently, 'don't speak of such things.'

'I'll show yer anyway,' he went on gruffly and dragged out the heavy chest from under the bed.

He went to the mantelshelf and took a key from under one of the candlesticks. With this he unlocked the chest and threw back the lid. Nancy came and stood by him and looked

441

at the contents: a large and a small jemmy, several lengths of rope, some sacks, a strong sheath knife, a set of picklocks and – oh God! – a brace of heavy pistols with ammunition, wadding and tinder. She drew back in horror and looked fearfully at her lover.

'Wot is it all, Bill?' she whispered. 'Wot does it all mean?' She was reluctant to have her worst fears confirmed.

'That's how I earn me livin',' he said simply. 'I'm a cracksman, a housebreaker. Me an' Toby, we're in it ter-gether. I keeps me blunt 'ere, too.'

And he stowed away his latest takings in a tin at the bottom of the chest, retaining two sovereigns in his breeches pocket. He looked up at Nancy.

'Didn't yer guess, gal?'

'I wasn't sure, Bill. I – I thought it might be summat like this. But the barkers, Bill. Wot they for? You don't use 'em, do yer?'

'Sometimes I 'as to,' he muttered, closing up the chest, and there was a silence between them.

Sikes had opened up a door into his private life, perhaps the most important one, and she respected it. No wonder he relied so heavily on her trust. Gawd, she thought, if I were ter tell wot I'd seen, 'e'd be dead come Monday. She looked across at him as he stood up, tall, strong, good-looking in a rugged sort of way. She could never betray him. To think that her tongue and the box beneath the bed on which they made love were all that stood between Bill Sikes and the gallows. She closed her eyes and saw him dangling at the end of a rope and a cry caught in her throat.

'Nancy! You all right, gal?'

She flung herself against him and he held her tightly, stroking her hair again. It needed a good brushing, he reflected. But Nancy did not seem to possess brush or comb, although during the day she would pin back her hair from her face with fancy clips. It was almost Christmas. He was flush with money. He would buy her a brush and a comb and she would look beautiful.

They sat by the fire, one on either side, Bull's-eye between them, and there was a companionable silence in the dingy room. Nancy resumed her sewing and Sikes sat for a while staring into the fire. He was well contented. He had done the right thing after all. He had brought the girl in off the streets and he enjoyed having someone to share his home with. No man is an island and though Sikes eschewed noisy crowds, he was basic and human enough to want company. He had been lonely for so many years now that the joy of having someone to come home to was almost too much to bear. His heart swelled with pride and felt fit to burst in his broad chest. He glanced across at his lover. The firelight caught the nimbus of her hair and he fancied she sat there veiled in spun gold. She was beautiful, he told himself, and she was his. The devil take any man who tried to steal her from him. He felt the anger stirring within him and smiled at his readiness to jump to her defence. This was a different Bill Sikes, he reflected. He'd never thought of any woman as he thought of Nancy. Whether or not he loved her, he couldn't say, not yet. He had not addressed himself to the question. But what he felt for her was certainly far beyond his experience and understanding.

'I spoke with Barney terday,' he said eventually, 'an' 'e says the landlord could do with some 'elp over Christmas. You int'rested?'

'Yes, Bill, I am. Jus' servin' in the tavern is it?'

He nodded.

'When does 'e want me ter start?'

'Yer can start ternight, if yer want. It ain't well paid, but no matter. Bet'll be there too.'

Nancy was delighted. She hadn't seen Bet since Sikes had taken her in.

'I'd like that, Bill. I'll go down when it gets dark.'

'I'll walk yer part o' the way,' said Sikes. 'I've got ter call in on Toby. I'll join yer later.'

They relapsed into silence and Sikes dozed off. Nancy dropped her work in her lap and studied him. In the fading light, she could just make out the dark lashes lying on his tanned and weather-beaten cheeks. Where had he acquired such weathering? Not in England, surely; and she thought again of the little box on the shelf. There was still so much she did not know about him. What of his family? Did he have parents living, or brothers, or sisters? She would ask him in time; it would strengthen the bond between them.

But now the light was fading fast and the fire was dying down. She reached across and touched Sikes's thigh, the corduroy warm and soft beneath her hand; she felt the firm muscle beneath. Sikes opened his eyes and smiled his lopsided smile at her.

'Gettin' dark,' he remarked and sat up, accidentally kicking Bull's-eye as he did so.

The dog growled and moved away.

'Go an' eat yer bone, will yer, you ole rogue,' said Sikes. 'Nancy, let 'im in ter the pantry, will yer?'

Nancy complied and drew the flimsy curtains while she was about it. Sikes poked the fire and raked hot ashes over it.

'There,' he said, 'that'll still be warm when we come 'ome.' He stood up and reached for Nancy as she passed him. 'Come 'ere, Nance,' he growled.

Momentarily surprised by his sudden passion, she hung rigid in his arms and he saw the fear of the streets in her eyes again. He gazed at her in wonder and she relaxed, but her arms were trapped by his embrace.

'Nancy, I still can't believe wot's 'appened,' Sikes said, his voice urgent and rough. 'You won't ever leave me, will yer? I mean . . .' He seemed lost for words. Nancy waited, smiling encouragingly. He tried again. 'I mean, this is just so bloody marvellous. All this. You an' me. Bein' 'ere tergether – all the time.'

Since Nancy's feelings ran in a similar vein to those of Sikes, there was no need for a reply.

SEVENTEEN

◆

It was Christmas Eve and The Three Cripples was very crowded and very noisy that particular evening, though few of the Cripples' customers had anything to be very merry about. The weather was cold, fuel supplies were low, jobs were in short supply and most folk had little ready money in their pockets. But it was an excuse for drinking and a get-together. There was an influx of strangers, too, who had drifted down from the Ratcliffe: several sailors, some with their bawds, others looking for fresh pastures.

Fagin sat alone at a small table, watching the sea of faces around him. Two fellows, well lushed with beer, lurched against his table, almost upsetting his gin.

'Here, take care, my dears,' he said, as he caught at his glass.

The men laughed and one of them leered into his face.

''Fraid we'll pinch yer gin, furriner?' he slurred.

Fagin ignored him and the two louts rolled away to make a nuisance of themselves elsewhere. He was used to taunts. He had spent nearly sixty years in this City and time had mellowed him. Though he remembered, wryly, how he had used his fists as a youngster when the local boys learned where he had come from and what he was by birth. It had taken him many years to repress his indignation, but now the names and spite just rolled off his back and he thought no more about them than if someone had cursed at the fickle English weather.

He saw Nancy pushing her way between the tables, her hands full of empty tankards. Fagin thought he had never seen her look so fresh and happy; and he had known her, how many years was it now? Twelve? Thirteen? My, how the years had flown. He was pleased in some ways that she had taken up with Bill Sikes; she would be a useful buffer between him and Bill, when the latter got too demanding over his money. Sikes had certainly done something for her and he almost envied their relationship. But he doubted its durability. He knew Sikes's temper and he couldn't see Nancy complying with that too often. No, he thought, there'll be blows there before long, as God's my witness.

He watched as Nancy and Bet stood huddled in a corner, their eyes wide and bright, their hands clasped in sisterly affection.

Yes, my dear, said Fagin to himself, tell her all about him. How he saved you from the streets. How kind he is, how he's bought you things. Pretty things. Maybe how good he is in bed. It'll be a different tale in a few months. I know his other side; how cruel he can be, how unreasoning. And God help you if you betray him.

He reached for his gin and his wily old eye caught sight of Bull's-eye planted foursquare at the top of the short staircase which led to the raised gallery. He stood there, surveying the rowdy scene, looked back for an instant, then scampered down the steps and disappeared underfoot. Fagin's eyes never left the stairs and within a few minutes, the heavily clad figure of Sikes appeared. He, too, took stock of the scene before him, scowling in disgust at the noisy crowd, before deliberately making his way to where Fagin sat.

He sat down and dropped his hat on the table, rubbed his hands together and blew on the tips of his fingers, which protruded from his mittens.

'Bloody cold out there ternight. Reckon there'll be snow afore long.'

Fagin eyed him. 'I've got a new idea. For you and Toby.'

'Oh yeah?'

'D'you want to hear my plan now, my boy?'

'I want a drink,' growled Sikes.

'Of course, of course, my dear.'

Fagin hurried from the table and returned a few minutes

446

later carrying two steaming tankards of hot gin, one of which he pushed across the table towards Sikes with his claw-like fingers. Sikes nodded his thanks.

'Wotcher want me ter do then?' asked Sikes.

Fagin began to lay out his plan to the younger man, sketching in the air with his hands and drawing on the table with his finger in the beer slops. Sikes never answered a word, and his eyes were wandering around the packed room. Quite suddenly, Fagin was aware of a change of tempo in the sounds around him. He glanced up at Sikes, but the latter's attention was focused across the room; his eyes, narrowed and smouldering, penetrating the smoke haze to where a scuffle had broken out. Sikes stood up and Fagin watched nervously. He sensed trouble.

A great bull of a sailor had clutched Nancy tightly round the waist and she was hitting futilely at him with her fists.

'Leave me be, you brute,' she shouted. 'I ain't fer sale, nor 'ire no more!'

'Oho, my fine gel, an' why not?' bellowed the sailor, groping at her breasts with his free hand. Fagin heard the hissing intake of air from Sikes. 'You always used ter be. Always willin' on the Ratcliffe when I was in port.'

'Yeah,' drawled another ruffian at his shoulder. 'Why shouldn't we 'ave our pick as usual?'

Nancy struggled in vain to rid herself of the men, but the big sailor had her pinned tightly on his lap. She could smell his foul breath on her face and the coarseness of his body against her.

'Come on, Nance, why you bein' all shy? Give us a bit o' the other an' we'll be quite 'appy. Got me three months' pay, yer know. Pay yer well!'

Nancy spat in his face. The man jerked back, releasing one of her hands as he did so and she brought her open palm across his face with a resounding smack. There was a cheer from the crowd.

'Leave me alone,' she shrieked, 'I've got one man now, an' I don't want none other. Certainly not the likes o' you lot.'

The rest of the Cripples clientele watched, fascinated, waiting for the inevitable fight. Most of them knew by now who Nancy's lover was and they didn't fancy the sailor's chances if Sikes was here tonight. They began looking round and soon spotted him, his face like thunder, the furnace in his eyes well stoked. They nudged each other and grinned.

'Who's the fancy bloke, then, Nance?' the sailor shouted at her, jumping up and holding her arms in a vice-like grip, so that she winced and the tears started to her eyes. 'I can't think 'e can be much of a man if 'e can make do with one gel, an' she a little whore like you!'

The distance across the room was not so very great, but Sikes seemed to cover it in a single stride, thrusting chairs and tables and drinkers out of his way, until he stood eye to eye with the big sailor.

'I am "the fancy bloke",' he said quietly through his clenched teeth, 'an' nobody – nobody – messes with my woman. Understand, sailor?'

The sailor, a heavy, black-bearded fellow with yellow teeth, abruptly let go of Nancy, narrowed his eyes at Sikes and then laughed. Next minute, Sikes had crashed backwards into the tables, knocking pots and bottles in all directions. He heard someone scream; he thought it might have been Nancy. Gathering himself together, he stood up, bits of glass and crockery dropping from his coat. Something warm and wet trickled from his nose and he wiped the back of his hand across it. It came away red and he cursed. He stripped off his heavy coat and flung it behind him. The room had grown quiet and the sailor was still grinning at him, sparring and waving his fists about, baiting him. Sikes moved slowly towards him, remembering his fight with Tom Seager, his fists doubled at his sides. Cautiously he moved in as near as he dared to his opponent. Then suddenly, his right arm shot out, straight into the teeth of the other man. There was a roar of pain and another crash of tables and tankards. People were moving out of the way, leaving space for the two men. There were cries of encouragement from the supporters of both parties.

The sailor, his mouth bloody and distorted, came at Sikes again. This time, he held a small, double-edged knife, a foreign-looking thing, which caused Sikes a moment's panic. But he caught the wrist before the sailor struck and the two men were locked in a frantic battle for possession of the lethal weapon, rolling, struggling, their bodies heaving, their legs flailing, their faces ugly with grim determination.

Nancy stood trembling, Bet's arm about her. She feared for Sikes. She knew he was big and strong, but she knew, too, from bitter experience, how strong the sailor was. Now she heard Sikes gasp in shock and saw with horror that the knife had sliced into his cheek and the wound was bleeding profusely. She made a movement forward, but Bet pulled her back.

'Are you crazy, Nancy?' she hissed. 'Leave 'em ter sort each other out. Don't you go interferin'. Can't yer see, Bill's provin' 'imself ter yer. 'E's claimin' you fer 'is woman. Before all this lot.'

Bet smiled into Nancy's frightened eyes and held her tighter.

The skidding sound of the knife across the floor drew their attention to the men again. Sikes had managed to free the weapon and had kicked it well out of reach. He and the sailor were up on the little gallery, locked in a vicious embrace. Sikes's head had been slammed back through the balustrading and now hung over the edge, wood splinters sticking out from his hair. The sailor's hands had closed around his throat. The watching drinkers gasped. Sikes's fingers tore at the man's grasp, but he could not dislodge it. In sheer desperation, he summoned all his strength, drew up his knees and flung the man off with a mighty kick. He staggered to his feet, groggily clutching the broken balustrade. As the bull made a final rush at him, he stuck out his fist, straight between the man's eyes. The sailor's face crumpled in agony and he slumped to the floor unconscious.

Sikes bent over, panting and dripping blood. He felt sick, but with a considerable effort he fought back the nausea. He was barely aware of the gentle hands helping him down the stairs and back to his table. Life resumed around him and he saw no more of the sailor.

Bet and Nancy sat him in a chair and Nancy did her best to staunch his wounds with a napkin soaked in spirits. Bet fetched a measure of brandy. Fagin leaned across the table and tentatively touched the bloody fist resting there.

'Nicely done, Bill, nicely done. You won't have any more trouble from him. What a wonderful display. Nancy should feel very proud of you.'

'Oh shut up, Fagin,' said Nancy, but not unkindly. She was too relieved that Sikes was still alive.

Fagin persisted. 'About the – ah – little job, Bill.'

'Fer Gawd's sake, Fagin! Can't yer leave the man alone? Yer can see 'e's faint with loss o' blood.'

It did seem as though Sikes was about to quit consciousness of the world about him. But he rallied enough to reply to the old man's insistence.

'I'll do it,' he murmured. And added under his breath, 'Yer greedy ole miser.'

Fagin swung away and slunk out of the tavern, leaving Sikes to the very tender mercies of Bet and Nancy.

EIGHTEEN

Between them, the two young women got Sikes out of The Three Cripples and into a cab. Nancy scrambled in after him.

'I'll manage, Bet,' she said. 'Thanks fer yer 'elp. See you in a day or so.'

Bet shut the door on them and leaned in at the open window.

'It's Chris'mas Day, Nance,' she breathed. 'Compliments o' the season ter yer both.'

Nancy smiled. She had forgotten the day.

'You too, Bet. An' Tom.'

Then she called to the cabby and they lurched away with a grating of wheels.

In the safety and privacy of their room, Nancy steered Sikes towards the bed, but he resisted.

'No,' he whispered, 'I don't want ter lie down yet. I'll sit at the table. Give us a swig o' beer, will yer? Me throat's fair on fire after that bugger's 'ands got round it.'

And he gingerly fingered his aching neck. He sank on to one of the wooden chairs and rested his bruised and bloodied head on his hands. Nancy fetched his beer from the pantry and then stoked up the fire. She glanced at the clock and saw it was half-past midnight already.

'Season's greetin's, Bill.'

He didn't reply for a moment, but she saw him fumbling in his coat-pocket. Then he took a long draught of beer, wiped his mouth and muttered, 'Come 'ere, sweet'eart.'

Nancy's heart leapt at the unusual endearment. He pushed his chair back from the table and pulled her on to his lap, gazing into her eyes all the while with that direct stare of his.

'Rum gal,' he murmured. 'Worth fightin' for. 'Ere, Chris'mas present for yer.'

451

And he laid a small parcel in her hands. She looked down at the brown paper package and then back at Sikes.

'Ain't yer goin' ter look at it, then?' he asked.

She laughed and her trembling fingers fumbled with the string and paper. The contents tumbled into her lap and she gasped in delight at the little ivory-backed brush and its matching comb.

'Oh Bill!' she cried, her arms about his neck. 'They're beautiful.'

She wanted to kiss him, to hold him really close again, but his wounds were too bad for that. Instead, she laid a soft, lingering kiss on his forehead and put her cheek against it.

'Thank you, dearest Bill. Now I can make meself look more respectable, so's yer won't be ashamed of me.'

He held her away roughly.

'I ain't ashamed of yer, Nance. I'm proud of yer. Yer the best thing as 'as 'appened ter me.'

For a moment, the barriers were down again. She saw him insecure and defenceless. She wanted him to tell her of his past. But she hesitated under that direct gaze and the moment was gone. He reached for his beer and Nancy stood up and began to unpin her hair. Sikes watched her as she brushed steadily and firmly at the tangles, the ivory flashing through her hair with each stroke. At last she was satisfied with it and sat down on the other chair to comb out the knots. Several times she hissed in pain as the comb snagged and tore at the long strands.

''Ere,' said Sikes presently, 'can't I do that for yer?'

He rose unsteadily and dragged his chair to her side and sat down again, taking the comb from her. She turned her back to him and he began drawing the comb through her tresses, clumsily at first, but with growing confidence and with infinite patience when he came to a tangle; so that it hardly hurt her at all. She closed her eyes and let the wonderful sensation which she felt flow over her, as his hands moved about the strands of her hair and brushed her shoulders.

For half an hour he sat combing, his pain temporarily

452

forgotten, until every tangle was removed and the floor was littered with little knots of hair. Then he picked up the brush and swept it through her mane, again and again, until it rippled down her back like a golden waterfall. When he was satisfied with his work, he turned her to him by the shoulders and smiled.

'My beautiful Nancy,' he whispered and he touched her lips and nose and cheek with his fingertips.

Then very carefully he laid his lips on hers and it seemed like the sealing of a bond. He felt her body almost vibrating under his touch and he knew he had aroused her. But he was in too much pain tonight and their passions would have to wait. He stood up and took off his coat stiffly. His arms were aching, his knuckles and ribs were bruised and his head was throbbing madly. He sat on the edge of the bed and Nancy came and pulled off his boots for him and drew back the bed covers.

'I'll bank up the fire,' she said. 'You lie down,' and she gently pushed him back on to the pillow.

He lay gazing up at her, as though he couldn't believe she was real. She smiled down at him and he thought it was his mother drawing the covers up over his tired body. He closed his eyes and felt again his mother's hand on his fevered brow and smelled the warmth and nearness of her.

Early the next morning, Nancy was awakened by an un-earthly brightness in the room. There was no sun, but when she slipped silently from the bed and stood shivering in her shift at the window, she gazed out on to a transformed world of white.

'Chris'mas 1835,' she announced to Bull's-eye, who had risen stiffly to his feet and stood by her side, wagging his stumpy tail in anticipation of breakfast.

Nancy pulled on her dress and stockings and wrapped her shawl about her shoulders. Then she bent over Sikes's sleeping form. His cheek had bled again in the night and there was blood on the pillow. She would have to find a proper dressing for it today. And the bridge of his nose now looked purple in the eerie light from the snow. His right arm lay outside the covers and she turned his hand so that she might see the damage to his knuckles. They were red and raw-looking; they had certainly taken a grazing last night. But it was the bruises on his throat which frightened her, great red and purple wheals, where the sailor's hands had squeezed.

She shuddered at the memory. An' ter think 'e did all that fer me! she thought. Oh Gawd, I don't deserve it. I don't deserve '*im*. I've never 'ad anyone like 'im afore. I just can't believe me good luck. Maybe one day 'e'll marry me. She studied Sikes's sleeping form, her head on one side. Nah, she countered, 'e ain't the marryin' sort. Still, 'e seems ter like me bein' around. Go careful, gal, an' yer might even get a babe out of 'im.

This latter thought was almost too much for Nancy to bear. For her it would be the culmination of all her dreams and desires. For the moment, though, such thoughts must wait their due turn.

She busied herself with the lamp and the fire and found some scraps of meat for the dog.

Then she sat and brushed her hair again and felt the softness of it. She'd get Bet to help her wash it one day. Then it would really shine. She pinned it back off her face and stood up. Sikes was watching her and she came and sat by his side.

'Well?' She smiled as she questioned him.

'Pretty stiff, achin' all over an' dyin' fer a pee,' he said, struggling out of bed and making for the slop-pail Nancy had insisted on keeping in the pantry.

'You want any breakfast, Bill?' she called.

''Course I want breakfast, gal. Burn me, a man can't live on beer. Give us a slice o' bacon an' a coupla eggs. Any bread left?'

There was and as he returned to the room, she cut two large slices which she toasted for him. He sat at the table, staring out at the white rooftops opposite.

'Real Chris'mas Day, innit?' he remarked. 'Snow don't usually come till later. S'pose they'll start them bloody bells up soon.'

The words were hardly out of his mouth, when they heard the joyful peal of bells from St Leonard's church, closely followed by the more distant sound of those of St Matthew's at Bethnal Green.

'Gawd!' grumbled Sikes, his mouth full of toast and bacon. 'Why do they go on so bloody long?'

Nancy laughed.

'Don't grumble on Chris'mas Day, Bill. The bells are 'appy. D'yer fancy a walk in the snow later?'

'Maybe.'

An hour later, well wrapped against the cold, Sikes and Nancy were about to step carefully out into the slippery, sparkling streets when they heard footsteps on the stairs and a peremptory knock at the door.

'Who the blazes can that be?' frowned Sikes. He called out, 'Come in!'

And in swaggered the Artful Dodger and young Charley Bates, smirking as usual.

'Compliments o' the season, one an' all,' they chorused together.

The Dodger produced from under his vast coat a plum pie and a bottle of port.

'Compliments o' the King o' Field Lane 'imself!' he announced loudly.

'Yeah, an' this is from us.'

And Charley handed Nancy a length of sky-blue ribbon. It looked new; she didn't think they had forked it.

'Thank you, boys,' she said softly.

And she gave them each a kiss on the cheek. They grinned and coloured and shuffled their feet.

Dodger continued, 'An' Fagin says to ask 'ow the Bruiser is terday.'

Sikes looked at him hard. It was an ambiguous question in the twilight underworld in which they lived. Did the old devil mean 'How was the prizefighter?' or 'How's the harlot's fancy man?' He was nettled. He didn't want the world to think of Nancy as a prostitute any more. They were just two lovers living together. But it was Christmas and he decided not to make an issue of it.

'Tell 'im 'e's on the mend,' he said quietly. 'An' thank 'im fer the wittles.'

The boys left and went clattering down the stairs. Their laughter echoed back for some time as they pelted each other with snowballs on their way.

Sikes turned to Nancy and took her in his arms.

'The walk and the puddin' can wait,' he murmured. 'So can the port!'

NINETEEN

A cold, biting wind blew through the City, throwing rain into the faces of those who walked its streets. Streets sodden with the filthy slush of melted snow, where middens were blocked with last year's leaves and the unmentionable mess overflowed on to the pavements. Streets, where tenements, which looked as though they had sprouted from the earth, now appeared to be fast sinking back into its bowels. Doors and window frames were swollen and rotten and, inside, walls streamed with damp and clothes never dried.

Such was the back end of January 1836. After the gatherings of Christmas, there was a stark return to normality. Faces were grey and pinched, money was tight, food and fuel scarce, and work even scarcer. The domestic rows in Old Nicol Street increased in frequency and intensity, as they no doubt did in a hundred other streets in that swarming metropolis; where husbands drank away what little they earned and wives struggled in vain to make ends meet for a large family of children.

Sikes stood staring down into the courtyard on one such gloomy afternoon. The rain was flung against the grimy pane and he was disturbed by memories of such weather in Macquarie Harbour. He shivered and wished the couple opposite would shut their noise. They had been arguing for the last ten minutes. Now a child had joined in; he could hear its pleading, piping tones. And a baby had started to cry.

Gawd! he thought. I 'ope we don't ever come ter that. Kids screamin' all over the place.

He turned to look at Nancy. She was toasting bread at the fire and he thrilled at the sight of her back and hips as she bent over her task. She stood up, her cheeks flushed, and put the toast on the table.

'There y'are, Bill,' she said, pushing a small basin of dripping towards him. 'This'll warm you up.'

Sikes sat down and spread dripping thickly on the toast. Nancy brought over two steaming mugs of coffee and sat down with him.

'I've got ter go out ternight, Nance,' he announced, with his mouth full.

Nancy looked at him. She was disappointed.

'I'll be away all night, so don't wait up. Lock the door. I've got a key.'

He was glad she didn't pry. But he was unaware of how desperately she longed to know where he was going, just so that it wasn't a secret, so that he shared things with her. But he never told her anything about his business, so she never questioned him.

'I'll miss yer, Bill.'

He leaned across the table and chucked her under the chin.

'You'll be all right, gal. Staunch-hearted lass. I'll be back termorrer. Meet yer in the tavern.'

And he pushed a couple of coins across to her. She toyed with the money, but her mind was not on drink.

'Bill,' she said tentatively. He eyed her over his mug of coffee. She went on. 'I'd like a babe.'

The eyes bore into her. 'Well I wouldn't!' He slammed his mug down, splashing coffee over the table. She flinched. It was the first time he had spoken sharply to her. 'Burn my body, woman! Isn't it enough to 'ave a roof over yer 'ead? An' now yer want ter fill the place with brats!' His voice softened a little as he saw the blue eyes fill with tears. 'No, Nance. Look around yer. Look at the squalor an' the argyments an' the misery in this place alone. Listen to it!'

He fell silent and Nancy could hear the voices shouting, children screaming and babies crying. She dropped her gaze, feeling rebuffed. She couldn't know that Sikes had suddenly been confronted with a mental picture of Elizabeth

Brewer with a child at her side – his child.

'No. If things were diff'rent, Nance, maybe we could. But not 'ere. Wot sort of a life would it be fer the kinchin, anyway? Yer'll 'ave ter ferget it, Nance. I couldn't live like that.'

He finished his food in silence and wiped his greasy fingers on his breeches. He pushed his chair back, so that it grated on the floorboards. Nancy winced. Sikes stood up and Bull's-eye leaped to his feet as his master fetched his hat and coat and dug under the bed for the chest. Nancy watched as he shoved the pistols into his belt and stuffed jemmies and rope and knives into the inside pockets of his coat. There was a wooden cudgel in the chest which she had not noticed before. He picked it up, weighing it in his hands, undecided as to whether he needed it. But he put it back in the chest and closed the lid. He pulled his scarf and mittens from his pockets and wrapped himself up against the cold. Thus muffled, he bent over Nancy and kissed her. Impulsively, she reached up and held him tightly round his neck.

'Gawd, don't choke me, gal!' he laughed. 'I ain't goin' away fer long.'

And he stroked her cheek and walked away. At the door he turned.

''Leven o'clock termorrer night at the Cripples.'

She nodded and he was gone.

The wrench she felt was out of all proportion, she knew. But it was the first night he had been away since she had come to live with him and she suddenly felt very lonely. She could go and visit Bet, but the weather was so awful that she dismissed the thought of going out.

She cleared away the remains of their tea and lit the lamp. It was almost dark and she drew the curtains and stoked up the fire. For a while, she sat gazing into its depths, thinking of the baby she wanted but was unlikely to have. Maybe life would change one day. Maybe he'd think differently and she'd have her wish. But she didn't hold out much hope. Her eyes travelled over the now-familiar room and lighted once more on the box on the mantelpiece. She took it down again and carried it to the table. The button and the hair did not interest her so much as the letter.

'W. S.' she murmured. 'W. S. It can only be Bill.'

She wished she could read the words at the top; who was it addressed to? The beautiful curves of the characters seemed to glow in the quivering lamplight and suddenly, she felt a tiny knot of fear beginning in the very pit of her being. Was this letter to, or from, another woman? Where had Sikes gone tonight? He wouldn't tell her and she had been too trusting to ask. Her face flamed and the tears started to her eyes. Suddenly she saw him as full of secrets. And maybe not all the secrets were about house-breaking.

Sikes was away several times over the next two weeks and Nancy's suspicions were never assuaged. The trouble was, he wasn't always with Toby. She knew, because she had seen Sikes's friend in the tavern more than once while Sikes was away. She had quizzed Toby, but he was close and evasive.

At the end of the second week in February, by which time Nancy had imbibed a great deal of gin, ('Just ter fortify me,' she told herself) she resolved to follow Sikes on his next trip and see where he went. On this particular evening, they had been sitting in the Cripples together until late. Nancy had drunk more spirits than she knew was good for her; it was so easy to slip back into the old habits, especially now, when she needed fortifying for what she was about to do. At last, Sikes kissed her and slipped out of the tavern. The place was crowded and smoky and no one noticed her small figure gliding like a shadow through the door in the wake of her lover, a bottle of gin tucked beneath her shawl.

Outside, it was a raw night and the streets were beginning to glitter with the first vestiges of frost. Nancy looked both ways and saw Sikes's figure disappearing at the top end of Little Saffron Hill. She hurried along, drifting in and out of dark doorways and threatening alleys, just keeping Sikes in sight. He strode on purposefully, unaware she was barely a hundred yards behind him. Together, and yet apart, they made their way through the maze of streets which led north-east. They came out into the silent square with trees and grass railings at its centre. At the far side, Sikes went down a narrow lane and turned left up a similar one, which bore the legend Grove Walk.

Eventually, Sikes halted outside the second house on the right and knocked on the door with his knuckles. Nancy, hidden in a nearby doorway, saw the door open and, framed in the light from the hallway, stood Toby Crackit. The door shut quietly and Nancy leaned back against the wall. She was cold, but determined to watch the house. She waited, shivering, for what seemed like ages, warming herself with nips from the bottle. Eventually, the two men emerged, laughing quietly, and set off in a northerly direction.

They *are* off on a crack ternight, thought Nancy to herself. But wot 'appens when 'e ain't with Toby? Where does 'e go then?

She felt depressed and drank some more gin. Its bitter warmth made her feel a little brighter and she staggered out from her hiding place, making vaguely for the direction in which she had seen the men disappear. Had she known it, she was but a few streets from home. But she failed to recognize any of its surrounding place names.

She found herself on a long main road and pressed on in the vain hope that she might catch up with Sikes and Toby. At the top, there was a great, dark building on her right. She stood and studied it, swaying, for several minutes. She knew what it was, but the name evaded her. And this was its back entrance, so it looked different.

'Nearly went there – with Bet. Ole Fagin took's in'stead. Glad we di'n't go there. Woss its name?'

'That's the work'us, miss. An' you look as though you need a night's lodgin' there.'

She turned and looked blearily into the face of a policeman.

'No. 'S'all right, really. 'M meetin' me – me – 'usband 'long 'ere.'

'Well, you hurry along home. This ain't no time fer young women ter be out an' about.'

461

The policeman went on down the High Street and left Nancy to lurch on up through a maze of back streets, where she became totally disorientated and lost. She felt frightened and lonely and began singing quietly and sadly to herself, finishing off the gin between snatches of popular ballads. But the words kept getting mixed up and she was beginning to feel sick.

Suddenly, she stopped, leaning against a broken piece of fencing. She felt an ominous wave of pain in her stomach and the sweat broke out on her face. She leaned over and vomited violently.

Afterwards, she felt so weak, she would gladly have sat down, but she kept seeing a vision of herself in a doorway in just such a state, with Sikes carrying her home. He wouldn't do it twice. She breathed in the sharp night air and clutched the empty bottle as though it were her sole companion. She forced her feet forward and began singing again.

It was in this sorry state, with the frost thickening on the canal banks, that she finally careered into two tall men walking speedily along the path towards her.

'God's teeth!' Sikes's voice was harsh and rasping as recognition dawned on him. 'Wot the blazes are you doin', Nance?'

She stared defiantly up at both men and wished there weren't four of them. Sikes on his own was quite enough for her to manage. She waved the empty gin bottle and smiled.

'I got lost, darlin'.'

Sikes gritted his teeth in a supreme effort to contain his anger. But even through her drunken stupor, Nancy could sense the ominous tension of his body as he snatched the bottle from her and flung it into the canal, which bordered the path. He seized her arm in a vicious grip and she whimpered. He spoke no more, but marched her, protesting weakly, into Kingsland Road, where they hired a carriage to take them down into Shoreditch High.

Inside the muffled darkness, she was aware of Sikes's angry breathing. Toby sat in an embarrassed silence and stopped the cab by St Leonard's church.

'Fagin's termorrer, Bill?' he asked quietly.

Sikes grunted and the cab moved off. They stopped finally at the junction with Bethnal Green Road and Sikes paid the cabby. In awful silence, he hurried Nancy through the alleys into Old Nicol Street and up to their lodging, where he flung open the door, lit the lamp and then locked the door; his fingers digging into her arm all the while, as though he would not dare let her out of his sight or grasp. He faced her now and she stood trembling, fearing what he would do. She felt ill again and was beginning to sober up a little. Sikes's face was livid, his eyes like a furnace, his mouth set in a cruel, determined line. He unbuckled his heavy belt and looped it in his right hand. With his other, he ripped the shawl from her shoulders and flung her on the floor. She lay there terrified and cowering, the torn shawl, the one he had bought her, lying like a great scarlet pool beside her.

For Sikes the darkness was closing in on him again. He saw his mother lying dead on her filthy pallet. Some demon from the deepest recesses of his tormented mind possessed him, taking control of his hand, the strap descending four times, hard and furiously, whistling down over her back and buttocks. A stroke for each of those he had loved and lost, so long ago. But most of all for she who had borne him and given him the only love he had ever known. He had been denied her love for so long. How could any woman presume to take her place? The blind rage lent strength to his arm and he was unaware of the pain he inflicted on the one woman who might teach him to love again. When he stopped, she lay in a piteous heap, sobbing quietly.

'Get up,' he said, putting on his belt again. She made no move. 'I said, get up!' And he dragged her to her feet, his fingers digging into her again.

His temper had not yet abated. She raised her tear-stained face to his.

'Now listen ter me, my gal.' He wasn't shouting, but there was menace in his words. 'I'll not 'ave another display like that. 'Ow the blazes yer got where yer did, I don't know an' I

463

ain't askin'. But you could've fallen in the cut an' no one would've bin any the wiser.'

Something told her that he had been badly frightened and through her pain she felt a little flicker of triumph. The thought gave her strength. But he hadn't finished.

'Nah, you keep yer 'ands off the bottle. It ain't good for yer, it'll ruin yer looks an' my pocket! An' if I catches yer in sich a state again, yer'll get the same treatment. Understand?'

She nodded miserably and he released her. He took some things out of his coat and stowed them away under the bed. She couldn't see what they were, but she caught a glimpse of silver. She remained standing by the dying embers of the fire.

'Yer'd better stick yer 'ead in some cold water an' then get ter bed,' called Sikes from the pantry, where he was busy filling the slop-bucket.

She went over to the ewer, but it was empty and she stood with it in her hands, staring vacantly at the green bowl. Sikes said nothing, but took the ewer from her and went downstairs to fill it from the pump in the yard. When he returned, she was still standing there. He poured some water into the basin and found a cloth, which he soaked in the icy water. And then, with utter tenderness, he washed her face and hands and smoothed back her hair from her face.

'That's better,' he said, his voice low.

Nancy slipped away out of his hands and went to relieve herself. Silently, she came back, took off her soiled dress and hung it over the back of a chair and crawled into bed beside Sikes. Neither of them spoke and he did not hold her in his arms as he usually did. She felt sore and utterly miserable. But she knew he was right to punish her and she loathed herself for behaving as she had. He trusted her; why couldn't she trust him? Well, she knew now that his night-time excursions were genuine business, so there was no need to trouble herself again.

But a little seed of doubt still niggled in the furthest recess of her mind.

TWENTY

No more was said about that disastrous night and in the days and nights which followed, they made love again with renewed passion. When Sikes was away, Nancy often used to visit Bet and they would talk of female things, the changing fashions among the rich, the latest exploits of one of their little company; or they would talk of their past and wonder at the luck which had changed their circumstances.

'Are you 'appy with Bill?' Bet asked Nancy one evening in early March.

'Oh yes Bet, an' I'm so lucky to 'ave me bed an' board. No more sleepin' on the streets. No more o' them awful blokes down the Ratcliffe pawin' over me.' She laughed nervously; she hadn't told Bet about the beating. But Bet, the older 'sister', who had known her all her life, sensed a discordant tone somewhere in her talk. 'An' Tom's good ter yer?' went on Nancy.

Bet beamed and her eyes crinkled at the corners as only Bet's could.

'Nancy,' she said, 'he's the dearest, kindest, silliest creature you ever did see.'

And they both laughed at this virtuous picture of the young rogue.

These evenings with Bet restored a certain balance to Nancy's life, so that she didn't become solely dependent on Sikes for company. And she felt almost as happy again as she had last autumn. Yet still the image of the wretched letter burned in her mind. And when on several occasions Sikes was away from home and she knew Toby wasn't with him, the old doubts began to surge again, no matter how she fought them down. She wanted to tell Bet, but she knew Bet would dismiss her fears as nonsense.

And then, one evening, in the middle of April, when the days were beginning to lengthen and the nights were less chilly than they had been, Sikes announced that he was going away for several days. Nancy's heart lurched and she fought back the rising tears.

'There's money fer food,' he said, slapping down a handful of coins, 'an' a *little* gin,' he added, emphasizing the word. 'There should be enough coal. An' Nance.' She looked at him, her eyes large and swimming. 'Don't do anythink stupid.'

She forced a laugh. 'No, Bill. 'Course not.' Then: 'Where are you goin', Bill?' she whispered.

He smiled down at her. 'That's not fer the likes o' you ter know,' he said quietly. 'Best you don't know nothink of my whereybouts.'

He took her face in his hands and kissed her hard and she wanted him then and there and pressed her body desperately against his.

'Not now, gal, not now. I mus' go. When I come back,' he promised.

She waited for his footsteps to sound across the yard. Then she turned down the lamp, snatched up her shawl and went quietly from the room.

This time he seemed in no great hurry and she could hear him whistling to himself. She darted along from doorway to doorway, hoping he wouldn't turn round. He was heading east, striding out along the Bethnal Green Road. She scurried along in his wake, trying to keep her panting breath to herself. Once, Bull's-eye, running along beside his master, stopped to sniff and cock his leg. His twinkling eyes caught sight of Nancy and he barked in joyful recognition. Sikes turned abruptly.

'Wot the 'ell you barkin' at, you thund'rin' ole tyke?'

Nancy jerked back into an archway, her heart thudding, praying that the old dog wouldn't come padding back to her. She heard Sikes grumbling at him again.

466

'I ain't stoppin' at ev'ry bloody tree we come to, yer know. Nah, get a move on, if yer comin' with me.'

She heard the click of Bull's-eye's claws, as he ran off after Sikes's fading footsteps. And she heard, too, a distinct yelp, as Sikes's boot made contact with the animal. Cautiously, she came out of her hiding-place and continued to follow at a safer distance.

Soon, the press of buildings became less dense and Nancy was aware of open areas between clusters of houses. They entered the Mile End Road and she guessed he was heading for Essex. She wondered how far he would walk, knowing he had given himself several days' absence. She was tiring now and the distance between them was increasing. At last, weary and dispirited, she gave up and leaned against a low stone wall to rest. The hot tears fell unchecked and for a few moments, she gave way to her grief.

She must go home. It was no good following where he had gone. A man of his nerve and stature might venture any-where, but a feeble woman on her own was in a vulnerable position. She wiped her eyes with the edge of her shawl and pinched her nose dry and set her face again towards the west.

It was dark, with only an intermittent moon, uncovered at irregular intervals by scudding clouds. Her eyes by now were well accustomed to the dark and she could see where her path lay. It was a lonely stretch of road and the trees had been cut back on either side for some distance, so that footpads and highwaymen had less chance to make ambushes upon their unsuspecting victims. But it lent the landscape a bleak and empty look and Nancy shivered and looked around her constantly. She passed an isolated farm building and in the distance a dog barked, once, twice, and was silent.

There was a sudden movement behind her. She gasped and hurried on. Someone was following her. She could hear his breathing, and feel the menace in his tread. She started to run. The stranger ran too. She stumbled and tripped along the rutted road. He caught her suddenly. There was a wave of stinking, beery, tobacco-laden breath across her face. In a sudden glimpse of moonlight, she saw his broken teeth and leering smile hovering above her. She drew breath to scream, but he clapped a hand over her mouth. She sank her teeth in. He cursed in pain and dragged her angrily to the side of the road. She struggled, terrified, suffocating under his filthy hand, as he groped between her legs. She clamped her thighs together, but he was too strong. And then with a raw, searing pain, he was inside her. Thrusting. Grunting. Sweating. Her body burned with pain. And all the while, her mind kept screaming out, 'Bill, oh Bill. Don't let this be 'appenin' ter me. I'm yours, Bill. 'Ow can 'e take me?'

She was still helplessly puzzling over the attack, when the man abruptly withdrew, buttoned his breeches and made off into the distant woods.

Nancy lay in a damp pool of pain, her dress ridden up, her lower regions cruelly exposed to the probing moonlight. She was beyond tears. Her mind had gone blank. For some minutes she lay still, the pain throbbing through her body, the hurt and ignominy coursing through her very soul. She began to feel chilled at last and slowly sat up and covered herself. For a while, she rested her head on her knees, hugging her abused body in an effort to comfort it and moaning quietly for her lover.

At length, she heard a horse approaching. She cowered down into the shadow of the bank and waited for animal and rider to pass. Then she stumbled slowly back towards the welcoming lights of London.

It was very late when she finally let herself in at the lodging house. All was quiet and the fire had gone out; she felt utterly alone. She sat down by the dead embers and let her battered body rest and her tortured mind drift in the darkness of the familiar room. Here, where she had been gently loved, cruelly beaten, but never raped. And now, thinking of Sikes again, the tears flowed. She kicked off her boots and clambered into the bed, hugging his pillow to her aching body.

And there the sun's rays wakened her the next morning, with a promise of spring in the air. She opened her eyes and felt for his body. Realization dawned and then the awful memory of the previous night. She sat up, shuddering at the picture in her mind which would not go away. She felt dirty. The ewer was full and she filled the big wide bowl to the brim and stripped off her clothes and let the chilly water run over her, cooling and soothing her, washing away the filth of her attacker.

But there was no washing away what he had left behind. A week later, after Sikes had returned, jubilant, from his successful Essex venture, only to find she looked wan and wouldn't let him make love, she finally had to admit what had happened.

'Bill, I'm sorry, luv. I can't let you. I – I've got the clap.'

He stood speechless, all his buoyant mood dispersed like a burst bubble. His brows came down in a dark line and she saw the fire leap in his eyes.

'Wot the blazes 'ave you bin doin'? Why, you little jade!'

He was shouting now and he lunged at her, seizing her arms in his vice-like grip and shaking her, spluttering through his teeth with rage.

'After ev'rythink! All I done an' said!' He couldn't get the words out. 'An' yer let some other bastard fuck yer!'

His hand fetched her a heavy smack round the face.

'No, Bill, no!' she squealed, struggling out of his grasp and leaping away towards the window. 'I didn't! I didn't! Yer don't understand!'

'I understand all right,' he roared and made a grab at her again.

She got into the corner by the pantry and watched him advance, her eyes dilated with fear. He was unbuckling his belt. There was murder in his face and Nancy shook with real terror.

'Please listen to me, Bill,' she pleaded. 'Please! If only you knew wot 'ad 'appened, you wouldn't be so cruel!'

Something in her eyes halted him and he stayed his hand.

'Well? Speak!' Sikes was deeply hurt already, but she knew she must tell him all.

'I wos curious ter know where you wos goin', Bill.' Her voice trembled. 'I thought you wos visitin' a woman. That letter in the little box up there.' She glanced at it now and his eyes followed hers. 'I wanted ter see where yer went. I follered yer – along the Mile End Road. But you wos too fast. So I come back. But I wos – I wos . . .' Something was choking her. 'I wos raped, Bill.'

The stark sentence cut him like a knife. He dropped the belt and the fire went out in his eyes. In one stride he was with her and she was safe in his arms once more. And the fright and the hurt were crushed out in his great embrace. He said nothing for a few minutes, only rocked her gently where he stood. But she could feel his body strung with the emotions inside him. When he released her, his voice sounded husky.

'Yer must see the doctor termorrer. 'E'll give yer summat for it.'

She nodded and laid her head gratefully against his chest once more. He drew her to the bed and they sat side by side and he put his arm around her and she leaned against him. For some time there were only the familiar domestic sounds of the room around them.

Then Sikes drew a deep breath and said, 'I'd better set things straight, afore there's more trouble.'

And as the evening wore on and the fire died down, he poured out the whole terrible story of his transportation, his betrayal, his losses, the letter from Spiring to his Sarah, and his dreadful treatment in Van Diemen's Land. It took a long time to tell. He spared her no details. She listened in pained silence.

When he had finished, he sat in gloomy exhaustion. Nancy rested her hand on his thigh, but uttered no sound. He spoke again.

'I ain't destined fer 'appiness. Ev'rythink I touch goes wrong.' He wasn't petulant, simply stating facts. 'I oughtn't ter keep you 'ere, Nance. It ain't fair. I'll bring yer bad luck. It's started already, 'asn't it?'

He turned on her such an expression of despair and sadness, that she wanted to hold him tight against her breast for ever. Instead, she shook her head slowly in disbelief.

'You ain't turnin' me out, are yer, Bill? Yer not tellin' me ter go? Not after all this?'

'No, Nance. But I'm givin' yer the choice. I've told yer. I'm a bad 'un, an' I shan't be any diff'rent till the day I die. But there's no need fer you ter share me bad luck. You can go off if yer wants to. I shan't stop yer.'

His voice caught and she knew it had cost him very dear to say all he had said that evening. She turned now and kneeled up on the bed and gently put her arms around his neck.

'Bill, dearest,' she said, her voice barely audible. 'I luv yer. An' I'm stayin'.'

He took her in his arms and they lay entwined on the bed until sleep overtook them. Waking in the early hours of the morning, Nancy sat up and dragged the bedclothes over them. She glanced at Sikes's feet and started to laugh. Sikes woke briefly and grumbled.

'Dam' me! Wot's in the wind now?'

'Yer've still got yer boots on, Bill!'

He snorted and turned over, taking her in his arms again and she sank into the warmth and security and the certainty that now she knew his past, life would be easier and all would be well.

TWENTY-ONE

The faint ticking of the clock and the occasional chink of weaponry as Sikes cleaned it were the only sounds in the room. The fire had burned low and was smouldering with a raw open heat. Nancy was seated at the table opposite Sikes, darning a hole in her stocking. Inwardly, she was in a turmoil of indecision. There was that which she must speak to Sikes about and she could not delay much longer.

She breathed deeply, her heart beating, and without raising her eyes said quietly, 'Bill, dear.'

'Wot is it?'

His rejoinder was gruff but passive and she deemed it safe to go on.

'You know I'd dearly love to 'ave a babe?'

He stopped in the middle of cleaning a pistol. He said nothing, but held her with his eyes. Nancy trembled inwardly, but hurried on.

'I know you wouldn't want littl'uns runnin' around yer feet . . .'

'Too right, gal. Any sign o' nippers an' I'm off!'

It sounded callous, but she knew his feelings.

'Well, we'll 'ave ter do somethink about it, Bill, or I'll be gettin' knapped.'

He slammed the pistol on to the table, making Nancy jump.

'An' jus' wot der you propose ter do?' His voice was menacing and Nancy feared an outburst, but he was still in control. 'I s'pose yer've got some clever ideas, 'ave yer? Somethink yer picked up on the Ratcliffe? Eh?' There was almost a sneer in his voice.

'Yes,' said Nancy, looking at him very directly. 'There's

472

somethink you can use. I know where to get them from. They ain't cheap, but if yer don't want me to 'ave a babe –'

'Wot the blazes are you talkin' about, woman? Wot "things"?'

'Cundums, Bill. They're made o' sheep's gut – an' tied on with ribbon.'

Now she had said it, it sounded faintly ridiculous and she dreaded Sikes's reaction. For a moment he stared at her, open-eyed and speechless, all trace of malice gone. Then he burst into one of his rare guffaws of laughter.

'Swipe me, gal! If you think I'm tyin' a bloody ribbon round my cock, yer've got another think comin'.'

And he went back to his pistols with a huge grin on his face. Nancy sat silent, feeling foolish.

'Yer'll 'ave ter do better than that, Nance.' And he started laughing again. 'I wonder if Toby knows that one?'

Nancy thought it very likely that Toby knew, and much more besides. These things had been around for centuries. They didn't always work and no, she couldn't really see Sikes stopping amidships to put one on. Still, no doubt there were others who had benefited from their cumbersome properties. But she could try another tack.

'Bill,' she said. 'There's somethink I can use – if yer don't mind.'

Their eyes met and the months of misunderstanding fell away for a few moments. He saw only love in her eyes and she noted the softening in his.

'Only if it don't get in the way,' replied Sikes.

Nancy shook her head. She almost hated herself for her thoughts. Her body was crying out for motherhood and more than anything she wanted to bear Sikes's child. The old Ratcliffe doctor had told her she was unlikely ever to bear a live infant, but she could not believe him. But Sikes wouldn't want her to be encumbered with a pregnancy and all that that entailed; nor would he want children about the lodging. He would leave her, or turn her out, she was sure. And she couldn't bear the thought of that. Yet she was also certain that deep down he loved her and needed her.

And so Nancy's days were filled with the preoccupation of preventing herself from becoming pregnant. And the fear of it and the fear of losing Bill if she did conceive were all at odds with her overriding passion to bear his child. She became nervous and jumpy, sharp with her friends, short with Sikes, which in turn fired his temper. She drank gin in an effort to abort any foetus which might be implanted within her. She allowed herself to fall and trip. Once, she slipped on the stairs of the lodging house and fell from top to bottom. She was not hurt, but lay there in a stupor of satisfaction until Sikes leaped down the stairs to pick her up. At night, she used a sponge device to prevent his seed from taking root in her and sometimes she even denied him her body. And all the while, her female instincts cried out to be satisfied, to be implanted, to produce new life. And so the heady days of their early love were lost. Sikes had struck her, more than once, when she had become petulant or shrewish, although he had never again taken his belt to her. He had become taciturn and surly. He rarely smiled these days, she reflected sadly, and the dog came in for a fair share of kicks and curses. Sometimes she felt that she and Bull's-eye were the scapegoats for all Sikes's misery and ill fortune of the past years. She sensed that she and Sikes were dragging each other down into a descending vortex. What had begun as a bright and shining passion, a new start to life, had deteriorated into something sordid and painful.

One day Bill returned to their room with a glowering face and a purple bruise around his left eye. Nancy wondered who had dared to cross his path this time. She greeted him with a smile.

''Allo, Bill dear.'

She went across and stood on tiptoe to kiss his rough cheek. He grunted and brushed past her on his way to the pantry for a jug of beer. He sat down at the table and began drinking at a fairly fast rate. Nancy stirred the saucepan she had simmering over the fire. The aroma from it smelled good and she was pleased with her culinary efforts. She dished up a large helping of stew on a pewter plate and put it down in front of Sikes. For a few moments, he sat staring vacantly across the room, neither eating nor drinking. Nancy watched him covertly from the fireplace, where she dished up her own supper, and her heart went out to him. He must have felt her eyes on him, for he suddenly found herself looking into those unfathomable depths. They held each other's gaze for a second. Then Sikes turned his attention to his food. There's summat wrong there, thought Nancy. 'E's in trouble, I'll be bound.

She sat herself at the table and they ate in silence. When he had finished, Sikes pushed the plate away and sat picking his teeth with a sliver of wood, his eyes sliding to the door every few minutes. At last, Nancy could bear it no longer. She cleared away the plates and fetched her shawl.

'Where you goin'?' asked Sikes quietly.

'I'm goin' ter see Bet.' Nancy kept her voice level. She was determined not to give him cause for anger. 'I promised her I'd see 'er this evenin'.'

It was a lie, but she had to get out, to escape this awful tension.

'Come 'ere!'

It was a command and brooked no infraction. She went across to him and he pulled her on to his lap and buried his head in the crook of her neck. But he remained silent and she felt annoyed with him. When he slipped his hand beneath her bodice, she pulled away from him. She wasn't going to let him have her when the atmosphere between them was so charged with mystery and distrust. And yet her body was crying out for him. She went to the door, afraid of her own feelings.

'Nancy!'

She stopped and turned. The furnace had leaped into life and his bruised eye twitched slightly. She shuddered as he spoke in the same calm, steady voice.

'When I want yer, I'll 'ave yer. Now, come back 'ere.'

Something was fighting inside her and it threatened to

overwhelm her. She must get out. She put her hand to the doorknob, but he was there like a shot, barring her way, gripping her wrist in his fingers.

'You're not goin' nowhere,' he snarled, his face very close to hers. She could smell the drink on his breath. 'Wot d'yer think yer up to, eh?'

Nancy began to whimper, 'Please, Bill, you're hurting me. I want ter go out.'

'Burn me, you'll do as I say, woman!'

She struggled and something snapped in her head. She shouted into his face. 'You're bloody drunk, Bill Sikes! You accuse me o' swiggin' gin an' you can't even keep control o' yer own drinkin'. Let me go!'

The blow from Sikes's hand sent Nancy staggering across the floor, where she lay stunned. Sikes came and stood over her, a wildness and pain in his expression which she had never seen before. She looked up at him in terror, thinking he would thrash her again, but he was fumbling with his breeches. She wanted him so badly and yet she had forced this abstinence on herself for both their sakes. He wasn't gentle, he was too pent up and angry. And although she couldn't have called it rape, he forced himself into her with no preamble. She cried out in fright and pain and desperation. But he ignored her. And she was thrown back into the nightmare of her humiliation on the Mile End Road earlier that year.

He left her abruptly, pulling her clothes roughly over her thighs, and flung himself on the bed. Nancy lay quite still for several minutes, the hot tears running down into her ears on either side of her face. She ought to hate him. She ought to leave him, to cut away altogether. But she knew she couldn't. Whatever he did to her, whatever he said, she would love him and stand by him.

She crawled to the fireplace and sat warming herself. She had no heart to go out now. She didn't want to see anyone. Perversely, she wanted to stay here with this enigmatic man of hers.

Sikes lay on the bed, his eyes shut, but far from sleep. He was already regretting what he had done. He had been so lucky to chance on this girl. He knew she adored him and was grateful for his protection. He knew he could trust her. He thought of those early days of their relationship, when he had experienced a joy of living he had never known before. Inevitably it had gone wrong, like everything else in his life. His bloody, rotten life, he reflected. Life had never meant him to be happy. It simply gave him a taste of the apple and then snatched it away again, leaving him angry and embittered. He wondered what he could do. He could leave London, but that implied running away. And it meant leaving all that he knew. He had no wish to repeat his exile. He could say sorry to Nancy. It would cost him dear. He wasn't in the habit of apologizing for his actions, and she would see it for what it was, a rough attempt at patching up. Better to leave the wound open, let the air get to it. It would scar over in time. Meanwhile, he would have to make a conscious effort not to hurt her any more. He could hear a dim voice from the very distant past: 'We all admired 'im. But 'is temper ran away with 'im. That's wot led to 'is downfall.' It was the voice of the old criminal in Coldbath Fields and he had been talking about Sikes's father. Christ! thought Sikes. Am I so like 'im?

He opened his eyes and looked across at the small form huddled by the fire. Now and again she wiped the tears from her cheeks with the back of her hand. Sikes felt bad. He must make an effort at reconciliation.

But once more his attempts came to nothing. There were voices down in the hallway of the lodging house. Men's voices. Voices which didn't belong to Old Nicol Street. Sikes leaped from the bed, dragged out the chest and extracted a pistol, which he cocked. Nancy half rose, her face full of fear, her eyes wide and questioning.

'Wot is it, Bill?' she ventured.

He didn't reply, but threw his back against the door, the pistol in his hand at the ready. The footsteps coming up the stairs stopped outside their door and an imperious knocking followed.

'Mr William Sikes?' The voice of the Law was ominous.

Nancy flew to Sikes's side and reached up to take the pistol. He moved his hand out of her reach. She could see the sweat on his face as he stared blankly at her and his chest heaved with panic.

'Wotcher want?' he called out.

'Are you Mr William Sikes?'

'Maybe I am.'

'We'd like to talk to you, Mr Sikes.'

'Wot about?'

'We think you might 'elp us with our henquiries.'

'Well, yer thought wrong. I ain't 'elpin' no one.'

'Mr Sikes.' The policeman on the other side of the door was being very patient, 'we'd simply like to talk to you.'

'Go ahead,' called Sikes, belligerently.

The policeman permitted himself a short laugh. 'This is 'ardly the best place to conduct a conversation. I think you'll agree.'

'You ain't comin' in 'ere.'

'Well, what about you coming out 'ere?'

It was Sikes's turn to laugh. A short, mirthless bark. 'Oh no. I know you peelers. You'll 'ave me in ruffles as soon as I set foot outside me own door.'

'Not at all, Mr Sikes. We've no case against you – ah –' he hesitated, 'that is, not at present. You'll be quite safe.'

Sikes knew he was in the clear for the moment. He thought he knew what they wanted, though, and he wasn't going to say anything on that score. Nancy made another attempt to retrieve the pistol. This time, Sikes relinquished it into her shaking hands, pushing it back to half-cock as he did so. Cautiously, he opened the door a few inches.

''Ow many of yer?' he asked through the opening.

'Only two of us. PC Cuthberts and myself. I'm Sergeant Marshall. We're from the Hoxton Police Office.'

'I know you,' said Sikes. He slipped out on to the landing and pulled the door closed behind him. 'Wotcher want, guv?'

PC Cuthberts took out a notebook and pencil and held his hand poised to write. Sikes gave him a withering look. The sergeant now spoke.

'It's a little matter about a friend of yours.'

'Oh yeah?'

'Yes. A certain rather well-dressed gent, who was seen leaving the premises of a particularly wealthy society lady about half-past three yesterday afternoon.'

Sikes's mouth twitched at the corners. What had Toby been up to? He folded his arms and leaned back against the doorframe. The policeman looked at him.

'Well?' he said.

'Well wot?' Sikes was not going to make this easy for him.

'Do you know him?'

'Who?'

'The gentleman in question.'

''Ow would I know 'im from all the other thousands o' swell coves in this 'ere city? Woss 'is name?'

'We thought you might tell us that.'

'I can't do that if I don't know which bloke yer mean.'

Sergeant Marshall tried another tack. 'If I told you that this gent's name is Toby Crackit, would you say he was a friend of yours?'

''E might be,' shrugged Sikes.

'A good friend?'

'Depends.'

'Do you – work together?'

'Sometimes.'

'What work do you do?'

'Second-'and business.'

The policeman nodded then looked at Sikes, his eyes narrowed.

'Not bootlegging, by any chance?'

A wave of panic swept through Sikes. Oh God, what had Toby done? Had he been seen? Had he been too free with the distribution of the bottles? He would have to be very careful how he answered.

'I don't know nothink about that,' he replied levelly.

'Have you seen your friend recently?'

'Saw 'im two or three days ago. Down the tavern.'

'Not since?'

Sikes shook his head.

'Do you know where he is?'

'Couldn't say.'

'But you know his address?'

'You know mine. I s'pect yer knows 'is. Anyway, 'e moves around a lot,' lied Sikes.

The sergeant breathed deeply.

''Ave you done with me?' enquired Sikes.

'I think so, Mr Sikes. Thank you. If Mr Crackit turns up, let us know, will you? The Law is inclined to look more favourably on those who assist in enquiries.'

Sikes opened his mouth to speak, but didn't trust himself, so shut it again. If they thought they'd win him over with an empty offer like that, they could forget it. He'd never let a mate down yet and he never would. Especially Toby. Peach on Toby? It was too ridiculous for words.

He watched as the two policemen clumped down the stairs; and not until their voices had faded across the yard did he go back into the room and lock the door.

Nancy had heard every word and stood looking at him, her hands clasped in anguish over her breast.

'Oh Bill, you 'aven't, 'ave yer?'

He ignored her and sat down at the table, his head on his hands. She looked at his bent head and broad shoulders and she loved him so achingly at that moment.

So he and Toby had been smuggling. It was not a line he was used to and he wouldn't know when the Law would catch up with him. No wonder he looked hunted, no wonder he was moody and secretive. And if Toby was involved with a society woman, where did that put Bill? Was he involved in some way, too? He was on dangerous ground, far more

480

dangerous than he'd ever been on before. But there was little she could do. Except to be there when he needed her, to love him and to stay close and faithful.

'Shall I find a steak fer that eye o' yours, Bill?' she asked brightly, as though the events of the evening had never taken place.

He shook his head.

'Can I go out an' see Bet, then?'

He grunted assent and she went to the door. He looked over his shoulder towards her.

'Mind 'ow yer go, Nance. I can't afford ter lose yer.'

'I'll be careful, Bill.'

And she went out with a lighter heart than she had thought possible less than an hour ago.

TWENTY-TWO

For a long while Sikes sat, just letting the panicky feeling drift in and out of his mind; waves ebbing and flowing relentlessly against his brain. He went back over the events of the past few weeks. Everything had gone so smoothly. He was sure that no one had seen him or Toby going back to the hovel in Essex. But it was pretty outrageous all the same, he thought. It was one of the best cracks they'd made. It was bringing in a steady income and they'd cheated both the police and the Customs men.

A small brig, the *Marianne*, had anchored off the Thames, up Barking Creek, and it was carrying a large quantity of good French brandy. Toby had somehow learned of its presence. His plan was to carry off some of the golden liquor and sell it to the underworld. It wasn't their usual mode of business and Sikes thought the risk too great, but somehow, Toby's insistence had prevailed and they had planned the whole thing one night, right down to the last meticulous detail.

They had rowed across to the ship anchored in mid-channel, when Toby knew the crew were in the pub leaving just two men on board as guards. They were playing cards and unaware of a secured rope and an illicit boarding party.

Sikes and Toby split up, so that they encircled the two guards and were each able to come up behind one of them. Sikes moved like a cat, for all his size, but as he raised his cudgel to strike, the other guard rose to his feet with a startled cry. Toby laid him senseless in a second.

'We'd better 'urry, Bill,' whispered Toby. 'They might've 'eard from the shore.'

Sikes led the way down into the hold. He stopped abruptly when he shone the lamp round. Toby cannoned into him.

'Wot is it, Bill?'

'Jesus! Look at this lot!'

Hundreds of wooden cases lined the hold from floor to roof. One or two had been opened and bottles of amber-coloured brandy winked at them in the lamplight.

''Ow much you plannin' on takin', Toby?'

'I didn't know there was this much, Bill. We'll 'ave ter take wot we can. If we take ten cases, that's an 'undred an' twenty bottles!'

'Yeah,' said the practical Sikes, 'an' one sunk skiff!'

'We could make a couple o' journeys.'

'No, I ain't comin' back. We'll take eight.'

'But –'

'Shut up, Toby, an' give us an 'and.'

Speed was of the utmost importance now. They heaved and grunted and roped case after case, lugging them up the hold steps and over to the bows of the brig. When they had their eight cases in the bows, Toby climbed down into the skiff and Sikes lowered each one on its rope to him. It was time-consuming, but the quietest way. They had to keep a watchful eye open on the shore and a sharp ear to the noises of the night. By the time their precious load was on board and Sikes had lowered himself into the waiting boat, the little skiff was very low in the water. But the tide was with them and carried them far up Barking Creek, to the tiny hamlet of Little Ilford. Toby had a contact here and they would be able to hide and store their contraband in safety, so Toby had assured his partner.

Sikes and Toby needed to approach several contacts for the disposal of quite so many bottles of brandy. Sikes made for his old fence, Rudd, the landlord at The Fig Tree, while Toby went off to Field Lane to see how the land lay in that direction. They would see Barney, too, at some stage. And Toby had another idea up his sleeve, which he wasn't divulging to Sikes at present.

Toby's contacts were numerous and varied. They ranged

from out-and-out scoundrels to society ladies. Caroline Harley was one such. Sikes wondered how he did it. It was, he supposed, the old charm. By the end of the week, they had cleared their first case of bottles. They had kept one bottle each and had had no difficulty in disposing of the others. But prices had varied. Fagin would give no more than three shillings for the bottle Toby planted before him, while Lady Harley considered her protégé's efforts worth a great deal more.

'Toby, my dear,' she purred, seating him on a brocaded chair in her private parlour. 'How many of these can you get me?'

'Quite a lot, m'lady, but they'll cost yer.'

Lady Harley smiled and touched his cheek. 'My dear boy,' she went on, 'I can pay you considerably more than your fence. And perhaps I can put a little other payment your way.'

She looked across at him. Coquetry did not suit her, but Toby was prepared to overlook her years if she paid hard cash for the brandy.

'Five shillings a bottle, Toby? And your own private supply of opium?'

He stared at her. 'But that's –'

She held up a small, plump hand, on which the glittering rings bit into her flesh.

'No, Toby. That's quite enough for you. Any more and you'll be spoiled.'

'But that's not what I meant. That's a werry gen'rous offer, m'lady. It's just that I ain't got no use fer opium. I'd never get rid o' the stuff.'

'I'm sure you and your friend can use it between you.' She stood up and sighed and wandered over to the window. 'I dabbled with the stuff, but I don't like it. I prefer the brandy. Much more mellow. But I'm sure you young men can make use of it. Sell it if you can't.'

Toby sat trying to collect his thoughts. A maid brought tea. For once Toby refrained from eyeing her. He was too concerned about Lady Harley's proposal. Sikes, he knew, would rather have ten shillings a bottle and no opium. But they could sell it if they didn't want it. It would probably make up the difference in price.

'Wot's this stuff like?' he now asked.

Caroline Harley smiled her secret little smile and said, 'Come with me, Toby.'

He followed her down a corridor and up a small flight of steps to a room near the top of the house. She unlocked the door and ushered him in. There was a strange, almost exotic smell about the room, whose walls were decorated with eastern wallpaper. There was only one small window and this gave a modicum of light, but there were no lamps and the daylight was fading. There were a number of oriental artefacts about the room and a low, wide couch in the centre. Tables were placed on either side of the couch and on these stood jars and pipes and tinderboxes. Toby stood and stared. Lady Harley took his hand and led him to the bed.

What followed gave Toby a taste for the drug and in the days which followed, he went several times to Lady Harley's, exchanging brandy and his favours for blunt and opium. The arrangement seemed to be working well. Until he was seen leaving Lady Harley's house by someone who was investigating the theft of the brandy from the brig, *Marianne*. From Toby's point of view, it was fortuitous that the police called on Sikes when they did.

Sikes sweated now at the memory of it. Toby must be warned. If Toby was found, then God only knew how far the implications would ramify. Sikes cursed the day he ever agreed to the plan. He should have known better than to trust to another of Toby's schemes.

And all that business with the opium! He had been angry with Toby for agreeing to Lady Harley's proposals. They could have both done with the money and he felt that Toby had let him down badly. He remembered how he had gone round to Toby's the day after the latter had been to Lady Harley's. He had been struck by something in Toby's manner which he couldn't name. Toby had ushered him into his room almost obsequiously and all but pushed him into a chair.

''Ere, 'ave a drag at this, Bill,' he had said, thrusting a small pipe into Sikes's hands.

Sikes had looked at him sharply.

'Where the devil d'yer get this from, Toby? You struck it rich or summat?'

'Let's just say, I've got a werry gentle contact. I pays 'er in kind.'

He omitted to mention the brandy at this stage.

'Wot on earth you blabberin' about? It's you as should be payin' 'er hard cash. Wot is all this?'

Sikes was getting angry. Toby stood sheepishly in front of his friend.

'She's a wealthy lady, Bill. A patron o' the arts an' a lot more besides. She's knockin' on a bit an' likes a younger man around. She's got a lot o' this stuff – don't ask me 'ow she got it, I don't know – an' she 'ands it over ev'ry time I gives 'er a knockin' an' – a bottle o' brandy.'

Sikes stared at him in disbelief.

'Yer mean, yer gettin' opium in exchange fer the liquor?' Sikes's voice was dangerous.

'No, Bill. She pays me fer the brandy, too.'

''Ow much?'

'Five bob.'

'Jesus!' breathed Sikes. 'You could 'ave 'eld out fer more; eight or nine, if you 'adn't accepted this stuff in part exchange. Toby, you really are the biggest fat-head wot's ever walked this earth.'

He sat and looked at his old friend in contemptuous amazement. Toby studied his threadbare carpet. Neither man spoke. Then Toby crouched by Sikes's chair again, proffering the pipe.

'It's good, Bill. Try it. It won't 'urt yer. You see.'

Sikes leaped from the chair with an angry swipe of his hand, knocking the glowing bowl from Toby's grasp.

'You mess about with that muck if yer want to, mate, but

don't think I'm goin' ter join yer. An' don't ferget,' he eyed Toby ominously, 'we wos *both* on that bootleggin' jaunt. *Both* of us!' And he strode from the room, crashing the door behind him.

Sikes had seen the smokers of opium through chinks in Limehouse doorways; seen the little pipes passed from one shaking hand to another; smelled the sweet, pungent aroma that hung over the human bundles huddled in the fastnesses of the dockyards. Bundles, not of ragged, poverty-stricken forms, but well-dressed, aristocratic figures, fallen to the same level as their poorer brethren. And he had known, too, those who haunted apothecaries' shops, who would pawn the coats from their backs for a phial of Kendal Black Drop. He had seen how it dragged a cove down, in whatever form, even more relentlessly than the drink. He wanted no part in such a practice. His gin- and beer-swilling were quite enough for him. He wasn't prepared to let his wits become addled, not in his job. But he worried endlessly about Toby. Not through any sentimental feelings of friendship, but for the hard reason that if they were to continue working together, Toby must stay alert and sober in every sense of the word.

He felt maudilin; ironically, he craved a drink. And he had to warn Toby that the peelers were on to him. He stood up abruptly, shrugged himself into his jacket and went from the room.

TWENTY-THREE

Sikes found Toby leaning on the bar at the Cripples.

'We 'ad visitors ternight,' he said, his voice low and pitched for Toby's ear only. Toby's only reaction was a slight glance towards Sikes. 'Peelers.'

Now Sikes had his full attention.

'Wot did yer tell 'em, Bill?'

'Nothink. But they see you come out o' Lady Wotsit's an' they're on to yer trail, Toby. Yer'd best lie low fer a bit.'

'Oh Christ!' breathed Toby. 'Who's bin an' split?'

'Well it ain't me, mate!' Sikes was immediately on the defensive.

But Toby's mind was elsewhere.

'I know wot's 'appened,' he said miserably. 'They've found the 'oard.'

'Either that or Lady H. 'as bin flauntin' 'er new bottles about,' added Sikes. 'Anyway, yer'd best get rid o' wot yer got. Bring it ter Barney. But don't go back ter Lady H.'

Toby toyed with his glass, tipping it in the hope that there was a dreg of spirits left. Sikes took pity on him and got Barney to refill it.

'An' you'd better get rid o' the hevidence of yer opium smokin' while yer about it, Toby. If they don't get you on one charge, they'll get you on another. So clear yerself altogether. Get yer winders open and throw away yer pipe an' any stuff yer got left.'

Toby looked like a man who had had his house knocked down around him.

'I shall miss it.' Toby sounded like a small child.

'Fer Gawd's sake, Toby. The police are on to you an' we

could all be blowed upon an' all yer can say is yer'll miss the bloody stuff! Wot about all that brandy? Don't yer think I'll miss that too? But I ain't askin' yer to 'ang on to it!'

He realized his voice was rising and stopped.

'No,' he said quietly. 'I won't miss the brandy. This whole business 'as started comin' between me an' Nance. An' I couldn't bear ter lose 'er.'

Toby looked at him, almost admiringly. His eyes were dilated again and there were dark rings beneath them. 'E's bin on the dam' stuff again, thought Sikes.

Toby tried to steady his wavering voice. 'She's a good gal, Bill. Yer lucky to 'ave 'er. Yer love 'er, don't yer?'

'Yus. I s'pose I do,' he admitted. 'Long as she don't peach on us.'

'She won't do that, Bill.' Toby had spotted Nancy in the corner drinking with Bet, and was watching her. 'She won't peach – unless she finds someone or somethink more worthy of 'er love than you.'

Sikes frowned. What in hell's name was Toby babbling about? The drink and the opium had got to his brain.

''Ere, Toby,' he said. 'You cut along 'ome an' destroy all the evidence. Go on. Don't 'ang about.'

Toby knocked back his gin and stumbled across the room and outside. Sikes watched him go and wondered how reliable he still was as a partner. He made his way over to Nancy, sat himself down beside her and slipped his arm protectively about her shoulders.

''Allo, Bet.' He greeted Nancy's friend with a panache which he didn't feel.

Bet smiled and dimpled at him and pushed her foot towards him under the table. Little minx, he thought, and turned his attention to Nancy, though he didn't move his legs away from Bet.

'Toby in trouble?' Nancy asked innocently.

Sikes shook his head. 'Nah. Not really. 'E's gone off now ter sort it out.'

''E don't look too well these days.' Bet held him with her

489

brown eyes.

'Not surprisin', the squalor we all lives in,' pointed out Nancy. 'I don't think Bill's bin too well either, lately.' She felt emboldened to say this, with Sikes's arm around her and Bet present for support.

Bet leaned across the table and gazed into Sikes's face. ''E looks a bit black under the eyes,' she remarked.

Nancy laughed. 'That's 'is permanent mournin' suit, Bet. You ought ter know that by now.'

Sikes was getting a little tired of being talked about as though he wasn't present. 'Come on, Nance,' he said gruffly. 'Time we was off.'

Outside, it was quite mild. She slipped her arm through his and they sauntered up Little Saffron Hill in companionable silence. Nancy dared to hope that perhaps peace might have been restored between them once more. She glanced up at Sikes, but his eyes were fixed on the road ahead. She wondered what he was thinking. If only he would talk to her sometimes, tell her what he felt and what troubled him. She squeezed his arm and laid her head against it.

At the top of the road, Sikes turned.

'Where's that bloody dog got to?' he muttered and emitted a loud, shrill whistle through his teeth.

In a moment, Bull's-eye's arthritic form appeared, running in a ridiculous waddle towards them. Sikes moved his foot, but Nancy caught at his arm.

'Don't kick 'im, Bill. 'E's only bin enjoyin' 'imself. Same as us.'

Sikes looked at her face, illumined by the soft glow of lamplight, and he kissed her there in the middle of the street, with the refuse of the City at their feet and late passers-by nudging each other and whistling at the sight.

When they reached home it was late and they were both tired, but he wanted her and began stripping off her clothes, slowly and carefully. It was not a cold night and there was a little warmth left in the embers of the fire. All the same, she shivered.

'Cold?' he asked, as she stood naked before him.

'No, Bill. Not really.'

She reached up and began to unbutton his shirt, while he ran his hands over the contours of her small body.

'I ain't never seen you with no clo'es on afore, Bill.'

She had said it shyly, tentatively. He didn't answer, but bent to pull off his boots.

'I'll do that,' said Nancy, kneeling at his feet.

They came off easily and she kneeled up, her face pressed against his thighs, her arms round his legs. He took off his waistcoat and shirt, unbuckled his belt and let them all drop on the floor. Nancy undid the fastenings at his knees and waist and pulled his breeches down. The warmth and nearness of him were overpowering.

'Stand up, gal,' he muttered, kicking his breeches to one side.

She rose to her feet and he held her close, so that she felt his hardness pressing against her. She put her hands round his back and suddenly pulled from him in horror.

'Bill!' she breathed. 'Wot's the matter with yer back?'

He drew her into his arms again, his face in her hair.

'That's nothink, Nancy. That's where I was flogged. Yer don't lose the scars of a floggin' like that.'

'My poor Bill,' she whispered.

Tentatively, she ran her hands over his back again. It was knotted and pitted like the floor of The Three Cripples. It frightened her, repulsed her, yet she felt morbidly fascinated by it. To think he carried such scars around with him, hidden from everyone. No one knew what he had suffered. Only *she* knew now how his fine body had been so ill-treated. She withdrew her hands and moved them slowly over his arms, his chest, his shoulders. She had forgotten her earlier violent treatment at his hands as she opened her body to him, willingly and unrestrained.

When dawn broke, they were both too sleepy to rise. Nancy lay with her eyes closed, not asleep, yet not properly awake, just letting the events of the last twelve hours drift across her mind. In that time, she felt she had suffered the final humiliation at Sikes's hands. Looking back, she was angry, outraged. And yet; and yet, when he had kissed her in the lamplight . . .

She looked across at him now. He was turned away from her. Gently she pulled down the covers and in the strengthening daylight she saw for the first time the angry red weals, the raised white lash-marks, hundreds of them, and the deeper, pitted scars, where the ends of the cruel cat had bitten into the flesh.

She lay staring and was suddenly aware of tears on her face. How could they do that? she thought. How could any man do that to another? No wonder 'e's so bitter about things. No wonder 'e 'as so little respect fer people. And in that moment, she forgave him everything and resolved never to leave him, no matter what he did or said.

TWENTY-FOUR

❧

Sikes was silent and morose that morning. It would be one of those days, thought Nancy, to be got through, somehow. She put a plate of eggs and ham in front of him and a large tankard of ale. He ate in silence and slung some pieces of fat at the dog. Afterwards he pulled out the box from beneath the bed and began going through the contents of his money tin.

'You ain't taken anythink from 'ere, 'ave yer, Nance?'

The question was bleak, a foreshadowing of something worse to come. Nancy shrank from answering. She stared at Sikes. What could she tell him? That she had taken a few coins to give to the poor woman across the yard, Annie's mother, whose husband beat her every night when he came home drunk; whose children were thin, emaciated little scraps; whose family would increase in size again in a very short while? Her heart had gone out to little Annie and by that route to the other children. Five of them, all under eight.

'I needed ter buy somethink, Bill.'

'Dammit, woman, I gives yer enough, surely?' He banged the lid of the chest down and fastened it angrily. ''Ow much yer taken?'

'Five poun'.'

'Five . . .?'

He grabbed her arm in what was becoming an all-too-familiar gesture. He would seize it just above her elbow, his fingers digging in and making the nerves jump and tingle. This time he twisted it, too, so that her body was brought up close to his own. His eyes were narrowed cruelly at her.

'Wot you bin buyin'?'

'I . . . nothink, Bill. I . . .'

He jerked her arm again. It had the desired effect.

'Them babes over the way. They ain't got no warm things ter wear an' they don't 'ave decent food. Not like you an' me 'ave. I couldn't bear it no longer, Bill, seein' 'em cry with cold an' 'unger.'

He was staring at her in disbelief. She ploughed on into his silence.

'If I 'ad a babe, I'd want good food an' clothin' for it. Annie's mother, she's got five. An' *I* ain't got *any* babes to love or look after.' She flung this last at him like an accusation.

'Fer Christ's sake, woman, don't keep on about a blasted brat! Every day you're at me! It's enough ter drive a man insane!'

The fingers dug tighter and he shook her with each admonition. His eyes glowed with anger and his mouth was pinched into a hard relentless line. Yet crazily, Nancy blurted on, as though she had not heard Sikes's words.

'I told 'er, if she needed more 'elp, she wos ter come ter me, because I knew 'er 'usband kept 'er short. An' I said as my man wos a good bloke an' kep' me comfor'ble.'

'Jesus! Wot 'ave you told 'er?'

His words roared over her and he seized her throat in a frenzied, convulsive movement. She clawed at his fingers; long, probing fingers, biting into her thin neck.

'Nothink, Bill.' It was difficult to squeeze the words out between those fingers. 'I ain't told 'er nothink. I wouldn't ever do that. I wouldn't let yer down, Bill. It wos only on account as she wos so desprit.'

'By God, can't you women ever keep yer bloody mouths shut?' He stared at her in disgust. Not hate, surely? 'I could kill yer fer this.' His voice was cold, so bleak and menacing.

Nancy began to sob in fright. 'Please, Bill. I wos only bein' kind to 'er.'

'Kind? To 'er? With *my* blunt? You must be out of yer 'ead, woman.'

He released her suddenly and she stumbled across the room to the chair by the fire, her hands rubbing gingerly at her throat. Sikes picked up his hat and coat, summoned the dog and stalked out of the room, crashing the door behind him.

Oh God, what was the point of trying to tolerate him? How could she put up with this for the rest of her life? Why not let herself become pregnant now and accept the inevitable? At least she would have the child. She would find somewhere to go, somewhere else to live. Perhaps far away from here. A country place, maybe. She could work, she wasn't afraid of that, and she could keep her baby close and pour out all her love on that innocent little soul. Love which, in time, would be fully requited. Surely that would be preferable to this living nightmare of love and hate, this living at the two extremes of human emotions? The thought began to take root quite firmly in Nancy's mind and she found herself in possession of an entirely new resolution.

Sikes strode southwards, knowing only that he needed to be alone. Inevitably, his footsteps took him to the river. He found a deserted spot at the top of Wapping Stairs and sat down on the damp, slimy step. The tide was out and the stench from the mud irritated his nostrils. Bull's-eye waddled down the steps and went scavenging.

It was raining hard and Sikes leaned against the wall of the stairs, which afforded him some protection against the wind. He turned up his coat collar and huddled within himself against the unseasonable elements. He needed time to think.

Where was his life going? It hadn't improved greatly since his return from exile; except that he was bringing in fairly regular cash and could live above the bread line. And then there was Nancy. He had thought she was so special, so precious in those early days. He had trusted her, he might even have admitted to feeling something more than affection for her. He thought they had developed an understanding on which to base their life together. Only now, it seemed, she was seeking to modify those criteria with her urge to get involved with others and this overpowering drive to have a child. He was fed up with her endless pleading to replicate herself. Why couldn't she be content with things as they were? Life was becoming too complicated. It had been so simple and straightforward before. Just himself to worry about. And the dog. He looked now to where the old rogue was worrying at something half-hidden in the ooze. He whistled through his teeth.

'Oi! Bull's-eye! Leave it!'

The dog glanced up and moved off, almost guiltily.

It used ter be just 'im an' me, reflected Sikes. Life were quiet an' peaceful, only meself ter please. It ain't like that now. I s'pose I ain't meant fer livin' with another.

He felt despondent at the thought. He looked down at his hands. Hard, strong, brown hands. He flexed his fingers. He'd nearly done her in that morning. It wouldn't have taken much. She'd driven him to the limits, really she had. He could so easily have tightened his grip and she'd have snuffed out like a candle. He pictured her hanging limp and lifeless from his hands as he released his hold. But her eyes still held him, reproachful, accusing.

'Ah, Nance, I couldn't,' he said to himself. Yet deep down he knew he could. Before long, something would give, something would snap, and he would regret his actions, whatever they were.

He turned west again and headed for Clerkenwell. The rain began to ease, but it had left deep puddles in the rutted streets. Passing carts splashed filthy water over pedestrians and Sikes finally arrived at The Three Cripples wet, spattered with mud and decidedly out of sorts. He had not felt so disgruntled with the weather since his journey to Shepperton.

He kicked open the door and barged into the gloom. Several folk greeted him but he acknowledged no one, ordered a large brandy at the bar and slumped himself down at the central table, where Fagin and Tom Chitling were already seated. They both looked up, silently eyeing their acquaintance. Sikes, in one of his moods, had to be treated warily.

'Hallo, Bill. Haven't seen you for a while.' Fagin was politeness itself. Tom Chitling stared, his eyes full of dread. His Bet had told him a thing or two recently.

Sikes addressed his brandy in earnest. Rain dripped from his hair and fell in dark pools on the stained wooden table. There was an uneasy silence, and he suddenly felt himself alone and unwanted in this populous capital. He took large gulps of brandy and closed his eyes. But always he could see Nancy's eyes staring at him in terror that morning.

'I should never 'ave frightened 'er like that,' he muttered.

He hadn't realized that he had spoken aloud. Fagin leaned forward.

'What have you done to Nancy, my dear?' He laid his hand on Sikes's wet sleeve as he spoke. Sikes shook it off.

'Oh leave me be. I ain't done nothink to 'er. I ain't done nothink to anyone. Yet,' he added, his eye ominously upon the old man.

Fagin shifted uncomfortably in his seat. 'She's a good girl at heart, is Nancy,' he said to no one in particular.

'Bet thinks the world of her,' Tom Chitting added, proud that his Bet should know a good woman when she saw one.

'Fancies 'erself as a do-gooder now,' grumbled Sikes.

Fagin's eyebrows shot up. 'That ain't good for business, you know,' he hissed.

'Dam' me, I know it ain't,' retorted Sikes. 'My hard-earned money goin' ter folks with a string o' brats.'

'Ah well,' sighed Fagin, relaxing a little. 'She always did have a soft spot for the kinchin. "Little Mother" Bet used to call her. She'll be better when she has her own, Bill.'

'She does that an' I'm away. Quick as yer like,' confided Sikes. 'Yer won't catch me 'angin' around fer no brats.'

He finished his brandy, then went to the bar to refill his glass.

'Oh there'll be trouble and strife there, my dear,' remarked Fagin to his young companion. 'You mark my words. Those two are as unstable as phosphorous and water together. Likely to blow at any moment.'

Tom's fears increased with a chilling of his spine. 'I'll be off now,' he said, rising. 'I'm taking Bet to see the new locomotives on the London and Greenwich Line. One day I'll buy her a ticket on one of them trains.'

He grinned and Fagin smiled at his boyish enthusiasm.

'You're a good lad, Tom. You look after young Bet.'

Tom disappeared and Fagin waited for Sikes to return from the bar. When he did, he had a half-bottle of brandy in his hand.

'Bit early in the day, my dear. Is something troubling you?'

The last thing Sikes wanted to hear was Fagin's ingratiating comments.

'I ain't talking, Fagin. So bugger off an' leave me alone.'

Fagin stayed where he was, humming softly under his breath, watching the level in the brandy bottle drop lower; watching Sikes's eyes become bloodshot and his body acquiring a slumped posture.

'She wants a child, yer know.'

The statement slurred out of the brandy fumes and Fagin was momentarily startled.

'They're all right if yer've got somewhere decent ter bring 'em up. But not 'ere, Fagin. It ain't good for 'em. I know. I seen my brothers all die off when they wos littl'uns. I seen wot it done ter me mother, too.'

He stopped and regarded the contents of his glass. Fagin noticed that the smouldering green eyes were overcast with a film of something brighter.

Sikes went on, his voice tremulous, unlike his own, 'I don't want that to 'appen to 'er. She couldn't cope. She ain't very strong, yer know.'

Fagin nodded his head. He knew how deceptive Nancy's frailty was. He was surprised that Sikes hadn't seen through it yet. Or perhaps he had and the man was trying to persuade himself otherwise. Fagin thought it more likely that Sikes didn't want the responsibilities of fatherhood.

'She talks ter people, Fagin,' went on Sikes. 'That worries me, too. She could come out with anythink.'

'She won't peach,' Fagin assured him. 'Besides, you're among your own kind in Old Nicol Street, surely?'

'Huh! Don't trust no one. That's my policy. It's safer that way.'

'Not even Nance?'

Sikes shrugged. 'I dunno.'

He lumbered to his feet and left the Cripples without saying goodbye to Fagin. His belly was afire with so much brandy and he had had nothing to eat since breakfast. The fresh air knocked his breath away for a moment and he leaned against a wall to recover.

Then he moved away slowly, using the wall for support. He felt strange. He was down, he was depressed, yet he felt extremely light-headed, as though he could have floated high above the towering rooftops of the City. Suddenly, unaccountably, he wanted Nancy. He wanted to bury his face in her soft flesh; he wanted to feel the warmth of her arms about him again; above all, he wanted to lose himself in the ecstatic delights of her body. It was the only thing worth living for at the moment. He had to get back to her, to recapture the joy that had been theirs last night. He saw again her naked body, slight and pale in the flickering candle light. He shivered.

But it was a tidy way home and he needed strength. He hesitated outside The Crown in Clerkenwell Green, then lurched inside the bar parlour, where he consumed another brandy. Temporarily fortified, he made his way ponderously across Smithfield, stumbling over empty crates and kicking aside the unspeakable remains of the morning's market. At the entrance to one of the great halls, he stood and retched as the smell of stale offal filled his nostrils. Passers-by looked at him in disgust; but the sight was not unusual, a man drunk in daylight.

It had begun to rain again and he stood for a moment to lift his face to the cool drizzle. He remembered doing the same thing years ago, one dark November morning. He had felt at the end of everything then. He walked on, his mouth bitter with the taste of vomit. He found a drinking fountain in West

Smithfield and cupped the cold clear water in his shaking hands. He splashed some over his face and his hands scraped against the rough stubble of his cheeks. He couldn't remember when he last shaved.

He looked around him. He shouldn't have come this way. This was not the way home. Not the way back to Nancy. It lay in quite the opposite direction. He wondered if his wits were failing him, and retraced his steps. By the time he reached St Luke's he had a raging thirst, which he quenched with a pint of beer at The Mitre, followed by a large whisky at The Three Tuns, just past the Lying-in Hospital.

Somehow he gained the haven of Old Nicol Street, where he rested against the familiar archway. He was sick again and as he stood leaning his head against the rough, dirty yellow brick, he was aware of eyes on him. He turned his head miserably. It was the child, Annie. Nance had pointed her out last week. That was before she had been handy with his blunt. The child stood watching him, her face solemn and concerned. She was wearing a blue wool dress with a little shawl tied round her thin shoulders. There were boots on her feet. Last time he had seen her, she had been in rags.

Realization suddenly dawned.

'Get away, will yer?' he shouted, the tears of retching still blurring his eyes. 'Clear off, you an' yer fancy togs.'

Annie turned and fled, terrified by the big dark man in the archway.

He staggered up the stairs and flung open the door. Nancy was there, but there was no joy in his homecoming. She was washing smalls in a bowl, her sleeves rolled up to reveal her pale thin arms. Sikes went over to her and stood behind her, running his hands over the front of her dress.

'Bill, wot on earth you bin doin'? You bin sick? Go an' 'ave a wash an' a drink.'

Meekly he complied. But something was welling up inside, threatening to choke him. And it wasn't nausea. He stripped off his coat, his jacket and his waistcoat and doused his head in cold water. He filled a tankard with ale and took a long

500

draft. He went back to where Nancy still stood, her arms in the frothy water. He ran his hands over her shiny arms and they came away wet and made wet patches on her blue gown when he put his hands on her breasts.

'Leave that,' he muttered hoarsely.

Nancy turned to him, wiping her hands on her apron. Sikes caught her face in his hands and kissed her hard. His breath was foul and she almost gagged. But she knew his mouth would soon be busy elsewhere. She slipped her arms round his neck and held him close. He began fumbling desperately with the fastenings of her dress, his breathing urgent, laboured. Nancy stood passively while he stripped her naked, a repetition of the night before. Only there hadn't been this urgency. He was muttering into her ear as he pushed her on to the bed.

'I'm sorry, Nance. Oh Gawd, I'm sorry, gal. Fer wot I done.'

She said nothing, but tightened her hold on him, one with him again as she rose to meet his thrusting and felt the enormous surge of his climax within her. She didn't care any longer if his seed should germinate in her. She felt a peace within her which she had not known before. Was this the moment of conception? The moment she had longed for? Would this mark the beginning of the end of the road for her and Sikes? A second of panic. Could she really let him go, fend for herself on the streets again?

He lay on his back, exhausted.

'Bill, wot if I'm knapped?'

There was no reply.

'Wot if you've given me a babe?'

The green eyes, not quite focusing properly, were studying her.

'You know bloody well wot, Nance. I'll be off. I ain't 'angin' about fer brats. There was one down in the yard when I come in. Starin' at me, she wos. One o' them brats you 'elped.'

'Little Annie?'

'Yeah. Cheeky little varmint. Wotchin' me, she wos. I can't bear kids starin' all the time.'

Nancy sighed and slipped out of Sikes's arms. She went back to her washing. The spent fluid ran down her legs and she felt uncomfortable. Women had a lot to put up with at the hands of men, she reflected. And some hands were stronger and crueller than others.

TWENTY-FIVE

◆

By summer Sikes and Nancy were spending less time at the Cripples and Sikes had been engaged on several small cracks on his own. He was making regular money now, which Nancy had not dared to touch, and he had not seen Toby Crackit for some weeks. He feared the peelers had caught up with his old friend, yet he felt sure that he would have heard soon enough if Toby was in trouble.

One morning in August, Sikes and Nancy had a visitor. It was stifling in the lodging house. Sikes had managed to shift the stubborn window a little to let in some air and they had flung open the door. His heart sank when Fagin's tattered red locks appeared in the doorway. Bull's-eye set up a sustained growling and snarling and Fagin hesitated on the threshold. Sikes was tinkering with the clock, which had stopped during the night.

'Come in then, if yer goin' to,' he snapped.

Fagin always managed to raise Sikes's hackles as well as Bull's-eye's.

'Call that dog off then, Bill,' retorted Fagin.

''E won't 'urt you, 'less I tells 'im to.'

Fagin looked doubtfully at the bared teeth and threatening posture and sidled nervously into the room. The dog growled again, menacingly.

'Lie down, dam' yer!' shouted Sikes.

The dog grudgingly obeyed. Fagin shuffled to the table and Sikes indicated a chair. Nancy came and sat on the edge of the table, her arm around Sikes's shoulders.

'Good to see you looking so well and happy, my dears,' Fagin said ingratiatingly.

'Oh shut up, Fagin, an' 'ave a shove in the mouth.'

503

And Sikes pushed a bottle of beer towards his fence. The latter held up his hands in mild protest.

'No thank you, my dear. A little too early in the day for me.'

'Ballocks!' exploded Sikes, with a rare laugh. 'You reformed, or somethink, Fagin?'

'No, Bill,' he said, 'but I've a little matter to discuss with you.'

Sikes cocked an eyebrow at him but said nothing.

'You remember back at Christmas, I mentioned a little job that needed doing?'

'Aye. I remember. Wot was it, then?'

'The perfect lay. But it will need more than two of you and you'll need a snakesman.'

Nancy felt Sikes stiffen under her hand. He leaned forward and the old look was back in his eye.

'I could do with the push,' he said, 'but I ain't workin' in no gang.'

'No, Bill, no. No gangs. I know you've had enough of gangs in your life.'

Gawd, 'e's pushin' 'is luck, thought Sikes. But he let Fagin continue.

'Listen, Bill. You, Toby and Nancy. And I'll provide the snakesman.'

Nancy sat bolt-upright, frowning. 'I can fork,' she said proudly, 'as well you know. But I ain't doin' Bill's job.'

'You can hold the cracking tools and loot, my dear,' smiled her old mentor.

Sikes turned angrily on him. 'You leave Nancy out o' this, you interferin' ole fence! Yer must be out o' yer mind ter even suggest it!'

'Wait, Bill, wait.' Fagin smoothed the air with his words. 'You need two on the inside for this job and a canary. And if you want to keep it in the family, as it were, who better than Nancy?'

Sikes banged the table with his fist. 'I tell you, I ain't puttin' 'er at risk. She can fork if she wants, long as she's careful. She knows that. But I ain't avin' 'er on a crack!'

Fagin shrugged. 'A pity, my boy. There's a great deal of silver there – and a lot of cash.'

He rose to go, but Sikes's hand shot out and grabbed his wrist.

'I'll do it, dam' an' blast yer. But I'm buggered if my Nance is goin' ter play canary.'

Fagin sat down again and began to explain. The house was a large one, with steps and portico and a basement area in South Square, west of Gray's Inn Road. Fagin had pre-empted Sikes and Toby's work over the past six or seven weeks by posting his own noses, his young spies, about the place and he had built up a very clear picture of the property. Sikes was furious when he heard this and would have refused to have anything further to do with the business. He and Toby always did their own reconnaissance. But Fagin calmed him down and went on to elaborate on the means of entry: a small window in the area. Hence the need for a snakesman and a pretty small one at that. He would open the door, once he was inside, and Sikes and Toby would lift what they could. Nancy's part would be to receive the goods as they were handed out through the area window. She would then bring them straight to Fagin, together with the tools, and if the men were caught, there would at least be nothing on them.

Sikes saw the sense in all this and finally, though reluctantly, agreed to Nancy's part in the job. The girl looked pleased. She felt Sikes trusted her completely now.

'Wot's 'appened ter Toby these days?' enquired Sikes. 'I ain't seen 'im these last few weeks. 'E ain't in trouble, is 'e?'

Fagin gave his oily smile and shook his head. 'He had to lie low after your little – ah – trip together back in the spring.'

His eyes slid from Sikes to Nancy and back again. He wondered if Nancy knew about the brandy and the opium. He wasn't sure and he wouldn't pursue that line now. Sikes was staring at him with a cold, steely gaze.

Instead, he went on to say, 'I think Toby has moved house. But I'm sure you know that.'

'I don't!' snapped Sikes. 'Where's 'e gone?'

'I'm not at liberty to say, Bill.'

Sikes leaped to his feet, seized Fagin by his coat lapels and shook him.

'Listen, Fagin. 'E's my friend an' I want ter know where 'e is an' wot's appened to 'im. You know ezackly where 'e is, don't yer?'

Fagin's eyes were wide with fear. He had tried so hard to keep the upper hand over Sikes. But the man was too strong for him, mentally and physically. The only hold he had over him at all was to slip the word to the police. And that might well bring them all to the gallows. He decided, wisely, to comply with Sikes's request.

'All right, all right, Bill. He's in lodgings in Seven Dials. He felt it was safer there.'

Sikes let him go, suddenly, with a short laugh.

'Hah! Flash Toby Crackit! In the rookeries? That's the best thing I've 'eard in a long time. Gawd, wot a laugh! I must call on our flash friend.'

'Yes, Bill,' muttered Fagin, nonplussed. 'You do that.'

He took himself off, leaving Sikes smirking to himself. Nancy smiled. Fagin might be a cunning old rogue, but he had certainly put Bill in a good mood and she was pleased. She went back to the saucepan she had been scouring. When it was clean, she chopped up some cold bacon and vegetables and tipped them into the pan with some stock from a basin in the pantry. As she stirred the cold, greasy mess, she felt a sudden wave of nausea and reached for the slop-pail. She retched, but nothing came. She leaned against the cold marble shelf and shut her eyes, waiting for the sensation to subside. Sikes called to her.

'You all right, Nance?'

'Yes, Bill,' she replied. 'Somethink I ate, I s'pect.'

'Them bloody eel pies o' Barney's, I shouldn't wonder. Enough ter make anyone throw up.' He came into the pantry, a mug of water in his hand. ''Ere, drink this, gal. Yer'll feel better.'

She drank gratefully, but he was frowning at her.

'You looks very pale, Nance. Go an' lie down.'

'I can't, Bill. There's yer dinner ter cook.'

'Dam' me, woman! That can wait. I ain't goin' ter starve! Anyway, I always used ter cook me own, remember?'

And he smiled at her and kissed her clammy forehead.

She fell asleep almost as soon as her head touched the pillow and when she woke, it was dusk. Sikes was not there, but he had tucked the bedspread round her and left a mug of water on the bedside table. She smiled. He *did* care about her, whatever his treatment of her. She felt better now and stretched out comfortably on the bed. But the knowledge that she might feel poorly again tomorrow dispelled her happy mood. 'It's somethink I ate, it must be,' she told herself. 'It can't be anythink else.' But she knew that it could be and probably was. Twice she had missed now and she had no real doubt as to what was happening inside her. She hugged the knowledge to herself. 'Just a little longer with 'im. Please. Just a little longer.'

Sikes had gone to seek out Toby Crackit, grinning to himself at the thought of Toby brought down to his proper station in life. He hadn't been back to Seven Dials since the day of his return from exile and he wondered if he would be recognized. He entered the rookeries by St Giles's church and sauntered at leisure through the warren of lanes which he knew so well, even after all this time. The smell was just the same, a mixture of rotting vegetation, stale water and sewage. Flies were everywhere and mangy-looking dogs rootled like pigs among the refuse. Dirty children, with scarcely a thread on their backs, squealed and laughed and jumped among the filth. Idle men lounged at every street corner and on every post and in every doorway. He could hear a fight going on up a side alley, two women screaming abuse at each other, while others cheered them on. What work was done here was mostly done under cover of darkness, as Sikes well knew.

There was a small passageway off Little East Street, called Monmouth Court. A tavern backed on to either end of it. Sikes thought this very appropriate for Toby's needs. He found the lodging house halfway down and knocked at the door. At least the high, close tenements here blocked out the sun and afforded some shade.

The lodging-house keeper shuffled to the door in his slippers and blinked like a mole at Sikes.

'Mr Crackit?' he repeated in a strained, thin voice. 'Mr Crackit? Oh yes, guv'nor. 'E's the one in the basement.'

Sikes was surprised. He hadn't even noticed a ground-level window. But then the windows were mostly the same colour as the drab, grey walls in which they hung so precariously. The old man pointed to a flight of narrow steps descending from the street. Sikes went down them and hammered on the door.

A familiar, but frightened voice called, 'Yes? Who is it?'

'It's me, Toby. Bill. Are you goin' ter let me in?'

There was a rattling of chains and a shooting of bolts and at last Toby's long, thin face appeared at the crack in the door.

'Come on, Toby. Stop messin' about an' let me in!'

Satisfied that it was only his friend who had come, Toby allowed Sikes in and quickly locked the door. Sikes looked at the room in some disgust. It was very small and dark and he was aware of an overriding smell of damp. The only light came from the window at street level, where occasionally a blurred pair of legs ambled past. A low, pallet bed, which looked as though it had come from a cell in Newgate, stood in the far corner, with Toby's greatcoat flung across it. On the table were some dry pieces of bread, several empty bottles and numerous mouse droppings. There was no grate and the only decoration in the room was a large patch of wet rot spreading itself inexorably across one wall.

'Burn my body,' he muttered to himself, 'you *'ave* come down in the world an' no mistake.'

'Oh no, Bill,' Toby hastened to assure him. 'No I 'aven't. Not at all. I'm just lyin' low fer the present. I feel safer 'ere.'

Sikes narrowed his eyes. 'So safe, yer wouldn't even send word ter yer ole mate ter say where yer wos! I wos worried,

Toby. I thought yer'd bin shopped. After all, if *you're* nabbed, things won't look too good fer me. The peelers ain't on to yer, are they?'

'Nah,' said Toby, relaxing a little. 'I just thought the ole lady might spill the beans.'

'But that wos three months ago, Toby. Wot yer bin livin' on?'

Toby looked miserable.

'Not much, Bill. Blunt's pretty low.'

'I should think it is! Come on, Toby. Come an' 'ave a drink an' some grub. Fagin's got a new crack fer us. 'E's left it ter me ter tell you fer once.'

'I can't, Bill. I can't go out. They'll see me. They'll get me.'

Sikes frowned.

'Who will? Who's goin' ter get yer?'

'Them. The coves at the end o' the passage,' and he pointed with a shaking finger in the vague direction of the City.

'Toby,' Sikes said sternly, ''ow long since you last 'ad any opium?'

'Since you tole me the peelers wos askin' questions. I 'aven't seen Lady 'Arley since then. I 'aven't 'ad so much as a sniff o' the stuff.'

His eyes were brimming with tears and his thin frame shook. He was breathing fast and seemed distracted. Sikes took him by the shoulders and sat him in a chair. It was dark in the room and he could barely see Toby's face, but he knew it bore a pained and twisted expression.

'Toby,' he said quietly, 'yer've finished with the opium. There are no more trips along the road. And no one is waitin' for yer. Yer must get out an' get back ter normal.'

The tears slid down Toby's face and Sikes guessed he was suffering in the wake of the loss of the drug. He must be firm with him.

'Come on,' he said practically. 'Come on upstairs. It's light up there. Much 'appier than down in this mole-'ole.'

He pulled Toby to his feet and led him, unprotesting, up to street level, where he stood blinking in the light which was trying to filter through into Monmouth Court. Sikes saw him clearly for the first time and was appalled at his friend's appearance. Was this really the same flash cove who'd bounced into his life ten, eleven years ago? The fellow who'd driven him on through such atrocious conditions to the fight at Shepperton? The friend he'd drunk with, whored with, cracked cribs with, sometimes even laughed with? He stood looking at him now. Toby's clothes were filthy and hung on his body as though they didn't belong. His thin hair had grown long and tangled. His face was the colour of parchment, with eyes huge and deep-set above his sunken cheeks. He had a ragged growth of beard and when he grinned self-consciously at Sikes for a second, it was obvious that some of his teeth had started to go black. And he stank to high heaven!

Sikes knew he must get Toby back to his former flashiness if they were to carry off a crack successfully together. And there was precious little time left before the day of the appointed job by which Fagin was setting so much store.

TWENTY-SIX

St Bartholomew's Day dawned bright and clear. The August
light filtered golden and almost mellow into the City. The
streets were full of bustle and preparation from daybreak
onwards. The celebration should, strictly speaking, have
taken place within the parish of St Bartholomew, but over the
years it had spread out across the capital, until there was
scarcely a thoroughfare or a green that wasn't making ready
for the night to come.

Toby Crackit arrived very early at Sikes's lodging,
nervously tapping at the door.

Nancy slid carefully from the bed and tiptoed across the
room. Her heart beating, she laid her cheek to the rough
wood and hissed, 'Who is it?'

'Toby,' came the reply.

Nancy's heart sank. It would appear they were to be
saddled with Toby all day. He was 'gen-teel' enough, she
conceded, in an odd sort of way. But he lacked the backbone
of her Bill. Still, she couldn't leave him standing outside their
room all morning. So she carefully turned the key and opened
the door a crack. Toby's long pale face emerged from the dim
landing. Nancy was worried. He didn't look like a man ready
to crack a toff's crib that night. She opened the door wide and
laid a finger to her lips. Toby slipped in and sat down by the
empty grate.

'Yer a bit early,' Nancy whispered. 'You want some breakfast?'

'Please. I 'ad ter come. I couldn't stick it on me own no
longer. I was that scared, Nance.'

Nancy looked at him sharply, as she laid and lit the fire.
This wasn't the Toby they'd known last autumn. She

wondered if Bill knew what the trouble was. Toby seemed a shadow of what he had been. He sat looking gloomily at the fresh flames which Nancy had kindled, glancing nervously towards the bed every few minutes.

When the fire had some strength in it, Nancy put a kettle of water over it to boil and handed Toby a toasting fork and a plate of sausages and bread. He might as well make himself useful, she thought. Her clatterings in the pantry finally woke Sikes.

'Gawd, Nancy. D'yer have ter make so much bloody noise? Wot yer doin' of?'

'Come on, Bill,' laughed Nancy. 'Time you got up. Toby's 'ere.'

Sikes sat bolt-upright, blinking in surprise at his unlooked-for early caller.

'Wot in Gawd's name brings you 'ere, Toby? I thought we wos meetin' down the tavern ternight?'

Toby looked uncomfortable under Sikes's dishevelled and disparaging gaze.

'I couldn't sleep, Bill. Worried about ternight. Yer know 'ow it is, Bill? You understand, don't yer?'

Sikes sighed and flung back the bedclothes. 'Aye. I understand.' He ran his fingers through his hair and stood looking down at Toby as though he would like to have removed him from the room on the end of his boot. 'I understand that you're feelin' scared out o' yer wits, an' yer want ter cry off ternight. Is that it? Am I right?'

Toby nodded miserably. Sikes leaned across Toby's chair, so that his face was very close.

'Woss got into yer, mate? Yer used ter be full o' spirit, game fer anythink. Nah yer like a bloody jellyfish, squirmin' at the first signs o' danger. Woss the matter with yer?'

He was angry. It was he, Sikes, who now took on all the organizing of their activities. Toby was following meekly in his wake. He supposed it was the result of the opium-taking. Well, it wouldn't do. If Toby went on like this, he was likely to peach on any of them without even knowing what he was doing or saying. Toby must be taken in hand.

512

'Nance,' Sikes ordered, 'fill this cove up with a good breakfast an' a jug of ale. We've got the day ter sort 'im out.'

Sikes went to relieve himself and Nancy filled a plate with sausages, eggs and a little bacon, which she placed on the table for Toby. He sat down to the modest feast and out of the corner of his eye watched Sikes swill cold water over his head and shoulders, and then put on a clean shirt. While he was buttoning it, he walked back to Toby.

'You ain't on that rubbidge again, are yer?' he asked quietly. Nancy was busy in the pantry.

'Nah, Bill. But I sometimes wish I was. I ain't felt right since I come off it. I get 'eadaches summat awful an' I ain't bin able ter drink much fer weeks.'

'Well, get that down yer fer starters.' Sikes indicated a tankard of beer which Nancy had placed on the table. 'We'll set yer ter somethink stronger later in the day.'

Toby finished his meal and drained his mug, while Sikes demolished his own breakfast and Nancy sat by the fire, her plate on her lap.

Presently, Sikes wiped his mouth with the back of his hand and said to Toby, 'You are *up* to this 'ere crack ternight, I take it? Yer not goin' ter do summat stupid?'

Toby laughed. 'I'll be all right, Bill. I can manage the crack. I know ezackly wot ter do. I just need a little fortifyin', that's all,' he added nervously.

They spent the next hour preparing their tools and weaponry for the evening. It was very hot, even with the fire burning low in the grate, and the two men were soon reduced to their shirtsleeves. Nancy went down to Covent Garden Market and purchased a quantity of cheap roses, with which to form the cover for her basket. When she returned, she found with relief that the men had gone out. The morning air had done nothing to relieve her mounting nausea and when she had set down her basket and put the flowers to stand in a bucket of water, she laid herself on the bed and tried to sleep. But the truth kept her awake. She knew for certain now that she was pregnant. She laid her hands on her belly. It didn't feel any different, but she knew that Sikes's child lay curled within her, growing, strengthening daily. She wondered how long she could hide the knowledge from him and so keep him with her a little longer. She thought of places where she might go to be rid of the tiny parasite. Places where old crones gave you draughts of bitter potions and poked about inside you with their knitting needles. She shuddered. Her maternal senses recoiled from such a thought. She had tried not to get knapped, but it was evidently meant to be. She would bear this child and the consequences.

She breathed deeply, and eventually, the sickness passed and she slept. She was awakened in the middle of the afternoon by the door bursting open and the two men staggering noisily into the room. Toby waved a hand weakly at her and collapsed into a chair. But Sikes came to her side and sat on the bed, leaning over her.

'Woss up, Nance?' His voice was slurred and he reeked of beer and tobacco smoke. Nancy blanched at the smell, but smiled and sat up.

'I'm all right, Bill. Just felt a bit tired. Can't do with bein' tired on the job ternight, can I?'

'Nah. But yer looks a bit pale, gal. Yer all right?'

He was concerned for her now, even through his drunken haze. But would he still care when he knew what she carried within her?

''Course I am,' she laughed, patting his thigh and wriggling from the bed. 'You two look as though yer could do with a sleep.'

'Yus. I reckon we could.'

Sikes stretched out his long frame on the space Nancy had vacated and propped his booted feet on the footboard. He sighed and closed his eyes. In a moment, both he and Toby were snoring peacefully. Nancy laughed and set about heating water to wash clothes. No point in wasting time waiting for dark.

The bells began ringing just before six and Sikes was jerked rudely awake by the noise.

514

'Wot the blazes . . . ?' he began, rolling off the bed.

'Bartlemy Fair startin', Bill,' Nancy reminded him. 'Yer've got work ter do, remember.'

Sikes stood up and stretched. Bull's-eye crept over cautiously towards him, but Sikes's foot shot out. The dog yelped.

'You can stay out of it fer a start. Yer'll be properly in the way, you will!'

He punched Toby on the shoulder and said, 'Get up, mate. Time we was off.'

Toby came sleepily to his feet. Then, after making sure they had everything they needed with them, the three set off for Holborn, leaving Bull's-eye to guard the lodging.

They went by Finsbury and Cripplegate and came out into the thick of the fair, where they were almost crushed by the press of people. Nancy looked wistfully at the stalls selling ribbons and trinkets. Had she not been helping Bill and Toby, had she not felt unwell, she might have stopped and enjoyed a half-hour in the noisy throng. As it was, she felt an unaccountable tiredness taking hold of her and found her feet dragging. More than once she lost hold of Sikes's hand and he stopped and waited for her.

'Come on, Nance,' he said, 'we don't want to 'ang about 'ere fer folks ter get a good look at us.'

And they would press on again, battling through the surging tide of noisy humanity. They eventually left some of the noise behind, as they turned into a dark and evil-looking street, then came out on to Field Lane and so on to The Three Cripples. Sikes had feared there would be few customers tonight, on account of the fair, but he was pleased to find the tavern full to bursting, the people coming and going to slake their thirst; a good cover for their own movements for the evening. They were greeted with nods of recognition and they wedged themselves into two high- backed settles on the raised floor of the parlour.

Sikes had planned the evening carefully. Toby had been loosened up with a good dose of ale during the afternoon and Sikes intended that he should have no more than a couple of brandies to fortify him for the rest of the night's work. He himself felt the strange elation which he always experienced before a crack. He was quite sober now and he, too, would limit himself to fortifying spirits only. Nancy could have her gin if she wanted, but he was surprised when she asked if she might have brandy instead. Barney came over with measures and glasses. He looked harassed.

'Bus'ness ain't bad, is it, Barney?' asked Sikes, as the first flow of fiery liquid burned his stomach.

'Doe, Bister Sikes, but I could do wid a hand. 'Ow about your Dancy 'elpin' out ternight?'

Nancy's eyes flickered towards Sikes, who hesitated momentarily.

'No. Not ternight, Barney. We're busy.'

Barney looked hard at him. Surely Sikes wasn't getting his doxy involved in the business? The girl didn't look too well anyway. He shrugged and shuffled away.

'Blast!' muttered Sikes.

'No matter, Bill,' said Toby.

He seemed suddenly to have shaken off his anxiety and looked more alert and ready for the job than Sikes would have thought possible earlier in the day.

'Barney's a close one,' went on Toby. 'Yer knows that.'

'I know,' grumbled Sikes. 'It's just that I'd rather no one knew we were busy ternight.'

By half-past seven, Sikes deemed it time to get started and they went out severally from the Cripples, meeting up again outside Fagin's lodging house. Fred let them in, cowering back when Sikes strode past him and up the stairs. He had not forgotten how Sikes had floored Toby Crackit last year and he feared those fists.

'Well, Fagin, where is 'e?' demanded Sikes.

Fagin thrust forward a very thin, very stunted boy of some eight years. The child stood looking up at Sikes's great height, but he was not afraid. He had been well schooled by Fagin and knew his own worth.

'Evenin', Mr Sikes,' he piped. 'I'm all ready, sir.'

Sikes cocked an eyebrow at the young imp and said sharply, 'Wot's yer name, boy?'

'Ned Green, sir.'

'Well, Ned. Yer knows wot yer ter do. An' not a squeak out of yer, or yer'll 'ave a napper full o' lead. Understand?'

'Yus, sir,' answered Ned, very smartly.

'He's a good lad, my dear.' Fagin's voice sluiced its way into the exchange. 'You'll find him very useful.'

Sikes cast a black look at his fence and the four thieves left the lodging.

By the time they reached South Square the light was fading and gas lamps had been lit. Toby and Sikes left Nancy and Ned in a passageway while they sauntered through and eyed up the buildings. The square was almost deserted. There were no carriages and it seemed as though Fagin's young spies had been correct when they reported that the house in question would be empty this evening. Being Bartlemy Fair, most of the other householders were out enjoying themselves, too, and only a few servants had been retained to guard the houses.

The two men walked quietly back to the passage. Sikes thought Nancy had seemed unnaturally quiet since their arrival at the Cripples, but he put it down to nervousness on her part.

'All set, gal?' he whispered.

She nodded and squeezed his arm.

'Be careful, Bill.'

He didn't answer but strode away from her, with the snakesman in tow.

Nancy stood at the top of the area steps, her basket of flowers on her arm, while Sikes cut the glass in the pantry window in a few seconds. He lifted Ned as though he were a paper doll and shoved him through the opening.

'Now. Quick,' whispered Sikes. 'The door.'

The small boy was heard fumbling and muttering at the area door, while Sikes and Toby waited outside in a fret of impatience. Sikes leaned against the door.

'Woss up, boy?' he called quietly, his voice rising above a whisper in his anxiety.

'I can't open the door, sir,' squeaked Ned. 'The bolts won't budge. I ain't strong enough.'

'Hell's fires! Someone'll pay fer this!' Sikes spluttered. Then he hissed, 'Ned! Open the front door an' then get back down ter the pantry as quick as yer can. Yer'll be needed there.'

Ned Green raced away and in a moment they saw the big front door open silently. The two men crept up the steps and slid inside, while Nancy stood on the area stairs, keeping a sharp lookout.

She waited nervously, an odd pain threatening her belly. Once, she heard distant shouting and was afraid lest revellers came into the square. But the voices faded. There was a light shining from a house on the far side, but after a while, the blinds were drawn and the only light came from a flickering gas lamp at one side of the square.

Presently, she heard Sikes call quietly from the broken window and he began handing out items of silver to her, which she stowed in her basket and covered with a cloth. Then she rearranged the flowers on top. When the basket was full and Sikes thought Nancy could carry no more, he put his hand through the opening in the window and gently chucked her under the chin with his fist.

'Good gal,' he whispered. 'Nah. Straight ter Fagin's. An' . . .' He hesitated. 'Watch 'ow yer go.'

The pain was there again, but Nancy smiled and blew him a kiss. Then she lugged her heavy basket away towards Field Lane. But as she slipped along the passageway into Gray's Inn Road, the house-owner's carriage turned into the square by way of an open area on its High Holborn side. The sound of hooves brought both men to the windows. Toby was in an upstairs room and saw the carriage arrive. He immediately climbed out of a back window, slithered down a drainpipe and was away over the yard wall, trusting that Sikes was behind him. Sikes, however, was trapped. He pushed young

Ned back through the area window and told him to run for his life. But Sikes could not fit through so small an aperture. He went to the door of the butler's pantry and listened. He could hear a lot of running about and shouting above him. Silently, he crept up the stairs to ground level and listened again, secreting himself in an alcove under the main staircase. The noise of the servants had drifted further upwards and he assumed they were all rushing about from one bedroom to another. He heard the little screams of dismay as the ladies of the house discovered the loss of their jewels and trinkets. Sikes grinned to himself. The front door stood wide open. The hallway was large. But it would only take a few seconds to sprint across and down the half-dozen shallow front steps and he could be away. He could hear no one at hand on the ground floor. With his heart pounding, he took his chance and ran for freedom. But as he reached the doorstep, a loud report rang out. A searing pain swept through his leg. And he collapsed down the steps and lay in a painful heap on the pavement.

TWENTY-SEVEN

Never before had Nancy experienced pain like this. It had grown and spread and seemed to be dragging her very being towards the earth, as though some primal force were reaching up to pluck the seedling growing within her. She staggered blindly up the stairs to Fagin's den, the sweat standing out on her white face. She dropped the heavy basket and slumped against the door, rather than knocked on it. Fagin himself opened it and caught her as she fell.

'Charley! Dodger! Come quick and help me! It's Nancy.'

The two boys rushed to his assistance and between them they carried Nancy to a chair by the fire.

'Brandy!' roared Fagin, 'and Dodger – fetch that basket in afore anyone helps themselves to the pretty contents!' He chuckled to himself. 'And young Tom, nip around and find Bet. Tell her Nancy's poorly. She'll likely need a woman's touch. I can't be doing with these females.'

He pulled a blanket from one of the boy's beds and tucked it round Nancy, while Charley held a small measure of brandy to her lips. This seemed to revive her a little. She smiled up wanly at them.

'Now,' said Fagin, 'one of you will have to go and check the square and make sure Bill and –'

He was interrupted by a desperate hammering on the door.

Dodger opened the door to reveal the scared and shaking figure of little Ned Green, the snakesman. He stood now, twisting his cap in his hand, his face grimed with tears of fright and exhaustion. He had run all the way from Gray's Inn Road to Field Lane and his thin chest heaved with the effort. Fagin peered at him in alarm.

'Come in, my dear,' he said briskly, 'and tell us how it went.'

The boy couldn't move yet, but he had to gasp out his story.

'Please, sir,' he stammered, 'the family come back just after Miss Nancy left. Mr Crackit got away by a back winder – I think – an' Mr Sikes put me through the area winder an' tole me ter leg it. I did – as far as the corner. Then I 'id an' waited ter see wot'd 'appen.'

His eye caught a movement from the fireplace.

'Bill? Is he all right? He got away too?' whispered Nancy fearfully.

The boy stared at her and then at Fagin, his eyes round with terror.

'Go on, my boy, tell all,' urged Fagin.

The child continued, his eyes flickering nervously from Nancy to Fagin and back again.

'Well – the fam'ly set up sich a to-do when they found the front door open an' they all ran inside, servants an' all. Then I see Mr Sikes at the top o' the steps comin' out. Next thing there was a bang an 'e come tumblin' ter the bottom an' the man come out with a barker.'

Nancy's hands were at her mouth and her eyes were huge and frightened in her pale face.

'Mr Sikes were clutchin' 'is leg an' the man an' the servants all jumped on 'im, like, an' the man sends one of 'em fer a peeler. An' – well – they puts the ruffles on 'im an' well . . .' The boy looked round desperately at his audience. ''E's bin shopped!' he finished.

The cry that went up from the girl by the fire struck fear into them all. Sikes would keep his mouth shut all right, but someone might start asking questions in other quarters and if Toby himself were caught, Fagin didn't hold out much hope for any of them. Charley went over to Nancy and put a comforting arm about her shoulders. The other boys stood about looking fearful and helpless, waiting for Fagin to tell them what to do. The kidsman and Dodger exchanged worried glances, while Ned Green sidled into the room and stood waiting. He felt safer here than on the threshold of the doorway.

'We need to talk to Toby,' Fagin said at last, 'and we need to find out what they're going to do with Bill.'

Fagin seemed oblivious of the distraught young woman in his care and he was still muttering to himself when Tom Chitling and Bet panted up the stairs and burst into the room. Bet flew to Nancy's side.

'Wot the 'ell's bin 'appenin' 'ere?' she demanded, turning angrily on them all.

'Eh? What's that?' Fagin's mind was on other things. 'Oh, she's not well, not well at all, my dear. Collapsed at my door. She needs a woman to look after her. No good me trying to do it, my dear.'

Bet turned to Nancy, who reached out her arms. Bet held her tightly.

'Wot is it, Nancy?' she said softly. 'Tell me.'

'They've got my Bill.' Nancy's voice shook. 'An' I've such a pain, Bet. I feel so bad.'

Bet delved into her pocket and handed Tom some coins.

'Get a cab, quick,' she said. 'I've got ter get 'er back 'ome, where I can look after 'er proper. Go on, Tom, run!'

Tom ran and was back in a very few minutes to say he had managed to stop a cab in Holborn, at the bottom of Field Lane, if they could get Nancy there. Nancy thought she might be able to walk. It wasn't far. She was gently helped down the stairs, the boys anxious and solicitous, Fagin flapping his hands uselessly behind her. With Bet on one side of her and Dodger and Charley on the other, she was almost carried to the waiting cab. Bet made her comfortable and climbed in beside her, pulling up the apron across them both. She knocked on the roof of the little vehicle and they moved off.

It wasn't very far to Old Nicol Street, but every jolt on the dry rutted roads and cobbled streets made Nancy groan and sometimes cry out in pain. She looked deathly white and sat with her arms clasped around her body. Bet had her suspicions.

'You knapped?' she asked simply.

Nancy nodded.

''Ow long?'

''Bout three months,' gasped Nancy. 'Oh Bet, I'm goin' ter lose it, ain't I?'

For answer Bet squeezed her hand.

'I'll look after yer, Nance,' she promised. 'Don't worry. 'Ave yer got a key?'

'Yes,' replied Nancy, fumbling in her pocket. 'It's 'ere. Bill's got 'is own. At least, 'e did 'ave . . .' She looked at Bet and the tears welled up. 'I 'spect they take ev'rythink away from them, don't they?'

Bet did not reply. She did not trust herself to answer and the cab was pulling up on the corner of Bethnal Green Road and Shoreditch High, which was as near to Old Nicol Street as it could get. The cabby, one of the more helpful of his breed, had promised to take them as close as possible. He got down now and he and Bet helped Nancy from the cab. When he had gone, Nancy stumbled through the alleyways and across the familiar filthy cobbles towards the lodging-house door. Halfway across, she stood for a moment, leaning on Bet's arm and looking up at the window of her grim lodging. It was truly her home now. But Bill wouldn't be there, not for a long time. He might never come home. The tears started afresh to her eyes.

'Come on, gal.' Bet was brisk and sensible and Nancy was glad to let someone take over.

Bull's-eye growled as Bet unlocked the door.

'Shut up, Bull's-eye,' said Bet sharply.

The dog recognized her and went back to his place of watchfulness by the fire.

When at last Nancy lay in the bed she had shared with Sikes for the past eighteen months, her whole being cried out in pain, for the end of her hopes, the end of her dreams, the end of her life with Sikes. She had known for weeks now that, one way or another, the end was inevitable, but that made it no easier to face. She felt very close to death.

By midnight, her pains had intensified and she went into a

high fever, sweating copiously and beginning to bleed. Bet had bathed her head and given her drinks of water but there was no more she could do and Nancy had lost consciousness. Bet was desperate and knew she must fetch the parish doctor. She went down to the lodging-house keeper's kitchen and found Mrs Waller dozing by the fire. She touched her arm and the good soul started up in fright.

'Oh my dear, wotever is it? Yer fair startled the life out o' me!'

She patted her heaving bosom, but there was no time for polite apologies.

'It's Miss Nancy,' said Bet. 'She's bin took ill. I'm goin' fer the doctor. Can you sit with 'er till I gets back?'

Mrs Waller had half-risen from her chair. But she stopped, frowning.

'Where's that feller of 'er's? Why ain't 'e 'ere ter look after 'er? Made enough fuss of 'er when 'e first brung 'er 'ome, though I've noticed 'e ain't so mindful of 'er of late.'

Bet looked at her very hard. She thought it best to tell Mrs Waller the truth. After all, they would have to sort out something later about the rent.

''E's bin shopped.'

Mrs Waller nodded knowingly. 'The perlice wos 'ere a few weeks back,' she confided. 'But I'm surprised. 'E wos always a quiet one, comin' an' goin'. Never knew when 'e wos goin' ter be there. Mindjoo, 'e always paid up reg'lar, I'll give 'im that. The only time they wos ever noisy wos when they 'ad a row, an' they 'ad a few these last weeks. Then 'e could be the werry divil 'imself. I heered them, y'know. 'E used to 'it 'er about a bit.' She leaned close to Bet. 'I heered 'im thrash 'er once, poor little thing. Only once, mind.'

Bet recoiled. Nancy had never told her that. But this was no time to be listening to a history of the couple's arguments. And she disliked the way Mrs Waller talked as though Sikes no longer existed. She led the way up the stairs.

'Wot about that dawg?' Mrs Waller and Bull's-eye sized each other up.

'I'll let 'im out,' replied Bet. ''E'll probably go lookin' for 'is master.'

Mrs Waller stood at the side of the bed, studying Nancy's feverish form in the soft glow of the oil lamp. She raised her eyebrows at Bet.

'Miscarryin'?'

Bet nodded miserably.

'Good job 'e ain't 'ere then.' Mrs Waller jerked her head in the vague direction of Newgate. 'Now you cut along an' find the doctor. Try the work'us first. I'll do wot I can 'ere.'

Gratefully, Bet left Nancy in the older woman's hands and ran off into Bethnal Green Road to find another cab. Her small stock of coins was running low, but she would spend the very last of them if it meant saving her dearest friend.

She found a cab and was soon stepping down outside the great grim building in Kingsland Road. She tugged at the bell-pull, the sound of voices drifted towards her at last, and the great door opened. The matron and a maid emerged carrying lanterns and came over to the gate. The matron glared at Bet through the bars.

'Wot in heaven's name d'ye want, girl?'

'The parish doctor – if you please, ma'am. Is 'e 'ere?'

'Wot d'ye want him for?'

'My – my sister. She's losin' 'er babe. She's very ill. Please, is the doctor 'ere?'

The matron looked at Bet in disgust. She turned to the maid, a timid, frightened little creature.

'That's the trouble with these girls. Live on the streets instead of earnin' an honest wage. Then expect the parish to look after them when things go wrong.'

The wide-eyed maid nodded in agreement. Bet was about to leap to Nancy's defence, but thought better of it.

'You're lucky, my girl,' continued the matron of the workhouse, unlocking the gate. 'The doctor's here, deliverin' a babe. So he might come to see your sister when he's done.' She led Bet into the building. 'You can wait here.'

525

She indicated a bench in the vast hallway, then disappeared into the darkness. Bet was left alone with her thoughts and a guttering candle.

She tried in vain to calm her nerves. Oh God, she prayed, please let 'im come soon. Don't let my Nancy die. The thought brought the tears to her eyes and she sought desperately for something else with which to occupy her waiting. She thought of what Mrs Waller had told her. It had disturbed her at the time and now she had time to think clearly about what the woman had said. Nancy had kept much to herself, that was for sure. So Sikes had been cruel to her. And they'd fallen out a lot. But she hadn't left him, so maybe it was not as bad as the lodging-house keeper made out. Such women were notorious gossips and would embroider any event to make a good tale to relate to their neighbours. But, reflected Bet, given Nancy's loving nature, she'd probably stand by Sikes, whatever he said or did. He was what she had always hoped for, all through those dreadful years on the streets. If things had gone wrong, Bet wondered, who was to blame? She knew Sikes had a temper. She knew he had been boated for seven years; Nancy had let that slip. That must make a man bitter and hard. Nancy had also told her how set Sikes was against a baby. But she knew Nancy, too. She knew her little displays of wilful passion, of obstinacy, and her penchant for the gin bottle. And she could see the two characters clashing. But still she wondered at Nancy's loyalty. She sighed and leaned her head against the wall and closed her eyes. Nancy must love Bill very, very much . . .

She was jerked awake some forty minutes later by the sound of footsteps and a man's voice, punctuated by the strident tones of the matron.

'I'm sure you don't want to be chasing off to some jade's lodgings tonight, sir. Leave it till the morning. These loose girls deserve all they get.'

The quiet voice of the parish doctor came clearly to the waiting Bet.

'No, Mrs Axbury. Tomorrow morning may well be too

late. I must go now. After all, it is my calling: to save life, if I can, as well as to bring it into the world.'

Bet leaped to her feet as the doctor came into view.

'Oh lor', bless you sir!' she cried. 'She's took real bad an' bleedin' all the while.'

The doctor patted her shoulder, while the matron looked on in disapproval. Then he handed her up into his waiting fly and they were soon rumbling back down the Kingsland Road. Bet recounted what she could of Nancy's condition.

'No man, I suppose?' The doctor's voice was kind.

'Oh yes,' replied Bet, carefully. 'Only 'e's away. On bus'ness, I think.'

The doctor smiled to himself and nodded knowingly.

'Well, here we are. You'd better lead the way, my dear. I get quite lost in these infernal alleyways!'

Together they hurried between the mean tenements, across the courtyard and up the creaking staircase. Bet opened the door and Mrs Waller opened her eyes very suddenly.

'She's wanderin' a lot, dearie, but I don't think she's no worse.'

'Thank you, Mrs Waller. I'll stay with 'er now.'

'Well, you call me if yer needs me.'

And Mrs Waller padded away to her own domain.

A brief examination confirmed their fears. The doctor helped Bet clear away the bloodied clouts and the tiny curled shape which would have been Nancy's baby. 'Ers an' Bill's, thought Bet. Oh thank Gawd 'e weren't 'ere ter see 'er like this. I don't know wot 'e'd 'ave done. She stood looking down at Nancy. The girl was thin and there were great shadows beneath her closed eyes. The colour had drained completely from her face and she looked as though her soul had already departed. Her hands lay quite still on the bedspread. Bet gently took one of them in her own warm, plump one.

'Will she live, doctor?'

The doctor was washing his hands. He came over to the

527

bed, drying them. He looked at Nancy for a moment. At last he spoke.

'Aye. I think so, my dear. But she'll be very weak for a good while yet. She must remain in bed for a week or two at least, to lessen the chances of bleeding again. Complete rest. Warm, nourishing drinks. Don't fret her with heavy food. Just a light meal when she's ready for it. I'll give you a draught to stem any further bleeding and she can take a little laudanum for the fever.' He hesitated. 'When is her – her man likely to be back?'

'I don't know, sir. It could be some time.'

'Good. That'll give her plenty of time to rest.'

The doctor collected his things together. 'Will you be able to look after her? She'll need constant nursing for several weeks.'

'Oh yes, sir,' replied Bet, smiling. 'I'll move in 'ere. An' Mrs Waller, downstairs, she's a good sort really.'

The doctor nodded and picked up his bag. Bet began searching in her pocket for money. The doctor laid his hand on her arm.

'No, my dear. I only ask a fee of my wealthy patients.' And he was gone, leaving Bet speechless and grateful and touched. Such was her emotional state, that she went to sit by the bed and laid her head by Nancy's shoulder and gave vent to silent tears. Nancy was sleeping more peacefully now and Bet herself was soon asleep by her adopted sister's head.

The morning was far gone when Bet was roused from her exhausted sleep by a quiet but persistent knocking. Nancy was breathing easily, the fever had gone and she was sleeping peacefully. Bet went softly to the door.

'Who is it?' she called.

'It's me, Bet,' came the familiar voice of Tom Chitling.

Bet opened the door and Tom slipped in. Never had she been so glad to see him as now.

'Dearest.' He spoke in hushed tones. 'Your work ain't finished yet. Someone's got ter tell 'er about Bill.'

Bet looked up fearfully at him.

'Oh Gawd, Tom! Wot's 'appened?'

'Well, I bin down the nubbin'-ken this mornin' an' Bill's bin up afore the beak. 'E didn't look too good. 'E wos limpin', so I s'pose that toff got 'im with 'is barker. Any'ow, there wos a lot o' questions asked an' a lot of argyment an' Sikes – well, 'e don't say a lot, do 'e? But they wos at a loss wot ter do, 'cause they didn't find nothin' on 'im. An' there wos no sign of anyone else. But there's stuff missin' so they know there's more than one o' them. An' they're 'opin' Bill'll talk. But 'e won't, of course. Not Bill.'

'But, Tom, wot 'ave they done with 'im?'

Tom examined the backs of his dirty hands and played with a loose thread on a coat button. Bet shook his arm.

'Tom?'

'A drag, with 'ard labour . . .' He felt Bet's eyes on him and met her gaze. 'An' a scroby. Ter see if 'e'll spout.'

Bet stared at him, uncomprehending.

'You know. A floggin'.'

Bet shuddered. Nancy had told her how Bill's back was scarred from the dreadful floggings he had received in Van Diemen's Land. Poor Bill, she thought.

'I won't tell 'er, Tom,' she said. 'The doctor told me she mustn't be distressed. It'd kill 'er. It'll be bad enough knowin' 'e's doin' a drag. We shall 'ave ter tell 'er that. But I won't tell 'er the rest.'

Tom nodded in agreement. Bet held his hand and looked at him, her brown eyes full of tears.

'I 'ope ter God you never get caught, Tom. I couldn't bear it.'

'No, Bet.' He laughed. 'I won't get caught. No fear o' that.'

'But Bill's clever, Tom.' Bet looked at him with meaning.

Tom was not hurt by her words. He knew that circumstances must have prevailed in a very unlucky combination for Sikes to have been shopped.

'I'll be werry careful,' he assured her and went out into the bright August sunshine.

Bet turned back to her patient and found Nancy awake.

She wondered how much the girl had heard, but it was with some relief that she received Nancy's first broken, whispered enquiry.

'Bill? Where is 'e, Bet? Wot 'ave they done with 'im?' Bet closed her eyes momentarily and Nancy reached out weakly to touch her hand. 'Oh Bet, Bet. Tell me, please. I must know.'

Bet smiled. ''E's all right, Nance. But 'e's in the stir fer three months. They couldn't really 'old 'im fer longer. They couldn't prove nothink. No swag, no tools. Just in the wrong place at the wrong time.'

Nancy seemed to relax.

To change the subject, Bet said, 'We've got ter get you well an' up an' on yer feet again, my gal. An' three months ain't long ter do it in.'

She laughed and Nancy smiled weakly. Then she frowned, as though at some sudden memory.

'I lost the babe, didn't I, Bet?' Her voice was small and steady, but tinged with sadness.

Bet nodded.

Nancy went on. 'I don't want 'im ter know, Bet. I think 'e'd thrash me fer gettin' knapped. I tried 'ard not ter get that way. All the things we used ter use on the Ratcliffe, you know. An' I drank an awful lot o' gin, Bet. But I gave up after two months. I couldn't bear ter get rid of the baby.'

Her voice caught and for a few moments her thin body was racked by silent weeping. Bet said nothing but held her hand tightly.

Nancy eventually continued, 'I thought I'd just keep goin' as long as I could without 'im knowin'. Just to 'ave a little longer with 'im. 'E'd 'ave thrown me out, yer know, Bet. Or taken 'imself off. Maybe 'e'll go anyway, but 'e wouldn't 'ave wanted no brats under 'is feet.' She slid her eyes away from Bet and spoke to the emptiness of the room. 'Yer know, this was the longest I'd ever carried.'

Bet squeezed her hand. Nancy turned her eyes towards her again. They were bright and brimming.

'I wanted that babe, Bet. It would 'ave bin somethink special between 'im an' me, even if 'e'd left me. But it wouldn't 'ave bin no place ter bring up a littl'un, would it, Bet? Not the den o' vice we all lives in. So maybe it's worked out for the best. Eh?'

The flood of sobbing which followed threatened to overwhelm her.

'Now stop it, Nance,' said Bet sharply, 'or you'll bring the fever on again. An' you might not come out of it so easily.'

'I don't care. I want ter die. I'm un'appy an' lonely.'

Bet grew cross. 'Fer Gawd's sake, Nancy. Yer've got me ter keep yer company, till yer well. They'll all come a-visitin' soon enough from the Cripples. An' none of us wants yer ter die. An' nor would Bill, if 'e 'eard yer. Gawd luv us, gal, 'e'll be out in three months. That's twelve weeks. It ain't so very long, yer know.'

She turned away and fetched the draught of medicine which the doctor had left.

'Come on. Get this down yer.'

Nancy complied weakly. And allowed Bet to administer a small dose of laudanum as well.

'Now,' said Bet very firmly. 'You 'ave another sleep. I'm goin' ter nip down ter Mrs Waller's ter sort out arrangements with 'er.'

Fear leaped into Nancy's eyes.

'Oh Gawd, Bet. The rent! 'Ow am I goin' ter pay the rent?'

'We'll manage. I'll get Mrs Waller ter run up a coupla weeks' credit. That'll give us a breathin' space. We'll go on from there when the time comes.'

She went to the door. Nancy called softly to her.

'Bet. You are good ter me. Thank you.'

Bet smiled and was gone. Nancy listened to her retreating footsteps, the murmur of voices and the closing of a door. Mrs Waller had no doubt asked Bet in for liquid refreshment. She would want to know all the latest tattle.

Nancy lay gazing at the yellowed ceiling of their shabby room. Shabby, yes, but it was home; his home and hers, too, and she loved it. She loved Sikes too, who had given her all this, and just for a moment she remembered how kind he had been when he took her in – how good he still could be to her, when he kept his temper.

At the thought of her lover, incarcerated in Newgate Gaol, Nancy wept again; tears of anger, frustration and sorrow.

'Oh Bill! Why? Why couldn't you be 'ere?' she wailed to the empty room. 'Why? When I need yer most.'

She beat her fists against the pillow and sobbed her heart out, until exhausted sleep overtook her once more.

TWENTY-EIGHT

◈

The shot which brought Bill Sikes to a crumpled heap at the foot of the frontdoor steps in South Square had not inflicted a great deal of damage, but it had grazed the surface of his thigh and was enough to prevent his running away. He lay clutching the wound and rolling about in an attempt to get to his feet. But when the house owner, a florid, busy gentleman with large side whiskers, descended on him wielding a smoking pistol and two servants laid into him with their canes, he knew the game was up and lay still until the peelers arrived.

They called a cab and Sikes was swept away to Newgate, to await sessions the following morning.

The progress of the coach was slow, since the streets were packed with revellers, and there were throngs outside the prison, too. Curious eyes followed him as he descended stiffly from the vehicle and made his way through the forbidding portals between the two policemen. He had wondered if he dare make a dash for it, but with his hands bound and his leg throbbing painfully, he doubted his chances, especially with so many crowds on the streets. His escape would soon be blocked. 'Fagin's boys ought to do well tonight,' he thought wryly.

The heavy door of Newgate banged behind them and they walked for some distance, their boots echoing along the passageways. At last, they drew up before a row of cells with heavy wooden doors and iron grilles in them and were met by a dirty turnkey. He was an evil-looking fellow, with decaying teeth and foul breath and an ugly scar over his left eye. He chewed at something in the side of his mouth and spat every so often. He and Sikes eyed each other. The police officer was brusque.

'Bill Sikes. Up before the magistrate in the mornin'. 'E's got a wound. Give an eye to it, will you?'

And he was gone. The turnkey gave Sikes a shove, which sent him sprawling on to the cell floor.

'Barker get yer, did it?' The turnkey spat and grinned, chewing all the while, his broken teeth giving his face a nightmare quality. 'Well. I've looked at yer an' yer look all right ter me, blast yer.'

And he gave Sikes a vicious kick with his boot and crashed the door of the cell closed, making a great do of locking it.

Sikes lay stunned for a few moments. The blow from the turnkey's boot had caught him in the ribs and for a while the pain was intense. Gradually, it subsided a little and he was aware of the growing silence, thick and overpowering after the raucous din of the city outside. It grew and grew, until his ears were ringing and he wanted to beat his head against the floor to clear it. Instead, he took stock of the situation.

Gingerly, he sat up, gasping at the pain in his side.

'Burn me if me ribs ain't cracked,' he muttered, rubbing a fettered hand cautiously over his bruises.

He felt his thigh. There was a damp and sticky patch and in the dark, he tried to pull away the material of his breeches from the wound. But it had already begun to congeal and it hurt him, so he abandoned the attempt. He groped his way round the cell with difficulty, but at last his hands alighted on a wooden platter with a crust of dry bread on it and a jug of water. He drank thirstily from the jug, though the water was not even as sweet as that from the pump in Old Nicol Street. He poured some water over his thigh and cupped a little in his bound hands to trickle over his bruised ribs. He picked at the crust and sat back in the straw, resting against the damp and stony wall.

How strange it was that Toby had got clean away, his pockets full of trinkets. He must have been aware of the returning coach well before Sikes, yet the coward had never given him a signal, never called out, but had legged it over the windowsill at the first hint of danger. The thought of flash

534

Toby Crackit, scot-free, with his pockets full of sparklers roused a fury in Sikes which set him shaking with its vehemence. But such impotent anger got him nowhere and as he calmed down, he thought of his Nancy staggering back to Fagin's with her basket of 'flowers'. He smiled to himself. She was a good girl and had shown no fear on the crack, although she'd looked a bit peaky and out of sorts over the past few days. He thought perhaps she had been worrying about the crack, or maybe it was just her 'poorly time'. Women were difficult creatures. He and Nancy hadn't always seen eye to eye and they'd had a few really explosive rows. But she had stayed with him, despite everything. He wondered why. But he supposed he was glad she had. He would miss her now. He wished he hadn't hit her. And he regretted taking his belt to her. It was all very well being sorry afterwards, but why couldn't he stop himself at the time? As he had told himself before, some things just made him blaze and he had no control over himself then. He couldn't help his temper; he'd inherited it from his father.

He leaned his head back against the wall and sighed. He wondered what tomorrow would bring. A few months in the stir. Maybe hard labour thrown in for good measure. They couldn't give him much else. They wouldn't hang him, because the crime was insufficient for such a punishment – at least, he hoped so. And they wouldn't . . . He stopped and sat up suddenly, a cold sweat of fear sweeping over him, churning his belly and making his heart thump wildly.

'Oh Gawd!' he moaned. 'Not the bleedin' boat again. I'd rather swing, burn an' blast me if I wouldn't.'

They couldn't send him away for a second time. He hadn't really done anything. He'd accosted no one and there was nothing in his pockets. Save the key to his humble home. And even that they had taken from him. There was no evidence at all to condemn him to such a punishment. But he was well known as a cracksman and they'd find a means of conviction if they could.

He wondered what Nancy would do while he was jugged.

535

And what if his sentence *did* take him further away? She would probably forget him soon enough, find herself another fellow, or go back to the streets. He moaned quietly to himself and cursed his misfortune. He cursed Fagin for dreaming up the scheme. And he cursed Toby Crackit again, too, just for good measure. If ever he got out of here, he'd break clean away from them both!

Reflecting sanely on it, he knew he wouldn't. He couldn't work alone. No successful cracksman did. He needed a second hand to act as stall or accomplice or even as a nose. Toby was good at that. And Fagin was the best fence around. He took his time, but he got rid of stuff and paid up in the end. The old mob, the fraternity of the Cripples, was like a family, in an odd sort of way. The trouble was that he knew that any one of them would peach, if paid enough.

He nodded off, weary and dejected. But his sleep was disturbed by rustling in the straw, by the pain in his thigh and ribs, by his confused thoughts, and by his fear of the morning's sentence.

When it came, the sentence of three months' imprisonment with hard labour was almost a relief. But Sikes's relief was short-lived.

'This man,' said the magistrate in a fat voice, 'is a well-known house-breaker. And though we can only convict him of being illegally on another man's premises, he may well give us the information we need to track down the rest of the gang who were obviously involved in this appalling business.'

The corner of Sikes's mouth twitched. Unless they were on to Toby already, they'd never find the so-called 'gang'.

'Therefore,' continued the voice of the Law, 'therefore, I recommend a flogging of twenty stripes.'

Sikes jerked to attention in the dock as though he had been struck already and there was a gasp from the public gallery. It was preposterous. They couldn't do it. It was torture. He knew that. He could tell them about it. They only tortured you in Van Diemen's Land. Surely? He gripped the dock in front of him and opened his mouth to protest. But the clerk of the court held up his hand for silence.

'Sentence has been passed,' he announced. 'Call the next prisoner.'

Sikes was hustled out of the courtroom, wondering yet again at that rocky edifice which was the British system of justice. Two turnkeys accompanied him, one of whom was the man who had kicked him the previous night. Sikes knew he could expect no mercy from them. They took him to a small cobbled yard in the Old Ward of the prison, stripped him to the waist and roped his hands to a tall wooden stock, erected for the purpose. The familiarity of his situation made his blood run cold. He closed his eyes. He could see the prisoners in Hobart again, feel the awful black cloud that had surrounded him during that most dreadful hour of his life. He waited now, tense, fearful, the sweat already standing out on his unshaven lip.

The flogging cove was called out and he strolled into the yard with no great haste, rolling up his shirtsleeves, passing the cat-o'-nine-tails from one great fist to the other as he did so.

''Ow many?' he growled to the turnkeys.

'Twenty o' the best, 'Arris. Ter make 'im talk,' grinned the kicker. 'Beak wants ter know where the rest o' them are. An' the goods!' He winked.

The flogging cove hawked, spat on the cobbles, spat again on each hand in turn, got a good grip on the cat and began his dreadful ministry.

Sikes thought the feeling would be familiar. The sharp initial pain, followed by the deeper, more intense agony, the pain which came in waves, heightened by the cutting ends of the lashes. Somehow it was different this time. This was England, the place he'd come back to from his long exile. And the pain seemed to be exquisitely greater. It was as though he had been betrayed again by his motherland. He couldn't blame her for his faults, but need she punish him so severely?

The flogging cove stopped. But he hadn't finished.

'Thirsty work,' he remarked.

He sauntered back into his office or whatever ghastly den he inhabited, and emerged with a half-bottle of beer, which he stood and drank very close to Sikes. He stared up at the square of blue sky above them and belched.

'Nice day,' he remarked.

No one answered him. Sikes moved his head carefully and looked at the turnkeys. They were lounging against the yard wall, hands in pockets, talking. The flogging cove finished his beer and Sikes braced himself for another onslaught. But the man merely strolled to a gully in the centre of the cobbles, tucked the cat beneath his arm and urinated. He came back, buttoning up his breeches, and called out to his companions, ''Ow many I done?'

'Dunno, 'Arris. Twelve? Thirteen? Ain't yer countin'?'

Flogger Harris laughed. It was not a pleasant sound.

''Ere, wot d'yer take me for, Jack? I ain't ever bin learned ter count!'

At which all three laughed loudly at Sikes's expense. Harris came up to Sikes and peered into his face. Sikes opened his eyes and returned the stare.

'You goin' ter tell us about your friends, mate?'

Sikes remained silent. They would never break him like this. They didn't know what he had endured in Hobart. They could never make him talk by flogging him.

'Well, we'll 'ave ter see if a few more'll 'elp jog yer memory!'

And he resumed his pastime with even greater vigour than before.

'Names!' roared Harris, between the strokes. 'Where do they live?'

Sikes screwed up his eyes and bit his lips until they bled. He would not give them the satisfaction of hearing him cry out. But he was worried, because he could hear strange sounds in his head and there was a darkness descending on him again. He tried to think of other things to keep away the nightmare. He thought of Toby, free and comfortable in his Hoxton lodgings, awaiting his share of the loot. But that was too depressing. He thought of his Nancy and hoped she wouldn't get to hear of this latest humiliation. How would she manage on her own? Would she go back to the streets? Or would she get Bet to share the lodging with her? No, Bet had interests elsewhere. He suddenly had an overwhelming desire to have her close, to hold her tightly. She would soothe away this pain. She was good at that. But she would fret over the state of his back.

Suddenly, it was over. He was sure he had had more than the recommended twenty lashes. At the final stroke, Flogger Harris grabbed him by his hair and jerked up his head.

'Think about it, chum. Yer might change yer fuckin' mind when yer've 'ad time fer that lot ter go rotten on yer!'

And he strode away, the lash trailing over his shoulder. One of the turnkeys threw a bucket of cold water over the bloody mess which had been Sikes's back and shoulders and the shock brought him upright again.

'Where's 'e to?' asked the second turnkey, as they half dragged Sikes back into the prison.

'Middle Yard,' grunted his companion.

The other nodded.

'Lucky 'im,' he said. 'Wot's 'e done ter deserve that?'

They knew that he would get better treatment there. The gaoler in charge was known to be a humane man, if a little simple by prison standards.

There was a row of low cells in the Middle Yard, with bars forming their front walls, so that the prisoners within could be watched at all times. The warden of these cells took one look at the mess presented to him and ordered a young lad he had with him to fetch a measure of cheap spirits, which he then proceeded to pour steadily over the raw flesh. Sikes gasped and tried to pull away, but he was held fast by his gaolers. The occupants of the other cells looked on with dejected interest. When it was done and the smarting had brought the tears to his eyes, he was thrust into a cell at the far end of the row.

He collapsed face down on the straw pallet in the corner and a wave of nausea and humiliation and anger swept over him. In a moment, however, all had gone black as he sank into merciful oblivion. The gaoler swung the iron door closed and locked it.

'I'll keep 'im there a coupla days, till 'is back starts to 'eal. Then 'e can be moved in with the others.'

The turnkeys looked at each other in disgust. He was soft in the head, this one!

''E's got 'ard labour as well, yer know,' said the kicker.

'I know,' replied the Middle Yard warden. 'You leave 'im ter me. 'E won't miss out on anythink, don't you worry!'

TWENTY-NINE

Daylight dragged Sikes back to a world of harsh reality. He had been cocooned too long in the velvet darkness of unconsciousness. He kept his eyes closed as the pain in his back roared over him with renewed anger. He felt fossilized into an immovable position and though his arms were numb, from their unaccustomed angle, he could not bring himself to alleviate the discomfort. He listened to the prison sounds around him. There were low voices and the rough hawking of men with bronchial problems. He heard a chair or a stool scrape on the flagstones and the sound of a knife clattering to the floor. Somewhere, someone was singing quietly to himself, while another periodically cursed his noise.

The door of his cell rattled and opened and he heard the rustle of a dress on the straw.

His gaoler said, 'Ten minutes, miss. 'Fraid that's all.'

Sikes opened his eyes, but didn't move his head.

'Nancy?' His voice was hoarse. 'That you?'

'No, Bill. It's me. Bet. I come ter see 'ow you are. An' if yer wants anythink.'

If he was disappointed, he wasn't prepared to show it.

'Got any blunt, Bet?' he whispered, still not moving. 'I shall need some in this 'ole if I'm ter survive.'

Bet felt in the covered basket she had brought with her and drew out a small leather bag which jingled with coins. She put it into Sikes's hand and his fingers closed over hers. Her heart fluttered for a moment. He turned his head slightly and looked up at her. At that moment, she wanted to reach out and touch his face with her hands, with her lips. He still had her hand in his.

'Where's Nance?' he asked. 'Why didn't she come?'

'She ain't well, Bill,' replied Bet. 'She's got a fever an' we 'ad to 'ave the doctor to 'er. But she'll do now. She's all right. So don't you fret over 'er.'

'Dam' me, 'ow the 'ell did she take ill so quick?'

He tried to rise, but the rawness of his back was too new and he sank painfully to his bed again, swearing between his teeth. He lay panting with the effort and Bet tentatively extended a hand and stroked his sweating brow and his close-cropped hair. They hadn't lost any time administering the 'terrier crop', she thought sadly, recalling Sikes's rather fine wavy hair. She could see grey silvering his temples and wondered, not for the first time, what he had gone through under transportation.

'Must 'ave bin somethink she ate, Bill. She 'ad pains in 'er belly and was ravin' 'alf the night.'

'I thought she'd bin lookin' a bit peaky these last few days,' remarked Sikes, more to himself than to Bet.

'Well, she 'ad us all worried, I can tell you. I thought it was all up with 'er, really I did.'

The sharp intake of breath warned her that she had said too much. But Sikes lay still again, except to say quietly, 'But she's all right now. Yer sure?'

'Yes, Bill. She's out o' danger now.'

'Thank Gawd,' muttered Sikes, perhaps the only time he had ever genuinely thanked his Maker for anything. 'But I wish I'd bin there with 'er. Poor Nance.'

He seemed to have drifted off into a reverie of his own thoughts. Bet studied him. He lay with a rough blanket thrown across him and she wondered what sort of a state his back was in. She wondered if there was anything she could do to alleviate his discomfort. Bet's unquenchable curiosity suddenly got the better of her. Gently, she lifted the edge of the blanket and pulled it slowly back.

'Don't!' said Sikes. 'You won't like it.'

Bet stopped, the blanket still in her hand.

'I want ter see 'ow bad it is, Bill,' she said softly. 'I want ter know if there's anythink I can bring ter put on it.'

542

'It's bad enough. But the gaoler's put spirits on it already. So it's just a question of time. It ain't no sight for a lady, Bet.'

'I ain't no lady, Bill.'

She pulled the blanket right back to expose the gory mess beneath it. She stared in horror and brought her hand to her mouth.

'Oh God, Bill,' she breathed. 'Did they really do this to yer?'

'Looks like it, don't it? Luckily I never 'ave ter see me own back! Cover it up, Bet. Or you'll be sick.'

Bet dropped the blanket as though she had been stung and sat back on her heels, looking pale.

'Poor Bill,' she breathed softly. 'Poor, poor Bill.'

'Ah, come on, Bet! Save yer sympathy. It's lost on the likes o' me. Wot yer got in the basket?'

Bet rose in a daze and emptied the contents of her basket on to the floor.

'Cheese, a coupla pies, fresh bread an' a bottle o' beer.'

She laid the items out close to his pallet. Sikes grunted his thanks. Bet stood over him, summoning courage. Then she bent and tenderly kissed his unshaven cheek. Sikes eyed her.

'Wot was that for?' he demanded, not unkindly.

'That was from Nancy,' lied Bet and hurried to the door, where the gaoler let her out.

Sikes listened to her footsteps retreating along the narrow passageway. Then he painfully reached out and began working his way through the victuals at his side. A flogging had never yet prevented Bill Sikes from filling his belly and it wasn't going to now.

Two days later, Sikes was moved to a communal cell, where his privacy was invaded by every known type of criminal on the face of the metropolis. He kept his money hidden close about him and was able to bribe his gaolers for measures of gin. This helped to restore him to some semblance of normality and he was soon put to breaking stones with his cell-mates. It was almost impossible to wield a sledgehammer or a pick without causing himself acute pain throughout every muscle in his back. But it would pass, he knew, and he had the fortitude born of years of hardship and oppression to see him through.

Bet came regularly to see him, while Nancy slowly recovered her health. She would come towards the end of the day, when the men had returned from the stone yards and were taking their ease in the cell. She was always a little frightened of entering the cell, since she had to run the ribald comments of so many of the characters there. At least Sikes would protect her if anyone should make a nuisance of himself. She tossed her head. 'Why should I need protecting?' she told herself. 'I'm perfickly capable o' lookin' after meself. Done it fer long enough on the streets, ain't I?'

With Sikes growing stronger by the day, Bet no longer felt she had the courage to administer the parting kiss, which she had bestowed on him several times. One day, as she bade him farewell, he reached out and caught her hand.

'Where's my kiss?' he demanded, his expression inscrutable.

Bet coloured. What could she say when he looked at her so directly? She wasn't left wondering for long. Sikes pulled her close, cupped her face in his strong, rough hands and kissed her very firmly on her pouting mouth.

'There,' he said. 'That's better. A man needs a bit o' woman's care when 'e's in the jug.' He grinned lopsidedly at her. 'That's fer Nance,' he said, staring at her meaningfully.

Bet laughed and took her leave. But she was frightened by her own emotions. And she couldn't betray Nancy, not after all they'd been through together. Not after all this, with Nancy still on her sick-bed. She walked home thoughtfully that day, glad of the breeze which had sprung up. It helped to cool her flaming cheeks. She felt guilty. She had encouraged Sikes in any number of little ways. But it had been just a game, to see if he would rise to the bait. Normally he was such an unemotional man, except for his anger. She had not thought he would show any spark of interest in her. But she knew she was young, she supposed herself pretty and Sikes was still very much in his prime. It was her own fault; she could see that now. She should never have played about with such fire.

When she reached Old Nicol Street on this particular occasion, Bet found Nancy much restored. She was sitting propped up on the pillows and a little colour had returned to her cheeks. Mrs Waller rose from the bedside.

'She's just woken up, dearie,' said the dutiful nurse. 'She's lookin' a mite better, wouldn't yer say, Miss Bet?'

Bet smiled and came over to the bed. She sat down and took Nancy's thin hand. The veins were very blue through the almost transparent skin. She was too delicate for the likes of Sikes.

'We'll soon 'ave you out of 'ere, luv. Another week an' we'll get you over ter Newgit ter see Bill.'

Nancy's face lit up.

'Oh Bet, I do miss 'im. 'Ow wos 'e terday?'

''E's fine, Nance. Sends 'is love an' a big kiss!'

'Garn with yer!' laughed Nancy. 'That don't sound like my Bill. 'E's more likely ter send me a black eye an' a string o' curses!'

And both girls laughed.

'Aye,' nodded Mrs Waller, making her way to the door. 'That sounds a lot nearer the truth!'

There was an awkward silence after she had gone.

'Wot did she mean by that?' asked Nancy in a small voice.

Bet shrugged and looked away, the laughter gone from her face.

Nancy reached out her hand. 'Tell me, Bet. Wot does she mean?'

'She's 'eard you 'avin' rows. She tole me 'e's 'it yer an' – an' that 'e'd thrashed yer. Oh Nancy, why didn't yer tell me about it? Why d'yer still live with 'im? Why don't yer leave 'im, gal?'

All this came out in a rush of desperation. Nancy merely looked at Bet with her blue eyes full of tears.

'Because I love him, Bet. 'E's all I got, an' 'e can't 'elp 'is temper.'

There was no answer to that.

The sound of voices arguing in the flat above drifted down to them and the squealing of children in the yard broke the silence of the room. Bet sighed. She mustn't let her feelings for Sikes get out of control. She was fascinated by him, but she wasn't in love with him, of that she was sure. It was just exciting to find out his reactions to her advances. But she could see them getting quite out of hand. And whatever happened, she must not come between Nancy and Bill.

The following week, swathed in blankets and shawls and cloaks, Nancy was helped down to a waiting cab and Bet climbed in with her.

'Here,' said Bet, leaning across. 'Let me tie yer bonnet ribbons for yer. The wind's got up terday. Yer don't want ter lose yer bonnet on yer first day out, now do yer?'

Nancy smiled and lifted her chin as Bet tied the ribbons.

'No. Bill gave it to me.'

'You're a lucky gal, Nancy,' said Bet. ''E gives you a lot o' things, don't 'e?'

'Yes . . .'

Bet could have bitten out her tongue. How easy it was to misconstrue a well-intentioned remark.

When they reached the entrance to Newgate, Nancy looked at Bet in fear.

'I don't know as I can go through with it, Bet,' she whispered, as they descended from the cab.

'Wot d'yer mean, Nance? Yer goin' ter see Bill, ain't yer? Yer want ter see 'im, don't yer? An' 'e wants ter see you. Wot is there to be frightened of?'

'I don't know, Bet. Maybe it's because I ain't seen 'im fer two weeks. Maybe it's 'cause I've got to remember not to say anythink about the baby. I don't like 'avin' secrets from 'im. 'E's got a way of lookin' at me so that I think 'e can see right into me mind.' She shivered, despite the layers in which she was swathed.

'Don't be daft, Nance,' said Bet. 'That's just plain fanciful. 'E won't know anythink about wot's 'appened to yer. All 'e knows is you've 'ad a fever an' you're better now. So don't go in there lookin' scared. After all,' she paused and laughed, 'yer do live with 'im, yer know!'

Nancy smiled and the two young women made their way through the portals of the prison. The gaoler who conducted them along the many corridors to the cell where Sikes was held was mercifully taciturn. He shuffled along and Nancy was able to match her pace easily to his, for she had not yet regained all her strength and she tired quickly.

Bet went in first and Nancy followed cautiously behind her. It was dim in the cell, although a pair of torches flared in sconces on opposite walls. Nancy looked straight ahead of her as she followed Bet to the far end of the cell, knowing that a dozen pairs of eyes were on her. Suddenly he was there ahead of her, struggling to his feet and holding out his arms. And the anguish of the past weeks fell away and she ran to him and felt the warmth and comfort of his body again. She couldn't speak, but just clung, her head laid against his breast; and he held her so close. Bet watched, her eyes full of tears. She had feared Bill's temper and Nancy's wanting a baby would drive a wedge between these two, but today their differences were cast aside. Sikes tilted Nancy's head towards him and kissed her, passionately. Some of the other prisoners made raucous noises and lewd comments. But the couple neither heard nor acknowledged them. They're in a world o' their own, thought Bet, almost jealously.

Nancy's fears had been stilled as soon as she stepped into the compass of Sikes's arms. Sikes, for his part, simply cursed the fact that he was still incarcerated and surrounded by so many watchful eyes. It seemed he was destined always to have his privacy curtailed in some way or another. But it was good to have his Nancy here with him, to have the comfort of her body so close, even for so short a time. He wished he was back in the cell he had originally occupied. At least there he might have got away with a more intimate embrace. But he must wait ten more weeks till he could slake that particular thirst.

There was a small bench against the wall at Sikes's end of the cell and he took her to it now and seated her on it, crouching in front of her, her hands in his.

'Are yer better, Nance?' he asked.

She smiled. 'Much better, Bill. I couldn't 'ave come 'ere terday otherwise.'

'An' Toby? 'Ave yer seen 'im since . . . since . . .'

'Oh, Toby's around, I gather. Bet's seen 'im down at the Cripples. Sportin' a very smart new coat, I believe.'

''E got away, then, the spineless funk? 'E ain't bin ter see me, yer know.'

'I should think 'e's too ashamed,' replied Nancy. 'Or too scared.'

She laughed nervously, but Sikes was not amused. He had been dismayed and hurt that Toby had let him down after everything. Nancy reached out and touched his face. She ran her fingertips over his closely cropped hair and shook her head sadly.

'Burn me, gal, it'll grow. At least it's easy ter get the lice out of it!'

Suddenly Nancy leaned forward and put her arms round his neck, sobbing against his shoulder. He said nothing but held her tightly. He looked up at Bet, who had come to stand by them.

'She's tired, ain't she?' he said.

'Yes, Bill. I'll take her home. I'll bring her again if she wants ter come.'

'No, don't, Bet. It ain't fair on 'er. I'll survive. If you can bring me extra wittles and some blunt now and again. Ask Fagin for the cash an' tell 'im Sikes'll settle with 'im when 'e comes out! That ought ter frighten the ole devil into coughin' up!'

Bet laughed and touched Nancy's shoulder.

'Come on, luv. Time we wos gettin' back. Bill's got ter go to the exercise yard soon. An' that's somethink 'e don't want ter miss. Ain't it, Bill?'

'Aye,' replied Sikes. 'You ought ter see us, Nance. Round

an' round that bleedin' yard like tigers in a cage. An' the guards stand an' watch us – in case we decides ter shin up the wall an' escape. Fat lot o' chance we'd 'ave. Them walls is twenty foot 'igh an' the winders is all near the top! Still, I s'pose it keeps us movin'.'

He was silent for a moment, his thoughts hidden from them both. Bet studied him surreptitiously.

'Come on, Nance,' said Sikes at last, disengaging the girl's arms from about his neck. 'You'd best go 'ome. You mustn't be ill again.'

He raised her face to his again and kissed her and watched as she went on Bet's arm to the cell door. As they went through, Bet turned and Sikes winked at her.

Wicked man! she thought.

THIRTY

Sikes sat in his corner and stared out defiantly at the company he was forced to keep. He hated them. Hated all humanity at this moment. He could feel something welling up from deep inside his chest, fighting to get out, screaming within him. He leaped from his stool and threw himself against the slimy wall of his prison.

'Hell's fire!' he shouted, at no one in particular, and beat his head and fists against the unyielding stone.

Several prisoners looked across in his direction and murmured among themselves. But no one approached him. They had quickly learned to steer clear of Bill Sikes. Uncommunicative, solitary, bad-tempered, he was a man not made for company.

For several minutes he stood leaning against the wall, his jaw working, his breathing laboured. At last, he flung away and sat down again. His hands were bleeding. He watched, fascinated, as the bright liquid welled and ran from the grazes. He felt a trickle on his forehead and brushed it away angrily.

When Bet came that evening, she brought with her a bottle of good port wine, two meat pies, fresh bread and a generous wedge of new cheese. Sikes was particularly grateful for the port.

'Good lass,' he said quietly, as she slipped the bottle behind the stool he had appropriated as his own.

She pulled some straw over it to hide its presence.

'I've got you some more blunt, Bill,' she whispered and slipped him a handful of coins.

Sikes put them with the bottle. There were too many pickpockets here to trust to his own clothing.

'That'll see you through the week,' smiled Bet.

Sikes nodded, but offered no further thanks. He suspected that the money had come from Fagin and he regarded it as only his due, his share of that last abortive crack. He leaned against the wall with his back to the other prisoners and Bet stood in front of him. It was the only form of privacy in this very public cell.

''Ow's Nance?' he now asked.

'She's a lot better, Bill. Wishes you were 'ome. I think she wants to visit you again. She's a lot stronger now.'

'It ain't a nice sort o' place fer a gal ter come visitin', is it?'

'No, but she won't mind that. She wants ter see you again.'

'Aye. Well, she can come. I'll be glad ter see 'er pretty face again. Not that yours ain't welcome,' he added hastily.

Bet smiled, but there was no corresponding reaction from Sikes. She thought he seemed even more morose than usual. Prison did strange things to a man, she knew.

When she made to leave him, Sikes laid a hand on her arm.

'You will come again, won't yer?' he asked.

'Of course, Bill.'

After she had gone, Sikes felt unaccountably lonely, as though his only contact with the outside world had been lost. He ferreted round in the straw and found the bottle. Good girl, she'd thought to uncork it and had jammed the cork back in. He pulled it out now and sat down on his stool. He put the neck of the bottle to his lips and began to drink, savouring the sweetness of the liquid. He took another swig and another. The warmth began to spread through his body and he felt life had improved a degree or two.

Presently, a couple of young felons ambled over to his corner and stood watching him. He eyed them through half-closed lids.

'Wotcher want?' he growled.

'A share o' your lush. Why ain't you 'andin' it around?'

'Because it weren't brought fer you, damn yer!'

Suddenly, one of the prisoners made a grab at the bottle. Sikes shot up from his seat and drove his fist into the young man's face. The lad's companion leaped to his immediate defence and struck back at Sikes, sending him reeling against the wall. But Sikes was quite capable of dealing with two adversaries at once and in a moment, both were floored and bleeding. But his precious bottle of port lay in the filthy straw, its ruby contents spewing out like blood. He stood staring at it with a disproportionate feeling of sadness.

The other prisoners had watched in silence, but one of them came over to Sikes and said, 'Bit 'andy with yer fists, ain't yer? That wasn't necessary, yer know.'

'You mind yer own bloody business,' said Sikes, 'and I'll mind mine. I ain't goin' ter stand by an' see me property nabbed from under me nose.'

He turned away and sat down. As he did so, his boot caught the little pile of coins Bet had given him and they gleamed bright in the light of the wall flares. The older prisoner saw the lustre and narrowed his eyes. He went back to his own company and spent some time in muttered conversation with them.

The following morning, Sikes struggled sleepily from his slumbers and broke his fast in silence. He thought back on the previous night's incident and wondered how he could avoid future recurrences. It struck him that his gaoler might well be bribed to find him another cell, a private cell of his own, where at least he could be away from the intrusive company he now kept. He felt about in the straw for the money Bet had brought. There was nothing. He thought he must have mistaken the place and searched again. But he saw the other prisoners regarding him and knew what they had done.

'Who's got my bloody blunt?' he shouted.

There was no reply. The heads turned away from him again. He leaped to his feet and strode over to them. Something gave way inside his head as he saw them all guzzling at their gruel. With a sweep of his arm, he sent several bowls of food spinning to the ground, where he kicked them viciously among the stools and benches, shouting, 'Just let me get my 'ands on the bugger wot's got my money!'

Several men jumped up and tried to restrain him, but he lashed out and struggled, cursing and fighting, catching more than one man with a blow on the jaw. In the midst of this uproar, the gaoler returned. It took several minutes and the help of half a dozen prisoners before Sikes was brought under control and manacled.

He sat on the floor, breathing hard, fuming, his eyes blazing, the sweat standing out in beads on his forehead. The gaoler went to the door and summoned two more wardens. When they came, he stood looking down at Sikes in disgust.

Then he kicked him hard and said, 'Get up, you. You ain't stayin' 'ere any longer.'

It was the best thing Sikes had heard since he had been flung in this cell two days after his flogging. He hadn't planned it this way, but it was a stroke of good luck none the less. He was removed from the public cell and marched away to another part of the prison. They turned down a very narrow, dark corridor and halfway along, his gaoler unlocked a door. The man tilted his head towards the interior.

'All yours, mate!'

Sikes stepped inside and the gaoler followed him, removed his handcuffs and locked him in.

It was quiet in the cell, private, and there was even a barred window, high up in the wall, which let in a modicum of light. He had a pallet to sleep on, though no blanket, and there was a small table and a chair. He ought to have felt pleased, smug, even; a cell to himself, away from the constant eyes of the other prisoners. And yet, there was something he didn't like. He stood quite still and listened. And then he knew. It was the silence. The thick, blanketing silence, which had driven him nearly insane on Grummet Island. For a moment, he relived the terrible panic of that week and feared he was

553

about to enter into a repeat of that most fearful time of his life. With a supreme effort, he pulled his mind away from the past and directed it towards the future. First, he decided, he would ask Bet to bring more cash and then, perhaps, the gaoler might be persuaded to let him have a supply of candles and tinder. That, at least, would give him some extra light. And he could have Nancy to see him, without the fear of prying eyes. They might even . . . No, he thought, he wouldn't humiliate her by snatching a few surreptitious moments in a sordid cell. That would have to wait till his release.

That night, he slept without fear. But during the days, he was constantly alert for signs of interference. Sometimes he would go days without anyone bothering him. Then it seemed as though they were looking for sport and he would be jostled in the yard and his pockets would be picked. He learned very quickly not to keep in his clothes any cash which Bet brought to him. Instead, he had to run the risk of leaving it behind in his cell and hope that the gaolers would not rifle through the straw for rich pickings.

Bet came two or three times a week and brought him good food and drink and occasionally a handful of money. And one day, Nancy came with her. Sikes was so surprised to see her that he stood wide-eyed for a moment when she stepped into his cell. Bet stood back and waited while they embraced with all the passion of their early days together. Then Bet took out the contents of her basket and put them on the table. Sikes had sat down with Nancy on his lap.

'Pity there ain't another chair 'ere, Bet, but the prison don't run ter luxuries!'

They all laughed, but there was a sense of tension in the air. They were each aware of it in their own way. Whether it was Bet's embarrassment at being a superfluous third party, or Nancy's wishing she had come on her own; or whether it was Bill's discomfiture at having two women in his cell, at close quarters and not being able to slake his growing natural need; it was difficult to say. They spoke of Fagin, of Dodger and the boys. Of Bull's-eye and how he was proving his worth by driving off unwanted characters at the Cripples.

'Ain't yer looking after 'im, then?' asked Sikes in some surprise. 'I thought yer'd 'ave bin glad of 'im, being on yer own.'

'No, Bill,' replied Nancy. 'Yer see, when I was first ill, I couldn't look after 'im. So Bet took 'im round ter Barney. An' I suppose I ain't given 'im much thought since.'

Sikes didn't answer. He thought she was being foolish not to avail herself of the dog's guardianship. But then, he never had understood women's ways, nor their flitterish ideas. He ran his hand over Nancy's thin body.

''Ere, yer've lost weight, gal,' he remarked. ''Ow *did* yer get that fever? Yer wos all right when yer left the square that night, weren't yer?'

Nancy looked down, her eyelids veiling the truth. This was the moment she had been dreading, ever since Sikes had been taken into custody. She hoped her voice was steady as she answered him.

'I wosn't feelin' all that well, Bill. D'yer remember, I 'ad ter lie down an' 'ave a sleep, the day of the crack?'

Sikes shook his head. He had come back in a state of pleasant inebriation that afternoon and he could not now recall what had happened.

'Well, as long as yer all right now. But yer'll 'ave ter get some flesh back on yer. She eatin' proper?' He turned his question to Bet.

'She is now, Bill,' answered Bet. 'But it'll take time ter cover 'er bones again. She always was a thin little thing, even as a mite. Thin but strong as an ox!'

And they all three laughed again.

When the two women left, Sikes couldn't help noticing the marked contrast between them. Nance was like a gamine off the streets. She was something which would slip through your fingers. Bet, on the other hand, was round and plump; not fat, but a pretty plumpness that roused a man's desire. Her eyes held him as she turned her head to bid farewell. He gazed after her and felt guilty.

The women came once or twice a week and Sikes looked forward eagerly to their visits, short as they were. He had bribed his gaoler into letting them always stay for half an hour, rather than the regulation ten minutes. Sometimes Nancy came on her own and Sikes was hard put not to take advantage of their time alone. But he felt it wouldn't be fair to her and she never seemed to encourage him. He guessed that maybe she was still feeling tired and lethargic from her illness.

The weary weeks dragged on. The weather mellowed into autumn and Sikes was finding it harder than ever to contain his anger and frustration. He greeted his visitors with disgruntlement and when alone, he would pace about his cell like a caged tiger, cursing and shouting at the four walls which surrounded him.

And then one day, Bet came to see him alone. She had gone back to her own lodgings now and Nancy was independent of her help once more. As usual, she made her visit in the evening. Sikes was sitting at his table, a tankard of beer in his hand, looking thoroughly dejected, thought Bet. He looked up as she entered and slowly focused on her face. Oh Lor', she thought, 'e's drunk. An' 'e won't like wot I've got ter tell 'im. She dumped her basket on the table and began unpacking the victuals she had brought, prattling on about how well Nancy was, how Fagin's boys had caused trouble in Clerkenwell and how her Tom had nearly been caught and . . .

Sikes grabbed her wrist. She met his eyes.

'Burn me!' he said softly. 'Wot you so jumpy for?'

Bet looked away, but she felt the insistence of his grip.

'It's . . . it's Toby,' she said at last.

Sikes narrowed his eyes. He waited for her to go on.

''E's fenced ev'rythink wot wos in 'is pockets after that crack. An' 'e's sportin' bran'-new clo'es. 'E's got a fancy mistress – some say as she's a real lady – an' 'e 'ardly ever comes down the tavern now. Quite cut us off, 'e 'as.'

As the truth spilled out, Sikes's face had taken on such a look of rage and madness that Bet was afraid to go on. His eyes, which had been smouldering ever since he had been in this place, burst into fiery life. There was much more she could have told him, but he suddenly leaped from the table, overturning his chair.

He picked up the tankard and hurled it against the wall, shouting, 'Dam' the bastard! I thought 'e wos my friend. Gawd, if I could get my 'ands on 'im, I'd kill 'im! Swelp me God, I would! 'E's taken ev'ry bloody penny from that crack, ain't 'e?' He didn't wait for her answer but plunged on. 'I ain't seen sight nor sound of 'im, nor 'is pickin's since Bartlemy Night. 'E ain't bin near this place. Dam' 'is bloody eyes. 'E's nothing but a yellow-livered whoreson!'

He kicked at the chair, picked up the dented tankard and threw it again. It hit the stonework with a resounding clang. Bet cowered by the door, frightened out of her wits, her hands clasped to her mouth. She watched in silence as Sikes flung himself against the wall, in what was becoming a familiar gesture of despair, beating his fists until they bled. His breath came in great sobbing gasps, but he was no longer shouting.

'Why me, Bet?' he moaned. 'Why is it always me? Toby got away with it easy once before. Now 'e's livin' in clover. I'm jugged up 'ere because of 'im, because of 'is cowardice. An' because Fagin's boys 'adn't done their job proper. It's always someone else's incompetence wot lands me 'ere. Ain't it? An' it was Toby got me shipped, yer know that?'

He turned his head and looked at her meaningfully. She thought he was being unfair to Toby, but she knew he was in a very dangerous mood at the moment and she refrained from comment.

'Yeah,' he went on, his voice rising again. 'You've got a proper 'ome ter go to ternight. I've got this bleedin' place. These bloody walls an' the rats an' the stink – an' the silence.' He strode to the door. 'I've got ter get out of 'ere,' he shouted and beat on the thick oak.

The gaoler, sitting a little way along the corridor, raised his eyes laconically.

557

'Shut up, Sikes,' he murmured. 'We've 'eard it all before.'

'You don't know wot it's like, mate,' retorted Sikes, 'being shut up in this place, day after day. It's the silence, the closeness of it all. It gives me bloody nightmares.'

He was no longer addressing the turnkey. He leaned against the door on outstretched arms, his head hanging down. He could sense the darkness creeping up again on the periphery of his vision and he was frightened. And when Bet stood behind him and tentatively put her arms about him, she felt his body shaking with anger and fear. Without thinking, she rested her head against his back.

But he didn't move, except to lift his head and cry, 'It's like Grummet Island. An' I nearly went mad there. This place'll drive me mad, too. I shall do somethink violent, I know I will!'

Bet held him tightly. She was frightened by him, but she must try to restrain his madness.

'Shh, Bill. Don't talk like that,' she murmured. 'Yer've got Nancy waitin' at 'ome for yer. Don't that give yer some encouragement? Summat ter live for? We're all waitin' for yer ter come back, Bill. Life ain't the same without yer.'

He was silent, breathing fast. She had touched some nerve within him and he turned in her arms and looked into her eyes. They were beautiful eyes, soft and brown. And he wanted her. He bent his head and met the lips lifted to his. He was seized by an uncontrollable urge, the culmination of the weeks of anger and turmoil and frustration. He fumbled at her skirts. Why so many blasted petticoats? He turned her round. Lifted her against the wall. She responded to his urgency, wrapping her legs about his hips. The darkness almost overwhelming him now. Driven on by blind rage. A frenzy of motion. Everything pent up inside him, poured out in a shuddering explosion inside her compliant body.

It was not until the madness had passed and he stood over her, breathless and gazing once more into her eyes, that they both realized with dismay that they had betrayed the one common factor of love between them – Nancy.

'She mustn't know, Bet. I couldn't 'urt 'er. She's bin bloody good ter me.'

He turned from Bet and fastened his breeches. Bet stayed where she was, her eyes closed. She had wanted Bill for so long. Now he had taken her, why did she feel unfulfilled? It wasn't for lack of a climax. It was something more. It must be what he was feeling now. That they had betrayed Nancy. She straightened her bodice and smoothed her skirts.

'I'd better go, Bill,' she said quietly.

He didn't answer and she looked across at him. He was staring at the grille in the door. She came to his side and put her arms round his neck, but he wrenched them away, saying, 'No. Not now, fer Gawd's sake!'

She followed his gaze and saw the door open. The gaoler entered and for a moment she could not understand Sikes's seemingly cruel rebuttal of her advances. Then she saw the reason for his anguish. Behind the gaoler stood Nancy.

''Nother visitor for yer, Sikes,' grinned the turnkey, somewhat maliciously. 'I told 'er you 'ad someone else 'ere, so she can't stay the full 'alf-'our.'

He shuffled away, grinning to himself, and locked the three of them in.

For a moment there was silence in the cell.

Nancy looked troubled, but Sikes did not think she suspected anything as yet. Bet had flushed bright pink and kept her eyes to the floor.

'Well, Nance,' blustered Sikes, 'this is a surprise. I didn't expect *two* gals in one evening. I thought it would 'ave bin a bit late fer you. You mind yer don't go catchin' cold, these chill evenin's.'

He went across to her and took her in his arms. When he kissed her and felt the thin body beneath her cloak, he thought she must see into his eyes and know what he had done. But he would not tell her. It would be his secret. There were plenty of other things about his past he had never told Nancy. It wouldn't be difficult to hide it from her, as long as

Bet played her part. But men kept things to themselves better than women.

Bet was collecting up her basket and bonnet.

'I'll see you again some time, Bill,' she said. 'Don't get too despondent. Time'll soon be up.'

She called to the gaoler and he let her out. Sikes and Nancy looked at each other. For her part, Nancy sensed that something had been said or done in this cell before her arrival. She wouldn't think the worst, because she thought she knew her man well enough by now. But when she had kissed him, she had smelled a woman's perfume on him. Very faint, but it was there, and she recognized it. Well, she told herself, Bet had probably given him a peck on the cheek. It was the sort of thing Bet would do, she was so generous, so good-hearted.

She saw the tankard lying on the floor and went to pick it up. 'Wot 'appened ter this, Bill?' she asked, as she examined the dents and scratches on it.

Sikes lifted his shoulders.

'You ain't bin fightin' again, 'ave you?' Nancy smiled and came over to his side.

She put her arms round him and was surprised when he did not respond. But she noticed that his body seemed tense and he was shaking, ever so slightly.

'You ain't ill, are yer?' she asked, frowning. 'Yer seem a bit feverish.'

'No, I'm all right. I 'eard about Crackit this evenin' an' I ain't got over the shock. That's all.'

It would be easy. She would believe him. Crackit's preposterous behaviour had covered his own misdemeanour. He supposed he should thank Toby for that. He would have been hard pressed to think of some other excuse, that was for sure.

'Yes,' said Nancy sadly. 'We were all a bit surprised at that. But yer know, Bill, it won't last. 'E'll soon be through the blunt an' then 'e'll come crawlin' back ter you fer another crack.' She looked up anxiously into his eyes. 'Will yer take 'im back? After wot 'e's done?'

Five minutes ago he would have said no, he'd rather shoot

the fellow dead with his pistol than have anything further to do with him. But now he realized how useful the cover of Toby's exploits had been and he would no longer hold them against his erstwhile friend. But he feared there would never again be that close camaraderie which they had known in the past. Toby had let him down too many times. From now on, Toby would be a business partner and nothing else. And their partnership would be a fragile thing. He stared down into Nancy's upturned face as the thoughts chased through his mind.

Then he said, 'Yus. I'll take 'im back, fer old times' sake. But it'll be on my terms, not 'is. I'll do all the plannin' fer cracks an' 'e'll do wot I tell 'im. 'E'll be a business partner, that's all. I ain't drinkin' with 'im no more.'

Nancy was surprised by the vehemence of his words. For a man to shun his lushing partner was an outright admission of favour forsworn. She was saddened. Toby had been so much a part of their lives. But she would never know the deep-seated resentment that had festered over the years in Sikes's breast and which he had endeavoured to hide up till now; a resentment born of the years he had spent in the penal colony, a punishment he had laid squarely at Toby's door.

When the gaoler came, Sikes impulsively took Nancy in his arms and kissed her fiercely. He released her just as suddenly and turned away. Breathless and surprised, she bade him farewell and went from the prison.

THIRTY-ONE

◆

Sikes slept soundly that night, contrary to his expectations. But when he awoke early in the morning and thought back over the previous evening's events, he saw with stark clarity that he had been a fool to allow himself to become involved with Bet. How would she ever keep her pretty mouth shut? Women talked about these things, didn't they? And God only knew what she and Nancy would discuss between them. He turned hot at the thought and got up from his pallet, feeling drained. But it had been good! Bloody good. She knew her job, that was for sure. Nance would never have done anything like that, not with him. And Bet had been so willing. That had surprised him in a way. He'd noted the brush of hands across the tavern tables, the playing with feet below; he'd winked at her, merely playing a game with her; and she'd kissed him when he had been at his most vulnerable. But he hadn't expected her to treat any of this seriously, certainly not to the extent that she had willingly taken his angry body into hers.

Well, it was over now. He would make sure that they didn't do it again. For Nancy's sake. Nancy. Nancy. The name kept burning into his brain. How could he have betrayed her simple trust, when he had demanded as much from her in return for his protection? Some protector he was!

But he would not waste his time and his energies fretting about a woman. Life was too short. He had another month to go in this place. He would exhaust himself with work and then perhaps he would, in time, forget this episode. And so he threw every ounce of energy he possessed into the daily routine of stone-breaking. Until his hands were covered in cuts and blisters, his shoulders and arms ached and his back had a permanent pain from the jarring of the sledgehammer.

Neither woman visited him again for over a week and in some ways he was glad. But he was short of decent drink and there was no more blunt with which to bribe the gaoler. When Nancy did come, it was some ten days afterwards. She looked chilled and kept her shawl tightly round her.

'Cold out there?' enquired Sikes.

Nancy nodded. Silence.

'It's always cold in 'ere. But I can still tell the temp'rature's dropped. Must be November now?'

She nodded again and there was another uncomfortable silence.

'Any more news of Toby? 'As 'is blunt run out yet?'

A shake of the head.

'Fer Gawd's sake, say somethink, gal, can't yer? Yer lost yer tongue? Or are you ill again?'

He was beginning to feel desperate. He frowned at the girl. She looked pale. There was a closeness about her, as though she had withdrawn from the world. Sikes was unnerved. He seized her hand and pulled her to him.

'Wossup, Nance?' He thought a bit of gentleness might not go amiss.

He was dismayed when she suddenly put her head against his shoulder and began to weep.

Oh Gawd, he thought, I can't take this. And aloud he said, 'Tell me, Nance. Wot's 'appened?'

She looked up at him, her eyes swimming, but flashing some of their old fire.

'You know full well wot's 'appened, Bill! You an' Bet! 'Ow could yer? My oldest friend, my sister almost. And my man. 'Ow could yer both do it?'

Sikes stared at her in horror. He wondered how she had found out. Surely Bet wouldn't have been so stupid.

'Yer don't understand, Nance –' he began.

But she turned on him, cat-like.

'Of course I do!' she spat. 'Wot d'yer take me for, Bill

563

Sikes? I promised I wouldn't betray you when you took me in. I proved ter you as you could trust me, didn't I? Didn't I?'

Her face was very close to his. He felt uncomfortable. Everything she said was true. He had no real answer to her accusations, but he wasn't going to let her get the better of him. He felt the anger rising inside him again.

'Don't you throw that one at me, woman. Wot about the time I caught you drunk, up by the canal? Wot about the time you got yerself the clap on the Mile End Road? 'Ow many other exploits 'ave you bin up to as I don't know of? Eh?'

He was really angry now and had risen to his feet. Nancy feared to say more. If she furthered the argument, she might even drive him into Bet's arms and even now she couldn't bear the thought of losing him. She stood trembling, studying his face. Oh God, she thought, how careworn he looks. He's suffered so much. I can't hold this against him. She came up to him and stood simply before him, aware of his tense body and laboured breathing.

'Bill, my love,' she whispered, her voice low and modulated. 'Why did you an' Bet . . . ?'

She left the question unfinished. She watched the fire burning in his eyes and feared what he would say. He seemed to be battling within himself, fighting to keep down the anger. At last, he spoke and his voice sounded unsteady.

'Nance, I didn't even think about it. I was that pent up an' angry. An' so scunnered with ev'rythink, I 'ardly knew what I wos doin'.'

Nancy looked at him, her head a little to one side. 'But I've seen the way Bet's looked at yer over the past weeks. I've seen the little things she does. So yer must 'ave known 'ow she felt about yer.'

She sat down on the chair, her hands playing with the ribbon on her bodice.

'You won't leave me, will yer, Bill? I couldn't bear it. Not after all this time. Promise me yer won't leave me?'

Her look was so pitiful, so pleading. He couldn't have refused her if he'd wanted to.

'No, Nance. I won't leave yer. I ain't seen Bet again, anyway. It wos somethink we done without thinking. An' I 'oped yer wouldn't find out.' He paused. ''Ow *did* yer find out, Nance?'

She looked at him, very directly.

'The gaoler,' she said simply. 'An' then Bet herself confirmed it.'

Sikes wondered how much Bet had said. He hoped she hadn't been cruel enough to go into details. At least they would have that little secret between them.

'Well, it's all over now, Nance. I'll be out of 'ere in three weeks. An' then we'll get back ter normal. Now, let's see yer smile.'

He took her face in his hands and she smiled up weakly at him.

'Can't yer do any better than that, gal?'

What was normal for them, Nancy wondered. A blazing row, a black eye, living off house-breaking, running from the Law? A longed-for baby and a secret miscarriage? Betrayal with her best friend? Once, their love had been enough.

But for answer, she reached up and pulled his head down to her mouth and kissed him hard and long. Maybe they would learn to trust again. It would take time but Nancy was prepared to try. She hoped Sikes was, too.

On the morning of his release, Sikes contemplated making his way to the Spa Fields Chapel in Clerkenwell, where he knew he could obtain a substantial breakfast. It was the custom of the time for the chapel to provide newly released prisoners with this commodity, but it was also the place where ex-prisoners could be met by friends and relations. Sikes didn't want anybody there, witnessing his release. So he had not told Nancy when he would be freed. Nobody really liked him, he mused; some went in awe of him; some envied him; many simply feared him. He didn't care what they thought as long as no one peached on him. That was all that mattered in his life. He knew that if he was caught again he would swing.

565

Almost certainly he had had his last chance. But life had to go on. He had to bring in the blunt. So there would be more cracks to make.

He made his way to a chophouse in Aldersgate Street. It was the middle of November and there was a chill in the air. The sky was clear, however, and there was no sign of the dank mists which so often beset the capital at this time of the year.

'Dam' me,' he said to himself. 'I'll 'ave ter find a hat.' His own had not been returned to him that morning and he was annoyed. His key they had seen fit to give him.

'After all, a man must be able to get into his own home,' remarked the police clerk.

The turnkeys, who had accompanied him to the front of the prison, laughed and one of them said, 'Wouldn't stop this one gettin' in!'

The police clerk was not amused and handed him his key in silence.

Breakfast seemed like a banquet after prison food. He ordered a great plate of eggs and sausages and bacon, a pile of toast and honey and a pint of ale. With all this tucked away under his belt, he felt well satisfied and on much friendlier terms with the world. He sauntered off into Petticoat Lane and eventually found himself a second-hand hat, which he crammed down on to his head with satisfaction.

At last he stood in the shadowy courtyard of Old Nicol Street, looking up at the window of his lodging. The curtains were drawn back and he wondered if Nancy were at home. His fingers closed over the key in his pocket. He rang the lodging-house bell and Mrs Waller answered.

'Oh, so you're back then, Mr Sikes. Pleased ter see you, I'm sure.'

She stood firmly in the doorway, her arms folded across her ample bosom, looking not at all pleased to see him back.

'We 'eard yer'd bin away fer a bit.'

Sikes grunted and made to enter. Mrs Waller stood her ground.

'I *will* be gettin' me rent reg'lar now, I s'pose?'

Sikes looked at her sharply. 'You bin paid, ain't yer?' he asked, frowning.

'Yus. Well. I 'ave. But not reg'lar. Young miss up there ain't bin able ter pay up each week. I give 'er credit on more 'n one occasion. Now yer back, p'raps yer'll sort things out?'

'All right,' muttered Sikes, annoyed.

His buoyant mood had been somewhat marred by Mrs Waller's revelation. He thought he had given Bet clear instructions for Nancy, right at the beginning of his incarceration. Well, that could wait. What mattered now was to get back to her. He strode past the lodging-house keeper and dashed up the stairs two at a time. Outside the door he stopped, his heart racing. Quietly, he inserted his key into the lock and turned it. It made a slight noise and Nancy called fearfully from inside, 'Yes? Who is it?'

He turned the handle gently and let himself in. His heart turned over. She looked so frail and vulnerable standing there in her shift, her hair loose about her shoulders, the ivory brush in her hand. He forgot what she was, what she had been. To him, at that moment, she looked beautiful and in his rough, brutal way he loved her.

Nancy's startled look gave way at once to sheer joy and she flew across the room into his arms.

'Bill, oh Bill! Oh I didn't expect yer so early. Oh luv, it's good to 'ave yer back.'

She clung to him, her head resting on his chest, and he held her close, feeling a rare moment of sheer joy and happiness.

'My little Nance,' he whispered hoarsely. 'Gawd, 'ow I've missed yer.' And then, 'I'm back now, Nance. Nothin' an' no one'll come between us any more.' At that moment he felt it to be true.

Not a hundred miles from the Old Nicol Street lodging house, a small undertaker's apprentice had run away from his master and was heading towards the great City of London. With every step he took, he drew nearer to sealing the fate of Bill Sikes and Nancy. His name was Oliver Twist.

EPILOGUE

JULY 1837

The big body hung lifeless, swinging gently under its own momentum. It was, perhaps, inevitable. He could not have lived without Nancy. He had destroyed her and sooner or later he would have destroyed himself. But Nancy had reached out and taken him with her two nights later.

It had been a horrific drop, enough to wrench a man's head off. Somehow Sikes's head had remained intact. There was blood, though, where the broken bones of his neck protruded. That same neck round which Nancy had so often flung her arms in childlike passion. His face was distorted in the horror of his final moment, his mouth a little open, his eyes staring, glazed, the fire quite gone out of them.

The Law, whom he had spent his life evading, pulled in the body through a lower-storey window. One of the young policemen was immediately sick, while two others hacked away at the noose, which had run up so smoothly and so tightly and cut off all that great vessel of life in seconds. They carried the body between them to a waiting cart. The officer in charge stood a moment with a canvas in his hand ready to cover it up. He looked at what half an hour ago had been a strong and healthy man in the prime of life.

'What a waste,' he murmured. 'Fine big chap like that.' He shook his head. 'I don't understand these coves.'

He sighed and hid the remains of William Sikes from public eyes.

'Where to, hofficer?' called the driver of the cart.

The policeman thought for a minute. Once, there would have been no second thoughts on the matter. He would have sent the body to the London Hospital for dissection. But they had stopped all that now. And the fellow hadn't been publicly executed. More an execution by misadventure, he thought grimly. Ah, well, it had saved the hangman a job.

'Send him back to his parish,' he said to the carter. 'Where did he come from? Shoreditch, wasn't it, or Spitalfields?'

'Oh aye,' replied the carter. 'I'll drop 'im off at the Whitechapel Work'us. That'll do, near enough.'

The cart moved away with its sombre load and the crowds began to drift home. They had watched a spectacular show that night and it would be discussed for weeks to come, over pots of gin and tankards of ale and polite cups of tea.

And so Sikes entered a workhouse for the last time. Reluctantly, the matron and master allowed his body to remain there until his burial had been arranged. The carter left a message at the undertaker's to that effect on his way home and the following day, Sikes's remains were laid in a plain, unmarked coffin and he was buried in a public grave in Spitalfields churchyard. The vicar had another burial to carry out that day. And so it came about that another, much smaller coffin was laid by that of Sikes. A few inches of earth separated them. But whether Death had joined them together again, God alone knew.

And Bet, in her anguish, lay immured in the asylum, waiting for her heart to break. She had loved them both and both had been taken from her. She had never understood what had been between those two. But whatever it was, she had never succeeded in coming between them. And she was glad. And the grass and weeds soon covered the graves and the mounds sank and no one knew who was there any more.

Far away on a hillside farm in Van Diemen's Land, on a morning of icy brightness, a small boy came racing across the farmyard, mud and slush spraying up round his legs. It was winter and he hated having to wear boots. He sat panting on the kitchen doorstep to remove them, before galloping up the stairs to his grandmother's room. He remembered, just in time, to knock on the door. At her reply he burst breathlessly into the sun-filled room.

'Look, Grandmother, look what I've found!'

He held up his grubby palm, cupped lovingly around his find. It was a small folding knife, the blade rusted into its hinge, the casing of scrimshaw work. He had found it half buried at the foot of the old stone wall, up in the hill field. He had rubbed at the surface and the dirt had come away on his fingers, revealing the smooth bone decorated with crude scratchings of ships. It was a glorious treasure to find and he would add it to the shells and stones and feathers and horseshoes in the box beneath his bed. But first he must see what Grandmother had to say about it. She was always so knowledgeable on such matters.

Betty Brewer took the dirty relic in her hand, turning it over. She wet a finger and rubbed it over the design and the three-masted sailing ship seemed to leap to life before her eyes. It might have belonged to any one of the many convicts who had come to work for them over the years. But there was something about the design of the ship, the ferocity of the incising lines . . . There was a mark at one end, very small.

'Fetch me my spectacles, Stephen, there's a good boy.'

Stephen lifted the delicate pince-nez very carefully from his grandmother's table and brought them over to where she sat in the sun-filled window of her room. He watched intently as she fitted them on to her nose and he held his breath as she half closed her still-beautiful eyes, endeavouring to discern the mark.

There was no doubt about it. The S was a little shaky, but the W before it was clear enough.

'This was your father's, Stephen.'

He could not understand why Grandmother spoke in an almost awed whisper.

'My father's?'

Grandmother gazed out of the window to the distant sea.

'Your real father's, Stephen.'

She knew she should have held her peace, but heavens, no

570

one surely believed that Edwin Jephcott was his father. She had promised silence to her daughter when Elizabeth had married Jephcott. But only until the boy was old enough to understand, she had added. Betty Brewer was a great believer in Truth.

'When you are older, I will tell you the story of your real father, Stephen. You are too young to understand now. Keep the knife safe, but say nothing to your mother. It would upset her too much.'

Stephen stood immobile at his grandmother's side, his eyes never leaving the knife still lying in her hands. How could he have two fathers? No one had two fathers. And then a thought struck him.

'Is he . . . is he dead?'

Betty Brewer gazed out to sea again. Was he dead, that strong yet broken young man who had briefly entered their lives? She thought of him suffering on the chain gangs, finishing his time. Of his sailing back to England. They had heard that news through a friend of theirs at the docks. Convicts returning to the motherland were a rarity. She wondered, as she had so often, what he had done on his return. How many other women he had seduced. She remembered his ardent gaze, his burning eyes and the disturbing effect his presence had had on her. She could so easily have fallen under his spell. Instead, he had taken her wilful daughter. And the girl's resultant pregnancy had been a godsent excuse to send young Sikes away. If he had remained she dreaded to think of the consequences to herself. But his sort were doomed in life. He was a bad lot. He would surely have gone to meet his Maker by now.

She transferred her benign gaze to her grandson.

'Yes, Stephen. I believe he is,' she said with certainty.

Stephen reached out and retrieved the knife. He walked away slowly, closing his grandmother's door softly. In his room he sat on his bed for a long time, just staring at the tiny incised ships, one on each side of the knife case. And he gently touched the initials at the end.

He wished he could understand what all this mystery was. Why Grandmother would not tell him everything, why he had to keep his find a secret, why he must not mention any of this to his mother. He sighed. For now he must be content. He had something tangible, something he could grasp in his small boy's hand and say, 'This was my father's.'

Child of the Phoenix
Barbara Erskine

The long-awaited new novel by the bestselling author of
Lady of Hay and *Kingdom of Shadows*.

Born in the flames of a burning castle in 1218, Princess
Eleyne is brought up by her fiercely Welsh nurse to support
the Celtic cause against the English aggressor. She is taught
to worship the old gods and to look into the future and
sometimes the past. But her second sight is marred by her
inability to identify time and place in her visions so she is
powerless to avert forthcoming tragedy.

Extraordinary events will follow Eleyne all her days as,
despite passionate resistance, her life is shaped by the
powerful men in her world. Time and again, like the phoenix
that is her symbol, she must rise from the ashes of her past life
to begin anew. But her mystical gifts, her clear intelligence
and unquenchable spirit will involve her in the destinies of
England, Scotland and Wales.

ISBN 0 00 647264 8

Waters of the Heart

Doris Davidson

A heartwarming family story by the author of *Time Shall Reap*

Young Cissie McGregor flees to Dundee with her step-mother, Phoebe, after her abusive, drunken father has destroyed their family. There, for a while, she finds happiness – with Bertram Dickson, son of the wealthy mill-owner who is Cissie's and Phoebe's employer. But, too late, she finds her new husband has not married her for love. After she bears him the son they've yearned for, he takes the first excuse to throw her out on the streets - keeping her beloved child . . .

Cissie has known the worst before. She will survive and she will win through. But while she builds up her own business and fights for the return of her son, she must finally confront the consequences of those events long ago in Aberdeen when her childhood innocence was shattered . . .

0 00 647321 0

A Distant Harbour
Jessica Blair

When the boats came in . . .

After a shipwreck robs Captain David Fernley of his wife, he can see no future for himself in Whitby, the whaling port where he has made, and lost, his fortune. But whaling is the only life he knows. Determined to change his bad luck, he starts anew in London, where he is offered command of the *Hind*. And where he meets Lydia, a woman who can understand the call of the sea.

Thus begin his voyages, which will take him to the Arctic, through treacherous icefields, to America and the fatal calms of the Pacific. But these adventures are as nothing compared to events in Nova Scotia and New Bedford – in which distant harbour David finds the one danger he'd long since forgotten . . .

Acclaim for Jessica Blair's *The Red Shawl*:
'A brilliantly researched book about Whitby, whaling and the havoc one woman could wreak on those touched by her ruthless ambition'   Elizabeth Elgin

ISBN 0 00 647912 X

The Charmed Circle
Catherine Gaskin

The Seymour family has everything – fame, beauty, wealth.

Julia, the youngest daughter, marries Jamie Sinclair, a Battle of Britain pilot, heir to a decaying castle in the Scottish Highlands. Through Rod McCallum she experiences another world, in Hollywood – the glitter, the corruption. Julia's sisters, Constance and Alex, are very different in temperament, in their yearnings, their ambitions.

But can even a charmed circle survive a murder trial which headlines across the world . . .

'Miss Gaskin is a born storyteller.' *Sunday Mirror*

ISBN 0 00 617728 X